Butter,
or
the Dairy of a Madman

A Novel in Two Books

Book One

Christopher S. Peterson

Fomite
Burlington, VT

ISBN-13: 978-1-959984-70-2
Library of Congress Control Number: 2024951188

Fomite
58 Peru Street
Burlington VT 05401

12-17-2024

For Ma

"There are only two tragedies in life: one is not getting what one wants, and the other is getting it."

— Oscar Wilde

Peki

The misshapen baby, living for nine months in a fetal position in a uterine universe, so sick and tired of placental nourishment, his umbilical cord acting as some strange antenna, suddenly falls down the rabbit hole of a birth canal and finds himself in the wonderland of this world. This, reader, is Spain in the Fifth Dementia, a dream dimension.

In this botch of a burg, a harelipped, humpbacked sadsack, Peki Zambrano, built like a fire hydrant, is a butter maker/shop owner, his establishment set up in what was once a petroleum jelly factory. He is a frequenter of casinos and brothels. He lives with his mentally ill mother, Marisa, in a gaunt building made of brick, glass, wood, and steel, a veritable house of horrors, with its accompanying cobblestone driveway and garage that could pass for a bunker, located in a funky neighborhood. After receiving from his doctor a diagnosis of syphilis, Peki pops mescaline and experiences a vision of Marisa castrating him. He holds his genitals like he would broken birds.

Peki and Marisa

The Charles Mansonoid Peki's laboratory architecturally resembles a run-down Moulin Rouge. Once upon a time, he was lost and found. He has vivid memories of Christmases at the orphanage: the pine tree, with its resinoid redolence, swaddled in lametta and cocooned in tinsel, with vibrant explosions of bulbs and baubles, and a glittering star on the tippity top. The whole affair was stabilized in a bucket of soil. There was the caroling and games, the holly and mistletoe, the parish parties and festive feasts. Priests and nuns often played cards and dice on the steps of the church. The celebration was a yearly miracle. Sills were glowing with candles. Windowpanes were constellationed by snowflakes. Abstract fruitage, antique lanterns, and paraffin lamps were strategically situated on particular surfaces of the residential institution. There were many angelic and astral ornamentations to marvel at. Bells jangled. Tunes were sung. Yuletide records spun on the gramophone. Huge plasticine effigies of Frosty the Snowman, Rudolph the Red-Nosed Reindeer, and adorable elves stood like sentinels around Santa's sleigh. A few staff members wore convincing polar bear costumes. Children tweeted in a chorus line, like warblers on a telephone wire, twittering in time to the pounding organ. The meals were indeed Lucullan in extravagance. The Argus sky was full of starry eyes, and snow banks were soft as cotton candy. Peki remained reserved, forsaking the opportunity to establish contact with the other foundlings. He made sure he remained out of sight and sound. He recollects mistreating a lashless and lipless teenager, the wheelchair-bound Oscar Jara, afflicted with muscular dystrophy, in the dank cellar. The boy had a skeletal face, twiggy limbs, paddle hands, and floppy feet. His head was permanently cocked at an unnatural angle. The kid could have been mistaken for an ashen goblin. It was common knowledge that he had a dubious liver and a defective kidney. Peki, complexion grape-purple with rage, was struck by his delicate peepers and jutting chin. It was practically a slaughter of the innocent. His aggressive force found an outlet, using the boy as a punching bag, slapping him with incredible energy and abandon. Later abuse happened behind swing doors. Peki was venting frustration and fury in equal measures, feeling vulnerable to his own random and destructive behavior which he couldn't understand. He pictured them as Jacob wrestling the Angel. The gymnasium-sized sleeping quarters held many cots in cubicles. The edifice was visually reminiscent of an enormous enameled cigar box. A plastic babe, an imitation of Jesus Christ, rested in a rickety stable in the lobby, the statues of Mary and Joseph protectively watching him. The surrounding environment suggested a Brueghel brumal scene. Doctors and nurses at the local hospital (the place always had a whiff of disinfectant) distributed presents to the orphans. Most of the gifts consisted of vehicular toys and stuffed animals. Peki received a bunny and a duck, both invested with personalities, and he adored them unconditionally. This one time he disemboweled a girl's elephant and monkey.... Blanca Luque wore a pretty christening shawl wrapped around her waist. Asthmatically breathing, he went to slug her but stopped dead in his tracks as if he were rejected by some deflector shield. He had an unfocused gaze, elongating his speech, and abbreviating his pauses for dramatic effect. She managed to adapt to this behavioral pattern. Her tresses flowed lank. She was eggplant complected. Even back then he was more sexually predatory than the Duke of Mantua in Rigoletto. His spoken language had exactitude and specificity, whereas Blanca's was florid and figurative. She was a bullet-headed, goggle-eyed, hook-nosed, breadstick-slender, salacious hoyden who, rumor had it, hailed from the rude provinces. She was composed in patience and caution, dignified and balanced, dealing with him. Her high-pitched modulation could shatter plate glass. She cut quite a decorative figure, possessing an androgynous perfection and conspicuous self-sufficiency he envied. It was a white-knuckle vocal exchange between them. His erratic conduct called his sanity into question. Flicking an imperious raven-feathery forelock, the teenage Lotharia turkey cock-strutted away. Silence in space imposed silence on Earth. The light shone brightly and sang soundlessly. Blanca was gone, never to be seen or heard from again...

Life, to Peki, is unfair. He should be in the royal box and not the cheap seat, so to speak. Incontinence (his) is the one torment in Hell that Dante inexplicably forgot about. He looks like a homuncular, hungover Rasputin, caricaturing himself when communicating his love to Marisa. It is difficult to make confidences to her, not knowing how she will react because she is so volatile. With a blank countenance, she shells boiled chestnuts at the sink. He is possessed by a physical and emotional attraction to her. Although he recognizes that it's wrong, he can't help himself. It doesn't come easy to bring himself to make contact with her. He is tolerant of her haughtiness. He has endured a lifetime of effacement and subordination to her and it is getting rather stale. His form of passive resistance to her rejections has taken shape over the years. He wants to be noticed, to be desired by her, but she seemingly goes through the motions with him. Currently, she regards him as though the sight of him makes her ill. Their private acts pull against public behavior. The relationship goes against the grain. The two don't falsify tricky truths, pretend their partnership is normal, and ignore circumstances. They face facts. She, a woman of uncertain temper, sitting cross-legged on the Quaker-gray sofa, partaking of bread and wine, appraises the cypresses and oleanders in the queer country beyond the city with absentminded scanning attention. She has a beetling brow, beaky nose, and sharp cheekbones, her intense, beady pies a pale blue. And she has a straight mass of straw-brown hair and pear-shaped breasts, dressed in a denim shirt, baggy corduroys, and platform loafers. Peki has a plentiful black mop and prickling beard and wears a herringbone tweed suit that could have been tailored in another galaxy, and a derby hat and shoes.

There is a leaden stream. A bifurcated path simmers with hazy heat. In the orangey effulgence, puddles are transformed into splashes of blood. The cloud cover conveys the impression of bruised flesh. Mist is an enveloping veil. The ample meadow blazes with sunflowers. Mother and son are perky as Punch and Judy. He imagines them as being a couple of Toulouse- Lautrec models, those quaint cafe habitués. They share coconut marshmallows and boysenberry yogurt. Shit only makes sense by contrast, he believes, the way a walk-in fridge feels warm when you've just spent a week in a walk-in freezer. Pornographic neckties with psychedelic colors snake dance. Unceasing smog, peculiar and precise, blankets and paralyzes the cryptic and perilous freeways.

The semi-furnished apartment is a series of repeated bland rooms, all painted battleship-gray. Marisa has an avian aspect and a bony body, her skin chalk-white. Draped in a bathrobe of cornflower taffeta, seated on the shell-pink couch with heaped and plumped pillows, she sees the preponderance of pedestrians on the sidewalk while gobbling dark chocolates, her "magic beans," and glugging a glass of bourbon, her disposition of hostile distance persisting. She remembers living for a period in America. She used to be a consumingly competitive rower in high school, this overcast dystopian oasis of modernist concrete slabs, motivated less by any kind of innate interest in the sport than the challenge of becoming Samson to beat Goliath. Wanting to surmount every obstacle, not just to win but to excel, in every way and at all cost, she approached the situation like a mathematical problem, frantically scribbling down equations, measurements, and times in her notebook to calculate exactly how to overcome her distinct size and strength disadvantages. There was a simultaneous physical and psychological deterioration, and a hallucinatory blurring of night and day. Her practice schedule was grueling. She pushed her body past its limit. She developed stigmatic wounds on her palms. Her athletic journey was on par with a religious experience. She took an analytic approach to everything. Her existence was like an infernal Nike commercial, where "just do it" was more akin to an omen of doom than an inspirational motto. Having an obsessive-compulsive drive, she occasionally did her homework in a spindly boat, one hand on an oar. She was continuously told by teammates that she lacked the right stuff. After all, rowing is a collective team undertaking, not an individual indulgence. Marisa's coaches, customarily taskmasters, became pushovers when it came to training their most rabid recruit. She was a breath of fresh air. However, her quest for perfection often came off as an indication of instability. The educational institution felt increasingly claustrophobic and sinister to her. The cuts and bruises on her were products of her hitting herself when workouts went wrong and her times did not improve. Her destructive conduct was directly linked to past trauma. She barely ate or slept, pushing herself to the breaking point in pursuit of athletic excellence. Her self-perception was defined by the brutality that she could endure while staying alive. A freshman determined to make varsity, she would skulk like some gynoid Gollum through the cavernous cellar, almost Brutalist and subterranean in design, with the glaucescent refulgence as if it were some watery purgatory, driven by her passion to succeed. She had a relentless thousand-yard stare and was never compelled to Freudsplain her actions to anyone. A voice in her head, muttering an inner mantra, was as compulsive and damaging in its way as the impulse to self-harm. Usually, she reckoned her victories as epic events worthy of public celebration. She was a pressure cooker of a human being, fixated with numbers, constantly making calculations and setting goals as though it might be possible to break the system by way of enhanced understanding. It all came to an end when, firing on all cylinders on the rowing machine, experiencing hours of powerfulness and exultation, she suddenly collapsed. When she regained consciousness on the floor, in a urinous pool, she mutilated herself and verbally accosted the cleaning staff. The basement was gloomed and gleamed. Marisa suffered a nervous breakdown and was soon institutionalized. The mental hospital was a crafty setting to her... Presently, she wanders into the kitchen, beholding the peacock rainbow. Buzzed on the booze, she experiences a lightening of the cumbersome heaviness of problems, dreaming of dwelling in a house a youngster would wish to draw with crayons. When she walks, it is half skip and half march. The conversation with Peki is mostly monosyllabic, discussing how imperative it is to exist frugally and avoid waste at any cost.

This is a killer world, with daggers drawn. Peki is grilled not unlike a turbot by Marisa. Her hair- tearing psychotic tantrums are incessant and uncontrollable. The argument goes up and down similar to an unequally weighted seesaw. Things have been dicey between them lately. He feels like a dummy and she is the ventriloquist with her hand up his back. He has an eggshell inflection. Her intonation is a cow low. Weakened by malnutrition, she wavers where she stands. Prescribed pills solve, at least for a spell, her plaguey issues. Off her medications, she is capable of being a monstre sacré — overbearing and splenetic. She imbibes Bordeaux and ingests oysters, saying his ass is wide enough to project a movie on, and adding that he is plump and moist as a Medjool date. Acid-tripping, he has chloral hydrate-laced whiskey with a joint soaked in PCP, in solitude and confinement, content with the knowledge that his existence is on the margins, unaffiliated and unburdened. He inhales and exhales, pondering the cosmos, understanding the idea that it's slowly winding down as the Big Bang turns out to be the Final Whisper. His brain is a state-of-the-art bomb that detonates, releasing dozens of thoughts that fulminate in turn to puncture indistinct targets with thousands of little metal fragments. He wallows in chemical dissipation, whereupon a hologram of StarKist's Charlie the Tuna abruptly materializes and announces that he has junk-food cravings and that he is employed primarily as a surf-rock saxophonist. A cartoony Arnold the Pig emerges from out of nowhere to declare that Chicken of the Sea is inessential. He keeps cropping up at random junctures, not unlike a hitchhiker, to slather nonsense over everything with an industrial-size trowel. The uninvited visitors transmogrify into animated cardboard cutouts. A doorway, leading to a funny foreign land, unexpectedly metamorphoses into a hula hoop. Peki feels twinges of guilt for neglecting his razor. His snaky mane makes him look like a manly Medusa just out of the shower. His eyebrows start to smolder. He wants to leave his uneasy compadres' orbit and follow his own star.

Later on, Peki, sick as a dog, finds himself getting tired of Marisa's matter-of-course indifference towards him. He fails to keep pace with her shifting moods. She is unpredictable, selfish, and petty, as far as he is concerned. He feels like a shock absorber in her company. He rolls himself a cigarette with pricey tobacco, listening to her interminable egocentric parabolas of speech, and thinking that she is flesh of his flesh, blood of his blood. Nothing and no one can change this. Trains clash by on the tracks. Peki feels as if society has let him down, and that it should be more welcoming to him. He is sick of working menial jobs to make ends meet, but he realizes it is a necessity until his mantequilla production career picks up steam. The bills are piling up. Marisa talks to herself, unaffected and unembarrassed, hobbling in heels, arms akimbo, glancing askance at the adjacent Renaissance brewery yard, a medieval courtyard, and a flight of stone stairs with wrought-iron balustrades, skirted by oregano, acacia, thyme, wisteria, and juniper. Smiling, she fantasizes that mother and son are Shakespeare's Antony and Cleopatra. She is fumed with alcohol and drowsy with warmth. The air is fluent. Doves make wing to the horizon. A lavender field is unvarying. Cockroaches make their agitated forays from the wainscot, skittering into the pantry. Marisa reads Peki's facial expressions as she did those fairytales in her childhood. Then she shrills like a trumpet before burning lichen and mushrooms in the tub, creating a hallucinogenic effect. She strips, steps in, and closes the curtain. Her laugh is a vulpine bark. Meanwhile, he has drugs to do and butter to make (with consummate esoteric skill). Coming down from his high feels like the net of comprehension has been torn down, draining the universe of most of its meaning. So, he smokes pot. Fear has noticeably crept into the metropolis like fog. Here are his latest preoccupations: paranoia and marijuana.

Roberto Sequeira

Ramshackle residences are in various states of faded monotony. Throng's features create an amalgam of aspects, the people as though they are collected to view a sideshow on the curb, in these imprecise, indecisive shadows. A crummy edifice is pyramidally shaped. A profusion of detritus in the gutters. The crumbling majesty of a chapel glistens with stained glass windows. Homo sapiens are in a compact mass in the square. The reservoir is restless. Canines of hail chew predatorily on the prey of the metropolis. Rush hour's practically cataclysmic. Streetlights are like dentists' lamps. Trucks the size of warships trundle along. Arrhythmic wheezes of wind. It rains, the incipient beginnings of a storm, and sounds like a tinny voice amplified through a microphone. Crooked buildings slowly sink into the ground. Crows lined on telephone wires have these voracious beady eyes, on stern watch, feathery shirttails nodding, their heads bobbing. Gang of rabble, grim-faced, well-groomed, foul-smelling, spill out of a beer hall, helter-skelter, onto the busy road. People bubble in a froth of activity. A flock of pigeons takes flight from a mournful park. Vehicular motors sob. Peki compulsively issues indecipherable verbiage, touches the erect kernels of his nipples, squints like he's skeet-shooting, and pictures Marisa's scaly soles as she skimmed lazily along, like a gecko, her expressions listless, movements dispirited. He drives decorated military officer, the suave, Herculean, crew cut, virile Roberto Sequeira, with a sandpaper voice, Adam's apple standing out not unlike a hernia, dressed to the nines, to his home base. He finds himself, on the highway, in disrepair, in the center of a whirlwind of humanity. His eyes are enlarged by the thick lenses of his specs. Roberto, with his offensive lineman's lollop, is about as terrifying as watching a middle-aged weekend warrior check off his to-do list at Home Depot. This thought goes unvoiced.

Jorge Machi

The dead whale of the sun is picked apart by fish of clouds. Scabrous ocean. Dismal, slouching huts on baking soda sand and in sorrowing gales. Gulls are enlivened monograms on the vellum of the vault. Postcard panorama. Jorge Machi, a drag queen, Peki's lifelong confidant, leases a crepuscular cave that is capacious and dank and reeks of a hospital for the impoverished for some reason. She looks like a cartoon character, fresh-faced, rosy-cheeked, elfin-eared, with a russet thatch under a Robin Hood cap, wearing a virescent tunic, ballet tights, torn at the knees, and floppy shoes. She abruptly resolves to dress in a magenta monokini and flirty fluffy pumps, come-hitherly sashays, bun flapping on her head as the wing of a trapped dragonfly. Peki peruses a profane paperback novel and Jorge reads a tabloid ragazine, a stuffed bunny rabbit resting on her lap. She denudes himself, and her flirtations pay dividends. To wit: she grabs Peki's tool like an elephant would a carrot. Her glabrescent, alabastrine keester shines like a polished teapot. Her craving is uncontrollable. She could eat this yummy piece off a toothpick spear! She coos like a pigeon perched on a still. She has the pallor of chalk and slides down him as water on a slanted board. Her voice is rough. Moon's not unlike the rusted and round head of a nail. Peki experiences an animalian ardency, the desire for her overwhelming. His panting sounds like sighs from a seashell. He strokes his soft and smooth integument. Jorge's teensy feet are redolent of poultry guts. What a peppy, fetching creature! Her sighs are mellifluous notes on the scale of his carmine mouth. She says she saw her shrink and went to yoga class. His arachnoid hand scuttles on her planar, ivorine tummy, muscular gymnast's legs, pert breasts, and cormous buttocks, her suspirations turning into wheezes. Her respirations with the sound of milk bottles in crates on a wagon hauled by old mules. Her perfect bum, to him, is a sugar-sweet peach. Her discarded scanty panties are dotted with menstrual stains. Her commas for facial divots drive him crazy. She is inconceivably gorgeous. Cellulitic dents on her upper thighs are like plastic pinholes in a telephone. He sees but does not believe. He trips, guffawing, with her, naked now, riding piggyback. Her belly is warm as an alcohol burner, shaven armpits slathered in deodorant. His hurtful wisecracks leave her with a haughty frown. She earns a slave wage, employed as a freelance stripper. Her stilettos are set on the backgammon tables with a few canvas chairs circumscribing them. She has insectile peepers and perpetually pouty lips. Her discouraged chops are palatially on his erectile cock. His constantly changing personality can be, for her, the equivalent of a needle turned malevolently in an infected wound. She's slight like a sparrow. She straightens out her wardrobe of maillots and sandals in the musty closet. Gusts sound like talking crickets. Without her, he'd be like a shell without the sea. She catches him peeking through the modest bathroom's keyhole while she wipes her fanny with toilet paper, and asserts he's a "disgusting ding-a-ling." Blood pounds in his coconut as waves slam against a wall. Impersonal furniture. Stone barriers in dampened despair. He swigs pinched port wine. His heart pumps as the dickens, expanding and contracting like a well-oiled machine. The sky's swollen with saturation. She impulsively admits her slumber has been, recently at least, rodentially light, and confesses she's horny as hell. The decor oscillates to the rhythms of the refulgence, which reveals its subtle imperfections. Sun's a huge loaf of bread baking in the oven of the empyrean. Bowed bed with ligneous splintering paws. She, insulted, bawls on it as a baby abandoned on a doorstep, and swaddles herself in an embroidered throw. The duvet requires reupholstering. Antique backgammon table. Surreal and cineral effulgence. Unsightly Oriental mat. Her sparkling teeth click as used knitting needles. Inanities of their argument with accompaniments of nit-pickings, and with generous injections of insults into the language. Jorge is inwardly hurt, outwardly confident, and struts like an emu. Indecisive illumination on the ceiling's plaster. Stinging sleet as strange acid. She calls him a "nin-compoop." Peki gropes for the hooch on the art nouveau bar. Pea-sized hail. Her pursed choppers are painted orangey. Inexplicable fulgor. Her stiff knee creaks like a corroded hinge. Zinc-silver overcast. His head coincides with her creamy stomachic concavity, the pair on the over-cush-ioned couch. She scours her calluses and bunions with a handy file. Sheets brumously drift. He has a resigned air about him. Cotton balls placed in between her painted toes, she walks like a lame egret. Photographs, framed in carved wood, depict faerie folk — her relatives. Silverish scin-tillation leaks. Bric-a-brac (ripped off from a distant bougainvillea) litters the joint. Her taut abdomen, unexplainably, feels spongy, noggin filled with helium vapor. Rufous arabesques of the dinghies bobbing in the horrendous harbor. She says he has an "infantile imagination." He exhib-its his incredulity. Her harsh comment hastens his departure into the kitchen, in complete chaos. An umbrella stand capably serves as a clothes rack. Kestrels' chorus of keening breaks out suddenly. Contorted features of her countenance, bogus tress a ball of saffron (in the intense splendor) as yarn unraveled. His manhandling of her prompts her to deprive him of the rimming she usually accords him. She thoroughly beautifies the premises. She puts on crumpled denim jeans and a frilly blouse. Her knockers separate like cells dividing. Frantic avian commotion proves distracting. Booted, blushed thus, she resembles a rose withered from drought. The very fabric of her person is torn. Her admonishing tones annoy him immensely. His expression of agonized distress. Her unex-pected submissive resignation to his (customary) uncontrollable sexual gluttony. He swaggers as a construction site's foreman. Romantic fire in the stove, vibratory and shuddering. He scarfs their bonbons while she fumbles lecherously at his fly. And he bounces awkwardly not unlike a crippled grasshopper. He's not in the mood. He flips through a porno magazine, fixates on the centerfold, and frets about their financial woes. He claims he has done some sporadic private detective work, only it's dried up as of late. Hyaline dermis of the mirror in the dinky parlor. A miscellany of mementos on the shelf. Ethereal serenity of the deliques-cent countryside. Peki paces back and forth between the solemn sofa and the writing desk. Intricate auditory mosaics of their echoing modulations. Pair of her floral-patterned bikini undies. His scrotum smells of moldy cheese. Moans and groans shatter into sharp shards. He's dazed by her curvaceous physique, delicate hands, and dainty trotters. Wilted flower of her forced smile. Long-limbed, lachrymose species streak down her cherubic cheeks. She cracks jokes and gestures dramatically like a tour guide. Her potent perfumes permeate the place. He can be temperamental over such piddly nonsense, making a ridiculous fuss! He's all bark and no bite. There are tingles in her wormy-wiggly toes. Attributed to the horrendous humidity, everything appears distorted, as though it is reflected in a funhouse mirror. Overlapping cruddy cotton curtains. He snorts several lines and she rolls reefer. Turbid lake. She meditates on universal tragedies. Weird bark dangles as loose flesh on the bones of folks who've lost significant weight. Her parenthetical dimples are on display. He masturbates in front of her and she is disgusted by his lack of decorum. Her cardiac organ barks in her throbbing temples. Firmament has a similar hue to smelted lead. Jorge's permanently goggled pies are more gigantic, snots runnier than fried eggs, phony bright blond hair fastened in a serviceable knot. Peki, prick throbbing, devours her like an owl a baby bird. The garden path has wilted plants. Moored boats. Lonely soccer stadium. She endures her physical and psychological discomforts. Moon's congealed in cirri. Jade lagoon's ripples visually remind one of winds running over grass. His histrionic phrases, pregnant pauses, and hard-on like a telegraph pole. He splits her as a prow does the surf. Rain has the sound of a running commode. She expected an indifferent, inert dick. Pollen's like trapeze artists' chalk dust. Her gait as a tightrope walker's. Absinthian pool, magnificent mermaids with glaucous manes cavorting. A tubular gypsy shoos away swarms of flies with a filthy hankie, waving it like a surrender flag. Showers sound like enamel being scrubbed.

Nightmare

The mechanized Medusa's serpentiform wires writhe and hiss with electricity as downed power lines. Deluge is like a second instrument taking up the breeze's melody. She is pale as a distant memory, watching the meanderings of clouds in the welkin, blue and serene as the Mediterranean. Her body is as responsive as a cello in rendering every modulation of emotion. Technology had broken the chrysalis and hastened her metamorphosis in the building that was structurally reminiscent of the Temple of Solomon. Pain encircles her head, stabbing into it like she's wearing a crown of thorns. Her eyes coruscate with undiminished luster. She advances, with timid and pious steps, near the drowsy waters of the public garden, in a plenitude of luminosity, and pays idolatrous worship to her makers with a lachrymose bow.

Cristina Caba

Afterward, his tensity too much to bear, Peki gets plastered at an unsavory taproom, abutting a funeral parlor, where he meets a juvenile prostitute, Cristina Caba, who looks like a pretty, although carbuncular, ostrich. She walks like a wounded wind-up toy and has turkey feet. The encounter is a pleasant one. She is attired in a tank top and hipster undies. She has this Tower of Babel hair and a Michelin tire mouth. She smokes pot and dances. Patrons' harsh words devour each other as ravenous hyenas. She flips through a fashion mag nonchalantly. She convinces him to go back to her apartment with her. He does. The place, an abandoned abbey ruin, is a veritable pit. She gloms the ruins of tuna casserole and he jumps rope. The ceiling's mildewed. She nicknames him Chickpea, puts on a sable smock, and gnaws on a baby pacifier. Calluses on her feet are like lemon peels. Paneling perspires dankness. The round ball of the paper lamp floats, lands, and is fading fast. He stretches his stunted arms, looking like a cricket loosening its wings. She clips potted plants and he swigs port wine. His heart rumbles like a tractor. She manipulates these buttons on a cherrywood bureau as checkers on the board. An unlit cigar is between her luscious lips, her countenance with concentrated cosmic insanity. He has got a bullfrog's belly. She has this foolish face, dull oculi, scar on her chin, and splotches on her anguilliform neck. Raucous laughter and shouting radio from next door. The liquiform rainbow is runny as the cosmetics of a weeping whore. A flushed toilet retches. Peki is sheepish. Cristina's eager to please, has a gutter-ish mouth. She's skinny as if she's sick with cancer, blasted by radiation. The town lights up as a nightclub. Airbags of his lungs distend and contract. Vermicular fag ends in the ashtray. Her armpits have a clogged commode funk. Flatulent fumes escape from his sphincter, not unlike steam from the aperture of Vesuvius. An exasperated fly circles, searching for an egress. Peki fixates on the folds of Cristina's frock. Her skin is probably soft like argil. She bends, as though to fellate him, like a plant's stalk in aqua pura when a sluice is opened. Her voice is resolute and emphatic, dreamy and unnatural. He paces to and fro as a sentry guarding a palace. Zephyrian sigh sounds as if it is issued from an indiscernible wight. He imagines sticking his blunt thumb into her gaping cavity. She is divine and gentle. Silken gloom hangs as though it's a clerical vestment. He clumsily plucks the strings belonging to her bodice like it's a harp. Her young flesh has a marbly smoothness. He is quite odd in his amatory proclivities. She is kind and tender. He gazes out the mullioned window, muslin-curtained, at the teeming degenerate city, a vicarage garden, garbage-strewn gutter, a structure resembling a monastery. His lust for her approximates a mania. He opines he is an unlovable gargoyle. He stares at her as if he is in a trance. Her hair is seaweed-straight, has ovaloid bosoms, and gets a glimpse of herself in the eighteenth-century looking glass. He sets himself to contemplating what the effective method of procedure is when it concerns the right moment to ravish her. He fusses with his flannel breeches, fixing them as he wants them to be. An expression reflects on his visage, wavering like the sun on ice. French clock on the mantelpiece tick-tocks relentlessly. Impulsively she tinkers with it. Anxiety-addled, his nostrils twitch. She curses. He tells her she has a bad tongue, but she's a little goose. She titters, spoons rice pudding out of the wooden bowl, and looks at him as though he's a cunning scamp when he pays her with coins. She gives him a faint grin and a reassuring nod. Her sanguine scarf streams from her scrawny neck like a jet of blood from a cut jugular. She drifts as smoke seeking an exit. He gazes at the love letter (how many admirers does she have?) on the coffee table like it's a death warrant. His face is contorted with shame and guilt. Why? He hasn't done anything wrong! The fireplace's corroded grate is evocative of a manikin's disembodied rib cage. He shivers as he emerges from frigid waters. Drencher jingles. Candles flicker. Laurel bushes line the winding gravel driveway. Peki gradually strips, peels free of any sense

17

of embarrassment, seats himself on the chair, and Cristina laughs hysterically at his disfigurement. I am miserable, he thinks. I'm wretched. He was never a man who attracted women. Furious, he strangles her. It takes too long to pass. She looks wet like she wept in her demise. Lying next to her, he brings to mind a deviant slug, in the flickering shadows as animated soil. Sitting up, he hugs his knobby knees with his wrists and bursts into tears. A flush suffuses his frontage. He puts on a petticoat, and hovers like a heatwave. She is dead. He sobs frantically.

On a creative instinct, Peki decides to include Cristina's body fat to make butter. He, in due course, spreads it on a croissant and hallucinates. He believes that this is the last vision of the victim before she died: Cristina is a child and swimming with her family. She submerges. When she surfaces in the water, everyone is gone and everything is silent. She looks up to the sky and there is a giant eyeball. A huge hand then comes and grabs the pool and folds it into a clear box. She struggles to breathe and wakes up gasping.

He puts the product, called Butyrum, on sale and it quickly sells out. Patient and resilient, he is devoted to his aims, however appalling and grotesque. His gray matter is a sacred temple of profane ideas. At work, in the acid shine of luminescence, he looks like a corpse at a wake. Pedestrians have the profiles you'd find in portraiture. He pictures them, in the aqueous air, as minnows unconsciously swimming in an aquarium in its vastity, and studies the psychic and physical natatory movements of these super-mundane aquatic creatures of the town. His body odor is redolent of wet wood. He has on a creamy lab coat, polka-dotted pajamas, and striped slipper socks. He's shaped like a duffel bag. Students, clumped together, create a gigantic octopus with tentacle-limbs on the chaotic street corner with its stony slabs. Peki is fed up with this stinking place. He crams his mitts in the pockets. The shop is like an abscessed tooth in the rotting gums of commercial structures. He wanders into his room as mist from a meadow, after wading against the current of the throng, and falls into a childish sleep of unparalleled serenity and security. The aftermath of having committed the heinous crime has been, for him, a vertiginous loop-de-loop alternating between relief and horror.

Peki and Marisa

Peki, gorging himself on baked goods, primarily the pastry, has a furtive desire to be left to his own devices, armed with permission from his Mama, and he resolves that he'll go to the shop's cellar to prep more Butyrum, determined to defy any ill-omened sidetracking of his plans. He visualizes rehearsing his repertoire of stabbing. He thinks of himself as a damaged evildoer and considers himself as being utterly unprincipled, with an unchanging contempt for any dissimilitude between life and death. His stream of urination parts into the can. He knows he keeps giving the detectives the slip. He's too clever for them. Hey, there have been hiccups here and there, a troublesome moment or two, with him getting away with his hind intact. His Spidey Sense, or killer's reflex, dependably warns him of the badges in the vicinity. Tomorrow is a blank until he fills it with something. The fuzz have been coming and going in ever-increasing numbers. He's got to be on guard. He hears barrelhouse piano playing, accompanied by hooting and hollering, coming from the scuzzy vaudeville area. The environment is not exactly welcoming. He feels held in this city, as if by witchcraft. Hootenanny is a-happening. He has thoughts of throat-slashing, decapitation, gutting, dismemberment, and skinning. He ties his shoes' laces like a surgeon's knot. The lab is where mantequilla miracles (beyond easy reckoning) are routinely expected, made through some desperate magic, the marvels manifesting oft. Butter-prep is like a productive calenture. His office and floor skills aren't the best, but they're not the worst either. His rickety establishment is Architectural Digest tour material, its every dimension and detail a reflection of his presence and personality. The store's prime location is not only ideal for scanning the streets for more potential prey, but also for keeping an eye out for the boys in blue. He has appointed himself as the official spotter, even going so far as to rip off telescopic equipment from an old observatory. Law enforcement officers show and he'll vanish not unlike an elf into the woodwork. Anonymity is a sacred condition. Pedestrians progress in their space and time by those brand new skyscrapers. He is tired of intimidating people glaring at him in revulsion as if he's a fubsy beast. They'll respect him in the long run. Poker-faced, he reels like a drunkard and feels as though he's being hallucinated by someone else. Transit here isn't rapid. Visibility, attributable to the smog, is limited. Portly gent in a bowler hat yomps on the jobless road in clockless illumination. The atmosphere produces a most peculiar haze. A police patrol wagon is parked in proximity to the variety theater and meat-packing plant. Plate-glass windows luminesce. Lake has diverse highlights, both natural and unnatural. Mammoth exhibition edifices. The throng at a pavilion makes a collected creature. Bellhops remind him of guards out front of the Parador palace. There's a muddle of summery bangarang and phosphorescence. The horizon is smudged white with clouds. Peki scoffs down a towering stack of waffles soaked in maple syrup. His life feels simultaneously dreamy and real. He is determined to rip through the fabric of the day. There are plots afoot to perpetuate further outrages upon society. He experiences a shock of moral horror when he thinks of the sins he has committed. His soul is black as night. He puffs on a stogy and blows a concentric ring of smoke, whereupon he has a consolation of muscatel. There's a slew of lurid headlines in the main local papers. His fart is a primal scream. He repairs the sitting-room, with its multiple stinks, the pearlescent emanation covering it with a nice glamor. Space is uselessly assigned in the apartment. Room, it is progressively revealed to him, is a precarious commodity. Marisa, dressed as a lady of flagrant repute, receives his kiss and caress (given with a certain celerity, swifter perhaps than the circumstances seem to demand) without a trace of apprehension, relieved to escape the tedium of vacuuming the dusky carpet (with extreme precision), obviously touched by his awkwardness, and ransacks her brain for a respectful response. Her respirations and gesticulations he takes the wrong way. It's as if he woke from somnolency to assert his individuality. He suppresses a smile, fancies he can hear her heavy breathing and remains for a minute in motionless indecision. His pulse thumps not unlike a bass drum. Her intonation wafts through the apartment like a winter draft. She fools elaborately with her wardrobe. He has the expression of a comedian withholding a rib-tickler's punchline. She slides like a serpent. The son bears the insults of the mother. He is sick of being the insultee. He is aware that he is wild-eyed and scraggly-bearded. Is his fractured heart unmendable? He glowers like a lad whose devilry is interrupted by an authority figure. He's sullen, unwashed, drowsy, starving, and flatulent. She quaffs rum. He studies her tits and ass. He needs to grab more than just shuteye… He imagines them humping in heaves like jackrabbits, one suctioning the other's tongue, their respirations making engine-revving noises, in the raunchy sexcapade. Whereupon they make out ravishingly. The maternalistic sextress fellates him, her head going up and down like a yo-yo. Her butt is plugged with his thumb. He pinches her chestnut-hard nipples and she skreeks. Then he vents couple-three raspberries. The chiaroscuro of their relationship requires her light and his darkness. There is a background choir of complaints from the drifters and squatters of the night. For the homeless, there aren't any crumbs for the picking up. They jabber in some incomprehensible lingo. Collegiate malcontents spill onto the sidewalk and harass ordinary folks. This is a shooting gallery section of town. Peki remembers his firearm is unloaded. Several helicopters hoist slabs of the sea into place like a jigsaw puzzle. His face will adorn t-shirts and lunch boxes. He's sure of it. Marisa is the yin to his yang. He pants like a puppy in a deli.

They smoke marijuana, drink rum, and eat charcuterie, then coax each other into unspeakable acts. Their perspiration pours in rills. Marisa's nates are soft and smooth as nainsook. Loose strands of her hair are like the tendrils of uncultivated flora. She relaxes into pleasantry and gulps a mug of claret. Her pansy-yellow, shabby-chic pantsuit enhances her spindly build. She reminds Peki of an aged priestess in some hallowed liturgy. His heat for her cools off. He disposes of the ham-and-cheese on a bulkie roll. He murmurs as if there's a deficiency in his vocal cords, an apology for interrupting her. And she shushes him; an instinctive interlocutress comprehending his meaning, independent of the words spoken. The key in which her voice is pitched is resonant. His voice sounds as though he's gargling nails. His double entendres become single. There's a quick interchange of glances. He snatches the starchy comestibles on the tray. Her features attain a harmonious expression. She prods clumps of coal in the fireplace with a silver poker, then winds the Geneva clock in an alcove, with its inviting character, its own environment, that adjoins the chamber. Her hands are semaphores. He scans the abstruse volumes on the bookshelf, under the mid-century cut-glass chandelier. His behind makes these gaseous, shrill bleats. Her boudoir's decor, best described as wide-ranging, is a combination of a toy store and bordello parlor. He appears on the threshold like a rising moon. Is he, spying on her, breaching a mother/son moral code? There is a foot-high stack of fashion magazines, a menagerie of stuffed animals, an arsenal of cosmetics, a phalanx of unguents, and a jewel box topped up with necklaces, bracelets, and rings, on the bureau. The mirror is defaced with goofy, girlish decals of kittens, birds, and mice. Silence is deafening. The wallpaper is cuckoo-flowered. The bedspread and pillowcases have incongruent Brueghelian imagery. Discourse occurs in bits and pieces, in wavy luminiferous activity, and not without confounding roundaboutness. He informs her that butter production is closer to a religious, not scientific experience. He has survived many laboratory mishaps, and experienced his share of null results. There was this one doozy involving an arc lamp, sandwich, and positive and negative electricity, pissing off the proprietors from adjoining premises, including the clockmaker's and gunsmith's. Rumors flew like summer skeeters… He thrives on being self-employed, meantime being romantically unentangled. The intervals of invisibility (making the mantequilla and not selling it) are essential. He'd prefer to remain in the background and stay out of the limelight. He is free as a bird! His machinery (most of it invented by him): wonders of the modern age. There's a jukebox, dartboard, and a pool table.

Cirri resemble Cracker Jack clusters. Webwork of waterways shimmer in the humidity. People, parasoled women and hatted men, are plentiful as fungi after a steady soaker. Picketers are dangerously fervid. A pot of minestrone simmers on the burner. Marisa has a tracelet of an amative moue. Brew-befunked, Peki's pulsating root is inflamed. His oral cavity is a heating vent. He has a taste in it as though he swallowed chimney soot. He wants to snap those bony legs of hers and make a wish. His chino pants have a pee-stain. She sucks her teeth, lights a stick of incense, and sniffs glue. Her long body has a vibrant dimension. She is a tad confrontational. The rictus of her rump shows through her unpigmented underwear as she meditates punitively on her sins, not unlike a disobedient nun, her mind filled with the vilest obscenities, sounding like a blithering idiot. He yearns to slather her entirety in hot fudge and lick it off. She is a splendiferous thinifer, bathing in the radiance. He can be a natty dresser, flashily turned-out when the opportunity presents itself, whereas her trappings exhibit an orientation toward the informal. She is in motion. He is at rest. His mood grows somber. His psychic tail is dragging. He has these episodic visions of being reborn, denuded of earthly possessions, liberated from civil encumbrances, on a directionless drift. He chumbles a vulcanized frankfurter and feels possessed by somnambulism like he's under some stultified edict. He waddles as if in a lapse of balance. A protest, hitherto peaceful, escalates into a general free-for-all, like a chemical reaction, as though inmates and keepers alike are running amok in the asylum, as if they're participants in an idiot's game, their shadows changing shape and size. The chaos is too advanced for the on-duty coppers to regain any semblance of order. The weather continues to change as if it's witched.

For Peki, watching the unicyclist and tenor sax player below is about as interesting as waiting for the grass to grow. His eyes are crossed and his tongue protrudes. His desire becomes desperation. His rubbery lips move inaudibly. The pictures, in his pocket, of her feet he'd surreptitiously snapped, are clearer than real. Stoned, he stands, at the doorsill, in disbelief, staring at the rubious sun and its inescapable glow as though it's conjured trickeration and he's a rube at a fair. Grazing cows disregard the townsfolk on the hillside. Policemen brandish their batons to ward off hellraising funseekers… Marisa reveals she is a fad diet addict, claims her bicycle has a consciousness and a personality, no denying it, can carry on a conversation, occasionally disclosing its deepest, darkest secrets. Her smile is almost cruel. She's a killjoy when she launches into the music-hall number. She looks at him as if she was betrayed. The fat is in the fire… Marisa, now bare as a baby, with febrile tics and wounded gaze, retires into the scullery, yawps, and yawns. Her vox is husky. She is a fabled Narcissa, the bees' knees. Towny overture blares. Peki sups the ambrosian tea. He considers himself an unromantic fattypuff grouchbag. She has an oversweet smirk. She rubs her left calf with her right instep. These phallic tenements are pornographies of architecture. Avenue of trees. Metallic brilliance. Vividly green vegetation. Parapet of a bridge. He feels not unlike a vulnerable animal requiring reassurance. She'd be shocked if she knew about his perversities, he thinks. She is outside the pale, wanting to be untouched and independent. He, shivering with excitement, or expectation, regards her with concentrated interest, experiencing the sensation that an unknown consequence is lingering in suspension. His stimulation makes his stomach feel sick. He catches the faint susurration of her deep breath. He starts to feel something of a fool. He attempts to hug this maternal figure before him, and she resists, her sonorous language, reprehending him, falling like a pole-ax on his ears. He bristles like a hedgehog. Phlox-whitish, his eyes and mouth are wide open as though to indicate sheer panic. She blows soap bubbles and pops one with the business end of a pencil. He salivates, surveying the sirloin (with sauce) and pudding she's preparing for supper. He is haunted, sleeping and waking, by reveries of Her. He smolders lustfully like he's on the verge of exploding into flames. He wishes to plow her furrow. Long arms of the law seem to swagger everywhere. Variegated raindrops — pointillism, but without the point. Stuffed to the gills, he hails a taxi from the safety of the curb by the refuse-filled alleyway. The car takes a hairpin turn and almost collides with a delivery truck on the thoroughfare and nearly flattens a dapper harmonica vendor. He climbs aboard and is borne away. The avenue is undeniably on the skew. The fiendish cab is more propelled into traffic than permitted entry into it. The pneumatic driver, looking like a pugilistic jockey, gnawing on an ear of corn and swigging hooch, acts as if he was anticipating the little person's summons. He asks his passenger numerous intimate questions Peki has no answers for. He feels like he's on an out-of-control carnival ride, that he is being taken off to parts unknown, maybe into the center of the Earth. The guy, under the influence, is dumb as an ox. He us appareled in gaudy athletic clothes. There is a resonant absence of anything even remotely personal in the wicked automobile. Oleaginous dust coats the dashboard. The metropolis is a mirage of an acropolis. The vault is lit up all spectral. A carrier pigeon overhead encircles the birch forest. Gales have moderated. It was a mild and ordinary day, to begin with…

The entire pastoral setting has an enameled distinctness commonly found in the work of particular old English painters. There is puerility in Marisa, lying supine, limbs outstretched on the fragrant turf. She feels the vibration of Peki's stride upon the ground. She leaps to her feet, sprints, gazelle-fast, and vanishes from sight into the elder. In leisurely pursuit, traipsing with boyish freedom, he dallies with his thoughts, shaping themselves, and loses her. He soon finds her, picking twigs, vestiges of her sylvan romp, from her tress, in the hollow valley and approaches calmly and coolly. She verbalizes hypocoristic names of exceptional poignance and purity to him that hover through the wood. He is moved. She removes her frock, displaying her starkness that, until this moment, has been concealed from him, like a flower that has unloosed its perianth. Something about the extraordinary loveliness of her form, provocative of lust, deters him from groping her. She is a possessor of senior prettiness, on a magical level, maddening to his senses. Her derriere dimples remind him of molar dents. Recognition of their relationship paralyzes any erotic potential. Her napped genitalial wraith is suspended over him, leaving him in elation. She sprawls on her front, chin propped on her palms. What would it take to break her spell? Pouches are established under her lamps. He gets a glimpse of her crimson sphincteric anemone. He's in petrified delight. Her frontal is ruddy from exertion, coarse crop of bleached mane a mess. He beholds her with hypnotized admiration. Birdsong strains swell and sink, the avian melodies floating forth from the leafy birches and beeches. The tributary teems with marigold and foxglove. He gazes intently and rapturously at her. They are together as the head and tail of a snake. Surreptitiously he glances at his watch, waiting patiently. The beauty of the state of affairs with her indisputably has to find its rationale in some progression of occurrences beyond the meager satisfaction of the fleeting moment, he thinks. Rolling onto her back, she regards the organic patterns of tree branches and plant leaves and the diverse elements of earth and water. The shade suppresses her pallor, like the pallidity of a corpse that lies in shadow. Dead-still, he vocalizes she should put on her things. She does. Her hand accepts his. They walk side by side through fresh shoots of hawthorn and reach a navigable lane. An estuary has a steel-grayness. Twilight has a blueness as though the sky has lowered. Heaven is a slate slab.

There's an unembarrassed quietness between them. The marinescape is in the background. Their steps are uneven and hurried as they gain access to the apartment. Peki pops a peppermint jawbreaker into his mouth, and feels a lack of energy. Marisa doffs her dress and dons a fur coat and hush puppies. She holds misfortune in her basset eyes. In her company, he feels not unlike a lost child that is suddenly found; darkness becomes light. In attendance on the stairwell, at the bulletin board, she smiles like a skull. The silence speaks volumes. O Mama, O love, he thinks. Her hair is styled and sprayed. Her grin is forced. He can tell. The birdie woman is all beak and talons. He experiences sensuous pleasure. He falls into an insane fancy, using his diseased imagination, with obsessive intensity. She has milk teeth, plum cheeks, venomous breath, chin vibrissae, a birthmark beneath her eye, and her derma layer has a grit tint. Dehumanized, he knows he is capable of enormities extreme. Is he a veritable psychopath hiding in selfish solitude? A heartless entity pursuing a goal? He feels like a waste product forgotten by God above. His silhouette is soiled. The leather wallet occupying his back pocket is thick as a fist. He believes he deserves to be taken out at dawn, blindfolded, turned to face a wall, and shot. He is disgusted with himself. Dull nausea overcomes him. His mind and soul are troubled. He plunges into tormenting, torturing thoughts. There are many disappointments lately. He's yegg-focused. She is keeping to herself and refusing to share with him. He pictures him as Orpheus and her as Eurydice. He hears them cooing, sees them giving and taking osculations and tactions. Actuality is the dreamer's alibi. There is a chaos of conflicting fantasies. Her sensuality is witchcraft. Her oculi are puffy from sobbing and want of rest. She'd pole-danced (her well-rehearsed routine involving farce and sadism) at the taproom in front of sleazebags the night before and wept afterward at the windmill, tempted to walk into the revolving vanes, in those pestiferous squalls. She plays the lyre, then the dulcimer, after skipping rope. He wants to gorge on her like a pig at a trough. Chalcedonic drops of condensation glint on the windows. Leven forms and fulgurates in a strident spectrum.

Withered leaves flutter down in the vacuum of a gust's departure. The weather is caressing. The Miltonesque megalopolis, in asterisks of showers, is being systematically gentrified within an inch of its life. Birds are songless in a prevalence of primroses on a verdant declivity on the marge of a deciduous forest. A stripped van assumes the shape of a scaffold in the yawning crepuscule, yet retains its steering wheel and front seat. Peki's ambition is to lift himself and Marisa out of prevailing disenfranchisement into community respectability. She is an illusion of miraculous existence. She makes the ground under his feet firm. He finds, in the repetition of each failure to get her, there is a mortification that confirms any subsequent effort would be absurd. The acidulation of nonsuccess eats at him. Futility has dried up the spring of endeavor. Lust is a virus, love is the cure. It is as though his mere presence seems to rip the stitches of her smoothed over, Franken-fleshed composed disposition. He bugles from his fanny and roars out a burp. His heart beats for her. He roams the rooms in maniacal pursuit of her. His perverse cogitations are scrambled. He sickens the oxygen with his breath. A bowl on the table sprouts a bouquet of lollipops. The afternoon is foggy and balmy with periodic sprinkles. His flatus sounds like a cross between pigsqueal and buzzsaw. His thoughts can relieve reality and refer it to fantasy. Inhibition will be forsaken. Problems at the workplace can be forgotten. There's an immense stillness in this enclosed place, their apartment, the structure pulseless and mellow. It sustains, heals. The amplitude of the quietness has a gripping effect on him. In her bedroom, vibrating with nervous energy, he feels like a Norman invading Saxon land. Its furniture, ill-assorted and incongruous, with the oddest objects, projects her essence. Her appearance from the wardrobe, into whose creation so much mysticism must have been invested, shocks something in his soul, a feeling not dissimilar to when he encounters a stunning work of art. His changeling madre, with preternatural powers, is a vampire-fanged, bat-winged harpy with pitiless eyes and hooks for hands, hovering around the gas lamp and quaffing cheap gin out of the bottle, and he is taken down a peg or two by the perfectness of form he sought. The core of his being dissolves in the shade, the experience leaving him soothed well beyond expectation. She's a reflection in nature's mirror. A moue touches the arcs of her chops. She is long, lean, and pale as a paschal candle. She's a phoenix raised out of flames. Would her bud open to leaf? He occupies a mahogany chair as she, black-gowned, pads like a panther. Sound has substance in the warm, crepuscular environment. A spiritual surf carries him along. She is a vision not of this dimension, contained in a commodious calico and wearing secretarial rims. Her olive complexion and magnetic mouth arouse him to the limit of his anxious endurance. His emotion: the spouting up of a white whale. The magic flute of her mouth blows encouraging notes. Her peepers glimmer like a pair of great gems. She stands in front of him and he automatically strokes her knee, like an affectionate automaton. His expression is simultaneously repentant and triumphant. He snatches at her exposed thigh, in scintillant spurts, and gives it a hurried kiss. Her phizog is practically vivid. She sports a mesmerizing smirk. Her openness encourages rather than deters him in the discourse. He looks at her with silent satisfaction. His body quivers like an aquatic specimen, stationary in the shallows, poked with a stick. Her person brings to his nostrils an odor that suggests mud. Waftures of tropical air. His cranium is a coliseum filled with combative ideas. He floats on a stream of cerebration. He hearkens to her with engrossed intensity. He smells potpourri. Her faults and qualities are captivating. They have put that dreadful quarrel behind them. Thank the Lord. Her shrill voice rose to a shriek. He had a sedate, matter-of-fact modulation. Her snide comments about his dwarfism rolled down his back like drops from a frog's as it emerges from a pond. She toes the line and he falls into his traps. Her cheekbones are pronounced, toenails bitten to the quick.

Their patter is incessant and excitable. She charms his irritations away. She punctuates a remark with a nudge in the ribs, and then she turns, with pained, pleading eyes, and avian-wittedly gapes through the misted pane at the grim midget food mart, on the meandrous, pummeled road, in the dismal nulliverse haunted by the ghost of penury. A jittery feeb with a ferox fizzog and red nose lurks in the lot. The hazy-mazy metropolis is astir. What will be the penalty for Peki's sins? Onanism or incest… Seeing himself living his life is like watching a train careen toward a fork in the tracks with too much speed and force for cataclysm not to feel imminent. He is sick of the burden of existence. His tears cease, sobs stop. He has tragic, lamentable lineaments. His brow is quite hot as he stares into vacancy, the gloam gathering. It is as though his universe is torn like it is made of paper. His mother makes his world solid to the touch. Lights of the megapolis (a grimy, Day-Glo inferno) twinkle. A taurine, gas-masked sprog with pendent teats slinks into a diving bell on the sidewalk.

Fat snaps and grease cracks come from the stain-colored, cubby kitchen. Marisa is a whirling dervish of efficiency, multitasking like a roadhouse hash slinger, going from fridge to cabinet to stove in a fluxional sequence of movements. She is sprightly and memorable. Her fingers are ablaze with rings pawn shop-bought. Pots and pans soak in soapless water in the sink. The joint is a puzzle that can't be put back together. Peki, presenting a lamentable figure, sitting in a low, vinyl chair at the uneven table, hitches up his trousers, studying her papier-mâché mush, the roots of his hair icy. Frustration only compounds his appetence. He scrubs his well-shaven chin and stares, in a transcendental gladness and astonishment at her physique and its forbidding trimness. She is the antidote to his poisonous life, the lotus that sprung in his swampy existence. She's hooded and nightied as though she's a member of the Ku Klux Klan, busy in culinary klankraft. It is gymnastic cookery. Carrying the dishes, she steps with an exquisite precaution, throwing a shadow on the linoleumed floor that arrests him, part of an accidental pattern of impressions. He gazes at her umbrose double with suspicion. Why won't she flush the toilet? On and off, he feels as if he is a patient in a lunatic asylum. She has made, with serene complacency, what proves to be the pleasantest meal he has had for some time. He experiences an astounding sense of peacefulness. Her presence accentuates it. He gives her his undivided attention, balloons up behind her, face beseech-side up. Mother and son exchange small talk. He is tired of compensating and compromising. She rattles a few plates. Her tress is now a nest and her body odor is olfactorily evocative of fried meat. He reminds one of a pintsized prizefighter with gypseian pies, or, for that matter, a small, whitewashed stone. His imagination active, he visualizes her sashaying, dishabille in an orangey negligee. He's been peeping on her too much. Obscure thoughts drift on the surface of his mind. A beam of hobish merriment manifests on his mug. Being in the remote room with her, his agitations are slightly alleviated. She proceeds in a capricious way. He scrutinizes the inscrutable and feels somehow remote, disembodied. She drives him to distraction. The sound of her footfalls recalls the creaking of wings. She looks like a puppet pulled by strings, conversing with him with weary politeness, starting appealingly at him. Nothing can disturb his contentment at this juncture. The atmosphere is deliciously smoky and hushed on this placid morning. Vaporously she wavers. A frown clouds her cast. Her personality gives pleasure to him, and he flourishes under its influence. Not being able to taste her sweet misaligned mouth (shut like an oyster shell) is a crushing blow. Her words ring in his ears. He ponders with fascinated interest her fundament and chortles in high glee. His winkle pulses as if it possesses an independent life of its own. Her sleek mane has a carefully brushed part in its center. She combed it. The crusty fan whines. Eighteenth-century prints are fastened to the unframed on the dingy wainscot. Hail is pumpkin seed-sized. Mall's a brick-and-mortar wilderness. A quirked edifice has a gimp gate. A hearse jounces past a capacious garden. Morbidly she goes hither and yon on inflamed feet and using chapped hands. He announces the butter business isn't a going concern anymore; there's profit aplenty realized in the recently upgraded mantequilla. She just nods. It doesn't hurt that he cheats on his taxes and pays the help subtable. He resists vocalizing that part. He is Aeneas with a passion for Dido. She's a flame in an opalescent cosmos. She is transfigured, immortalized. She fills his emptiness. Their eternal bond is shaping itself. They've been going to the movies, wining and dining (sparing no expense), taking photographs, swapping gifts, gamboling in the wanton air, enjoying dancing and music... Is she conceding, or is he conquering? His countenance is rubberized into a screwy expression. He is garbed in a puce-hued habit sufficiently volumetric to cover his deformations, subrationally needing her. He adores her rat-a-tat-tat chuckle. He's committed to keeping the more sinister elements of his character a secret. She clicks her tongue. Her jet orbs shine with inexpressibles and hold the promise of dreams. Starlings, in the celestial sphere, fly, unindividuated, in a loony figure-eight, then swoop up and nosedive in a plummet to hell. Cirri open for the sun to shine. Sparrows carom over the myrtles spread out in a rolling lea, not unlike tiny kites. Marisa struts away to prepare the gooseberry preserves, sipping Asti Spumante out of a juice glass, pulling in her wake the heat of Peki's fire. He wants to feed and water their relationship and have it grow. She is a riddle he knows he can solve. She arbitrarily despoils her body. He takes stock of the situation. He has the sensation of being on the bourn of a psychogenic maelstrom.

Peki's Journal

I'd tempered my braggadocio and machismo and chose to accept humility. There was famine, disease, and savage air assaults. Liberation armies attempted to corral an unruly mob thronging a public square at curfew time. The stench of death brooded over the demolished city. Spain was losing the nameless war. Germany was winning, driving us beyond the border, out of their homeland. America and Japan were acting as referees. An ancient monastery was reduced to ruin by the unrelenting bombardments. She, a piteous sight, filthy, starving, and ragged, idled on the balustrade, patched with lizard-green mold as if she were a Proustian patron in an opera house box. She was a midget, a malformed Venus, and had the fixed look of a dead cat. She cleaved the oxygen with a shrill cry. I gazed without blinking. I climbed up with a simian nimbleness. Her body gave off a faint odor of musty linen and rotten leather. She was unkempt and painted. Her locks were disheveled, visage, plastered with rouge, riddled with pockmarks. Her breath had the saliferous tang of brine to it. My pallor was faded and I had livid lips. She made these flaccid, viscid, muffled sounds, lifting her dress, offering her sorry merchandise. A blue lobster was crawling out of her shaven vagina, which resembled a chunk of rotten meat. She handed me a bouquet of withered flowers. Whereupon she dropped them and rubbed my wrists like a masseuse. The flesh of her belly hung like clothes too big. I bolted, laughing, wanting to weep. The fetid alley reeked as though it was composed of a hundred effluvia.

Glad Mermis

It is an anthropomorphic trash bag that smiles nonstop, with a vox like a soprano singing while gargling shingle.

"All right, what happened?" It asks.

"Not now. I don't want to discuss it," Peki answers, dumping the dead body into the tub. Marisa toils (dejunking upstairs) like Sisyphus, only with a better outcome. Glad Mermis croons a rude strain, turgid and unmemorable, and shouts a friendly insult at Peki, who cringes.

Lead a Butter Life

Healing powers
Butter has the power to heal bruises! Yes, really! Next time you have a contusion, rub some butter on it and watch the magic manifest before your eyes. The scientific secret is this: the phosphates in butter keep your skin vessels from breaking down which, in turn, prevents bruising and any significant swelling.

Squeaks-be-gone
Is that squeaky ceiling fan of yours driving you nuts? Instead of selling your house, simply grab some butter from the fridge, rub it on the squeaky hinges, and voila!

How cheesy
Have you ever had a block of cheese go moldy because you couldn't eat it fast enough? Instead of tossing it, cut off the hard rind and spread some butter over what remains. This will prevent the cheese from getting moldy. (Same goes for onions!) It's a literal lifesaver if you're a passionate dairy fanatic like me!

Behold, butter buffing
Butter can make tarnished things in your household shine bright again. How about that scuffed leather shoe of yours? Or your nice wood floor, with that unfortunate stain? Grab a paper towel, apply some butter onto it, and then rub the affected area with the towel. Let the scuffed item sit for a while and wipe clean – it'll look like new!

Boiling point

Instead of panicking when that pot on the stove starts to boil over, calmly drop in a tablespoon of butter and all that roiling nonsense will come to an instant halt. No more steaming stovetop messes or kitchen hazards.

No more bitter pills to swallow

Ever have trouble swallowing a large pill? Lightly coat that big ol' tablet with butter and then wash it down with a glass of water. The butter will smooth the pill's ride down the hatch, making it a lot easier to ingest. And let's not forget butter's delicious aftertaste!

Sticky situations

Next time your kids "accidentally" get gum in their hair, don't stress. Rub butter over the tangled locks, let the hair absorb the oil, and then gently wipe the butter away with a cloth. Presto! Butter is also perfect for liberating hands from glue or sticky syrups. Just rub a little butter on the stickiness, wash your hands and dry them with a towel.

Body butter

If those dry winter months have your flesh and nails looking and feeling rough, go the body butter route. When dry, cracked skin is craving moisture, butter is a great substitute for lotions. It's also the perfect fix for dry and brittle nails. Just rub some on your nail beds, put on some cotton gloves, and let the butter soak in. After a few hours, your nails will feel brand new. And guess what! You can even use butter as shaving cream.

Jewelry fixes

There are few things in life more frustrating than trying to untangle a necklace or bracelet. But you can rub some butter on the entwined sections and use something pointy to help slide any knots out. If you are trying to remove a ring from a swollen finger, apply some butter to the finger and carefully slide the stubborn thing off.

Keep onions fresh

You can keep a half-used onion fresh by rubbing butter on the cut surface and wrapping the leftover onion in aluminum foil before putting it in the fridge.

Dissolve tar
If you ever happen to get tar on your hands or clothes, smooth the butter onto the tar and it will dissolve instantly. Then you can wash it off.

Shine leather
With a soft cloth and butter apply a small amount of butter on your leather items and polish to a shine.

Hand softener
To keep your hands soft and prevent them from drying, smear a small amount of butter on your hands, rinse off with soap and water, and work it well into cuticles and fingernails.

Shaving cream
For a nice, close smooth shave, spread some butter on wet skin and let the blade glide over your stubble for a close shave.

Remove wax
f you have gum in your hair or wax from your beauty treatment you can rub some butter on the problem area and wash it off with soap and water.

Hair Conditioner
For shiny and healthy hair, shampoo your hair then put a little butter through your hair, comb, and rinse with lukewarm water.

Snow way!
If you apply butter on the blade of your snow shovel, it will help prevent snow from sticking to it, making your work easier when trying to shake away the excess white stuff.

Arianne Orts

She is simultaneously multiple things, like a sphinx. Fresh as a daisy, she pounds down martinis, poured out of a canteen. She's grim and tense. Arianne, in her mid-to-late teens, is carrot-topped, fresh-faced, pug-nosed, snail-shell-eared, and big-boned. She has mournful eyes. He wears a greasy threadbare suit and tie. She is dressed in a frayed jumper she bought at a pawn shop. She admits she's a runaway, escaping from an abusive household, her drunken uncle, and cruel aunt first-class teachers at a prestigious private school. Her siblings, three brothers, and one sister were domineering. Life has dealt her some devastating blows and she has withstood them. Peki comes across as mild and harmless, furtively scoping her suet. He pictures the new jerrybuilt butter-churn that he constructed, the contraption looking like it was a prop plucked out of a steampunk movie. He's always looking to improve his knowledge and skills with mantequilla-making. He is even enrolled in evening business classes at university. These courses are of paramount importance. He educates himself when he chooses. It can be difficult sometimes, succeeding in a city rife with starvation, desperation, and disease, the poor all around. The establishment apparently operates itself, the flow easy and natural. When there are setbacks, he confronts the problems head-on. He's a pertinent part of the real working class. He is wise as a serpent. Peki and Arianne skinny-dip in the sea and sunbathe on the far-stretching sand of the wild beach. Fair individuals stay under protective umbrellas. She talks to him in a slightly combative tone. He knows that she knows that his peepers are on her burly body. She enjoys being admired and confided in.

He confesses he believes in anarchy, that authority should be abolished, and everyone would benefit from disharmony. The disorder will accommodate the public. He's an advocate for violence in society. He makes a brash speech and beats his breast. He carries things to extremes... She rises like steam from a train and steps gingerly, squiffy, dodging the caked dung, sits slumped on the shore, and wriggles her bum. He has the sensation of nonexistence, being unreal, the simulacrum of a manikin, flesh, and blood in a state of dormancy. The pills and liquor only serve to intensify his perception of abstraction. She is seated on a rock, staring at the saltwater, not unlike a mermaid. She's a youth with an adult seriousness. He experiences a voltaic prickle of a charge in his groin, staring at her. They talk and walk on the otherwise quiet trail, and observe rare birds and bugs. Bats hang from branches of the elms like furry fruit. Cloudlets form and unform. She can be equally amusing and annoying. A cinnabar streak in the empyrean gets concealed in a cirrus. Sauntering sardonically, she fesses she believes that fairies exist. They bumblingly negotiate the wooden stairs that lead to the stable loft where she has been staying for a spell. She elbows the ramshackle door open. He pinches her waist and tickles her back and she giggles and bats his mitt away. The wallpaper — rufous berries. An expensive tapestry has paradisal verdure. The ceiling is painted blood-red. There's a set of spindly chairs, high and low shelves of books, and a woven rug on the dark floor, in the narrow room. There are minimal furnishings. They have beefsteaks for supper. The two share a silent, passionate hug, mouth to mouth, belly to belly, both on their knees beside the iron bedstead. He rubs her abdomen as she ties her long, lank hair into a ponytail. His pies are hungry. It is an awkward encounter at first, disrobing clumsily, both blundering and blushing, but they soon become amiable and unabashed. His hands seek and find her private places. And she suspires, clutches her shoulders. He fingers her hidden cavities. Her cunt, below her bulging stomach, reminds him of a trout lying under a stream's shelf. She smells of sour milk. He stinks of rancid fat. Persistently and consistently he feels her up. Specks of dust float in the air. Human odors are tenacious. He is another person with her. She is a brawny beauty. When she thumbs him in his feculent orifice, he feels as if he receives an electrical shock from a live wire in his core.

They don't discuss what they're going to do, it simply happens. Peki is so happy to be here with her. He's over the Underworld of that metropolis. The lovers are monsters, hissing, spitting, and gnashing their teeth, during intercourse. He fucks too fast. Expressionless, Arianne suggests he slow down, and pace himself. She straightens his crookedness. Afterward, under the influence of cannabis, she toasts them crumpets. He crouches between twin uneven pillarets of literary volumes, holding the paper plate of a treacle tart. He is sure he will have daydreams and nightmares about her. This is their utopian universe. He is in dire need of rest and distraction, these past weeks spent in an excess of despair, dealing with Marisa, in addition to the scathing criticisms he received from a former rival in a magazine article review of his store... There is so much of her he cannot apprehend with his limited senses. He sports a satyr smile. Although bulky, she's harmless as a dove. She takes significant pleasure in the power of her newfound independence. It'd be annihilating if she ever found him out. It is imperative that he keep her in the dark. He rises like smoke from a chimney and strays into the pasture. A donkey cart is out front. Peki is narcotized, feeling bodiless, his 'form' transitory and fading, and he chants a chunk of Latin, in a thinner, and subsequently thicker, irreality. He has a dreadful vision of the cops, as beasts, catching him and burying him alive. He will be living, dead. Hey, he's still in a reasonable temper. Arianne's blubber is too plentiful to pass on...

The cumuli separate and the sun shines so clearly to their sight it's as if they've adjusted binocular lenses. The firmament is eft-colored. Peki and Arianne, in a clump of gorse, are alive and well and going about their purposes. He draws his strength from her weakness. She is quite naked. His vermiform winkle writhes like a worm getting skinned. He tells her splendid stories, some true, some false. She succumbs to his charisma. His existence is full and complex and he conveys this articulately. She is neither trusted nor distrusted. His intentions are left unmentioned. She declares her hopes and fears. This is a dreamworld in which she doesn't wish to be awakened. They hold hands and swing them. They are such a unique pair! Their behavior is unreserved, unaltered by an observing presence. He fancies experiencing her. They unwind in a hammock after the lunch of chestnuts and blackberries they brought along in a satchel. He explores her body and investigates her personality. They revel in the peace and quiet. She is like a dryad he met while wandering in the woods. She has intelligent blinkers and large knuckles. Their flirtations are anything but innocent. Her lips are open and his blood races. Ozone wafts. Illumination filters through the leafage, breaking into myriads of lucent particles, creating a mosaic on the ground. Raindrops glimmer in the sunlight. The transpicuous aqua pura laps at a pebbly strand. Woolly sheep munch on cliff-side spinney. The weather becomes soggy and the lovers take refuge in a cave, imposing and imprisoning. Arianne spreads a blanket on the dirt floor. Primitive chalk drawings decorate the stone walls. There is a sum of curiosities and naughtiness. Insects are busy on the earth. This is the couple's magic world, where the stillness seems to have movement. Brightness flares through the foliage. Peki describes tales in detail, potboilers mostly, the plots complicated, as though she's an audience or his muse. His fingernails are grimy. In the cobweb-silver barn, they bowl and then bonk in the hay. Her bottom belches out foul fumes. Her bunghole is reminiscent of red coal. He tunnels further in and deeper down, quick and slow. She has Ivory feet with cobalt veinlets. Her mouth is ostensibly permanently pursed. Her nudity enchants him. Her midsection shivers and contracts and expands. He studies it intently. Ghostly white, it hangs invitingly. Gently he smacks her shaven genitals. Her erectile nipples are wine-reddish. Tenderly he bites them. He grips her horsy hips and she makes a short, guttural sound like a farmyard hen. He mounts her from behind, whereupon She promptly kicks off the foolish flip-flops. The nooky is halting and humpy. There's a rushing and roaring sound in his ears not unlike breakers on the beach. He tongues her pucker and she gasps. They stretch the lovemaking very far. She pants and squeaks as they fornicate in a sort of flurry. His voice is dropped and serious. Her stout physique makes her remarkable in his estimation. Sodomized, splayed, it is artery-freezingly unpleasant for her. It's painful to be penetrated there. The sexual experimentation is extensive. She is stocky and sensual, with bladders for breasts, sturdy arms and legs, meaty hands, and beefy tootsies. Pumped hard, she bares her teeth. Their rhythm falters when she, flushed crimson, half-laughs, half-cries when he licks her anus. His blood rises in his face when she reaches back to cup his cock and balls. Her posterior is perfection. She is bent over and reamed. His prong makes its way inwards and downwards and she wiggles and grunts. She stimulates him appallingly. His stamina is creditable but his finesse is nil. She grins and bears it. The nape of her neck is lanate and vulnerable. She bellows and shudders. He treats her like a life-size wind-up doll. He skewers her crap-encrusted rectum. A strapping giantess, she could be mistaken for a pro wrestler. Incredibly, she collapses into cachinnation. Her skin is solid and she has a sensible countenance. She has this fine towy fuzz on her tailbone. He yells he's sick of being the butt of mockery, tired of the spite, grasping the boiler of her rump, his being a burning furnace. They copulate with abandon. They climax together and lie tragically on the straw in the flax-pale fulgor. Her flabby middle is clay-clammy. Her breath is acrid and her feet have a cheesy fetor. Their hidey-hole is cramped yet cozy. Arianne, composed and dreamy, gets out of the swimming costume and smart cap and into a dressing gown (the hue of a judge's robe) and beetle-black sporty slides, leaning on the folding table. Peki delights in seeing the slight sag of her tummy. Physical attraction floats like dandelion seeds. She is barefoot again and rearranges her limp, strawberry mane. She is like a creature of the deep who took on human form. He wants to flay her buttocks. He has the sense she's a wicked thing, dangerous and wild, which turns him on. She has a vulpine lollop. Her fiery physiognomy is egg-shaped. She has bumps and bruises all over from their shagging sessions, seen because of the oil lamp on the rocking base. Her long hair glistens. She gestures precisely, turns around, and, standing on a heap of sacking, clasps her ankles. And he rims her russet sphincter.

The stench of his pewie is asphyxiating. The whopper stinks of something unspeakable. He sure can be a nasty little turd! Arianne coughs and expresses repulsion. Peki, complexion bereft of bloom, waddles like a woman in labor and takes a slug of tequila from the chipped pottery mug. His manly beard and mustache are dull and bushy. He's fed up with being the single object of people's venom. His pies are puffy from too much alcohol and not enough sleep. He admires and desires her.

She sweeps up moldy crumbs. They converse incessantly. Her company is appreciated. Alien and grungy, his visage plaster-pale, he is curled like an unborn baby on the creaky couch after violently vomiting into the can. The wet weather is harsh. The duo lives not unlike fugitives. The spiderwebbed pane is ill-fitting in the structure, with a crocheted drape over it. The floor is uneven. Arianne massages his hunched, unresponsive shoulders. Peki is nauseous. He has grief and rage inside. She puts the bowl of forget-me-nots on the dresser. His condition has severed their connection. He's got to get back on track; he's gone off the rails. She makes him a screwdriver with insufficient vodka and OJ. He is odder and jerkier around her, and with a vacant gaze. On the cordless phone with his store manager, a capable older gent, he encourages the termination of a youthful employee, a major hazard, and is satisfied with the latest profit numbers that just came in. The master plan for building his business is working out. What he accomplishes with the Butyrum creation cannot be taught in his view. It can only be acquired with ceaseless practice. There are amateurs and there are professionals. Arianne prepares tomato soup with onion and barley. Peki assesses her sebaceous surplus. He could use scissors as a weapon… Her undies are in holes and she's discalceated. She glugs homemade rotgut out of a jug. She moves around the kitchenette fast. She is sexy, and more. Shampooed, her hair is a luxuriant mass. Her figure is rounded out. She shows no sign of noticing him gawking at her as she ponderously struts. Stomping about, she is a miracle of economic movement, considering her girth. Her gait belies her heft. He's clad in a monk's habit. He feels as if his stomach is an octopus, his intestines its tentacles, the cephalopod mollusk quivering through the water. They eat oysters and discuss Goya. She gives him a measured glance when he exposes himself. Their routine is developing casually. An arachnoid lady, with a frizzy postiche and multiple opalescent oculi, spins silvery threads on the side of a wrecked Art Nouveau edifice, adjacent to a Sicilian palace. She is prettily dressed and a tad grubby. Arianne is impassive and still as a statue in the blond bracken. She is spicy and desirable. She increasingly impresses him. Peki stares at her with silly and touching fondness. They celebrate the flaming season in a swelter of intercourse. And he thereupon decorates her supine form with flowers in the thicket, so she suggests Botticelli's Flora. He values the intricacy and delicacy of her vagina and compliments her cast-off clothes, which pleases her at a certain subliminal level. Her smile is sweet, albeit empty. She gesticulates as though offering a benison. Stirred, he surveys her thickset physique. He could care less about the trim, twig-limbed, fine-waisted fairer sex. Her cream-colored derma layer is exquisite. They jaunt at a rapid pace along the rivulet. A blush mounts from her ample bosom to her bull's neck. He is not lovely to look at. He wonders whether he arouses her indifference or revulsion. They fall into each other's arms, torsos grinding with gratifying urgency. Without hindrance, they flourish. Their spontaneity is deliberate. They are passionately mechanical. Before, her loneliness was unbearable. Now he's here. It is good. They fit together splendidly. Arianne is sublimely placid. The galootress is gorgeous. Peki scrutinizes the slackness of her midriff. She undoes his belt. He unbuttons her blouse. He can't keep his mitts to himself. Her dugs are profound in their presentation. Her clever fingers feel his rod and relieve it. He comes with a full-throated call. He rests his brow intimately on her shoulder and desperately whispers he "steadily adores" her. She sprawls in the long, roughly mown grass, garbed in her knickers, and flexes her stubby toes next to the formal garden and unkempt hedges invaded by brambles. Her wrists, in the limelight, are acceptable. Her heavy face is nice. They surge not unlike waves of the sea. He peels her down as if she's a dressmaker's dummy. Shadows are sinister. She squats, cross-legged, shapely thighs and fleshly calves stubbled, mane flying. He performs cunnilingus on her, and she becomes irked by the constant repetition. Hers is a sham-orgasm.

Sunburned, on this squally noonday, Arianne, swathed in grayish-white sheets of paper towel, like dripping bandages, some strips indicating bindings, sticking to the adhesive lotion slathered on her ruddy skin, could be mistaken for a plaster sculpture of a human being. Her inactivity is unacceptable to her, mooning aimlessly around the room. Unemployed, she is anxious. He wouldn't dare hire her, even for a meager clerk or cashier position at the shop because he knows what he will end up doing to her. Peki is cocooned in a quilt. He recollects his memories as he might dream, endeavoring to find meaning in the images. She's a puffy-lipped cutie-pie with damask soles. The drizzle makes hissing sounds like a hot blade coming into contact with liquid. A building in the distance is in a turmoil of construction. He removes her wrappings, as per her request. She ambulates as though she is sleepwalking playacting. With her, there is much life and light. He's glad to get out of the miasma of his previous existence and glow in her aura. He doesn't miss that filthy city one iota. Her blinders glisten with magic. Her public hair is golden not unlike sunlight, upper thighs transparent as ice. She is ripe as a mango. She has fresh flesh and a captivating self-consciousness. Arguments rage and love is made. She experiences fear and desire, aware of the vagaries of his temperament. She firmly and rudely rejects his brassy, ballsy overtures. The two are going through a contentious period. She doesn't mind being alone. She is paralyzed with shyness when he mentions the ideas of bondage and sodomy. He can't keep his perverse fantasies to himself! Their hanky-panky, in his opinion, has felt time-restrictive and unreal, their verbal communication unnatural. Peki reflects on the collection of curios in the cabinet. The sink is a dreadful mess with all of the dirty dishes. Arianne plaits her honey hair (excessively long and not very clean) in a mane, feathery lashes cast down. She has on a sky-blue tank top, lacy panties, and serviceable but worn slippers. She is quite attractive and well-shaped. She has such a sweet and innocent front. Coupling with him over the course of the week, she has felt like an amatory apprentice, as if she's learning the ropes. There's a smoochy interlude. Her beanbags are creamy-colored, nipples salmon-pink. She hunkers down and reveals an unexpected flair for fellatio. His mop blows in the gusts coming off the brine. He pats her back. He earns his keep by entertaining her. She is his "buxom babe." He feels as though he's been held at arm's length lately. Sometimes it seems as if she is making fun of him… He makes more overt advances and she vehemently rebuffs him, on the pretext of checking provisions. They have fruit punch, coleslaw, lobster salad, and macaroons. Then they make tender small talk, dance, joke, and flirt. He goes swoony and feels a jump in his loins. He concentrates furiously on her foot and imagines his head lurking under it like a fish under a stone. Arianne approaches hares and pheasants in the plowed meadow. And she contemplates pike and trout in the crystalline stream. She is knock-kneed and pigeon-toed. Her cellulite looks like pallid belts of turf that were stabbed by predatory beaks. She is perfectly proportioned in his book. Peki listens to the euphonious birdsong in the copse and on the hillocks. Like a wild thing, he picks up her distinctive scent. He skillfully approaches the recumbent demi-goddess, emerging, snuffling, like a badger in the evening, to lose himself in her nether regions. His intent is unalterable. He comprehends her needs and limitations. Both suffer injuries and setbacks during the funny business, as though it's a gallant battle, each striving and struggling to gain an advantage. She becomes calm and quiet, feeling like prey for the hunter. He is cunning and pertinacious. He shudders and ejaculates, keens in ecstasy, and rolls beside her. They companionably converse, and exchange views on the planets and the constellations, in the reeds and buttercups and petalous confetti on the banks of a river. She espies a marten and a raven at various points in the discourse. She arises and wades into the delicious brown-green water. It is warm on top and cool under. He is fixated on her and touches his member with a precautionary palm as if the appendage hurts. She splashes, making, in the coruscation, a rainbowed crest, and the floating lilies scatter. Snarling and sneering, she calls her cantaloupes "the ugliest abortions." She has swings of mood, copes with spells of black depression. He understands she has a difficult disposition. His squidge makes this sluicing sonance. Winds whip. Sun is achingly luminous in the draggled cirri. She is in over her haunches, waist-deep now, arms moving like a windmill. The currents are treacherous. Her hands slap on the surface like paddles, trunk lurching, steps mincing. Ultimately, they smoke hash.

Arianne, in the midsummer sun, inhabits the bed, seated upright on crisp sheets and a blanket embroidered with numerous mutes shades, her abdomen, in this position, washboard-semblant — ruckled and ridged. Peki grins evilly at her. And she glares and grumbles. He realizes, with a sudden shock, that he hasn't seen Marisa in over a week. He isn't longing to return to the pother of the metropolis. A glint of interest in her appears in his eye, beholding her husky beauteousness. She is endlessly fascinating, angel-faced, veiled in perspiration. He drinks and smokes and explores her. She's adrenalized and afraid. He has the sensation that this is a reconstructed reality, an artificial paradise, feeling as though this is land beyond the ocean and desert. She is an amazon in a negligee, seemingly sculpted in marble and bronze. She's a chimera being coaxed out of inertia. He possesses a loitering suggestiveness and wickedness. His fizzog is intent in the swirling smoke. He's self-assured and eager. She is agreeably avoirdupois, her integument olive in the red-gold emanation. Their voices are earnest and ironic. Egg-bluish vista. Peki is strung up in the unconsummated tension between them. He wants to taste those nectarean juices of hers, to witness her flushed with pleasure. Arianne snickers when he grips her hips. He sniffs her armpits, not unlike a hunting hound. She receives a voltaic prickle in her groin. He smells the fragrance of potpourri as she applies mascara and rouge. He envisages her wound in filigree vines, her shape shifting in the fulgor. He imagines himself as being a knight, her a damsel. She gazes into the vacant and unknown. She has an instinct to be secretive. He craves her apertures, protuberances, and clefts. She looks, unfocused, in his direction. They squabble lucidly, and with wit and exasperation, while she cooks the meal, consisting of beet stew and boiled yams, on an alcohol burner. She looks like a living statue at the Louvre. Neither side will concede. They're twitchy and harsh. She accuses him of being "corrupt and a corrupter," to which he replies he is into "venereal variation," and "orgiastic excess." They dine.

The two dawdle on the bottle-green grass by the channel waters. Amethyst welkin. Solid crags and medieval towers, baroque and rococo, and a Jacobean country abode, melt into mist. The couple visits a puppet theater (the saga scenes are virtually Shakespearean) and a toy booth in town, en route to picking up supplies. There's a display of gigantic dolls' houses, with glass and pagoda roofs, the market exhibitions idiosyncratic and exorbitant, flamboyant and artificial. A miscellany of aesthetic delights, such as a rich collection of historic art and woodworks of Hungarian ash with copper inlay, are on display. There are countless fashionable men and women. Factories belch perceivable pollution. Next to a telephone kiosk, Peki abruptly delivers a tirade, disconcerting and incendiary, creating a serious situation, and Arianne, confused, pulls him away. Acid-tripping, he notices the Versailles-ish fountain spraying liquiform diamonds. Buildings transform themselves into sapphirine and topazine hippogriffs. Vehicles transmogrify into chariots. Variegated cumuli turn into shimmering serpents. Citizens surf on waves of pavement. A rainbow is pouring molten lava. Decrepit shadows of malign spiders scurry across the street. The LSD is an animating force. An omnibus is drawn by a dozen zebras. A cyborg transformista with turquoise pigtails and wearing Prada heels is helium-voiced, larger-than-life, towering on forbidding mechanized prosthetic stilts and barely balanced on a colossal plinth. A phantasmagorical diorama serves as a backdrop. Her burp rumbles like a bulldozer in a pachinko parlor. Her queefing sounds like Kevlar-coated reggaeton, trap-influenced grooves spleen-crushing, rhythms shuddering violently, crisp, clipped percussion arrayed into loping dembow beats swimming with plangent synth melodies, plunging bass, and turbocharged hissing breath… With swaggering confidence, she adopts a sing-song tone that bounces like a slow-motion yo-yo and overflows with sass. Her spoken-word performance sounds like processed vocals that screech like loosed balloons and blat like deliquescing kazoos. It's a swarming, sludgy sound, like a beehive in a tarpit. Her clarion falsetto could shatter glass. Her intonation is a Windex smear over a precip-spattered piano and bear-trap drums, then changing into a lovely little synthesizer lullaby, like a music box from the future mixed with ambient techno. She is pop-primed, fierce, self-possessed, a being of her own creation… Peki is surprised and delighted when Arianne flashes her brassiered boobs in the side alley, in proximity to the Viennese eatery and quaint estaminet. His nerves are chock-full of electricity. She wishes to talk about birth control. He can't even think straight. He is worried he has recklessly introduced syphilis to her body. The sides of his hair flap like wings. Their reflections are repeated, in many angles, in the store windows, making a faux infinitude of the pair. Her rounded rear is visible in the clinging cotton garment, a garnet miniskirt. A cloud of midges is over her head. The police are snooping about. It is stiflingly hot, and, standing at the municipal library's fence, he feels like this is Rodin's 'Gates of Hell' masterpiece. He decides that she cannot be any part of the massive mission in his life, the whole vision, which is to conquer the kingdom with mantequilla. This place is a pickpocket's dream come true, with all of the mortal congestion.

They coexist in their mutually imaginary universe. Peki is alternately neurotic and grumpy, tied in a moral knot he can't undo. Muddle-headed and madder than most, his behavior switches from ludicrous to horrid. Gloomily he swigs cognac, feeling like a boor and an ignoramus, strange fruit with a silly shape. He glances askance at the ceramic clock, decorated with pouting cupids, clustered with glazed bees, and stag beetles in regular intervals, on its carved pedestal, studded with roundels of crystals. The sage-greenish vase beside it on the shelf is painted with dragons, fauns, harpies, dolphins, and dragonflies. So much artifice and enchantment... He considers the gamine to be compelling and arousing. There are angry cerise blotches on Arianne's paunch, ones she tried (unsuccessfully) to hide with a powdery substance. She demonstrates with mime sucking him off to shake him out of his doldrums. He's homesick, missing his Mama. She is his other half, his second self. Without her, it's as if he's carrying water in a sieve. He chuckles and pantos climax. She is bright and gleaming, ingesting sherbert out of a little glass and imbibing lemonade out of a pond bowl, wrapped in a whine-stained coverlet. He envisions them conjoined, in their otherworld, in an exact visual reproduction of copulation. Peacock-blue horizon. Clouds are moth-grey. He envies her, for she is lively and sociable, lovely and excitable. Resentment (on his part) is already setting in. She inhabits his dreams, whether he is awake or asleep. Her overpowering sensuality has a poignant effect on him, negative and positive. His frozen serpent thaws. Her face is reddened, body dampened, holds a cushion with Japanesey flowers on it. She takes off her celadon socks, her large feet strawberry-pink, and with the sickly stink of orris root. She is breathtakingly attractive, he thinks. Her guffaw is deep when he tweaks her behind. Putting on a polka dot jumper, Arianne flushes like fire when he attempts to coerce her into performing a sexual act she finds disgustful. It includes feces and urine. She thinks he's a monstrous pervert. Suddenly, she can't stand the sight or stink of him. Peki wants to shove her anemone brooch up where the sun doesn't shine. Her glabrous pudendum reminds him of a tulip denuded of its petals. He resists the temptation to describe the nightmare he had about dying and dead geriatric males and females in various states of dress and undress, and children in extremis, in a conical pile. A rangy, bony-faced vampiress, wearing a frock coat and beret, head tilted at an awkward angle, fingers clenched and toes balled, shone palely. Her hair was dark and straight and she scowled. Her fangs looked fake, like plastic. Her bare legs were splayed, skin like putty, slit showing, eyes bulging and wistful. She situated herself diagonally across a jointed mannequin with no sex in a pavilion. She had a sharp nose and serrated lips. Her ankles and wrists appeared to have been lovingly chiseled. Apes, mermen, mermaids, and warriors smiled and sprawled. She had the lifelessness of an unanimated automaton. She was damnably discomfited, had these wild jerky movements, making stabbing gestures. Her back arched, and her tresses flowed like a black kahuna. Was she a denizen of the underworld or its ruler? Her rattling respirations sounded like dried leaves in breezes. Meanwhile, the swarming forms of the blessed and the damned writhed, howled, pursued, and fled. The entire scene was like Dante by way of Pasolini — a filmed pornographic 'Circle of Hell.' The corpse with canine teeth metamorphosed. She had a death's head, flaccid breasts, a bag of stomach, shriveled bottom, and withered limbs... Arianne is alert and benign. Peki adores her attitude and build and sulky phiz. The space flares with lamplight. He's assertive. She is amiable. There's a confusion of mephitis: food, feet, breath, and gas, not to mention bodily odors. She plunks on an ample sofa adorned with cabbage roses near the huge mirror. He tends the furnace, primitive prurience on his brain. She inhales and exhales tobacco and pours herself some champagne. He bends before her, feeling the weight and warmth of her bosom. The fuck is sensible and efficient. And he comes quickly. She is unaware of the danger of his disease. Her pleasuring herself revives him in no time. She holds his scrotum like the apple from the tree of the knowledge of Good and Evil. He's a fork-tongued snake staring with satisfaction. Her mane crackles with electricity, gyrating lewdly furling and unfurling on the soiled mattress, illumined by the magic lantern on the low table. The room has become a theatrical box... Peki clutches her and she's compliant. Arianne is a resplendent and voluptuous ingenue. She's incandescent and unconsumed. His blood is magma, chest an oven of a holocaust, oral cavity a hell-mouth. She covers herself with a shawl with a frilled hem, rolls over, and drifts off. She snores loudly.

Arianne is suffering from multiple sclerosis and opioid addiction. She's wearing a handed-down, reasonably sober, shepherdessy smock embroidered with blossoms that doesn't fit her exactly; it's a bit tight. And she has on these dove-hued baskety clogs that are too small for her big feet, destroying them with scrapes on her heels and abrasions on her toes. She doesn't care; she is partial to the style. Peki's comments about her appearance are complimentary. She is a provocation to his sight. He guzzles stout. She approves of his presence. She wishes to be used, manhandled, desired passionately, and made love to. She swallows sherry. Larks sing in the dismal marsh with its dun air. Waters are mirror-calm. Trees are windblown. Her gait is a hastening march, getting the supper of crab cakes, potato salad, and scones with gooseberry jam ready. He admires her culinary achievements. She clears up, padding around nude, and sits on the upholstered chair alone to sew. A haze of grit hangs in the place. He puts the wire net on the window to keep out the flies, bored to exhaustion. Sediment coats the pane. He hallucinates her as a griffon, the creature quite threatening. She is an obscene chimera, a faceless fantasm, ecstatic when she chances upon her favorite recipe for jelly. With her, his metamorphosis is complete — the grub has turned into a butterfly. The lavatory is an echoing empty sarcophagus. Arianne has a catty smirk, stands proudly naked, balanced on chunky legs, has red rubbed blotches all over her, made by him. She looks at clothing as being oppressive, and confining. A somatic need possesses her. She polishes off the cream soup and sugar cookies. Peki imagines her as being a mighty china doll. He regards her with mild curiosity and produces a condom like a conjuror. She titters. She's extremely pretty and brimming with exuberance. She is just right. He's in awe of her. She looks like a Flemish painting of a saint. She observes his observations. She droops perfectly. Intercourse is vital at this delicate point in the frantic foreplay. He makes the suggestion. She nods in agreement. She is satisfied that he is interested and interesting. They break the day with rumpy-pumpy. Several of her spoken sentences go unfinished, trailing off as he boffs her. She stares up at the whitewashed ceiling. She expects something different and secret and isn't disappointed, contorted into extreme positions, every hole, crack, and canal exposed graphically, during the sexual congress. He kisses and caresses her upper and lower lips. She's on her back, thrusting her pelvis up, her butt tongued. She promises that her pussy will be kept open for him. The repeated penetrations are economical and precise. Male and female organs separate and join. Their positions are possible and impossible. The coupling is gentle and brutal. Their energy is ferocious. Arms and legs waver, torsi thrash. Peki defiles her milk-skinned body in the dusty light. Distress flickers across Arianne's countenance when he nibbles on her nipples. Pleasure for both is intense. His hand slides under her botty, not unlike a dunnock scuttering under a shrub. Her corporeal solidity delights his imagination. Disadvantaged, held down on the dusky carpet, she is unsettled. She expresses surprise when he smacks her bingy with his palm, the flab jiggling like Jell-O. He takes a second to put an enamel pendant in her navel. She shrieks self-consciously. He's dulled, or dimmed, on account of inadequate radiance. She stretches, majestically splayed, and smirks kittenishly. He conducts the coitus. She is an angel and he is a demon. He performs miracles on her genitals, orally and digitally. Her smashed tootsies, shoebox-sized, have bunions and lumps. Worked up, she speaks fervidly. There is something improper about their intimacy, she deems. He's her lord and master. He still has on the unlaced clodhoppers. He withdraws his prick for a moment, his prepuce pointing like an arrow. She frowns and murmurs when he enters and exits her cunt with bunched fingers. She is neither pleased nor unpleased. Her axillae smell like suede. When it comes to her sweet spots, he is uncannily accurate. She's aroused and disturbed when his indexer contacts her pucker. She has the expression of someone considering an objection... Later, they take bicycle rides and trudge in the cornfield full of heat and humidity, finishing off the freshly baked brown bread, under the griseous overcast. A canescent, thewy farmer greets them civilly. His tractor chugs, with a series of spluttering petroleum flatus.

Time ticks on. Peki, the maestro of mantequilla, staggers into the gloaming, silently and without warning, and vanishes, leaving as suddenly and mysteriously as he had come. He needed a change of scenery and felt trapped in a cage. He's got a lot of responsibilities that require his attention. The disagreement with Arianne lacked any such sugar to help its medicine go down, so the entire dispute was a bitter, nasty pill. The two needed to have a little talk concerning his impending departure. He left a loving note and latte for her on the nightstand. His return is inevitable.

Sparkling stars are insect eyes. Moon's like a bubble of blood. The forest has a fairytale bewitchment. Human crush like army ants in the city. He is the goose that lays the golden eggs upon which Marisa depends. With a mind for butter-making like an intricate mechanism that works to faultless perfection, rarely does he put a foot wrong, taking inspiration from the history of the spread to bring one of the greatest products ever made to the market. He treats his Butyrum (THE game-changing gateway drug to the fatty edible substance) as a living organism, and, when he gets to the lab, he reaches through the wooden crate to press the sticks and tubs as though ensuring they are still alive. The commodity represents creation and new beginnings. The cranked music has a mix of moaning guitars, thumping bass, pounding drums, winding melodies, and a groove so insistent it could induce delirium. He slithers about the stage, supporting various vats, like an escapee from a Bob Fosse dance routine.

Bernard Dib

The scrotiform-faced, octopus-brained roof-fiddler, named Bernard Dib, a spastical lummox and sensitive soul of socialist persuasion, has skin that is green as jealousy. His upper atmospheric excursion is fueled by nepenthes. The stench of butchery from the poultry shop finds him. Factories regorge smoke. Streets swarm with the citizenry. Sun's the open mouth of Hell. The festive town is smeared with smaze. Next to the fire escape that has something of the makeshift about it, Bernard trains his juggling eyes upon the subject of his curiosity: a charming dumpling of a mime, that practitioner of the gesticulative art, wearing a revealing costume of vivid magenta, pork pie hat deliberately aslant, ostrich-feather boa, and rhinestone-encrusted ballet slippers, Inessa Zadorov, putting on quite a show in the fish market for an oohing and aahing audience. Her inexpensive perfume is introduced to his nostrils. She notices his expectant gaze. And her smirk is not unmischievous. He wants to get closer to her than her own shadow. Then he gobbles vision-producing shrooms on the sly and soon remembers that last night he slumbered inside a snake that had slowly swallowed him whole in the foggy forest. Thankfully, the reticulated python left him undigested. The darn thing served well as a sleeping bag! This event took place after the kerfuffle with the Cactus Kid and his hippopotamine henchwoman on them thar adenoid-looking hills. A bad wind blows from his backside. In stomachical distress, he unbuttons and unzips his trousers in preparation for a lavatorial charge. Litter is adrift, in fitful gusts, in cloudy patterns in an earthly empyrean of the parking lot. Leafy trees are atweet with avian badinage. Thunder sounds not unlike cracks of doom. Stars explode like those gag cigars advertised in vintage comic books. The circus sea becomes crowded as colorful ships of all kinds arrive and depart. Lunarly whiffle ball gives new meaning to the term 'moon shot.' Following Inessa's performance, in urticating, aureate light, Bernard approaches and tells her of his adventures as a spitballer assassin, describing, in detail, the special straw, an ingenious invention really, with its cylinder, piston, and spring system for compressing a charge of air to send forth small-caliber shot of balled, saliva-sodden, poisonous paper at the intended target. A pimped-out gasbag was his conveyance of choice on certain clandestine missions. After bumping off the gonzoid blind lifeguard, he swore his liquidating days were officially done. He feels self-conscious about his unkempt beard and fulvescent gnashers. She has a mass of fair hair. Finally, she punctuates her silence with speech, in garbles of a foreign tongue. Her voice is booze-and-cigarette affected. He realizes now that he took a wrong turn in the sideways timeline. Peki promptly introduces himself.

Isis Mensah

There are hookers of all shapes and sizes to satisfy any preference, going in and out of the massage parlor, which is an adobe house. Some, fiery-tongued, are positioned in a row as vultures lining a scarp, the flock of floozies dedicated to public service. The oldest is maybe forty, the youngest fourteen. A chicken stalks on the corner, clucking and pecking at crumbs left on the curb. The fleece on Peki's chest is flattened by the weight of his perspiration. His innards feel like ground glass, trailing a thickset mulatta, Isis Mensah, a whore. He looks like he's chasing a blue plate special; but not the perfunctory kind from some random diner in suburbia — we're talking Aunt Meg's special here. Round about midnight, in an isolated district, his nightstick wallops the back of her neck and she crumples. Stunned, on her hands and knees, she whimpers. He lays into her, knocks her around, and pounds her to the ground, with its lush verdancy. He crouches, leans forward, yanks her head back by the hair, and quickly slashes her throat with a switchblade. Her eyes bulge and roll and she makes these horrific gurgling sounds. He has the urgent need to chunder when she writhes and shrieks. He rips off her tunic, slings her onto the woodchucks, and pins her. She begs and cries as he penetrates her, causing her passage to expand. She is nothing but a diseased sow to him. She's in incomprehensible anguish. His lower lip quivers. He stops thrusting. Sweat trickles down his temples. She seems astonished and confused. Her lamps are clouded and his are glazed. She is paralyzed in shock and agony. An expression of wonder flashes on her face. She emits a guttural croak, whereupon he whispers words of comfort to her as she dies. He sidles swiftly and quietly away, ducking into the shrub. When he returns, he squats and strokes her plump but unprepossessing tit. Her nombril is hidden by pleats of flab. The flesh of her fat thighs is coarse. She's got dainty feet. Spasms of regret ripple through his heart. Her calves have impressive muscularity. A quiver of terror races up his spine. She has amber eyes, a broadish nose, full lips, and frizzy fro, dyed ginger. He watches her perish with a sense of desperate awe. He topples backward and begins to blub. He sits on a log, retching, and shivering. She was an avid reader of risqué romance novels. The clientage sought her company as if by gravitational force. She was exotic and naughty. He studies her like he is deciphering runes. Her phizog is alien and impersonal. He experiences dyspepsia and disgust. It is a gruesome sight. Isis's bleached teeth gleam in the moonlight. Peki knows he's a brutal barbarian conducting a bloody campaign of violence in the community. When he set out that evening, he wasn't sure what he was going to do or how he was going to do it. What he was certain of was that he had a relentless determination to obtain more human fat, a precious and prized commodity, to produce more products. Profit is of paramount importance. The pain he inflicts, although regrettable, has a point to it. His exploits cause carnage. Desperation spurs him on to such inconceivable extremes. He attains feats of unfathomable lunacy. He violates and mutilates her. And he carries her off, carefully, as a kidnapped child, wrapped in a blanket, already ruminating over his next move. He starts with every single noise he hears, stumbling through the dense darkness of the jungly region, the victim's hand incessantly hitting the same spot above his kidneys with his every tramp. She grows heavier, and he holds her, doggedly, on his shoulder, during the horrendous trek through the suppressive territory. He soon falls asleep against a citrus tree, among pedigree horses grazing in the pastureland. He awakes during the night to a goat nudging him. He shoos it. The kid canters a couple of yards in comic surprise. With excitement and guilt, Peki caresses the ankle of Isis. He trips, regains his balance, and breaks into a trot, afraid of the day dawning. A perspiry torrent pours down his brow into his eyes, blinding him. He's a land mine, waiting to be stepped on, and exploding. Life is war. The death of an innocent is collateral damage. The recent events have conspired to disrupt his domestic and social existence severely. He swills rum out of a canteen and is seemingly battle-torn. He is a wunderkind enfant terrible, alive and killing.

Emmeline Knickerbocker

Emmeline remembers kissing her alluring cousin on the balcony. He became as still as a corpse. The fixity of his stare could have penetrated steel. Her complexion was crimson with arousal, body tremulous with fervency... The firmament has something sublime in its softness and clarity, a certain simplicity and grandeur. Several clouds move in concentric circles like the ripples of eddies on the surface of the ocean. She is the manageress of a place of ill repute and looks like a paper knife of a human being. Boughs are reminiscent of limbs deformed by arthritis. Cyanic waves suggest an undulatory range of knolls. The field is rich and vibrant in hue from the dew's saturation. She struts on the sidewalk like a panther. Her sweaty hands, with their silken texture, are smooth and slippery as water lilies. She possesses a bewitching beauty. Anthropoid salmon swim upstream on the street of the city. Ideas flow in her mind, not unlike leaves down a waterfall. She's half an angel and half an animal. She can be more emotional than cerebral. Her cheeks are a pair of milk-white spherules. The air has a purity that is spirituous to her. She talks to herself, her inflection as delicate and exultant as a nightingale's song. She nourishes bitter grievances and harbors black thoughts. Would he again be deaf to her overtures? Emmeline imagines he is Romeo and she is Juliet. She's starving for solid viands. Oily puddles look like scales of sardines. The countryside suggests a watercolor by a master. She sees Peki, his powerful physique impressive. The sound of his footsteps is audible, and she auscultates it. Shivers are sent through her entire frame. The rhyme of the language and the rhythm of his square-toed shoes are not devoid of significance. The effect this has on her is unsettling. She is an elemental thing. His patience in waiting for a potential victim for human fat has dwindled as a candle melted to its holder. This nonstop rollercoaster ride is getting old. He stubbornly struggles with his conscience not to allow his guilt for committing these appalling sins to prevent him from proceeding as planned. Her ambulating is recollective of automatic motion. And he imagines clobbering her. He buzzes like a hornet and she bleats like a sheep. His nails press into his palms. She has a warm glow about her. He helps himself to a slice of bread and butter and an oblong bottle of ginger beer. Cogitations shoot in his noggin as stars through space. What would it take to be with her? The sluice of decency raised, the flood of indecency following... Peki lowers his guard down like a drawbridge over the current of inhibition. He pictures absorbing her like an anemone an aquatic tidbit. He is shunned, whereas she is, chances are, sought after. Unfair! His eyes are languorous with enchantment as hers are candescent with excitement. His forehead is knitted into a frown. They are each other's true love, he thinks. He evaluates every move she makes. Emmeline has wavy hair, a sinuous waist, and boyish hips, her haunches hanging like a drowned person's clothes, deep-set somber orbs, and a mouth like a knife-cut in white cloth over cardinal crystal. He stares at her like a dog at its mistress. She's an unbelievable attraction of ephemeral glory. He would not miss a date with her for all the riches in the world, his pleasure at the prospect poisoned by the image of his mother in his noodle. His muscle twinges are like nettle-stings. He has spasms of anger and disgust in this agitated twilight. His sobbing has the sound of a vivisected cur. He looks into vacancy, face a dusky red, peepers with a dazed, ensorcerized aspect, the pot and booze mounting to his brain. He has a rugose neck, gnarled shoulders, knotty back, and is in a semi-comatose state. The humble den recalls a shipwreck, or it was damaged in an earthquake. He consults the barometer, keeps a weather eye wide open, worried that a storm could threaten the workflow. He has a bone to pick with his Mama after she gave him an over-the-top dressing-down, saying, emphatically, that he was a dipstick and had this Machiavellian guile. Her irregularities of conduct are unacceptable. With her, he's like a lion-tamer who gives the impression that he's intimidated by the animal. She is a problematic reef in his maritime life. The smack she put on his cheek constituted a thank-offering for him abiding her. His whole manner exuded a clement gravity. She senses things with extraordinary keenness. A film beclouds his pies. He has gone astray and cannot mend his ways. He is not in a situation of self-denial — he is cognizant of the vileness of his comport-ment. Self-tyrannous, and shocked by his ungodly tactics, he flagellates himself with a cane. He is a public menace no one knows about. He ventrilocates Marisa's voice.

Jorge

Trails from a planes are like pale scars from pregnancies on the abdominal azure. A bellboy, this robust ragamuffin with roseate cheeks carries a vase with a feather duster, a cheery visage suffused with ironic curiosity. Coiffures of cirri. Electric currents of excitement charge through Peki and Jorge, defacing the Stalinesque edifices. Ill-bred Jorge, all flirt and flooze at this particular point, dressed in a fake fur coat, rosy boxers, and bra underneath, torn fishnet stockings, and clogs. Peki finishes spray painting graffiti against the government while Jorge bitches about the fact they've been reduced to reserves in the cell group (that doesn't exist). They are insignificant small fry, longer big fish. She says their diminished status is a problem that needs to be nipped in the bud. She becomes comically kittenish. Her heavily mascaraed eyelashes remind him of insectoid legs. Narcotized, her doe's oculi droop. She writes sarcastic slogans on the brick of a Swiss Bank. Her cigarette smoke swirls slowly. She gets sadistic pleasure out of busting his balls. Greasy tumult of walkers and drivers. Habitually he searches for his shadow, can't believe it's gone. It was a penumbral potter that modeled his slender shape in ebony. Jorge frolics beside him, on the grubby cement, rubbing his face in it. He has long since considered his to be authoritarian, he pathetically tied to it, ball and chained, pitifully powerless. Well, good riddance! Yet... he feels a sensation one experiences after an amputation, dealing with phantom pain, but this is a sort of spiritual ache. Rebelling is on par with pupils playing pranks, to him, honestly and truly, student shenanigans. This is a Mickey Mouse operation, more or less. Hey, they consistently make valuable contributions to the cause. The two are productive radicals, not incompetent washouts! They're capricious, surely, in their innovatory improvisations. Thin morning mist leads to thick afternoon fog. Crows disperse as if chestnuts shaken from a tree. Conoid lambency, as though from a film projector. Confused, changing cumuli. Tranquilizing, saliferous winds. The perfumista's fufu enters his nostrils. Her ass-cheeks give him a hard-on. She sensually shimmies, creates showers of pixie dust, and snorts away, getting high on her supply. Politics is a serious subject for them. Drab streets. High, Jorge individualizes the garbage cans, counts them carefully. Somber twilight is soaked with horrid humidity. The duo romp in furious joy in the trashy alley. Her fingers possess the precision of surgical pincers. A cross-eyed, emancipated, geriatric vagrant's frontage is fissured with wrinkles. He hugs a vacuum cleaner and sips consommé, stares at them like a hungry pet at its owners, Rasta hat hanging as an elephantoid trunk. She doffs her jacket and dons a poncho. Her saponaceous sweat oozes. She flitters, definitely, as a nervy parakeet in a noiseless flutter. Power lines. Barbed wire. She tells Peki of her nightmare, in which these feathered human torsos cheeped and hopped with hybridized mythological beings. Her axillae have the mephitis of garlic. Borderless beach beckons. Weeping willows. Sawdust sand. Sapphire sea stretching. Albatrosses are aghast, attributable to the barrage of bathers.

Peki, the amateur sleuth, is hot on the trail of his shadow who was kidnapped by the dastardly pirate Captain Roberto, who looks like the lead flamboyant thespian dressed in a corsair costume on a theater production poster. Peki meets his informant, the mutinous Luis, once Roberto's bosun, squat as an owl, cutting a diminutive, bulbiform figure, appareled in rags of buccaneer regalia, in this seedy, soulless taphouse on the waterfront. He acts as the master of ceremonies. His alienated blinders and periodontal problems. Floating debris of patrons drowned out by rock 'n' roll blasting from the vintage jukebox. Diving bell of a makeshift elevator. Mingled odors of liquor, poverty, perspiration, bad breath, and fear. His phlegmy, crackly intonation sounds like it's sent through a staticky loudspeaker. He plasters oily strands over his bald pate, spreading the wealth, so to speak. He's staggering-drunk, and, goddammit, gas churns in his intestines. His physiognomy is as a basset hound's. He gazes at Peki like he's a mutant scorpion. His perspired and peakish phiz conveys the impression of being wrapped in cellophane. He reeks of cheap foo foo juice, from, and haust, rocks as a skiff, hammered on whiskey. His gold earrings wink sarcastically. Parakeets in the honky-tonk establishment are free to fly. One lands on the cash register and poops on it. Anthropomorphic, coy pink flamingo waitresses in aprons and heels strut and serve. Buoys blink not unlike eyes. Parrots and toucans chatter on bony branches. Luis... the schmuck's enormous, ill-fitting footwear's comical, perhaps pathetic. He has a defeated demeanor. His flaccid pecs, sagging gut, and double chin (turkey wattles) have the consistency of instant oatmeal. Marmalade monkey on a leash quickly climbs a fig tree in perhaps arthritic agony. Tattered tent. Wild peacocks and their anguished calls. An ancient angel with orbiculate lamps and garbed in burlap orders a shot of sambuca from the saintly bartender and slugs it. Harsh and tarnished furnishings. A mauve mule canters and hinnies. Peki's trusty dagger dances in its leathern sheathe Jorge stole for him from a department store months ago. Liquescent fury of his eyes. Blurry forms in the luminosity. Dealing with him, Peki has the serious voice of a school teacher scolding a misbehaving student. Luis, timid as a termite, quivers like a leaf, gaze permanent as a subject's posed for a portrait, scampers like a besotted puppy, only doesn't get very far, Peki doing his best Dostoyevsky by shaking his fists and flying at him. Luis ends up betraying him, selling him out to the authorities (in exchange for immunity), Lost Brat mercenaries Cubby, an itty-bitty battalion of sprogs attired in overalls as uniforms. Peki flees but is soon arrested and jailed by his former comrades.

The War

On the massif, Peki was feeling like a midget Moses on Mount Sinai. Below was a Hieronymus Bosch hellscape. He escaped his labor battalion to exist precariously AWOL in the uncompromising wilderness. He was undeterred in the undoubtedly aggravating truth that he was a coward. In the military, he was a dewdrop in the sea. He soldiered on, in spite of the many unwonted trials and tribulations of life during wartime. He was always being deliberately furtive. He was somatically, spiritually, and emotionally crippled from active service. He felt as if he were perishing from starvation, despair, and exhaustion. Every so often he encountered groups of desperate deserters. He managed to survive by stealing from a disfigured field. The nearby village substantiated its financial and ethical collapse in its very appearance. Buildings tipped in drunken angles. Roads were dilapidated. Stores had next-to-no products to sell and people had little money with which to buy. Most of the shops had been looted. A park was unused and unmaintained. There was this permeative sweet malodor of rot in the air. Death supplanted life. The dejection was apparent in the expressions of the denizens. Sheep were taken by the brigands. Shepherds were helpless to prevent the thievery. The outlaws were not unlike packs of animals. Wrapped in a copious black cloak (as to be almost invisible in the darkness), delirious and jaundiced, Peki barbecued a blue jay on a stick and picked the bones clean, and drank a goat's milk. He'd been improvising his meals whenever possible. He counted himself lucky that he was still alive. His failing health required urgent medical care. He was skeletal and mad and he cursed God and man. He had weapons but not much ammo. He suffered continuously from fear and worry. He saw a mirage of Marisa standing like a heron in the water. She sang lullabies in a low voice, sending them to the moon. A male acrobat and a female juggler performed for him in the shade of the pines and planes of the wood. They were feeding on locusts. Soon after, Peki slept unsoundly in the hollow trunk of a mighty tree. The songbirds kept him irritably awake. He accustomed his eyes to the tenebrosity. There was a drought. A fountain was silenced. Due to the deluge, Peki sought and found refuge in an isolated shack with a flat roof, iron-grilled door, and latticed windows. In the stuffy room, he discerned a hefty young woman with unnaturally white skin, her frontal painted with cosmetics. He paused mid-step and swallowed hard, watching her with anxiety. Hana (her name) had a pair of empty, doleful eyes. Her flesh was ingrained with dirt and her nails were scuffed. There was something in her deportment that betrayed purpose. She smiled wanly and beckoned to him with simulated salaciousness, dancing with a pleasure that was profound. The place was composed of old furnishings. He wished to lie with her. At last, he summoned his courage and propositioned her. Nervous, her fingers twisted together, expressing gratitude for his company. She called herself a worthless whore, and added her diseases were incurable. She was ugly in a comely sort of way. She was motionless and timeless. Her face had pride and kindness in it. He put a hand on her head, as though in benediction. And tears rolled down her cheeks and splashed onto her bust. When she wept noisily, he moved to comfort her. Her chest and shoulders heaved with sobs. Her vox sounded as if her larynx was coated with grave dust. The certainty that he was going to get laid was uncertain. They smoked opium. She indicated her surroundings with a grand gesture. He had the sensation that he was sheltered under her wing. Sloshed vermin in tatters passed by her property. Hana's feet were dry as leather. She told him that she had suicidal thoughts, such as wading out into the ocean and drowning, and added her family was dead, because of a bombing raid, and she buried them under the stones among these tombs. She longed for justice and vengeance. Her mouth tasted sour, like wild cherries. Her vagina smacked of vinegar, and her backside had a copper flavor. Intimate, on the cushioned bed, they were akin to a couple of entwined vines. Pumped, she wailed as though she was straining in childbirth. She momentarily paused, like she was waiting for the baby's cry. Sexually satisfied, they parted as if they were sundered, like a pot that fell on the floor and broke into two pieces. Later on, fellatio eased the farewells. He whimpered like a whipped puppy when he came. He spoke, his intonation sounding as if his throat was full of ground glass. He experienced a dire quivering in his soul. The Devil ruled the world.

Peki and Marisa

He, with a deprecatory turn of his humongous, box-shaped head, scans every detail of her appearance with enormous, spectacled, El Greco eyes, animated in their hollow sockets. She reminds him of something unapproachable, solitary, with an expression of a hag asleep. Seeing her, the flint is struck, sparks fly, and he is ignited, crackling and spreading. When she neglects him, it feels as though she has jabbed an icicle into his heart. To be ignored by this unparalleled maternal being… Would they both thrive under separate roofs? He is fed up with her studied games of indifference. He feels pulled to pieces. She gives him a radiant glance and helps herself to a lingering slurp of a flask of brandy, pours out liquiform notes of words in symphonic sentences. Her mop flutters like a flag (one he pledges allegiance to) in the breezes. She sucks on a snow cone (dessert after dinner) and optically measures the shrimp's littleness. She is twice his height. She gazes at him like a preacher at a sinner. With a Puppetoon intonation (and movements), puss in a perpetual sulk, she flings out a series of lame excuses. The short fellow, wallowing in a shamefaced, damnfool silence, is amazed by the keen gravity with which he takes her conduct, her moods a phenomenon of ebbings and flowings. She is a skeleton in its ossuary. Ice-cubes jingle in her stemmed glass of Jack Daniel's. His ankle socks are stale. He has a starched pallor and quarter-sized ears, standing at bullseye-omphalos-level with her. She gestures like an orchestra conductress, with a menacing moue, glomming a hunk of herring and a cayenned egg (making a medley of mastication) at the magnificent food table. She's cute as pie. His raspberries are brought out not unlike pistol shots. A scent of apples hangs about his attire. An embroidered backpack weighs upon his stooping shoulders. Cloris Leachman's novelty semi-hit version of Iron Butterfly's 'In-A-Gadda-Da-Vida' is on the transistor. Sun's the exact hue of a pomegranate. Cumuli interrupt the welkin. Botanical chromatic clamor. Mountains roll to the celestial sphere. Bluebirds are perched on a fencepost. Cloudlets school like herring. There sure are enough streetcars. Kids choir on by. Creepers squiggle up and down the sides of these hearth-hued edifices. Buildings rise up like redbrick islands. Trams arrive and depart. Marisa has a fine figure and an unappealing countenance. Miffy, her silence has a resentful edge. Peki produces an immature snicker. He pecks at the hotdog like a chicken in the yard and observes her like a fox would an unguarded henhouse. The telephone rings loud. Gales have hostile intent. Riverboats hoot. Saffron luminescence bounces off trolley tracks and bridge rails. Mother and son are sidekicks, both dedicated to a code of behavior that would be considered, in most circles, unconventional. His arousal is like a charge gradually increasing upon a condenser plate, his being jolted in a surge of energy. Her stare possesses an intimidating potency. She looks at him as though he is a trespasser on rigidly preserved private property. He lets his eyes slide on her slight curves. His adoration for her is irrational and depraved. She looks like an animal that's wary of humans. He regards himself as being a sad case madly in love. He is horrified; she is the woman who had given him birth. Does she even give a fig about him? "I'm nothing," he mumbles almost incoherently. What is this queer attraction he has for her? It's so contrastive to the allure when it comes to the sluts. He takes good care not to reveal to his mother his secret as to the desirability of her. Her protrusive conk is out of all proportion to the rest of her fizzog. He tells her that living, for him, is getting behind the mule and plowing; it's a trudge through sludge. She is all sugar-and-spice and unconventional. She's just being herself. Is she disconcerted by the intrusion in the dingy, high-ceilinged dining room? He feels awkward at having been caught observing her. He gives vent to a sough of sorrow. Her cabbage-colored complexion is so made-up her visage has a clownish semblance. She bites into a wheat cracker with a turtle-ish snap. Her falsies slip. Her forehead is flaky like an Italian fresco. She is vulpinely snouted. Her perfume has a petrol smell. She clacks her dentures. He imagines her duff is punch bowl-rosy from self-flogging. Her thatch is frazzled. She inhumes a suspiration. The little man feels as though he's permanently adrift of the Dead Sea of daily distress. Her distilled essence seems to exude equally from every nook and cranny of the place, like a sort of fragrance. His thrill in beholding her is unsubduable. She wanted to be alone after their ad libitum supper party. He relishes listening to her voluble voice. She projects a kind of hypnotism on him. Her armpits are redolent of smoked oysters. He wishes he was received with more warmth. His heat goes out as if she'd extinguished it. He can hardly hear any mortal sounds save for his pumping heart. Spacious eventide engulfs the pebbled beach. The weather's moods vary. Cirri surge back with a perceivable increase of visible whiteness. Church bell's doleful tolling: leaden bongs. A serpentiform lubricity of thought slithers through him. He hopes she fades from his mind. Can she hear his salacious whisperings? Her cleaning up commences, entering her labors with alacrity in the forlorn apartment, containing a dreary collection of furnishings, its emptiness worse than its squalor. The lair looks outraged, violated. She rotates like a top. She has no end of energy. Her flesh possesses the pigment of moonlight. She curvets on an arc. She is a prime example of a case study of extremes. Her prat protrudes like a poodle's. He's seated like a pharaoh, mitts on his knees. The effect the sordid city has on Peki's senses is ghastly. He feels not unlike an abortion of mediocrity. He is often in despair, thinking everyone despises him. Marisa is silent for a space. Then she calls their crash pad a "slave-galley." And he, dressed in Lorax pajamas-with-feet, mounts the hobbyhorse on the uncarpeted flooring in the tomb of a den. She has a faint mustache, abridged pubes, and lithe legs. She puts on gym shorts with a zipper-fly and faux garter stockings that resemble butterfly nets. Pedestrians are a wandering cast of poltroons, at the mercy of the elements, he opines. He feels like a man-made monster, and imagines shoehorning himself into the throng and disappearing. His digits waggle demonstratively as if they are finger puppets. His tears flow and reflect the refulgence. The sky appears to be made out of zinc. Clouds haunt the heavens, persistent as ghosts. In the laboratory, he parks himself in the leather-cushioned chair, augmented with a footrest, he stole from a nearby barbershop one orange dawn, his thoughts lost and found. He imbibes scotch and ingests biscuits. It's as if the place is alive, with a voice and a soul. It gives instructions and he takes dictation. The joint could be mistaken for an alchemist's cave, with its shelves, benches, and tables cluttered with bottles of strange liquids and jars of powders, sci-fi magnesium lamps, massive contraptions, colossal machinery extracted from a steampunk novel, gigantic crocks and keeves, a weird electric generator connected to an old bicycle, an assortment of tanks and meters, various ovens and burners, and other miscellaneous stuff too difficult to accurately describe. The spiders stay put in their webs in those darkened corners, looking on in stupefaction. Peki moves with purpose, not unlike a journeyman walking through a big town for a job. He's focused like a sharpshooter. His actuation is the result of a furtive imperative, as the force of gravity. He revels in taking his sweat and turning it into mantequilla. He prefers to work odd hours. His frustrations are sloughed away. He listens to the surf's lullabies and hears the ocean's rhythms. Squalls are meaner than usual. He notices the shotgun, a suicide's amigo. A single shot and it's adios, muchachos. Apocalypse Next.

The blue is promising precipitation. Shapely cirri occupy it. An infant caterwauling in its baby carriage, in conjunction with the pernicious sidewalk bustle, contributes to vehicular commotion. A Doberman pinscher on a leash in a driveway barks professionally at passersby. There are dynamitic blasts of thunder, its percussion making Peki's crowns judder. He is seized by an oleo mania prevailing. A version of himself is reflected in the kier. He resembles a beer barrel. Packaging the product, he has become unconscious of the o'clock. He's looking forward to a little taphouse time in the end. Once in a while, he toils with an absence of thought. He reminds himself he has to remain unknown to the levels of the law. He's not interested in becoming a particular favorite of the militia either. They might lie in wait to shoot trespassers on their hilly territory, including him because he goes there regularly to commit cruelties on his targets and operate on them then and there. He, black-faced from the slag, battered a Falstaffian fellah to death just last night in the fathomless, windless, and quiet dark. A hawk hung high in the air, on the lookout for rodents. He partook of ice cream at a soda fountain, later on, the unholy mounts served as a backdrop. What was stupid was when he sucker-punched a yuppie in a sweater, leaving a backlot wingding. The price he could've paid… the total cost… he can't even think of it… He's the type of murderer who enjoys watching it happen. He is no lazy son of a bitch, sniping, picking people off from a distance. He tends to prefer the up close and personal way. The corpses are piling up. His nature is no secret to him. He is well aware of who and what he is. He'll soldier on, but making sure he stays off the roads. He is (proudly) in prime killing condition. Although he's cutting short countless lives, he's providing sustenance for society, thus countering the bad with the good. There's an undeniable balance. He honors his commodity with every slit throat, spewing artery, and punctured armpit, putting on a punishing showcase for himself as he slaughters residents like a buffet of brutality, blazing through the body count. He's enslaved to his art form, devoting every breath of each day and night sleeping and waking to make mantequilla. It's on par with being born again, creating Butyrum. It has, he'd reckon, taken up a good part of his personhood. He possesses an insane fanaticism when it concerns his product. Hard labor is a badge of honor. He doesn't give a rat's turd about the competition. According to the numbers, he is pulling ahead of the pack. Numerals tell the truth. They don't lie. Cumuli are illuminated from within. Sage treetops explode skyward. He could easily pass for a grease-bearded roustabout fresh from the pool hall. His existence is blooming like a poisonous blossom. When he woke up this morning, with its unmerciful whiteness of effulgence, he knew that whatever the day held in store for him, it would include butter. Rays go by like protracted ricochets. Bugs fly like lead. He experiences shortness of breath and waywardness of mind. He must replenish his opium stash. It is imperative. He can't remember where he put the Chinaman's number… He downs his Hennessy Cognac, spots her at the foot of the long flight of wood stairs. She is straight-faced and apparently nitro-fuming about something, to the point where steam is issuing from her ears. Or is it light trickery? Quick as levin, and without warning, he rushes upon her in the ill-lit living room, grabbing her, exhibiting his predatory roguery in the genial horseplay, the maneuver entirely successful, by main force, and a wrestling match ensues. He has been hunting her like a dog. A slow blush gathers on his countenance. There is desperate clutching and scrambling. He acts all pissy himself, a strategy that works unfailingly as a domestic lubricant. He has an urge to unburden his heart, and impart an essence beyond himself. She ventilates a torrent of drivel. Their eyes meet. They hold each other's gaze, the two overtaken, synchronously, by awestruck recognition that only they can comprehend. He holds her tightly against him. She is in a heightened state of receptivity. She has such a youthful vitality! "You are possessed by the devil," she mutters. "You use human beings as chess pieces." He hugs his deep-breathing mother, with her alabaster, flexile body, lovely bosom, and slender hips... so inspiriting. She wriggles in his grasp, crying and kicking, fighting in vain to break free. His hopes for bedding her corrode to fragments. Clung together, they rock with a motion that makes them dizzy, flushes brought to their throats. A fine silence falls on them like noiseless sprinkles. They stay motionless, stare at one another like a couple of wooden beams bearing the weight of the same ceiling of reality. Marisa has peaches for cheeks. An expression of bewilderment shows in her fixed gaze. She looks like a child about to cry. She soon wearies and surrenders. He grips her wrists and she hardens her body, pulls her hands away, and draws her trunk back. Peki, pride hurt, releases her and hands her a pack of cigarettes and a book of matches. She lights one, inhales, and exhales a trembly ring of smoke. His brain whirls like a leaf on troubled water. She doesn't have the remotest conception as to how rare her sexiness is. His ardor for her is born of ardency. Her blinders look like antique marbles. Flushed from the ludic struggle, she brushes her rough abundance of silvering hair, standing on the Chinese rug. Her clear-toned inflection is infectious. She, vague as a virus, excites his senses. He's dominated by licentiousness, washing over him like an insidious solution. She is no innocent, taking into account her coquetry. His pisser rises like a storm-driven eely fish aroused from a mucky rill. She is the apple of his eye. In her company, he feels like a minnow near a pike. His fantasizing is this prolonged orgy of abhorrent evocations. His cardiac organ beats like a water pump. She munches a maroon, orbs conflagrant with bitchery. Her tress looks like a fright wig designed by Klimt. Her prat is as supple as a tobacco pouch. Her breath has the fetor of a terrarium, armpits ill-smell-ing. She opens another bottle of JD. She's stone-blind and has a digestive indisposition. Language is an arrow out of her pontifical quiver. The brightness of the day is congruous with his mood. He sits like a sapient fakir, snots shining in his nares, in the swivel chair, and folds his hands as if in prayer, as though in supplication to her. She's paper-thin, with twigs for limbs. He gets a glimpse of her long stretch and gulping yawn. Lovesick, stimulated in the vitals, chatting her up, making moves on her, he knows he will pay the price in action and consequence. He is up for kissy-and-huggy-poo. She is old and tired as a wish. She finds mystic drama in a casual occurrence, discovers revelations in diurnal events. She has premonitions and descries miracles. Her glare is eviscerating. She has a Gorgon glower. She's pigeon-toed, eyeglasses low on her nose. The imi-tation-Thraco-Roman wall-paintings are masterpukes in his estimation. A decrepit barge is slowly drowning in the harborage. Burglarious splen-dor steals through the blinds. Dust on the sill is not unlike puffball powder. Wind sounds like the humming of a seashell. The overcast, veil-ing the vault, is a congregation of clouds, low-hung, and pearl-white. She presses her diary, with stiff pages (turned, they make a musical of crepita-tions), biscuity odor, and bisected spine, to her chest. There is nothing unwritedownable whatsoever, she thinks. Her privates sting from encoun-ters with curious fingers and thumbs of patrons at the Sphincter strip club the night before. Gongoozled by sameyness, she handsprings in manic rhythm to the Coltranean jazz cranked on the phonograph. He, in an upright position, in the shimmering scintillation, is enthralled, vora-ciously cro-magnoning a pastrami sub. She's a toothsome turnover displayed in a sweetshop. She is clad in a ruffled maroon skirt (momen-tarily revealing her bare buttocks, like twin flabby faces full of welts, the havoc of cellulite, and a bad case of pimples), a matching brief shirt (chastely buttoned), and saddle shoes. His fire is fed with her. His enceph-alon revolves like a wheel with spokes of ideations, picturing a play-world of romantic adventure with her. Between life and death is an umbilical cord, he believes. He floats on the water of emotion, its depths, unex-plored, unknown. Shivering sensations travel through his nerves. He believes he is a man-beast, an anemic centaur, in an Eden of reddish leafage, grass blades, river reeds, anonymous weeds, dykes, ditches, holly trees, bramble bushes, and apparitions of swans, and he wades into a turquoise pool, surrounded by brown earth, quenches his thirst, leaves behind the barrooms and music halls. He welcomes the coming on of night. The barrier Marisa put up between them may be unscalable. He takes mincing steps, guzzles the befruited, canned beverage. His head is filled with angst and his heart is filled with fondness. He feels as if he's being tortured alive. His fart is a crack of doom. He is hungry as a bear. The odor rises like a poisonous fume. Her voice sounds far away, as though she's underwater. Feeling panicky as a vampire at dawn, he could burst into tears.

Peki, with an expression of imbecilic vacuity, after a substantial supper (of bloody beef, mashed potatoes, and some apple slices thrown in), serious as a hangman, feels ripples on the surface of his stomach like the rising of shoal darting to the top of the water. He has been betting (and winning) on boxing matches, horse races, and football games. His business is a religion, and he is the priest of butter, bearing the product. There's the sacred text he studies, commandments he follows, and a liturgy that is pertinent. Work, he thinks, produces wealth. He has an interview at the office this afternoon for a shift boss position. There will be straight-and-no-double-talk. He's constantly making moves of a professional nature. There have been employee docked hours, customer ejections, and accounts frozen. He's calling the shots. He doesn't want any buying and selling associates, no multiple snouts at the trough. He relishes being in charge of hiring. He can be a blunt individual. Before the mantequilla explosion in sales, he was exploited to the last, slaving away, never getting a fraction of what his toiling was worth, waged in occupations ranging from bricklayer to carpentry. A working stiff, with sweat and soreness, he took any job that happened to be available. He has learned lessons and suffered injustices. And so he creates, unaccompanied, dummied up, and poker-faced, his nose to the grindstone, the pedal to the metal. Dirt-beige light. His fart blasts, cracks in the fabric of air and time, ruthless and bone-rattling. If his madre discovered what he's been up to, would she fink him out? She ever and anon treats him like a donkey dropping on a mountain trail. He works solo, enjoys being a loner, around the clock. He's swift and deadly as an avalanche in taking folks out for their fat. A breeze is an uncaught breath. Living for him — a dog in a dogfight. He is unable to sit still. He has significant aspirations. He is no marginal rank-and-filer in the margarine trade. He takes the subject of his establishment very seriously. He polishes off a loaf of bread, tosses off a cup of coffee, and puffs on a Havana. He remembers the other dusk and the carnies entertaining the bank robbers and anarchistic bastards on the dusty slopes when he, Peki, was predatorially a-prowl. He loitered out in the vicinity of the electrical plant, waterfall, sand-choked arroyo, and rushing creek, and rolled a cigarette, leaning against a boulder as though he was waiting for someone. A buck knife was securely sheathed under a pant leg. Once he got the knack for killing, which didn't take long, he was off to the races, with, initially anyway, hit-and-miss results. Befogged and blinking, he, a blotch-complected dipsofreak, revels in erotic musings. In his existence, it seems as if every relationship shits the bed. Is the coincidence in all actuality a pattern? His gray matter is liberated from its disconcertment. These libidinous ideations ooze in his slimy brain. He pines for dark, incredible intimacy with Marisa, picturing them involved and interchanged. His eyebrows are snarled. His smile stretches from here to there at the prospect of reaming her. He yearns to verbally express himself but his tongue continues to trip. His heart sinks fathom deep into his chest. She is so lovable, his precious. He aches, and longs for her. She is world-reversingly amazing. His excitement is high-voltage. His pleasure is pain. His love for her is true, certain and unshakable. Cupid's arrow is poisoned. If he came on to her, would she fall laughing or run away screaming? She'd probably resent him pretty quick, hold it against him. She drives him just nuts. He has a desperate need to be respected by her... She puts the come-hither on him, bringing about a gourmandizing makeout sequence between them. She goes down and he goes up. They passionately hug. Whereupon they waltz and swirl, swing and whirl, his urgent mitt rummaging optimistically for her heinie. He sucks her suspirations. Diabolicating ardently, they are embraced, engaged in a long French kiss. He is hot-blooded and altiloquent. He cannonades her tuchis. Her anus is a ruby rare. It's a warm and illicit scenario. He pinches her nipple clothespin-fashion. In a drunken idiolect, his wordulations are monarticulated. He asks questions that don't get answers. She shock-absorbs his bulldozing body. Soughs are accompanied by coos. They clutch in an ebullition of carnality. Their cries, in contrapuntal, echo, make a mockery. There's a rolling in her peepers. Wheezing manfully, she is mussed, her honeysuckle-hued smock bunched and disarranged. There are pinwheels in her eyeballs. He makes a battery of gripping. Their vertical actions become horizontal. They're noisy, at a primordial pitch, and aglow, during the inter-dimensional intercourse, their sexual misadventures... Drapes, with bell-flower design, billow in and out. The clock bongs. Oxygen is beebalm-lubricious. Gusts carry the unmistakable smells of barbecue. The illumination is as white as elder pith. Wispy clouds appear out of nowhere, not unlike a conjurer's doves. Her pies are dreamy with a lassitudinous self-satisfaction. The room, a solitudinarium, where there are no consequences, no expectations, is blanched to ghostliness. She takes refuge in herself, looks beatific, resigned to reflection, surveys the impossible, paradoxical chiaroscuro, and holds a paper cup of Hawaiian Punch. She seems further away in time and space. Her blinkers star-shine. She idles gracefully. He pittypatties in, his serviceable shoes squeaking. He spots artifice in her artful deportment. Thoughts of his are pieces of a puzzle. His beard wags when he childishly tugs at her jersey's sleeve, jesting with her. He has the voice of a toad, hovers around her like an unsplendid, indivine cherub. His lamps bounce like a juggler's. He gooches her in the gut. She punts away her sporty slides and stares at him like a schoolgirl bully, having a dry, stern modulation. She gets a vulpecular gleam in her eye. His acquire a squint. She's as cold as wintry fulgor. His tallboy of Foster's Lager is still held by the zero of the six-pack's plastic. He chug-a-lugs its contents. He brought it for reinforcement. She is the bough, he is the root. She's the straw that stirs his drink. She hurls her invectives like javelins. Her physiognomy grows grimmer under a cloud of curls (from a perm). She has a defeated poise. Her mien is as stiff as a mask. She is a slinky, browbeating individual, casting jocose looks and issuing brutal jeers. Her microaggressions and nagging implorations are meant to control and dehumanize him. She's a button-pusher. Their interaction is awkward. Marisa disrespects him with a smirk, and makes him feel alien about his deformities. She can be, alternately, a stilted automaton and an impassioned firebrand. Already tipsy, Peki knocks back a tulip glass of gin-and-bitters with an unsteady hand (looking like one of a monument-maker). The spirit is uncommonly good. He has a roaring vox. His guffaws greet her insults. His mind is flustered with alcohol. Conflicting impulses flicker through him. He manages to master them. He willingly vacates the beer-stained squab for her. Fuddled, she ensconces herself, speaks in shaky tones, and subsides into an intermission of composed coma. She has the stink of tobacco smoke and horse dung. She hobbles in heels as if she's on stilts. He makes shambling progress into the orifice of the pantry, and attempts to bring together his wandering wits for an adequate retort to her unfair criticisms. He wants to burrow into her like a mole, peck her on her peaky, wrinkled dial. Her stretch marks are ones of distinction, like the prize ribbons on a well-bred horse. She pads, dink-toed, into the parlor. His vascular organ's pounding could make the earth tremble. He gets a sniff of tar and paint. Aware of the appropriateness of Marisa's ensemble makes him realize how badly he is dressed (in long johns), which causes him a great deal of vexation. Foliage is dew-drenched. People on the street are, to him, marionettes on a stage. Spate is cider-sour. A tram clangs and whistles like a whirligig. There are so many automobiles and aeroplanes! Peki remembers the brawl he got into at the tavern the other evening. There's a fortune-teller's tent set up on the curb, sandwiched between the vendor stalls and hawker booths. Nomadic scroungers come in a wretched conveyance into the neighborhood, an electro-Babylon. He, with absorbed interest, watches the proceedings in undisturbed security and sees them in inferior and ignominious incandescence. His temples' veins thrum noticeably. He tries to straighten his shoulders and cannot. He fears his personality has turned into a multiplicity destitute of a nucleus. Crickets chirrup. He has a penitent's lacrima. Gloom's as black as the Devil's pocket.

Following odd bird Marisa's coprophagic break, having lapwinged in her buffy nightie into the bathroom like it was a lighthouse, a summoner beckoning her with its beacon, Peki says, "Mama, that is so disgusting."

To which she responds, "Consuming feces is normal behavior in some species. Certain cannibalistic plants are coprophagous. A surprising number of animals eat poo. A momma dog will cram down her puppies' excrement because they are unable to eliminate on their own. This happens after she licks her babies to activate the defecation reflex. Ingestion of shit also keeps the area clean. Fly specks contain much undigested or partially undigested food. It will regurgitate some of its stomach contents after landing on a potentially edible, solid substance. The regurgitated liquid dissolves the substance and creates more liquid for the insect to suck up. And foals. The crap it partakes in introduces microorganisms to the gastrointestinal tract. True. They're needed to switch from a milk-to-forage-based diet. Pigs, those opportunistic carnivores, devour doo-doo. In medieval Europe, porcines were used in toilets. It was built raised, and the porkers lived below in a chamber, gobbling the human waste. This practice still exists in some developing parts of the world."

"This is all so very educating, but it's still frigging gross."

Her legs are longer than a Monday.

There is a touch of precip and a toasty torpidity. A train quail-whistles, its brakes hen-screeching. Peki, limp and relaxed, chariots swinging low, drinking a highball, is caught in the current of Marisa's magnetism. His pink handkerchief hangs out of his checkered vest's pocket like a weary tongue. His cerebrum is a loom weaving ideas, a sickle to harvest thoughts with. He takes his prescribed valerian. She, pensive and dour, pronounces untypical syllables. Their disagreement has misresolved itself. She leads and he follows. The drawing room has funeral home decor and stained glass windows. Terrified loneliness has taken possession of him. Marisa, an egoistic lady, delicate and damaged, has a sea-gray derma layer and a pursed-up bazoo. She is horse-faced and sharp-lipped, wears a cyan turtleneck sweater and tanga briefs, unfurled over him like an umbrella. Her mirth is measured. Erasers of her paps are erectile. She could sweet-talk a mouse into a trap. They belong together but are unable to connect. They are suitable for each other as the two halves of a sleeve ripped from a shirt they cannot fit into. Her rake-lashes bat. He sees her in full color, CinemaScope, his gumball greymatter begrenaded by narcotics. Hallucinations give him the fantods. Orbs bright as klieg-lights, she sways, sips the mint julep, harmonizes to Sorrell Booke's butchered recording of Donovan's 'Sunshine Superman' on the stereo, and hums the last chorus. Singing, she sounds like a mynah. His organ swells. Her kitty-upcurvital kisser is sensual. Farcically he jigs, howls like a coon, imagines waddling on her like a drunk duck on a June bug. Her head, blowing him, jerks back and forth like a woodpecker's. And he rides her like a camel. Venereal monkeyshines on the pot-liquor-green couch. Her mocking reptiloid eyes glare at him. Her feet have a mundungus malodor. The carton disgorges milk into an earthenware cup. She puckers her brows while adding rum, experiencing a heightening of her spirits, calm as a cured demoniac. She swallows, in stellar obliviousness to him. Peki's perishing passion begins steadily to revive, despite her giving him little heed. His preputial part pulsates like the tip of a tapir's proboscis. His desire is aroused. The blasted sex suppression is kicking his ass. His overtures have been continuously rebuffed. His burdened encephalon is like an overcrowded platform. She fires off derisive remarks point-blank. Her disdain solidifies itself in unprecedented tangibility. His receptivity makes him a perfect target for her ridicule. She is troubling to his peace. It's as if she's turned into a different person overnight. There is an unappeasable rivalry between them. She is in full command of the situation and gives him a penetrating look. Her smile is strained. She's as fickle as a feline. Her oral cavity is like a sluice gate. And it's open. A brownish rash running on her throat is like a muddy streamlet. His face droops wearily. Her line of attack annoys him. With the vindictiveness of defeat, he gets in his vocal jabs. He has a remorseful sensation, as though he is responsible for starting the argument. They're not unlike ancient rivals confronting one another. The heated encounter has a horrid effect upon him. She gospelizes, with hewing hands, like some ensainted evangelizer, pulling no stops. The loop of rope around her neck is like a gallownoose. She has an expression of the hysteric. She is an attitudinarian, a gynecocrat. He gets a smell of cheap cologne and roasted chestnuts. The war of words is disorganized, disjointed. She appears rigid as if she's a dummy that's been set up (with difficulty) in an erect position, looking like she could topple at any second, and speaking as though she's in a trance. He gazes at the snooty outline of her scornful profile. She is like a wicked witch in a fairy story. He feels like he was thrown under horses' hooves, trodden into the ground, depleted from the squabble, murders, and work. He knows that emotions course under her icy surface. The spat is about fate and chance. Peki's brain operates at top speed. He's engaged in the conflict. The perplexities of her behavior fret his mind. He raises his shaggy eyebrows at her unbelievable temerity. A truce is called by him, but antagonisms are renewed in no time at all. Marissa acts as though she cannot bear the sight of him. The dispute is a waste of energy, he weens. How can he untie the knot of spitefulness? He feels extreme discomfort, and distaste. She gives him a sort of nausea. Then she starts to rearrange furniture and flowers in the waxlight. She makes a mad mystery out of daily life. The ram mutton is in the oven. To his vision, she assumes an attractive figure. She makes sport of him. She plays polo and cricket. He draws his rubicund rictal expression to a discreet distance, going at a snail's pace, feeling vulnerable, out of his element, like a jellyfish stranded, high and dry, on a rock, vacating the room without fanfare, out into the jostling mob of residentiaries in the lobby. He speaks in tongues. His countenance is blubbered from weeping. The acrid, ammoniacal redolence of the spritz pricks his nostrils. Identical twin rapscallions, male and female, have bowlcuts and Punch-and-Judy profiles, flesh veneered by a tanning parlor, both rigid as pipes, are coked into fidgets out front of a honky-tonk. Homo Stupiens are everywhere! The stormy sky spits its wrath. The protracted human intercourse has wiped him out. Bazillions of impressions bombard his consciousness. He catches his reflection in the door's glass: rutabaga-shaped dome, doorknob-round sneezer... He's dressed in his duded-up duds. His Cuban stogie makes hellsmoke. His balls feel like cracked acorns. He looks like a frog ready to jump from a lilypad onto the riverbank. I am becoming exactly who I am, he thinks. He has the morals of a Tomcat. He is a species unto himself, nature's fuckup, an unsalvageable narcissist. He's hemorrhoidal, homicidal. Avian caroling.

Peki, ebon-cloaked like a prophet, resolutely tightening the canvas belt, reeking of urine, round his waist, experiences mental distress that one has when one impels oneself awake from an intolerable nightmare. He is ill-complexioned. An inundation of color flows into it. He copes with cramps from too much smoking and drinking. The megapolis shimmers in waves of summer heat. Sea usurps the semblance of sky. Strikers, a rank file, picket on the pier. A cop, bald as cheese, with ample, jutting ears, weasels his way through the demonstrators, and gets caught in the vocalic crossfire. It is warm and windy. Marisa, flapping around not unlike an injured gooney, with a premeditated simper, has disproportionate lineaments. Animation is established in her stolid features. Initially rejecting his advancements, she gives him a blunt, ornate smacker to his chops, full-on, her lips sap-sweet, and he protests weakly. He is dejected, for she is taunting him. She can be treaclyly nasty. He's horny and confused. Libido succeeds bewilderment. Her being ignites the avid flame in his heart. Her resistance could extinguish it. She is longed-for. She's a wonderful enigma. Her eyes are popped. She has grassy breath. She is lovely and sulky. To him, she's neither old nor young. He is like Pan, the goat god, his tumid shaft quavering in anticipation of... Losing her would make him suffer a hundred deaths. His existence, with her, is like chess: he'd sacrifice himself, a pawn, to save her, the queen. He adores her, and desperately. His fantasy consumes reality. Deposited on the cutesy sofa, in an italic position, he crosses his bowed legs, sinks like an anchor into the cushions, brow with centripetal furrows, and gazes at her as if she's a target he's sizing up. He has a compactness of individuality. He articulates like an auctioneer, his malerect rod with its pangs. His chogey sounds like dishwater gurgling through a pipe, making itself audible to her ears. Her feet are limp off the ankles when she saunters on the Dutch tiles, in a charade of elegance, a masquerade of inattention. A wall is put up between them. She, an antihuman worldling, between heaven and earth, rows a spoon through the pot of porridge. Her beak is shaped like a shoebill. The tatterdemalion shrew cackles at his embarrassment. Her intonation is cruel and flat. His fiery oculi, big as begging bowls, flash at her. Getting her would be another string in his bow. He optically inspects her with equivocal intentness. Their duologue takes a turn for the worse. His insinuendo gets her irked, obliging her to jerk her knee. They castigate, accuse, and contradict in the objectionable flat. They are like ventriloquist and dummy, speaking simultaneously. Together, they are odd and perfect, even and imperfect. Their metallic shouting subsides. Separation and reunion happen within an hour. They've found their composure. To err is to be deaf, dumb, and blind. What wasted time. It was an enormous misunderstanding. Standing on the Libyan rug, cruciform like a windmill, Marisa looks out of the lozenge-shaped pane and affects an assortment of facial tics and bodily twitches, gothic globes rimming with bitter tears. Peki's ruminant jaws grind. He appraises her as if he is an art connoisseur assessing the perspective of a painting. His weather eye is kept open. Light is like clarified honey. Reverie-inducing drencher. Clouds are harbingers of rain. The atmosphere is comfortless. Skeeters zither. Nondescript, unpretentious edifices are unconfined and unpersonalized. Finches and grackles shrug off the soaker. A freight train rockets on the railroad. Booming, bone-rattling thunder. Artificial tussie-mussies are kept in a jug. Capably he plays the tabla and has an archlucifer leer. Short-skirted-and-pleat-bloused, and barefoot, she dances quite corybantically, glancing audaciously steamily at him. Her phiz appears to have been carved out of a crag. Spellbound, lechery glistens in his concentrated peepers, distracted by her bold leaps and bounds. Perspiry beads stand out on his forehead. Breathless, his pies dilate, trap wide open. This is a rhapsodic upended province, protected by paneling, effectively preserving their mutual reclusion. He verbalizes the fact that she tickles his fancy. Her sweet yap ripens to a smile. He's converted into an attitude of lapidified stupefaction by her indecent pirouetting. He groans like walked-on ice. His bup has the sonance of a blackbird's tweet. Her vixen eyes goggle at him. Her integument is white as a toadstool. Her performance brings a prickling sensation to his groin. She would ruin his life if she left him. He is damned; smitten to death. Her hair is neatly divided by a straight part. He's under amatory anesthesia. He wants to ram her. And he takes to his heels, with a beaten-puppy look, glancing at her crouching form, spent, like he is a stevedore who emptied a vessel's container, swinging off in clumsy haste, with a man-monkey swash, under the sickle of a moon. He spots a nest in an elm. Thrushes are perched on a branch. He wishes to dissolve like a liquid in liquid, to expel her from his obstinate preoccupation. He hurries away, his brain beset with a burden of tumultuous cogitations, and he croaks like a frog. Redd Foxx's psychedelic rendition of Devo's 'Girl U Want' is on the radio. Peki eases himself gradually, like a scuba diver, back to the surface of the city. Marisa ocularly marks him with a sigh of relief, unashamed delight. She's left on her knees, hands clasped on her lap. She can't refrain from talking to herself, the chatter sounding like a parakeet. "I think aloud, therefore it's better to be alone," she mutters, her grin fading as quickly as it had come. Her cry is disembodied. Her voice settles into silence.

Butter Addiction

I've built my butter business and I resist getting crocked on my own stock, so to speak. I know this is blasphemous, but I often bite the bullet and purchase other companies' brands. I don't mean to brag... I have no real competition. There's mine and everyone else's. Butyrum stands above the rest. In terms of quality, it is on another level entirely. Nothing comes close. The tide will never turn. Trust me. All I can picture lately is mantequilla. Cheesy as it sounds, it makes everything better. My continuous enthusiasm for butter is unlikely to end well, but you know how it goes with addictions. There's the inceptive honeymoon stage, and then there's the I-shouldn't-be-doing-this-but-what-the-heck-phase. Perhaps my body feels it is in danger and has gone into its most atavistic response: fattening up in anticipation of famine? Or it could be I have this awful affliction, or maybe even fat-gorging worms?! It might be that I'm shopping for groceries online, and since they limit purchases to two, something in me always wants to hit the maximum. I always buy a couple of slabs of mantequilla. Whatever the reason, my dependency shows no signs of subsiding. I haven't been able to guilt myself with health consequences, nor, to my shame, the starvation of others that I see regularly on TV and read in the papers. Bottom line is, once I consume butter, my brain flows well. My journal, for example, is fueled completely by butter. I'm unable to go out much, I don't store unhealthy nibbles at home, and am generally pretty frugal (no shopping binges, ever). So butter seems to have become my only escape, reward, and refuge. I've told myself this can't go on, but each time I'm writing, my body goes on cruise control.

Even now, I have butter clumps on a plate beside me, their yellow, soft, salty goodness a constant temptation. Someone needs to intervene. I've perused this entry, and it reads like a half-humorous call for help. I'll probably need to start a seaweed/sunflower-seed /dried fruit variety of habit or a sound meditation method to get me out of this one. Until that happens though, I'll be here. Eating healthy breakfasts of nuts and cereals, vegetables with every meal, working out the best I can. (And stealing mantequilla off the cake. I guess this my version of a meltdown?

Julia Losada

A gangly fish vendor, Pedro Losada, with a Doberman Pinscher's mug, tubulous choppers, and an ill-humored scowl, visits the shop and purchases a box of 'Butyrum' for his whalish wife, Julia, for their anniversary, requesting that it be delivered on a certain day. A week goes by. At the address, a rather modest home, Peki, dressed in fancy slacks and a polyester shirt, is greeted at the door by Julia. She invites him inside. She's garbed in a gauzy gown, her orange nest of a shock filled with vespine pins. She has this piggish snout and sweaty mustache. His myopic eyes are stung, pricked by refulgent splinters. He strikes her as an unremarkable character, haggard from lack of slumber. Oxygen is like translucent, greasy butcher paper. He reeks of cigarette smoke and has filthy fingernails. The odorous sum in the place is sickening. He has a distinctly somnambulant gait. Nervously he puts his thumb under his armpit as though it is a thermometer, stationary, like in a languid torpor. Her blinders are puffy from a nap, having slept in a bog of moist blankets. Excess effulgence from an energetic sun shines on an uninhabited tenement. He wants to push aside the veil of fatigue. Her fat face is deformed by the fishbowl lenses of his glasses. He makes the guttural sound of a shot-putter. In the humid house, he feels like a polyp in an aquarium. The oral cavity of a bedroom has tonsils of twin beds. Wallpaper's tobacco-colored. Heat visibly rises like a soufflé. Julia shuffles in fluffy slippers. She offers him a meal of meat, soup, bread, and wine and he hesitantly accepts. Peki's words are like dried, pale bones. His sarcastic oculi, the size of bottle caps, widen like a madman's, mouth moving as a marine corolla. He's sluggish with booze. Porcelain Buddha is zazen on the mantelpiece. She lists not unlike an ocean liner in the aloe-hued radiance. She gets into a lotus position. Winds have the sound of infantile sighs. He whispers like he's confined in a confessional. Her intonation lingers, independent of her, and drifts off like a cloud. He seems almost stupefied as if he's a soldier standing at attention before a commanding officer. Venetian blinds make these zebra stripes of shadow. His inflection is ossified. She's bleary-eyed, her mop now messy, and she walks akin to a beginning skater. Leaves with holes are like lace fans. His brain spins like a windlass. The aroma of starch impregnates his civvies. She changes into a cochineal cardigan and color-coordinated panties and fuchsia puddletons. He optically, and prudently, measures her butt from a distance, as a lunarly rock. Railing's reminiscent of an iron spine. She says he has the face of a handsome giraffe. She vents torpefied flatus. Her respiring sounds not unlike a tablet fizzing in a glass of water. Their friendly back and forth, discussing diverse topics, is like a verbal puppet show. She removes the swampers. She has a husky modulation and a digestive rhythm to her vocal cadence. Her drink looks like iodine. He lets her idle, squamiform, chubby heel wander over his foot at the Formica table, and permits her ham hock calf to rest on his knee. Under normal circumstances, he would've recoiled as a fired rifle. Petaline tongues lick the grungy panes. There's assorted junk. Julia cants and he gawks at the gap in her globulous haunches. Her leprose crack. Peki's mongoloid brow beats. He moves like a guerrilla commando. He has a newborn's teary eyes. Verminous critters have invaded the district. It's quiet as a museum. The hexagon of a window, with a crocheted drape, is filmy and opaque. He clutches the banister on the spiral staircase. Luminescent needles pierce his eyeballs. An equestrian statue has a flaking lichen of rust. She is a redheaded hog sipping bubbly, achromatic like bleach, out of a snifter. Whereupon she soaks her used sanitary napkin in it, lids opening and closing as oysters. She stamps like she's squashing cockroaches, rowing with the currents of the alcohol, her dandruff as rice-cake crumbs, one chin piled on the other, heaped in pleats, speaking in a cemetery voice. His hamster's mouth quivers. Then he stares at her varicose veins with an assassin's eyes. This insistent, incomprehensible oral diarrhea squirts out of her rectal chops. Her plenteous cutis seems elastic, insubstantial. He releases gas from his ass like air from a punctured tire. He has the impulse control of a refrigerator magnet. She is en route to the kitchen to get dessert when he cracks her on the cranium with a baseball bat. Spread on her side, the echoes of her bovinely lowing resound through the rooms. He wears a desperate expression, similar to that of a cornered cat. Her skull crushed, blood gushing like a niagara, she mewls in misery, and moves on the dusty parquet as a castaway on the tide of an island's beach. It's a punchy smashy affair. Uncomfortable intimacy. Peki manages to drag the granite weight of her bulky body down the hall and outside into the gurgling deluge and strains mightily to fit it into his spacious trunk. Julia's suet has a specific sponginess. Her exposed chunky nates suggest, optically, glabrate badgers. Snail-slime snot oozes out of his nose. The vault drips like a faucet. Clusters of cirri are confused. His panic dissolves like vapor. He climbs as an insect into the driver's seat. The key turns painfully in the ignition. The weary vehicle stutters and reluctantly starts. He drives away, fanning out a brackish puddle. Moon flutters in the cumuli not dissimilar to flame in a kerosene lamp. Raging persecution of the downpour. The stars are as those dots in a game where you've got to connect them to create an image. Buildings, in the smaze, are ostensibly unfinished drawings, sketches done in charcoal crayon. Filament volutes of cloudlets. Automobiles propel themselves on the main road pell-mell. He uses her adipose tissue for another batch of margarine. Eventually, he puts it on vegetables and trips. He embarks on an indiscriminate murderous spree, dumping the casualties in a peat bog when he's finished with them. Business booms and the body count goes up. There is an unexpected swirl of customers spinning in the store! Sun bursts like a boil over the sooty chimneys. His heart is coal, its glow dying out. Moribund wisteria. He's reduced to a paper cutout (in the intense emanation) against the acneous wall. He partakes of a cappuccino, inflaming an infected molar. Morning and afternoon merge as a couple of naked beings. The flea market is set up on a tennis court. Bumblebees' buzzing sounds like lawnmowers. Lidless sewer is an abyssal yawn. He feels like an injured rodent that has crawled into this location to die. Carnivorous growls of zephyrs. The plane's like some massive pigeon. Stocking the refrigerated shelves, he croaks as a gull, ostensibly putting pieces of a puzzle together.

He spreads the mantequilla (with Julia's fat in it) on an English muffin and eats it. He has a vision of her lying in bed. Her feet begin to itch. Ultimately, they begin bubbling and little spots appear, and grow into pus-filled boils. Then, they turn into tentacles, each about an inch in diameter on her soles, thrashing and waving around, whereupon they die and dry out, into dead scabs.

Junkie

The day's gloomy as night. Her recollections of the previous week are now nothing more than pen scribbles written in invisible ink on the paper of the past. The apartment is so squalid even the vermin have relocated. She peels the leech of a Band-Aid from the festering sore on the crook of her elbow. It was stuck there for quite some time, seemingly sucking the blood. Serious infection. Fucking syringe. The struthious junkie once had magnolia flesh, face with the roundness of a ranunculus flower. Her derma layer is not unlike modeling clay and her bare feet are tough as certain hedgerow fruits. She sees her pudic, strabismal eye reflected in the puddle of piss on the floor. Her stream of consciousness is reduced to nothing more than a series of separate rivulets. She'd fluttered to the party, attracted to it like a moth to a lucent window, where she scored. High, she feels like Nike, heroin her manna. Her black hair is ruffled as a raven's plumage. She cradles the puppet, a quadruple amputee, rocks a chair, and reads Homer's 'Odyssey.'

Guadalupe Lira

The skies open. Peki bumps into the busty and curvy girl on purpose on the dirt road on the outskirts of town and calls himself "unforgivably uncoordinated," after profusely apologizing. She has this sort of hay-sweet body odor. Her copper-chromatic hair, piled exorbitantly on her head, has the scent of honeysuckle. Her breath is redolent of papaya. There's something special about her winsomeness that makes him feel pious, Lord forgive him. Guadalupe seems worldly-wise, in spite of her relative youth. She is on the verge of nineteen and addicted to sniffing from cans, paint tins, peroxides, and hair dyes. In life, she's lost in the woods, wandering around aimlessly in a futile search for familiar land-marks that never present themselves. She decides, following a moment's hesitation, to countenance his company while she walks home. He tries to court her, trying to convince her that he's a great catch. He is motivated, naturally, by the adventurism of the amorous kind. Putting it succinctly: he's bent on banging her. And he has mantequilla on his mind. She's got some good baby fat on those big bones. His imagination runs fever-ishly wild. He is tempted to seize the bull by the horns and tell her the truth. They traverse the muddy floor of the valley. For him, with her, the copse is paradise. She's an angel who fell to earth. He is in heaven. She's conscientious and principled he discovers. The perpetual drizzle drifts. A trio of ravens looks taxidermized, perched on a branch. During a down-pour and windstorm, they find shelter in an unoccupied tin shack. The weather causes a crisis. The vacant room has an odor of dried herbs. Peki strokes the silvering strands of his beard. Leaping at the chance to tag her, he begins unclothing her. Guadalupe stands still. Her blank expression betrays her trepidation. Her armpits reek of orange and chicken. He waits to launch an assault on her command. He will take unilateral action with her directive. He attacks her with precision. Her pallor brightens when he exposes his nether parts. She has a saccharoid modulation. His vital piece of intimate equipment is operating with no fundamental faults. He feels her breasts and buttocks, their substantial solidity and weight, in his hands. His woody supports his chinos like a tent pole. She has the hottest tail in the world. His chopper rises and swells at his will. It is as though he has mastered the art of charming a snake. The sensation, in itself, is stimulating. He's desperate for ardent appeasement. His prepuce nods like the oscitant head of an alky. He admires his impressive boner. She blushes crimson as he plays with his tumescent organ. She miaows not unlike a pussycat and pulls a sour face. "Suck my thingummy," he wheezes. She engages in the act of fellatio. She expects cunnilingus later on. His apparatus is functioning just fine. She grins coyly and gives him a calculatedly sexy sideways glance. He tuts irritably when she uses too much teeth. She is becoming so adept that he is already fantasizing about a repeat performance. His trigger finger is itchy, longing to enter her orifices. He wishes to sodomize her in the time-honored tradition. His push-button virility she presses. He has the exceptional capacity to be erected at the drop of a hat, and for a length of time that he fancies. He fondles her with no finesse. He resembles a devil. Her haunches evoke cabbages. She squats, in this semi-nude, seductive pose, at his genitals, furrowing her brow in an effort of optical examination. Molested, her heart sinks, and her face falls. He takes a deep draw of his cigarette and blows the smoke. He sees demons and thinks he has an infestation of worms under his fingernails. He wonders if he is out of touch with reality. Fucked, she flaps her arms so fast that they blur like a hummingbird's wings. In the yard, he bludgeons her on the nape of her neck with a truncheon he found in the shack. Stunned, she reels on the mulch, staggering in drunken circles, not consenting to die. He watches with utter fascination as she defecates and urinates, stumbling about. And he circumambulates like some grounded and hungry vulture until she collapses into a brackish puddle. His winkle resumes its repose in his slacks. He hangs her by the feet and beats her. She wails as though because of parturition. Whereupon he hangs her by the neck and disembowels her. The taste of her is fresh upon his tongue. The entrails he extracts from her he tosses aside for the animals. He fills her stomach with stones and drops her like an anchor in the quag's murky water. He ruminates. His murderous ways have already been set in motion. He's a one-man death squad, roaming the city and countryside, liquidating members of the civilian population. His soul is beyond saving. Once he's started he can't stop. The Butyrum is like the Blessed Virgin — no one knows whether or not it is immaculately conceived. His is a personal crusade for butter knowledge. He hails himself as the "savior of the spread." He is handling his accumulating influence in the field well. Through circumspection, timidity, or incompetence, his competitors make themselves noticeably invisible. When it comes to these adversarial companies, it's as if he's a guerrilla terrorizing the peasants, raping and pillaging them. He demands privileges and provisions with the assistance of obvious threats that amount to extortion. He will never clean up his act. He makes no bones about it: he is an exploitative employer. He distributes equitably the profits of production when it concerns his Mama. His frequent coughs produce clots of blood that congeal on his handkerchief. The abdominal pain is excruciating, and he downs a veritable pharmacopeia of painkillers. His brain is unclear. He washes in the drenching rain that saturates the region. His midsection is swollen as though he is preggers. He bounds along a trail like an idiot. Then he buys himself a pair of alligator flip-flops to make himself feel better.

Andrea Osorio

Peki has covered an enormous distance on impossible terrain, coming across Andrea in his travels. She has huge, strikingly amber pies, a cute pixie cut, and an elfin form. She cuffs him spiritedly, sportively about the ears, and bites his throat. His demented, salacious grin gives him an equine expression. With his paw, he swipes at her keister and dodges her kicks. He plants a kiss on her cheek. His stelliform peepers glisten. Her voice is borne to his hearing as if by special distribution upon the airwaves of the heavenly etheric liquid. On psychedelic mushrooms, her spoken language sounds the same backward as it does forward to him. She has lidless eyes, nostrilless honker, and a lipless mouth. She mimics his every move, not unlike his shadow. She has the fragrance of strawberries. She is so lovely that it breaks his heart. He's convinced that he's parasitized by a fungus. Shaken with fear, his yap quivers, and his orbs fill with tears. She looks dismayed and astounded. He visualizes despoiling the velvet darkness of her derma layer. Her smirk of mischief materializes. Vehicles clatter and roar on the thoroughfare. Peki becomes prey to the predator's suggestibility. He believes this accidental encounter may have been arranged by a higher power. Their mutual attraction is a revelation. Andrea tantalizes him with exquisite foreplay, sending shivers up and down his legs. They drink wine and make love. Her pelvis thrusts when he tickles her perineal fuzz. His behind has an acute sensitivity when she smacks it with an open palm. Fingers travel to every anatomical nook and cranny. She sounds like a plaintive oboe, he like a tripping bassoon. His glans makes contact with her cervix. Both are on the edges of their seats in this venereal drama. She squirms deliciously beneath him and ambushes his tush. He is petrified of premature orgasm. He humps the mound of her pubis. Quick as lightning, they thunder to contractions. They romp, with breath-catchingly brief increases in velocity. She caresses his testicles until he squirts his jizz. They climax in unison. He feels like a matador triumphing over the bull. People are disappearing, she says. They are evaporating away. Citizens seem daily to diminish. Perspiration breaks out on his forehead. He experiences the enervation of post-coital funk. His tumescence returns after a short while. His mind whirls with the indecency of his thoughts. His madness is unmanageable. She smirks brightly. He is listless and empty-eyed. With pleasure, he watches the birds scrapping over the chunk of bread he tossed, in an avian carica-ture of rugby. He finds himself in the past, present, and future. And he contemplates the rolling mist. Condors ride the updrafts in an incessant quest of carrion. All is right with the universe and nothing is worth fret-ting about. His heart leaps in his chest when he sees a tattered scarecrow with a pathetic phiz and infected lamps. His rags visibly crawl with ticks and lice. The town's stench has become ever more intolerable. The stink of deliquescence is so awful that it is a rare sight indeed to behold a window ajar. Electric fans usually hum polyphonically throughout the neighborhoods, many of them pointed directly at places where a draft might enter to counter the miasma. Folks would prefer to suffer from the unbearable swelter than the nauseating mephitis. The dispossessed, living in makeshift cardboard shelters, are forced to deal… Some of his victims reside beneath the opaque waters of the river, their feet encased in concrete, contributing to the fetor. Adding to the misery, crime escalates and the innocents sleep with one eye open. The criminal underclass and disaffected youth maintain a stranglehold. The police are disinterested in doing anything about it because theirs is a thankless job. Why bother? Peasant life in the countryside is one's best bet to survive. The ferment-ing acid reflux maddens him. He hallucinates a mule, retching pensile strings of saliva, its legs swaying back and forth inches off the dirt, its pizzle winding around his neck like a lariat. His intonation bongs with the mockery of a gong. Words emerge from his trap as balderdash. Will hell on earth change into a Garden of Eden? Lizards float in clouds of pungent smoke, squealing and gibbering, adjusting the racket as though to achieve emotional effects, vocally tinkering with the sonorities, taking into consideration the range and limitations. Several sulk and hide in a chasm. The noise unfolds and he follows. It gets difficult for him and he gets lost. A disembodied, rotund belly has a spiral navel. A sinuous tongue licks this wrinkled pudenda. He is cognizant of his human fallibility. He's puffy-eyed with exhaustion. And he drifts into the delectable obliteration of slumber. Waking up is a blithesome exhilaration. When he turns on his heel to leave, he's mobbed by baying rakshasas who rake him with their claws and chomp him with their fangs and taunt him. He searches his pockets for drugs to banish them. He comes up empty. Andrea isn't around.

Peki and Marisa

Life, for Peki, is sometimes like a crustacean trying to claw its way out of a pot of boiling water... Marisa is magnificent and seraphic, framed against the window, the sun behind her like a halo. She gambols, speaking nonsense. She longs to touch the cirri. He, looking like a tubby crow in his black robes, watches her with consternation. He clutches at her clothing, his mind seized with incertitude. Her countenance contorts. In possession of lordly confidence, he attempts to quieten her by using a soft voice, anticipating her curiosities to engage. Pleasure glows in his stomach as if he swallowed effulgence. She gapes in disbelief, then scowls, deeming it beneath her dignity to make a fuss. She endures arthritic aches and existential problems that she can't alleviate and discuss and suffers from futile aspirations. She can be deep and silent as a well. He imagines the refulgence spinning into yarn and made into a bright dress for her to wear. He pictures a cemetery, bereaved families tending to the graves of their loved ones, cleaning headstones, leaving bouquets, and sobbing over the dead. He is at fault. He's to blame. His being feels numb and tingly. He shudders and has halva. She has the lokum. His respirations sound like the rattling of birds' bills. Resentment rises in his breast. His ears ring, eyes full of sorrow. He will save his emotion for later. He lays the flat of his mitt on her diaphragm. She forces herself to calm her breathing. Her world stops spinning. He inhales her perfume, its fragrance similar to resin, and exhales. He masters himself, relinquishing his grip on her hips. The train plumes with steam. Stars visually suggest glittering specks of grit in the cumuli. The gay club, called the Succulent

Sphincter, is tilted askew by the settlement of pavement. A leprose starveling loiters. Peki remembers waking in a sweat of terror, heart tired out from pumping. He had a dream of chancing upon a deceased Marisa, her body distended and deliquescent, in a patch of weeds in a church's courtyard. She was being desecrated by cherubs with desiccated pink poppies in the wisps of fair hair. She murmured the Jesus prayer in the indifferent pastel light, looking like it was filtered through shutters. The little angels had olives for oculi, tomatoes for cheeks, white cheese skin, and loaves of bread for buttocks. Abruptly, she became animated and tutted when they relieved themselves on her. She patted their fundamental in parodic reproof. Whereupon the intimate quiescence had its own garrulity. Two of them, an Asian male and female, stood self-consciously beside and behind her, their heads bent not unlike modest virgins, their hands folded together, while she was playfully mauled. They cast their peepers to the ground. Their mushes were full of concern and sympathy. The Caucasian cherubs were busy and she was confused. One Eastern Indian, broad-bellied-and-bottomed, kicked dirt in her face to blind her and then ate her out. Gales of childish guffaws from three African Americans ensued. Her pigtails recalled old ropes. Her tongue was cut out. The assailants munched their way through the obligatory apertures of her anatomy. Slumbering, he guessed the baby angels arrived on earth from heaven without a history but assumed they were cast out of the celestial city and wound up one wingbeat away from hades. Afflicted with a spontaneous and ungovernable impulse, they insulted and abused her. A couple of them orbited her and collided with each other. Still sleeping, his heart grew heavy and sank. Their tiny wings poised, they wore peculiar moues and had fanatical twitches of the eyeball. An eagle whistled over the backside rock roses. The rubicund sun reddened further. A bell tolled sadly. A wrought-iron railing was rusted, the brick wall lopsided. Storks squabbled. The cherubs beat her with a scourge. Marisa made a sign of the cross and scolded them. And she grinned and pissed herself. She was like a shark who found itself swimming with a school of mackerel! Her bare heels kicked, casting aside spitfuls of ochreous soil. Perspiration pearled on her brow, and her chest rose and fell arrhythmically. Her attackers were consumed by a violent curiosity. They dug into her, their passions transporting them, sounding like a herd of beasts wailing, burning in the wilderness, so absorbed in her orifices that they scarcely heard her moans and groans. She wiped her damp forehead. They brushed at her bosom with their fingers, as though it was a relic they were excavating or exhausting and clearing of dust. Their mellifluent singing turned into a dreadful keening, sounding like a flock of wounded birds. They held her chin reverently and kissed her nipples fervently. His Mama reminded him of death's mockery of a living lady. He was more fascinated than horrified. The nightmare was enough to keep him bilious for a month.

Peki dispatches a raven-haired siren and a mousy brunette after a rough night in the karaoke booth with these Power Rangers-style superheroes. A bucket of vomit on the bar had a mind and voice of its own.

Showered and dressed, Peki's bearing is proud, his mustache and beard well-brushed, his galoshes gleaming with a fresh coat of polish. He marches with practically military precision. Marisa, meanwhile, is livid with righteous rage, circumlocutorily going on about the rumors circulating concerning their relationship, a "friendship-with-benefits." She has conviction in her indignation, parading around, almost hysterical. "Human beings are ignorant and mean-spirited," he declares, "loving rubbing salt in one's wounds, squirting lemon juice in others' cuts." He stomps in a bold passion. "They remind people of their misfortune and disappointment." His modulation sounds as if his larynx is made out of dead leaves. He swings a glass bottle of Jack Daniel's Tennessee Whiskey like a priest his censer. "These are symptoms of a societal disease that's incurable." Well, she wishes that the neighbors' scandalous suspicions were nipped in the bud. Her flesh is whiter than snow. She knocks back raki. Her throat is constricted with emotion. She scarfs down the koliva. His digits remind her of the stubs of pale candles. She turns in idiotic circles. She softens his stony heart. He seems to exist in an unceasing state of longing for her. She frowns. A department store is completely demolished. The sun flickers sorrowfully in a claret cumulus that spreads like a bloodstain. Visitors depart in a pack from the cubical complex. Marisa indulges in creating another asinine episode, as though in some pointless behavioral experiment. Peki adjusts the spectacles on the bridge of his nose, fantasizing about the pure tongue in her oral cavity. She puts the finishing touches on the honey pastries in the kitchen, yakking about the "advanced learning" of her "elementary education." Her intonation has this crackling quality. She crosses her pies and hops. Faltering, and with interjections from her, he tries to tell her to relax. He attempts to maintain his patience, to no avail. She suffers from insidious loneliness. He helps to fill out her life which is vacant at its core. When things are going wrong for her, she needs someone to show her the right path. She screws up her orbs in an imitation of a zombie. "Forgive us our daily bread," she says, "and lead us not into temptation." To call her nutty antics a self-parody would be an insult to parody and to selves. She calls him bad names a few paces away, such as a "Mephistophelean demiurge." Blood beats behind his lamps. His lips are grimly tautened. She slides her feet into these embroidered slippers with a lack of enthusiasm. He figured she'd be seduced by the fabric and stitching... There is a deep silence. Serenity is in the air. The sprinkles jingle not unlike bells on surfaces. Weatherwise, there are sinister omens. Gridlock is a mundane struggle. Luster is starting to fade. Laundry items are mixed promiscuously together on the floor. The room has the dank malodor of a cave. Pigeons cock their heads and crane their necks in agitation on the ledge. Marisa's diminutive container of tequila is curiously concave on one side. She is becoming peevish at his vexatious attitude and obstructive manner. Beholding her, Peki can't help but feel a sense of wonder. Her eyes are beginning to shimmer. She sighs through her nostrils. Off her meds, she feels like a dove released from its cage. She talks in pig Turkish and dog Danish, twisting her mouth and raising her eyebrows. He looks pityingly at her, cramming a sweet cake into his yap. The tray on the counter supports a treasure trove of sticky desserts. He settles into a chair. Jubilant, she jumps up and down. She starts to develop the idea that she doesn't want to be a captive bird anymore. He persuades himself into believing that she will shed her silliness like a snake does its skin and become calm with the due passage of time. Her accursed flip-flops are not only too tight, they're contorted and limp. The cheap sandals bespeak a humdrum existence. She regards them with a sharp loathing. There's a comely intimacy between mother and son. Drapes reek of rotted grave clothes. The burg glisters with neon lights. Linnets wheel skyward from an almond tree, flying higher and higher. In this sector of town, there is torpor and decay and medieval harlotry that boggles the brain. The district is replete with bars and brothels. Riffraff runs amok 24/7 as if persecuted by insomnia. Protesters of all ages chant about exposing governmental corruption and abusive power. Peki deliberately turns a blind eye and a deaf ear. He is just endeavoring to cope with his vacillating paranoia. Several college students are arrested, ill-treated by the police officers, accepting the handcuffs with dignity and aplomb before they're loaded onto the wagon like cattle by the authorities. Bullet shells lay glistening and dangerous on the hot cement. Peki harks back to burying the gals in the flesh-devouring earth, in neglected undergrowth, the declining rays pressing its warmth into his uncovered back. He yenned for moral support. He made sure that he kept a proprietorial and protective eye on his business with his phone's special camera. He heard sibilant twittering as he shoveled. He patted the dirt using a spade when he finished.

Peki, clad in a viridescent kurta and oriental pajama, is wound fairly tight. His mustache and beard gleam with fresh pomade. His mane is clean and brushed. Marisa feels moribund, marooned, believing that she has been expelled from civilization because of subversive activities. His intention is not to die for her, but to live for her. There are stretches in which she shuts him out, and he thus feels as though she is a lover of the purely theoretical variety. Not only is she neurotic, but she can also be naive as a chick straight out of the egg. It turns out that his expeditions in the megalopolis and country are for murderous purposes, and the citizens are being terrorized and killed under the pretense of Butyrum production. He refuses to countenance disruptions in the process. He won't be hamstrung by law enforcement. He develops his perverse sanguinary gifts through practice. He swears allegiance to the product and kisses his sacred knife reverently. He thinks of himself as being completely indestructible. His employees are paid a pittance. And he capitalizes. He is an important individual, today and tomorrow. Irrelevance is unacceptable. He's growing weary of the false or exaggerated reports about the homicides in the newspapers. He pictures a number of the more recent victims. May they rest in paradise. He ponders over political corruption and inefficiency. Marisa listens to the enchanting and enspiriting sounds of birdsong. She dresses in a teddy like it's a uniform. She says, "What if we get caught?" And he replies, "Who cares? People should mind their own business!" "But what we're doing is indecent," she adds. "Folks enjoy cutting you and pouring vinegar into the wound," he responds. This type of lasciviousness is over and above. She has seemingly absorbed his perversion, like a clay cruse that soaks up water. His salacity is contagious as lice. He recollects the two of them sneaking out into the fields, fornicating, snorting, farting, and hinnying as horses do. Their heartbeats sounded like the clopping of hooves. Peace was upon them. His hardness softened. The penis in his pants was not unlike a carrot laid up for winter. He was bruised from his homicidal pursuits. He champed a piece of straw. The megapolis is destitute of vivacity. It is a place that from birth and death is an interminable time of misery. The region is paralyzed by impoverishment. Poverty is reshaping the nation. There is a lot of clutter and bedlam on the roads. Mother contacts son hesitatingly, as if afraid of soiling her hands attending to her sullied boy. Peki is a pest, like a flea in her ear, or a gnat up her nose. He can't bear to see such grief in her. Marisa whines like a dog when he tries to embrace her. He is small. She's slight. She pushes him away with a few words of reprimand, her inflection sounding strangled. Often she feels as though she exists with his foot pressed on her neck. He's nothing but trouble. Settled into the divan, she cracks pistachios on her lap. Her pretty body drives him wild, and her ineffable despondency perturbs him. He has every reason to be happy, being in this woman's company. Lusty, he pants to regain his breath. She stands, ominously silent. He realizes she is just toying with him. Hardhearted, she makes him feel like a considerable burden. She finds it a strain to maintain a placid front. The river disappears into the sea. A sandbar materializes in the bay through the mizzle. Tourists walk behind their guide as if at a funeral. Dust hangs over the macadam. Plants are withering. Quaggy patches of muck are on the sidewalk. Peki formulates a plan to get her into bed. Marisa converses with every semblance of coolness. There is defeat in her carriage. In this life, she is making progress but still is in pain. He sucks on melon seeds while she organizes her footwear of many vintages against the massive wall. She squeals with delight, fluttering her papery hands, her bracelets jangling together. He could just hug her to death! She adopts a self-approving expression and pretends to preen herself. She's raving mad and he adores her. On the balcony, she admires her reflection in a puddle below. Her vox cracks and wavers as her fingers work at the prayer beads. He is faithful as a shadow, following her wherever she goes. He smiles seraphically, yearning to pinch the elongated lobes of her ears. He beams with satisfaction, leering at her, discomfited in the crepuscule. She makes funny eyes and purses her lips. She adopts a pleading tone when he grabs the crook of her elbow. He imagines her bouncing him on her knee — a haloed Mary with her Christ Child. He is unsteady and faltering from the legacy of his drinking. She smells of patchouli. They hear an extraordinary flurry of loud and exuberant catcalls coming from the street. They acknowledge the immemorial turbulence of the metropolis. It is a pauperizing, demoralizing economy. It's a vile, hostile environment. The calefaction makes their diaphoresis a glue. She tactically retreats into the pantry. Dawn's showers were sweet. Dusk is gentle, in terms of temps. He renews his affectionate assault on her. When he gets in her hair, she brushes him out.

Tita Egidio

Peki knows he is breaking down his health by the constant carousing. Meanwhile, Marisa is blown by mental illness from one problem to another. He yearns to unveil his heart to her. His loins long for her. He needs to meld with her. She is the missing part of himself. He deems himself amusing of comportment, accomplished in business, excellent, and enthusiastic in the techniques of murder. He concentrates a lot on his clandestine life that devotes itself to plots of Byzantine complexity, whose aim is to restore relevance to margarine. Sometimes he gets nervous in thinking that his establishment is a sorry structure built from hacked flesh in the name of mantequilla. He can't help but get carried away by his creative impulses. She's puce-lipped and fair of skin, and lean and sinewy, with the long beak of a bee-eater. She lights up the gloom of a room with her presence like the moon. She is a woman worthy of his current state. He's wearing patent leather shoes of the highest quality, a frock coat, and buff chinos, dressed like a thoroughly modern gentleman. His facial hair is trimmed. He smokes grass copiously and admires the scenery: his madre. Her urine has the scent of rosewater. She swallows a shot of rum with a theatrical flourish and sighs contentedly. She is optically riveted to the floor as if anticipating finding coins there; or perhaps she feels like she's lost in a dream, searching for something, but she doesn't know what it is exactly. He's disconcerted by her unfocused blinders and is infected by her stillness. She is unresponsive. Emotion stirs in his breast. She snatches at flies to feed the pigeons in the park. He does mental arithmetic, calculating the amount of profit that might be expected from the latest batch of Butyrum. No person is a proper person if they don't use butter. He works day and night to produce the stuff, and yet cannot meet the demand. He's lucky. It is maybe more important than having genitals. His hunger for her is forbidden and punishable. He could care less. He sees the terribleness of his licentiousness. He starts to dictate the terms. The city is crawling with cops, most of whom have more than adequately mastered the art of ruthlessness. It's unsafe for anyone to travel these mean streets alone. Aegean-blue welkin. The roads buzz with vehicular activity. A train at the station makes ready to depart. The landlord discusses issues with a bunch of his tenants. Mizzle has the fragrance of cinnamon. Peki remembers the barbarous herbage, his dreadful blisters, and the affliction of fatigue, in addition to the searing desert and lush jungle. It was a long, boring, and wearying trek... Pancake foundation covered Tita's cratered countenance, the result of a childhood encounter with smallpox. He was hardly four feet tall, approximately Peki's height, reddened from sunburn from top to toe. He was riding bareback along a dirt path, with his pony's saddle on his shoulders. He was transporting spices and cloths. The sour-faced wretch had an abundance of adipose tissue that had Peki salivating. He had a shaved head and a ring through a nostril. He wore hand-me-downs. He was all in trepidation and trembling, talking in a funny baby tone of voice. He wept a bit and anxiously tapped on his chest with his knuckles when Peki, hard as a rock, withdrew his gat from its holster hidden under his Hawaiian shirt. Tita had a sheepish expression when Peki told him to strip. Peki slapped him across the face and kicked him in the shin. Tita went wobbly and nearly collapsed... After the buggering, he began to cry and flap his hams as his sodomizer rubbed his hind. Peki lit a cigar, took a drag, and cautiously deposited it in the guy's ass. Peki was already familiar with his anus, backwards, forwards, and sideways, having penetrated it with his preputial aubergine. The devil inside his head coaxed him. Tita's blinkers popped out and his mouth was opened wide. He was crestfallen. His brain stopped working. Fellating Peki, he looked as though he was repeatedly salaaming on his knees. He paused in the blowing as if to gather his wits. Reamed again, he whistled not unlike blackbird. He was a peculiar character, Peki thought. Caked in sludge, Tita looked like a cross between a leper and a corse. Peki's strands were like bindweeds, winding round Tita's throat and creeping over his back. Straddling his tailbone, he grabbed him by the scruff of the neck and twisted his ears. He decided then and there that he'd only be satisfied if he came a second time, and he would be at peace. It never happened. He kept giving the fellow instructions and directions that he had difficulty following. It was as though Peki spoke in a language that Tita did not recognize. Drizzle smelled of hot metal. The thrushes wouldn't shut up. Tita appeared mildly outraged when Peki impaled him with the dagger. He floundered in circles like a drunken dervish on the grass. He said he was "rich and respectable" before Peki smothered him to death in a dungheap. Peki was on him like a mad dog on a big bone. Killing a human being isn't easy, even in the best of times, he felt. Spent, Peki, with rats, slept on coiled ropes on the wharf. Sailors flirted with trollops on the pier.

Monti Mera

Peki's poisonous hangover forces him to upchuck into the gutter. His eyes squint against the sun. He has become a notorious and inveterate lush. Although short in stature, he is robustly built, and thus nobody messes with him. He generates turmoil and indulges in the shameless exhibition, refusing to lower a raised fist. His skull throbs, idly looking at a vulture on a garbage can. He perspires as if in a fever. His gait is unsteady, vision drifting in and out of focus. His limbs feel as though they're operated by a series of unseen levers. It's like a nail was hammered into his cranium. And his maxilla aches badly. He has a vile migraine and a short temper. On all fours, he barfs again and says something inarticulate. Pedestrians are attracted to the maudlin brouhaha, entertained by the spectacle. The mob is like a pack of hyenas. He wheels around and glares at the crowd with contempt. The people, gawking in malevolent pleasure, disperse, tiptoeing around him as if he's sleeping and they don't wish to wake him. Peki composes himself and lurches away purposefully, in the direction of the apartment, his apparel in disarray. It is impossible for him to tally the number of murders he has committed, or to reimagine how these killings were perpetrated. The homicides are receiving much publicity. At this rate, it will become a holocaust. Will it be commemorated by the nation? Will monuments be built? Calendars be marked? Religious and public services held to pay tribute to the lives tragically lost? He muses on his megalomania and psychopathy, the expense of effort to financially sustain the shop… The sky whites with clouds. He finds to his irritation and frustration that his labors have ruined his chances of getting laid. He just hasn't been home much. Mother and son copulate in privateness and swear oaths on the Holy Bible. Marisa thinks of his butter production as tedious hocus-pocus. She doesn't question his astute business sense. The name Peki is synonymous with mantequilla. Monti, his Mama's former lover, the dashing military man, was shot and wounded in a firefight in the hills against the revolutionists. The campaign was a half-baked affair. He had gathered the troops in the barracks and led them into battle. He was grandstanding, at the front of the infantry regiment marching into the mountains to confront the enemy: the local villagers who took up arms to rage against the machine. The nature and intentions of the operation were to seek and destroy and take no prisoners. Honor would be satisfied and peace restored. He was simply following orders. Mistakes were made. Signals got crossed. He was characteristically and unfailingly heroic. Mission accomplished, he returned injured and triumphant. He saved four soldiers' lives and was promptly decorated. The tide of war carried an opportunist officer into a territory in which the foes' ranks, supplies, and ammunition were significantly depleted. Monti was punctilious and vainglorious. Other than his undeniable courage, Peki saw no evidence of quality to redeem him. He was keenly aware of his superiority over the inferior "midget," browbeating him, threatening him implicitly with the things he said. He was seduced by power. He was dependent on status. His riffs on patriotism were aggravating. He was undeviatingly adherent to his mongrelized country. Existence is arduous and risky for Spaniards in the Fifth Dementia, living side by side with many diverse races. Monti never succeeded in impressing a skeptical Peki, who regarded him with disdain. Marisa met him while working as a pole dancer at a seedy joint. She was infatuated with him with such passionate adoration it made her lachrymose. Whenever he'd visit her, he would squeeze her so tight her eyes would bulge, her mouth pucker, and her ribs would nearly crack. From her person sprung a rill of joy. She bit her lip one noon in her boudoir when he kneaded her bosom. She glanced at Peki and closed the door. He strode up and down the room, protesting, being shut out, burying his face in his hands, and continuing to complain. He was so begrieved it was as if she had passed. He promised himself that soon enough Monti wouldn't be alive and intact. The patrolling of the parlor was accompanied by obscenities. His stream of consciousness was turbid. He made a gesture of impotence. His words were throttled by sobs. Tears trickled and saliva was strung across his teeth. His voice seemed to fail him as he paced in the darkened hall, shaking his coconut, in spiritual and moral pain. His form glittered in the half-light. His knob grew heavier in his mitt, experiencing a sudden surge of arousal at the thought of them in bed. He bowed his head, feeling the soft pulse of his breath on his chest, endeavoring to suppress his agitation. He clenched his eyes shut, choking with convulsions. The shutters were open. Goldfinches peeped in the fig trees. Overtaken by tiredness, he gave up pleading with them to come out, or to let him in. He couldn't deal with what was occurring. It was far beyond his control. They were romantically involved, overtly and in secret. It tormented him that she despoiled and defiled herself. Peki abducted him and tortured him in a granary (Blashill-Buskas Inc.) before slitting his throat with a carver. Fate be fucked. He wasn't going to wait for divine malice to pour down on him with disgrace. Monti was huddled instinctively in a fetal position, bleeding from the sanguineous smile. The idea of violation germinated in Peki's intention. His shirt and breeches glistened with blood. Then, to his surprise, he wondered whether or not he should take him to a surgeon and save him. He knelt and kissed him. Whereupon he rested his brow on the victim's sternum. His coughing sounded like clapping. The mountains were not unlike somber fortresses. The grim plains stretched into infinity. He was affronted by the sordidness of the neighborhood, stepping over sedated addicts, skirting obsecrating beggars, as though he was a master leaving a chess match, not wanting to disturb the pieces on the board, in the teeming alleyway. His devoted shadow was in tow. This hell was a mockery of heaven.

The War

Peki has a dream in which he pilots a sperm-shaped craft into a space uterus and enters through an airlock that resembles a geometrized vulva. He arrives in the massive chamber of a penthouse tower. Then he wakes and blazes a blunt so thick he uses fireplace tongs for the roach clip and dredges up a memory from long ago: he was neck-deep in the proverbial feces. In reality, he was up shit's creek, becoming submerged in a brook flooded with waste, hiding from a marching German division. He struggled to hold his breath in the murky aqueous realm and made peace with the idea of death by drowning. He swam to the surface. It was sheer pleasure to rise from those filthy waters, very nice to let the oxygen fill his lungs. His heart made knocking noises that reverberated. The brigade was gone. He crawled to the banks, covered in clumps of crap like the hull of a boat encrusted with mussels at the bottom of the brine. He was relieved to abandon the insect-infested jungle, and take a break in the clearing. His cogitations were disconnected. He was over his head in excrement. The discourse with himself was adrift. He was sinking slowly in the oily waters of confusion. Extreme exhaustion was brought about by exertion and dismay. He was delirious from an infected monkey bite. He thought for a second that it might be easier to die than live in this chaotic climate. He was bitter about the war until he began to fight it properly. His commanding officers, a bunch of boobs really, made an infinity of mistakes big and small. They were multiplying. The errors. He thought it'd be outrageous if he was reprimanded for innocently and magnanimously inflicting atrocities on the peasants, male and female.

He blatantly displayed a lamentable lack of scruples. He was out of control and more often than not no one had any idea what he was up to. It drove them crazy. Certainly, he wasn't out on civilizing missions. He relished embellishing his reputation for hooliganism. He was an Iagoid schemer. Allied battleships in the port maintained principled impartiality and cautious impassivity. There was a throng of humanity desperate to leave. Peki was horny. This was a law of nature he would obey. He sprang to attention, catching the sight of a girl, and appraised her loveliness with disciplined admiration. He was inspired by his libidinousness to commit an unwise act of assault on a young woman, named Jun, who was taking optical inventory in a raisin harvest. He took her by force to what was once a pretty playground but had become a place of bones and metal and timber and piles of ash. He was determined to frogmarch her to her demise. When they ran into a Spanish unit, he explained that he was interrogating the lady, accusing her of supplying weapons and ammunition to the enemy. For extra seasoning, he added that she didn't possess a legitimate license for a hunting rifle. They moved on without a word. He forced her at gunpoint to denude herself down to her camiknickers. He was prodigiously overendowed with sick and salacious ideas as to what to do with her. Her firebrand personality pissed him off. Whole villages were wiped out by the melees. Peki threw her onto the ground and jammed his foot in her crotch to expedite the removal of her panties. Jun seemed genuinely perplexed. She was a sweet virgin, and he violated and defenestrated her. She had a cute face and an excellent body. It wasn't a gigantic fuck-up because his nincompoop superiors would never find out. She shook and sobbed while he attacked her. He attempted to communicate his feelings and spouted foul language she did not understand. Fondling her… these were addlepated antics. It was an exciting occasion, digitally exploring her exposed orifices. It went all downhill from there when she started kicking and screeching. Gibbering like a lunatic, he stomped on her torso, tore at her flesh, and perpetuated unimaginable horrors upon her person. He engaged himself in an electrifying spree of self-congratulation and singing patriotic songs, irritating the birds beyond measure. Mayhem was everywhere. Buildings were razed to the ground. Farmers labored on their land. Peki treated her as if he had harbored a grudge against her. He felt he was entitled to express himself picturesquely. Jun tried valiantly to fight him off. She seized the chance to bemoan this barbarism. He called her a "dumb bunny," a "slant-eyed tart," and a "lackwit rattlebrain," as he molested her. He said he wanted to "play poky hole" with her, but she just cried and trembled. He made no distinctions between race and religion when it concerned the fairer sex. He beat and raped her, whereupon he gouged out her eyes, broke her teeth, split her lips, and cut off her ears. He nursed her, stroked her, and whispered endearments to her as she perished. He held her bare feet, not unlike a botanist would rare exotic orchids. The city was ruined and impoverished. Jun was so disfigured when he was finished that her own family wouldn't recognize her. Peki regarded her for some time. Tears came to his eyes. He was on the cusp of vomiting. He was stunned by what he'd done. How could he be so cruel? His military uniform was blood-splattered. Twitchy, he was thinking that he made a terrible mistake. It was too late to correct it, for she was dead, lying on her side. He wanted to be a sensible man. At twilight, in town, he cheered and waved a Spanish flag out front of a bawdy house until some idiot sniper fired a shot at him. He ducked for cover. Then he casually returned to the barracks like one would go home after work. He perfected the art of alienating himself from his fellow soldiers. He had lobster and crayfish for dinner.

Peki was shellshocked after the firefight. It was a dizzying, almost hallucinatory experience — akin to being thrown into a washing machine and mercilessly churned for hours. He felt like a tumbling barrel. He managed to outwit and outface his enemy, a Kaiser expeditionary force out for blood, by pretending to be a traveling circus performer, clowning around, pulling off backflips, cartwheels, and somersaults, to not insignificant applause. And he explained to them that the Spanish uniform was his jester getup. The patrol clapped and hurrahed. He skipped rope using barbed wire. For a short time, there was an excess of joy. The troop's cheering exposed an inevitable undercurrent of sorrow. It was a momentary distraction from the daily horrors. The unit went on its way. He was a deserter and was afraid he'd be put on trial and convicted and executed.

He had a strong feeling that gossip was spreading among the men about his disappearance. When it concerned his position in the military, he was disinclined to seriousness. His brothers were probably glad that he was gone. He laid down the steady beats for his infantry brethren to march to. Sporadically he would throw in intricate polyrhythms to trip them up. He was becoming a human being of alternately lesser and greater irrationality. He was abject and shaking. He witnessed heartrending and pathetic scenes with the dislocated families. He came across a multitude of soldier and refugee cadavers on the roadside. He endured a long and desperate slog. Japanese civilians were on a death march in an overgrown field. The region looked like Paradise was transformed into Hades. Having arrived in it, Peki felt that it was attempting to accommodate and incorporate him. There was rampant destitution and injustice on account of the warfare. Hope was evaporating. He was sweating and shivering. He could barely drink from his canteen. Although tired and sick, he was surviving. He wept with relief and burst with pride… His trudging and actions were without trajection and consequence. Unsureness ate at him like cancer. He appeared aged because of the toll taken on his health by wounds, both physical and psychological. He was skinnier and more disheveled than ever. His limp was pronounced. The injuries mounted. He had problems breathing. The issue was not helped by the continual smoking, a habit that had him hooked. His carriage wasn't erect. His hump saw to that. Madness contributed to his metamorphosis. Houses were dilapidated. Areas were depopulated. Animals were gone. The desire to see Marisa again made Peki's throat constrict, his heart ache, and caused butterflies to flutter in his stomach. He kept picturing his beloved in his mind, and he had a kind of quivering sensation all over his skin and felt a sort of hunger and restlessness. She enjoyed adorning herself, employing aromas to satisfy him. She was composed and perfected for his eyes only. His energy dripped away, drop by drop, traipsing on the desert terrain of scorpions, lizards, dust, and stones. Endurance washed out of him by the effort. His longing for his madre was pain. His chest hurt from heaving. His intonation was ragged and his speech was muddled and his gait was more peculiar than usual. He feared he wasn't right in the head. He'd lost a couple of teeth. He wanted to get back in balance. He sat on a rock and sobbed, rubbing his face with his hands, imagining his Mama caressing his nape and kissing his cheek. He experienced yearnings in his groin. He uttered words in his language. He meant to say everything. In his craving for his mother, he found a potent source of emotional and spiritual strain. His slumber was often turbulent, and he had no magic medicine to yield him improved sleep. At night he had these recurring dreams of her in a hundred infinitesimally disparate versions, involving her being gangbanged by recruits in a galley. Folks he encountered were on the edge of hysteria. His articulation was simple and direct. On a dirt path, he was besieged by a group of orphans in tatters, begging him for food. It was a bewildering and impossible task of working out who to feed first. He was well-provisioned. He had much stuff to spare. His inflection was thin and dry. The children held their hands out beseechingly, palms upward, their faces trained toward him. Everyone got something. He accomplished this feat with patience and pertinaciousness. Suddenly, a few of them were plunged into extreme states of fervor. Several were confused. Peki was stunned and silent. The kids, encircling him, talked and gestured wildly. Rooting through his rucksack, he contacted objects of sentimental value, such as pieces of Marisa's jewelry and photographs. He waved his arms and shouted to attract the attention of the foundlings. They had to leave. It was too dangerous to stay. They refused to go. This was their home. Some of them were crazed, some retarded, and some fugitive. He tried to marshal the youths, to get them moving. You couldn't stand still and expect to remain alive. Those were such straitened circumstances for the poor humbled souls. He struggled for optimism over pessimism in the place of despair. The lenses of his spectacles were cracked and smeared.

Piper and Darwin

Marisa's boudoir is bare and functional and pleasant enough, a haven for her with satinwood walls. The furniture, shaped out of walnut, is anomalous and redundant. She studies assiduously the ash-whitish overcast. She is being refractory as a camel. Peki wants her to be dutiful and obedient. He gazes at her adoringly. His peepers are evocative of chunks of glowing coal. He invades her body in order to touch her heart; however, he reaps nothing but sexual gratification from the assaults on her being. He's graceless in his motion, quick and nervy. He is a human powder keg. His glare coveys, to a staggering degree, his minacious disposition. Even she's often taken aback by his intensity. She is tensed as if for the attack. His unprompted hissy fits frequently develop into violent paroxysms, eventually restoring himself to some semblance of sanity. Her melodious voice has a remarkably civilizing effect on him. He was a wayward and incorrigibly savage child, and from his infancy, she knew he was destined to meet his maker in the worst way. He has an absolute lack of principle. He was disowned by most of his immediate family for his evildoings and forced into near exile. Lessons were never learned. He was devastated by the dismissal, feeling humbled and dishonored, experiencing stabbing pain in the gut. He was discouraged by the disgrace. He was demeaned by his relatives. He vowed never to forget. As a kid, he derived an exhilarated malicious satisfaction from urinating in a teacher's soda can... Marisa's walk is like she is trudging knee-deep in clinging mud. A sweat of anxiety breaks out on her brow. Seated on a low stool, he sparks a fatty and glances at her bony, angular feet. His oral cavity is as dry as summer clay. His affection for her is sacrosanct. Her recently shampooed tousled mop is superb and glossy. Horrendous agitation takes possession of her mind. He had disposed of a youthful couple, a sardonic ice queen with a nasal modulation, insouciance personified, named Piper, and her significant other, Darwin, a gent with a thousand-mile stare and who was as hairy as a Tibetan mastiff. Peki has been on a homicidal rampage, going through the megapolis like a hot knife through melted butter. He was a hunched figure with bowed shoulders to the pair, peregrinating in the thorny scrubland. He appeared disturbed when he spoke to them coarsely. His heart pounded unevenly, so he had to periodically catch his breath. Depraved thoughts were burning into his brain like acid. And he said something indistinct. After shooting the male with a Webley, then handcuffing, tasering, and pepper spraying him, he drew his dagger, the curved steel blade shining, and thrust it hard into the female's midsection. Dispassionately he watched her sink slowly to the ground and slump at the foot of a conifer. He slashed her temple, leaving a nasty gash. Then he crouched, grabbed a hunk of her tresses, and pulled her head back. She had a fine physog. He sniggered bitterly, heart clenched like a fist. He kicked her in the neck, sending her toppling sideways. He felt like a marionette, the imperceptible strings controlled by an unseen entity, and manipulated into doing these awful things. Piper cowed and trembled, got a glimpse of her beloved Darwin, lifeless in the bed of tulips. Death was fast approaching her. His cerebrations were disconnected, dabbing, with a napkin, at the blood and spittle that frothed in the corners of her mouth. She whimpered desperately, tears streaming down her cheeks. He was puzzled for feeling sorry for her. He admired her resignation. He recognized her loveliness and anger. He couldn't see fear. His motive was meanness. It was no longer about mantequilla. He acted as though he was behaving basely for a righteous cause. There was a buzz of bug noises. Peki fumbled at his fly, failing to unzip it after a number of tries. Piper glowered at him and smirked. He didn't experience shame when he exposed himself to her, his seemingly ventriloquized vox shaky. The first blow to her jaw was delivered halfheartedly. The second, to her chin, had this destructive intent. He pummeled her, baying like a hound, grinning with gleeful cruelty in the malevolent barbarism. He took advantage of the chance to beat such a beauty. He punched her to a pulp. She made a cryptic remark as he belted her senseless. Abruptly, he stopped to examine her expression. He parted her thighs. Battered into semi-consciousness, she turned her head, like it was tilted by invisible hands, or out of modesty. Her gasps were rhythmic and agonized. Dying, she wished she was never born. She was apparently detached from the fury and anguish. She had the blended bodily aromas of vanilla and musk. He stoned her. His access to viciousness subsided. Whereupon with a heavy, unwilling heart, he strangled her with her scarf. He kicked at her crumpled form. She was gone. He saw what he did in his wickedness. He ached and stung all over. His virescent cloak flapped out behind him in the zephyrs. He looked into her empty, half-closed eyes, and scrutinized her lips, stilled in mid-breath. It registered that he was a maniac. It wasn't just about the Butyrum. He was left in heartsick solitude, depressed and appalled by what he did.

Early Butter Pots and Size Standards

The butter crock has evolved over the years. Historically, a butter pot was a different type of container. It was a large, cylindrical, or slightly bulbous vessel, taller than it is wide, used to store dairy products and carry butter to the markets. Large Norman butter pots date back to at least post-medieval Welsh borderland kiln sites. They were cylindrical vessels with or without a handle, and often with internal glaze.

An example of early butter-pots, made in the 1640s, were unearthed in Burslem, the center of the butter-pot industry from the earliest days. The Burslem pots were well made of common clay, without glaze, and were marked in "rude letters" Cartwright on a relief two inches in diameter. This was the warranty that the pots were of the proper size.

At that time shysters tried to hoodwink the butter-buying public by various means: false bottoms, or too heavy or too lightweight wares to insure proper weights of butter to the ultimate consumers. Finally, in 1670 Parliament passed a law that these utensils had to weigh not more than six pounds, had to hold fourteen pounds of butter, and were to be of hard quality to prevent them from absorbing water from the butter. To ensure and/or enforce the law, surveyors (inspectors) were hired to spot-check the contents; so rather than depend on weight alone they used an auger-type "butter board" which was inserted obliquely to the bottom, removed, and checked/tested to assure that the butter the same all the way through. This was, after a fashion, an early-day pure food act.

Potter Frank Gosar's grandmother told a slightly scandalous story from her childhood in Slovenia about a butter pot. There was an old woman in her village who made clarified butter to sell. She'd save the cream from her cows, churn the butter, then melt it on the woodstove and pour it into her old grey stoneware crock. Once a week, on market day, she'd go into town and sell butter by the scoop to all the housewives there.

Well, one day she sold all her butter early, before noon, so she had a little time to go looking at the other stalls in the market. In one booth she came across a lovely big pot, all painted in flowers, with handles on the side. She thought, "If my butter sells so well from my old grey pot, think how much faster it would sell from this pretty new one." And she bought the pot.

You know what's coming, of course. The next market day, nobody bought any butter. The city women just giggled and pointed, and wouldn't tell her why. It fell to the gatekeeper at the end of the day to explain to her what a chamber pot was, and why it wasn't the best container for displaying and selling her butter.

Womb World (Featuring Chutcha Yip)

After a bad trip, in sooth, Peki ends up in this uterine cosmos, its fetal denizens getting around on snake-slithering umbilical cords. He happens on the dinky and winning and albinal Asian teen, Chutcha Yip, in the placental dankness, under a shining vulval moon and clitoral sun, shining concomitantly, in a venerable clump of trees. She Is wearing a fetching native outfit that's unstained. She's a bold spirit decorously dressed. They chitchat at a magnificent swing, with its ligneous and ropy authority, in the dark air. Embryoid folks make haste. A Roman centurion in leather skirting grapples with a paper skeleton with bat wings. A phantom steer vanishes. Drugged, the dwarf sees everything dimly and distorted. He measures and values her youthful beauty. Her life story has narrative tension and no conclusive denouement. Her personality is natural and infective. He studies the smooth sheet of aquamarine water. Their emitted language rustles with a flirty suggestion. He wonders whether this is an imagined world. He feels as if he has somehow 'developed' here. The impossibilities are possible. He sees a widening, psychedelic horizon. The coral-pink sun is irradiant in the iris-blue sky. He has the sense that unreality is in collusion with reality. He follows her like a sheep would shepherdess. She spills the beans about having titchy birds for pubic hair. They make their own nest on her genitalia. She feeds them worms. Peki is impressed and discomposed. Chutcha has this byre body odor. Her feet stink of singed cabbage. In her little place, stark and ambrosia, she nurses and sings to him while he recovers from a hangover and withdrawal symptoms (from H). She is currently unencumbered by habiliments, reading recipes in a Rolodex, as a nun might prepare for her vows. She is milky white, pretty, and petite. His repressed energy builds. He feels like a sweaty, hunched lump. His appetency stirs, aroused by the angelic sight of her. There are bursts of unbridled hooting between them, interspersed throughout the otherwise curiously serious and elaborate discussion. He notices her axilla rash (an evil side effect from frequent shaving). He isn't the least bit surprised; she has such delicate skin. He tells her he is a long-distance runner and high diver. She doesn't believe him for a second. He gets a whiff of talcum powder. The two swap anecdotes that sound not unlike classical dramas. He brings up the subject of sex. Her half-hearted response and near-apathy were anticipated. He expected to be misunderstood. Has he behaved in an undignified manner? She led him on. She acts as though he has done her a great and inexpiable wrong and that he must atone for his sin. He has an artist's eye, picking out this anatomic detail and that on her shapely figure. More than just his eyebrow is raised when he studies her. In his embrace, she is confined and floundering. She finds out soon enough that he has an almost pugnacious approach to lovemaking. They get smoochy. Their bodies are inadvertently positioned in an imperfect parabola. Their incompatible passions swell similar to floodwater, drowning them. The plaster walls are white as new. The joint is clean as a whistle. Moon glares down as if in judgment, beheld through the hall window. Downpour resembles steel mesh. Peki's blood burns. He wants to rip her asunder. Each kiss is inevitable, every touch lovely. Male and female both are forces, not dissimilar to eruptions, or conflagrations. It is an unchoreographed dance in bed. Chutcha supposes that his sense of self-worth is wrapped up in the achievement of intimacy. Her voice is choked with emotion. He's exceedingly vulgar and rough. And she is stunned to the quick, as though some ceremonial travesty has occurred. She's absurdly captivating and compelling. Then, after the congress, she fixes a repast of shepherd's pie and custard, her fine lips pursed in concentration.

Chutcha manifests like a mirage in the blare of calefaction and coruscation, hops like a Mexican jumping bean, doffs her jammies, clips her pubical flock, and they fly the crotch. Whereupon she dons a clinging houndstooth bodysuit and high heels and lies dead and inert. Her crash pad, located in a structure of brick, glass, and steel, on the blighted corner of a city block of pervasive queerness, is a series of prismatic cubes. Shirt buttons, pants zipper, and belt buckle meantime are being undone. Peki takes a short off-angle step to gain quicker access to her ankles. Though not exactly planning to gut her into the beyond, he harbors doubt about exercising restraint if the urge arises. He's darned sure she has no interest in acquainting herself with the sanguinary. She has an elf's pointed ears. She shifts herself into a pose he reads as bashful. The vault is bleak and cloudless. Pedestrian traffic is diminishing. Emanation drains. Oxygen thickens, as before a tempest. There's no mercy in the mugginess. Considering his abbreviated height, he could be mistaken for the Baby Jesus. He finishes his glass of tequila and chases it with barley wine. He is strong as an ox and ready for anything. There is an abrupt dip in the dialogue between her and him. Chutcha falls silent, and Peki figures the verbal portion of the program is over, that the action should start pronto. He realizes that days and nights have elapsed, claimed by concupiscence. The thought of returning home crosses his mind. They both speak at once, kneeling on the Prussian-blue couch. She's like some mythical being. She is employed as a topless waitress at a nearby barrelhouse. Her circumstances are pinched. He guesses she twirls the umbrella for style points, or distraction, revealing her ex-boyfriend was a tax inspector. Her voice maintains a satin contralto, fessing that she frets about becoming demented and senile, she wants to travel abroad, and can't wait to say goodbye to this damned cosmic uterus. Rain has the stinging malodor of chloroform. With the winds, the windows' shades belly. Peki spoils her purity, moving on her, in the uncomfortable armchair, like a ghost passing over the Styx. Will there be a price to pay? If so, is it buyer beware? Strung up about intercourse, Chutcha shakes uncontrollably — a nervous reaction. She sobs, swaying to and fro, on the cast iron-headed bed with cotton blankets, gasping for breath. With her, he gets his release and respite from the barbarous regimen. The coupling goes round and round in a romantic mist. She has a poignant, sour, lopsided smile, and vents an unrequited suspiration. Her oriental eyes sparkle. He has an oily modulation. He straight-shoots: she's got the goods. He whispers to her as if it's a password to gain him entrance. Clammy-cheeked, she puts her knees up to her chin and he grasps her haunches. She surrenders, defeated, abandoned to the anguish and degradation of sodomy. He heedlessly assaults her, his whining turning into hoarse rage. She moves her toned arms and legs, not unlike a compromised swimmer in choppy waters. His hair hangs in limp threads. She cries, as though a tap is turned on. She feels like she fell and doesn't want to rise again. For her, the sex was a disaster, a capitulation, an acceptance of degeneracy. Climaxing, wet-faced, he howls like a wounded wolf. She gathers herself up. On her bare feet, she staggers as though her balance is gone, bringing her shadow with her as she moseys in the apartment. Salty tears brim in her blinders and film them, then run down her neck in warm streamlets. Hiccups shiver in her throat. She's exhausted as if she'd jogged a marathon. Vista looks like clouded glass. Fetal tennis players compete on grass courts. Blinds are drawn halfway down the dusty panes, the sun glaring. Chutcha feels faint as though the polluted air is an anesthetic. Deluge is an endless rolling scroll, a disorderly, repetitious screen. Peki is sorry for causing her agony, even if it was unpremeditated. Her harmed flesh was uncomprehending. She is ill-equipped to handle such maltreatment. He's concerned for her well-being. She brightens his darkness. They enjoy the peace and quiet, drinking tea and eating toast, seated on the mud-colored, tubate sofa. Chutcha's hands are folded and composed in her lap. Peki's nose interprets the precipitation as smelling sharply of ether. He remembers Marisa telling him, in a mild, castigating tone, that he's overambitious, overextending himself, overreaching, in making and selling mantequilla. What a crock! She swore he wasn't doing himself justice, added he was a great disappointment to her. Butyrum is his life and work. He vocally fought back in a sedate, defensive timbre. He has found his place in society. He is aware of her needs and problems. She was confusing his best interests with her own unfulfilled goals. He was furious and frustrated. He is wise in his responsibilities. He has overcome countless setbacks, surmounted many obstacles. She insisted failure is important to build character. The clarity of filthy images of her soils his mind. He believes this is not the normal thinking of someone firing on all cylinders.

Chutcha is a comely and complicated creature, spread cunningly and voluptuously before him on the single bed, her hand lazily lying on her monumental abdomen. Peki's mouth meets her knee. Her uncovered foot, with its tindery dryness, glides past his breath. She has a desire to be seen. He touches her intimate parts. She doesn't strike him as an exhibitionist. Not at all. Her adolescent face and physique are fine and glow with health. She's sure of herself. She has sherbet and wafers. Her nipples are chestnut-glossy with sweat. She has a chipped tooth and pipe-cleaner limbs. Her asscrack is lined with frizzed fur. She is agreeable and seductive. A bowl of wax fruit calls attention to its artificiality. Her pinkie fiddles coyly with his discreet fly, her head bent submissively. She licks her bow lips. Her neck swerves not unlike a swan's. She is subordinate and hopeless. His digits are snaky sausages on her stubbled shin. His manhood rises in his sopping jockeys like a fish in water. He looks mesmerized at her. He'll remember every detail of the commingling, chapter and verse. She ascends as he descends and she is engulfed. Their sexual congress is like a shocking initiation into individual completeness. Their brows clash like the horns of rams, bodies mixed. Pounded, she focuses on his Roman nose and tightened chops. She has a gleaming puce pageboy haircut, the bangs uneven. He palms her tit like a priest would cup a Grail. She trusts him with her juvenescence. The tonguing and fingering of her orifices are unpredictable and unexplained. He kisses her lips, oral and vaginal. Pumped, she issues incomprehensible nasal syllables. He twists her arms and legs like bits of wire and manipulates her integument like modeling plasticine. Their spasmodical, frenzied fornicating diminishes. She is in feeble perpetual motion like a lobster. His hair is streaming rat-tails. He comes with a satisfied sigh. She makes a singing sonance when he squirts his jizz. He plops on the foamy pouffe, leans over, and pats her shoulder, trying to be nice following the destructive tumble in the sheets. She acknowledges his questing buns-bound stare and titters. The pair attempt to be open and honest, and keep everything aboveboard, each taking turns to perform the pertinent function of communication. She's an incessant talker and he's a captive hearer. Her mop is a damp mat on her scalp. She catches his blinker. And he takes a seat on her tummy, arms wide, like a boy riding a bike with no hands. She is dying of thirst, unable to get up because of his solid weight. He rocks from side to side. A blush rises from her chest up to her throat in the cruel fulgor. Seemingly, she is in a trance. He has no interest in snapping her out of it. Intercourse, he thinks, is the truly significant triumph of the human species... such intricacy and simplicity... With her, he feels as if he has been searching his whole life for something and has found it, in this current state of ecstasy. Chemistry. Affinity. Compatibility. Attraction. A miracle. Or is it the speedball? He lets the situation evolve. Drencher sounds like shaken chains. The confab burgeons in vocalic jerks and bumps. She flashes a glass grin. The two are effective storytellers. He's still as a mouse, smirks apprehensively, scared stiff perhaps to take the plunge. Sitting like a brass Buddha, he gazes at her skeletal armature. Overcast is storm-gray. Music, a muted heavy metal, is on the boom box. Rain tinkles. Silverware on the countertop recalls instruments of slaughter. His moue glittery, he slips into a Japanese wrapper. His floppy hat looks like a robber's stocking. Making a meal out of the candy bar, her movements approximate the balletic. She has a round, rosy bust. Her cheeks are flushed. Fuchsia sun. Soaker sounds musical. She sits in a lotus position on the jade-green coverlet, shining with youth and glistering with sweat. She has the pearly flesh of raw scallop. His oculi are mobile, lively, as though they're on little stalks. She puts on maroon overalls. Precip is a blotting-paper hiss. Her speech is accompanied by gestures. Thunderclaps sound like distant drums through a loudspeaker. A trolley sibilates. Venous-blue celestial sphere. The ocean is cobalt and copper. The illumination is orange-henna. The couple has a quick brunch of succulent noodles. Banal, jazzy muzak plays. Sleet plinks and plunks. A stick of incense burns in a porcelain pot, delicate and elegant, situated on the display case, lacquered in wood, appearing to belong in a museum, holding these neat miniatures and ceramic objects. Now in her ebony and ivory bra and undies, she reminds him of a Rorschach mannequin made by a folded inkblot. She prepares a lunch of steamed oysters, beansprouts, and spring onions. He pictures Marisa's derma layer, hanging in folds and pouches, countenance engraved with crisscrossing wrinkles.

The ocean is the color of dark slate. Pavement's puddles look like bean sauce. Heaven, over the placid panorama, is cornflower-blue. Viridian seaweed glistens on the shore. An embryoid crowd streams urgently onto the beach. Chutcha, potato-pale, is extraordinarily cute in her lapis lazuli socks. Her limbs, after utilizing a dull razor on them, are bandaged like mummies. She takes a spoonful of bamboo shoots and blurts out she suffered from bulimia, starving herself down to almost a coat hanger. She was in a very depressed condition. The gamine was evidently possessed by inordinate self-loathing and absorption. She sedulously annihilated herself and was obsessed with self-inflicted bodily horrors. She went through Sturm and Drang. She's clever, complex, and wickedly provocative. Peki is violent and controlled. He imagines Marisa's phiz, mapped by creases. She can be pigheadedly misdirected. Is it misguided tenderness that he cossets and nurtures her? She is his anchor of sanity in an insane world. The ingenue waters plants and says she twice overdosed on codeine. He helps himself to a bowlful of pure rice and scrutinizes her from top to bottom. His ramshackle diet is tedious. His gullet feels as if there's liquid boiling in it like it's a cauldron. Narcotics have soothed his busy brain. Over these last months, worry has cancerously grown in his private self. He is afraid he will get busted by the coppers. A waterfall of words plunges into a pool of subjects. She is dressed in a cadmium hospital gown, fastened at the back. The gal is as peaceful and kindly a person he has ever met. His eyes are sleepy with pills and cannabis. Due to his dwarfism, his pings and pangs are worse than ever. The aches and pains are becoming more unbearable. He wishes his chronic discomfort could be wiped away like a stain. His mien is watchful and canny. He discovers she caused a scandal at school, with a few educators, male and female, respected educators with whom she had relations. He understands — she is irresistible. There was so much dirt flung and hatred dispensed and venom spewed, and thus she dropped out. Splendor is ocher. The upper atmosphere has an iridescent haze. Her peepers are slits between puffed eyelids. She picks at grapefruit segments, shining with juice, on a saucer. She loves the sweet sourness! The room is enshrouded with dusk. Pipes throughout the tenement wail. Cardinal moon. Lake is clear as crystal. Cirri are black as ink. He caresses her fishy skin. She surveys the pine forest at the mountain's ridge, rainbow's bright ribbons of hue, flowery orchard, an ornamental garden inside high walls, and luscious cornfield, under the sandy-saffron sun. Pigeons roost on the outside ledge. Boulders on a knoll evoke the knuckles of a giant's fist. Sand seethes with the unborn babies like an ants' nest. Dense smoke drifts on the duck pond. Chutcha cooks and washes in the nude, on the move like air, earth, fire, or water. The sight of her is enough to mitigate his prevailing boredom. The soles of her feet are salmon-pink. He experiences an aesthetic pleasure in optically inspecting her glorious nakedness. He wears her vermilion peignoir. She dances recklessly, her exquisite young body flung about freely as though she is in front of flaring footlights. He grinds his gnashers unconsciously and accompanies her instrumentally with bongos and tubular bells, catering these rhythms to her graceful movements. When she takes a breather, he eats her out like a boar digging its blunt snout in to find truffles. He sucks, making a soughing noise. Stable as a stone, she gazes at his semi-erect horn as if it's a gross worm, with its bald head and cyclopean eye, creeping toward her mouth, unrelenting and slow, the vermicular thing lolling and loathsome, its progress dreamily unreal. His scrotum, looking like cabbage, has an unspeakably foul stench, similar to melting rubber. A sick, paralyzing uncertainty seizes her. She is frozen not unlike a mouse before a viper. The prepuce is rimmed with a gummous discharge. Her pies glow not dissimilar to coals. He stares at her like a stoat at a rabbit. Scintillant shafts are tongues of flame. He masturbates with her head, hurriedly and messily. Her stomach is queasy. She has bad breath, smelling, he'd surmise, of charred rind. Yes and so he fucks her on the featherbed. She pants and squeaks like a pig. Her cutis is viscid with adhesive diaphoresis. Suddenly, she crawls as though driven by mechanized necessity, and he promptly scrambles after her. His need to hump her is some biological need, like the recurrent return of the turtle to the sea to breed. He is stubbornly persistent in pursuing her. She gets a glimpse of the reflection of his ugly fanny (giving off an odor of roast pork) in the pane and gags. She feels crushed and withered. He experiences exceptional delirium. With her, he feels rescued and restored.

The spat causes vague discomfort to the combatants. Bickering, the scenario looks like a puppet performance you'd see in a park. They're circumscribed by seaweed-green verdure, proceeding past the wooded ravine and up the egg-shaped knoll. Peki treats the circus peanut candy like a hoarded treasure, lapsing into a resplendent reverie. He realizes the responsibilities back home are piling up. He has a caustic grin. Chutcha shakes her head and shrugs her shoulders with a semblance of sarcasm. A zone of hostility is established. Their visages are furrowed during the heated exchanges. She pretends to pout. The two come to the understanding that holding back in the quarrel is advisable, only they stay alert. Her burp provides amusement for both parties. The evening is clouded and thick. Bats are unseen and everywhere. Limestone mountains. Wild terrain. Soaring pinnacles of rock. The weather offers not security but fear. Pond's color isn't mitigated by the fog. Shadows are solemn and awful. Drama recommences. Sprinkles are just on the edge of hail. The couple starts downhill, headed for the streambed. Peki's fingers seek the uncertainties of her private parts. He catches her with both speed and surprise. He puts his dick into a mouth that doesn't want it. He finds no resistance beyond the expected. Chutcha struggles on her knees and considers praying. He turns this into a sexual spectacle as if he is a carnal Christ in a passion play. In this compromised position, in the public garden, she wishes to crawl into a hole in the earth. She believes she has the right to feel the wrongness. She feels as though her dignity isn't real, or recoverable. Her sulk strikes him as a mockery. She insists on being difficult. Silence pulsates. He experiences the unexpected delight of his feet contacting hers. She gags, her tonsils losing all sensation, fighting against forced entry. She is prey submitting to the predator's demands. He's about as tender as a street brute. He has a refined appreciation for her anatomical perfection. The oral going is slow. Arousal comes to him as if from a special stimulative providence. He studies the musculature of her slim limbs. Her face supports his weight as he makes these corkscrew motions, deepthroating her. She's inert as a corpse. Gusts carry her strangulated cries into their vast indifference. The space they occupy is an atmospheric sensorium, the oxygen itself with an appetitive nature. Chutcha's expression is like she is waking to an awareness that a dong is between her lips. She suffers for an undefined time. Peki is delirious in his bodily painscape. She inhales and exhales. Desire, his, throbs. Showers purr. Leaves twitch in the breezes. Mist collects in the olive grove. Banners of cirri fly proudly. Blue of the empyrean begins to reassert itself in the cloud cover. The temperatures are remorseless. Birds glide not unlike ghosts. A vaporous sheet covers the nameless valley. She's pitiful as a broken animal. The lovers detach themselves from the day and attach themselves to the night. There's an accretion of trash on either side of the ancient bridge, with its pure arch and severe contours. Patches of light. Winds wail. The firmament seems transformed, as though by a dark art. Things between them have desperately deteriorated. Equally distressing, for Chutcha, is the discovery that he has, simply and unaccountably, disappeared. The air is warm and still. She cuts up peppers, onions, celery, and carrots for soup. Then she, in a committed dither, cooks.

As a matter of fact, Peki merely needed to clear his mind, getting out and gaining a modest amount, gambling at the tables. He is entitled to relaxation. Chutcha's queef is a shrill tessitura. She has a brunette bob, neutral nails, and no makeup. The great amatory wheel spins. She decides, at the last second, that his hind is better left unexplored. She pauses to get her bearings, her mien specific, not unlike a statue's. Driving her hard, on the oriental rug, he shouts her name over and over. She makes a significant personal effort in keeping her expression free of irritation. One feels like a part of the other. Thunder sounds like cymbals repeatedly bashed. The welkin is a celestial blue. Mike Ditka is on the stereo doing, wretchedly, The Beatles' 'You Can't Do That.' Peki considers himself an angel, or devil, of destruction. They make these goo-goo noises. Chutcha stands, partially clothed, an element of nakedness waiting to be granted admission into material existence. Carelessly radiant, she walks and talks in the nicotine murk as if drugged. Nude, her skin smells like snow. He gazes at her as though she's a cosmic revelation. He's possessed by a waif he cannot control. She embraces him with arms and legs. Her midriff reverberates like a struck gong. Cunnilingus is executed with an absence of hesitation. Her fair arms and legs are spread on the floor. They devote themselves to a coital dance. Combined, they are like a locomotive recklessly barreling along in a tunnel without lights or signals. She smiles tightly. They drown in the breaking waves of desire. He experiences a sober joy of being fellated. His vascular organ pounds fiercely. They are ardent dervishes. There's a promise of orgasm on a scale he's only now coming around to contemplate. Her discipline, in blowing him, is impressively unbreakable. Peering at him closely, she discourages anal analysis. Her noodle-narrow torso doesn't go unmolested. He looks for the opportune moment (to phallically penetrate her) to present itself. He trusts the laws of probability. He is coition-crazed, dizzy in the dalliance with her. Climaxing, he crows like a rooster. Rectally probed, she sounds like a discontented animal. When he's done rag dolling her, she's left queasy and resentful. His behind blasts out a flatulent admonishment. The skyline is incandescently incarnadine. This is a sacred place in the orthogonal building. The to-and-fro of her domestic life is on display in the noontide brilliance. He daydreams that she is his destiny, and utters this aloud. He wants to spend as much time as possible drinking, smoking, chatting, and coupling with her. He feels like a lovelorn imbecile. He sups fruit syrup, spiked with absinthe, out of a carafe and thinks of blood, arterial, capillary, and venous. The domes and spires can barely be seen through the black smoke. Unremarkable azure. Rain beads drop like pigeon shit. Peki enjoys the vista and subsequently stares at the red roof of a flophouse, spice bazaar, gas works, beer hall, pot bar, indigotic shade, and the plum and pomegranate trees. The city is dull and modern, seething with people. There's enough clag to confound any living thing. Feral punk rock music blares from a packed tavern — anthems of anarchy. Hookers' tits and asses appear from time to time for sale to potential clientage on the muddy street. Mizzle slurs. He swigs no-name rum, imagines the hail is shrapnel. The dark hours wane and he regards the carmine dawn. The molecular products of the narcotics lay claim to his brain cells. Here is a district of hardship and misdirection.

Overcast is a menace to the integrity of the upper atmosphere. Vaporous wraiths drift over twisted trunks and drooping ferns. Oxygen smells of condensation. It is gloomy and dank. An electric vibration quivers in his loins. Peki pounds espresso and sniffs blow. He promptly disrobes and literally gazes at his navel, shining in glorious splendor. His sobbing sounds like Aaron Neville warbling while gargling gravel. He drops a hint that he is horny, only she does not pick it up. His pride is hurt. Should he just say something point-blank? He restrains the impulse and stays silent.

He won't plunge into that deep and dangerous pool. Profane inspiration is a rising tide that draws its imaginative waters from gulfs of thought, leaving no obscene idea unsubmerged. Many vivid impressions are taken in. Chutcha has cast a magnetic spell on him. He enters into an inadvertently comical flirtation with her, trying to be spontaneously affectionate. Sexual matters have relapsed into a state of suspension. And he is surprised at his patience in this situation. He derives moments of ecstasy from fantasizing about her. He thinks intensely and excitedly of her. He's aimless in a masturbational haze. His pies gleam with sardonic mischief. She is reserved, remaining uncommunicative. She wears a girdle under her habit. He notices the ironic glint in her peepers. He worships her as a deity and presents himself as an offering, or a sacrifice. He moves in the humectation like a fin cutting through a crest. He feels like such an ugly duckling next to her! She observes his frowning brows. She has a mock-tragic air about her. Her smirk is a teasing indulgence. They proceed as if through an unseeable, imponderable medium. Periodically the two encounter idlers. A flock of fowls meanders in a patch of paisley. Vernal spate. Flowers, leaning earthward from the spritz, look not unlike forlorn survivals. Flakes of gray clouds suggest, visually, ash. Birdsong is delivered in modal scales. Uproarious collision of wave and boat. Skein of channels. The celestial sphere is a cinema screen where pictures move and narratives unfold. Aroma of myrtle. Peki makes a faint grimace. His fizzog grows flinty. Chutcha's laughter ripples when he repeatedly pinches her derriere. She endures it like a rock withstands the surf. She's lovely and thrilling. She traces the lines on his kisser with her agile fingers like a sculptress tactilely going over her work. She gives him a long, hard, penetrating glare, tilting her pretty head to one side. Whereupon there's an unexpected vocal paroxysm, a verbal outburst that shakes him to the foundation. Blotches appear on her cheeks. She bites her under lip, making dramatic gestures. He trembles like a leaf in a zephyr. A tender, whimsical smile settles upon her countenance. Her chortle sounds hollow. She quickens her steps. His bones feel as though they're melting. He experiences an indescribable entrancement, visualizing her nude. She is an extraordinary person. Her presence bestows on him a delicious peace. He wants to fuck her mouth. He listens to her murmurings as if hearing a message. Soil is sodden beneath their feet. Attentive to pitch, she sings a familiar pop tune, near the rapids of the river and bare rock. He has an urge to run up and bite her on the rump. Destiny awaits him. He realizes she can't accompany him to wherever he is bound. It's his path and he has to walk it on his lonesome. He must carry out his duty to the pale yellow edible fatty substance. Departure should be recognized as a reality. They pass these precarious abodes, dwellings of the impoverished. There's a vague odor of seaweed. Peki abandons himself to rumination: he must make mantequilla to be at all operative in society. He thinks of nonexistent butter, in the world of the not-yet-created. He is out to prove that his Butyrum is the planetary product, a property of the universe. He goes back and forth, in and out of reveries, surrendering himself to this satisfaction, in a partial vacuum. He puts on his monk's robe and contemplates the cosmic struggle between darkness and light. Chutcha studies a thrush. There is a convergence of bodies in space and time. Crickets chirp them to lunacy. There isn't an excess of water in the reservoir but a deficiency.

The hot weather is ruthless. It exhausts the pneuma. The rooks in the cypress trees have stopped cawing. The arbitrarily assigned minute's worth of spritzing brings a semblance of relief. Immigrant workers, mercilessly exploited, in wine country look deeply unhappy. Ravens appear to be in unthinking migration across the sky. Peki, bananas on angel dust, hallucinates the foreman has elk antlers and boar tusks. A pawpaw orchard turns increasingly chaotic. Streams of folks, inextricable, swell in an area unimaginable. Thunder thumps in the distance. Lightning evokes firelight during wartime. Eagles patrol the monochrome horizon. The homeless wander the hillsides. He is afraid Chutcha will be swallowed by fate and crapped into oblivion… The environment, he senses, has this conscious force. Bumblebees change into buzzing bullets. He vents a battle cry. A limbless man and woman, reminding him of human slugs, wriggle in the muck and wildflowers. The downpour is a sustained barrage, the hailstones becoming howitzer shells dropped from an unseen enemy from above. On the crooked, complicated trail, at a stagnant ditch, he yells they should vacate the premises. Squalls roughen the surface of the sea. She watches him in numb captivation. Booms sound like the footfalls of giants. Allied planes fly in formation. He is petrified of the lethal din. Roiling pea soup is cordite smoke. He wipes his wet eyes with a sleeve. Alert as a lookout, she just wants to sit and talk things out. He's ready to embrace his end. His bad trip is getting worse. He fears they are dead ducks. Rain's respite offers them choices. The leven is fluorescent cyan. A sheepdog looks like a shaggy bear. Peki and Chutcha find shelter in a deserted thatch hut, miraculously intact. She lights candles. He finds ginger beer, ouzo, salami, and eggplant. They use Dixie Cups postcards for plates. The sudden quietness is welcome. They snarf down raki in comradely companionship, permit themselves hours of slack to recuperate. With calibrated gentleness, she takes his shaking hand. He wrinkles his forehead. She's in flirting range. Their kisses sound not unlike bat and ball making contact. He invites her attention to his crotch. His erotic mania he cannot contain. She appreciates his unit in detail, flashing her all-purpose grin. After a heartbeat or two, she mouths his member. She bites and he barks. She puts her cheek against his chest and dozes. Winds make harsh shrieks. The ocean is furious. Desolate peaks. He multitasks, scavenging for kindling and scouting to make sure the coast is clear. Rumors abound in the region about the rash of killings. No homicide case has been solved. Nothing. Nada. There aren't even any suspects in custody. The public is getting antsy. The citizens demand results. Hearsay echoes in alleys. Speculation ricochets off buildings. Everyone everywhere has their theories and suspicions... He is proud to be self-educated, and well-schooled in the art of murder. Down in town, in the predawn gelidity, Peki and Chutcha roister on the esplanade.

The road waits for Peki to hit it. His departure surprises Chutcha and doesn't surprise her. Before he was to set sail, if you please, he suggested that they have a bon voyage toast with some bubbly and merriments. The sorry saga, unfinished, was aborted in the bedroom. He felt like a shitheel for bailing on her. Their parting was chilly. Her stairwell echoed with the steps of the departed.

Theodosia Lash

Surfaces sparkle in the lambency on account of the dust. Peki thinks about the government, an administration not inclined to reach for a rectitude beyond its self-interest, as well as the tribal allegiances and opportunistic feuds. The populace becomes fractious, unrest grows, because of mistrust of the officials. Elections these days are mass protests. Bedlam and babel are normal and natural. Authorities arrive and quell any disturbances. The regime, although shrunken and weakened, stays strong. The empire is still the hub of the societal wheel. The false idols are imbecilic, incompetent devils of specious nationalism. And they are morally stunted. Their customs and habits will never change. The cosmopolitan sheen faded years ago. The metropolis is one of colorful chaos. The wired trolley, so packed with passengers, a heap of perspiring humanity, it's fit to burst at the rivets, and jolts its laborious way for considerable distances. Air's thick and heavy. A tram slows to a snail's pace on the tracks. Errand boys steal a sedan chair under the full fire of the sun. A golden-vested capuchin monkey clutches a pink parasol in a sooty puddle. A ruminative Ethiopian eunuch, pattering with parcels, looks as pompous as a camel. Songbirds fall silent, exhausted by their nocturnal serenades and expeditions. Somnolent mutts foul the sidewalks almost as much as the pedestrians. There's plenty of push and shove of the throng. Peki is not in the best tempers, queasy from carousing, and left in a condition of irritable disrepair. His legs need loosening. Inexplicably, his forearm bears toothmarks. His clothes are creased and stained with vomit and impregnated with ash. His pubic hair feels like it is a rat that stuck fast to his scrotum and died. He watches the gently wreathing cumuli, contemplating fireproofing the storeroom for the merchandise. He is more than just singlehandedly holding his own against the unionized companies trying to monopolize the butter trade. From him, there are no low blows to the competition. He is an important personage with nonamateur integrity. He's in a position of influence. He's devout in his religious observance of mantequilla making. He remains steadfast in his faith. The Good Lord has blessed his enterprise. A cast-iron cauldron, inlaid with nacre and ivory, is supposed to be delivered to the laboratory today... Despite the diligent din, he broods, breakfasting on yogurt and latte. The neighbors have given into the suspicions aroused by the rumors that mother and son are involved in an unsavory amorous entanglement. Gossip is the great deceiver of reason... Peki muses on entering the lowly streets. Hanging out on the squalid corner were false prophets, card sharps, fortune tellers, pickpockets, abortionists, counterfeiters, pimps, and prostitutes. The sewage channel had its varied and ghastly dreck. Distorted cripples hobbled on crutches. An individual required a bodyguard in that place. He was both exhilarated and unnerved on this side of town, the melange of different cultures and raucousness of it all. Beggars clamored for coins. The harbor was clogged with vessels of diversiform shapes and sizes and in all states of repair. Gulls shrieked. Cargo was moved by brawn on the jetty. The oxygen seemed crowded by the racket. Emaciated felines and canines rummaged through piles of rubbish. A dead chicken lay swelling on the cobbles, encircled by corvids. It was late at night. Theodosia was a smutty-faced, snotty-nose, crook-backed cutie with auburn bangs awry, hugeous, hypnotic eyes, pomegranate mouth, and a pudgy frame. Her rictus was apparently open and honest. He longed for her with a desperation that is akin to thirst in a factory. She was filthy and flaunting. A sexual deviant catcalled from a doorway. There was a stilted and unbalanced exchange between the gnome and the girl. He overlaid his inner insecurity with a carapace of outer calm. She had the ocherous teeth of a hardcore smoker and drinker. Her snout looked like it was flattened in a fistfight. The topics of conversation kept changing. He could tell she was highly strung. She endured his hyperactive behavior and vocal bombardment, leaning her elbow on the particolored paneling, pocked with bullet holes. She plucked an oud. He had some misgivings about mounting her. As a present, he gave her a bouquet with a hidden serpent. Snakebitten, she doddered and attempted to take deep breaths. On her like a jackdaw upon a carcass, he crammed a rare lethal herb into her mouth and made her swallow it. Her belly hung like a disused waterbag. He puffed out his chest. Dying, her lips worked soundlessly, chin flecked with spit. A musky odor emanated from her. Her stomach exploded and she suspired and perished. The last sights she saw were his beetling eyebrows and hoggish mustache. He delivered an inconsequential monologue. After taking her adipose tissue, he sank her in a weighted sack in the sea.

The War

Chafed with boredom, Peki yearned for his madre's companionship. He imagined her composing her visage with makeup. She was his destiny. He was a liability in battle, so he was kept on the sidelines instead of being on the playing field. He was a cheerleader. Time passed in an endless cycle of drills. He was an accomplished snare drummer, and yet he still felt useless. He served his country faithfully, helping the cause whenever he was called upon. The environmental suspense was unbearable. He was very thin, reduced to a specter, a shadow of his former self. He was a living creature, out in the middle of nowhere, surrounded by the mass of contorted and decaying dead, his brethren. The military authorities gave him the morbid task of disposing of countless bodies. The carrion birds and vicious rats fed night and day on the fallen heroes who lay otherwise undisturbed in the grasses and bushes. Some were skeletons in shreds of uniforms. Many incomprehensible atrocities had been maliciously committed against the soldiers. One patch was eerily uncluttered as though it was sacred ground. He was stabbed by the pain of sorrow. The temperatures were atrocious and his diet was execrable. Cadavers made an unidentifiable, incomplete, and anonymous pile. Meanwhile, armies reorganized and regrouped at base camp. Peki was ragged and wasted in the last of the light that illuminated his work, putting his deceased and decomposing brothers in a heap. He beheld them disbelievingly and with a desolate heart. They were massacred by the Germans. It was like a firing squad on a large scale. There was so much despair and shells. His comrades were disintegrating. He chewed melon seeds and gave a soft coo of pleasure when he shat in the shrubbery. He spoke to himself in a croaking voice. His head was a chest full of thoughtful treasure, only he couldn't locate the key. The dried perspiration felt like salty crystals covered his crawling flesh. He stank of piss. The usual clarity of his mind became opaque. He toiled, dragging corpses. The migraine was like red-hot rods were driven into his temples and nape. He was battered and famished. He endured convulsions and delusions. He wheezed as if demons were throttling him. His fingers and toes went numb. He slaved away in the bright moonlight, grungy and tired. He thought that the politicians were leading Spain into ruin. The Krauts were getting the upper hand in the conflict. The Japanese were relegated to referees on their home turf. Peki acknowledged that the local population could hardly wait for the combating factions to drive each other out. Unity was split on both sides, demoralized on account of the sheer volume of deserters. Troop and supply replenishments were important, yet nothing was happening on that front. The fighters were left high and dry. Peki wrote furious and detailed letters to his superiors, pleading for weapons, ammunition, and other miscellaneous provisions. He got no replies at all. He was awkward and quarrelsome, in person with the higher-ups. He served under them. He did as he was told. He wanted them to resign and be replaced. There were spies everywhere. Units were essential to salvage the disastrous operation against the Jerries. His side was in dire straits, left in a desperate, diseased state, ill-equipped and undermanned. The situation was hopeless. The Kaiser advanced. Spanish forces would be destroyed if they retreated. They stayed entrenched, refusing to surrender to the enemy. Hungry and thirsty refugees lurched and looked like zombies, feet bound in shreds of fabric. When an officer checked on his progress, Peki struggled to remain stoic. His was not a complaining nature. He acted as though he was on the last frontier that marked the boundary of a new world… At one point, he beat a mob of homeless people back with a whip, wielding it with immediate and dramatic efficacy. And they withdrew from the engagement. He gasped for oxygen as if the air was sucked out of the cosmos. He dealt with diarrhea. He was temporarily blinded and deafened. His distended abdomen was causing him significant agony. This torment was appalling. He talked at length and brilliantly to himself, in his customary highfalutin style. Flowers forced themselves out of the earth. Bulbuls began to sing. Peki's shoulders shook when he wept. He had no one to comfort him. His gut was swollen. It was filled with fluid as though it was a waterskin. His breath was foul. His eyes were brimming with blood. He babbled. His pallor was turning yellow. He sprawled on the weeds in anguish, drifting in and out of consciousness, and suffering horrific cramps. He mentally strained to grasp moments of lucidity. His brow, warm by fever, made it feel like it was branded with an iron. His skin had sunken over his bones. The sickness was vile. Gurgling sounds came from his throat. Nausea pushed rhythmically in his gullet. He believed he was fading off. Was he slipping into a coma? The spasms in his midsection were like the contractions of birth. The breezes, bringing some semblance of relief to him, blew more and more infrequently. Peki clutched his head between his hands and started to whine. He proclaimed his misery to the vacant vault. He was defeated by malnourishment and labor, not to mention a kidney infection and the Spanish flu. He rose and stumbled. Finally, he collapsed onto the forest floor and slept, in a twist, next to a spade, shovel, and an ax. He dreamed he was marrying Marisa, with whom he had the misfortune of loving since childhood. He woke with a start. He had many graves to dig...

Bamidele Awoniyi

She smiles ironically. Her chiclets remind Peki of Tic Tacs. She has a curiously strangulated voice. Her eyebrows meet in the middle. She's neither tall nor squat. The epicene person is stupendously angulous and has a prominent Adam's apple. Bamidele's flamboyant attire emphasizes the trappings of femininity and masculinity. Puffing demonstratively on a crack pipe, she is a bizarre and loquacious creature, unfamiliar and not unpleasant to him. She was reasonably educated in Nigeria. This freakish being possesses such natural authority! His cheeks color. He has a distinct feeling that he's being teased. Will her bestowed favors prove to be a fiasco? His head swims a little. The madam struts with a kind of dramatic skill, smirking playfully while applying some cosmetic touch-up, using a compact mirror, to her countenance. She says she detests tedium and insists that it is tantamount to death. She sports a merry expression. She's an ebony lady with satin skin and long, black, shiny hair. She shakes her skinny hips as she salaciously sashays on the Moroccan rug. The Negress visibly suppresses her mirth. She delicately smokes a slim cig. He is pale as the moon. She sips the glass of java coyly. He cannot resist her, so he chooses her. She is for sale. Does she have the goods to justify the expense? He acquires her. He tweaks her tummy and she pulls a grimace. She's fragrant as a rose, her breath has the aroma of an apple, and her flesh is sweet as honey. She sings delightfully. He experiences an unbalanced serenity. The garrulous androgyne is disorientating and appealing, reclining on the cushions. She is semi-divine. His animal instinct kicks in. He is mesmerized into a state of vulnerability. The masculine/feminine sexpot's bellybutton is a knothole. The soles of her feet are marble-white. Her full lips are painted blood-red. And she grins indulgently. He imagines making love to her... The bordello's well-appointed room's flooring supports furniture (situated in a sort of ordered abandon) of no mean manufacture. This house of ill fame is not unlike the majestic home of a well-off merchant. He can't conceive of a soul ever becoming bored or lonely in this brothel. Oxen-like bouncers are on sentry duty. They convene in the corridor, chattering in monotone. Several patrol the premises, keeping a watch on life. A plump, pretty Arabess saunters with significant dignity, swaggering perhaps a bit too much. Her skimpy raiment is smart. She sweeps along the hallway. Her perfume has the scent of lavender. She seems like a sweetheart. Oil lamps, fixed to the primarily carpeted walls, spill a claret luminosity. A tamed partridge, plainly indignant, puts up with the johns at the staircase. In the altogether, Bamidele's bony fingers wiggle, her body uncomfortably bent double in the poorly illumined, richly furnished chamber. She moves languidly. Peki is titillated by her spherical tits and the slight mound of her stomach. He admires the elegant curve of her neck, the contours of her back, and the sensual tapering of her slender thighs. He is short of breath. He experiences a sense of profound wonder. Her attractiveness demands a different type of arrangement, one involving binds and gags. She slips out of his grasp to swig a viscous liquid from a thermos. He appreciates her boyish/girlish beauty. A silver chain is about her ankle. Although dark, she glows somehow with the light of life. She makes these obvious observations about the weather. Her exuberance raises his spirits. She wishes he were less grave. Thanks to her personality, it is granted. The ticking pulse of the mechanical heart of the grandfather clock resounds. The gynandrous intersexual woman's intonation sounds uncertain. Peki's inflection expresses sympathy and mordacity, witnessing her in a state of perplexity. Her stern is round and fine. He feels a tad light-headed. His melon thumps. The potent tobacco, polluted luminescence, and the atmosphere itself fuddles his intuition. His temples throb. His thoughts are disconnected, the impressions fuzzy. He finds just about everything about her refreshing. But he has Butyrum to prepare. The stock is dwindling rapidly. His throat and groin ache with desire. Tingles travel up and down his vertebrae. At her booty, his aim is uncannily accurate. She encourages the sodomy, to his surprise, and showers him with endearments. His mind is awhirl with carnal ideas. He is momentarily dumbfounded. He catches their reflections in the concave mirror. Entered repeatedly at the rear, she shudders theatrically, grunts once, and rolls her eyes. She yeowls. Her violator grips her waist. She wails, showing signs of hysteria. Her tears are irresistible. Rammed in the anus, she speaks in hushed tones. Her African accent is endearing. The rain smells like charcoal. A beslobbered sloven makes a ruckus in the horrid town's center. A brawl breaks out between a few men. The horde of rancorous kids is overbold and impudent. This place is a nightmare. After spewing his spermatic load, Peki looks around, as if for an escape route. He vanishes just as neatly as he'd arrived. Has the flow of fate veered off course? He braces himself for a destiny to come.

The journey back to the apartment is hardly pleasurable. Trouble appears in the louts' eyes. He regards them as a city dweller does campesinos. Peki is trepidatious concerning them. He lurches and sways on the sidewalk, finding himself missing the sublime feeling of being mounted on his madre. A bloom of longing blossoms in his loins. Her pubes — like the fur of a faun. He pictures her and his heart bursts. Loveliness radiates from her face, creating this lucency like a nimbus, or an autumn moon. He reflects on his goal to ardently attain her, summoning up his linguistic resources. He respires heavily. Clouds fill up the entire sky. He ambles unsurely through the noxious alleys. Now and then he comes up against the slumbering form of a wino. One recoils in alarm. Demonstrators practically antagonize passers-by with their trenchant criticisms of elected officials, offering their newfangled concepts. They are talkers and dreamers. Peki gets a twinge of apprehension, spotting the police up ahead. It isn't sufficiently dark enough to light the posts' lamps. Drug addicts lead oblivious lives. A moonbeam casts his face into the shadows. He encounters more hoods with disturbing frequency. They are infirm of purpose, hence the hanging out. He chews toasted pumpkin seeds irascibly, stomping on the warm road. He is affronted and appalled at the volume of lowlifes. He threatens a belligerent unfortunate by swearing to cut his throat or knock his block off. His nut-brown integument, dingy duds, and gnarled hands betoken a laborer. The adversarial companies operate within gratifyingly complicated systems of secrecy behind the scenes, in a cosmos of arcane oaths and medieval vendettas, the opponents dedicating a ton of time conspiring against each other. Peki, on the other hand, prefers things to be clear and direct, to know who exactly his enemies are. He takes unerring action to achieve his objectives. He is seizing his chance at glory. He's installed in his career and keeps a close eye on the competition. He knows he's destined for greatness... Suddenly, he is struck by the majesty of the skyscrapers. The heat is so searing he feels as if he is burned to a flake of ash. Brilliancy is broken up into dapples because of the foliage. Swallows sing. Heaven is damselfly-crimson-and-maroon. Peki takes a shortcut through the cemetery, treading on the stiff grasses, experiencing the sensation of peace, and the place's sacrosanctity. Numerous gravestones subside at angles, interspersed with pristine and upright ones. He feels the abstruse dread of being buried here. His casket would be so minute it'd scarcely hold an infant. Will he be a useless and forgotten nobody under the earth? He dismisses the thought from his brain. He wants to be comforted by the softness of civilization. He's adrift on the streets as though in a dream, auscultating the nightingales projecting their cantatas from branches, walls, and roofs. He buys a hat and suit and changes into them in a public restroom. The sun is unplacatable and oppressive. The evening is leech-black. Mosquitoes gorge on his blood. Ruins of a Roman theater. An intimate jumble of shops. He sees minarets of a mosque. Cirri stretch as far as all possible horizons. Twilight is exceedingly sultry. Peki is stupefied in horny, holy wonder, beholding her in a romper. When he arrived, Marisa met him at the threshold. She poked fun at him delightedly for his dapper appearance. She never takes him seriously! He speaks with the exaggerated alertness of someone wasted trying to sound straight. Talking to her, his tone of voice sounds as if it is somewhere between entreaty and desperation. He has the unnatural ability to seduce her, regardless of the circumstances surrounding them. His toothache fills all of his skull. A lancinating pain rushes into his molar when he chomps on a cookie. He's afraid he belongs in a lunatic asylum. He marshals his impulses. There is almost a sob of self-pity in his modulation. The universal excruciation of mankind is being deprived

of coition with one's mama. Light seeps through the chinks of the shutters. Peki has Scotch and opium. He is tempted to tell her about his
incessant bouts of crapulence. He wants to supervise an onanistic exercise designed specifically for her. He loves conducting these and being in
charge. He prepares in-depth plans and orderers. He's persnickety when
it concerns the details. She is periodically vexatious to him. They discuss
the crushed uprising. Sometimes he is disillusioned and depressed. Only
she can get him out of the doldrums. She looks at him as romantic but
unintellectual, and thus he is uninteresting. She recognizes that his business is gaining traction, and is piqued at not having been invited to the
party. Drizzle is like gauze. There is a certain something that makes Peki's
heart lift when he discerns her. Marisa's movements have more to do
with encouraging enticement than preventing it. Lately, she works hard
at being lazy. Her favorite hobbies are drawing in the dirt with a stick and
catching grasshoppers with her bare hands. Her orbs sparkle. Her smell
is an amalgamation of frankincense and rosewater. Is her allure a curse
or a blessing? Her arms are as long as her legs. She has yellow stains on
her hair from cigarette smoke. He feels homely and unwanted. Her body
makes his head spin as if he's been drinking alcoholic beverages. He is
enormously impressed by her. Her phiz glows like a lamp. He feels on top
of the world with her companionship. He sweats as though he's seated in
a steam bath, and envisions his grubby skin being sloughed off. She huffs
and puffs in the swelter. He gawps at her, wide-eyed and open-mouthed.
Is she a present or a reward? It's like a stab in the heart when she doesn't
pay attention to him. Every once in a while he gets scared that he's going
to lose her. She's his addiction; he's got to have more and more of her. He
is her slave. Really. He is mesmerized by whatever she does. Sometimes
she treats him not unlike a prince, other times like a pauper. Stars are
scintillating cruciform scars on the sky. Often Peki lies awake listening to
the nightingales' arias, his imagination and balls burning. He's proud and
pleased with himself when he captures her interest. Marisa's sweet when
she's spoiled. She doesn't know whether to laugh or cry or be pleased or
unpleased with his doting. She is an exotic, aged princess. She composes
her physiognomy with makeup. He steels himself to be persevering. He
experiences hotness in his gut as if he gulped the sun. He goes into a

kind of hypnosis. His nostrils flare with each breath. He winds up in this undesirable situation. The promises extricated from him by her, and the restrictions introduced, are unwarranted, and as yet he has received no osculations or tactions from his mother at all. Impatience on his part at this point would sever the Gordian knot. The alternatives are to sit tight or give up. She has an unending list of requirements when it comes to sexual congress. It gives her a sort of teasing pleasure in keeping him waiting. She has the air of a frightened hare. He is agitated and lubricious. Her whining wrinkles the oxygen. His sighs smoothen it out.

Abby Domen

Abby Domen, a sentient human trunk, as fat as it is hairy, lounges in a lawn chair in the yard after providing calisthenic consultation to a neighbor. The avant-garde, modernist architecture of the residence behind it, reminiscent of Robert Mallet-Stevens, is large enough to accommodate an indeterminate number of torsi. Peki favors it with a squint and one-sided smirk. It seems to have the attention span of a famished squirrel when they chitchat. Is it a trunk of sensualist persuasion? He is red-faced, seemingly ready to explode, but he's aroused by this weird entity. Is it a case of hormonal or homicidal rage? It is a comic book collector of about average obsessiveness. It buys and hoards, despite the demands driving prices through the roof. Everything kept in storage is in mint condition. The country has fallen into dismal times. This doesn't curb its splurging whatsoever. He feels like such a simpleton next to it and can't fathom why exactly. He wishes to reach and occupy it. His belch has the sonance of a gunshot. It's the strangest damn thing he's ever seen. Though high strung, it is all right... Before long, he finds himself clinging carnally to the slab of flesh. He made his move after an hour of indecision. Automatically it responds to his advances. It is calm and solid when he comes on to it. He removes its apron with its orientoid motifs. It is smooth in some spots and rough in others. Its behavior is a tad flighty, he thinks. He looks it in the nombril. They make sparks, like trains. The parlor is dim and balmy. Peki is bewitched by his new power: sheer dominance over his submissive. And he unhesitatingly humps the lumpen dumpling in the room, plaster from the damaged ceiling sprinkling them, contemplating halting the obscene recreation. He recognizes himself as a master and Abby as a servant. Unexpectedly, it resists his affections. Then it abandons its struggle, with an almost apologetic air. It talks dirty, filling the atmosphere with foul language unfit for the sensitive reader. It is as though the god of torsos singled him out for special attention. He pours his heart out. His pecker slips into its umbilical mouth and he begins pumping. Time becomes extradimensional. Thrusting is frantic, too fast to even register. Voices are loud. The place is chaos. It's like he's riding a bull. He refuses to get thrown off. It bucks not unlike a bronco. They shake in a frenzy, in blind velocity. There's a series of rapid thumps and a good deal of moaning and groaning. His cock is like a locomotive loaded with dynamite and deployed at desperate high speed against the creature. It is pillow-soft. The chunk of skin is just the dearest thing. It's still, as if acceding to a penance. It coughs and retches miserably. His shaft feels like a stovepipe, electricity running down it. His orgasm in the omphalos is like a blast in a mine. His screech, climaxing, sounds like a steam horn. Worn to a frazzle, he takes a nap on the futon. It sees to its chores. A fleece-clouded sky. Abby totters around, breathing heavily in the white-gold radiance. Midday, it rests its hirsute bulk on his shoulder to rest. They keep like this, quiet and unmoving, till the din of night rouses them. Peki stares into its spellbinding bellybutton and French-kisses it. He wakes with a start in a freight car, banged up from the activity with Abby, but nothing too serious. Realizing what he has done, he panics and flees. He's got to get his backside back to where he belongs — with Marisa. Fine showers commence. Reality, for chrissakes, has gone straight to hell. He remembers how immoderately, and at what length, he coupled with it. He must avoid the hoosegow no matter what. He feels as though he is inching a bit closer to the edge of the abyss. The hemisphere appears radioactive. Existence is a shifting abstraction. Sun hammers the street. He feels as if his soul is a barren badlands. He hightails it for the apartment and his mother, far from this. He is subjected to a sensation of dread. Yet he turns back. They eat tacos and drink margaritas.

It is a cavernous decommissioned chapel. The architecture is beautiful. The place has a handsome library of extravagant, Borgesian range and diverse curiosa, a testament to an uncommon fecundity of brain: preserved exotic insects, Venetian millefiori glassware, objects rare and fascinating of all imaginable varieties, old wrestling and bullfighting posters, and ravishing Matisse and Picasso nudes in pencil. The walls look like Escher woodcuts. A hot afternoon cools into the evening. On the narrow single mahogany bed, in an elegant room, Abby Domen's optic navel is half-opened, the sweat pooled in it reminding Peki, round the twist on blotter acid, of unshed tears. It considers itself a torso in residence. It is cold. He's warm. These dirty mental pictures go through his drowsy mind. He's caught in the grip of an exalted apprehension. He has to offend it. He must hurt it. He beholds, or believes he does, these waxwork Kali kids with hourglass shapes, prosthetic arms, and plaster legs. Their feet are booted. Oily puddles on the floor glisten not unlike fresh blood. The luster is contraceptive-colored. Clouds metamorphose into ultrasound pictures, the cherubs in a fetal position. The rainbow's colors are somewhat subtle. The lily-white thing, on the citron duvet, embroidered with Tudor roses, repels and attracts him. Abby looks like an enormous dandelion head. To his total amazement and embarrassment, Peki experiences bodily excitement. He commences, not inexpertly, to stroke it, his sex stirred. Then he removes its umbilical metal ring. His whispering sounds tired. They embrace decorously, tum to tum. Overcome by emotion, he takes it into his arms, holds it, and wants to make love to it. The sheets are unlaundered. He caresses its mussel-dark nipples and munches on its chest fuzz. It is a complicated creature in its simplicity. Scabs on his elbow and knee are like carapaces. Water drips. Light pulses. The two getting intimate on the goose feather mattress in the vaulted vestry, in a curtained-off space, and he discovers it has endured real pain and suffered human harm. It copes with medical issues. It has dealt with much hardship and solitude. It is wholesome and innocent. It arouses his desire. It's unmistakably demure and sweetly virtuous. It glistens with sweat. He is proudly naked, feeling dangerous and dirty. Abby, recollective of an animated Arcimboldo portrait, a portion of one anyway, tightens when Peki enters and exits its umbilicus with his root. He sucks on its breasts, evoking a baby feeding. They are in full flight. He thrusts in its nombril in a deliberate and considerate way. It is designed and fearful. Pumping in and out of it, his voice is small and shrilly. They have intercourse on a seventeenth-century birthing chair next to the carved bay window and under a rood screen. The copulation is awkward. The trunk heaves and struggles like a fish on the hook. A wave of cramps washes over its stomach with him pounding on it. It acts as though it's having contractions, its water is breaking, it's withstanding long and horrible labor... Coitus is fraught with difficulties, as you might imagine. He clutches its rolls of flesh and grunts. Its writhing movement looks as if it's a disagreeable effort to him. Climaxing, he grabs its tits and howls like a baby. It attempts to read his expression: amazement or puzzlement? It doesn't know. He is a hangdog with it, his overactive cerebral imagery... He puts the mohair jersey on it and bumps into the dressing table. Is it at the end of some tether? When he walks, his ass wiggles like an armadillo. He has a coldish fug that won't shift with a dozen Lemsips. He looks beaten down. Exhausted. Defeated. And he takes a fluid bath in the tub. He feels like his blood pressure has improved. He relaxes into this narcotized, unencumbered peace when Abby, the wandering soul, drifts into the lavatory. The orgasm was incredible. That is the truth of it. It rises from the soap suds not unlike Aphrodite from the foam. It breathes lightly, stomach bruised from the coupling. It has a unique, lovely tummy. Ripples are visible on its flesh. He hops like a woodpecker to entertain it. Drugged, he has the sensation that he's sultry-skinned and with silky lashes. He is barefoot and short-sleeved. Possessed of immense determination, he runs hither-thither like a servant to satisfy it. He imagines it as being a prince, or even a princess. The bust is flawless. It behaves as though it is faintly bored. He doesn't want to emit anything unwittingly foolish. With a slight lift of his cracked lips, he says he's enjoying himself greatly. Its navel is deep and distant. The Blush-pink moon is in its gibbosity. Peki washes, towel-dries, and swaddles it, whereupon he slips a hospital nightshirt on it and pats its back. Abby feels constricted, but composed, in the material. He has a mien of baffled adoration. He revels in these delirious days. He is a changed man. They practice ballroom dancing. Their waltz is clumsily executed, his unaccustomed feet blundering, making him feel inadequate. He claps and laughs following the polka. Stepping properly, he gains confidence. They make a charming and homogenous couple!

Pressed together, they quickly pirouette and float. This is another world. Rhythmically they sway. He rubs, cuddles, and nuzzles it with shameless vigor. He's good with thought-reading. It is exquisitely pretty, masculine, and feminine. It is propped against a scalloped cushion. He falls asleep and dreams that his back is straight and stiff.

They met cute at a pinball parlor, looking like some medieval manor, situated in a nondescript strip mall, that was incessantly beckoning to the empyrean. Peki thought that Abby, in an aureate aureole, had a radiant, magnetic charisma. It tried out different priorities and personalities… The firmament is of the richest metallic blue. Sun appears at infrequent intervals through the cumuli. Mares and foals pace in a paddock. Doves settle on the ledge and preen. Gales sound like the monotonous cries of howler monkeys. The swimming hole's saltwater is a lachrymal flood. A crowd of people: a horde of army ants. Flies bite. Thrushes chime. Rain and wind sound like swishes of hay. There are traces of dirt and crushed leafage on the checkered floor. Abby makes a suggestive gesture. Peki returns from the previously-untrodden wilderness of his mind and rises to the occasion. He attempts to be a rational being. It has a mischievous spirit. Pyretic, it is under his ministrations… or torments. It has fever dreams of a kindly presence, and his absence. He sticks the thermometer in its oral-omphalos to take its temperature. It smells of poultry. The idea of a romantic union with it pops into his noggin. He wants to believe that he's desperately needed. Would he be easily forgotten? He remembers being flat broke, penniless, and without prospects. Those days are a distant memory. His hands are folded in his lap. He learns that it is a quadragenarian and noble and wields power. It was once a mine owner who invested shrewdly. Its siblings died in infancy. It is a living thing, wondrously made. Narcoleptic, it tends to nod off without a moment's notice. The spate has an ammoniac whiff. The pond finds itself with a plague of frogs. Peki chomps on a carrot loudly. Then he doffs the friar gown, frayed and musty, and dons a loose jacket and baggy trousers that stink of dung and piss. His mouth buried in a frondescent beard, he kisses it. Both are seated on a hard oak bench. He is substantial, it thinks. Solid. Abby's ocular nombril is modestly cast down. Its derma layer is satin-whitish. Blood rushes to his head and he nearly faints. He is piercing-eyed. It is a remarkable creation, extraordinarily designed, evidence that a Creator actually exists. He's instinctively and physically drawn to it. It's brilliant and he's drab, is his opinion. His pink tongue moistens its navel. It seems timid. It can be placidly evasive. Sometimes it puts up an invisible barrier that he is expected to surmount. It looks delightful in a tee-shirt of red damask. It flaunts itself with impunity. A cirrus of magic dust attracts and nauseates him. He deems himself a careful observer with a casual eye. Its perspiry belly reminds him of viscid dough. He envisions them lying together in a canoe on miles of iron-gray aqua pura. He bows politely and smooches its umbilicus. And he shrivels in an ardent fire. He licks his false milky teeth. There is an encouragement to converse and he obliges. "I am yours to command," he says. The plain study is stone-cold and hexagonal-shaped with perpendicular-styled panes. A roof-light is located in the center of the ceiling, which is carved with designs of flowers, foliage, and fruit. An arched bookcase and collecting cabinet are leaning against the wood paneling with pomegranate wallpaper. Someone's salvaged treasures are packed in a walnut chest. Welkin is pale lavender. The ocean is an iridescent green, visually evocative of a vast scarab. Cloudlets are whitish as wool. Abby has an air as if it has an atmosphere of its own. Peki braids his beard into a sort of dangling bell-rope. He soft-footedly comes and goes into the den. Seen out the window — endless structural sameness. Clumps of his hair are stiff like dead leaves. He discerns a lofty tower surrounded by swarthy demons and stupendous serpents. Acid churns in his gullet. Bile sprays up into his throat.

Peki waddles more than walks in the copse, pretending he is a scientific explorer, or some primitive hunter, in a virgin tropical jungle. He expects to encounter wild people, naked savages, in tribal villages… He wears a voluminous, jet-black robe with a practical cowl, strolling through the meadow in a great fall of summer rain. Finally, he sits on an elm stump, on a muddy bank, amidst the bryony and hawthorn, under a canopy of foliage, and fishes for minnows in the stream to have for supper. They swim busily. Grass and twigs and stalks and sticks float on the placid surface. Dirt bristles with a convoy of ants, minute and rapid aggressors.

Some carry grubs and cocoons. Gaudy insects dance in midair amongst the weeping willows and white poplars. This is truly Paradise. The mass of herbage is suffocative. Water is alive with movement. There's a turmoil of aquatic energies. Spoiled verdure. The incarnadine velvet curtains are partially drawn against the sanguine shiny sun. The spritzing sounds like the hissing of sizzling skin. A fire is lit in the hearth. A pile of hydrangeas Peki had picked on one of his nature rambles is on the footstool. He enjoys these refreshing outings. Abby sometimes joins him (strapped to his back, not unlike a backpack, by a special harness) and sometimes does not. He is immobilized by torpor. With a canny, calculated expression, he consumes large quantities of sherry and port, lounging on the deep couch, with a nest of cushions, embroidered with butterflies, oriented towards the window. Opiated, he speaks in a fading voice. His nerves feel torn. Next to it, fitted in a corset, he feels like a limited being. It has a cashmere shawl draped on its back. He has barley water and scones with jam and a selection of macaroons. He's vacantly amiable. His spirit is desolate. He feels as if his soul is a pit of horrors. A break from his murderous activities is necessary. He's been killing indiscriminately; color and race are irrelevant. Thunder sounds like a gunshot crack. Lightning is terrible and terrifying. Abby's pure pain rarely dulls. There's tremendous tension in its diaphragm. It thinks Peki's bare butt is moony-bland. Its chest hair is plenteous and lustrous. It is well-fleshed, has countable rolls, and bloom on its dermis. He applies a cold compress to its aching abdomen and recites poems off the top of his head. His complexion is chalky, face unsmiling. He rubs the transparent jelly from the corners of his peepers. It is stationary on the table, covered in baize. Taking care of it is a labor of love. He wipes its belly button with a cloth dampened with witch hazel, cleaning out the lint. It hopes that it's not overburdening him with tasks and that he's comfortable. It is currently not committed to the conversation. Significant imagination, his, is lavished on sexual fantasies. He gives it his complete attention. It is a docile creature. Often it speaks only when spoken to. It's tumefied and glossy. It is good at keeping still. He experiences a sensation of electric forces charging through his entirety. He gets a prick of pleasure in massaging its flocculent midsection. The thing is flaccidly unexercised. It is watchful. Its cotton top is severe and unornamented. His amative overtures are rejected. He gives up the ghost and wants to curl up and die. It breathes in and sighs out. He decorates its stomach with vegetable dyes. It is as though it is a magnetic field, pulling him here and there. With a delicate frown, he clings to it like a creeper to a tree (trunk). They are interlocked like cogs in a watch. He is grinning and diabolical. His limpid pies rest on it. His tone is neutral, talking with conventional complacency. He's part-clothed. It is rosy-breasted and olive-backed in irradiance. And it thrashes like a curious fish, held by him. His equipment is electrified. It gasps and becomes inert. It remains angry red. Its tummy is a fiery fuchsia. It opens and closes its tremulous optical umbilicus. Is it flushed with ire or elation? It blushes pinker...

Together, Peki and Abby are like cells in the body, two parts of one whole. Its navel softens into a smile, rocking itself in the chair. He kneads its paper-pale midriff. It belongs to no place on this planet. The torso is wrapped in wreaths of bluebells and primroses and pretty pearls. With the tip of his forefinger, he traces the perfect arch of its omphalos, its chestnut-hued, hardened nipples. It extends the invitation to him to fondle it. His grin is stretched from ear to ear. He fears that his life will go out should he leave. It is a worthy partner. It's a sympathetic individual, one with a kind heart. He observes it sharply, searching for signs of possible boredom. It seems to be as satisfied as ever. He's gratified, seated alone with it, companionably, on a low bench. He puts an arm around it. He must have it or perish. It can be ambivalently impenetrable. Carelessly he pinches an inch of fat and it flinches. Its cologne has a jasmine aroma. There's an erectness of his tonk as he tastes the nectarous drink. He plays around with it with a succession of squeals of fascination and revulsion. His hands are about its waist, thumbs tickling its ribs, and gains vicarious pleasure in doing so. Then he organizes the chapel with exemplary industry in the brimstone-yellow scintillation, wearing nothing save a starched cap. He bobs to it in worship when he passes, hurrying hither and yon. It looks on dubiously. He is dedicated to his chores. It's swathed in grass-green crinoline. He feels as if he is relegated to a between-universe, being here with Abby and being there with Marisa, connected to them. Its spare tire is set in annoyance, feeling neglected. Its attitude is full of a charge of meaning. It is in distress and he comforts it. Despite the differences between them, they trust each other. Sometimes, however, he has neither patience nor discretion when it concerns the trunk. He waylays it on the stairs after lunch. Tawny-orange splendor comes through the glinting glass. The air is alive. The oxygen is insectilely chromatic. The bugs are living jewels flittering in undulant patterns. An ingenious hornet nest resembles an inverted chalice hanging from the rafter. Clouds of pollen drift. Abby Domen, warmed by the rising sun, is in a buff-pigmented bodice trimmed with tartan ribbons. It spreads its fragrance. Peki's body throbs with desire. Vim beats in his veins and stings his senses. It fesses that it is lucky to have him with it. It stares at him as though it can read thoughts. Sexing it… this is the reward he promised himself after running around like a maniac to maintain his business and care for his mother. It is gorgeous and good. It shows great courage just by existing. There is affectionate benignity in its gaze, situated under the halation of a lamp. Outrage takes over when his mitts molest it. Now it crawls like a caterpillar. Ultimately it will fly like a butterfly. This transfiguration will occur in a moment of it is a bright heavenly body or a portion of one. He is pallid-faced and bleary-eyed. It sits in a wire basket, auscultating his slippered feet and swishing skirts. He feels as if he's sucked into it, not unlike a boat into the drag of a whirlpool. He envisages the preputial part of his tube in its nombril like a bee in the throat of a floret. In his embrace, it looks like a moth trying to break out of the pupa. The polished floor reminds him of a bestilled pondlet with a reflecting surface. He appears preoccupied and serious. Colorless grass. The domed roof is leaky. Flora is vigorous. The marble statue of a nymph on the front lawn is overhung with trailing vines. There's a pair of goldfish in a shallow bowl. Climbing plants and twining branchlets are supported by a wrought-iron grille. Brilliantly-colored blossoms are bedded on the side of the yard. Palm trees stand here and there out back. Silver moon is in the otherwise empty sky. Peki is stolid and expressionless, thinking about home. His madre must be frantic.

"What is your name?" Abby asks.

"Will Cumb," he answers, whereupon he absconds.

Home

Peki is back in the apartment, deep in the predawn hours, before he even knows it. The minutes are organisms, creating an event of life that can be measured in time. Light has chance encounters with shadow. Marisa haunts the place like a ghost. She's dressed in a rubber suit, looking like some sea monster in a semi-miraculous manifestation, drinking gin and eating macaroons. He prepares himself for everything that her presence might hold. He keeps his eyes and ears open. She sits in a folding chair, enormous oculi quiescent. Will she give him the bum's rush? She has a somber and unreadable aspect. Her expression suggests she is under hypnosis. He fails to hide his lecherous intentions. He finds her irresistible. His lechery never fades. A smirk occupies his rictus. Mosquitoes hum in the vicinity. She is quiet and does not move. His tail snarls and sputters with flatus. His mane is snarled, frock filthy. She appears to be a lady in need of assistance. He reads her like a devout person does a religious text. He is confident he'll crank himself up to normal speed once he rests up for a spell. With the illumination, the furnishings seem etched in chalk... Marisa puts on a navy shift, wraps an afghan around her shoulders, and sleeps on the divan. Peki watches her with an erection. The outlook for intercourse prospects isn't promising. Color leaves his face. She shifts onto her side and he admires her milky tochus and dark crack. He puffs on a butt and blows a smoke ring that shivers as it expands in midair. He flicks ash into the turtle tray. He reaches into his boxers and masturbates. Her mop spills off the cushion, stomach exposed. He strokes himself, imagining her caressing herself. She slumbers through the disgusting activity.

He realizes what an unprincipled pig he truly is. This is an act he cannot believe he's committing. The grand finale is unreal. Coming, he emits half a growl, splooging unapologetically on her toned thigh. His orbs are steely, taking a gander at the skein of waterways. He wants to be the great and powerful in the mantequilla kingdom, a force to be reckoned with. Success is a fantasy that constantly teases him. His tension rod is vibratory. Sozzled, he walks as if he's on a high wire. His cogitations are comparable to those of a prophet. There's fading light and treacherous shadows. He feels as though he'd traveled here, from Chutcha's pad, not unlike an Argonaut crossing a continent. He hears the muffled grumble of her gut. Her intentional insouciance toward him is becoming less bearable. She's busy as a circus midget, sashaying, stacking the antique crockery in the cabinet. Her grocery list is written in her spidery script as though it is presented in a deliberately indecipherable code. She saunters in a dreamy glide. A tremor of excitement passes through his loins. Her impenetrable visions, images drawn in pastel and ink on pieces of paper, are disturbing. Her mood improves when he pays attention to her. She swabs the decks, fore and aft. Stars look like torches streaming in the orchid-purple heavens in a continual current above a complex, unmappable country. Guano stains the paving stones. There are stagnant puddles. Levin blazes over the whole range. A mystery of masonry partially obstructs the salt squalls. The wet sand is wreathed by the motor exhaust. This vessel is dismasted at the jetty. The storm drives folks indoors. Peki remembers the goose-stepping troops of the Third Reich.

Stringbean

A lanky giantess with alabaster flesh and twiggy limbs is in a state of catatonia, standing upright, gazing blankly into the middle distance, and emitting a series of nervous grunts and teeth-clicks, after magically coming out of an oak tree. Her nickname is Stringbean, a war-damaged misfit who suffers from catalepsy. She was a gunner on the front line and was discharged after a permanent concussive injury. She snaps out of it, in the iron-grey curtain of precip. She has piss-yellow hair, vague blue eyes, and is clad in this emerald-green knitwear and rust-hued boots. Peki is dumbfounded. He was just delivered here, courtesy of Chutcha. Their discussion stays on a trajectory for a while and then, like a brakeman throwing a switch, the discourse is shunted off to a separate but plausibly parallel track. He regards her as a genuine oddbod. She's employed as a nurse at a sanatorium, secretly euthanizing patients who will not recover from their wounds. Is she less an angel of mercy than a bringer of death? Woolly cirri. Waves are sluggish in a vaporous veil and the sand is seeded with shells. Stringbean waddles not unlike an albatross. She's an imaginative being, her head in the clouds. She sips bubbly and chews almonds. She is bovine, whereas he is a fierce force. His shaft rises in his breeches like the snake in blind John Milton's cavernous skull. She has spent much of her life soul-searching. Phosphorescence flickers fitfully. She thinks of herself as a Typhoid Mary, an incorrupt infector, an unknowing killer. Lately, she has been lingering in a void of inactivity. They decide to take a dip in a water tank. The poor galootress, who had an impoverished youth, is subject to sudden seizures and spasms and is learning the language of whales and the songs of porpoises, and is a connoisseur of passion fruits. Tall and thin, she towers over him. She has a voice like nails on a chalkboard. Thoughts gather in his cranium like starlings. She is a liberal-minded, ingenious, amateur narratologist who specializes in fables, and is a frequenter of coffeehouses and bookstores. Her breath is evil-smelling, body odor redolent of stale smoke and alien sweat. She says she feels, in the banalest sense, like a redundant woman. He watches her make an ostentatious of her jerky progress on the seashore. She is a pasty pythoness with slack-sinewed arms and legs. In her existence, she explains, she often feels as if she's a prisoner trying to break her chains and escape from the dungeon. She has many natures and snores and farts. She has fake teeth and laser-corrected vision. She is neither beautiful nor virtuous. She's always alive with new ideas and inspirations. Stories are exchanged. She recently recovered from bouts of influenza and tuberculosis. A thread of misfortune is woven into the tapestry of both lives. The two pause at a willow-bordered river, momentarily becoming spectators of a winding bridal procession. Stringbean looks at him as though he is some ghoulish apparition, a stalking spirit, curdling her blood. She is consumed by despair and revulsion. Peki has a burning sexual need. He wraps his pygmoid arms around her illusorily unending legs. He'll die if his lust remains unconsummated. She brings him back to her place, a quiet and reflective flat in a modern edifice, constructed of cement, wood, and glass, that is connected to a hillside, in which she savors her solitude. She lapses into a fugue state, going glassy-eyed, and appearing to lose time. She is silent and still, as though frozen. On the footstool, she reminds him of a statue on a pedestal. And she treads, making no sound on the floor as if her feet are shod with felt. Preoccupied with self-assertion, she crouches and smooches Peki's mirthless mouth with a thrill and a shudder. Their told tales gallop. They go from being clothed to uncovered in the twinkling of an eye. She stares at his unit like Macbeth at the feast. Making love, patience is shown between them, the roles of domination and submission consistently changing. Stripped of sheets, the coupling is like it is to punish, correct, into willed oblivion. The copulation is conducted, bizarrely, between comedy and sentimentality, with vim and vigor. When she ejaculates, she says he's a lord and she's a lady.

He swoons, uncomprehending. There is power in their gripping. They are so tightly embraced you couldn't tear one from the other's grasp. They enact their pleasures with verve. She wheezes asthmatically. Their stoppered and stunted energy is unparalleled. The conclusion of the coition is splendid and satisfactory for both parties. Emotions are relieved. He lies on her like lead. The lamp's light glitters in her eyeballs. She is still and silent. Skyline is stone-colored. To him, she's a pillar of salt, a grasshopper of a human being. Her swollen globes are red-rimmed. She is flat-chested, crack-lipped, and hook-faced. Is she a product of hallucination? He's not so sure... It is as though they are seasoned performers, dramatically swapping anecdotes. Peki's beard is a silvering sable. Her skin's texture is like it's fashioned out of clay. They converse about Pasolini the filmmaker and spring anemones. She calls his pencil the sword of Damocles. There's a polished gleam to his dermis. He gazes at the row of generic baked figurines on the mantelshelf. Ocean rages in the squalls. He feels as if he's a disproportionate troll, and that she's perfectly proportioned. The thermometer reads she has a slight temperature. They embark willy-nilly on a gabfest. Stringbean gets up and goes into the kitchen. Her buttocks protrude behind her, her breasts splayed. He is impelled to shamble after her. The slippery slope to orgasm has been further greased...

With the property's innumerable passages, it's like a minor maze. Balconies, one above the other, are carved with carnations and chrysanthemums and edged with resplendent mosaics. There are hidden rooms and secret spots. Peki feels blind as a mole in the gloaming. His blood is hot and his body is powerful. The migraine makes his head feel as though it's being stabbed with ice splinters. He is tempted to dive into the small underground swimming pool below. He experiences delirium tremens. He dances like a bear, only he is the size of a cub. Stringbean digs into the stuffed peppers and shish kebabs he had prepared on the trestle table. She'd barbered her axillae's tufts temporarily but now they thrive anew, like mown grass, growing in much thicker and luxuriant. Her skin is soft as a baby's. He gapes at her columnar legs. She is austere, not unlike Artemis. She strides stiffly into the kitchen. Her bosom is ripe, bottom full. She's supple and sensual. A damselfly buzzes against the smeared pane. She turns into an animated plaster

Venus. Blood thrums in his ears. She is seemingly kind of cardboardy, motionless on the Turkish tiles. His veins hum. She transmogrifies into a many-armed Hindu deity, in the network of undulatory refulgence, tinkering with the dumbwaiter. Her form sparks with flashes of fire. He can't move a muscle, on her large, hard bed, until he comes to himself. He has the sensation of being more alive than ever before, exhilarated as if he'd evaded fate. His heart and lungs pump. He won't glance at his reflection in the elegant mirror, afraid he would behold a pappose brute. He feels sort of weightless and vanishing, as though because of water pressure. His nerves: pure energy. It is like his destiny is in his own hands. He imagines the apartments as being Aladdin's caves, full of twinkling treasures and magical carpets. She sits cross-legged on the rug and gulps brandy, flaunting and subtle, out of a tulip-shaped glass, encompassed by dangling lamps. The sea absorbs the azure. In her seated position, in the indigoid shade, dishabille, her knockers resemble fleshly witchy hats. In this box of space, he gives her nipple an experimental tweak and she winces. It's high noon and she's feeling low. Inside, she channel-surfs on the television — a sizable lozenge with a rectangular screen. Images, moving, flicker and dance across it. Outside, the rush of traffic. He has a cup of delectable yogurt, and raspberry fudge. A whiny skeeter expends enormous energy in attempting to leave the premises. Long roads are sort of reminiscent of red deserts. Stringbean is transparent as water, solid as the earth, heavy as a rock, and invisible as air. Peki's breadbasket, from the acid reflux, is a furnace of fire. The java, spiked with schnapps, is unbearably strong and sweet. He imagines soaping her torso, shampooing her mop, and eventually toweling her off. She's unexceptional. Well-preserved. She is wan and wonderful. The harbor has an excremental malodor. Effulgence is the color of beeswax. The marble street has porticoes. There is an Egyptian temple, a Seventh Wonder of the Ancient World, with sphinxes under its arches and lions at its gates. Date palms line the front. Genies and winged antelopes and bulls are before a brick wall. The city is a sewer, and It is putrefying. Roses, climbing on a cedar, have thorny stems. A Greek building, architecturally certain, constructed of eclectic materials, its pillars curious, made of brass and stone, is imposing in its vastity. The Tree of Life holds these geometric flowers with insipid colors, petals expanding and contracting. Malachite brine shimmers. Stringbean wears a fluttering paisley sari, sterling bangles on her wrists and ankles. Peki, dressed in a tan tunic, shows her in mime what he expects her to do. Struck by a primitive fear, she mechanically nods, grave and noncommittal. Forcefully he insists. She laughs loudly and kneels like the faithful at a holy shrine, or like a Muslim in a mosque. Darkness slides over them. The seeds are sown. The flame will consume. Stakes are raised when she rejects his advances, ensuring maximum tension and, ultimately, pleasure. The possibility is the delight. Her countenance is distorted into one of discomfort in the acid-gold lances of coruscation. He gently pinches the taut integument of her thighs. And she cringes. He takes her hand, slightly electric, her pulse pounding, like an extracted still-beating heart from a patient's chest by a surgeon. Her perfume's scent has a combined scent of cinnamon and sulfur. His feet are of an olive hue, the soles scaly, their nails horny. A vein throbs in his temple. His speech is harsh, emitted in a language she can't identify. It is incomprehensible. Expletives? Parrot feathers float up and not down in the sea-green emanation. Peki presses his huge head against her shoulder blades. Then he osculates her sharp cheekbones and tactions her doughy middle. She is larger than life. Next to her, he feels extremely tiny.

The moon, this pale evening, has gone red as a living heart. The two are verbally going round and round, as usual, the subject being sadomasochism, the debate heated. Stringbean hugs herself as if for warmth, even though it is sweltering. Meantime, Peki enters a state of attention to her bust. She senses and sees it. It's disagreeably evident he's titillated. His hands reaffirm their allegiance to her abdomen. His chuckling, far-reaching, is soul-stabbing. She sits on the stool nearly paralyzed. He speaks in unsolvable riddles. Maybe it's the speed. They blither a mile a minute. Manhandled, she angles her head and raises her eyebrows inquiringly. She can't manage to mentally process his mysterious visitation, as though it was the result of some magical force. He is a ravening wolf in sheep's clothing. His hands disengage themselves from her boobs. The sexual road branches into unsuspected side streets. There are confusions in the intersections and rotaries. Accidents happen. Detours interrupt. Who has the right of way? He's insatiably drawn to her. He goes for her crotch like he is endeavoring to grab a weapon. Lust, to him, is a corrupt form of love. They're unappeasable individuals in an unforeseen coital tempest. The structure is gale-beaten. Menacing clouds. The metropolis is scarcely comprehensible. Stringbean moves deliberately, unhurried, in the pantry, an outsize, dead-white, seraphic figure. Watching her, Peki, seated on the hassock decorated with grease stains, tilts like a ship at sea. His libido comes to life. An argument arises and soon enough they fall speechless again. Her feet drag on the floor. The fulgor points in its accustomed direction when the blinds are lifted. He studies the arachnid webwork in the ceiling's corner. He looks at her pretty intently. She could squash him like a bug if she wanted to. She searches for a cooking utensil as if she's in danger and is looking for a firearm. She acts as though she has been sentenced to hard labor in Siberia. Her complexion has an unhealthy shade of yellow. He is pudendum-possessed and drinks incessantly. He declines food and accepts liquor and smokes. Muttering to herself, she rattles around in the kitchen preparing tostadas. He is still a stone. His will to screw is pure, his modulation uninflected. The mumble of thunder at the horizon. The vault's hue deepens past blue. A fountain sparkles in the courtyard. The shopping center seethes in exuberant commotion. An eagle soars like a song. Meaningfully she gazes at him and his schlong rises into active status. She throws off the appropriate items of apparel. Everything here becomes chaotic. There is a delicate balance of intimate interests. Emotions are severe. Bubbles burst. Cirri account for a quarter of the visible horizon. Illumination is blood-orange. The brownish river roars under the bruise-colored vista. Unlimited blackness of the murk. Stringbean is at her barmaid job. Peki flagellates himself and swills wormwood-intensive vermouth, wishing to acquire the ancient powers of flight by quoting passages from the Scriptures. Ichor seeps in the gloaming. The clock on the wall works backward. The lane shines not unlike a stream. Exotic beetles have a taste for the vital fluid like mosquitoes, skittering onto his shredded back to feed. Rain tends to fall unpredictably in the miles of dark. It's a cascade of electrical noises. Terns perch on the boughs of firs. Skyscrapers extend, sheer and unexpected, out of the fogbank. Petrels swoop to snag fish out of a shallow creek. It looks like live-action replays. He hears the humid breathing of the meandering brook. He imagines this is a secret city, a hidden land, contaminated by age, afflicted by time, a sleepless conurbation dedicated to manufacturing, dense with industry, its creatural citizens feeding on one another. He is blind drunk. These incandescent effects last long. Peki is blithely deranged, ambulating about like a holy wanderer. It is as though the carpet has gone to quicksand. The wiring in the power supply of his gray matter melts. He's feeling blasted off the map. He gutturally sings into the unhopeful, bleak dawn... until a throaty bass vocal accompanies him. There is no one else in the sacramental room with him. He stands alone. There's no other human of any kind. It's his sphincter. Using a cosmetic mirror, he regards his pucker with profound curiosity. It has a tremolo to its trill. He notices that night has been reincarnated into the day. Shrooms send him off on outrageous internal (and external) odysseys, visually, auditorily, and spiritually stimulating, and equally entertaining and enlightening. Appearing stricken, as if beyond redemption, he speaks, deviating from the local language. Then he flies into the sky, perhaps destined to never land.

Smokestacks sprawl under an aerial flotilla of spherical airships. The celestial sphere is crowded with cumuli. Brilliance leaks from the day. Cocks crow. An ocean liner, the shape of a watermelon, is clockwork slow. A musical crescendo comes from somewhere. Landscape emerges in the mist like a photograph from a developing bath. The upper atmosphere has an apocalyptic shade. Peki's behind emits gaseous gasps. He views the automatic restaurant adjacent to the virgin woods. A huge cat, lounging on the mailbox, looks like a dog in disguise. The dwarf wears a mourning frock. Though alive, he feels dead without drugs, thoroughly zombified. He looks more haggard than usual. His mane is a capillaceous spilth. He announces he suffers from a range of conditions, somatic and emotional, these ailments incurable. Breezes rise. He loafs around the flat. Stringbean is dressed in an ingenious garment: a lace chemise. They've passed, for the most part, a pleasant morning together. She is slender and sensual. She's the oxygen he breathes. He thinks she is a desirable package, albeit a lanky one. Her porcelain integument invites aggressive attention. He considers himself a gent who cuts her some slack. With her, he wins more than he loses. She has a curious pallor. Stuck by luminous needles, she mucks about with the elaborate java-maker next to the vaseful of flowers. They sound like a couple of chattering fools. Canvases of abstract art lean against the plaster paneling. Leven flickers across the empyrean, not unlike reflected water-glare. He notices the occluded lambency of the cloudy afternoon. Consciously cruel, Peki wants to sodomize her and makes little secret of it. He takes care to look dejected. Stringbean appears to be preoccupied with her shadow. He wishes to obtain her tail as if it's something to be negotiated for. She proclaims she has tidying up to do. Her eyes don't meet his. She, in the fractional luminosity, is flushed, in disarray. Her feet are exquisitely stockinged. She glances nervously, not gazing steadily whatsoever. He can give her the chills. Narcotics find their way to his brain center. Her blond coif is drastically cropped. The hairdresser at the salon was merciless with the scissors. Their sportive routine recommences. They pump in a passional frenzy in the phosphorescent phenomenon. All hell breaks loose in her hazardous bed. He can tell her heart really isn't into it. They settle down. Their banter is lighthearted. He sticks to her leg like a fly to flypaper, fingers becoming intimate with her nether regions, whereupon he stares at the syringe and thinks of a vein. A few pigeons waddle on the perilous window ledge in the nacreous luminescence. He contemplates the idea of the Butyrum being distributed into the greater market of the wide world. He's glad to be out of the subterranean laboratory. A break from the business is doing him some good. And he becomes cosmically inspired… Her ethereality is emphasized in the declarative brilliancy. The Rouge on her cheeks is smudged. He allows himself a brief moue. A polyhedral chimera bumbles in the countryside. Night transudes darkness. Stars glitter across the firmament. A cheap motel's neon sign glows radioactively. Feeling as though he's locked up in the pokey, Peki's presence disintegrates into absence.

The infernal winds blow the draggled shoes, till now hanging by their laces, off the tram lines, and they illusorily stride, with a march tempo, down the road, as if in magical migration to a more salubrious climate, a tropical retreat for footwear where they can rest and dream of new feet to cover. Perhaps even a little therapeutic polishing will betide. The racket of the underworld is unremitting. Plenty of pedestrian traffic is on the cobbles of the street. Peki's gait is a commanding creep. There is a beastly pigment to his complexion that connotes illness. His besotted behavior, with the customary vile virile exhibitions, yelling threats of bodily and facial insults, is growing increasingly insufferable to Stringbean. Her nodding and shrugging are turning into tics. She's encircled by the ring of routine. She vocalizes in measured cadences that are the backbeats to his revved-up motormouthed rhythms. Trying to get along with him, for her, is a thankless task, and requires discipline, like mountain-climbing. She is in nothing save for a velvet hat, sport spectacles, and kid boots. He finds a perverse fascination in getting her riled. She admires herself. He ogles, and gulps counter-soporific, and illegal, tablets. She resolves to give up communication as an unproductive indulgence, an invalid use of her time. She's tempted to bid him a jaunty arrivederci (because of his nasty attitude), the most effective expression of a fond farewell that she can muster. He's brutal and simple. He beams mindlessly upon her. His verbalizing has a Teutonic candidness. Steam horns and tourist chirping are distracting. He has this damnable tickle and stricture in his throat. She has a tightlipped moue. Though they occupy the same room, it's as if they're seeing and talking from across a chasm. His farting is bull elephant thundering. Heedlessness of commerce surrounds them. Sanguineous scintillation gushes like blood from a gaping wound. Peki forsakes the typical chary protocols of courtship, his fervid approach stunning. He staggers toward her as though for shelter. And he comes on to her with a not untheatrical flourish. His smile's fierce as the weather. Stringbean's resistance to his advances: obstacles to be braved. His thumb addresses her asshole and clitoris, his free hand dividing her bum and clam. He fingers her alternately considerately and rudely, at angles unfamiliar to her. Coupling, they become a composite being with its ardent aspirations. He porks her savagely from behind. Their respirations sound not unlike rapid wingbeats. He fesses he sometimes feels like an exile in his own land. He feels at home in these recreational elements. Her cerebrum lobes relax. She delivers herself into adumbrative abduction, from the streaming sunshine, making the meal and pouring the mead. He seizes her bottom. She utters she hasn't been slumbering too frightfully well. Their conversational resources are already depleted. If he insists he must leave, would she try to persuade him to stay? Dusk darkens and takes on a soupy warmth. The megalopolis reeks overwhelmingly of garbage. Boats whistle in the bay. Citizens seem to have a vague ceremonial purpose. Cumuli have individual countenances. Scenes on the sidewalk shift. Belltower looks like the ruin of an ancient fortress, barely standing, built before history. Gusts are unending breaths. Uproarious deluge.

The marketplace is aswarm with shoppers and school kids. Shoreline approaches infinite length. Lifeguard chairs are arpeggiated along the sand, stationed, ostensibly, at every vantage. Umbrellas on the beach suggest, visually, a chain of islets. Gulls multiply beyond counting in the parking lot. Peki, on PCP and wolfing down chocolate bonbons, regards, with a most peculiar eagerness, the nubile dewdrop in a maillot and espadrilles out front of a droning seedy pub. He calls her, under his breath, a busybody in a wasteland. She is under the gaze of his lens, this outlandish optical device. The day is deep. Swallows harmoniously pivot. His suicidal mania is severe. He acknowledges the splendor's simplicities and the sofa's cig burns. The drencher sounds not unlike drumbeats. He stares at her duff as if it is a familiar face. Stringbean's towering white figure stands like a young birch in the forestial flat. She discourses on the virtues of being her and his ears perk up. She is clad in excruciatingly tight denim shorts (brevity producing inviting effects) and an unspeakably nauseating tie-dye tee. He squints. She's stylish. He has intentions to kiss and stroke her. He is afraid that she will provide venereal slim pickings. Her irregular walk looks like a set of exercises or lively dance steps. He's obsessed with perverted thoughts, giving her the swiftest of once-overs. His paranoiac behavior is getting to her. She is a phantom fading in the full beams of luster. In this environment, possibility expands. She's a sprightly youthful creature who can bewitch everybody in her path. She lists, port and starboard, his appearances ahead and astern. He wishes to stroke and smooch her organ and prat. His forehead is corrugated. He is smitten, privately and publicly. Her fleshly hips swivel at a sweetly enticing angle. He's dwelling in a condition of idiocy, lurching uncoordinatedly in the pocket-size parlor, making a complete fool of himself. He tugs at her belt loop with a smidge of insistence and a predatory grin. He is ungifted in the seductive arts. His oculi are so glassy they appear to be artificial. He doesn't know whether to adore or assault her. His heart will be broken forever if she doesn't fuck him. She glares at him as though ready to settle an old score. He perspires because of a fever. He hounds and begs her for sexual favors. Her belch and nostril-picking help moderate his boner. He blinks rapidly. Inebriated, she serves him a lunch of eel and prawn and ultra-carbonated sage-flavored soda pop. He jabbers, never pauses. His language sounds like it's something she has to learn. He knows he's made of flesh, blood, muscle, bone, semen, excrement, urine, psychosis, visions, drugs, and intoxication. She sips her raki and flashes him a look. A shrug of her brow informs him he is in business. He drifts over and gropes her as if to inform her that he hasn't left his lecherous ways far behind. Her blue eyes and blond hair… amazing. She sucks him off as though it's for career advancement. She pulls out a tampon. Her period is a bloodbath. He shows admirable restraint in holding himself back from hitting her. At close range, he notices the unevenness of her pubic fell. She dispenses a detailed inventory of quibble. It dawns on him that she is drunk. Her ass wags. Night's fig-black.

Kiddingly, enervatedly, Peki points a finger, extending it, like a little person version of Michelangelo's David. She pulls it and he farts. Stringbean's mouth is round and rosy. She has a serviceable and agreeable figure. She is flushed, as if from a steam bath. Her neck is a veritable ivory tower. Her derma layer is pearly-white. She has an appendix scar. He ranges the splendid parlor like a tiger until she takes his head, holding it as though to absorb his cogitations by cerebral osmosis. Her complexion is clear as the sun, her butt fair as the moon. She appears to be out of another world. He strokes her slim arms and legs and caresses her flat belly. She is a creature of the body, whereas he is one of the brains. He's maddened with the desire for her. She articulates in a deprecating tone. The aroma of sandalwood emanates from her. His coiled sex stirs like a snake. They share, impermanently, a complementary existence. He's afraid of falling asleep and waking up to find her gone as if she had never been. She is both his liberator and jailer in one. He is free as a falcon, flying. She is sweet-breathed and slow-witted. Though loosely built, she's not exactly awkward. She enunciates in a monotone. Vibratory sensations travel from his phallus to his encephalon. Her peepers catch the light like stones in the intestinal murk of the pantry. She stares at him as though to hypnotize him into carnal compliance. Dust is like pool chalk. The racket (construction) is hellish. Weather's stifling. Tenebrosity gathers. Stringbean is menstruating, bleeding pretty good. Her stomach has a simmering quality. She fixes smoked turkey, Cesar salad, fresh figs, and an Arabian sorbet for them, her brow knitted in rumination. She is in nothing except for a striptease performer's G-string and halter top. Her globoid bust and fundament are lovely and rich. Judas Priest, are her fingers and toes long! Peki just wants to find favor in her eyes. He is all over her like a horny beast, going in and out of her cavities as he pleases. Her breaths come in gasps. He bathes in her sweat and thumbs the hollow of her collarbone. He feels like his participation is an inadequate act. Kisses glance, words peter out, anatomies are formless. Intercourse makes conversation virtually impossible. They are thunder and lightning in the hay. Their pleasure and pain are indistinguishable. His spectacles get knocked sideways and she titters. Seemingly they pluck endearments from the oxygen. His tongue creeps on her throat like a centipede and she snuffles. He experiences epic difficulties in attempting to fit his tool into her sphincter. His tube never gets nervous in tight places. With cautious brutality, he shoves her face-first into these flower-splashed pillows on the ottoman. It is as if this sanctuary is exempt from time itself. She turns languorous and enfeebled under his unrelenting assault on her flesh, barely able to lift a hand or a foot. The breeze is alive. Peki's work-roughened hands diligently work on her like a potter making a pot. Stringbean has a searching look. Her feet are warm and dry. She shifts, trying to shrink herself to accommodate him, alas, to no avail. He is condensed in a kinetic blur of skin and hair on top of her. They speak their own language. She decides on a whim to finger him on general principle, getting him to wiggle, shout, and cuss. They jack erratically into mutual, and memorable, climactic detonation during a nameless hour... The post-coital rap in the sack is relaxing for them, the idle chatter tidally ebbing and flowing... He sees her weeping and wringing her hands in front of the demisted looking-glass following her shower. Something goes funny about her expression. Her eyes start out of their sockets. Her slender, curious-shaped thighs, the color of silky sand, are unparted. Balanced on his elbow on the chesterfield, in a comma position, he removes the flask's domical stopper and ingurgitates gin. He's mortally bored and ardent for action. He possesses a restless intelligence. She moves, drifting off into a reverie, her flaccid midsection rippling and her flabby hips juddering. She is formidable and poised, fashionably disturbed, and has bodily graceless-ness. She feels uncleansably filthy. She has a long face and dignity in her movement. He puffs on a Havana and notices the bruises on her back, acquired no doubt from their last session, perusing them as though her integument is a document depicting the suffering she underwent. He prefers she forget the whole matter. Peter Rabbit nibbles on a carrot on the beige carpet. It's the psychedelics, Peki thinks. The mega Sockburn Worm, with Peter Lorre's face and the paws of a possum, materializing, convinces him. Cartoon fish thrash on the ceiling like they're drowning on a dock. Platoons of prosties collect on the corner. Clubs in the center of the megapolis are just hopping. Clouds disappear not unlike fleeting dreams. The camera is mounted on the tripod like a machine gun. The daily parade of pedestrians is spectated by him. He feels like a sinister critter. He's a practitioner of perversion, faithfully dedicated to it, a cleric of this dirty religion. He is envious of the fact that she dwells in such a transcendent structure. They communicate with walkie-talkies. The fur-niture is aesthetically acceptable. Stringbean is a heavily opiated fellatrice.

Peter Lorre Sockburn Worm

On psychotropic drugs, Peki downs a bottle of Jagermeister and watches the rubious-argent dawn. Camels roost in trees. Fishermen metamorphose into haystacks. Plants' leaves turn into elephants' ears. The lake recalls a sheet of molten glass in the pouring effulgence, its surface frilled by gusts. A rainbow appears to have been painted by William Hogarth, over the non-natural, uncompromising summits. The visible piping is the longest boa constrictor. Cobblestones bound the driveway. Sun's shocking pink. The reservoir is somber, weedy, and reedy. Clusters of petunias and geraniums encircle it. Stringbean has paddle-sized hands and feet. Asleep, thonged, she grunts. His hard-on points at her pussy not unlike a divining rod. The edifice in which she rents is an irregular oval triangle. The lit sleet's like glinting crystals. She is eminently cuddly. He reveres her face and figure. Bare belly petted, she rouses. They shapeshift, lovemaking on the kingfisher cobalt davenport in the spick-and-span room, the intimacy with intimations of infinitude. They swim over and around each other like playful dolphins in the depths. The duo takes turns getting lost and found, under the branching candelabra and gilt-edged mirror. The upholstered sofa is one of fire and they cavort in the flames. It is a mini magician's stage for conjuring tricks. She flexes her abdominal muscles while he pecks her on the yap. Their bodies chop and change. Sexing is a strenuous exercise, an intense engagement with immense and important problems, of geometry, apprehension, chemistry, stamina, psychology, and physicality. Her squished titties look like twin torpedoes. Stuffed Muppets are assembled on the vacuum cleaner. The vault above is poppy-pigmented. His boner shivers akin to a conducting rod with the air's electrical forces. She writhes like a flounder stuck in the sand and dying to reach the safety of the sea. The heavy-headed man's mane reminds her of an exorbitant toupee. He has an apish aspect. He has sores and scabs on him and he has a disagreeable odor. She soughs, butt-plugged. He is quiet and powerful. Her tress is fanned on the covers. She spreads her gangling arms and legs. Coming, he croaks like a monstrous bullfrog. He has infantile dreams. The azure's hue harmonizes with the ocean's. Afterward, they sip sparkling wine. Stringbean declares her self-respect is the size of a pepper grain. Peki's heart is wrung for her. She shakes the paperweight, with an English pasture and enrapturing castle, and creates a snowstorm. Raindrops on the windowpanes dissolve like tears. His cutis inclines to the albino. He feels as though his deterioration, inside and outside, is accelerating. He knows he's an organism that will return to the inorganic — the soil — from which he originated. She announces she had plastic surgery and hair implants. His pubic hair resembles a hedgehog. The celestial sphere looks like turquoise milk with the salt-white cirri. Peki leans on the multi-hued cushions as she makes his mop into a mass of dreadlocks. It is blandly easy for her. His mephitic stench is in her nostrils. Her mind is muddled by spirits. He gazes at her and snorts. Stringbean smells like her lavender lotion. Her breath is redolent of marsh grass. His dried sperm on her groin is like icing on a cake. They're side by side, apparently held in suspension in the dull oxygen. She mysteriously deliquesces. He both believes and disbelieves his senses. The wen, unreal, rushes. This is a dog-eat-dog land with extremes of hot and cold. Skyline's dragonfly-electric-bluish. Cumuli are the color of baked mud. Frondescent arc's against the powdery-hazed horizon. The moon is a slumbering embryo over the bald crags and ultramarine waters. He paces like an excited panther. His dermis is ashy and suppurating. Thinking of preparing a new batch of Butyrum fires the neurons in his cerebrum to a crucial occupation... when the Sockburn Worm shows up unannounced in the velvety blackness. It has petechial peacock eyes that rapidly and repeatedly blink, its bugged oculi, one crimson, the other vermilion, dimming and brightening like they're lamps being flicked on and off, and also expanding and contracting. Coiled, it unwinds itself like a rope. Its skin is midnight-pitch. It has a diamond-shaped head. Its tail, swarthily scaled, flops. Most folks would run screaming, but Peki, curious as he is courageous, stands his ground. He isn't going anywhere. Its flickering forked tongue is salmon. The thing's slinking is entirely serpentine. Its stalactitic fangs morph into human incisors. The pitch darkness is lustrous and liquid. The creature slithers swiftly across the floor and wraps itself around a snoozing Stringbean's waist, lewdly erects itself, and flirtatiously beckons him. And Peki, entranced like Mowgli by Kaa in Disney's 'Jungle Book,' hunkers over it and is instantly penetrated. Vista is similar to a Möbius strip.

"Fee-fi-fo-fum," Peki vocalizes, beseeching peepers horrible, reeking of spoiled pork and cigar smoke. Illumined water on the grated window makes it look like the Milky Way. A shutter bangs. Rays are refracted by the panes' grime. Life and light are seen on the sidewalk. Sea and sky shine compatibly. Stringbean champs on a croissant and a peach, wanting to slide into unconsciousness. She is garbed in a cheesecloth garment, clinging and knee-length, imported from India. Her nails, finger, and toe, are polished with a vermeil varnish. She smiles tentatively as if satisfied with herself. She has enormous and pretty feet and hands. His whang is pulled to her rear like a needle drawn to a magnet. She brushes him off in the pinkly pale refulgence. She casts her eyes down modestly. Her mouth is glossy. She reminds him of an Amazonian princess, stomping around the kitchen. Her probing questions receive almost-answers from him. Dwarves are notoriously irascible, she thinks. She carefully inspects his stalwart build and solid limbs. He must be going soon. Butter calls. He grumbles and sulks, knowing he's got to leave. He wishes he was handsome. He looks mangled and mashed. God has made him a midget and he despises him for it. He feels like an unregarded person, a miserable shadow in public. He is a mare and she is a filly. He's all brawn and she's all bonny. He is percipient and she is ungainly. She scrubs a copper pan with steel wool in the sink. She is an oddity, alluring in her otherness. With concentrated skill, she chops onion and garlic on a board on the counter. He fillets the fish. His heartbeat sounds not unlike hailstones hitting a roof. He sups the sweetmeats while she slaps, erotically, dough.

Kittens chase parakeets on the patio. Stringbean moves with ill grace. Her large legs are reminiscent of plodding oak trees. Her pies are slitted, cumbered with culinary duties. She's a chef analyzing the essence of creation. She understands the multiplicity of the natures of sweet and sour, salt and pepper, margarine and oil, sugar and spice, and grasps touch, taste, smell, and texture. She has such fine, transparent flesh. Peki pays attention to the wheat and rye loaves in the oven. He praises the flavor of the raisins. She wields a knife and a ladle like a warrioress would a spear and a shield. She excels at the stove, frontage compressed in absorption. His amorous attentions are ignored. He gawps at her down-drooping embonpoint and backside. She is gentle and soft. Her flaxen cap is slicked back. A few wisps and stands have escaped from the salon gel. Her composed countenance yawns. She has this vulnerable fragility about her, despite her volleyballer size, which seems easily breakable. The blush fades from her narrow neck as though it had never been. She has a color that has no color. Her chiseled cheeks are evocative of bone china. Her fingers and toes remind him of white rose petals. She has faint facial dimples. Her head is perfectly balanced on its sturdy stalk. She directs a blank stare at him. She feeds him well, with nourishing dishes. Presently, she's procumbent on the couch, swathed in muslins, her revealed back unmoving like the surface of still cream, visualizing herself natating in the virescent depths of the drink. Her frontal is expressionless. She gazes rather indifferently at him. His cue to skedaddle? He sits on the recliner. She is a picture of languor. Is she going through one of her customary coolings, like the earth, or is she heating up, like global warming? His blood humming, being electrically charged, he impulsively bites her haunch, and it feels like a burn to her, strangely painful and pleasurable. He's hard and hot like sunny stone, clasping her pointy boobs. He is alive and crackling with energy like levin. She deems him dangerous and threatening. And she rises to reconnoiter the cupboards. Her calves are spiderweb-veined. He is in an alert, dreaming state... It is a full moon with slaty shadows. Peki, appearing livid and squashed like a newborn, traverses a meandering river, running red and rapid like blood through the body, trudges through a deciduous coppice, and clomps across a grassy prairie, en route home. He hoofs with caution in the wind and rain. His strands float in the zephyrs. Stars wheel and glitter. There's a nip in the eddying air. The hike lasts a day and a night. Bugs make whispered music. On the spur of the moment, he commences this weird leaping dance, tossing his hippie hair, skipping manically, pointing at the town in the distance, and doing cloddish handstands and somersaults and turning cartwheels under the blackest of skies, the encompassing darkness insistent and relentless. He cannot wait to return to the diurnal grind of murder, mayhem, Marisa, and mantequilla! The sensation of stripping and sprinting wild is delicious.

Peki and Marisa

Her lobe is noticeably denuded of ring. Her negligee is one of insubstantial chiffon. Her permed tress is a thicket of curls. The dank oxygen's thick as a motor lubricant. Marisa has an intriguingly unfocused gaze. Her slippers are floral in theme. Peki's roving eyes don't come to rest on anything else but her. His slept-in clothes, kasha dinner jacket, peacock-blue tee, and taupe trousers, are wrinkled. Although he's negligently groomed, he is, at least to a certain degree, presentable. His cologne is unambiguous. Slyly he flirts with her. She is astonishingly beauteous, knocking back screwdrivers at an astounding pace. She's still fairly lucid, making these deep-fried potatoes. She is like some angel of the amorist, taking him under her wing, looking over him. He glances askance at the aniline-teal ocean. Cumuli are Congo-ivory. City's a-seethe with the citizenry. She communicates to herself things like reincarnation and karma, lingering through another glass of Hennessy. He breathlessly witters on about his cretinous peers, their caution and contrivances, the new gammy hire, compulsive relationships, and raised rents, effectively exhausting her patience. He is within earshot of chirpy music made by a street ensemble, the time signature unknown. Although smitten, he curtails any contemplation of a continuance of overture, well aware of the diminishing returns. He barrel-rolls off the sofa and opens a package of no-name crackers. Her wardrobe provides a wide selection of colors, styles, patterns, sizes, and levels of formality. Roach traps are deployed all around the place, not unlike mines. Marisa inspects the number of abrasions on her abdomen. He wonders whether she looks better from the front or behind? Both. He wants her face-first on his tarse and ass-first on his kisser. He partakes of opiated powder. He is in love's grip and cannot get free. Drinking and drugging a lot isn't helping one iota. Her maquillage becomes blurred thanks to the perspiration. Her lip is bitten and her sighs are staccato. Silence is intolerable. Then mother and son bicker seemingly without end, the floor a portion of strategic ground. There is an unidentifiable racket. Her makeup is lopsided by sweat. Her integument is titanium-whitish. She's a cupcake a little long in the tooth. He smokes a slender cigarro, eyeballs spinning in their sockets like roulette wheels. She practices yoga on the mat, performing the exercises of turning and stretching, the more advanced moves quite contortionistic. She looks at him through bogus lashes. He has been feeling uncommonly isolated and could use her company. Against his better judgment, he accompanies her into the boudoir. He mixes champagne with absinthe; a spiritous concoction. And after executing a gleaming smile, she mysteriously vanishes in the marine light. The room is resonant with presence and absence. He's got to fly. Pertinent matters have arisen that the bibulous Peki must attend to, such as getting soused. He has a taste for brutality, and is out to maim or kill. Frankly, he has lost count of how often he has committed murder, without compunction or fear of consequence. He is out the door. She watches him leave. He's been dumping the dead bodies in the mapless, fetid forest. He more accurately waddles than runs from his troubles, determined to drown his problems in the sauce. Moon's sour orange. Defectively, eccentrically dressed, he peregrinates through the town, seeing so much human suffering, and experiences vague alarm. The sea pulses. His beard and mustache are disarranged. There is centrifugal carousal a-happening in a sports bar. It has a saloon-type atmosphere that's enticing. He threads his way through the patrons in their jollification. The noise picks up markedly. Chuntering is general and prolonged. Here is an escape from the civilized world.

Marisa is tawny from the outing under the sun. She is agile and lean, feeling rejuvenated. She feigns ignorance of Peki's covetous gaze. The predator keeps a respectful distance from the prey. For now. She inhales deeply from the kef stub and exhales expressively on the wrought-iron balcony, wreathed in morning glories. She nibbles on japonica, elbow against the redbrick wall. Wearing his whites, he brings her flowers, cigarettes, and chocolates. He's dressed in a fisherman's smock and work boots. She is an older woman with ruinous lineaments, a self-possessed lady in a wide-brim Parisian hat, floral lace hiphugger underpants, and a plush half-zip hoodie. He gets more glimpses of her feet than he can accurately account for. She's a receiving antenna of a human being picking up his avid frequencies. She fits the geraniums and myrtle in a decorative urn and puts them on the mantelpiece. She is his type. He's interested in her romantically, not platonically. She is ravishing, gnarled, and dimpled in the slim beam of coruscation. He is acutely hungering, his bodily passion unbelievable. She ignores the attention. The scar on her stomach is a pink certificate of her appendectomous history. When she reaches into the overhead cupboard, the materializations of her navel are multiple and successive. He grins not unlike a rogue. She flicks a stray wisp of hair away with an index finger. She doesn't look a day over fifty. He smears mud on her scanties. She screams bloody murder. She's at the end of her tether with his juvenescent pranks. He drives her crazy. He has gone too far. He settles into an impression of himself. He is revealed in episodes of emanation, with depressing clarity. Rough and raggedy pack of street children move through the miles of Venicean water mazes, the labyrinthine segment vermin-infested. Seminotorious smugglers unload their cargo. This sector is getting too hazardous with all of these unwholesome characters... Peki awakens, sprawled in the back room of a student hovel. What a bender. What decadence. Experimental paintings are exhibited on the cheap paneling, the art verging on brutalism. Hungover, he feels like Lucifer banished to Hell. The experience of going from there to here, a pomegranate orchard, is on par with advancing from a lobby into an arena. He is out to commit unholy offenses on the public. He imagines the shop as being a house, the employees as apostles, the city as Jerusalem, and he's the Holy Ghost. Insomniacally adrift, he promises himself he'll put in a full night's work and sleep during the day, proof of his business dedication. He thinks of the mass-grave-to-be, filled to the brim with the bodies of his victims. He is the essence of evil, an entity of sinister intelligence subsisting in an irreversible blackness. He considers himself a breed of magician, making folks vanish like a coin behind the ear or a card up the sleeve. A patch of mist glides past. Bleeding-red slice of heaven. Bone-white clouds. He chomps on quince in the creeper-scarlet shafts. Recently he's been going out in the killing spree, with vibrational impulses, covered in cloaks and masks, looking like the freakiest damned thing, acting as if he's a wounded soldier demobilized from some unknown war and seeking shelter in obscurity.

Bells peal across the inordinately populated metropolis lit up like a birthday cake. After the acid trip in the subterranean contra-borough (such queer geography!), saturated with fog, in the fourth-dimensional space-and-time, fed up with the surface world, getting around in a rented futuristic buggy, unconcerned about his destiny, the cirri ostensibly variegated explosions, virtually everything hallucinated, Peki edges into a semblance of semiconsciousness. His brain interprets himself as a Pygmy in a lucid dream in which he walks through solid walls. It is so leaden he relies more on hearing than seeing. He is haloed in bugs in the dank gloom, using a scalpel to remove the suet from a deceased dewdrop he'd butchered with a cleaver (not before penially plowing her tonsils) creekside, the aqua pura a filmy green. The circumjacent land is a mute revelation. A sewage-treatment plant looms. The generous megalopolis is behind him. She was called Luna, her uncommon prettiness promissory of heartache. She was swan-serene and wore tortoiseshell rims when he saw her entering the tannery where she worked. He waited patiently, or loitered menacingly, at the fountain for her to exit. When she finally did emerge, in a surge of employees, he followed her, sleuth-stealthy, readying for the perfect moment to ambush her. The outfit she had on, with its transgression of brevity, beyond the restrictions of the tasteful, contradicted her characteristic (excessive) modesty. He bounded with athletic alacrity, not unlike a mini Adonis, and used his abnormal power usually reserved for the possessed to knock her senseless in the stubbled field. His inexhaustible capacity for cruelty was on display. He took a breather from the abuse to enjoy a bottle of lager, grilled pork tenderloin, and boiled sausage that were packed in the Bugs Bunny lunchbox. He looked like a snake up on its tail, entranced by an imperceptible charmer. She had hay-hair, parted in the center, smoke-colored eyes, and a sallow complexion. Defiled by his fingers, wrackingly weeping, she admitted she was kidnapped in a raid years ago and sold as a slave. His ferocities caused her significant distress. She had transcendental pubes. He was erotically smitten. She was on all fours and he smacked her breech with a bamboo stick. Then he shoved her onto her back and forcibly penetrated her. He sexually stabbed into her as though to bisect her, to impale her soul. He was vicious and delirious. Compliant, she cried. Lying still in the moonlight she reminded him of Snow White in her glass coffin. Her reedy neck was fascinating. He persisted in assaulting her, sucking on her pointed paps like they were ice cream cones. She was overrun and conquered, struggling with no success. He'd coerced her into doffing her gear and donning these exotic pajamas and slippers with Asian prints, swearing he wouldn't hurt her anymore. He rudely whistled when she changed in the fantastic foliage, sobbing uncontrollably. She was screechy-voiced and was a brave and modern gal. He said she was a "faithless harlot." Whereupon he explained that his mission in life was to lure people into premature demise and use their fat to create the butter. He fessed he was a man of decidedly mantequilla-mystical inclination. She shrieked that he was a "perverted invertebrate." The cognizant gnome knew this was a ploy to distract. His cauliflower ears quivered. He suggested a midget effigy staring with sightless eyes. He treated her as though she was a subspecies of another race. He cranked himself up to carnally operating speed. He had the sensation of being damned, a prisoner in the underworld. He seemed to be irrationally celebrating himself in a lethal way. Spruces and eucalyptuses swayed sensually. A watchtower came into view in the drizzle... Peki cuts into the belly and bum with the blade and carves the chunks of blubber like he's a sculptor. He feels ancient and unique. There is no one, anywhere, like him. He crouches, taking in her cadaverous image. He sparks an Austrian butt and dances the polka, a tone-deaf lunatic in vulgar song. Shaggy and filthy, he even creeps out the mad dogs, who watch from a safe distance in the bushes. God has forsaken this goosey girl, he thinks, combing his huge, unkempt beard digitally. He must have other priorities, turning his attention elsewhere. He gazes at her like she's an apparition he's trying to make out. Face creased into a frown, he wraps the corpse in a velvet curtain. His indifference to mortality is evidenced. Marisa is at home recovering from a nasty bout of jaundice. He's worried about his mental instability, or lack thereof. Peki: now you see him, now you don't.

Marisa is a divine being revealed in brilliant beams refracted by the stained-glass cupola above. She has a breakfast consisting of an omelet and porridge. She is a mother of many mysteries. She has a mat of mop and red-rimmed blinkers. A late riser, Peki looks like a robed, boxy acolyte with an enigmatic facial expression. She smiles grimly, orbs twinkling. He squats at the oxygen tank, equipped with a breathing mask, and dispenses a nice volume, the gashead getting a brief high. She has a chilly glint in her oculi while he searches for booze, a fool's errand at this juncture. She goes lickety-split for the platterful of treacle. He grudgingly settles for a stein of warm, uneventful ale, balanced on a thinned deck of tarot cards, The Hanged Man on top. She fixes him with a pop-eyed stare. He wipes his mustaches with a wrist, and recollects hunting down the antique dealer, who also happened to be a counterfeiter and forger, and ditching him, but not before ravishing the guy, then gutting him. His aching bones feel as if they were gnawed on by rats as he slumbered. He has mischief written all over his mien. He gazes at her as though he can't grasp the concept that she's real. She gives him the once-over when he quaffs expressively. He takes a lively interest in her. She has such fine flesh. She observes his warped cranium with an untrained eye. He is not up for a domestic to-do. He regards the calamitous aftermath of her morning meal and suspires tragically. He is so debilitated he feels like a fable's dwarf, toiling 24/7 in a mine, pushing and pulling overloaded trucks. He has an equine stink about him. He engorges himself with a currant bun beside the blue lamp, ermine flittering around the bulb. She defies elderly woman fashion fore and aft, kept in a tight-fitting, slate-hued corset and kid gloves and shoes, and surveys the vaulted ceiling, as though it was transplanted here from a church's crypt, ornamented and etched with cherubim and seraphim and hawks and doves. Peki feels like some poor sap wanting some nasty. Sporadically shit gets so intense in the digs that he feels as if he is a gnomic missionary sent onto unfavorable shores, hostilities imminent. Marisa's blinders are downcast. He gets a gander at her tush. There are more than a few anatomical aspects of hers he appreciates. Her nervous constitution is not in evidence. Evening gathers, along with a proper soaker. Fog thickens. Drops of rain condense on the sill that has these Arabic motifs. When he was a kid, he used to imagine that his chamber was an Arabian Nights cave, his belongings ancient treasures with necromantic properties. He slept on a stone bed, rice sacks piled on it to make a mattress, roll of habiliments, tied with a string, serving as a pillow. The room was not unlike a tomb. The tapestry on the drywall had toads, birds, fish, beetles, and snakes, woven by his Mama. He slouches in the seat, a French gilt chair in an ornate style. Their taste in furniture lately is eclectic and extravagant. Windows are modified by dirt. Their pad is a habitation of singular monstrosity. She treats him as though he's an obtrusive guest. She mentions nonsense about bondage and torture. He pictures the crimson berry of her bunghole and gets a ramrod. She worms her way through the busts, materials limited to marble, with biblical and classic themes to them. She exposes herself to arouse. He adores her every wrinkle and wart. He pictures her as a captive demoiselle, appealingly juicy, contained in a pleasing system of restraint. Lumberingly he crosses the expanse of mosaic flooring. She has a very nice shine to her skin. The horrible city is a corrupted version of the Big Apple. The pebbly quadrangle below is bleak and hushed.

Peki's horniness must be met and not magnified. He is grim and ghastly, dressed in a checked nightshirt. Marisa is acutely aware of his intentions. She will provoke his indignation if she refuses him. She wears a peignor with Broderie Anglaise trimmings. She submits herself willingly to sexual service. Her hand begins to move, as if without volition on her part. Dutifully she takes up his shaft and tugs to empty it. Her skin quakes, slippery with a sheen of sweat. She feels alternately hot and cold. Her flesh pulsates crimson. It's as though she's a water diviner and his dong is a forked hazel twig held over a field and it suddenly rises and writhes in her grasp. His rod twists, rears, bucks, and wiggles between her passive fingers. She has a throttled voice. She's alert, experiencing only dread. The thing is like an eel. She looks at it like it's a dagger. Her receptivity he thinks is indicative of his animal magnetism. She is wan and slimy. Her bosom quivers. The self-inflicted cuts on her arms and legs criss-cross not unlike a child's scribbling. The sun flares fitfully in the clouds. The tendons in Marisa's neck are rigid. Peki's eyes boil under his broad brow. His pallor has an opaque pearly pigment. She strokes him very deliberately and carefully. The two making out, her earrings fall like figs from a shaken tree. Her breathing is labored. He reproaches her for a lack of zest in jerking him off. A teary flood inundates her face, overwhelming her. Their emotions are separate, yet fused somehow. The poor woman lowers her head, for she wants to play her part in the salacious dramaturgy, but she's afraid. His snaky tongue slithers into her mouth. She utters a series of harsh, grating sobs. She has sharp knees and pasty flanks. His nates tightly clench when she repeatedly yanks his stiffy. Her belly and back are heated and flat as plates of molten glass. She gives off a bright light. There is the struggle of the involuntary. He pictures his penile clapper swinging in her vaginal bell. Spewing his seed, he sings at her on varied upsetting notes, hurting her ears. They usually have a couple of drinks after their exertions, and this time is no exception, and discuss, in-depth, the session that just transpired. Mother and son have unrelated difficulties and should hold each other for the warmth of comfort, he believes. Does she view their relationship as something touch-and-go, built on sand? She talks dreamily. Oviform stars in the colloidal cirri — frog-spawn. Peki notices the note written on the board in chalk, the characters schoolgirlishly spheric. He gazes at the oceanic plains. Marisa mops her perspiring forehead with a handkerchief. She is stationary as a statue. He finds her facial expression touching. Her cheap jewelry is strewn on the desk with the lit candles, the arrangement like some makeshift shrine to domesticity. She beholds the little man, a white wasp. His mane, with strand extensions, is like a horse's. The environment has an ominous serenity. She glides like a ghost. And he concentrates his agile mind on her, endeavoring to rein his rampant imagination in. Feeling the prick of desire, he is tempted to grab her and propel her towards the ample futon, covered in a rufous eiderdown, pushing her like a sow into a sty. He mounts and pumps, unregarding. There's an explosive rumbling in his stomach. He emits a throaty snort. His loins ache. Her lineaments are superlative. His lust burns him to the bone. He makes his fantasies fade on the grounds of inverisimilitude. A miniature Vesuvius of fireball candies (glued together by her for an art project) falls to pieces on the coffee table when she accidentally bumps into it. His cogitations are visionary and tragic. He waddles as if enceinte and commences a rambling speech. Their conversation is the verbal equivalent of a parlor game. She dances and shimmers like the yellow flame of a gaslight. She thinks he's possessed by a malignant spirit. She encourages communion between them with elements of cautious normalcy. Kids are blowing bubbles outdoors, reminding him of a corpse sinking in the water with a trail of globulous air pockets… Guilt bears her away from him, but not before she tickles him. A walk will benefit her. So she gets a move on.

The end credits for the rerun of the American sitcom, 'Everyone Loathes Raymond,' are on the television screen in the drawing room. Peki thinks: a man shall leave father, and shall cleave to his mother, and they twain shall be one flesh, thusly butchering the Swedenborg quote. He glooms and equivocates in his head. He feels like a beast with a humped back. He longs to experience the delicious sensation of deliquescing into his madre. Their love, he opines, is a state of innocence. For as long as he can remember, he was bound and determined not to lead a lonely life on this planet. Being resigned to his fate was not an option he ever seriously considered. As a rule, he tries to be wholly truthful with himself. He clears his throat with a phlegmy "hem." Whereupon he mumbles market observations and comments to himself on the power of his mantequilla. Their mutual affection and co-existence are critically important to him. She's his one true significant other. He is dressed in a beryl cloak. She has a glass of sherry, and he has a decanter of port, suffering from opioid withdrawal symptoms. He hated it that she was committed by the state to a lunatic asylum years ago. It tore his guts out. She used to screech, straitjacketed, confined in that padded cell. She thought her sanity was irrevocably gone in that bedlam. The institution was controversial in the staff's handling of the patients. It was a place of sorrow and sin. He considers the condition of his brain and body, on crack and Valium, and has concern for his welfare. She's hysterical. He is self-assertive. They are fiercely attached. He is confident in this fact. He recognizes it with an ever-strengthening certitude. She's the best part of him. Their relationship is rendered timeless by his myriad mind. Marisa's smiling eyes, in the fulgor, sparkle not unlike rubies. Her covering, a teddy, corresponds to her nature, and is an expression of her sensuality. She is resplendent in the illumination. She struts around, in an exhibition of spiritual levity, wayward in a copse of cerebration, and pauses for effect. She wears these stilettos, despite the carbuncles and the distended, painful lumps on her feet. Her build is anorectic but well within the bounds of sexy. She's frank. He is devious. She glimpses him sizing her up. Her gaze is questioning, perhaps challenging. She is behaving like some hostess. Her complexion's color is lively. She lives in her private universe, and precisely. He envisages himself taking a lumbering leap onto her lap and scrubbing like a puppy at her bust. Her perfume, aromatized with antiperspirant, invades his nostrils. And he makes a wheezing noise. He has a purply face. Will her hands be welcoming or rejecting? She lights the oil lamp while he pokes the dying fire. Elms look doleful in the downpour. Marisa is chilling and rebuffing. Her repudiation of his overtures is aimed to hurt. Peki is morbidly sensitive to being shunned. He's thoroughly convinced that she revels in his disappointment. His advances have a kind of male forcefulness. Her resistance has a sort of female directness, causing a flurry of impotent rage. She resists, as if under moral oppression. She can be insensitive, just like the dead. There is dramatic tension in the atmosphere. She smells his redolent cologne. Her circulatory issues are making her ill. She has undefined feelings. Her lips are anxious. His shakers are damp with diaphoresis. He treats her like a mixture of princess, child, angel, pet, and deity. He worships her passionately. They share a nervous hug. She smirks amiably. She views herself as a country mouse and him as a city boy. She pretends she is a Byronic heroine and he is a handsome prince in a fairy wood. The weather's watery. With her companionship, he is elated, in both eye and ear. Light and shadow brawl silently. The breezes sound weary. Marisa satisfies his sexual appetite in ways he previously thought were inconceivable. She is the object of his desire. Her tongue and touch are delectable flames. Her form has the cold weight of water. Peki puts urgent kisses on her mouth. She catches her breath beforehand. Her timidity is endearing. She notices his hands and feet are shaped like fat fish. His countenance burns brightly. He's calm and still, seated next to her in the saffron-hued armchair. This love affair is thrilling! She is fatigued. She may retire early. She has a leaf-mold malodor. Words are woven and caresses are knitted delightfully into the discourse. She is with him, close and wonderful. Oftentimes, when he's laser-focused on the butter business, in solitude, she lightens the mental load. He bursts into ardency. The radiance behind her is like a nimbus. There are vibes of anticipation and apprehension. She has a modulated intonation. They share the sacredness of the moment, their ardor unrepressed, the couple apart from reality, and withholding the hour. The crash pad is their earthly Paradise. They possess a two-sided gray matter. She laps and smooches and sucks and strokes him into orgasmic oblivion. Stars are brilliant as diamonds. They prate, vocalizations quick and decisive, till the break of dawn.

The exterior of the apartment edifice evokes a venerable Franciscan monastery dating from the sixteenth century. The Spanish-style roof of the structure is supported by quarry stone columns. The interior is simple and unpretentious. Adobe walls are covered with stucco and whitewashed and decorated with glyphs of Peki's design. The cedar beams give off a pleasant scent. The gorgeous garden out back grows luxuriantly, calling to mind paradise. Flowers issue these lusty fragrances. The damp pavement metallically gleams. Imposing skyscrapers apparently hold up the empyrean. Marisa dramatically raises her eyes heavenward as if appealing for aid. He remains silent and in suspense. They play their respective roles with elan. She suffers a slight dizzy spell, in all probability due to her tenacious activity. Her long, lean face and straight, fine-drawn figure bring him out of his self-absorption. He is disquieted by her current indifference towards him. His uneasiness vanishes when she acknowledges his existence with a vampish expression and speaks in an affected tone of voice. His long-suppressed desire to be intimately involved with her is finally about to be realized. He studies the beauty mark on her right cheek. Following her, he reminds her of a puppy nuzzling its master's hand, dying to be petted. Her icicle-cold-and-pointy glare stabs the air between them. Her moue effaces as though by magic his concern that she's ignoring him. She looks at his perpetually melancholic visage. He talks directly to her. She listens, aloofly. He doesn't feel like her son, nor does she like his mother. They are a male and a female. He is a small man and she is a tall woman. It is nearly impossible for her to hide a grimace of disgust at his obsequious behavior. She gives him an affable grin. He's optimistic that they will sleep together today, but her distance casts a shadow of pessimism over it. She keeps him on tenterhooks. She is secretly planning an imaginary escape route she would take to get away from him if he grabs her. She keeps to herself, her inexpressive physiognomy providing no clue of what her inner feelings are. This is a domiciliary nightmare she is resigned to never awaken from. It is his wet dream. It is an especially bright and balmy noon. Cirri depart from the firmament. A line of street hawkers resembles a colony of industrious ants. Reticent and stern, Marisa is wearing a homespun sundress. Peki's clad in an embroidered jacket and painter's pants. He is adorned with costly jewels. The force of desire finds room in his groin. He wants to receive affection from her like a field receives moisture. Rapturously he contemplates her fanny, the way a composer does his masterwork. Her state of mind is reflected in her attitude. She treads with firm and unfaltering steps. She tinkers with the vials of medicine and tubes of pomade situated on the bureau. Excitement goads him. He demands attention from her. He yearns to have her fiery kisses ignite his lips. He wishes to stroke her contours, the curves of her knockers. His mitts avidly seek her hips. The love he has for her is immense. His feelings are pure and lofty. Libido presses him to caress her cutis. He has pledged to take care of her and respect her. These sensations he's experiencing are intense. The son wants to be one with his mother. Is it an outrage to yen to unite his deformed body with her lovely one? Her nonchalant approach to interacting with him is dampening his spirits, shaking his soul. A motley mosaic of beggars makes the rounds in the market square. Vendors mill about. Marisa's plenteous graying hair is caught atop her head. Peki barely gets a glimpse of her semi-nudity as she changes, offering to his vision her profile. She is surprised and indignant when she catches him spying on her. A conical, impeccable breast is crowned with a nipple. He readies himself to receive those flawless butt-cheeks but restrains himself. A profound, unspeakable fear causes him to hold back. What would she think of me if I were to tell her how I feel about her? He asks himself, only doesn't answer. He deems himself a perverted, incestuous jerk. His shameless and immodest advances are unfair to her. He combats the irresistible attraction by sheer force of will. Her youthful appearance defies age. Full of resolve, resisting his overtures, she's not unlike Eve overcoming Satan's enticements. With her, he is like a moth circling a candle's flame, drawn to it, but afraid of getting burned. He is tempted to sin. She looks at him as though he's an individual of ill omen. She attempts to prettify the place and make it more inviting. Her naked feet have this sweetish smell. He's drowsy and languid. When his palm contacts her heinie, she reacts as if a red-hot brand touched her. In the boudoir, lying on the bed, she hears the disturbing chirping of countless crickets. She watches dusk invade her room. The heat of his hand is still on her keester. A raging storm hits. Right now, the thought of the establishment settles in the corner of his consciousness. He sits in the umbral gloom.

Marisa is illumined by the silvery light of the moon. Peki studies the delightful body of his Mama showing perfectly clearly through her negligee as she sashays smilingly into the kitchen. His horniness is pent up, like the scents of blossoms are stored up, awaiting the evening to be given off, maddening the bugs with their fragrances. She is delicate and loving. He envisions her labial lips as being the fleshy leaves of a gillyflower. He pictures her vulva opening like a lily, spreading its petals to receive a ray of the sun. An acute twinge in his pisser foretells an ejaculation, he surmises. She has a pacific dial and a pensive stare. She appears to have lived a long and difficult life. Her lineaments express precisely what her soul feels… She fusses with the curtains in blue damask. Everything there is about her form seems to have been deliberately developed to astonish and arouse him, especially her umbilicus, twisted into a capricious knot. She has such a graceful build, very svelte. Her enormous eyes practically take up the whole of her face. Her mouth is pink and puckered. She has an animal's charm. Her presence reflects the absence of his life. She exudes a carefree spirit. She's his reason for being. Their interaction has the air of a bitter rite with a tragic association. He winds the gilt clock, feeling not unlike a good-for-nothing, on the surface a sad figure. The continuous and irremediable degradation of his health is attributed to his indulgences. He is bloated, with a puffy puss and double chin. And his eyelids are tumid like the rest of him. The fact is, he feels stone-dead. His fits of coughing are becoming more and more frequent. The poppy tea she makes for him to ease his insomnia hasn't been effective recently. He has let himself go. He must put a stop to it. The frivolous and absurd diversions of debauchery are the main reasons he is falling apart. The drugs and alcohol are also contributing factors as to why he's shitting the bed. He is disoriented, directionless as if the compass of his existence is cracked. He's smart and skillful when it comes to stealing, making Ali Baba and his Forty Thieves look like rank amateurs. He has to get back to that. The realization that he has been slacking off at work gnaws at his vitals. Frustration has come home to roost because of the messing around. This is punishment for him forsaking his responsibilities, opting instead to have a fun time instead. He's paying with interest. He conceals his discomposure. He feels as though his energy is leaking from his person, like a cask with a hole in it. He is the reason for his pitiful state. He has the periodic sensation that his gonads are arid rocks and his weenie is a storm of impotence. Framed engravings and paintings, severe and somber, hang everywhere on the blank, austere walls. These creative works wouldn't look out of place in a palace. The sexual appetite… Peki's gluttony is primarily placated by strumpets and gigolos. Marisa is aware of it all and chooses to look the other way. She knows of his dubious reputation. She is his lover and his friend, important to him as the heart in his chest. Without her and the business, he is like a bird without wings. She's the breath of his life… He demands a lot of her in bed. Her burden is the obligation she has to uncomplainingly satisfy him. Every once in a while she treats him like a celibate stripling. The tedium between their sessions torments him. Sometimes they play games of cat and mouse with each other. Excited, operating the oven, her temples throb, and her cheeks turn red. Her new dentures are cream-colored. He is as close to her as her shadow. He's serious and silent, wanting to squeeze her like fruit to extract her tasty juices. He chats her up, only it's on par with trying to get water out of a stone. She strums the strings of authority in the crib. She possesses the power, winning the fights, and dispensing justice. She is prepping the roast goose, resembling a pagan deity. She's adorned by the moon's wanings and waxings. She scrubs her greasy hands with a sponge so hard it's as if she's skinning herself alive. She is coiffed and fetching. He rubs his throat with cologne. She's erect and elegant, attracts and intimidates him. She is more inebriating than the intoxicants. He flatters her with these gallant remarks. He can see them, frisking about, playing lovey-dovey games with avid dexterity. With her, he's ecstatic at being alive. Her derriere looks fresh through the frilly, filmy material, her loose middle illusorily harboring a new life. Ardent blood, an implacable plasma, runs through his veins. He grabs her, but she slips away like water through his hands. She is proud and reserved at the stove. Welkin's tulip-purple. A woolly dog chases a rubber ball. The swelter is suffocating. Trees are dropping their leaves. Sun's a vermilion dreamy eye with luminous lashes.

Elania Cokes and Alejandra Lelu

Her diarrheal streamlet rooster tails in the shrubbery. Elania, a transsexual stuck in the early stages of transition, the circus acrobat with a cute raven bob, dressed in her red costume and black slippers, spits a glob of tobacco juice in a vomitous parabola and emerges from the Earth's curvature, or, to put it exactly, an isolated clump of willows, and adroitly avoids the pavement pizza on this corroded day. The air gradually accelerates into a gust. Summer is somehow sentient. Overcast is one of tarnished silver. She wallows in moral squalor, maintaining her control through the killing of the innocent and she continues the devastation she inflicts on the community. She thinks of the cadavers by the uncounted dozens she's responsible for. Her actions are indicative of a criminally psychopathic disposition. She has been using cudgels and machetes as tools of the trade lately. She is a death merchant and these are her desirable weapons. There is the suggestion of a city in the smog. Wind's a fierce whisper. The bawdy house's colossal construction, in this twilit hour, seems as if it was designed by Pieter Brueghel the Elder, the structure settled anciently under fate. Elania is a ghost choosing her haunt. The place is situated canalside next to a patisserie. The block is a hotbed of the illicit. She shows up at the front door in a state of discernible eagerness. The darkness naturally acquires substance and depth. Glistering stars become blotted out by the cumuli. Her optical illusions are manifold. The moon is in its opacity. She's a power supply possessing enormous energy. She fancies an espresso and rolls. Alejandra the zoftig fizgig, bereft and lesioned, with flaxen ringlets, in the precarious umbras, a receiver of stolen property, scarcely contained in a cami and thong, is so beguiling, in the watery dusk of the parlor of sin, that Elania is not surprised in the slightest to find herself with an erection. The shade, sorrowfully embrowned, dominates a corner of the room. Vinegar fumes sting her nose. Her lips glow pinkly as though from within. She sips a glass of beer. Her heart pounds in a sub-audible ostinato of arousal. Alejandra has the eyes of a dead fish, her mouth resembling a damaged rose. Her bare feet reek of hops in a kiln. Her body odor smells of mayonnaise. And her breath is quite corrosive. She arouses Elania's blood. Her breasts and buttocks are impervious to gravity. She blossoms alight in the opium smoke and clucks like a hen when she spills a little vino on the carpet. The stain is glandular shaped. Her shadow is correlated with her anatomy. Elania drifts in a dream around the Arabesque decor. The raddled baritone, reminding her of a fluvial creature that customarily lies below and is brought to the surface, in the barbershop quartet on the cochleate staircase, glouts at her. Alejandra regards Elania as if she is strangely creeping around in the hesitant night. The light in her eyes is not unlike a beacon. Illumination is a cryptic insinuation. Cirri blear the moon, suspended over the mirror-still moat. Elania is suddenly translated to her back as if by some nefarious agency. In the hallway's desolate lucency, Alejandra is like an animal seeking freedom from captivity. Her armpits have the redolence of flowers out of season. Elania wrestles her down to the floor and mounts her like she's a horse, but she bucks, unseating the unwanted rider. Then she gets up and confronts her. Whereupon she launches a blind and desperate kick, landing in Elania's balls, which of course sends her flat onto her ass. Alejandra's inflection has an aggravated edge. Kneeling and weeping, she plucks a ukulele, producing chords, creating linear notes, improvising a catchy melody. This is Elania's cue to leave. She feels like a childish clown. Her decapitated twin sister's head abruptly appears, kisses her on the cheek, loops the loop, and does a figure eight with a porcine squeal, like a balloon, its knot untied, and disappears. The shore is held hostage by the sea. Peki poleaxes both of them, Alejandra in the sumptuous disaster of the library, and Elania in the gramineous intricacy of the coppice. He extracts their fat at fog-swept, finely-set masonry near a footbridge. The murk has a wondrous momentum. A tower's carillon startles him. The larks wheel in their synchronous ascent from the glebe and vanish. He is convinced that the tenebrosity is conscious, considering him, but for what purpose? His mane is blown into a tangle. His brow tenses and relaxes. Worn to a frazzle, he wishes to be enfolded by sleep. He stumbles away, struggling to breathe. The dawn's sun is metalized and oblique. Peki, weary of thumbing through the stack of invoice copies, leaves them, along with the illustrated magazines, on the cabinet in the office and roams comfortably the streets of the gigantic metropolitan area, with its plentiful noise and confusion, weaving through dealers and sharpers and prosties and tourists. His establishment was rhapsodically reviewed in one of the main local papers this morning, and he is just pleased as Punch. He can't shake the nagging certainty that he is the subject of forces set on his demise. He feels as though he's headed toward his own destruction. His homicidal velocity is speeding up. He has got to throttle back. He wants longevity in the game. His new shoes, made out of shark leather, are really stiff. He threads his way through these nocturnal sluggards and opulently turned-out putas in the unendurable swelter. Every so often he considers the idea of moving to another place, getting married, having babies, and changing jobs… He has learned to trust his intuition. Heck, he's going gangbusters. His dreadful villainies are taken right out of the melodramas. He has disposed of people. What's done is done. One can't put the smoke back into the cigarette. He cannot change anything. He experiences a sensation of being displaced in time. The sky looks not unlike white celluloid. Shadows have solidity and sharpness. He remembers the scarifying nightmare in which he heard the voices of everyone he'd eliminated pipe up in a diabolical choir, the score dedicated to him. He plugged his ears with his fingers. Gnats rise in a plaguy pall. He meets a tough-talking, wild-haired, kink-necked, semi-feral pixie-punk rocker-chick, named Annabelle, at a popular snack bar. She's pale as an angel and distant as heaven. They sit at a window table with their lattes and scones in the vilely mucilaginous atmosphere and its brilliance-bearing oxygen. She gazes in a direct grim sensuality. Cosmetics enhance her splendor. They are engaged in animated dialogue. Rain gives the impression of being in everlasting descent. He pictures adoring her shaved pussy with his tongue, grasping those exquisitely muscled legs. She is splayed on her front, on a bedroll, rear-end eaten out, the endearing lady singing sonorously... She is a mark of his murderous intent. Her dermis is like nearly-transparent vellum. Her rump is probably hard-as-a-rock. His heart hammers. Annabelle's intonation is one of cool sarcasm. His sinuses are stuffed. He palms her knee. She throws a glare at him like it's a dagger. He feels as if he's a failed impersonation of himself. Rays are refracted by a large number of signs. She has a tobacco-stricken inflection. Boys and girls, carefree and clean, breeze briskly along the duck-green firth, laughing and talking. Peki bows under the weight of stress. His mind is incommunicado, his heart benumbed. A statue evokes Al Jolson or a lawn jockey. There's a loud sound like a pterodactyl scratching itself. He is losing his grip on reality as quickly as one would lose sand in their hand. The vault has lavenders and siennas.

Glad Mermis

"You fucked up, didn't you?" It snaps. "What did you do?"

"Don't start on me," Peki responds. "Please. I'm not in the mood."

The first glint of the risen sun, high in the heavens, strikes Peki's eyes, narrowed into slits, looking like knife-cuts in a piece of paper. He had drifted off in the cushioned oaken chair with its high back and curved arms. Togaed, in the Ostrogothic, low-arched chamber-turned-lab, with its arrow-shaped, stained-glass windows, he disposes of the minced mutton, barley loaf smeared with oleo, and elderberry wine, devouring with the air of an individual satisfying a gnawing ravenousness, the motions of his jaw odd. Alcohol sutures his insecurities. Sobriety tears the stitches out. He proudly evaluates the stack of mantequilla bars stacked in the refrigerated chest. He hopes his popularity will become overpowering. He more than dabbles in the black art. It is darker than pinewood ash. With roving eyes, he surveys the scattering of substantial cabanas lining the pavemented path in the misty daylight, the virgin holt that clings to the bevel of a promontory that terminates in the town. He suppresses his soul and his mind is perverted. Glad Mermis' 'mouth' trembling is a substitute for a moue. Peki's breathing sounds like zephyr whistling through a chimney.

Abigail Rodriguez

Peki sheds his clothes, pretending he is an aborigine hunting her, Abigail, this ponytailed, adorable minor, with a blowpipe with poisoned darts. He moves at an undulant lope, raising plumes of dust with his strides, hot on her heels. Clouds are shimmering white and the sand is a scintillant yellow. The shore is in desolation and the mountains are spectacular. A gigantic condor wheels on an upcurrent over a glistening peak. A luxuriance of flowers in the meadow. Metallized-appearing morphos glitter. Lugubrious fish swim in delicious water. He evades semi-wild peccaries and envenomed reptiles, clambering over red rocks, trudging through alien plants, and traipsing on desiccated grasses. Sun is resplendent. He's feeling empty, like a tree stump hollowed by lightning. He stays out of sight of the encroaching army of washerwomen, marching and singing through the barren scrub, with baskets of laundry on their heads. Abigail is taking a shortcut home, parting ways with her nerdy bestie, through the cataclysm of bushes and mire. She chews on an avocado, loafing around a creaking windmill and cherry tree. Peki remains composed during the trial of his patience. He is waiting for the right moment to strike. She goes at a prodigiously unhurried rate of progress on the appalling road. He is grim-faced, a picture of dejection. He's the powder keg and she's the spark. He rushes up and grapples with her. He smashes a liquor bottle over her head and kicks her to near death, expending his anger on her. When he is done booting her, no one would be able to tell who she is, she is so disfigured. Infectious insanity contaminates his brain. The sickness of depravity spreads throughout his being. Is this morbid bloodlust thinly disguised as occupational survival? His approach to killing hasn't reached new heights of ingenuity and sophistication. Tactics are improvised, and perfected by experimental practice. He has a firmness of incentive, and an unshakable vision. He's not unlike some satanic entity that jumped the gates of hell to wreak havoc upon the inconceivably vast tracts of land. The viciousness, barbarity, and obscenity of the whole affair are getting out of hand, he instinctively thinks. She is beaten and bleeding, lurching along, grabbing a fence, powder blue cheerleader uniform ripped to ribbons, mind revolving with incomprehension, eyes filled with tears, swollen phiz smeared with sanguine, screams terrible in the verdurous cascade. He runs her over like a freight train. She looks like a deer in the headlights. She turns around, suffering on the enormous palm, and gazes catatonically at him while he pokes a pile of fresh canine excrement with a stick, mulling over a strategy he may apply in the disposing of her. She pleads, in a nasal drawl, for him to leave her alone. He shakes and squeezes her. Then he tears off her soiled outfit. She is stout and shapely. Her sculpted brown legs are drawn with veins like they are maps of rivers. A teen with a generous heart is a rara avis in her social circle, and can easily dam the flow of selfishness in the clique. She never rocks the boat, not wanting fall in and splash the others. She's honorable and hospitable. She comes from a respectable family. Earlier, she had cheered indefatigably and undauntedly, with wondrous spirit and infinite pain, to invigorate the fans in the bleachers and the players on the pitch, despite her soccer team getting blown out in the rivalry game. She was a fiery spirit. She thrived in that environment. It gave her stability and direction. She conceived of cheering not as a means to war but as an instrument of peace. It was unfailingly interesting to her. She was the logical choice as captain, given her character, but she was a long way from being the best. She is smart, fit, and strong. He makes a beeline for her crotch. Her belly and bottom are tight not unlike drums. He mounts her backside and covers her mouth with his mitt. A bat whirls and squeaks, setting on the rump of a mule. Effulging stars are like magnesium flames. Vegetation is exhausted and enfeebled from drought. Thunder cracks and leven dances. The moon glows an inferno orange. An unexpected storm sounds akin to bombs and shells. The city's like Hong Kong, with its 'Tron'-ish neon lights.

196

After melting Abigail down into tallow, Peki cuts the rest of her up into small pieces, puts them in satchels, and heaves them into a garbage receptacle. Assorted law enforcement leaders make impassioned speeches before the press and cameras, expound theories concerning her disappearance, and publish photos of the missing Hispanic girl to post on every available surface. To him, they are just grasping the chance to hog the limelight. Search parties scour the entire area. Her parents weep and beg for their daughter's return. He is the demonic blaze of brutality and inhumanity burning the bodies and souls of the innocent and guilty alike... He listens to a 1950s doo-wop track while showering and jacks off.

Peki's soliloquy is topped up with abstruse quotations, acting as if he's an integral part of the intellectual elite, resolutely expressing his opinions. He gets irritated by interruptions from Marisa, the telephone, and visitors, mostly vendors. He inspects his ragged, grungy fingernails. She had summoned him with the annoying electric bell. Intestinal rumblings of pipes. Whitewashed domiciles glimmer like snowbanks. There is a bizarre racket outside. People push, shove, and shout. The sky has the grayness of winter water. He feeds Turkish Delight to her, ensconced in the squabbed sectional, informing her that his establishment has not only hit the target set by his projections but has surpassed expectations. This is more miraculous than the parting of the Red Sea! He is relieved to know the human fat in the product has no undesirable effects. He dreams of her stuffing his mouth with bonbons, toying with his nipples, tickling his testicles, and giving him a spanking, with verve and vivacity. Will she give him one of her serpentine hugs, affirming her affection? It would be q character-developing and constructive occurrence. He'd find himself at the Gates of Heavenly Bliss! He craves an experience of a romantic nature with her. Would she masturbate with him? If she were chaste, would she give her virginity to him? She has her share of sorrows. He thinks he's sadistic and stupid, irredeemable and worthless. Her feet are propped up on a washing basket, tam tilted at a jaunty angle. She has powers of persuasion to induce him to do anything she wants. He adores her olive flesh and sensuous mouth and hates her vile temper and recurrent drunkenness. She's stubbly about the shins. He can be both jealous and curious when she would be conversing with a customer on the sales floor, and he would take in breaths sharply behind the counter, at the cash register. He even sees the new hire, a fifty-something gentleman, mild and reserved, devout and compassionate, as a threat. He could, with his presence, light the place like a lamp. He wouldn't wish harm to his worst enemy. Although soft and sentimental, he is prone to periods of glumness. Peki has a worn-out appearance, plonked on the homemade coffee table. Visions of Marisa spring unbidden to his head. She looks waifish, garbed in a T-shirt, dungaree shorts, and espadrilles. She's got a lovely body and missiles for knockers. She is sexy, sitting around in idleness. He tolerates urgent pressure in his bladder and bowels. He is the proud proprietor of his shop, and it cuts him to the core to witness his mother spreading margarine, whitish like lard, with the texture and consistency of butter, on a slice of wheat bread. He wants to bash her brains in. His trap is set into a scowl, the corners turned down, a frown deepening. He quaffs fiery spirits and pulls the covers over his head in bed to block out the sounds of her mastication. She has insensibly wounded him. His peepers glint with disdain. This is an insult that only a peck on the cheek could satisfactorily avenge, with the irreproachableness of an Old Testament God. Colossally incensed, his blood pressure skyrockets. He's so furious that he can barely breathe. He is ashen pale. His hands twitch unmanageably. He had committed himself to a lifetime loyalty to the cult of mantequilla-making. Lord, he's been getting away with murder. He considers the laws of probability and the inscrutable mechanisms of cosmic justice. Her pies are glazed and unfocused. She has got a sinewy leanness and tight lips. He flatters her, but she doesn't lose one iota of her polar intensity, lost in the outer space of her irreality, talking to herself in subdued tones. He fantasizes about pinning her to the wall and kissing her, quelling his timidity and carrying out what he is afraid to do. Whereupon they can become locked in an embrace. Would groping her countermand her impulse to flight? He is besotted with her. He gasps as though he dragged a bull by the horns for miles. Lean toward me, he thinks. Put your head on my shoulder. Let me sniff your hair. We can clutch each other. We'll get bombed at a fiesta. We will make love with ravening abandon, our bodies ablaze with fervency... Her steps are cautious and unsteady.

Luis

Luis, now brazenly smebbin, totally teed, curses his former crewmates, a shitload of assholes, steering the jalopy through a slalom of construction cones. The chill and clamminess conspire to crystallize and make a coldish, condensational atmosphere. He studies his engraved copper ring and, with clinical objectivity, studies the brown freckles on his hirtellous forearms, currently dotted with diamondiferous diaphoresis globules. He plans his pelagic projects, and plots thalassic ideas, all too grandiose, ones he knows damn well will never come to fruition. He digs into a bag of supermarket peanuts. Potato chips, meanwhile, churn in his gullet. His migrainous pulsations in meterage to the city's surrounding racket. Enveloping threatening darkness. His jaws are like scissors. Slippage of his falsies' plate. He is a pariah. Unemployable. Broke. Busted. A forever loner. He soughs between swigs of gin. He pops prescribed pills for his astronomically high blood pressure. His dunlop, fuzzguton. Prospect of a heart attack is probable. His double chin has the chromacity of a toad's pansa. A broad's boftt. His fune rises and falls as the mercury column in a common thermometer. Hairs on his tootsies are like the bristles of a hedgehog. He glances at the scribbling on the slip of paper, holds it with his cigar-shaped digits like a shutterbug a still-wet picture, and hates Peki and Roberto even more. He's got to blow his fuse. Then there are hot flashes. Luis scratches his itchy pyab, like the needles of a cactus. His chapped choppers are distorted by the filmy rearview mirror. He stops the vehicle and gets out, dizzy, queasy, and barfs colloidal chunks on the passenger-side seat, ears ringing as alarm clocks he cannot shut off, flushed fotch striated by scab-colored light, abdominous area basaltic layers of blubber. The Octopod moon has tentacles of phosphorescence. Stew-hued vault. His outbreak of goose pimples, tingly forestial manscape. Another vomitous surge in his venter. Canted, and sick, his physique makes him appear to be a leg-short chair with plentiful padding. Ulcerous residences. His dubious teeth detach slightly. Gas surreptitiously escapes from his sore sphincter. His sandpapery retching. Grease-black night. Inordinately towering projects. Leafy tongues lap the dew. His ox's appetite proves to be detrimental to his health. Din of transit tumbles. Orgasmic zephyrean hisses. He imagines his anus is staring straight ahead with resentful suspicion. Copse's blaring quiescence. He wipes his lips with a soiled handkerchief. He's red from gagging. Precipitation is like searin. Vista's the color of gums. Driving rage of the deluge. A goateed old-timer in tatters under the verdurous awning of a laurel is dazed in a mild stupor, perched birdlike on a park's bench. Optic moon us riveted to Luis. He rummages through the clutter of cogitations in his attic. He has the sensation of being bruised, overripe fruit tormented by a torturous sun's relentless beating. Lindens shake as if because of pain. His eyebrows are like gauze pads. He pisses, milgate a sporting faucet. His reverberating heart. Acknowledging he's off his rocker, he remembers his roller skates and electric train set. He urinates as though a nurse instructed him to at a medical exam. A geyser of puke bubbles up. His build is square like a public photo booth, tongue out of his trap as a strip of a shot through the slot. Reflux in his innards is like roots pushing up stones of a walkway. He'd prefer to have a catheter applied to him than to remain in this deplorable condition. Piceous Mercedes with pockmarks of dents on the quarter paneling. Shrubs in a shivering fit. His regurgitations ebbing and flowing like the tide. Frantic waves of boughs as though they are hailing cabs. Lassitudinous drafts ruffle the bounding main. Launched, lighted drencher is like a Niagara of bleach. Arsenal of charms on his chintzy chains and their tinny chinkle. His motion like the handicapped trying to balance on a pogo in a quagmire. His shrinky dinkey in his ham as a whiting with its tail in its mouth. The boner makes a beeline for his pot. Migrainoid ache is diminished to a long-distance sensation. His stoic smirk, discolored modulation, words a whorl in midair. Entangled clothes and a collection of junk in the trunk. Antediluvian takeout. He carps monotonously, fulgurously framed like he's a pic. He is dressed as a piratical plumber. Gales sound like caged and mocking canaries. His collar bones are protuberant. Sporting the empty mien of a stuffed mammal. Periodic fits of a creatural shindy. His fossil eyes and podgy body. Elms gesture like roadside vendors exhibiting their wares to passing drivers. Everyone he talks to balls up his opinions and throws them into the wastebasket as if it's mumbo jumbo. Acidic chompers gnaw at his ventral stuffing. His harmonium moue, hillbilly blinkers, a cicatrix crossing the rotten apple of his cheek. He has this spineless, faraway vox. Winds are sharp like knives. Leaves fall from trees as though scabs from skin. His hamass saddlebag-sags. A powdery spray of dandruff is inadvertently shaken from his head. Worried thoughts dash as mice in a basement. He cannot placate his demonic alcoholism. His waxen blinders, crapulent caramel making his drawers feel like a candy wrapper. Thunderous azure bangs like pots and pans slammed by a shrew. Luis hallucinates a transvestic Roberto wrestling with a gigantean crocodile. The extremity of his inner turmoil, unremitting angst. He thinks he's built like a tire, has a retiring disposition, a simple Joe Shmoe lacking ambition. His tokus, with the tarf, begs its pardon. Poor standing of his dookie toofs. His glazzies are glazed like he just woke up. Ginormous shabba. Glorious gimpies. Walkering, he is evocative of a kid awkwardly jumping on rocks across a creek. His mind is in a permanent state of confusion. Listless disarray of the heap's interior, the exterior a tad better off. Vacant spectacles. His practically typhlotic fageyes muculent, existence hopeless, hapless. Acneously flaring (with stars) heavens. Breezes huff and puff as though they're blowing out birthday candles. He, lacerated by splendorous swords, wets his whistle with a homemade rotgut. His sardonic, infantine grin could aggravate a nun. Vigorously cracking his knuckles, absentmindedly articulating what he's thinking to himself. Beast of sobriety anticipates his arrival, conniving in a gloomy crevice. Monkey of addiction determined to remain on his back. The radar of his melon automatically turns. The core of his essence in the shell of problems. Scruffy young adults, with the grace of grasshoppers, wield signs and yell, hold up posters in a hubbub of demonstration, fanatically in support of socialism, humanists with a militant zest. Immobile cirri. Wrought iron railing. Porcelain frog. Tosca aria blasts from a boombox. Born-again Christians and their sycophantic solicitude. An Afro Saxon suave not unlike a tennis instructor, with a moose's eyes. His asexual cologne with the malodor of disinfectant in an excessively antiseptic suite. An anorexic adolescent, shock as if it's a beetle, chin bristling with peach fuzz, bustles like a waiter. His ominous friendliness. Shade is a divested ecclesiastical investment. Marine wateriness of dawn. Vaporous cadaverous corona. Moon-galvanized cumuli. Weather-beaten firs. Back behind the wheel. With effort. Engine sounds like grinding jaws. Anemic turf. A Bluey vermicular thing in a brothy puddle is like a thrumming vein. Leathern pouch of his nargberries, spoilt cherry of his rectum. Mist is a membranous series. Mozzies prey on his flaccid shape. His flabby chest's beslobbered. Paper sheet of sand. He glugs a can of emphatically bad brew to alleviate his anxieties. His grubby trousers are slipping. Lariat lines of vinage on a battered trellis. Suet of his neck bundled by the shirt's collar. His puke is not unlike embalming fluid, nut drooping as a mongrel's. He sprawls, and reminds you of a cruciform bug. He's bestilled like a paralytic. Tin-tinted tributary. Luis perambulates as a puppet. His prickly eyebrows are like the li'l' legs of a centipede. Hobbling is akin to an injured goldfinch. He had long ago lost his enthusiastic smile, the exuberance of the sailing ship. Resinous scent. His carnation-white derma layer, nodulous fingers. He digs an improvised latrine, and experiences a productive BM. Stars in the overcast are like lighters intermittently flicked on and off. His spreading rash makes him feel like a shack covered in climbing creepers, meager gums with the kiss of death of infection, and it's bothering him. The clunker glides. It needs gas. Motor grunts. Orchard's fabulous fragrance. Farm paths. The wreck's dust and disorder. Cardboard skyline. His suffering constitutes the center of the universe. He searches for his lost soul. He wants to play checkers. Will he manage to put the pieces of his totality together again? Dismantled dummies in a fountain, transparency of its coursing as an unending petting. Hydroplane of a brook. An apricot-aproned robin. Sun dies in the clouds like a candle burning out. He feels like an ancient Egyptian mummy, considers his entirety a squalid specimen, benumbed as if his life is anesthetized, and fears that the feeling of who he is will never be revived. His felt-cloth suspirations. He was a street performer for a spell, a misshapen homunculus playing the barrel organ for a maniacal ape for peanuts. The eschar on his knee he peels with the curvaceous claw of pinkie-nail as he would a tangerine. His ham takes refuge in his BVDs. He croaks and clucks, shifting like a cockatoo on its perch. A shrill chorus of cranes. His flesh is like crinkled cellophane, sleeves as wings, and he's about to take flight. He fidgets like a hen on its roost. Miserable oil refinery like a loner, an individualist. The estuary shines as hair cream. There's a comedy of errors. To wit, fender tag with an amazonian towhead...

Thaddeus Coolwhip and Circe Belotti

Everything pales in the light. Ideas, he thinks, are ripples in the water of the mind when the wind of inspiration blows upon it. Hungover, he feels like a living and breathing organism that has inexplicably transmogrified into something else entirely. His halibut face is now deformed with emotion. Thaddeus Coolwhip resembles a cross between Tom Thumb and a shapeless dumpling. He walks in the shabby room like he's carrying on his broad back a weight beyond what he can bear. He woke up on the wrong side of the bed, threw a Rumpelstiltskinian temper tantrum, made a zany of himself, running over the harlots he'd hired as a lawnmower over weeds. He glared at them like the Big Bad Wolf at the Three Little Pigs. He always feels cornered, like a fox hemmed in by hounds. Overcast's ice-white. Mass of citizenry moves like surf. His skull seems sawed-off. The down-and-out building has a slate roof. Sun's a knowing eye. Circe Belotti, the picturesque strumpet, is as unstable as a child's sand castle and moves like a claymation character. She has these raptorial eyes, a falciform nose, and a carmine gash of a mouth. Desire burns through his body, forcing its way out, like a dragon escaping from its cavernous prison. She is whippet-slender and dizzy like a coal mine canary, with this Katharine Hepburn semiquavery inflection and untweezed eyebrows. Her thelerethism is obvious. He sips the first-rate port out of a cut-glass decanter and eats the bagel and chicken livers like an otter. His hands and feet have a Biblistic thickness. Dog-snouted, he vocalizes, intonation sounding like a screechy drill. He has the malice of Iago. He shuts his yap like he's closing a vault. Sounds of burglarious activity are heard coming from next door. Spilled soda on the counter shines oilily. Walls are adorned with framed paintings. The watercolors are striking productions. He considers himself to be a capable connoisseur. The black-draped palette looks like a place of execution. There are serviceable plastic plants. Thaddeus coughs and sneezes. He has banana skin and moon pie-round rear end. There's a cannikin-clinking of hailstones. Jays are glossily blue. He suddenly speaks, and has the intonation of a misplayed oboe. Feverish, he watches the drifting gulls, and imagines Homer's ghosts floating up from Erebus in 'The Odyssey.' Coasting clouds, to him, are "Powerless heads of the dead." Her bare, incurvate stomach is satiny to the touch. Their kiss is as a seal of union. Peki, who'd spent the night in a sleeping bag, sedates and drowns them in the tub.

Peki consumes naan with Butyrum containing Circe's adipose tissue and has a vision of her hiking in the woods with friends, when she hears this blood-curdling scream and a "HELP ME!" coming from somewhere in a claustrophobic cave. She walks tentatively towards the noise and finds a billygoat with a human face, and it shrieks "HEEELP MEEE!" in this pain-stricken voice.

The War

There were tonsil-tormenting screams and banshee wails of the wounded and dying men-at-arms. Peki was utterly appalled by the sights all around him. The town was mostly empty. A sorry bunch of civilians remained. They had strange dress and customs. Unexplainably, some had high spirits. He ate raw snails and drank spring water among tombs and rocks — a perfect place for a deserter. He had hardly been able to get any rest at night for fear and worry. People were disturbed by his appearance. He milled about with peasants in the square, fussing and fretting along with them. They fanned out and spread up a knoll. Refugees were preparing to depart. They subsisted on scraps. He wanted to relax in their company. He continued a conversation with himself. He had gone mad. He was clearly in an agitated state. Stress reduced him: he was skeletally thin, his meager hair was oily, and his ebony oculi sank into his wizened visage. His gums, teeth, and tongue were in a bad way. The villagers were not reconciled with his grotesque grin and horrifying expression. His demonic air frightened folks. They looked at him as if he was a bogeyman, and pitied him because of his physical deprivation. He grunted incoherently, dancing and gesticulating, and venting weird piercing cries of joy. "Everyone dies," he declared. Then he made impatient beckoning motions with his fingers to an elderly lady. He commanded emphatically and imperially. She hesitated for a moment, caught between a reluctance to step forward and the necessity of flight. Whereupon she scrambled away up a stony path. He was becoming an irritable and cantankerous character. There was panicking and hurrying when the explosions commenced. A blackbird sang beautifully from a branch. Thunder snapped. Lightning crackled. Sun was slightly blurred in the clouds. Fog bloomed not unlike cordite blossoming from the barrel of a fired gun. Peki serviced his weapons and rummaged through his rucksack, with one eye asquint, for ammunition. He needed to lock and load. His rifle and pistol conformed to his requirements. They made him feel more of a soldier. Plus, he relished hefting their weight in his hands and seeing their shine. He managed to shoot a deer, hare, and goose in a fairytale forest. These weren't exactly significant feats of marksmanship, but he got meals out of them. Assessing his sober and tattered military uniform, he thought of how he caused many innocent victims, male and female, to suffer from the many varieties of masochism he inflicted on them. He traveled on a goat track, his heart thudding. He decided to lay low for a spell and was committed to the idea. He conquered his trepidation about scaling a summit by a stupendous effort of will. At the top, he raised his arms as though in surrender. Being AWOL, he felt like he was dishonoring himself and that maybe he had made an irretrievable mistake. It wasn't too late to return to the ranks… He used a walking stick. His helmet sat securely on his head. He received respectful greetings from passers-by. He attracted flies. There were fine days and inclement ones. A cemetery was desecrated. Was it the Spaniards or the Krauts who were responsible? Peki broke down the door of an abandoned house, in which he located a bottle of red wine. He popped the cork and started guzzling. He destroyed holy books and religious ornaments. He put a box of crackers to his nose. His face lit up. He pinched precious and practical items. Drunk, he rounded up a group of pigs that were left behind and herded them squealing over a precipice. He told himself that the action was approved by the Almighty above. A geriatric couple fornicating in the bushes aroused in him simultaneous feelings of longing and revulsion. Their combined body odor reminded him of roasting pork. He wandered off, thinking of what he'd done to people with various degrees of disquiet. He was barely tolerant of the interminable deadening events of a disenjoyed existence. While smoking in a courtyard, he saw a wild dog lying on its side on a patch of weeds. Its coat was entirely white, except for a greige spot on its chest. The thing was just skin and bones. It inhaled and exhaled rapidly. Saliva dribbled from its gaping mouth. Its pink tongue lolled to one side. Its respirations were hoarse and irregular. The creature's stomach was reminiscent of a bellows, puffing in and out. Peki was disconcerted. He wasn't too keen on putting the poor canine out of its misery. It began to wheeze. Should he strangle it? Shoot it? Drown it? He didn't know what to do. It smelled of dust or death. He lifted it onto his lap and rocked it back and forth, akin to a nurse for a newborn. It was too sick to understand what was going on. The animal blinked slowly and growled feebly before he smothered it with a shirt. Suddenly, it stopped breathing and its head fell. The sun dried the blood on the bricks. He hugged it tightly for a very long time. He wrapped it in a cloth and brought it into the woods, where he dug a shallow grave with a spade and buried it. Leaves fluttered in the sea breeze. Peki thought of Marisa and had a mystical sense in which no complete bond could ever be severed. He had so much grief and guilt. Spain was winning the war. Germany was losing. And Japan was in the middle of it. On their turf, no less. He was journeying to nowhere in particular. The stains on his tee were tears.

Peki and Marisa

Robustious Peki resists being a nothing. He isn't a nobody. He's togged out in a polyester indigotic ensemble. He is trying mightily not to fall apart. He's buried beneath a staggering burden. There's so much paperwork (invoices and so forth) to be sorted and filed. He has been haunting the overpasses and catwalks for quarry like the wind. Coming and going from the store and apartment, he feels like a soldier trooping in and out of encampments. Their building is dingy and ruinous. He had terminated, without ceremony or common courtesy, a fella of the Nippon who'd uncharacteristically used profanity against a staunch shopper, the cussing vigorously expelled from his mouth. He seeks a companion to engage in buttery debauchery. His Mama is the ideal candidate. He is grateful to God for her presence in his life. He winces in dental discomfort and mumbles aggrievedly. Cloudlets are not unlike sheep's wool. Teeming jetty. Cars career at speeds excessive. Sun has a blinding shine. A construction venture is in progress. Empyrean lapses back into anonymity, attributable to the overcast. Showers taste like the dregs of old joe. He smells sulfurous combustion. Marisa frowns, wanting to retire to idleness in a tower as Griselda, her inflection disenchanted. She dances on the pole like a flag on a mast. The reedy lady complains to no one in particular, strides from left to right almost faster than the eye can follow, angrier than a maddened wapiti. She is more erotic than maternal. The vermin scramble for cover to somewhere else in the hemisphere. The sexual frisson makes a magnetic field, irresistible and erratic, pulling them together. They are supercharged in a voltaic frenzy, both assaulted by pruriency.

Some of their discourse, in a shared waking dream, conducted often as not under their ceiling, loses its knife-edge, the two going round and round. They argue in the abstract. He struggles to maintain his composure, utters the most generic jocularities to lighten the atmosphere, and she scornfully guffaws. She has a red-faced glunch. Her tone is barely tolerable. The beef, labyrinthine and bitter, slowly reaching an incredible intensity, is about their varying and clashing decorative tastes. Proper communication commences. The dispute is resolved amicably. Apologies are exchanged, and reiterated. He drones like a transformer coil. Her face is irradiated by an enigmatic smirk. They hug to make up but it's a chilly parting. She is frustrated on account of her not getting the telegraph operator gig at the Deaf and Blind school. She sputters like an electrode. She believes the students could see and hear her. Cooking whiffs of a chemical procedure. He feels concupiscently electrified and somatically calibrated. The neighbors' noises are really hard to associate with any radix in the material sphere. Astounding is the birds' abundance in the firmament. Seascape is storm-illumined. There's a considerable population in this metropolis of some size. The soaker is a brutish cascade. He gazes up into the welkin's reasserted vacancy. Peki and Marisa mutter and shuffle, preparing the gumbo and mousse for supper. She walks around barefoot and he's not disappointed. She is bent over the stove in palpable perplexity. Hail looks like pearls of quite uncommon iridescence. Sprinkles have a resinous scent, a fragrance maybe reminiscent of conifer. Stevedoring on the docks. A vessel lies offshore. Cabbagy cirri. Horizon is busy with them. Wage earners are like worker ants. Panes are acned with sleet. Battery of towering waves. Weather, owing to global warming, is fraught with instability. Thoughts float in his dome as specimens in a jar filled with formaldehyde, in this polar environment. Wasted, he feels like a jellyfish perishing upon the sand. Dirty laundry is ankle-deep on the floor. Open compartments of her shoe-holder contraption remind him of mandibles. Slivers of light inch along as glow worms on the chipped floor. A truck cruises with a submarine's sluggishness and making a slew of noises. Cars are like cows in a manger. Moon's a hugeous head. A van whines not unlike a boat run aground. She rises from the matting like a geyser, has an irradiance like that of certain insects to attract others of its species. Her head tilted back because of a nosebleed, her honker seeps like a lava cone. He believes he's Romeo and she's Juliet, that their love is not a fleeting vagary but a veracious predestination. She appears shaken, as though she staggered from a railroad wreck. She is a scab covering the wound of him. Scarcely lit darkness. He cleans the crud out of his eyes using a gaudy rag. She has the blank expression of a mannequin in a store window. The timid sun emerges through the cumuli. Her derma layer is damp as shower tiles after a hot bath. Ebb-tide clouds over the crests of cypresses. The clearing sky is like a photographic image emerging from its solution. Air's as olive oil. His pulse quops. His heart whumps like gas in a heater. He disregards the hysterical transistor in the devastated room. Hail's mini meteorites. His nape burns. Surf laps the shore like a tongue. His jaws grind horizontally like a horse's. She is Andromeda, chained to her addiction. He's the Argonaut who'll save her. She reddens her mouth and cheeks with lipstick and blush, and blackens her lashes with mascara, maintaining she is a hermaphroditic flower who shall remain infertile. Astronauts ride motorcycles. Cloudlets drift like dead fish. Peki licks a lollipop, thinking or reading erotic poetry and perusing obscene photographs. He is hellishly unhappy. His lungs are like a pair of harmonium bellows. Waiting for him to bring her the downers and uppers, Marisa was like an orchid anticipating the hummingbird to convey pollen to her. He sucks in and expels oxygen. A tenemental building's occupancy has become sparser. She's an animal who spurns the notion of being domesticated. Firework pyrotechnics at the carnival amount to explosions with mass entertainment objectives. Roman candles burgeon over the structures in hues by the hundreds.

Peki corkscrews and ping-pongs through the crowd. His head spins like a Tibetan prayer wheel. Rutilant dawn gives the impression of being fateful. Wrappers are risen by way of gust. Unexplored reaches of the celestial sphere. Cloudy sky looks like an ice-scape. Rain lashes out of the heavens. Wilds of telephone wires. Horizon holds a spectrum of tropical pigments. He feels as if he's adrift, in a helical curve, in a vastly resonant space, then sucked into a sort of intraplanetary vortex. Skyline is a wide-open mouth screaming silently in the calamitous birth of daybreak. Marissa stands, still as a wax figure, wearing a simple, loose dress of a cream color, on the semicircular balcony, apparently suicidally crestfallen. She receives inordinate observation from him. He finds himself embroiled in a byzantine codswallop with her of the household. He glances askance at his mammoth cranium, its reflection thrown back at him by the framed glass. He has a tortured headspace, like a tragic hall of mirrors that seems endless. He shines as with sweat. For a detailed description of the mother's' narrow escape from his growingly barmy attentions, her son with his unconscionable connivings and ardent villainy, you, dear reader, would have to be adept in the rarest art of reading the mind. Her approach to dealing with him: he is to be presumed randy until proven otherwise. His advances (closing in on her awfully rapidly) are evoked in her anxious memories. He abases himself before her denigration, realizing the astuteness of submitting himself for domination and allowing her to proceed as she pleases, for she is central to the development of means to send him into ecstasy. Daily verbal skirmishes between them are fought among anomalous antiques, these clashes, also amid unreportable carnage, undeclared and imperceptible to the world at large. Both attempt to gain the advantage by vocalic brute force, the combatants caught up in the resolute departure from reason on the untamed domiciliary frontier located in a remote corner of the universe. She strums a mahogany mandolin and stares into areas that don't include him. He floats on the noontide to time's flow and imagines her pubic hair as being an unmapped wilderness. She is lapped by fulgurous tongues. They disagree none too politely. She thinks that the Planet Earth is a plane surface. He endeavors to get a glimpse, even at a degree of indirectness, of her cleavage and settles for the crescent of her countenance, the cords bulging in her neck, at a three-quarters view from behind. A sea stink permeates the place. Her armpits reek of reproduction. They quarrel all but eloquently. Knickknacks are weapons readily identifiable. Beer bottles are lethal debris. They are far from the outpost of rationality. Crepuscule is notable for mental distress and recrimination. The speaking trumpet might come in handy for either one of them. Precip hisses like flame. Sibilant sounds of the drafts. Mizzle is like chalk dust. He promotes his lewd program, his motivation not in any way opaque. He is drawn to her by a wildering carnal passion to the abysmal brink. She sports the disdainful smirk of a parrot. Her inexpensive cigarillo's smoke thickens the oxygen. He experiences scrotal shrinkage. She is his incomprehensible idol. Her insanity makes him appear a model of sanity. He pants like a frustrated hound on the hunt and gazes at her as though he recognizes an intimate acquaintance. She looks at him as if he is a toy designed to amuse her... He's convulsive with sinister lubriciousness, his voice tiny and plaintive. Afterward, they resume their activities. She preps tomorrow's midday meal. He scans the drab wastes below and keeps an alert ear to her movements. Empyrean-piercing high rises. An aurora incandescently interrogates the firmament. Fog froths and glides. Marisa disappears and reappears in clouds of dust. Dusk is relieved by the brown-shaded lamps electric and gas. An edifice reminds him of a kind of castle, with metalliferous parapets and turrets. He peers at it through a spyglass. Sunlit ocean. On the same wavelength, mother and son share pheasant, muffins and jam, and pudding. Her earlier castigation for ill-defined wrongdoing is engraved upon his brain. Pedestrians, intrepid innocents, scurry not unlike disturbed ants in the sun's yellowed glare. Thunder has the sonance of dry-throated coughing. Sea-green foliage. Coruscant colonnades. Sheets of the downpour. A conical roof supports a weathervane. Heavenwide pulses of pigment. Buildings are like ancient fortresses. Kirk has an onionish ovality. There are contrary winds. Skyscrapers suggest cliffs of ice in the titanium-white effulgence. Steadily brisk traffic. A diner has a queue out the door. The long line of drooling clientele becomes enlivened by the merest fraction of mortal repositioning. Vehicles are in potentially perilous transit. Shorn knolls. Aromatic breezes. Buff refulgence, slightly muted, moves in a wriggling restlessness, fails by a visible margin to be bronze. People are wordless as animals. A steam siren's shrill cry begins to abate. The lab, a subterranean workshop beneath the surface, a melancholy place that is a haven from the upper world, never to be grazed by light, is Peki's private realm of eternal rest. Radical scientific apparatuses, these fantastical doobries and thingos, occupy every available cubic inch. A separate room recalls the spacious control cabin of a great craft. He settles down on a granitic Mongoloid odalisque. His establishment is the genuine article, the substructure of substantiality. Police galore have put him at loose ends. Insomnia has wrapped him like an overused bath towel. He is an unsleeping soul of uncomity. He has poor impulse control. He guesses a steady appetite for unceasing destruction and gruesome kills keep him slim, trim, and grim. He feels as if he has arrived from some unsensed excursion. He sees flitting fairies, alternately melts and freezes, and imagines Marisa as an amphibious creature, swimming nude, graceful in the emerald water as any porpoise, after ingesting edible fungi and imbibing absinthe. His blinkers are protected by a pair of ingenious goggles, dropping the needle on a turntable to play 'Can I Have This Dance for the Rest of My Life?' by Anne Murray. He is satisfied in knowing he can clog up the city's drainage system with the blood of his victims, many of them knifed, gouged, raped, neck-snapped, strangled, baseball bat beaten, pitchforked, head-hammered, throat-rammed with fluorescent tubes, and so on. Stab-stab-stabbity-stab… He lives, of course, being the very quintessence of evil. Peki Zambrano is a nightmare dreamer, a mover and a shaker. He thinks of being estranged from his former colleagues, remembering when personal animosity and professional resentment bubbled under the surface, eventually boiling over into passive-aggressive brinkmanship and mass resignation. Relationships became strained and terse. Things went from bad to worse. Distance grew between them. There was so much criticism and hostility… Presently, with his establishment, he feels like a robber who had pulled off a heist, a sensation that, despite all the uncertainty and despair, he has gotten away with it. He will always up the ante, and raise the stakes.

The light shining on Marisa makes her look like she's bathed in gold. Her perfume is discreet for a change. She tells him these fantastic tales, rendering him spellbound. She is not only lovely but likable. Her skin is white as cotton. She's soft-textured as if she's made of thin paper. Her long neck is splendid. He considers her private parts as being a flor de maravilla, or wonder flower. Her tummy is smooth as a teen's. He has been feeling shipwrecked in an ocean of liquor and despair, so her storytelling provides a welcome interlude from the unbelievable stress. He can't exist without her. He'd be driven mad. The idea of it is a sharp pain. The thought weighs heavily on his heart. He is fearful of losing her.

She speaks without so much as pausing for breath and he nods like an automaton. It's hard for him to get a word in edgewise. He has a knot in his larynx and can barely utter a syllable anyway. She dispenses incoherent speech, one sentence following the other in a rush that pretty much makes no sense. In a happy mood, she stretches her arms (creaking like those of a windmill when driven by a gust) out wide to greet the gentle lambency. His throat clogs when he tries to talk to her. So this is infatuation. Truly curious. She has been of passionate interest to him for years. His tongue comes out of its paralysis. And she admires his erudition. She sheds her attire. Starkers, she feels freer and more relaxed, and as though by abandoning her apparel she has also renounced the rigid protocol of domestic etiquette in her behavior toward him. One addresses the other in a familiar form. He heads toward her as if she leads him by the legs. He gets her in his clutches to devour her. She wriggles out of his grasp. She's not unlike a coral snake: she can be unassertive, but if she bites you and injects her poison, there is no antidote, and you will have a few hours to live. Her lust for life is contagious. He is confident she will not be long in granting him favors. Love-smitten, he has an idiotic expression. The price for sleeping with her is hefty. His affection for her grows like a mushroom in soil. He attempts, in vain, to optically absorb her anatomic details, to discover her somatic secrets. She whirls round and round, with mechanical elegance, on the steep staircase that leads to the terraced roof, like a ballerina figurine on a music box. She has always been a tireless dancer in a bell jar. Staring at him, her eyes seemingly see farther than what she is focused on. She believes he is a monster in disguise. He reminds her of a devious gnome that escaped a picture book. Her oculi sparkle. Her face appears withered. Gloomy and somber dusk. The rain cascades like a waterfall. Gray sky, dreary drizzle. Peki remembers his recent victims — blacksmith, milkman, laundress, butcher, chimney sweep, tavern keeper, street musician, florist, cabinetmaker, town crier (his tongue was instantly removed with pliers for obvious reasons), watchmaker, confectionist, and seamstress — using a mallet to pound them with vigor, and not without a certain gracefulness. Murder, for him, is like magic. Killing is precise work. Pleasure in slaying innocents is accompanied by a tinge of sorrow. The mantequilla has become a staple of the diet of most people in the country because of its exquisite taste and fair price. There is no reason why he should conceal his pride in practicing such an esteemed craft. His fame will soon spread like Butyrum throughout the world. He will become the protagonist of brilliant writers throughout the land, his character as popular as a legendary prince, captive princess, wicked witch, and an indomitable dragon. His product will draw plebeians and aristocrats alike. He doesn't lack for customers. The town is undergoing a feverish butter boom and he is at the forefront. Marisa, hearing voices, looks around, apparently afraid of being assaulted. He stays at a prudent distance. Fortunately, he doesn't take leave of his senses and fondle her. He could couple with her from sunup to sundown. He's ravenously hungry for her. For frantic, hallucinatory sex... She attracts him as a magnet does iron. She is an integral part of him, like a wick in a candle, barrel of a gun, or string of a crossbow. They follow each other like the beads of an abacus. The rose window, recently installed, is radiant. Twin towers, squarish and imposing, ostensibly float above the megalopolis. The river, near the tilled field, glissades like a humongous boa constrictor. The smog clears and the city extends itself in every direction. The market is mobbed. The stench of trash in the dangerous neighborhood is intolerable. An equestrian statue is made of plaster and bronze. The slice of pliant bread has a faint acidic flavor. Peki recalls the handsome fishwife, who lived in the basement of a print shop, adjacent to a stonemason's, a hardworking young lady surrounded in the cellar by secondhand machinery and various old-fashioned equipment, that he ruthlessly gutted. He got a whiff of the aromatic varnish she had used on the polished surface of the commode. The redolence was penetrant and agreeable. Dying, holding his wrists, she begged him to stop stabbing her. He wanted every piece of her, to hoard her not unlike a miser. He dilated his nostrils to take in the suggestive inky smell. Stripped of her boiler suit, the impressive sight of her made a deep impression on him. Her flesh was white as milk. Her heels were the exact color of aged wine. He contemplated the panorama, the thicket of sycamores and eucalyptuses, for a long time. A barge was anchored in the harbor. Swallows swooped, in sync, looking like they'd lost their way.

In the catacombs beneath the cemetery, Marisa is so picturesque, such a colorful figure, yakking about "reaching a ripe old age." The leotard appears to have been painted on her as if she was born wearing it. It's a fabulous fit. The getup is daring. Brazenly she shows her form off. Her pedicured feet are in Dutch clogs. Numberless skeletons are indifferent, the skulls perpetually grimacing and blindly glaring. Peki reeks of a thousand devils combined with waste matter. He alone could enrich a meadow. He has possibly the weirdest discussion with her that he has ever heard with his ears in his entire life. He realizes how much he has in his existence. He's thankful for the blanket on his bed, food in his stomach, water with which to slake his thirst, a roof over his head, clothes on his back, shoes on his feet, a toilet to sit on, books to read, butter to churn, and, above all, a mother to snuggle with. His guts feel gnawed by rats. He wishes to dispel from his senses the frightful remembrances that devastate his brain. His shot at seduction is a qualified disaster. He spends his magazine of compliments in a rat-a-tat speaking style, but she barely pays any attention. He just keeps missing the mark. She looks at him and doesn't see him. She conceals a yawn behind her purse. Her weariness of his schtick is appreciable. She musters all the patience in her possession in putting up with his overtures. He makes one last effort to contain his annoyance. She is smooth as a mirror, whereas he looks like shattered glass. He's a strange sybarite to her, and homelier than a spider. In his company, she gives free rein to her anxiety. Her body odor is comparable to that of damp earth. She sports a mute smile. He's an onanist constantly searching for gratification. He can no longer suppress his irritation, venting in a loud, solemn voice. She yatters, and he gazes at her as though she's vocalizing in a language he can't understand. Tense, she is cognizant of the verbal traps he sets for her. It's like, by harassing her, he's trying to drive her health away. She is like a theater directress and starring actress in a play production of her design, the staging impressive, the set splendid. She creates stupendous effects and considerable commotion. Her significant achievement distracts the audience so that it doesn't listen to her delivered lines, comprised of lamentable rhymes and awkward dialogue; however, she does express herself with fervor. Nevertheless, his attention is taken by her. She's an intimate part of his mortal coil. His madre fills the unendurable emptiness that always assails him. Her breath whiffs of fresh woods when they French kiss. Their tongues are agile. He pulls up the sports bra that has kept watch over the most beautiful breasts, firm and proud, that he has ever seen. Circumspectly he bites their nipples, savoring them. Her flesh glimmers like dew. He longs to penetrate her pudendum, the entrance and exit the beginning and end. Desire, for him, has never felt so destructive before. Enthralled, he can scarcely retrain himself. His spoken language caresses her bosom while her hand strokes his dick. He can visualize them intertwined, commingled, once and forever. He talks to her in verse, intriguing her, reciting lines as if it's a mnemonic exercise to fasten in his memory the poetry he's been trying to interpret. The strikingly diaphanous passages soothe her. He is like a roguish and shrewd dramatist utilizing wordplay to seduce her. It is problematic for her to remain standing. The trembling in her legs is intense. And nervousness consumes her. His whispering lulls her like a wet nurse singing to an infant and gives her the courage to continue jerking him off. He goes to hug her and she flails her way out of it. Her pleas are repetitive. He wants to banish the sadness from her soul and awaken the happiness lying in slumber in her spirit. She has been gloomy, and secluded, as of late. Vigorous blood channels through his veins. He resolves to revive her libido. Chords of her musical modulation soak Into his consciousness. A nerve twitches in her right cheek. She provides substance and form to his fantasies. In a lightning-quick flash, he embraces her again. She stays stationary, tears flooding her eyes, the lachrymal liquid cleansing her pancaked visage. He is like a sponge, absorbing her. Unexpectedly, she slips out of his grasp, not unlike a fish just taken out of the water. He feels as vacant as a public square in the wee hours. Her gait on the dirt floor is wobbly like she's on the cusp of falling into a faint. Mother and son get above the ground. The rented house resembles an inn. The miasma of this block is legendary. The floating fruit and flower garden is out front. Birds cheerily warble. Pedestrians in the distance are not unlike tireless, tiny ants. Jasmine bursts into blooms. The runnel murmurs. Ivy climbs the trees. Marisa properly prepares the crepes. Laughter comes to her lips. She beams a winsome grin at Peki. Motes of dust dance in a shaft of luminosity. In a grave vox, she tells him off, along with a mocking gesture. Thoughts of her sweeten his feelings for her, but sometimes he becomes embittered. A throng of people reminds him of a swarm of bees. He is deep in moroseness like a philosopher in cogitation. He boasts that his fame will spread over Europe like his beloved butter over a muffin. She thinks he's overconfident. The firmament is an eloquent vision of black nothingness.

Nightmare

Light bullies shadow. The girl, with an avian brain, beanpole body, and knotted face, makes these strange noises that are disarmingly unnatural, her cerebroid bird pecking at scraps of thoughts in its cranial cage. Her best friend, a wrinkled boy who looks like a furless primate, has a harp for ribs. He skillfully plucks the bony strings and creates weird music. His speech is slow and suspended. Their squat house, with a slate roof, over-furnished and with a tang of vinegar and tobacco, is situated in a leafy suburb. Wind sounds hair-raisingly scary as if some lost soul is singing in the dense gloom. It is enough to make the blood run cold and the skin crawl. Then there's is a glacial silence. The rhinocerine man, with a horny nose, strokes the glabrescent, humongous cat, with its Dracularian fangs and icicle claws, in the wardish room. Whereupon the bald and stout Ghost of a Genius, with this vacant stare, wanders noctambulously in the zoological garden, carrying a varnished wooden box, a substitute casket. Suddenly, a sallow, infantine creature, with a pear-shaped head and impassive expression, sits up and starts screaming as a meemie. Curiosity reigns. The home's occupants are now at the window, spermatozoan rain-beads swimming on it. The baby begins to spin around like an excited dog. Stars are like argus eyes in cloudy wings. They're watching the world.

Pickens Happymeal

The variegated raindrops on the windowpane are like Pollockian paintdrips on a vitreous canvas. Pickens Happymeal has a caricatural malangularity. His brain's empty as a noose. He is a Marabou stork of a young man. An effete, self-maiming sourpuss, mesmerizingly egoistic, he has a sock puppet's blank gaze, paralytic mind, the beak of a nose, mismatched, acned cheeks, viscid grin, bat-handle wrists, board belly, and underwater modulation. Sometimes he seems detached, not unlike a somnambulist; or he's stuck sempiternally in an amnesic state. He relishes being single. There's no key to the door of his heart. He is so sick of the knock-down, drag-out fights with lovers, male and female. He's a dead end of a human being, a hapless waste product who has a vagabond's indirection in life. He's one of those guys who'd perish and leave no more of a mark of his existence on the world than a bug leaves on a pond. He has no dreams to realize. He is bereft of a master plan. He wears a secondhand sweater, ripped jeans, and flip-flops. His egret feet reek of cod. He enjoys telephone calls, Scooby-Doo, public benches, fast food, and thrift shops. He dwells in a ramshackle edifice with its rabbit warren of dilapidated apartments, sleeps on a recycled mattress, and uses borrowed blankets. A fly is cast in the room. The downpour sounds as death rattles. Thick, humid oxygen is like damp rubber. He puts up a punk pretension in a social environment. He's tired of slaving for peanuts, selling cosmetics, and bagging groceries. He is considered by many to be underadvantaged and overconfident. He's a maladjusted daytripper. Rainbow is an extravagance of color. Pickens thinks of the classic rogues' gallery of exes: Gladys

Doty was dreadfully anorectic, looking like a retail store mannequin with an abnormal nose-to-mouth ratio. She had a fish-eye stare and barnyard/cayenne stink. She was partially deaf and had a ferret face, badly clipped bangs, psychoceramic eyes, gummy smile, setose chin, etiolated integument, and pipe-cleaner limbs. Braces zippered her buck teeth. She lived in a structure that suggested a monolithic file cabinet and worked these entry-level jobs at sterile tech companies. Oh, how she dug futuroidal films, electronic gewgaws, and mechanical gizmos! She'd been dealing with intestinal parasites. She felt like she was on the last frontier of sanity. She walked wobbleheadedly and puffed on cigs as if she were attempting to send smoke signals. She had proportional turpitude and hopelessness. She bore the stamp of the damaged. Her nipples were like pencil erasers, ass flat as a flapjack. She was lonely not unlike a field in winter, feeling as though she was a failure, and compulsively stretched, appearing pretzelesque. He eventually hooked up with her gal pal, Marge Barnstorm, with Tourette's Syndrome, bucket-shaped head surmounted by an avocado-hued coiffure, peepers round like pocket watches, plainness of phiz, balloonish body, bollard-arms-and-legs, sandbags for nates, derma layer soft as bread dough, and the gait of a pelican. She continually panted like the air was methane gas. Her dewlap was barnacled with zits, the goth tats hit-or-miss. She had inner mayhem and outer stoicism. She loved pizza, bowling, cacti, wrenches, bunnies, and, with an unsurpassable omnivority, read skin mags. She was evocative of some sullen bovine creature, talked in this tranqued-out manner. Anatomically speaking, she was all arc, Gladys all angle. Pickens rips the stale baguette in two, remembering Orville Zartoonian-Smythe, an attention-addicted, suffocatingly clingy, insolvent rageaholic with pert chops and zombielike self-preoccupation. He resembled a goosey girl and possessed a rodentine/timbery smell. The glistering flecks in his rheumy pies were as teeny-weeny homunculi floating in a hyaline jar filled with formaldehyde. Their smooches were more like bonks. The breakups barely register. "Meta beta big and bouncy," he says, regarding the leaf-dappled, tree-lined lane, the unsorted heap of coins on the cheap dresser, opining he's slender and breakable as a breadstick. What's he doing? Where's he going?

Peki strikes up a conversation with Pickens, with his pretty kisser and impertinent air, in a nearby noshery, appraising his feminine character-istics with every conceivable mark of consideration, everything that is masculine about him nullified. Pickens finds his aristocratic affability and artificial inflection to be irksome. He tries to connect with him, a labor in vain, the need coming by spontaneous propulsion. He sees his true colors. He listens to him with a sufficiently respectful quality. The ill-hu-mor aroused in him by his companion's behavior doesn't go unnoticed. They putter in a patch of clover. The welkin imitates the ocean, like a flower that assumes the aspect of the insect it seeks to attract. Peki's voice hits the note of a tuning fork to his trained ear. He's a Don Quixote who has tilted against scores of windmills, and worries his acquaintance will nip in the bud any chance of them venereally commingling. He wishes to devour him alive. He utilizes comradely language and a jocular affec-tation of camaraderie. The cordiality is conspicuously fake. He thinks of giving himself an advantage, if things get out of hand, of suggesting a diplomatic action, expecting him to counter with an act of war. With an eye to the future, should he lower his sights, and cut his losses? He's grown weary of being swept into the gutter by people. He studies him inquisitively like he's confronted with an artistic masterpiece. He brings him to his chest with the power of a suction pump, addressing him as a scholar speaking to an ignoramus. A metalline breeze sounds like a blade being sharpened on a grindstone.

Peki sports a sapien smile, and pictures his rail-thin Mama, a woman of the world. The household has become hostile territory for the two. His life is a Racine tragedy. He wants to believe she's this glamorous seductress, a statuesque stunner, her eyes glinting like jewels. She is the light shining upon the darkness of him. He would allow himself to be dragged from his death bed. To her, there is a foundation of resentment on which to build. The lab is as mysterious as the Temple of Jerusalem. Rainwater channels through the eaves, obedient to the designer's original orders. He's soaked with perspiration, like he was plunged, dressed, into a bath. And he mops himself with a handkerchief, migrating, in his head, to another hemisphere… He whines, with distended nostrils, not unlike a wild boar, and it turns into a resounding roar. He'd pounded Pickens into a pulp.

Peki slathers butter, with Pickens' fat, on coburg, and devours it. He sees Pickens waking up in the middle of the night in a cold sweat. He looks up to see a gargoyle hanging from his fan. It just dangles there, glaring at him, and he is frozen, unable to move.

Butter Tub

Along with the changes in butter making wrought by the advent of creameries, there developed also a change in the type of bulk package. The firkin began to lose ground and early in 1863 white ash 60-pound tubs were introduced in the west. They found such favorable acceptance that it was not long before they came into quite general use. In the east, the spruce tub was favored probably because Vermont and northern New York State butter were packed in 20, 40, and 60-pound sizes made of that wood. The tub came into general favor as both dairymen and creamery men became shippers, their product finding its way to markets such as New York, Philadelphia, Boston, and Chicago where it was sold through commission houses and brokers. There were some variations in the size and style of such packages which becomes understandable when it is recognized that the dairymen had to take into consideration the fact that his butter must go forward every week and accordingly he was governed in the size of the package by the amount he would have to ship. In the Chicago market, the 40 or 50-pound ash tub was preferred by this type of shipper whereas the creamery men, whose chief business was to manufacture butter in large quantities, adopted as their favorite package the 60-pound, 5-hoop, hand-made, clear ash tub, well put together, without glue or nails. For years, there was a controversy between the east and the west as to the relative merits of ash versus spruce tubs. As the years passed, suitable white ash became increasingly scarce, and some of the tub manufacturers turned to the Sitka spruce and Douglas fir forests of the Northern Pacific Coast. These woods were relatively free from the flavor and made attractive containers. The early made tubs contained five wooden hoops, but in 1917 the use of three galvanized steel hoops for the tubs and a galvanized beaded steel rim for the tub covers was introduced, and they replaced the five wooden hoops. The original size of the tubs was 56 pounds — the "half firkin" container for the "fresh ends" as formerly quoted on the New York market. For economical and progressive reasons, savings in the cost of manufacture and handling, the size gradually crept up in capacity from 56 pounds to 57, 58, 59, 60, 61, 62, 63, 64, and 65 pounds. Pioneers in the manufacture of butter tubs were the Creamery Package Manufacturing Company originally founded in 1882 and the Elgin Butter Tub Company founded in 1886 located at Rock Falls and Elgin, Illinois respectively. The use of the tin fasteners replacing the earlier ten-penny nails for holding the cover to the tub was developed in Elgin by the Elgin Butter Company as a means of utilizing the waste tin of the Illinois Condensed Milk Company who manufactured all their cans and cases for shipping their product. Incidentally, a Mr. C. W. Gould has been cited as starting a cheese factory in Elgin about 1860 (the Illinois Condensed Milk Company factory having been erected in 1865) and later engaged in butter making using as tubs for shipping his product, containers made of flour barrel staves cut in half. Australian square boxes, containing 56 pounds were introduced when creamery men began to consider the prospects of foreign markets but they never became popular in the east although they were used to some extent in the Central and Western sections of the country. Boxes of other shapes and sizes come into moderate use, especially where butter was to be cut and otherwise molded for prints. The most common and constant complaints against butter packed in tubs, boxes, and pails before 1890 pertained to woody flavor, mold contamination, and difficulty in stripping tubs. The common method employed in efforts to control these defects was to soak the tubs, boxes, or pails in salt water the night before they were used. The following morning they were rinsed out with scalding water and then with clear cold water, after which the butter was packed at once. Every effort was made in packing to eliminate air holes and when the tub or pail was full, it was placed in a cool place so that the tops might be chilled. When taken out, a little brine was poured over the top surface of the butter in each tub and a white "dairy" or "butter cloth" put on, the cloth having been cut the size of the top. The cloth was then smoothed on top of the butter and salt sprinkled on and rubbed around and around until a thin even paste covered the cloth. When the butter was so covered, it would generally reach the market with a smooth and bright surface, as the cloth would strip clean. Paper and Paraffin put in an appearance. The next step appears to have been the use of paper liners — Paraffin paper having first been recommended and used for such purposes. One of its staunchest advocates was quoted as follows: "I have experimented with paraffin paper and know what I am talking about. Last year I stored 6,000 tubs. Every tub was lined with paraffin paper. When I took the butter out last winter there was not the slightest taste of wood to the butter. The flavor was as good on the edges as it was in the center of the package, and the paper gave us no trouble adhering to the butter. Further than this, the paraffin paper I used did not color the butter or make it dark in the least." The reference to the paraffin paper not discoloring or darkening the butter may seem rather strange to the reader but in the 1880s and 1890s, paraffin was not as highly refined and free of odor and color as our modern product. In 1889, W. F. Brunner interested Mr. Sol Wheat Hoyt in the possibilities of vegetable parchment as a liner for butter tubs. Sample liners were sent to the Fairmont Creamery Company for investigation and were found satisfactory according to Mr. E. F. Howe. Incidentally, Mr. Howe had begun to use vegetable parchment sheets for wrapping pound prints of butter in 1888. Apparently, his experiments with vegetable parchment marked the beginning of the almost indispensable use that vegetable parchment now enjoys as a wrapper for butter and other fatty foods due, of course, to its grease-proof character, insolubility, high wet strength, as well as its odorless and, in fact, tasteless properties. Parchment because of its peculiar and distinctive characteristics, contributes as an important prerequisite to our modern butter packaging methods.

Sappho

The wild woman, hardly a member of the upper crust, thinks of writers and publishers and how they consume one another, like corpuscles and microbes, and by their conflict secure the vitality of artistic existence. Birds drift as petals. She fixes an ecstatic gaze upon them. The reddened sun appears to boil with rage. She looks at her faint mustache in the cracked mirror. She belongs to the avant-garde and is currently composing a magnum opus about a vulgar beach. She gloms creamed eggs and honey cake. The sky's salivary glands, that is, clouds, are oversaturated with moisture, and some drops of spittle trickle from its immeasurable mouth. Gusts waft the aroma of zinnias. To her, cerebrating is not unlike a game of billiards, the cue of inspiration striking the ball of an idea that plays off the cushion of her brain. The celestial sphere's hyper-secretion intensifies. The wind seems to be suffused with life, blowing with deliberate intention. Peki spies on her from a bluff. Her mannerisms are worthy of the stage. Abruptly, she strips and flings herself into the viridian sea as Sappho, and feeds the peacocks in proximity to the presbytery garden, talking to them in a nasal twang. She has a charming quality of mind and wants real teeth. Peki departs surreptitiously.

Filip Krafth and Jovie Webfoot

Cloud is the silver in a filmic sky. Sun's white as a rose. Filip Krafth, the professional dumpster-picker and street-sweeper, lives in a rented room, cellar-damp, directly above a strip joint that's about the size of a peep-show booth. The cadaverous, Mephistophelean landlord leaves after a war of words. Filip is a sawed-off, razor-boned runt with feldspathoidal flesh, the mien of a malamute, and the eyes of a cartoon tomcat. He reeks of goat cheese. There's something of the Faustian about him, with his passion for the supernatural. "I've sunk to greater depths," he says, putting on his porkpie hat and probosculating upon his situation, sucking on a cinnamon stick like some infantilized hydrocephalic creature, feeling the climate of exhaustion in having to deal with his latest girlfriend, the dit-zoidal creatrix, Jovie Webfoot, standing with an erect posture in an aurora of lamplight, a gender bender who, verily, resembles a walrus wearing a tent. She has multiple personae. She depends on booze to think as a dust particle needs air to float. She's a budding pianistress with pinwheeling eyeballs, uneven nostrils, the skin of a shark, and a whipped cream voice. This stink exudes from her like a sheen. He appears comically disgusted. She is a shallow and ephemeral mendicant, hormonally accelerated, and not exactly the sharpest tool in the box. Her fuchsia feather boa hangs on her neck like something that was strangled. Television, to Jovie, is a calmative. It hampers dreaming. There is an interlude of morbid silence. Her parfleche earlobes glisten with sweat. She's a human nightmare. Her walk is more of a crow-hop. Her tea-colored incisor is tapered as a blackboard pointer. Showers sound not unlike frying eggs. He beholds the broken curb, the padlocked businesses. He chomps on the spinach roll-up as a water buffalo, suffering in the unmercy of sickness. The donut tastes like drywall, the jelly as tallow. Jovie's bronchial chortle drives him bats. Chrissakes! She gets a buzz out of theatrical productions, loud music, crappy romance novels, and random "rumpy-pumpy." Their relationship, paradoxically, unifies and diversifies them. The foreplay earlier was a knot, one loop engaged with the other, thus dynamizing the whole sexual shebang. The deluge's chords drown out the gust's melodies. She's got a severe speech defect. Her antic behavior is maddening. Her gum-chewing sounds like rubber glove-snapping. Filip can't exist in this world, as a bacterium can't live in honey. They are ambuscaded by Peki.

Peki partakes of the anpan with margarine made with Filip's fat and trips. These fist-sized sempervivum are growing out of Filip's armpits. When he pulls on them or tries to tear them off, they bleed profusely.

Luciana Leal

An overweight, snub-nosed indie, a drama queen and grave-robber, a tutor and nanny, a sweet young thing wearing a guard's rig, called Luciana, lives in a solidly constructed, Arts and Crafts-styled, shacky abode with odd-shaped windowpanes and eaves, an oaken door, twisted stairs, and plenty of nooks and crannies. The place is in a dilapidated state, renovation is required pronto. Peki saw her at a street stall at a godawful hour, obviously cock-eyed, and, radiantly attentive, he offered to walk her home. She mumbled and nodded. He felt like a boy who'd hunted and caught a rabbit. Her skin was soft as soil. He glances askance at the archaic water clock and conducts her, gin-soaked, past the lurid plaster statue (purchased illegally from a museum official) into the necrotic-yellow living room, a sensation of bohemian decor. A menagerie of uncanny ceramic creatures, aesthetically brilliant, is situated on the mantelshelf. Brightening marginally, she turns up the gaslight. Her orbs are bugged and speculative. He has an expression like she took a potshot at him. She is strikingly homely-lovely, with unwound mahogany hair, and huge and nut-brown blinders. There is something loose and wicked about her that thrills him. She has impressive buns and calves. She looks absurd and gorgeous. The chaos of cirri converges. A rainbow oil painting is luminescent in every color of the spectrum. He's so dirty it's as if he came out of the earth, not unlike a zombie. He smells of tobacco. He is in a minacious and explosive state of mind, riled like a baited bear. He feels like filth is ingrained in him. Her spoken language he does not even recognize. She's paranoid and screaming. He attempts to calm her. The two sparkle like crossed wires. She looks at him with a haunted stare, speaks in a distracted tone, and insists the magic mirror shows the past and future. Her laugh is more akin to a bark. He makes a sour face. She deftly evades his flirty grasp. He recollects the chain of events that led him here in minute detail. He is groggy, having overslept; a serial killer's hex. He's worn out like a galley slave. She keeps her own troubled counsel. She narrows her gaze and murmurs as though in code and he can't decipher. She sashays, carefree, flaunting herself. The garish dining room's clarity is painful in the walrus-ivory illumination, its tastelessness bold. Luciana's an angel, if not of death then of nonlethality. She has cowslip-yellow teeth. Peki is ravenous. She's an alien. She wishes to satisfy her craving for solitude, in the dark and dust. There are vibes of tension and wariness. He is content as a fly on feces. His life has been so hectic it's as though time is no longer a force. In a tranked narcosis, she strips, the peeling compulsive, clumsy, and daring, divests herself of the woolen garments, slips on see-through lingerie, fishnets, and high-heels, and drapes herself across the couch. Her paralysis is pleasurable. A pot of coffee cools next to the bag of syringes and crack pipes. She is redolent of roses. He says she's a sleepyhead and she smiles cattyly. He cuts a slice from the slab of fruitcake, its starch and sugar outrageous. He is surefooted when on the edge. She's unrestrained, acting as if she's an entertainer aware of her audience's expectations, obligated thus to put on a show. Her now-naked feet have the foul odor of vegetables, both disgusting and fascinating. He has an urge to get on his knees and lick them. She could easily be an Edward Burne-Jones model. There is a tweet, coming from her, dishearteningly distinct, of a bup. She dribbles saliva on her chest. His beard is in direct violation of the law of physics. He dozes for a while in the wicker chair. He wakes because she shakes him. She declares she is a "freethinker and an anarchist," swaying to flute and fiddle music on the radio. Her voice is rich and rings out. She announces her parents came down with croup and died last year, adding she got seriously ill but recovered. She needed a change of air. She ended up befriending a talking parrot named Lou, who regrettably passed recently. Salaciously straddling a nursery rocking chair, she declares she's "financially comfy." Peki does a fairy rollick as if it's part of a play. Luciana deems him shifty and irresponsible.

Her belly button reminds him of a white worm popping out of a pallid apple. Her stomach is sackish. Her intonation becomes creamy. She has perfectly stubby fingers and toes. He bends his head as though reverently. She is dragon-fiery. He cannot control the recrudescent impulses of his homicidal nature. He barely feels connected to the outside world. He knows full well he is in the acute phase of drug-and-alcohol addiction. Her anxiety ratchets up to an alarm. She speaks to him as if he's a baby, which pisses him off a lot. His sphincter tightens. He turns her around like she's a mannequin and hugs and kisses her tummy. When he tongues her nombril, she wriggles in his embrace and shoves him away. They grapple in the fox-reddish fulgor and fall through the screen. On the grass he ragdolls the heck out of her. She issues a choked, wailing cry when he wallops her in the solar plexus with a roundhouse left, and follows this up with a right jab to the ribs. He slaps and mauls her. Her midsection is pig-pink from the blows. She has a fierce fizzog. He has animalic energy. She can't hope to compete. She makes strangled sounds. She has waxily smooth flesh. He wrangles her into a mass of liquescent mud in the backyard and drowns her face-first. Whereupon he, wide-eyed, determined to deliver her from this place, drags her into the hawthorn and hazel hedges by the duck pond in the woods of yew, dry-humps her, biting her shoulder with the strength of a bull terrier, and emits semen. He assesses his ruthless handiwork. And he hallucinates a willowy brunet shepherdess trying to tame an uncooperative peacock in a flowered field. He talks to himself without seeming to pause for breath. Chloral hydrate-addled, his heart drops like a stone, gets a sniff of melted chemicals coming from ovens and chimneys in town. He plays Richard Strauss's 'Salome' on the stereo system. The sky is streaked with several colors of the purple family. The moon resembles a stylized human brain. He sports a Cheshire grin, and sits on the rug for an onanistic interregnum, picturing himself as a runty fakir on a fantabulous carpet. He experiences a delightful tightening of his innards, and scrubs the deceased girl down with a sponge on the bathroom tiles. She is doorpost-plain and narcissus-pale. He stands stock-still and stares. She has plum-pigmented soles. Her cutis is clean and pleasant. Before taking out her fat for the Butyrum, he puts on her fluffy, mulberry-hued slippers, clasps her

Fauntleroy lace collar, and fucks her corpse between the toilet and tub, working himself into a rhythm of elation and a soaring, gloopy ecstasy, calling her a "gone-wrong wench." She has weight and warmth. Then, after covering her cadaver with a robin-red, voluminous, sumptuous shawl, he, wearing long johns, peeks into the billiard room and paneled library. In the cellar, with this sink and a pump, he fetches soap and a towel and washes. He tends to his wounds, scrapes, and scratches, he got from the scuffle. A loft can be reached by a ladder. He climbs and rests on the handcrafted kid's wooden bed, musing on esoteric and astral matters. The sun is snagged in the boughs. Wondrous drawings (hers?) illustrate the walls. Owls call and answer, possessing the night and quietude. Peki sees about supper and a plan. In the kitchen, jets of flame from the stove's burners are blue as the Pied Piper's eyes. He heats the leftover lamb stew. He finds pumpkin pie and blancmange in the fridge for dessert. He gorges the dinner in a shadowy alcove next to a party lantern. He believes he is careful and clever. He will never get caught. She must've been exceedingly privileged, he opines. Probably spoiled rotten. No way in hell could she afford to maintain this property. He takes a long country walk, through a raggedy region of neglected fruit trees, with snarled branches, brambles, lichen, bramble, and moss, watching out for wasps, to clear his tormented mind. He trudges through a salt marsh, crosses a herbaceous border onto a curling lane, and bimbles between sand and sea. Beachgoers arrive at intervals, from near and far, on this flaming day. Fish-shaped leaves swim in place in the zephyrs. His pupils are overdilated and his lungs burn. He doesn't take the relatively fresh oxygen out here for granted. The wild garlic is pungent. He knows he's hardened for life. He is glad for this respite from that brick-and-mortar wilderness with its ten million inhabitants. At any rate, this is an exciting excursion. He pictures Luciana's waist, lion-colored muff, haunches, and ankles. His prick is stiff as a narwhal's tusk. An image of her nude opens a trapdoor in his perverted noggin. He fantasizes she's gangbanged by these gnomic and elfin folks in a frenzy. He envisages her with dragonfly wings and wiry antennae. The vault is butcher-blue. He picks pansies, poppies, crocuses, and daffodils for Marisa at the bank of a flushed river. Sullen fires of campers flicker under the waxing, truly circular disc. Verdure makes deep Wells of shade. He has nits in his mane. Insects hum. He has got to get to the store; he is opening and closing, the manageress on vacation…

Agnes Cheezwhiz

The topsyturvification of her existence began with the first popped Xanax, and the wheel of misfortune stopped, or so it seemed, then and there. Taking drugs, for her, is like a mental dialytic procedure, that is, pulling wastes of thought out of her mind without removing the cerebral substances her brain needs. Agnes, the wannabe sextress, is church-mouse poor, has a vulturous visage, lean like an intravenous pole, stiff as a nutcracker soldier, with dyed-brindle mophead hair, the eyes of a gorak, elongated ears, lopsided mouth, columnar neck, arms the shape of slats, legs not unlike stilts, and feet as the business-ends of shovels. Her axillae are redolent of acetone. Her jaws are vise-tight. She has a deficiency of subcutaneous fat and pancreatic enzymes. She ofttimes vaults life and lands in fantasy. She is so thumpingly dense she requires written instructions on how to pour water out of a boot. Her complexion is unmarked like a blank check. She has a lack of vision and a public persona that has usurped her actual identity. She has already gotten over her roosterish guy, Kyle Marsupial, a loser who'd blundered into her life. Things worked for a while, the welding making sparks. He used to hold her as a sailor would a mast on a ship during a storm. She felt like she was Lear and he was the Fool. Her relationship pursuits have been abject failures, mostly due to varietal misdecisions on her part. She listens to a tape cassette of Tiny Tim, the ukuleleist, totally digging it. A shadow creeps like a sable lizard. These gusts sound not unlike Gregorian chants. Sycamores, on the embankment, are dignified in the flavescent light. The humid air feels like a purifying medium. The foliage has the camo hues of regimentals.

City looks like an illimitable jukebox, with its full spectrum of colors. Agnes uses a phonograph record for a dinner plate. She's an assemblagist when it concerns junk. Her daydream is an aurora borealis, with these radical rosy-ebony streamers of imagery. She is occasionally overobservant and hyperalert. Her cross-eyed, neurotic roommate, Vera Toolshed, with uncountable compulsions, almost always stinking of poultry, a frottage practitioner, distributor of pop-cultural claptrap, and tarot card aficionado, has a pyramidal tress, this angelic phiz, and elephantine body, her head constantly bobbing as a fellatrix's. She is transfiguringly attractive. Even Dante wouldn't dare describe her physical appearance in too much detail. And she could charm the horn off a rhinoceros. Agnes revolves around her in the subleased pigsty like the moon does the earth. Oh, she abrades her nerves. She's a butt for Agnes's blagues, delivered with malicious intent, inspiring, as a result, animosity. The frigidification of the place is because they just don't get along. Their exchanges verge on the vaudevillian. The bathroom smells of sewage. Agnes studies it as a rebus. She's athirst for change like an anarchist is for carnage. Her reflection is sustained. She wishes her problems would deliquesce, as ice blocks, the portions melting and sliding off. An overripe pear is turning. Agnes promises herself she'll never be a laughing stock again. She finds herself mired in quandaries. Vera waits in the wings, ready to enter, like the disarranged room is a stage, and she is an actress in a play production, revealing herself as if a kind of showcase. She is the cause and Agnes is the effect. She's the copy and Agnes is the original. Agnes sings the praises of tip-top Vera, to be nice. Peki ambushes them, hacking, slicing, and dicing, using a samurai sword. The joint suggests an abattoir. He, bathed in blood, intones "how-d'ye-do" to them. If he winds up getting apprehended, is a death sentence the appropriate punishment that's adequate for his crimes? He discharges a triumphant tirade. The cesspool malodor overwhelms his sensitive olfactory organ.

Peki gobbles the lavash smeared with Butyrum containing Agnes' adipose tissue. She is driving down a specific street in her hometown. Ahead of her, she regards a pedestrian crossing the road. As she approaches, she turns... and it is also her. She drives over herself.

Nevermind

The line between reality and irreality is often blurred for Peki. He's struggling with confusing concepts, absurd ideas which clash, and high-flown flights of fancy that continue to ground themselves of their own accord. He feels disappointed, indeed defeated. Faded buildings surround him in this shitty city. His torpor is as if it's caused by a fever. White-hot fulgor burns his exposed skin like brandy does the throat. He imagines his arteries are hard and hollow as though they're grapevines. The rhythmic purring of the rubescent river. Music made by a forlorn cello from somewhere he cannot pinpoint. Fetor of fried food amalgamated with a grungy ashtray. Circus performers execute their well-rehearsed routine in the town square. A scant crowd accumulates. Clowns in baggy, striped, and checkered clothes balance on unicycles on a high wire, polka-dot parasols teeter-tottering on their deformed craniums. The audience stands enthralled in a semicircle in the commodious courtyard. Albinotic acrobats contained in leotards in a whirl of somersaults and cartwheels. A nauseating stench of an alley. Asphalt, requiring paving, is patchy with avian and canine turds. Slate-blue funnels belch. Passers-by are In melancholic resignation. Wharf's warehouses. Creepy-crawly gridlock is a segmented vehicular centipede slinking along. Devastated town is shimmering unfocused in vaporous eddies. Diminishing savan. Sun pokes its head out of a cumulus like a cuckoo from its clock, in slo-mo. Numerous street sellers and their broad gesticulations and booming voices as carnival barkers. Unexpected Mehul jingles like a shaken piggy bank. A bland fellow in standard shirt and slacks toddles, mustache as prickles on a bush. Peki remembers fragments of the narrative of the stage play, entitled 'Nevermind,' that Jorge wrote, directed and starred in: Quarky Wendy Darling, an aspiring actress with a vulpine visage you'd find in an Aesop fable, hardly dainty and not without defects, lives in a flat with brothers, goughy John and rute Michael, and their St. Bernard nursemaid, shaggy ole Nana. Her cogitations feel not unlike dominoes haphazardly strewn. In the shabby apartment, John and Michael, still in their pajamas, are gamboling, neighing like threatened horses, Nana trying, futilely, to rein them in. Penny candy in a hyaloid jar on the coffee table is seemingly their main source of nourishment. She observes them, and gazes as a calf. John chugs like a loco locomotive, Michael huffing and puffing. They're transmogrified into a frenzy of flames commanded by playful urges. Stars are sparks spat out of the sky. A driving dairy truck as a noctambulant toad. Her annoyance has lingered into the afternoon, putting up with their infantile, trivial outbursts earlier this morning. Their diametrically opposed approaches to daily life are obvious. She is so weary of their farfetched poppycock. Her expression is like she's receiving Communion. She's the black sheep of the family. She succumbs to temptation, joining in on the joyous rumpus, and instigates a pillow fight. The trio flail as desperate castaways stuck on a deserted island and spotting a ship. She is afraid their sibling relationship could flop at any given moment. Their friendship is fragile and unstable. They argue about their rinky-dink rebellions against the powers that be. Her coconut trembles like a boiling pot. Roiling clouds. Innumerable papers, windblown, sound as leaves rustling. Gravel percolates under the flattened tires of a psychedelically airbrushed trailer. This place is a mystery. John claims he's a revolutionist caught in a castrating environment. Her uneasiness eats at her viscera like acid. He suggests they can pass out anti-propaganda pamphlets. She puts on her favorite poncho, panties, and sabots, reminds him they're not living in Neverland anymore, and emphasizes this fact. They should scandalize society, he announces, ignoring what she just said. He has a fighting militant spirit, but does he have the pertinent backbone and necessary conviction? The three are butterflies born of caterpillars in a cupboard. He ridicules her "fashion sense," the vastity of her vocabulary, and she smokes as a factory to spite him. They could create a cell group, he announces, handing out illegal flyers. Resuming the rowdy-isms. Screw the ruling class! He shouts, tackling Wendy. Michael rubs his pansa, pinches his pipik, and combs an exasperated Nana.

Breezes sound like children suspiring in bed. Cirri vanish as water down a drain. Muddled dance of brilliance. Insectile cuirasses of cups. Wendy, in a gothic townhouse in wartime/torn London, confronts her parents, George and Mary, from whom she's been estranged for years, and an altercation ensues. It emerges she was physically and psychologically abused by them. She storms out onto the boulevard, sobbing, feeling like a marionette, strings manipulated by an imperceptible puppeteer, tugging at her arms and legs, depression impregnating her gait with a saddened sluggishness, beleaguered by anxiety and melancholy in equal doses, a kind of cosmical conundrum expanding and encompassing her entirety in concentric circles, and is noticed by Peki, impotent and inse-cure, who consoles her. It's a case of love at first sight. They converse and connect. A date is set. She chews her gum as a cow does its cud. He chomps on a carrot like Bugs Bunny. A gust: animalian breath. The veranda is enclosed by a balustrade. She is like a hidden meaning in his life he is compelled to decipher. Horizon is inhabited by cumuli. Winds asthmatically wheeze. Sun emerges as a penis from its sheath. Noon's anti-septic splendor. She's wrapped in a towel with a transparent shower cap on. They twist like amateur contortionists. She does not know where the essence of her existence begins or ends. Humectation is as tumescent as a globose-gravid labonza. Scraggly birches branch out veinously. Average hotel room's counter laden with whiskeys and candies as cocoons. She trots, nude, the multitude of anklets and bracelets tinkling metallinely. Horsed, he daffily waddles like a penguin. A wizened mang with a bald crown slick with protective lotion and squirrely skeleton under sagging dermis sits like a termite-ridden log on a chaise longue and feeds a pack of mutts. Peki's pulsing penile piston. Reaming Wendy, his rod advances and retreats. Wobbly furnishings. She, plowed, feels as if her pupa and brain have changed places. Plump chairs with oriental motifs. His respi-rations sound as though he's blowing rapidly on a pitch pipe. His pencil mustache, elastic mouth, embalmed-rodential rictus. His socks look worm-eaten. She has a lovely weasel's face. Lustrous leather shoes on the canvas stool. She exhumes a tortoiseshell cigarette case from her sequin purse. She was, at first, charmingly shy like an eel. His erection is like an automobile's antenna. His digits tickling her ribs makes you think he is plucking a harp. Ecstasy in his eyes. He is contented as a seal. She appears pallid with insomnia. Concupiscent coos and caws. Bodily impressions on the spread like footprints in the sand. Near naked, (traipsing in her chonies), she arouses the alarming ardency within his perspiry loins. The magical mystery of her russet muff. Satin birdies of her feminine hands and masculine feet. Detective novel with an airbrushed cover is seductively splayed on her lap. Her sphincterial cinnamon pastry swirl is exposed. She parades as a striptease dancer. She is already adept at perceiving him, like divining the lining of a jacket through ripped fabric. Her lactescent stummy is smooth as silk, whisker biscuit ajar like the mouth of a baby bird waiting for the worm from its mom. Forgotten laundry expands the hamper. Dead-animal attire. Moon's a childish eye searching through the gloam for parental guidance. With Superman's X-ray vision, Peki pegs her. He has candor and culture. He holds her skinny neck like a chicken he's about to pluck. Blood in his skull makes it feel like a herniated testicle. Ovaline sun is blinded by clouds over the blob of the burg. Their carnality is a carnival devoid of a crowd. The cadence of a resident quarrel. Siss of surf. Malodorous refuse. He plops recklessly on the amberous aureole of a hemorrhoid pillow and mutters as a strummed zither. Conurbation's decayed serenity. Ripples of her bluk like those on the surface of a well's water when a stone is dropped into it. Their (contained) human odors drown out the city's fetor. They snooze on the cot like eggs in a chicken coop. Maroon splotches gradually develop on them as they feverishly pound. Oblong objects on an aluminum shelf. A plate of nauseating pork beside salt and pepper shakers. Rhapsodies of conversations below on the corner. Hitherto smoggy environment meticulously comes into focus. The corroded pipe is an IV dripping. Hyaline tarantulan candelabrum. He gets scarlet ears from guzzling a glass of bourbon. Her fadoodle and burgundy-blotchy chest from the bonkers doinking. Cig stubs on saucers. Crescentic slices of melon. Discarded dishes of pudding. Her statuesque lamps with substantial elation, aerial ambulation like that of a ballerina. Wendy is stuck in a post-coital coma. His torso hits hers like a bomb. And she remarks it'll take hours to clean up the crap strewed around. Her intestines are akin to burning wire. His scrotum shrinks as the flesh beneath noctambulous operculums. Milky brilliancy. Pearlescent lily padded millpond. This yota hiccups on the lumpen asphalt. A bakkie guns it. Honeycombs of the citizenry's hinds wag. Wavering echoes of gales, getting louder and quieter. Moon's a fish's boiled eye, bugging and blind. Specter of stormclouds eliminates itself. Indigotic surf is rife with floating foam and fibrous pieces of wood. A plastic surgeried giantess with plastic titties, conspicuously bored and disenchanted, traipses. Smazy profile of the block. A dilapidated lighthouse bats uncertainly in the eddying pea soup. Pigeons take wing with lazy indifference. Wendy's face is drawn with fatigue. French fries are left in an ashtray.

The metropolis is swallowed by a throat of pollution. Speechless people, veiled by a drencher, peregrinate, drift as rudderless ships. A schwasted biggith with a fof and teefers bitches. Hullabaloo of collegial millions. They thrive on disturbing the peace by quoting unpopular playwrights, poets, philosophers, and novelists in an unintentionally humorous intellective march. Plentiful plagiarizing. Competent and presentable prosties and their come-hither inclinations. Rancid rage of the nearby dump's miasma. Rays are refracted by effluvium. Pachydermic garage and hulking oaks. Medieval church's bell chimes. Ammonial soaker. Blighted city. Cumuli crawl minerally incrementally. Lamp's upside-down hoop-skirt-shaped bulb tumid with light, its filaments like wriggling insectival antennae. Peki flies into the spacious pantry of his new crash pad, piloted, illusively, by Wendy, that tall redhead with petaliferous lips. It's so sultry it's as if the wen's submerged in a swamp. Her sough sounds like a priest's parp. Crepe-colored celestial sphere. She, looking as a comely ugly duckling, serenely leafs through a sketchbook while he sedulously shaves. She admires his aging actor's cast. The opalescent sheen of the overcast. The digestive rumbling of thunder. Nictating lightning. She's self-conscious when it comes to her cylindroid thighs and spider webbing of varicose veins. Coked severely, her oculi are telescopic. Her molluscoid mouth. Proud chesterfield. Pumpkin seeds spilled on it. Her vart sounds not unlike a punctured tire going flat fast, wades through the slime of sogginess. Before she met him, she felt as though she were a plank, the mussel of desolation nibbling at her. Blood gallopades in her cranium. She is drawn to him like a moth to an illumined pane. He crucifies the pop tune on the fancy stereo. Glass-bead precipitation. In garters, Wendy walks with a bit of difficulty in the high heels. Sterling silverware is scattered on the ceramic tiles. Velvet drapes, Persian carpet, and a bizarre assortment of knickknacks. Her pantyhose bunched in corrugations on the hassock. Squid-pigmented wallpaper. Peki's antiquated shorts. Union picketers vociferate. A pimp with chromic teeth sics his pit bull terrier on a reedy john; hardly a civilized method of resolving a monetary dispute. Mosquitoes multiply in mere minutes. Mizzle is sulfuric acid. Peki's penial heat-seeking missile. Wendy's furtive molest it. He harbors the hope she'll penetrate his keister, rub it like she would running a cloth over the polished surface of a car. He divests himself of the sweater and slacks. A monstrous minstrel plays the accordion, and capably. Dreary hollister, frequented wawa, popular packy sto. An obelisk occupies a granitoid plinth on the esplanade. Dead-end alleys. Glass of azure is cracked by cloudlets. Her pristine paws approach his behind as an undetonated bomb. His larynx floods the ample parlor with cacophonous chords of cries, thumbed thus by her, his snarl exposing uneven, sparkling zubies, face fluorescent. Her minge fringe glistens with diaphoresis.

Butter Geek

There's not much in life that can't be made better with butter. Ain't this the truth. What's not to love about butter's rich, creamy and delicious flavor? Plus, it's so versatile, that it will enhance the taste of anything, from a simple piece of bread to the fanciest gourmet steak. You know you're a total butter nerd when...

You're always prepared. Your fridge is always stocked with butter. No matter the meal, butter is the one topping that tastes good on everything. It doesn't even surprise your friends when they catch you eating butter straight out of the fridge.

You spoil your dinner – on purpose. Let's be real. The only reason you go out to restaurants is for the (bread and) butter. Then you "accidentally" leave no room for the main course. "How rude of them" to taunt you with beautifully textured, perfectly soft butter that you can't resist.

Butter always comes first. Cooking a meal? The first thing to go in the pan, the pot, or the baking dish is always the butter!

You have a list of butter idols. Julia Child, Anthony Bourdain, and the queen of butter herself, Paula Deen are your culinary heroes. You've bookmarked every recipe and relate to their butter obsessions on a deep level.

You own at least one butter candle. Is there anything better than the smell and sound of butter melting in a pan? Nope. That's why you have a secret collection of butter candles. Butter fanatics can bottle up their favorite scent and save it for a rainy day — they can buy them or make their own!

You daydream about butter sculptures. You're mesmerized by the fascinating art that is butter sculpting (and too bad sampling the artwork is frowned upon). At the same time, you're torn thinking of all the other ways you could've used that butter.

You worry about non-butter lovers. It doesn't make sense to you when someone says they do not like butter. How is this even humanly possible?

You have a to-die-for collection of butter dishes. Yup, one for every occasion. Who needs a shoebox full of keychains when you have so many fun ways to show off your favorite cooking staple?

You get excited about the little things. You do a little goofy dance when your favorite brand of butter is on sale (Butyrum!) or when they announce a new butter flavor (have you tried my Garlic & Herb Butter?).

You like bread with your butter. At the end of the day, what's better than some good ol' buttery toast? Using butter that's sea salt flavored, unsalted, garlic herbed, or pumpkin spiced… It doesn't matter the flavor, a buttery muffin always wins.

Peki and Marisa

The conurbation is brought low. It is a wen best to be kept clear of. The presence of an advertisement zeppelin is in its gibbosity. Poison-green herbage. Rust-red sun. Industrial-gray overcast. It was a cloudless and windless noontime. Volant birds wheel. Zephyrian melodic susurrations. An omnibus, reminiscent of an ark, proceeds with ominous slowness. The Rainbow, multicolored, is overbright. A cathedral is indistinct in the murk. Skyscrapers linger against space. His gape remains directed solely to her, no matter where she moves or stands. Peki, not feeling right in the head, garbed in a sporting suit, straw hat, and razor-toed, patent-leather shoes, leans on the door of oak and iron, in the morgue-yellow reful-gence. His eyeballs are ashine with goo. He is so white he looks like midget-shaped light. His hemp makes a rolling fog. His daymare is an exhibition of a bacchanalia with ballet dancer participants, their tutus and slippers cast aside, breathlessly, nubilely, and demonstratively flounder-ing on a marble staircase. Almost debilitated by lientery, innards in a state of mad disorder, just reaching the john would prove an Odyssey. Marisa has parched-by-life skin and a long gray mane. She takes a dram from the foamy stein, getting a head start on alcohol quenching sure to persist into the night. He utters her name in repetition in the echo chamber of the side room, tidy and dustless, the drapes and upholstery in deep hues of puce and malachite. Pre-convo passions are running high. He, unsteady on his feet, visualizes them diving into the saturnalian pool of iniquity. She reads a dime novel and has zero interest in relations with the outer solid world. He is twinkly-eyed and cranked up, bonkers as a bedbug. She's a turkey buzzard of a human being, a total whackjob, but he cuts her some slack. She, in an effulgent episode, admits she feels cooped up, lives an idle, shallow existence, and needs a change of domicile. Nonsense. She's just being daft. She acquaints herself with pachisi. Sun over the stand of maples and walnuts diminishes as if a gaslight's hidden valve is turned off by an invisible hand. Vista is jagged with stars by the uncountable thousands, from his perspective. He's been scrutinizing the upper atmosphere for a while now. Street toughs lecture fitful vendors, utilizing a vernacular of unease as though they are violating the vague rules. Futuristic scenery is an unlit mystery. She polishes utensils at the arcuate table. A clock ticks for them its time. He broaches the subject of them rationing their liquor supply, leading to a funny confab. Peki envisions her as a trapeze girl, dressed in a sequined spandex leotard, spotlighted and swinging upside down by her knees forty feet above a transfixed audience, their cig smoke undulant, in an acid-green palmetto tent. She is floridly faced and emotionless as if obliged to perform. She is spellbindingly splendiferous! The finale involves an interaction between her and an ill-behaved wildebeest, both christened in champagne. The unadorned, terra-cotta apartment building has an aspect of abandonment. There's a plentiful amassment of lowlife specimens in tenancy. Ambiguous babel comes from next door. A symphonic brass, percussion, and woodwind section rip through a lengthy fanfare of a European operetta or musical drama. Installed in her spherelet of self-absorption, she meets his gaze. Her shadow is in possession of her. Glances are exchanged. She commits indecent exposure — his fantasy taking on substance. Her posterior is a portal into another dimension. He takes a keen interest in her behind and bosom. They lead entirely unsynchronized lives. She bends over and pretends to inspect the sizable inventory of margarine sticks in the refrigerator, bringing him to a state comparable to one of drunkenness. Her expression is one of naughty expectancy. The megalopolis, immeasurable stylized wreckage, with an abstract aesthetic, is in a condition of sorrow and wreckage. This is not a place known for its kindness. It is wholly defective. Its inhabitants, their innocence lost, pass for dreams. Gritty municipal workers, with exemplary discipline, sweep the sidewalk, weaving in and out of the city folk. He has turned into one sadistic son of a gun, he thinks. He has sworn an oath to himself to never harm the enfeebled and unprotected.

Anyone else in urban civilization is fair game. He is a creature and this is his home territory. The nights, on account of his murderous sprees, are thoroughly unpleasant. And the days aren't much better, the town reverberant with a panic fear. The killings are constantly occurring so you cannot even analyze or examine them effectively. He's reborn, purified by fire, inflicting his unconditional wrath on the public. He takes his victims by surprise; they never know what hit them. Their bodies turn up in the most random places to confound prediction: alleyways, junkyards, cargo ships, waterways, rooftops, bridges, tunnels, railway stations, etc. Peki makes sure he doesn't let homicidal patterns develop. He strives to keep the law off-kilter. He feels as though he is a being with supernatural powers, unremittingly unleashing it on the populace, terrorizing the multitudes. Most rock concerts and theater productions are canceled (tickets in most cases refundable). Many cinemas, restaurants, and clubs are closed until the perpetrator of these flagitious offenses is caught. The politicians are egesting bricks. The authorities are flabbergasted. Bulletins posted virtually everywhere implore people in broad letters to 'Stay Indoors During Twilight Hours!'... He continually hears the chorale of despair. The population density works wonders for him. Cops pose on the corners: all window dressing. Maritime clag makes the boats semi-visible. Dourly cinereous sky. A seltzerish mist shimmers. Mother and son play cards and shoot dice and later pancake batter-wrestle, got up in skimpy swimmers, in the bathtub.

There is a mental montage of domestic drudgery in Marisa's mind — soaking pots and pans, rusted drains, and knuckles tensed around a scrubbing brush. She's doing her daily chores. She is barefoot and unkempt.

It is as if the region is the target of the storm's spite. He, out of eyeball range, spews his jizzmatoid juice and sinks into a sickbed of desolation. Then he listens to the unmistakable sound of unquiet walking in high heels. Hit with an agonizing hangover from the rotgut (he's a devotee), Peki feels malaria-racked and wishes to return to the encompassing embrace of his mother. He hopes for domestic ease. And he wouldn't say no to a warm shower and home-cooked repast. Nausea leaches his lust away though.

Seething gridlock. Inescapable, vile smog for one to breathe. This construction site pounds uproariously. Townified frenzy. The sun, an intense orange and lemon, declines over the peaceful, spruced valley. Eventide creeps across the megapolis. He remembers depositing the cadaver in a disused mine shaft, a mile deep, surrounded by barren ground, after raping and robbing the sheep-herder, a handsome young man, on a marked grave. He stood above the steep void. He is satisfied that no guilt has taken the unpitying edge from the ebullience of his murderous deeds. There is no ugly or painful truth he is forced to live with. He's balancing an imbalanced universe, righting the wrongs made by the cosmos. His descent into the abyss is on par with going back into a black womb. The law would love to nab him, string him up, or shoot him down. For the authorities, it is nothing but a wild-goose chase. They have no leads. They've got zilch. The cases are unsolved. The long-sought killer is still at large. Yes! The Butyrum unavoidably depends on death-dealing acts. He doesn't discriminate, dispatching lowland peeps and mountain country folk to sea level individuals, a hunter identifying prey, resisting getting all general about his approach. He has created so much excruciating anguish. He realizes his deathly actions are not conducive to public placidity. He, a premiere harmdoer, has far too much work on his hands. The perp has no sympathy for the vics. He's in it for the fun, for the thrill of the stab, choke, club… How did he ever get to this point in his existence? He is a hombre trying, for the life of him, to not succumb to weariness. His gastrocolic condition is sad… Marisa, dressed in an unlined, cap-sleeved merry widow and velvet slides, looks like she comes forth from a lucid (and wet) dream, and he is stoked up to working heat like a poked farm stove. A queer euphoria suffuses his system. The woman, of immoderate lovely homeliness, happens to be of prime interest to him. She's caught in the beam of his admiring eyes. Light occupies the panes. Shadows fill the room. Scintillation declines, departs. She glares at him with an unspoken loathing. Hyped up and freaked out on banned substances, he is apt to see and hear things that aren't really there. She has flesh that reminds him of fine clay. Short-tempered, her inflection is toneless as a cicada. She becomes confessional, blurts out that she's "under unaccustomed pressure," the residence is a "house divided," and that their "conflict is explicit." She can be reassuring as a three-alarm fire. She's been taking amphetamines, tranquilizers, marijuana, Vicodin, Percocet, and abuses heroin. Badges engage in fisticuffs with strikers at the steel mills after the Union and scabs mixed it up, and spilled into the closeby steak house parking lot. Relations worsen. The environment is tense. It's like mortal combat between a couple of full-scale sides, each with its chain of command and tactical goals in this civil war. Posse-size militia units, armed to the teeth with army-issue weaponry, hired guns, professional and amateur, move in from the creekside trail to keep the peace. Mounted police make the rounds in the aspen-filtered radiance. The skyline sprouts fulgurant plumes of many pigments. Badmen hardcases, roughnecks if you please, irradiated by the rays from civic sources, have these unfinished-business miens, bustle about. Anorak chickadees are vibrant as visions. Tourist scum, unwelcome visitors, overwhelm the area. Motorcycles snarl on the strip. People run like hell, behaving not unlike basket cases when the rain starts. Apocalyptic azure over the mountain peaks. Wrecking balled structure is an urban Stonehenge. Its destruction scared the bejee-zus out of mother and son, as it would've anyone with their wits about them, both mightily relieved when the demolition was done. A tramcar leisurely trundles. Peki's grateful for the comforting simplicities of the crash pad. He is in an experimental frame of mind to make mantequilla. He feels as if his arousal is a living organism, growing by the minute, assessing Marisa's abdomen like a husband his beloved wife's pregnant belly. His heartbeat has the sonancy of a drumroll. Remaining free… is it stupid luck, staying out of the pokey? He inhales energetically on the ganja, slowly exhales, and pictures penially plunging into her throat-way. Strong gales feel like he's hit by compression waves. The wallpaper's repeating patterns change into new and vivid panoramic vistas. Shaking his head vigorously. He has the sensation of being out of his body and glissading, without a worry in the world, feeling unbelievably mental. He wants to cop a snooze. He bethinks himself of the mayor's myrmidon, in a T-shirt and knee-britches, an emo he'd mown down with an Uzi in the boscage, the caca on his botty not offering a deterrent to further interest in his person. Peki left him to the critters, forgetting to pile rocks on the defiled corpse. Bathroom's similar to a cargo hold. After putting on a sack suit and jogging sneakers, he departs the commode in some haste. Aromatized candles are lit. Tarot pack left on the air conditioner. His peepers glint with dew emotional. An edifice echoes with desertion. Thunder is a deep rolling growl of doom. Heehawing hoedown eventuates. His duds display laundering inadequacies, including urine splotches, shit stains, food streaks, and butt burns. The window is blurred by his breathing. The scent of the silver woman's soap, a musky fragrance, stirs him. They whoop it up, in the fierce luster, belting out a tune in clashing keys and tempos, the notes bearing components of enthusiast jubilance, the harmonically complicated choruses ineptly sung. Unexpectedly, her testiness gets ratcheted up. He sits on the steamer trunk. She calls him a "squarehead squirt," says he's a "madre corrupter," and that he has "dangerous tastes." He has an ineradicable scowl on his facet, a retinal Perseid meteor shower, and a seasonal event, occurring in his pies. He should buy opiates from his dealer, preferably without incident this time. The crackbrained Jew, notoriously unprincipled, practices his trade to flagrant excess, unsuccessful on a few occasions to retire from his stupefacient drug-dispensing vocation. Vicinity is asidle with aspirant agitators, end-of-shifters, alky-joyous nihilists, easing snakewise. Brothers and sisters share the same struggle. His pupils are reduced to pinpoints. Her algid verbiage comes gusting like a winter gust. The expression on his frontage is set like stone. He is self-schooled in the ways of restraint. They are not on the same psychical frequency. A patch of fluorescent phosphorescence touches her instep. She is flustered by the vehemence of his need. He resents her because she has inflicted damage on his self-worth. She's an expert in the field of intimidation. She can be simultaneously desirable and contemptible. He is demoralized. Coruscation drains away. She peruses a week-old copy of the paper. Her pernicious moue is meant to wither what little self-esteem he has left. And his anima shrivels. His fingers contact her wrist. He ignores her flinch. Is their love a two-way situation? Her shadow takes a part of him.

Peki reclines in a well-tended wicker chair with a trio of battered, dirty-brown cushions in the paneled dining room that smells like fusty books. On psychoactive substances, he sees unnatural nonentities, vibrant hallucinations with terrible energy, haunting his vision, curling into the air like smoke and diffusing themselves. He can't ground his soaring illusions. His liver is acting up, bothering him immensely, as though he is some Lilliputian Prometheus, the glandular organ ripped at by a rapacious bird. He manages his unmentionable pains. His raven hair is unkempt. Marisa, sitting at the table, gazes blankly at the fricassee of chicken on the plate. She squirts her supper with lemon juice. She feels as if her life in the city is like rot in the earth mold. He is motionless as a man turned to stone by a genie, staring abstractedly at her. Her fingers are crooked claws because of arthritis. He studies her like a mathematician attempting to solve a difficult equation. He smiles broadly. His bland brow is creased. She absentmindedly appraises his unpresentable apparel. He suggests they visit the park and a museum tomorrow. She nods sagely. Would her despair be alleviated by his cheerful company? Awkwardly he enfolds her in his arms. A smidge of sparkle has returned to her. And she doesn't know whether to laugh or cry... Leaves rustle brittle in the branches of the trees. The apartment is Marisa's prison. In this place, she feels like a root growing in a grave. Her eyelids are swollen. Her slumber was uneasy, attributed to blood constriction. She tossed and turned in the ghastly moonlight. Peki had lurked in the dark depths, watching her flipping and flopping in a nest of coverlets. She drowsily awakened from a semi-sleep and he came up behind her and fell in step with her en route to the bathroom, putting a firm hand under her elbow. She could scarcely bring herself to grope her way to the lav, overtaken by a dizzy spell. Her symptoms were marginally relieved by the prescription medicine. She trilled on the toilet. The flush sounded infuriated. The oxygen undulates and buzzes with bugs. Bleak breezes. A steady flow of undirected talk. Marisa's comments about him are mean, her mockeries disproportionate. There's no reason to beat around the bush. Does she view him as an object of pity? She aims a poisonous dart at his heart when she behaves like this. Peki copes with the shocks and sorrows. She is all froth and fuss, fits and starts, fizz and furor. She has an urge to clout him and at the same time protect him from the blow. He wants her head to warm his breast. Their relationship is a ship that's going aground, a squall set in. He believes they are what each other needs. His oculi are intent.

Marisa has such an interesting physiognomy. Peki pays her a compliment. Sometimes he feels as though his admiration is an embarrassment. She considers herself lanky and unlovely. Her feet, dusky and leathery, catch his attention. She warbles not unlike a nightingale. He beholds her mane's dangling strands, lustrous and multitudinous. Her long frontal is vacuous. Her legs are a good shape, taut and elegant. He thinks of his many vices and wonders if there are any virtues left in him. His existence is a whole slew of intricate muddles, a seemingly never-ending series of scrapes. He considers the Butyrum as his masterpiece, and the machinery to create it as his monuments. This last week it's been nothing but working and brooding. Oh, and fucking. The fire is slowly sinking. Marisa is encased in eccentricity. Peki looks at her sharply, allowing his fantasy to imagine her nude. He deals with the unappeasable longing. She's a contradictory creature. He wants to be a permanent fixture in her life. She is a trembling human flower. He puffs on a pipe, his shoulders hunched, speaking as though at a lecture. Flushed, his face is red-raw. She can be a callous flirt, heartlessly teasing. She calls it being "abruptly charming." Between them, thoughts are spoken and unspoken. He suppresses his emotions when it comes to their souring partnership. He wishes they'd shuck the seed corn of stubbornness and get it on…

Marisa stands mute as Peki's hand speaks silently to her cheek. She howls like a baby, refusing to be comforted. Whereupon he pulls her like a magnet. He is as sturdy and stumpy as a tree trunk. His blood springs and slams. Her osculations and tactions burn like ice. He feels like a frozen reptile warmed by her body heat. Her husky intonation falters, weakens, and strengthens. When he releases her, their equilibrium is restored. His heart in his chest flutters like a thrush in its nest. In this joint, there is a cool quietness of the tomb. He breathes rapidly and rhythmically. Her liquiform intonation bubbles up to the surface of the convo. She has chalk-white derma layer and coal-black eyes. Hands and feet move like flotsam and jetsam on the surf. She flitters like a fretful mosquito and recites poetry to herself. She is so homely-comely and despondent. He pictures them in conjoined bliss, two-in-one, the carnal passion substantial. She sways in front of him like a snake before the charmer. Is his rapturous devotedness, insane idolatry, ridiculous? He feels like he's in the late stage of exhaustion. She is trembling and morose. Her cosmetic foundation makes it appear as if her countenance is caked with clay. Her gait reminds him of a person walking for the first time after being bedridden for months. She treads hesitantly, imperfectly. Motes of dust hover in lances of emanation. Peki masturbates, parched lips parted, and roars like a lion when he ejaculates. Marisa looks at him, accusing and unappeased. Her flesh is smooth and sweet like a bonbon. She sits, in her shift, gray-white like mist, on the pine chest, in the velvety black shade of the study. Her mind is everywhere and nowhere. He senses she's far away, lost in her wilderness. His stubby digits, the tips sullied mahogany from the nicotine, fumble at his collared shirt's buttons. His breeches are besmirched. His shakers are puffy. She is seated and staring vacantly into diminishing infinity. He thumbs her ear as though to feel her hearing. She's rigid as a rock, her integument clammy and chilly to the touch. He has a dark daydream of smothering her with his generous backside. She walks on the floor like an angel on a grave. Her fingers are long and sinewy. Her callused heels are rough as cheese-graters. She sure is anxious and elusive. She strides and prowls. There's an atmospheric stillness. He snuffs out his Cuban cigar. His respirations rustle as if his throat is packed with birds. His clothes have powerful aromas of horse-piss-and-dung. The corn-yellow fulgor dwindles (because of the adjusted blinds) like a guttering candle. Marisa's head lolls like a lily on its stalk. She preens herself on the barstool like a dove on a windowsill. Then she doubles over from stabbing stomach pain as though she were jabbed in the ribs with an icicle. She inhales and exhales with difficulty. She sees her reflection in the plane of glass. Her feet, purple-veined, are vulnerable and naked. Mother and son verbally communicate, next to the dresser, using their special language, the words hanging over their heads like clouds. There is a sudden gust of her breath's odor, reminding him of corruption. Peki possesses an admiring love for her womanly and manly aspects. She has a feminine sensibility and masculine energy. She's androgynous and gynandrous. Pallid moonshine. Inky night squirts as if from a squid. Peki wishes to pull her back into being, gazing at her with protuberant orbs. Marisa's attitude is an impenetrable fog of vagueness. He feels like a salted wound of a human being. Light gives way to shadow. She stares at him in the face, like death. Verses are akin to voices in her head. He takes to her like a duck to water. She humors him. He protects her. He ambulates. Insects hum assent. He imagines applying his eye to the orifice of her kaleidoscopic asshole where his face rotates. The fecal bits turn into snow crystals. She bears his weight. A spasm of abdominal anguish contorts her expression. He is as inanimate as a side of beef. The moon is curled. Stars sing scintillantly. Hailstones fall like scattered seeds.

Vanesa Grao

Day's beginning to night over. The city has the lights of an amusement park. Its din massacres his hearing. His mouth is a disdainful gash. Rousties on the grounds are like ants on a hill. Constellation of cars are aligned in the outer space of the parking lot. A disjointed concert of engines enters his ears and exits. Fireflies make ellipses. Vapor's like tear gas. Swarms of reflections go on and off the muddy pools. There's widespread discontent. He wants to blow this joint to kingdom come. Rain sounds like a cascade of earthenware crashing on tiles. Skeeters sting with homicidal insistence. Air's suffocating and adhesive. From the suppurating sore of poverty seeps a mucoid sorrow. Foggy smoke. Cotton candy cirri. Papier-mâché people meander, and have the mass movements of a mob. They live with death daily. They circulate, chatter. Peki possesses a regal rigidity, like the king in a deck of cards. He sucks on a sardine. Employed temporarily as a laborer at a carnival, Peki borrows bagpipes from a corpulent clown and plays for the new hire: an enormous bearded lady, named Vanesa Grao. He's dressed in an obsolescent getup. Charmed, she invites him into her gaudy trailer. Her great girth practically erupts out of her flamboyant flamenco outfit. Her heels are too high. Masticating a Caesar salad, her chubby cheeks (with brushstrokes of blushes) go up and down like the buckets of a waterwheel. The rhinocerotic lady has cylindroid curlers in her goatee. His entirety shakes as if with ague. He feels claustrophobic like he's being held in a subterranean dungeon. He fondles his knees as though they're sated testicles, his blinders flashing like miners' lamps. Ulcerous tumescence of the moon.

Her guffaw is free and easy, dancing in all directions, the pimples on her alabaster neck akin to champagne's pink bubbles, soma with a vegetal fetor. Her abundant lard gleams and she articulates like an actress repeating her lines, the material she knows forward and backward. She thumbs through an old family album, fingers as mollusks, amplitude quaking like she's suffering an embolism, blinkers like glistening drops of grape jam, in the opaline illumination. Peki sees etheric eidola and dazzling homuncula, tiny bodies ruddy as blood and with peaky heads. He imagines maddening Marisa, Madonna-glacial, a wraith of a woman, a bewitching, animated scarecrow with bony hands. She is the apple of his eye. If he loses her, who would heal his wounded heart? He covets the idea of grasping her narrow waist. This image tantalizes him. His pulse quickens and his throat dries, thinking of her trim torso. He cannot be evasive with her. He vows to be increasingly forthcoming when it comes to being around her. He wants to be the inseparable companion of his Mama, and become her other half. He used to relish auscultating her stern voice. She can be doting when she wants. This dilapidated dump has rosewood flooring and paneling. A cock crows. A dog barks. Phlegm rattles in his throat, sounding like milk cans in a carried crate. His approach to keeping his career going: shoulder to the boulder and pushing it uphill with all his might! Spell of stormy weather. Sickly fruit is in a ceramic bowl on a rickety table. Blotched pillows are on the flimsy pallet. His burning lamps suggest gas flames in glass globes. Black bear rug. Miserably battered decor. She is distracted by his mobile eyebrows, the guy treading hither-thither on the ashen carpet… Wind howls as though it's hunting for something. Furniture appears to be cowering. A kaleidoscope of astounding colors passes before his vision after he sneezes. He wishes to compose himself for a siesta. Mid-Victorian windows. His forehead is the size of a letterbox. Greasy cushions. He fusses with his fly with blind fingers. His ludicrous galoshes, hooded slicker. He snuffs up her vaginal redolence, reminding him of harbor, with a rapturous sniff. Ocular stars blink. Puddles are ink-black. Meditatively he scrubs his shins with his grubby digits. He has a reptilian gaze. She is grossly overfed. Hailstones click as knitting needles. He is a runty rogue with a hoarse vox. He folds his plump paws. She thinks the humpbacked scalawag is funny-looking.

They huddle, as if from an indiscernible threat. Phloxes in a vase on the counter smell nice. Lozenge-shaped panes. His confident strides are characteristic of a commander. His adrenaline is not unlike a magnetic fluid coursing through his system. His self-worth is something like a metalliferous deposit he'd have to quarry out of himself. He experiences an ecstatic quiver, a phallic buzz. He believes he loves, Roberto hates; he is good, Roberto is evil; he's creative, Roberto's destructive. He has an orgasm of a cognitive nature. A cosmic ripple expands through the planet's rondure. Peki, a gnomic entity unique to himself, is wearing a snug-fitting tweed three-piece, with a morbid odor, and buckled, polished shoes. His breath has a composite stink, one of rotting toadstool and musky herb. Fungoid growths between his toes cause itches he is impelled to scratch. Crows clamorously croak. His fart reeks of damp leaves and the breath of Death itself. He's been heretofore willfully withdrawn. No more.

Vanesa's axillae are freshly deodorized. She wanders as a hippo in a zoo's enclosure. Her lingua franca sputters. Peki follows her, and hangs on her, not unlike a tail. He has the lackadaisical dodder of a roly-poly person. Day-Glo signs tenuously pulsate. A welter of penumbral shapes struggle. The ceiling is concave as a uteritis. It is mouse-gray. Advertisement posters are everywhere. Her pudgy feet stink of broiled lamb. He is bantam as a choirboy, has an ecclesiastical modesty, and skitters like a scorpion. He's awkward and timid in her considerable company. Drizzle crackles as tissue paper being crumpled. The cumuli circle like a phantom merry-go-round. Disconnected racket in the musty oxygen. Her ruminant bones make this grating sound. She is scarlet-faced from liquor. He's tight and tense. Precip sounds like a record player's needle scraping in the disc's groove. His manikin form scuttles like a spider. She floats along the floor, not unlike a swan on a pond's surface. And he compulsively touches his pectoral. It has the brassy coldness of a doorknob. The dumb waiter, with a doghouse-ish opening, vomits a tray of saccharine comestibles. Noises jab him like knives. Ceremonious laughter breaks loose. His joints crack and creak as if they're crunched in a vise. His rictus looks like a monstrous mask in a magnifying mirror. Her expressions are vague and intriguing. He has fierce, hungry eyes. Her visage is painted with makeup. Sleet has the sound of clinking bracelets. She lights a joint with a recalcitrant match. Her halitosis is horrible. She has the breath of a diegetic. His existence has lost its meaning and sense. He looks like an alien from outer space. His labored respirations sound like whirlwinds, volatile thoughts a whiplash. He has these automatic movements. A trump card is an improvised napkin for his chunk of fudge. He stares at a taxidermized owl, the geometrical hedges. Her powdered phiz has an involuted topography of lines. She is like some thickset saurian soaring over him. Time's a nuisance. Life is a ritual at this point. Empyrean is speckled by flints of stars. His ligamentous squeaking as mattress springs. He experiences, alternately, hot and cold flashes, and deals with these indescribable cramps. He walks like an ape. The television set is the size of a threshing machine. Her nails are talons. Peki is tyrannized by Marisa's schizophrenia, her incessant needs. He leans at the grain-beige paneling like a prisoner about to be executed. His baby bird's heart patters. Vanesa holds knitting needles, not unlike drumsticks. Umbrage playing hide-and-seek. Firmament explodes as an aneurism and a squall starts. She tosses dice on the coffee table, making the sound of castanets, her voice loony, pleased as punch. He thinks of Marisa's lunar cheeks. Mizzle tinkles like chimes. Lactescent luminosity. Chestnut welkin. His gut's grumbling has the sound of lowing reindeer. He's indifferent as a mannequin. Her limbs wave like elephants' trunks. He decides, off the cuff, to suffocate her with a cushion. The scene is reminiscent of some surreal madcap slapstick. He taps immense reserves of strength in doing the deed. His purposefulness tilts the scales of possible success in his favor. Her muffled pleas for mercy die away to faint tones... then dwindle to nothing. Whereupon she goes completely limp. His eyes suggest black holes in a rock face. Is he a devil who cannot be exorcised? He has made drastic decisions regarding desperate actions. Second-guessing affects him. Is he careless? Is he leaving forensic clues behind? These are not cautiously-laid schemes. There's no detailed planning. Everything's been improvised. These are impromptu eliminations. He has dragged bodies across wide pastures, along broad roads, and through deep ditches and dense woods, to properly dispose of them so that they will never be found. Umbilical vines vibrate in the winds. He has fought against society's system. He was losing, now he's winning. He washes thoroughly, using a bar of cedar-aromatized soap, at the china basin set on the swivel chair. The water is lukewarm. He picks a cauliflower ear. He presses his flocculent knuckles against his bulging Adam's apple. Saffron grass glows with dew in the autumnal air. Peki pictures touching his dong like a tongue does a hurting incisor. Transparent curtains are as well-washed lungs. He gargles with mint mouthwash, and it sounds like his piss sloshing in his bladder when he ambles. He applies butter (with Vanesa's fat content) on a grilled cheese sandwich and experiences visions. His brain explodes as a mine.

Vanesa's last vision, seen by Peki, after wolfing down the challah, daubed with her butter: she is six or seven. There's this hideous, wrinkled hand sticking out of her bedroom wall. It has blotchy, gray skin, and the nails are yellowed, pointed, and cracked. The thing beats on the floor, accompanied by a thudding drumbeat, commanding her attention, and drawing her to it. She grabs it, and it pulls her through the paneling and into a cage hanging in a cavern. Below her, an unsightly crone is stirring a cauldron full of bubbling goop. The hag maniacally squawks. Vanesa is meant to be the next ingredient.

Nightmare

The lidless eyes of headlights are like those of a maggot displaced from its original accommodation and seeking safe haven. A gale sounds like the howl of murder. Into the murk there now projects a presence that is teratoid and intolerable. The pygmean man's pockmarked and freckled face works spasmodically. He has a slobbering mouth, straggly beard, and dirty neck, lingering at the foul canal lined with plum trees. He reeks of raw gin and gingerbread. There's an ominous quiescence. His Adam's apple jerks up and down. The broodings of his mind produce abominable thoughts. Hairs on his ears grow like fungus on cheese. Suddenly, he becomes still, like some nocturnal animal sensing danger.

Nevermind

In Nevermind, a timorous string of steady creek, turd-tinged, with sludge at the surface and stones at the bottom, has make-believe fish. Mozzies are in ellipses of hyperactive flit. Vibrant birds abscond. Cinematic eve. Harsh, inquisitorial sun. In a Mussolinian structure, with dimly-lit rooms like lairs in alabaster corridors, the nursing home-sterile foyer replete with dry and determined bureaucrats, an obese operator, at the switchboard situated in a cramped cubicle, is divided from another by a flimsy partition. Her inflection sounds distracted and distant, hallow and disagreeable. In the main area, subservient subordinates, nondescript clerks, robotically type documents at their varnished desks, looking like mannequins you'd usually find in crummy shops' display windows, these workers with neutral expressions. Running Nose, an American Indian, and leading official, with a beguiling countenance, petite body, pup's eyes, ossiferous intonation, and a hard-boiled personality, acting as though she's part of a class that's regularly exploited, in her office suggesting an interrogation chamber of some crappy third-world country, with an incomingruous saloon mirror, token faux modern masterpieces, distinctive landscape watercolor, narrow davenport, and generic file cabinets, the sneaking light filtered by the diaphanous curtains, offers to release Peki only if he can capture Roberto, who should be brought to justice for his countless crimes. A Chopin Nocturne spins on the vintage turntable. A shadeless lamp flickers. The place is even equipped with a room service-type buzzer he notices. Nerve-grating noises come from the hall. Oppressive silence. Her personal bodyguard, bouncer-burly Injun

Chubby Chief. His asthmatoid respirating. Peki ultimately agrees to the terms of the deal, hawks a loogie on his palm, and shakes hands with Running Nose. He eventually locates Luis, the bifocaled, poor sap, the miserable microbe with a paramecium's encephalon, absorbed in sweaty suet, inches of ash bending precariously at his butt's end, facially red not from rage but, instead, alcohol, lingering at a bar, and beats him senseless for selling him out. He leaves a napkin with an address written on it for him to pass on to Roberto, that vain, vile, pompous swine, a foppish prig, preening villain, with his long, curly wig Charles I would've worn, who, assuredly, is looking for Luis. Peki had stolen a portion of Roberto's treasure and plans on trading it in return for his shadow.

Marisa Found

Peki has had enough of the shitty episodes in his everyday existence, his life's consistent lethargy, the unmatching bargain furniture, and the overall garbage of the populace. He's liquefied with loneliness and fatigue. He thinks of Vanesa's shoat's eyes and anemic jowls, in motion like a weary sloth. He doesn't stand pat when it comes to business. He will not resist change. He'll budge. He believes you will go under if you don't adapt to trends and refuse to modernize. Luminescence expands and contracts as a digesting intestine. He slurps his lobster bisque out of a styrofoam cup. Squamous glaucescence of the brine. He is too deep in these occupational waters. Hail hits the asphalt and sounds like false teeth clacking. He remembers Marisa flopping like a crippled butterfly. Her feet were like those of a crane. Her arms and legs were remindful of strings of spaghetti. She's sexy when discalced. Spate and squalls stop, as if both sides agree to a peace treaty. Fly of leven unzips. Upon returning home, he discovers Marisa naked, bloodied, cut, and bruised, cringing and whining on an upholstered footstool. She's drunk. He notices drops of tobacco juice on the floor and recalls Roberto chewing the stuff. Turns out, that Roberto came here to taunt him further and was confronted by his mother. Trams stream by. Skeletal scaffolding. Parade of persons. Spritz is like damp dust. Cranes and tugs are bunched on the pier. Peki puts out his products on the sales floor, dividing them as though they are precious spoils, in proximity to the archaic cash register. He counts the scratches on the skylight.

Roberto

Roberto, slanky, with an Ichabod Crane schnozzola and Dudley Do-Right jaw, in the lamentable motel on a muddied road, slumps, lollygagging, on the florid settee in the ocherous luminosity. Brochures on the austere reception desk were like cards on a casino table. The minuscule, uniformed, Asian guard was bulging as a peen in erectility. He had on a toupee, tie, and holster belt. A whirlwind of turtledoves. The pitch periwig is lopsided on his glabrate skull, moving slow and slippery like seaweed in the toasty draughts. Tacky furniture is brownish from too much smoke. Moroccan rug has the hues of scurvied gums. His body on the bed bent like a folding blade. The cirri unravel like frayed civvies. Botanical surplus. Cypresses are muculent with dew. Interrogative tones of discourse. The mellifluous ferocity of the gales. Ill-defined, puerile persons in the umbra slinking as slugs. Shrubbery's shoulders shrug. Bombastic bickering. Ravel's 'Bolero' gets cranked to deafening volume. A couple of stars are the disengaged eyes of a registrar. The impersonality of the decor. His slack limbs waver like kelp in water. Precipitation is akin to pus. Hesitant honks from horns are interspersed with insistent beeps. Condensation coats the shingles. Shipwreck of a pawnshop. Tuxedoed Eastern Indian. Wet stuff spits not unlike jets squirted from those gag rubberoid bulbs. Drapes are painters' palettes-semblant. Bald plateau. Epileptic empyrean has a seizure, and foams with flooding rain. Meadow is funereally somber, smooth, and flat as a stomach. He's hygienically attentive. Renny tipped. Dinosaurian yugos, bimmas, stulos, beaters, jaaags, oreos, scoobies, benzes, and minivans, with headlights for peepers, lumber through the prehistoric metroplis, watched closely by Romulans.

Plumbing periodically burps its gases. He picked this dive, by the way, to remain out of sight, off the grid, as it were. He regrets the decision. Useless sports rags gathered in the walnut cabinet with its glass doors. It's eerily tomb-quiet, at least for the nonce. He hears scraps of ardent dialogue. The stocky Eskimoid janitor, with a dulcet modulation and in Franciscan sandals with tire-rubber soles, was too chummy to abide, told unfunny jokes with ambiguous punchlines. Sun pops through the cumulus like a navel out from under a tee. He sniffs a line of Bernice using a tightly rolled gallah off the coffee table. The firmament shakes spasmodically. Languid glissade of traffic. Trafficators malfunctioning. Suicidal sweeving. Mouth of the welkin is wrenched wide. Street spam. Fulgent fraction the nucleus of glimmer inhabited by an inert roach. A helicopter hiccoughs over the highway. His breville sounds like clattering cans on a newlyweds' jalopy. He pulls a packet of dipsky out of his pocket with the alacrity of a magician, brandishes a pint of kossu. Krunked on drooze. Stickiness as soup. The snoose tucked snugly between cheek and gum. He wants to lie like a log for a month. No seafaring adventures, raping, and pillaging for a while. Fireflies flitter like fanned embers. Sporadic mizzle. Effulgence has the resonance of a butterfly's wings. Oppressive mustiness is almost suffocating. The pool is like curdled milk. Shore of mire. Oceanic ovations. Noisomeness stain-spreads. Millimetrical chiggers, male and female, stark white, as troglodytes, lingering at a conservatory entrance. The lugubrious pace of passers-by, undeniably anonymous, verily indistinguishable. Succession of turquoise waves. Rain-parturient stint. He lounges like a lazybones. Quivering distress of the row of willows. Compact quietude. Rundown avant-garde theater. Crate brims with baubles and trinkets and such (from Davy Jones's Locker) like an excavated colossal creatural cranium. Ethanol breath of his bup. Manducating on gangker. Thunderous drumroll. Lightning's pyrotechnicsnarenon display. Bombazine briefs. His charcoaled, Armenoid unibrow, carbonized larynx, disdainful yap, neck like a water-ravaged rope, wilderness of a darn darwin sweater, inflexible attitude, and imperative uppishness. He is a floofer who loves his chush. Wilted-fleshed Roberto has got an impressive chestal thicket. Breakers have the sound of bursts of audience applause, the combers in unanimous frenzy. Swathed in a teal towel (worn like a toga) he looks as a merman reeled into the honey wagon, the bathroom like a ticket booth. A passage from 'Carmen' on the glistering gramophone. He tends to his ablutions with the sterile expertise and economy of a nurse. Lizards of refulgence slither on the wood flooring. He masticates cope. Decrepit furnishings. Brilliancy is she'd serpentoid skin. Ceiling is the pigment of dried tobacco. His purple pantaloons are secured by clothespins. Lusterless vegetation. A g-ride hacks in a phosphorescent nimbus. His ludwig, or hairhat, is seemingly electrified in the waftage. Shampes, nautical-themed, on his spindly arms and legs. The clouds dissipate into smithereens. Unintelligible phrases are issued by a hobo. Syrupy puddles. Dandelion heads bow politely to one another. Brine pants with fatigue. Phlegmatic gurgles from the piping. He sits on the springless seat, mummy fingers and toes flexing, and scarfs the stale cookies that had spent an eternity in the cupboard. His varied heraldic rings have plenty of brilliant bling. He's tuckered, tired of voyaging. Bathmat's like sandpaper. Roberto's gorilla salad's dead insecteous legs, slong a limp hose, heart raging like fire, tread comparable to that of a chary stork, his mind laboring like a mole. Gypsean nubile nymphets, craving, clearly, unconditional adoration, with ponytails, olivaceous integument, caper in florid mailots. Pleats of the crests, folding and unfolding. His sweat smokes as lye. Hispanic maid with a raven's voice has the physique of an exclamation mark. He magpie-squawks at her for interrupting his train of thought. His crispy socks are rolled like tubes of toothpaste. Skeletal slate of the shutters. His plune breaks free from the jock. Mesas appear to dissolve into the cover of cloud. His scrutinating, mucilaginous orbs. Horizon is furrowed with grooves of cloudlets, ostensibly a thinking forehead in its immensity. A break to recharge his batteries, and regain his inspiration for pirating, is essential. Worries grow on his brain as moss as a boulder. Designer desk lamp. Auto pandemonium. Blades of grass are osseous phalanges. Lightning bugs are itsy-bitsy paper lanterns. The stubborn insistence of the gales' siege. Housekeepers and landscapers are correct and mannerly. The elevator is inoperable. The eyelets of his clodhoppers are the size of bottle caps. Blowtorch flame-tips of glow flies. Infernal calescence. This lettuce-green joint is shaped like Noah's ark. Staffs of skeeters, notes sorta snively. The morning had inflated, and the afternoon had deflated. Will Luis, built like a hard-boiled egg and with elephantine ankles, sniff him out as a doggie distinguishing its master? The Tom Thumb's obnoxiousness is exasperating. Fireworks exhibition of fulguration. These llamas perform an irrational sketch in a slate-grey veldt. Heaven's cobalt begins to darken not unlike a pupil when one falls asleep. Combustible chiaroscuro. The day comes from the night as a patient from a coma.

Roberto's father, Sergio, resembling a rotund, strunk Errol Flynn, a voracious reader of pulp mags, with a carnivorous intonation, abused his authority in the household. He looked like the figure of a clay friar in later years, or a bulby newborn. He had tree trunk legs, and arms as boughs. Roberto felt not unlike a fragile eggshell whenever in his presence, he could crumble at any given moment. His diminutive inflection. He'd stare with spellbound appreciation, managing to maintain his composure, blood jaunting. Their house was a hellish hive of dysfunction, the place permeated by loudspeaker music. Sad hexagonal rooms had livid walls. Woolly, humongous hedges. Neglected yard. His mother, the elfin Irene, who spoke in squeals and squeaks, voice the equivalent of needles jabbing your ears, resemnling a schwilly Esther Williams (with dyed platinum bowl-cut) if she let herself go, belonged to a traveling vaudevillian troupe, and dressed as a toreador with a cardinal rubber ball for a schnoz, dunce cap, and floppy galoshes, her comedy routines ceaseless, executed daily, operatically belting (God, was she capable of hitting those high notes), slapping and kicking, to everyone's dismay. Her gristly fingers and toes and the fleshy mesh of her feet as a duck's provoked profound disgust in him. She toured the circus circuit and was a temp bank teller, but her slapstick antics rarely went over well at the branch she was employed at. For practice she would form a ring of lawn chairs and tie her son to a target and throw knives and use a bullwhip and shoot arrows from the bow, traumatizing the lad. If he got steeched (on the verge of a coma), customarily sneakily, he could be in a (preferred) state of drowsy resignation. She rehearsed her repertoire religiously. She would wear voluminous Japanese robes and slippers occasionaly. Her drugstore makeup was a paste of cheap cosmetics. And could she employ a powder puff! Cracks would materialize in the foundation, like ones in a cement wall. To him, her perfume was RAID and he was a fly. Her odd orangutan fetish, interminable moue, voluptuous get along's pace, wine-rich sweat, long, glittery, artificial lashes, like peacock tails, global jumms, and elephantine wrinkliness of cellulite he always noticed. Her countenance would fragmentize, as though pieces of a jigsaw puzzle, detaching themselves once it was, at last, finished. Her radical tittoos, frumby. She sought refuge in the saunas at the Turkish bath. With her metallic braces, her woolly dentata suggested birdseed. At the workplace, she acted as a heartburn-affected jester, with her funny faces and spastic movements, pretended the clients were critics critiquing her, until, finally, she got canned by her squint-eyed, dim-witted boss, an uncouth creature with an asymmetric countenance and sour simper, much to her husband's chagrin. She had a thorough commitment to her artistic duty, like some dedicated civil servant, making the necessary sacrifices to the mission of self-expression. His wife was self-defeatedly eccentric. The habits of the married couple were wacky, to say the least. There were interregnums of hostility mixed with interludes of tenderness, sexual dissatisfaction, flaunted infidelities, umpteen separations, and untold marital misunderstandings. Fettling, Dad climaxed as clockwork. Mom imposed her verbal imagination through a convoluted network of self-indulgent verbosity afterward. Her illegitimately prescribed cheaters were thick as manhole covers. She, the quirky bird, once tore her face away from his as a moth's wing from a lepidopterist's pin. Sepulchral quietness. She had a vacant character, and he signified a sulky teenager. He was wearing long johns. She was nightgowned. He fumbled in fingering her as if he were using chopsticks (for the first time) on sweet and sour pork. Helter-skelter flickering of resplendent lances. She loped like a shooed-off turkey, but not before he lethargically diddled with her, again, on the couch. His pinky was an avid corkscrew up her butt. She was a certifiable neurotic, a bonafide bohemian he handled with considerable calm. Her bangs were blunt. He chose to wallow in the mire. She changed outfits with the semi-occasional voracity of a chameleon switching its colors. Roberto's emotional upheavals were unreal. Sergio was a strapping gent, a tower of power, a road-grader, a skilled saxophonist in a local jazz band that played the coolest, happening clubs, and was a part-time stonemason when gigs were sparse. He gazed upon his scrawny and meek boy, a castaway domestically adrift, contemptuously. Irene was vampish, vampiric, blew on nuggets, spun around as an aspiring top, sank her fangs into Roberto's neck, and sucked on him on the cartilaginous spiral of stairs. The sun inflamed the cirri. Her scapula was like a folding fan. She smoked her fair share of yam. Dice was her favorite. He got a glimpse of her rubious, hirsute sphincterate rose when she scrubbed herself with a bar of sample-sized soap in the steamy shower, her pendulous buttocks castigating one another when she moved. Then she pulled off episodes of handstands. Splotches of her rouge. Croned, her Dutchboy a chromoid jellyfish splattered on her skull, she moved as though she was a cockatoo winging, or natating, through a window washer. The gaseous form of her fades. He was a perpetually pebbled, sensitive youngster and clinically depressed in the uninteresting domicile. He felt useless not unlike a burnerless stove; or like a fungus on a riverbank. His shameless subservience. And his fakir's dfc, cowpoke's hands, basketballer's feet. No moobs here. Too many unpleasant incidents piled up in that loony bin. Linoleum was carpeted with her skimpy lingerie.

Roberto, blood stopwatch-ticking, brushes his glistening camel's teeth, puts on his cartoonish pierrot-suit of camel-hair nightclothes, and hits the hay. Skittering hamsterish pitter-patterIng of his heartbeat. Kinky cord of the terra cotta telephone. Gargantuan cop patrols. The jumbled mass of crap on the Formica nightstand is like the emptied contents of a woman's pocketbook. Visceral sounds of the ocean. He tosses and turns in the sack, pops a tranquilizer, remembers that traitor Luis's hemorrhoidal minger, smelly stocking hat on his head as a filmed Roman lawmaker's crown, the cursed mutineer's fotch vexed by warts, "surag" whiny like a trombone, avoirdupois, amorphous anatomy, and these disconnected buccaneering events in the way different vocalizations mix. Visual and audio. His goose is cooked. Roberto is going to derive significant and perverse pleasure in prolonging the son of a bitch's suffering. He'll hook him as a butcher would a slab of meat and chop the beef up, with stupendous control, and magnificent execution, on the block.

Possibilities are virtually limitless. In the bowels of the building, he hears too much. A bum in a leotard proceeds sluggardly like a deep-sea diver. Leaves dangle from trees as the roots of hanged men. Identical high-rises raptly watch. Asthmatoid drink's tide. A far-flung bevy of boats. He conks out. Accusatory silences of twilight. Stars nictitate like fish's fins in crystalline aqua pura. Soundless scream of space. Putrefacient-plum vault. Santa Claus beards of cumuli. The tumult of a tempest. Piping babbles. Humidness is akin to eczema cream. The draft is vibrant like a cello. Gloaming crouches. A viscous odor emanates from his planate der-rière. Sewer stench swirls around as a smoke ring. Discotheque lightning. Off-the-wall mob of stevedores makes a hurly-burly on the docks. These openmouthed peacemakers osmose. Carnival streamers of clouds. Storm's deafening roar: Last Judgment. Daily tricks, nightly sleights of hand. Countryside, in the roiling smaze, assembles and disassembles itself — a purportless puzzle. The courtyard is comparable to a drumhead. Gloppy shellac of his spittle. He feels gobbled by the quadrate trap of a haunted house. A hurried multitude of denizens. Excessive and unpitying heat. Roberto finds the spheroid Smee in a tavern. He looks like a cartoon character on a bubble gum wrapper, and exists in mortal sin. He feels like Captain Bligh, and Luis Fletcher Christian, both on the Bounty. Luis, glomming rock-hard doughnuts, and croissants not unlike pumice stones, bleats and gives him the napkin. His bitonal skrieks. Thunder sounds not unlike cymbals clapping. Stars are spurs. The Captain wolfs down cheese appetizers, sinks his hook into Luis' nuque, and drags him screaming to the ship. There, he makes him walk the plank, a monstrous octopus waiting in the topazine water below.

In a realm where Nevermind and Spain are mysteriously merged, Roberto travels to the address: a zoo, situated, inexplicably, in a slum's godforsaken neighborhood. Peki and Jorge are there, holding hands and watching the animals in their cages. The Darlings are indulging in a saturnalia in a paddock. Peki wonders whether or not Roberto is a figment of his imag-ination. They get into a hassle, a fight breaking out, even their shadows, handcuffed, chained together like Sydney Poitier and Tony Curtis in 'The Defiant Ones;' or as Hammer and Anvil from Marvel Comics, engaging in fisticuffs. Roberto stabs Peki with his sword; however, when he goes to finish him off, a familiar, taunting ticking of a clock distracts him and he pauses, when Jorge pushes him into the crocodile tank and he is eaten alive. This is the end, hook, line, and sinker.

In the butter biz, Peki is an unapologetic jackass of a hero, a James Bond if the spy had attended Delta Tau Chi instead of Eton.

Ragnhild Thorsby

The nude, rumbustious occultists, male and female, twist and turn in the stormy convoy, suggesting a coital frenzy, riding the tempest like a tidal wave, going to their Sabbath, frolicking mid-flight, to and fro, with palpable eroticism, wrapped in the ecstasy of the moment, after fornicating with the devil, in the form of a goat, the bacchanal held in their secret place in the petrified woods. The dead, along with monsters and animals, are an integral part of the orgiastic madness in the weltering sky. A beldame, with her aged features and pretzeled anatomy, reaches for her carrot-topped, feminal protege. This is a caress of passion. Ragnhild, her skull shaped like a butcher's cleaver, with a Joan of Arc haircut, tormented hen's eyes, and ondine visage, gerbil cheeks overrouged, wears a conoid gnome hat and fruit-colored, misfitting clothing that looks almost edible. The twenty-something elfette is thoroughly wasted, goose-stepping while eating lunchmeats and drinking daiquiris, with her mooseish, incandescently pretty, bugle-bosomed lover, Stine Lode, passed out on the palette in the garbage can-gray and sedum-pink loft. The club across the street, hopping and slamming, is intimate, sophisticated, and smoky. Stars have a metalline shine. Clouds open like Chinese paper umbrellas. A voluptuous, redheaded witch, named Berit, naked as Praxiteles' Aphrodite marble sculpture, has an anserine aspect and ice-blue eyes, her slender hands stroboscopically flittering. She has materialized out of nowhere. She has a strangulated voice, spewing glossolalia, leaning her flying broom against the wall. She moves like a liquid. Her curly mane resembles the flame from hell. There's an abysm of silence. Ragnhild, now in her chiffon panties and leather bra, notices the brazen intruder has lilac veinal tributaries on her wan calves and a diamond toe ring. Suddenly, the trespasser titters and pony-struts exhibitionistically, delivering diabolical hissing, sucking, and kissing sounds, whereupon she magically levitates and rotates like a pinwheel, raking across the ceiling like lightning, startling the shit out of Ragnhild. Her heart sinks and her stomach convulses. She absentmindedly drops her underwear and brassiere like a tree does its leaves, perplexed in upside-downness, face a blank of detached zombieism. Her snow-white skin shines with sweat. Sphincter-looseningly nervous, she gazes at the Wiccan woman's pliant, pale body, perfect back, ductile belly, and helical nombril. She squeaks when she's goosed. Berit's fingers flicker, making these lewd come-hither motions, orbs currently with a jewel luster, narrowed in an avid squint, and she limbo-walks. Darkness encompasses everything. Ragnhild sprawls on the floor, pelvis rising and falling, her being orgasmically trembling. Her excitement has the weight of an avalanche. She has fallen apart, wayward in the blackout of arousal. Her nipples are hard and her feet are dirty. Serpentine sweat slithers down her sides. Is the seductive sorceress planning to steal her soul? Is she in the grip of a hallucination? Giggling girlishly, Berit slowly bends her head backward, crown contacting her scapulae, palms mimicking the touching of her crotch masturbatory-wise, furious oculi sprinkled with sparkling retinal fires. Then she leans forward, pears of her breasts swinging not unlike bell-clappers, fleshly hips shimmying, supple thighs shaking. Ragnhild sits up. Berit, wild and hot, expression intense, obscenely gyrates, sensuous mouth agape, does splits, crawls on all fours, and provocatively rolls, tresses thrashing around. A demonic vision, she snarls and squats, cavorts about, grinds like a lap dancer over Ragnhild in concentric circles. Ragnhild holds her gut as if she was shot. An ache pierces her brow. Her reality is corrected by trickery. She feels as though she is becoming less sane with every passing second. Her closed eyes open in disbelieving inattention. Phosphenes swirl like embers. Her cardiac organ pounds not unlike a concert drum. There's double-talk between the two. An amorous arrow penetrates Ragnhild's thunderous chest. An impenetrable gloom hangs like sable drapery. She feels empty like a sock puppet without a hand. Her pride has gotten lost in the worship of the sexy necromancer. Why won't Stine wake? Is she that soundly asleep? Jesus fucking Christ! She haws and hoos and dispenses saturnalian shouts. The brooding fog is as unfathomable as the deepest beyond. With a whinnying screech, Berit abruptly whirls and is gone into thin air. The dawn is sterile and pulseless. It changes shape and dissolves. Just so. Ragnhild opines that love is a torturer, lust is an executioner, and that death is a virtue, life is a vice. 'O, how much more doth beauty beauteous seem,' she thinks of the Shakespeare quote, 'By that sweet ornament which truth doth give.'

Peki knocks at the door.

Darkness is Peki's light. It shines on him as a sort of benediction. He is afraid of living and dying. And he still feels incompatible with society. His existence doesn't register. What is he to do? Before the Butyrum, there was nothing but a series of dead ends; now there is the open road. Life can be unendurable and pointless. Headachy neon lights are too much to bear. Ragnhild is gone. Forever and ever. Her roommate as well. He brutally ambushed them, with extreme fury, his rage desperately uncontained. He opened them up with intemperate slashes and stabs of the sharp blade in a spate of lunacy. He believes he is a mental case with blood on his hands. He hopes he is never forced to confront the consequences. The irreversible implications of what he has done, and not on a sudden impulse, scares him. The finality of it frightens him. He could go for an efficacious tranquilizer and stiff drink... The smoking gun is the vat of butter. His hold on reality has slipped. Are the police lying in wait? Will the authorities spring a trap? He fancies himself a genius Rumpelstiltskin, only instead of spinning straw into gold, it's mantequilla he churns into cash. Depthless upper atmosphere. Inscrutable gloaming. Ghostly brume. Seesawing angst and anger rise and fall within him. He longs for oblivion. His chest feels as empty as a cenotaph. Is he simply being moody? He should start again, rebuild his life. His breathing has the sonance of croupy wheezing. His countenance is lined like cracked crockery. The sea's fizzing sounds not unlike a radio that's lost its tuning. His azoic eyes gaze at the stumbling drunks and puppety prosties. They gab. His dervish shadow kind of whirls. Conscience slaughters his soul. He took unreckonable amounts of codeine. A pigeon-kneed pimp with Harold Lloyd spectacles has the cinereous flesh of a fish and sugarloaf-looking middle and beercan-shaped butt-cheeks. It appears as if light and shadow have made a pact with each other to coexist. He moves into the underworld like a person being pursued and thinks of his Mama's diary, which is a written portrait of herself, and an honest autobiography. He knows he shouldn't have read it. Her virtuoso instability can be endearing. He imagines her long, prehensile toes… He feels like a bird seeking a cage. The storm in his mind is untrackable. Doppler radar of his grey matter isn't functioning properly. There is an almost sacramental silence. The tenebrosity is transfinite nothingness. He's fractured with despair and mute with sorrow. He is a candle in the tallow of misery. Metronomic clanking comes from the nearby metro. He has the sensation he is living in multiple realities. The strings of his existence remain mistuned. He feels like he's a piece of clockwork running down and needing a winding up… There's a faraway fullness to the empyrean. The moon, at its apogee, is in conjunction with the taupe clouds. He hears the vague sounds of conversation. A godwit-slender slattern with a bland mug hiccoughs like a calliope and crow-hops, swigging martinis in the wet wind. He feels like a human form without weight. Night transmogrifies into day. Tide shrills over the shore. Peki moves swiftly, scurrying like a squirrel as if to get away from himself. The megapolis seems irregular, interminable. He drinks hard liquor and eats fried rice at a diner. Later on, he begins to feel ill. The buildup of earwax is bothering him. He has unholy thoughts. The city is a deformed mess. A rummy, white as paper, with sly eyes and a buzz-cut, has the intonation of an auctioneer. Glow flies are frenetic sparks arcing. He marches robotically, staring catatonically.

Carton Packaging Of Butter

It goes without saying that the invention of the Peters' package as well as those of the Howe silicated carton and the Vavra high gloss paraffined carton opened up new opportunities for the merchandising of butter. The individual packaging of crackers got underway rapidly because of the consolidations that Editor Willson referred to. In addition, a development of considerable importance was the building in 1900 by the E. G. Staude Manufacturing Company of a shell carton machine. (U.S. Patent 730,410, June 9, 1903) for the Heywood Manufacturing Company, Minneapolis, Minnesota, which machine was to make two-pound folding cartons for Quaker Oats. According to Bettendorf, this machine took the printed board from a roll and cut and creased the cartons at the rate of ninety per minute. Staude later built and patented similar and improved machines for Cream of Wheat Company, Minneapolis, Minnesota; Ralston Purina Company, St. Louis, Missouri; Shredded Wheat Company, Niagara Falls, New York; the Larkin Company, Buffalo, New York; Fels and Company, Philadelphia, Pennsylvania; Postum Cereal Company, Battle Creek, Michigan; and the W. K. Kellogg Toasted Com Flake Company, Battle Creek Michigan. By 1909 the machine had been improved so that it would cut and crease "wet" printed stock from a web, strip the waste, and deliver two hundred box blanks per minute. It is this type of machine that is used for very long runs of cartons, printed or unprinted and glued or of the unglued over-wrapped type. The butter industry was not prepared to undertake the mass production of cartooned butter at the start of the 20th Century as the means for so doing were not available either in its production facilities or in the supply of the paraffined cartons themselves. Automatic molding, wrapping, and packing of butter prints were unknown although the industry was on the threshold of a tremendous expansion not only in production but in the development of its art. Such mechanical aids as the combined churn and worker (and incidentally 40 years later the "roll-less churn") mechanical refrigeration for processing and storage, pasteurizing equipment for batch and continuous operations, cream ripening and holding vats, neutralizing practices to enhance keeping quality and reduce churning losses of fat, and transportation and marketing were all waiting for their advent. Then too, in the production of cartons themselves, their fabrication from virgin pulp and their volume manufacture as well as multi-color printing and modern attention-compelling patterns were all developments still to be envisioned and created. To convey some appreciation of the momentum that the creamery system did generate following the turn of the 20th Century, we have only to point out that in 1908 more patents were issued for butter churns than for any other device. The Continental Creamery Company and later the Beatrice Creamery Company were able to take advantage of the potential markets for their Meadow Gold Butter in the Peters' "Inner-Seal" package as well as they did only with the most strenuous efforts. According to Tom Borman, at the time general superintendent of the Topeka, Kansas plant of the Continental Creamery, "some of the prints were made manually with punch blocks after the butter had been permitted to chill and firm up." Oftentimes the butter was cut from the tubs using a former machine designed to cut one-pound prints from tubbed or boxed butter. The scraps were then collected and prints were made up with punch blocks. Continental Creamery first used the 'Inner-Seal' carton with a manual operation later using a cumbersome machine designed by Mr. Peters, which performed the entire operation mechanically and increased the production enormously. This machine which had been designed and constructed rather hastily required almost constant attention and supervision by a trained mechanic. Nevertheless, the success of Continental and Beatrice in discovering and establishing a market for cartooned butter, served to interest other factors in the industry to serve the apparent demand. Early in the 1900s, the Blue Valley Creamery

Company of Chicago, Illinois spent considerable money in inaugurating the production and distribution of pound prints packed in cartons in the markets they were serving of which the City of Chicago was a considerable one. Fairmont Creamery Company of Omaha, Nebraska was not slow in realizing the marketing appeal of carton butter, and early in the 1900's they also prepared to meet the mounting demand, as did other creamery organizations.

Peki and Marisa

Peki has a rooster-in-the-morn type of energy, out of the typical nowhere. He'd stayed late at the pool-and-gambling parlor, his favorite illicit refuge, a dim, sunken chamber, the building painted celadon, and with corrugated roofing, the joint racketing with patrons and hirelings, jammed with gloating winners and sore losers. The place played catchy tunes from olden times. Although in a foul mood, considering other contests of wagering, he presented himself as pleasant enough. Working the slot machine, his espresso cup held neutral, he was ready, at any customer's first funny move, to cover his ass. If the atmosphere got too tense, he would know exactly when to vamoose, and with the utmost promptitude. The rental property is like he's ambling through a waking dream. Marisa's hip is near his hand, but he makes no gesture toward it. He is a trooper for keeping his dirty hams off his madre, he thinks. There are incremental alterations of the shoreline in the fume. Turquoise and crimson empyrean, threatening storm, in the clouds, is warped into an arc. The drencher has thunder and lightning thrown in. Loud intrusion of rush hour is irritating. Cannabis and pills, all as yet unstashed, are strewn about the carved wood coffee table, acquired on sale at Sears and Roebuck, surrounded by pieces of non-store-purchased furniture. Peki already misses being in the health resort of her bedroom, with its sage-and-fawn color scheme. Her vibrator, he ascertained, is pretty constantly in use. His mirage-reflection manifests on surfaces glassy. At the stuccoed apricot wall, Marisa is washed in a pale fulguration. She's not a tough one to figure out. She is composed and spacey, at the stove, concocting the venison chili on the burner. For her, watchfulness rules. The two were frolicking earlier, stomping up the stairs and busting guts. She sings a hymn in this vibratoless voice. Her weathered frontage beams away. Spell of silence. Creaky percussion of the branches of the cottonwoods inhabited by zephyrs. His ears ring like school bells. Palming his pocket flask. Cirri thicken and levin pulses. He stumbles into the pantry to get the can of olives. Pearl firmament. Her flesh is of the waxy gray, all limbs and sensuality, light as a sigh, stepping gracefully, baby blues ablink, prepping the collation for the next day. Her respirations remind him of the sounds of a brook brought by a breeze. The illumination, let in from the lifted shade, avalanches on them. He sincerely hopes that her serenity is contagious. She is his mama, his confidante, looking sexy, shelling peas in the fractional fulgor. She gets a glimpse of her son in a sidelong way. She looks like she was in a concentration camp. She's a sun-ducker, a classy cracker, to him. He remembers he has a whole list of important to-do items he must check off shortly. Is there even a remote possibility of romance? In her underthings, dot & lace strap panty and underwire contour bra, her near-nakedness is a certified miracle. Now and again he wishes he had a kind of personal kill switch, a convenient mechanism to flip off his raging hormones. She peels onions this dismal aft. He soughs expressively, lips pursed lopsidedly, and wears a stricken mien. She seems to be having an entertaining interior conversation with herself and an exterior one with him. Her body, liberated from clothing, is free to claim association with the exhibitionistic. When she puts on the apron, protecting her puckered tummy, he becomes so despondent you'd think it was the end of the world. His forehead creases with serious thoughts. Her mouth is just this side of a smirk. The wrinkles of her brow are ironed out by the uncertain incandescence to the smoothness of a teenager. Erect, he struggles to tinkle into the throne, the sonancy not unlike chimes brushed by a gust, whereupon he trips, observing a sex doll, resembling his mother, an evanescent mirage, floating, with these go-go-dancer holograms, dark-eyed, blue-haired, and pink-skinned, above the sandy floor as in a stereopticon view, the population of sun-beaten cacti and rocky jewels in vertical and horizontal attendance, out front of an industrial temple in the ambery haze of a desert. The glassy welkin shimmers with watery reflections. Trees are scarce. The rodential corpses are in dissimilar states of pickat and putrefaction courtesy of the turkey vultures, those birds of death. Denizens betake themselves with their interpretation of the night. Rude constructions are made of adobe brick. The megalopolis is like a religious painting of Hades preternaturally enlivened to scare the pants off potential visitants. The ambience of atrocity reigns supreme. Firearms are discharged from somewhere nearby. A public sexual act is occurring under an awning, ovine nymphets the performers, wearing items of feminine (one) and masculine (the other) apparel. Their patently abominable behavior is boldly showcased. It is an erotic exercise in transgression. Sights are shown to him. His swagger is apish. A lurid vapor collects here and there in mounds during this advanced hour. A little girlie brunette bites her nails and flickers on and off like a broken projector image on the corner. Marisa is cloud-whitish. Ardor, a presence, swells inside him, and he becomes gravid with it. His pulse throbs. Stifling day and night. He has the absolute power of life and death, usually reviewing, as a predator, members of the immediate population of identified prey. Lately, he has been leaving the carcasses for the buzzards, carrion avians perpetually circling overhead, dignified and longanimous. He'll do anything to avoid an encounter with the cops. The megapolis is one of loose morality. He belongs. Shaken and ashamed, in the roofless ruin, she, an African American, wore a shapely tangerine dress, he remembers clearly. She said she was packing: a .38 Special. Her lips tasted like pinguid ashes. She had a skull's rictus and blank eyes. Her frontal was hard like it was some marble mask. The phosphorescence was funny enough with its antics. She reminded him of an underweight, longevous, phthisical Billie 'Buckwheat' Thomas from 'The Little Rascals' in dirty drag. The sprinkles had the odor of turpentine. Aquamarine sky and mauve cumuli. The wind tended toward shrieking. Peki was the living opposite of the dead lady before him. She indefatigably blew and thumbed him. He was pre-human in appearance, according to his image deformed in the brandy bottle, the simian grin a real standout. His glistening glower unnerved him. He was almost without breath. She took her sweet goddamned time masturbating and fellating him. She told him, between sucks and strokes, that she went on a picnic and then to a parade. She whispered, sounding as if she were reading him a bedtime story, sending him off into the safe passage of dreamland. Felt up, she looked on with differing degrees of disengagement. She shuddered… the symptom of a condition? They both knelt, stripped, his back against the blood-reddish paneling gone to dilapidation. She paused, as though observing a moment of silence. She suggested a damaged and redolent cadaver. He had a thunderous vox. She was disinclined to further coition that alkaline eve, glided away giggling as if the coital shenanigan was a jape and he was the target. Shade was an artifact of the coruscation. Her gait was like she rolled as if she had wheels instead of feet. After ejaculating, he shelled out the pelf, and resisted haggling. Beside the unusable church organ, she sounded loot, akin to some sermonizing street preacher. Shadow illusorily reassembled the broken emanation. He had a semi-stiffy. A fruit orchard was in the rear of the structure, prob abandoned centuries ago. She struck him as being bestially rendered in the dusk. She complained that she had a cargo of contraband and ventral cramps.

Her unexpected arrival in the daylit room of gloom strikes fear into the hearts of the murine inhabitants and they instantaneously disperse. He'd experimentally made a new batch of butter just for drill, filling the laboratory, a subterranean mystery, with sebaceous disaster. The porky stripling with the bowl haircut paid the price. Alas, all for naught. A chemical embellishment was introduced into the accustomed flow of creation, opening entrances elsewhere. He finds himself, in spite of his failure, to be in a particularly serene state. He is sensible enough to grasp that right now practice makes perfect, and all he needs to do is to continue to plug away, one clumsy step at a time. The messes are manure piles he's been able to dig his way out of. He spent, or wasted, time on preparing the new stuff. No playing the ponies tonight! This is a city harrowed by homicidal crime in the name of mantequilla. People are imperiled because of him. To the edible fatty substance he has sworn his deepest oath. He immerses himself in the delights of evil, eradicating human beings to keep business hopping at the shop. There is an ever-increasing supply of the product. His opinion on the murders — he helps the innocents depart the material plane. There are villains and heroes in society. He believes he is both; a two-in-one deal. Lightning-glazed skyline. Sheep sail over a fence. Marisa's measure of bodily movement readily indicates itself as a means of impacting Peki's conduct. He radiates in frank admiration. She is a High Priestess in her subleased tower. To keep his hams off her heinie... how problematic it is to observe the basic imperative... It's a frightfully awkward situation. He has the appearance of an individual in relief, being home at last, getting goosebumps off of the thought of it. Stoned, she maintains a straight face, noonlit. She says he's a "fashion failure." Tweed-smocked and combat booted, he wants to sink his pearly whites, or corny yellows, into those hot haunches. She inhabits attractiveness as daunting as her maternal role but intensifies the challenge for him to couple with her. She offers (unsolicited) wardrobe advice. He heeds it, doffing the linen overgarment and donning mystical robes. He is a seeker of certainty. He's a Serpent in the Garden of Eden. He sparks weed and tokes and soon starts to feel strange, a sure sign of an impending high. Her bondage teddy is fatally inappropriate. He looks pointedly at what she has on, which isn't much. She's comfortable wearing next to nothing at all. Doing yoga on the carpet, momentarily posing, evoking a wannabe contortionist, she is genuinely puzzled by his observation. She gathers appreciative glances from him. His joint is accounted for by the smoke and the smell in the air. He acquaints his lamps with her boobs. She does a newspaper's crossword, and completes the splits. Her anatomy is subject to weird modifications due to the refulgence. If incestuous interest is a hereditary disease, transmitted from one family member to another, passed generationally like a baton, from whom did he catch it? His natural father? Is there a cure? Effulgence leaches color from the immediate surroundings. Shadows slink with sinister patience. The miniature park is packed with males and females, the young and old. They pop up from nowhere, drift by, in full view, ostensibly without destination, and vanish. Is the wacky backy spiked with a hallucinogen? Mist is like the veil of maya. Rainfall sounds like rhyming codes. A flowering tweeny streetwalker of unestablished gender is accompanied by a bulky pimp, pallid as plaster, recalling a magazine illustration come to life, serious expression doubtlessly meant to warn off flippant folks, in the violet gloaming, as if their fates are bound, incapable of separation, passing through the greater macrocosm like spirit presences, around the block of flats in this troublesome world. Birds sing at different pitches. Marisa presents him with an unintended gift: her rump, one of seraphic agency. Peki has pathological impulses he cannot properly control. He is appreciative that he is in the company of his striking mother. His aspect is one in which hopeless torrid fixation can't be discounted. Draped fabrics in Eastern Indian designs in the plant-abundant den. A peach, and enchanting, she claims his focus and disturbs his dreams. Her tresses, subdued by mousse, are pinned, leaving her nape bared. Her undergarment is simple but not too severe. He simmers toward his boiling point. She has a steady and speculative gape. Seaside umbrellas bring to mind multi-hued mushrooms. Nondescript pub next to a canal. Peki has already invested minutes in the seduction necessary to obtain her much-coveted body. Marisa is within his sphere of influence… There are unaccountable whooshes and voices in his coconut that are difficult to distinguish. This is a dangerous and dirty part of town where not even the vermin will dare venture. It has become a literal shambles. The wen is in municipal crawl out of the province of landlines. It's been reported that gang executions are being carried out in the appallingly primitive conditions of the projects. Corpses are piling up at alarming rates. Breathless hush. She appears impervious to the effects of time's passage after the facials, perhaps immune to the aging process altogether. Time doesn't bother to touch her. Her maquillage is worn as in schismatic observance. He inhales varied fumes and exhales. He groans with an inflection of almost celiac discomfort. His hardened peter wigwags like a gauge needle, imagining fingering her diligently not unlike a lock-picker. Her chesty globes are like cricket balls. He frequently feels like a faithful second banana. The two act as opposite poles of temporal flow between Heaven and Hell. Passions are running high. He sniffs glue and his head spins. Hours are consumed. He is fed up with her unbending refusals to mate. That she is wholly humorless is no laughing matter. Obviously opiated, she smiles condescendingly at him. Currently, she favors sexy lingerie and serviceable shoes. His mute fascination. He'd welcome any excuse to share her companionship. He ambulates in curious exhilaration. Pistol shots echo in the electrical dusk. Extreme and merciless mugginess. The rozzers are quotidian frights discernible. It is utterly imperative that he watch his step; there are multiple chances for error. He cannot afford to slip up now. Citizens serve superbly as a nescient species of camouflage. Peki's cocainized brain whirls. He got wrecked before he was completely awake. The ebon Egyptian cigarette is dampened with a queerly luminous green liquid — absinthe. Is he on an ill-marked path to his destiny? The rumpus outside becomes inaudible inside as though the windows are shut. Soft sound of water dripping gets gradually louder. He inspects his coat's cuffs. There is an actorly polish to his self-presentation, garbed in a snow-white lab ensemble, about to return to the vast workshop, the realm of flasks and funnels, boilers and barrels. The backs of Marisa's thighs are dented as if by years of shooter assault. The moon shines, inevitable. No dice. Shot down in flames. Those fortunate enough to have close family and friends might find it difficult to understand what it truly feels like to be alone, he thinks. Especially at a time when the sense of belonging is both encouraged and incessant. With her, it's like the gravitational pull of a planet that he can't escape!

Yuto Kobo and Ashdance

Yuto is a dumb ox cross-dressing former sumo wrestler, a man who now considers himself a woman. On the stage of a disused playhouse, she, garbed in a boiler suit, performs a number called 'Ashdance,' a comical musical take on 'Flashdance,' in which she imitates the character of Ash from the 'Alien' film, spinning in circles like the malfunctioning robot, spewing Peki's semen from her mouth like the milk in the movie. Irene Cara's 'What a Feeling' blares from a boom box. Her rotundity tantalizes him. Akin to a cartoon fox looking at an existent turkey as being one cooking in an oven, he gazes at her and sees a crate crammed with bars of butter. He believes, triumphantly and unquestioningly, in the resurrection of his establishment, and the Butyrum everlasting. He envisions the earth stacked with sticks and heaped with tubs. His senses are stirred, the gnome rapt, into the ponderous performance and its inescapably sensual nature. He used to think that personal and professional relevance was a laughable impossibility. That mentality is gone. Nude, on all fours on the platform, she recalls a massive white cow, teats and all, in a pasture. He grunts and chuckles. Her inhalations and exhalations are problematic, understandable given her elephantoid size. The stabbing starts and stops in spurts. He is in a waking trance. His chant of grief is primitive and straightforward. Rhymes ramble inexorably on. There is a repetition of impaling with the bowie knife in pure concentration. Her peepers look not unlike shriveled moths. The deluge plashes down. The light is low. Yuto moans like the sea. She reminds him of a beached whale. Peki's mind and member are stimulated by the sheer quantity of flesh, the redundancy of suet, at his disposal to make mantequilla. Her fingers and toes are like frankfurters. His nerves prick. Her blood puddles. He'd introduced himself to the permed orca in the trendy art gallery downtown. He was skulking down the streets during the day searching for the right victim. They were drawn together, both being eminent outcasts of their time. He saw her and knew he hit big-time paydirt. He butchers her with the knife. In terms of blubber, this is the jackpot. He has no problem stepping over the threshold of fantasy into fat fact. He reaches empyreal altitudes of thought. It sounds like the Discovery Channel. Peki slays in a romantic glow. His back is goose-pimpled. Yuto squeals like a sow. He carves her big belly as if it's a Yuletide ham. He pictures them as doomed lovers. The porker wails. There are transcendental aspects to murderous behavior. The blade plunges into the massive stomach and viscera spill like eels from a pail. She shrieks like a dolphin. She makes a last, desperate plea to have her life spared. It goes unheeded. She is swiftly approaching annihilation. Adrenaline soars in him while he slices her vast throat. She makes a sickening gurgling sound. The pool of blood expands on the floor. He thrusts the metal into her breast as casually as pushing a button into a shirt's slit. There's no real need to overthink the process. He acquits himself well enough in the art of killing. He has this craftsman's work ethic and expertise. He experiences a suffusion of affection and hatred, the synthesized feeling unpleasant and inadequate. He imagines they are intimately connected with sensuous pleasure. He dispatches her to death calmly and coldly, appalled that he should even entertain the idea of necrophilic activity. She was alive, she is dead. They would've never loved each other... Peki repents in agony. Mirages appear and disappear. There is no language, only lament. He torches the place. The hellish flames glimmer. He sounds like a crying infant, feeling as though his soul is blowing in the wind, and getting wet in the rain. He's ensanguined in tooth and nail. In society, he feels like he is a mistletoe, that parasitic plant, on a dying tree. Life and death, in his opinion, are merciless abstractions.

The room was a beastly lair, a dark pit. Thingamajigs lined the mantelshelf. Yuto was snow-white and stock-still, in a shapeless greatcoat, fanatically neat, and naked underneath. Her nostrils were cavernous.

The atmosphere was electric. She peered down at Peki. It was as if she couldn't move a muscle, except that she could use her throat to swallow. Her blackish hair was all curls. His fingers pried into her rear's orifice, like roots searching for a vantage in the soil. She was stupefied like a cow at the slaughterer's. The air was heavier with an approaching storm. Her cellulitic thighs looked like milky, breeze-ruffled puddles. Her hands and feet were humorously incongruously tiny in comparison to the rest of her anatomical enormity. There was apprehensive quietness. He vocally smoothened her ruffled feathers. She could be mistaken for a corpulent cherub. There was humiliation and glorification in their coition. He blew her like a champ, kneeling before her, not unlike a prisoner in front of the inquisitor. Both had been through bad times and were glad to share the good times. Sky was lapis-blue. Yuto was heavenly, and Peki was earthy. The fleshy purse of her chin quivered, uttering thin whispers. Her gaze met his. Her penis shivered and shrank and squirmed in his mitt. Her voice sounded strangulated. Swears were flung like arrows. Her tits joggled. She was open-mouthed. She was larger than life. Her derma layer was gray-ish-bluish like damp gault. His fart had the sound of a papery squeak. Giving oral, he shook his head like a surfacing swimmer, made these chok-ing sonances, gripping those ham hock thighs. His lips moved numbly as if shot with novocaine. He sounded like his breath was being sucked out of him. His melon jerked, and his spine arched. Her heels drummed. His pies were wide open and unseeing like he was in the presence of absence. He grasped the blush-pink, plumpy limbs, lapped the shaven sac, and puckered up to her scarlet hole with its sable hairs and rich, decaying stink. His filthy imaginings were becoming realized. They were joined and made a single person, intensely joyful in exchanging bodily fluids, indulg-ing in the fleshly feast, and subsequently had Earl Grey, steaming and aromatic, poured from a china pot, and sugared biscuits piled elegantly on a plate. It was a miracle meal, relished in the benign lamplight.

Horizon's colors are ash and plum. The dusk lurches ferociously. An alba-tross stretches its wings on a bluff. Peki has many worries and wicked thoughts. Though he feels a twinge of regret for his homicidal actions, he knows he is making something tasty out of the horror of Yuto's demise

— butter. By being unmade, she will make something else entirely, Butyrum, that potent narcotic. He has a conscience. He's got aim. He envisages churning mantequilla like molding clay into human form. His remorse, a hurtful lucency, fades like a dwindling fire. He feels like a bird kept in a globoid cage. His being is vacant darkness at its core. A suspiration rattles in his larynx. His brain is inflamed by brandy. His scrotum is wound into a tight ball. Alpine-green brine. Iron horizon. Fireflies make the gloom spangly. Celestial-blue estuary. His gut turns like a potter's wheel. Potholes brim with standing water, suggesting, to him, eyes with standing tears. He listens to an accordioned version of Cream's 'Toad' through headphones, plodding on the wetted pavement of the sidewalk. His oculi gleam under bushy brows. Tendrils of strands hang limply. He yearns for the scent of his mama, her fragrance like no other in the whole world. His sobs are carried off by the zephyrs. His skin creeps over his skull. A battle of conflicting cogitations rages in his cranium. His knuckles are white. American Indians exist peaceably among the spirits of their ancestors, so perhaps he can live among the spirits of his victims.

Evening browned and blackened. Yuto, gutted like a fish, stared in uncomprehending excruciating pain. She was an avoirdupois angel, beautifully bulky and true, a bulging mass. Peki defiled the lumpen cadaver from dusk until dawn. The playhouse became a pleasure house. The hot sun was followed by a cold moon. Storefronts had bulwarks of grillwork. Mazes of alleys. Slaty crests of the sea. Teal vault. Gusts commanded the strings of the soaker. The fire he had started bellied and flared in the distance. Smears of smoke stained the vista. Leven came in flickerings. The moon had spinning threads of light emanating from it, so it looked like a grub creating a cocoon. A taxi had borne him away. The sounds of Yuto's screeches were close and distant at once.

Peki is being brought home on the wings of the wind, floating like a dandelion seed through the woolly clouds. He's sure he's equal to the stress of uncertainty in finally seeing Marisa, but her ill-temper daunts him. Her modulation is liquid-sweet. There are foul odors in the apartment. He is self-conscious about his loathsome appearance. Does his disheveled

291

condition make her nauseous? She's lean and lively in his arms. He buries his face in her tummy, hands clutching her tush, and he issues a whirling cry. She is spume-whitish. He holds her like emotions. They kiss and touch and talk. And two are entangled in one.

Aoife the Mermaid

Peki discerns a mermaid struggling on the shore. Her name is Aoife. She has a proud, pretty face, fine ivoried teeth, winding hair like brunet silk, flat breast, nipples like fat rosebuds, and cyan scales. Her huge tail thumps on the loam. She tosses her head, cries like an owl, and mewls like a cat in a sky-high voice. Her torso is deathly-pallid. Her eyes remind him of cold green jewels. She is bruised and broken, with a large bloody gash on her belly, just above the umbilical coil. She's shrill, calling to him, crouching on the cement wall, in an unfamiliar tongue. His vascular organ bangs in his chest. She has a comforting gaze and smells of the sea. She wears a nice seashell necklace. He picks her up and carries her through the streets and the square and up the hill and into the forest, instantly contending with brambles and gorse. Hauling her, he emits an "oh" and an "ah" in wonderment. He begins to lose his sense of direction. If this is a test, he feels as if he is failing it. Frustrated, he begins to weep. She tries to console him in a dry, creaking intonation. The rays are split into lucid needles through the foliage. Sun's like yellow glass. Cirri are gray as ashes. Leaves shiver and branches clatter in the breezes. The celestial sphere is mackerel-puckered. Vegetation is malachite and jade. Butterflies swoop and dip in the dappled light of the glade. Peki is an incurable optimist, firmly believing that he'll find shelter for them soon enough, as they enter a clearing in the verdurous depths. Airy arms embrace them. Dirt rises and flies about in tiny sod-fountains as he trots. He skips and jumps in the unforgiving brush. Twiggy fingers of the beeches and laurels tenderly touch their faces. Spate and glancing splendor. Streaming cumuli. Pitted and scarred boulders. The ground is sodden. He has the feeling that they are headed somewhere and going nowhere simultaneously. Whereupon his feet make more wavelets of soil like they're water. He speaks to her with a flaky inflection. Boughs sway in a beckoning manner.

Peki pours water from his canteen all over Aoife to sustain her. Brilliant birds. Mysterious moths. She notices his feet are swollen in the serviceable sandals. He pushes on, fatigue affecting him, deftly avoiding the poisonous thorns. Fishpools and climbing plants. Sighs of showers. The soft moss of the coppice is a welcome change from the grit of the trail. They nibble on a variety of berries and nuts. A river races. The lambency flecks and streaks the aquamarine surface. Hail tinkles like broken bells. Aoife's mouth opens and shuts tremulously. She croaks something incoherent. He's exhausted, but she urges him on. They are shelter-seekers in the midnight-blue crepuscule. He hops and scurries, bolts and stumbles. She beholds the grasshoppers and bumblebees. She communicates in husky whispers, interspersed with rasps and gulps. She auscultates the harmonious chirruping. Patches of sand in puddles are reminiscent of drowned islets. Peki and Aoife encounter witches, wrinkled and wormy, out front of huts. Their voices are unrestrained, ululating, and interminable. Their buttoned shoes are encrusted with mud. Insects crowd around their heads and rest on their shoulders. Hoary wizards exit their caverns to gawk at them. He makes it a point to be courteous, not wanting to be turned to stone or confined to a vault for being disrespectful. Being a statue or a prisoner would not suit him. Huge scorpions hiss, waving angry pincers, deadly tails at the ready. One's claws snap and it tries to sting. A few of them rear up menacingly. He complains, striking dejected notes, despite their progress in the wildest wood. He rushes headlong on the dusty road. He eludes the venomous serpents and the nest of vipers on the rocky paths. Peki and Aoife travel extremely fast. They come across deer, fowl, and hares. The sun is a bright eye in ghost-gray clouds. In no time find themselves caught in a sandstorm.

The shanty, conveniently located in the mountainous region, is a sturdy and commodious residence. Peki knocks quickly on the solid wooden door and waits. No one is home. The sides of the structure are ranged with bold herbal exotics. Peki and Aoife stare at the periwinkle place in wonder. It is so peaceful he is half-loath to disturb it. He marvels at the craft with which it was constructed. She's gentle as a fawn, and mumbles, "We go together like bread and butter." Beams are brassy and shade is long on the seaweed-green grass. The weathercock goes round and round. The gloom grows. Once inside, he plops her, bluish with cold and reddened with heat, in the oval-backed armchair in proximity to the noble stairs, and covers her in a complicated shawl. She settles stoically into the cushions and gives a shudder. Her countenance is slightly shadowed. He tours the premises, the chambers bland in equal proportions. The furniture bulges. She fits herself into a pastel crimplene jumper, chanced upon in the closet. Stars blink and shine. The spritzing has the redolence of just-burned sugar. The surrounding forest is delightful and dangerous. Peki digs up meat and wine. He asserts his presence in a place echoing with absence. Candles burn steadily on the sills. After he stitches up her stomach and dresses her in an olive, waist-length gown, they sit on a rainbow-colored carpet by the log fire in the fabulous cottagey brick chimney and play cards, taking pleasure in each other's company. Aoife is lively and wholesome. He smooches her chin in the flickering firelight. Then he applies disinfectant he found in the medicine cabinet to the nasty wound. It was self-inflicted, she sheepishly confesses. She was kicked out of her aquatic kingdom because of "questionable behavior" and felt compelled to commit suicide. She once operated a magic loom that created magnificent tapestries that would animate on walls. She was only moderately efficient with the thing. She bends voluptuously, stretches, and yawns. He looks composed and expectant. The parlor is festooned with furnishings. The pair discuss their problems and pleasures. Gales howl outside.

Peki brushes his woolly beard. He has bloodshot eyes and the hot breath of a flagged dog. Aoife murmurs he is "versatile and intricate." She has a throaty intonation. She shines, warm and enticing. His dome right now is a crystal ball shaken to produce a blizzard of thoughts. He's quiet as if his lips are sewn into silence. He imagines her swimming in the ocean's deep, whirling, and twirling in exultation... The two swill sharp cider and glom fruit tarts, both in good spirits, becoming acquainted, and eventually get snug and tumbled in the blankets on the mattress. The spacious room has the aroma of ripe apples. Her creamy-white tummy injury is healing surprisingly well. Gossamer threads left by spiders glisten. It's as if the cabin's history is somehow woven into the web. Overcast swallows the skyline. Thunder hops and rolls. Squalls sound like wailing babies. The storm is savage and hectic. Wisteria and jasmine are plentiful. Peki sweeps. Aoife scrubs. He churns the cream. He bakes the bread. Her clumsiness is lovable. She sips amber tea. He fixes his whole attention on her cute visage and compact build. He puts on a blaze ear and dungarees. Together they prepare a malt loaf and a walnut cake. They're vigorous-voiced. Words flow and ultimately overflow. He draws the chintz curtains, chops in a down-droop, afraid of inertia assailing him. He can't get too content; he has a business to run. The oven has given up. The stove had gone to pot probably long ago. The geriatric dishwasher bustles and natters. The abode is stifling with legal (and illegal) smoke. She is seated at the low table and assesses the college garden, sunken pool, and compost heap in the backyard. She puts in multiple bead earrings. The downpour has the sonancy of the rustling of wood shavings. He laps the fringe of cappuccino froth from the cup, then he drowses and rouses. She admits she's feeling decidedly better already. Her well-cut bob is decisive, extravagant, and mannish. She clips his pepper and salt mustache. They converse about the serial drama, 'The Edge of Wetness,' their opinions unapologetic and contradictory. Sleet on the roof sounds not unlike the tapping of an egg with a spoon.

Aoife is eye-lined and smooth-skinned. Peki grins decorously. It is also casual and deprecating. Coupling, on the bed, draped anachronistically in loose quilts, under the window, they sound like the clattering of antique pistons and hinges in an ancient contraption. She displays almost saintly patience when he fails to sexually perform. Whereupon he manages. They scream like avenging angels when they climax. She shakes with emotion in the manically complex blankets. He mentions his work but leaves out the gory details, the silly messes he's gotten himself into. The sheets are stiff and clean. The alarm clock ticks on the bureau. A linen basket is reprimanded to the corner. Frisky zephyrs. Rain makes scratchy sonances. Lindens and birches are wavering and threatening. The incandescence simmers on the landscape like it's on a desert. She soaks for a spell in the bathtub. The lovers shag in the small hours. The bower has practically no character. Aoife shakes with emotion. And Peki experiences elation. He, in a V-necked pullover and boxer shorts, falls into an uneasy slumber, wrapped in the goose feather spread. He wakes to see Aoife slithering down the hall, along the wall, slow and halting. He hears her keening. Her mane is cut into a mop of darkish flame. His state is altered. Her hands pat the floor, her tail slip-slapping. She arches her back, trunk strained. She curses and collapses. He passes out... and comes to in the kitchen, the pots, pans, dishes, glasses, and food scattered on every available surface. A powerful stench of rotten fish assails his nose. Clumps of her tresses look like dust bunnies on the countertop. He vomits into the sink. What happened? What did he do? Did he fry or bake her? He makes these awful belching noises. His body aches intolerably. He shakes. His pallor is sludge-gray. He is suffused with unreasonable fear. He pukes again. His flatus sounds like a hunting party's trumpeting. He cannot remember. He recollects the quail eggs and the pomegranates... He consults his memory and his conscience to assure himself that he's blameless. He endeavors to finish the mental jigsaw. Its pieces turn like the lozenges of a kaleidoscope in his mind. He makes his frustrations vociferous. He has a career devoted to the betterment of butter. He craves influence and status, to step up on the social scale. What is his next course of action? To vamoose, naturally. Stars in the smoky topaz sky glimmer like pearls in aqua pura. Fog veils the bay. Peki stares at the basin, ill-disposed for a dip. The wind sings not unlike a siren. It is over. It's the end.

Roberto

Peki is summoned by Roberto, that acneous, modelesque, hulking volcano of virility, prodigiously intimidating, to take him to the airport. The
framework of the fire escape is akin to osseous metal. Marisa, in mocha
jamas, fights with cook/bakeware. She switches over to chopping lettuce.
She's as punctual with food preparation as a cuckoo in a clock. Their
relationship is undefinably intimate. Her ankles scrape like springs. Hazy
horizon. He is inert, indifferent at this juncture. The construction site is
engulfed by gloaming. Vaginous stink of low tide. A marzipan-hued sea.
He is lightheaded as if his coconut is a bubble about to float away from
his body. Squat gypsian erections. Gnats flit like fairies. She is root-whit-
ish, with an apathetic aspect, her dandruff as grated cheese, and plunks
on the cane settee. She has a pea brain and melodramatic gestures. His
toupee clings to his dome like a spider. She holds an accordion of mail.
He observes the supernatural continuation of the pea soup. Orange sun.
An Asian amputee in a turban and with a challenging expression shows
his stumps to passers-by. Scintillation butters the pavement of pestilential, mazelike avenues. The tongue of scum laps the macadam. She
advances as though she is a sneakthief. He experiences these tingles and
tremors in his being. His piles are giving him fits. A trolley car moves
not unlike a ferryboat. Her elbows on the bureau prop her up. Vines on
the trellis remind him of veins arrayed on a tumor. Din judders. Sludge
brims in the potholes. She is always in a clumsy hurry! Her crow's-feet
seem exaggerated somehow. Her breath has this nasty malodor. She spins
a silky smirk. Traffic's choking and coughing are deafening. He envisions
the cumuli, with lightning, as being like word balloons for comic strip

characters. He digitally traces his receding hairline. Colors radiate out of the rainbow. Marisa has irregular, unpleasant lineaments, and reeks of burning rubber. She has a compromised liver. She once had a case of meningitis. An overhead lightbulb pulses. Peki scrutinizes the acacia bushes, grillwork gate, and the leonine statuettes. Whenever Roberto pays him, Peki feels like a dog given a bone by his owner as a reward for doing a trick. En route to catch the flight, at a rest stop, Peki, feeling as if he's on the cusp of exploding like a firecracker, spikes the stoned Roberto's drink with a sedative. He shoots him with a pistol, execution-style, on the outskirts of town.

Eating pasta with margarine made with Roberto's suet, Peki, caked in dried blood, has an illusion of Roberto assaulting Marisa, and he mimics masturbation. Bathed and refreshed with meat and brandy, he gives a toss to his head. His compkexion is egg-white. He looks like a softened waxwork. He's bruised and broken and has demonic visions to contend with, venturing into unnatural dimensions of human existence. Panic-stricken, his knees knock. He, scant of breath, mouth agape, the worse for drink, throws incriminating evidence out like a desperate passenger in a sinking ship and buries the bag as a canine its bone. After that, he sups substantial tea under an intense sky. With the human-enhanced butter, he enjoys his repast with zeal. Show him a red line, and he will cross it.

Peki's hallucination has Roberto, as a boy, hiding in a closet when a ghostly Asian girl jumps on top of him and pins him to the floor. She commences pulling out his hair. He attempts to call for help but he cannot move or produce any sound.

Aitana Hothouse

Her sorrow has an echo. Aitana, a ballerina and gossip columnist for a tabloidal mag, is maleducated. The air smells of leaking battery. Subway station, in the heart of the seaside town, is white-and-brown as a public toilet. She is meltingly attractive, with the body shape of a porpoise, hair flat like paper, jet black unibrow, unspoiled, searching eyes, and a blunt nose. She possesses the kindness of a woman who is at peace with herself. She is empathetic, often feeling the suffering of others. She's a luculent ironist who mistrusts the wafer-thin government and has no faith whatsoever in authority. She manducates a wad of gum the color of Tuscan plaster. Her long legs are left unshaved, with a few days' growth of stubble on them. Mercury glass upper atmosphere is silvered with cumuli. Drizzle has this urinose odor. Aitana has had many ups and downs in her life. She was vaccinated this morning. She thinks of her beau, Gael, built as a torpedo, prematurely balding, ponytail not unlike a bell-rope, head tending to the ovaline, face with an unobtrusive homeliness, and popcorn-yellow teeth. His smile is warm and appealing. He's learned and glib of tongue. She is quiet as a lamb. She's passion-inebriated, and intoxicated on the ichor of his image in her mind. She wishes he came included with instructions! Ha! The relationship has its fair share of snakes and ladders. With him, there's physical pleasure, whereas without him there's mental hardship. They are two elements remaining apart. They'd argued earlier, their words as knives, sharpened on the whetstone of determination. An ascending and descending scale of uncertainty exists. Apparently, Gael was alluding to the hiccups in his life too elaborate to be related, he was stuck in the ruts, waiting till doomsday to get out of them, he was in a tangled accretion of dilemmas, and his equanimity was compromised by multitudinous influences. Turmoil was distorting everything, his sensory perception was off, and his nerves were disordered. He felt as if he was losing all sense of direction. He maintained a mild and leisurely approach to living. She was suffused with the blaze of an internal flame, imbued with the conviction that he'll succeed. She knew that once she was out of the picture, she'll forever speak to his imagination. She was an awkward and beguiling thing. In other occupational endeavors, he knocked on many doors without seeing any open. He said she wasn't exactly a model of virtue, and complained that his rheumatism was flaring up. She was dropping with fatigue. Following the succulent repast, she pulled out a needle and thread, a Bach fugue playing on the vintage turntable. She was sheltered in the dwelling as a mollusk in its shell. Shutters were hermetically shut. There was a trace of tipsiness in Aitana. Gael expressed himself in peevish tones. Stock Exchange had resoundingly collapsed. He withdrew out of sight like a thief in the night. It suddenly dawns on her that all of these thoughts are used to come to one conclusion, like thousands of spermatozoa being spent to fertilize a single egg. Estuary is gray as an eraser. Ocular sun has an incipient cataract of cloud. The citizenry, in the fulguration, is spectral. Love annuls her ache and anneals her soul. She walks through the world as a dreamer and visualizes squaring a circle... Peki butchered the couple with a machete in a field of beetroot, close to a ravine overgrown with bracken, elders, and willows... The magnet of their magnificence drew him to them, dallying on the sepia-hued, leafy slope. Was there sadism in him? The pungent stink of their entrails pervaded the oxygen. His ferocious impulses overtook him. His bugged lamps had a hydrous rheum. He had a hankering to violate the corpses. Would scruple intervene? Would he act what he thought? He felt like a scum-beetle, moved like an automaton in the thaumaturgic breezes, whereupon he salaamed as Sinbad the Sailor. He wanted to disassociate himself from what was happening. He experienced shock. He had the cunning of the crazy. Clouds raced. He spluttered and spat like a candle. Then he pounded them into pulp with an iron bar. Gusts blew obliquely across their bloodied faces. He hung like a sloth from a bough, penis throbbing like a divining rod twitching at water. His body was in spasm, muscles tightened. His bared behind resembled a cracked bell. Wind made a storm. He held her ungainly ankle. She mumbled something, the gist of which he caught only psychic vibrations. He envisaged opening her organ to its utmost stretch. Her comely, composed features attracted him. He derived no iniquitous pleasure from butchering them. He wore convict's clothes, galloped away like a horse, hooving the sludgy ground, the muck flung apart in the dyke-mist. A flea derived comfort from his pubes. The undersea subconscious ebbings and flowings he was conscious of. He was ignorant of the ways of privileged people. They befuddled him with their behaviors. He obliterated any traces of them. He was no executioner of the innocent. The precip was discontinuous and the zephyrs were recurrent. The fog was like a screen between himself and the supernatural. There was a tropical downpour. Branches of the hollies were as extended gaunt arms by the blighted water. His mouth was agape and slobbering. He had lupine teeth. Tract of hedge and brackish grasses. His mouth was as round as the letter O, pictured himself perishing like an asphyxiated gnat. He was feeling like an embryo tree eaten by a grub. Traffic made about his ears a reverberant bedlam. Pollen was powdery as sawdust. The symbolic essence of the heavens was remarked. It had far-horizoned import. He felt reduced to dirt under the heel of his deed. Was he a homicidal maniac? His countenance was indented with a grin. A roofless and windowless structure was once a shelter for sheep. He was a sapling gathering the lichen and moss of problems. He was untouched soil. Gales rendered his muttering inaudible. He screamed at the top of his lungs. His hackles were raised. His self-inflicted cuts opened and closed like a fish's gills when he sprinted. He'd gone on a flesh-scourging rampage that afternoon. He was weary, his affairs pressing on him, weighing him down. Marisa was an imaginary goose with ruffled feathers in his dreamscape. He adored her beyond measure and restraint. His hysteric cachinnation seized upon his sentience. He wiped the crime scene clean, busy as a beaver in a dam after a flood. He retired to ponder, long and hard, on his interests, personal and professional, and surrendered himself to an orgy of cogitation. Plans sprouted from his encephalon not unlike shrooms. His emotional pendulum swung. He had slumbered a disrupted sleep. Rain repeated rhythmical patterns. The metropolis, with its weather-stained buildings, had its surplus of sorceries.

Ragged clouds blotted out the vigilant moon. Its flow was diminished in their obscurings. The lab suggested a chemist's shop. The wraith of his mother wandered in the shadiness, her spirit taking palpable form, with a voltaic force, exerting a startling impact. Would she break his heart? He built himself up after she tore him down. She brushed him off as vapor dispersed by a draft. The saurian Marisa had slunk in the cobbled yard. His imperishable infatuation survived doubt. He had the hankering to wrap his marbly limbs about her, to give himself to her without compunction. She reeked of sweet straw and sour piss, sitting sewing and wearing nothing save a woolen shawl. Her skin was smooth and pale as whitewashed stones. She was an engaging sight. He advanced and retreated, as though in a kid's game. Her movements were mysterious, as in a ring-of-roses dance. His made was a dream he dreamed. He feared his lust would outsmart his self-control. He clutched the bowl of cereal's leftover milk like it was Christ's blood and he was afraid of spilling even a drop of it. Would she embrace him to her heart? He imagined opening her as the gate of heaven. He held his tongue. Beams and rafters moaned and groaned. She could offend him to the quick and rake his axons. There existed between them a gulf. They belonged to separate categories of being. He pictured himself as being a louse crawling into her. His maffling sounded like piffle from a childish jingle. Irrational ideas surged to his gray matter from the darkest depths. The tide of temptation was rising. He suffered in service to his ambition. He hugged his febrile pillow and tossed and turned in pervy avidness, looking not unlike a plump infant in his crib, swaddled in quilts. He resided on a funny farm! He woke, his disturbed shuteye rendered a distant memory. His mop was ruffled and his nightshirt was rumpled. He lost himself in repose.

Peki's goes on a head trip after the brioche drowned in Aitana's butter. Her eyes abruptly flutter open. She, on her bed in the room, feels breath blowing on the back of her neck. She rolls over to her side. A hooded figure, face shrouded in blackness, stands there, watching her. When she attempts to cry out, the figure snaps into the air and quickly floats back into the wardrobe. It sits, glowering at her until she falls asleep...

Peki and Marisa

Peki's aches and pains are so severe he fears he will never escape from them. Blubbing in the lavatory, he sounds like a donkey braying. He feels as if he were poisoned by noxious herbs. He washes away all traces of his latest homicide. He'd asphyxiated a chemist, resembling a tubulous tot, who was devouring a bag of chestnuts, his peculiar profile seizing his fancy. Winds shepherd the flock of clouds. Presently, he has the point of vantage, gauging Marisa, looking carved in granite, a tilt to her posture, in the next room. She negotiates its breadth. In repose, she relaxes the tension within herself. She's rooted to the spot, implanted there like a tree. It's as though she is improvising her role in a dumb show, a part she ardently rehearsed, with a lavishness of preparation, introducing new mannerisms, the scene etched with a surrealness. His curiosity emboldening him, he moves closer, not unlike an animal by auspicious hazard, in the rose-pink splendor. He ogles her with a quirky fixity. He wishes to hear her caressing tones. They were at daggers drawn a while ago. Every verbal blow in the tiff struck home. Her disposition changed as if she were touched by a wizard's wand. She sensationally vanishes, as though in obedience to the dictates of a voodoo virtuosity. The joint is an indescribable dump. Broken Venetian blinds. Sun's a queen of hearts head. High, these elegant swans circle on a merry-go-round behind her veinal lids. Mildew of alcohol rots her brain. She is stricken with the incurable ulcer of dolor. Her fart reeks of unwashed armpit. Her chuckle is musical, filamental like a wig whacked against a vibraphone, whereupon it gets rattly, the cackle does, the sound not unlike dentures somersaulting down a flight of stairs like a Slinky. Neighborhood din. Gazebo'd to the gills, she decides to tackle doing the dirty dishes stacked in the sink. Their apathy towards the pigsty of an apartment is obvious, the accumulation of rubbish more or less overflowing. Crackly rock music's playing on the artifact of a radio, it unfathomably heroically working. Lambency leans wearily against the dingy panes. Triangular mass of gnats clusters. Ducks are poised on a beryl pond. Numerous nameless trees. Continuous complaints of rush hour's cars. Schoolchildren are alert and lively. Peki, slizzard, dressed in dungaree overalls, garbles his words, envisages her pussy plantation. His gnawed, stubby fingernails are examined. She slips on a stylish skirt, moving like a mechanical doll. Bloodstain of cloud cover. Confused messages of the gusts. He envisions her pudendum opening and closing like a rare underwater plant, their bellies rubbing against each other as if attracted by an active, avid magnet, guttural intonations smothered by soft derma. His moist flatulence's odor seems to have risen out of a pail of spoiled bait. The luminosity's pigment changes from tangerine to raw egg white. The two quarrel over abstract expressionism concepts. His lechery is triggered by a mysterious inner mechanism. The turquoise coverlet is at low tide. Haze is like burst vitreous particles. Words spoken by her sound incomprehensible, compromised by faulty bridgework, countenance afflicted by nervous tics. She feels useless like a stringless violin. He stirs a piña colada with a straw. She, creeping as a caterpillar, feels oddly exiled from her person, divested of herself. A cockroach cautiously skitters across the floor. Peki pictures them as being lovers, their impatient and impassioned kisses and strokes... Marisa's pedo with the sound of chorister cachinnation. The tenement looks distinctly two-dimensional. Hideous cascade of the deluge. Parking lot bustles like a subway station; or, for that matter, like a hall at election time. Unjust insults of the weather. Vault's the color of brick. She squinches as though she's peering through a tiny camera's lens. Her ajada, knotty poo peck. Sparrows soar with sedate ceremony. Herbal whiff of her cough lozenge. Gouts of the couple's lascivious grunts. Her physiognomy is as if it is deformed by febrile delirium. Geometric gunmetal gray thicket of her pubes. Bathing-suited, flip-flopped, she ingests a Valium and imbibes brandy. Prehistoric weaponry stashed in the closet is discussed in-depth. Busy lobby is like an animated Mexican mural. Zephyrs are hesitant whispers. Spate of the pair's spit and exclamations and mutterings continues. They divulge resentments and disappointments in their wild relationship. She's seated on a wicker basket, comely as a calendar model. A potential storm keeps stalling. Thankfully. In terms of cumming, it is indeed equal opportunity. Stars are like micaceous flakes flittering in the hiemal welkin. He refuses to conform to the systems of society, ideally preferring to revise them to suit his practices. She is this antitoxin that protects him against the disease of the public. His mitt substitutes for a visor on his brow to screen against the scintillating sun. Without notice, she manifests, prettified in a cerise chemise, prinking herself like a bird preening itself, flings a spontaneous "hello" at him. He bombinates not unlike a bumblebee. Her insectan gyrations are spellbinding, engaging his focus afresh. Several minutes elapse. The laws of conscience prevail over the rules of impropriety. Marisa's a rare bug and he's the captive flower. The possibility of their concupiscent conjunction is probable, by providential chance and observing botanical canon. Her companionship affects him as a healing tonic, restoring his verve. Her frigid modulation is taken up an octave higher. She remarks his turgescent waistline. Peki gazes at her like Ulysses did Athena. She has shunned him. She doesn't want his company. He is as cunning as a climbing plant in this household. He's intent on making improvements on the butter product, with an apostolic fervency. The theoretical will become material.

With capable employees holding down the fort at the shop, Peki has a great deal more time to devote to his murderous pursuits, bringing about an irremediable barrier between him and Marisa, attributed to his unavailability. She has too often saved him from foundering in the mire and he overflows with confidence. She is the solution that cures his suffering. Occasionally, though, she is a wretched woman, and he finds himself at his wit's end. Her outer shell of coldness covers an inner vulnerability. She can be either a supernova or a black hole. He feels bad for her: he was such a distinctly ugly baby, not at all a child prodigy or darling of the ladies, but he could run like the wind! There are certain instances in which he sees her and experiences the glee one feels when one accomplishes a long-desired aspiration. She's his malady and remedy. Her latest disparaging comments passed over him like water off a duck's back. She was authoritative and paranoid, not unlike a ship's captain sensing the sailors' mutiny below deck. The tête-à-tête with her recently was atrocious. She sipped nectar and scanned the 'Arabian Nights,' sitting at the baccarat table, saying he was a "spoilsport." They had lounged around like a pair of lovers. She dipped the croissant in the coffee and stood up straight on end like a snake. She presented her face and form to him. She was not bait he was tempted to bite, not nearly tempting enough to reel him in. There was an impassable crevasse between his libido and action. She attempted to seduce with a bag of tricks, countenance a comic mask. She smoothed away his difficulties and removed obstacles. She imposed her will on him. His cherished dream of being with her could be realizable. He clung to her like he was a sculptor taking an imprint of her figure. She was a fresh flower, one he studied like an expert botanist, and whose fragrance he breathed. He could easily look at her and listen to her for days and nights. They filled a space. Their disagreement came to its culminative point. He will not be her whipping-boy any more. Should he, by hook or by crook, compel her to shut up next time? Her chronic psychosis is irrepressible. He has profound pity for her. He always felt estranged from his family, living in exile from his native land, and submitted himself to solitude. He doesn't miss his dull relatives and tedious acquaintances. He emerged from the cataclysms of destructive friendships over the years. He has grabbed hold of his life, taking the bull by the horns. He arrives in the laboratory as if by judicial summons. Tonight he is confining himself exclusively to making more product to put on sale tomorrow. His occupational goals smack of military objectives. He wants his business, and his name, to have extraordinary prestige. He believes that the success of his company would encourage him to improve himself socially. He resists the idea of slackening his pace when it comes to the killing sprees. Is he skating on thin ice? He had a narrow shave the other evening, after being spotted by a minx with too much makeup on. The jocund fizgig, all furs, heels, frills, and lace, eyes like almonds, nails as claws, flesh with marvelous opaline transparency, sauntered by these bums on the curb as a doctor past expectant patients in a hospital, the luminous coastline in the background. Common herd was massed together in the gathering gloom. The drencher splashed her like a wave crashing upon a rock. An engine driver, rubicund-complected, had blunt features and a tomato head, his attention arrested, fondled her with a frenzied zest. She maintained a proud posture of erectness and wore symbolic shoes. She was, truthfully, celestial, combed her cropped hair. She had a raucous voice, a toothbrush mustache, and a love of ostentation. She was a fabulous inhuman creature, and, going by her feathers, was an avian of another genus. He scurried like a squirrel. A bird rhythmically beat the air with its wings. The value of his wares — priceless. Peki plods like he's wearing a suit of chainmail. His eyes shine as reflectors. He clips his Vandyke beard, gnawed by forlornness. Morbid doubts nag at him. He is useless without the store, as a soldier who is posted at a desk and not at the frontlines where he'd be productive. Water leaks from a pipe like drops from a cistern. The taurine roar of thunder. Summer season is in full swing. The beach is peopled. Are his dubious ways and sullied reputation known to Marisa? Does she think he is seeking to corrupt her? He dreads like the plague the thought of encountering his hypochondriac Mama in here. He imagines them linked, arm-in-arm, in geometrical rays, a phosphorescent phenomenon. He's her disciple. He swears to become her master, inspiring her respect. His acidic stomach turns like a mill wheel, reading the headline on the front page of the newspaper: Manhunt Underway For Serial Killer. He does not want to attract undue attention. If the hounds of authority pick up his scent, he'll put them off it somehow. He feels cankered, putrefied. He twitches, as though by a reflex, in the decomposing luminosity. The monotony of the firmament is broken by crawling cirri. Lately, he feels like he's been existing in a universal theater well-stocked with actors and settings. The narcotic mantequilla enlarges the scale of the environment, and magnifies the proportions of Homo sapiens.

Marisa poisons everything in his life. Impecunious, against the eight ball, Peki was never lacking in ambition or talent. For years he did backbreaking manual labor, slaving in the glassworks and claypits. Does he have too many irons in the fire? He knows he's ill-made and on the small side.

Empyrean loses its cumuli, as metal put in an acid bath loses its qualities. He manipulates his machines. She is hidden in the folds of blankets like she's lying in furrows of dunes. Bees sound like violins. Cherubic lutanists, ones you'd see painted on the ceiling of an Italian cathedral, flit like flies, wallpaper as a Japanese print. Ocean's bluish bosom heaves. Boat's mast is like a church steeple. The city is filled with the tumult of its citizenry under the flesh-pink sky. The downpour makes a quagmire of the earth. Water resembles a meadow. A steamer smokes like a factory. Existence, for Peki, is like a squall, against which it is useless to struggle. He finds himself in monotonous spirits. He's pale as death. What he would give for a spell of contemplative relaxation. Scenarios in his head play as Judeo-Christian tragedies perpetually in performance. She appears to be less alive than other people, or she's a perfect imitation of life. Her face is haggard and leaden in the dawn's premature heat and humidity. In a tunic, she tidies herself at the mirror and assumes a joyous air, dispelling his doldrums, holding herself rather stiffly perpendicular on the chessboard ceramic tile. He puts on his smock and bestows on her profuse flattery. She grins ear-to-ear. He has an apoplectic blush and there's an alteration in his speech. When it comes to her, his dastardly mistrust takes a concrete form. He was not raised to abide by the rules of regular folks. His relationship with her profits from the ruses which he has adopted wholeheartedly. He wants to believe their connection is like a wave, crumbling before reaching its vertex. It cools off. His fart expresses the jarring emptiness of the room. Her vocabulary is defective. Cabbage-green aqua pura. Throughout his existence, he has felt like prey chosen by predacious life, that it's a matter of time before he's taken. Sun breaks through the clouds, restoring brightness and warmth. Cluster of crows' cawing sounds not unlike a rallying call. An age-old parish has a pepper pot turret. Painted and powdered, she plays, with a barrel organ, a Viennese waltz. She has the aroma of geranium. His heart misses a beat. He remembers them going on the donkey ride yesterday, the fresh air doing them good, and sea-bathing. He feels a jab in his groin. Tangible particles, specks of dust, are revealed in a luminescent beam. Her piercing voice arouses in him an excruciating unease. Hail sounds like the chords of a celebration. Peki imagines Marisa in a straitjacket. He wonders if he's overanalyzing his nervous ailments, as a sufferer misdiagnosing his symptoms. Does she have the capacity for deceit? He feels like he's not even fit to be thrown to the dogs. Her ebony dress is like a bishop's vestment. He experiences an ebullience in observing her. Sometimes it's like he's a superintendent of the apartment asylum, and she is the lunatic inmate who has her key to the institution. She respires as if she is recovering her breath. She was domiciled at a defunct chapel for a month. She ran away like a little girl. He searched near and far, over hill and dale, under the wild heavens, rested for a while on a heap of turnips and heather in a fully, had an orgasm of contemplation, the infinitesimal, parasitical Marisa burrowing into his consciousness. He was transfixed by the careless grandness of the briny. He missed her desperately. She was found sleeping in an oaken pew by a thewy contractor. He has a goblin's grimace. Her laughter has the sonance of equine whinnying, as if in response to the punchline to a cosmic joke. With her, concerns and fears fall away as the flutter of autumn leaves. He undergoes a satisfaction of senses, his bestial lineaments beaming, for once not feeling like a leprotic imp. She laps up compliments as a kitten does spilled cream. She reverts to her ossuary of a boudoir with its bizarre furniture. Pregnant silence. Peki feels an electric tingling throughout his entirety. He sniffs the air like a seal. They mumble during discourse as though it's a segment of an immortal custom, reciting what sounds like gibberish, probably having a disconcerting effect upon the ears of neighbors. He's rocked by verbal blows dealt to him and he reels. Nails of insults are hammered yet deeper. Invectives, spontaneously generated, strike like thunderbolts. The rhythm of his respirations accelerates. The horizon is piled-up with clouds. The town is rainswept. Her intonation sounds not unlike a screech owl. His breath fails him. He recollects rubbing and rinsing after the slaughtering. He went home as an injured animal makes for its den... Prone on his mattress-sarcophagus in the sepulchral bedroom, a scooped-out cavity, he wept like a boy, unintentionally making funny faces in the dim lamplight. His muttering sounded like ritualistic incantations. He used a zinc ointment to treat his eczematous condition in the silvery stream of moonlight. The vista was disencumbered of cloudlets. He brushed his bushy beard. After the consecutive argumentative battles

royal, her inflection is flat and toneless, the wisp of smoke from her cigarette like the fanciful letter of a tragic tome. Being his mother, eccentric
and wayward, is a potent weapon for her, and she takes full advantage
of it. Her title is a crucial and singular one. His fondness is violent and
feverish. He is dedicated to her with a piquant zeal. He thinks of Roberto,
a man of Herculean proportions, colossal egoism, and immense status...
dead and buried. She is long-necked and snake-smooth. She prolongs his
tantalized elation by dancing and singing in her chiffon nightgown. Her
breasts protrude wantonly. He listens with all his ears and sees with all
his eyes. She sets his sensory faculty on fire. Her company can offer transporting satisfaction. She's supple as a serpent, adept at the art of coquetry.
She diminishes his sorrows. His phiz is molded by them, his body bowed
by them. Her words can wound, though, rend his heart. Their alliance
annihilates time and space. He has spasms in his loins and he glows with
stimulation. He interacts with her like a thespian who has learned the
ins and outs of his part and is improvising as the scene unfolds, adroitly
taking his cues.

Shadow disincarnates him and light reincarnates him. Rainbow's a roar
of coloration. Peki's trade is flourishing. He was on the brink of ruin. He
had the feeling like his potential was being frittered away, promise erased
by endless setbacks. He'll progress from relative obscurity to a blaze of
glory! He has several cards up his sleeve. He sits in the center box of
the wardrobe. Marisa acts like this is a dress rehearsal for a play in some
fashionable theater. He succumbs to her allurements, left in an attitude
of rapture. Eroticism is embodied in this entertainment. She insists it's
a "charity concert." To him, it is more like a mystic rite. She gave him a
dressing-down earlier on, insisting that he was selfish and cruel. And he
was shaken with sobs, felt as if he were game that was cornered. He was at
the bottom of the food chain, on the lowest rung of the domestic ladder,
and she would never let him forget it. She was quite distant. He was
shrunken. Everything he was, with her, had dwindled. She couldn't take
the trouble to conceal her derision. His attention was drawn towards her,
into a central concentration. Drizzle tinkles like a bell. Bowl of pottage.
Stray cinerarias. Lacking in inertia, Marisa announces masturbation is

second nature, sex being the first. She has come to his rescue, saving him from the barrenness of soul, and restoring his spirit. She has tightened his loose screw. Tears stream from Peki's eyes. She is the container and he is the contained. Engaged in making more Butyrum, it was a titanic struggle, like he was an epic poet endeavoring to wrangle language for breakthrough verse. Making margarine, he tightened the slackened reins of his focus. The previous homicide looked as though it was a blackly comedic, sadistic skit. He stews about leaving clues behind, picturing evidentiary, circular waves moving out from the crime scene and reaching the walls of his establishment. The heat of worry begins to boil. Her character has tremendous value, her personality with an inventory of assets. Intermittencies of illumination. The weather system consists of these sequences of spritzes, without any solution of continuity. The image of his Mama recedes in his mind as a dream. It is stiflingly hot. He longs to feel her arms around him, smothering him with smooches, his heart bulging to the breaking point. Purply dusk. He feels totally out of step with civilization. People are mostly petty and trivial. He resolved, at a young age, to never walk the straight path, instead seeking to put one foot in front of the other, to take either a right or a left at a fork in the road. He studies her like he's absorbing every particle of vision. His lamps lock on hers. Night has dominated day. Stars are effulging pinpricks. Cirri weave the azure. Pea-souper dazes the depth of the megalopolis. There's a rancid, vomitous fetor. She is designed for his sight. Something approaching bliss passes through him. Is she a blessing degraded to a curse? She satisfies his visual gluttony. Bouquet is a gush of resplendence; botanical technicolor. Marisa attracts his admiration. The megapolis conducts a raid on his eyesight. She looks like a spellbinding sleepwalker. Rumor of their involvement spread as popple. Although she's wight-pale, her felt integument confirms her corporeality. Contacting her, it is like he is sampling her molecules somehow. Peki shudders with satisfaction. She speaks with a lisp and has ocelot eyes. Her cerebral development is incomplete. Her company replenishes his vivacity. She realizes he is highly strung. He's worn out and ready to drop. His reserves of strength are weakened. He is revived as a flower put in water. She's the talker and he's a hearer. He would never offend her opinions. He feeds on her nervous energy. His prophet's beard is surmounted by a flat nose. His views on their nation are diametrically opposed to hers. The demon of desire drives him. She is heart-shatteringly fanciable. He's finding it increasingly difficult to disguise his arousal. His work is far from his thoughts. She is a rare bird! She has put him off its scent, like a hound on the hunt distracted in tracking the fox with the arrival of a mutt. She wields the domiciliary scepter and sits there like a fairy godmother. She's an unknown species, born of magic. He has his pleasures and regrets. If he's ever convicted and incarcerated, would she believe in his innocence, cast a shadow of doubt on the verdict's legitimacy? Soundness? He's resigned to accepting whatever is in store for him. He has traveled a significant distance to reach his present position. A crack in the cumuli covering the sun is like a fissure in a pupil. She is impressed and has a warm regard for him. She knows he has unorthodox tastes, profound megrims, and is inclined to be flighty. She has an affectedness that becomes her, throat harnessed in imitation rubies and sapphires.

Butter Up!

Butter is as old as Western civilization. In ancient Rome, it was medicinal — swallowed for coughs or spread on aching joints. In India, Hindus have been offering Lord Krishna tins full of ghee — luscious, clarified butter — for at least 3,000 years. And in the Bible, butter is a food for the celebration, first mentioned when Abraham and Sarah offer three visiting angels a feast of meat, milk, and the creamy yellow spread. Butter's origins are likely more humble, though. Rumor has it a nomad made the first batch by accident. He probably tied a sheepskin bag of milk to his horse and, after a day of jostling, discovered the handy transformation so many generations have noticed and learned to apply: churned milk fat solidifies into something amazing. The oldest known butter-making technique still in use today is remarkably similar: farmers in Syria skin a goat, tie the hide up tight, then fill it with milk and begin shaking. Although some of the earliest records of butter consumption come from Roman and Arabian sources, Mediterranean people have always favored oil in their cooking. Butter, it seems, was the fat of choice for the tribes of northern Europe — so much so that Anaxandrides, the Greek poet, derisively referred to barbarians from the north as "butter-eaters." Climate likely played a key role in regional tastes, as the cool weather at northern latitudes allowed people to store butter longer than Mediterranean cultures could. By the 12th century, the butter business was booming across northern Europe. Records show that Scandinavian merchants exported tremendous amounts each year, making the spread a central part of their economy. Butter was so essential to life in Norway, for example, that the

King demanded a full bucket every year as a tax. By the Middle Ages, eaters across much of Europe were hooked. Butter was popular among peasants as a cheap source of nourishment and prized by the nobility for the richness it added to cooked meats and vegetables. For one month out of each year, however, the mostly-Christian Europeans got by without their favorite fat. Until the 1600s, butter-eating was banned during Lent. For northern Europeans without access to cooking oils, meal-making could be a struggle during the weeks before Easter. Butter proved so necessary to cooking that the wealthy often paid the Church a hefty tithe for permission to eat the fat during the month of self-denial. Demand for this perk was so high that in Rouen, in northwestern France, the Cathedral's Tour de Beurre — or Butter Tower — was financed and built with such tithes. Across the English Channel in Ireland, butter was so critical to the Irish economy that merchants opened a Butter Exchange in Cork to help regulate the trade. Today, barrels of ancient Irish butter, which were traditionally buried in bogs for aging, are among the most common archeological finds in the Emerald Isle. In France, butter was in such high demand by the 19th century that Emperor Napoleon III offered a large prize for anyone who could manufacture a substitute. In 1869, a French chemist won the award for a new spread made of rendered beef fat and flavored with milk. He called it "oleomargarine," later on shortened to just margarine. Across the Atlantic, butter consumption started with the pilgrims, who packed several barrels for their journey on the Mayflower. During the next three centuries, butter became a staple of the American farm. At the turn of the 20th century, Americans' annual consumption was an astonishing 18 pounds of butter per capita — nearly a stick and a half per person per week! The Great Depression and World War II challenged America's love affair with butter. The turmoil brought shortages and rationing, and margarine — now made with vegetable oil and yellow food coloring — became a cheaper option for American families. Butter consumption took a nosedive. In addition, dieticians and the USDA began promoting a low-fat diet in the 1980s, and butter became déclassé. By 1997, consumption had fallen to 4.1 pounds per capita per year. Since then, butter has staged a comeback. Researchers have discovered that the ingredients in old-style margarine are significantly worse for heart health than the saturated fats found in natural butter. The news has lured more and more Americans back to their buttery traditions. The passion for delectable cuisine is bolstering consumption once again as artisanal butters appear in chilled grocery cases across the country. And at top restaurants around the globe, chefs are doing extraordinary things with this millennia-old food, creating an exciting new page in the history of butter.

The milk of most mammals contains a mixture of fats, proteins, sugars, vitamins, and minerals suspended in water. The water is denser than the fats. If whole milk is allowed to sit for a time, the fat globules, in the form of cream, will rise to the surface where they can be skimmed off. The thin fluid that remains after the cream is removed is called skim milk, and it was once fed to calves and pigs. Today it's fed to diet-conscious humans. When a quantity of cream or whole milk is agitated, the yellowish fat globules join to form a solid mass of butter. Historians speculate that butter was discovered when some desert nomad threw a goatskin full of camel milk on the back of that same camel and lurched off across the desert. When he arrived at his destination, he was astonished to find a congealed mass of what we now call butter on the skin. Evidence of butter was found in King Tut's tomb and it is mentioned several times in the Old Testament.

Probably from the beginning of dairy husbandry, people who milked cows set aside part of the milk in containers while they waited for the cream to rise to the surface. The process could take 12 to 36 hours and, with no refrigeration, the cream and milk frequently soured by the time it was finished. The resulting cream was not only thin and often sour, but also could pick up objectionable tastes and odors. Meanwhile, the soured skim milk wasn't much good as feed for young stock. Although cream needs to be 'ripened,' or slightly sour, in order to make good butter, that made from tainted or overly sour cream was inferior in taste and often smelled bad, bringing much lower market prices. Dairy work consisted of milking and making cream, butter, and cheese. Women traditionally did that work in Europe, and the practice was often followed in the New World as well.

Even if women didn't always do the milking on U.S. farms, they were usually responsible for separating cream and churning butter. Of course, there was more to making butter than churning. It had to be rinsed several times to remove all the buttermilk. Then it was lightly salted and worked (or kneaded) to evenly distribute the salt, remove excess water, and make the texture smooth. The butter was then ready to pack into a container.

During the 19th century, many farmwives supplemented farm income by selling butter. They churned every day or so, or whenever enough cream had accumulated. The butter was stored, layer upon layer, in a wooden tub, kept in a cool cellar until it could be taken to a nearby country store. As can be imagined, the quality of the layers varied widely. When 'goin' to town' day arrived, the farmer's wife put on her hat, loaded the tub of butter into the wagon or buggy, and set off. At the country store, she presented the butter to the storekeeper, who assigned a value. Country storekeepers in those days were a shrewd bunch, and they had to be to keep ahead of their equally shrewd customers. Our man was as canny as anyone and knew that the bottom layers might be bad or that the good wife may have mixed in a quantity of lard to fill the tub. So, before giving the woman a price for her butter, he tested it. Using a butter borer, which he pushed through the layers to the bottom of the tub, the grocer extracted a core of butter. The test consisted of a cautious sniff or two, along with a quick lick of the tongue along the length of the sample. The column of butter was then replaced in its hole, the borer withdrawn and the top smoothed with a finger (this may not have been standard practice, but it did happen). Once a value for the butter was agreed upon, the farm wife could take the cash, although many merchants issued tokens for future use at the store. More often than not, the lady 'traded out' her butter, receiving needed items in return. The story is told of the farmer's wife who brought in some chickens and a tub of butter to trade for a list of items she needed. She gave the store clerk the list to fill and proceeded to look over some new dress goods that had just arrived. On her list was "1 roll of butter." As she returned to the counter, she saw the clerk reach for the tub of butter she had just brought in. Quickly she cried, "Oh, I don't want any of that – I want some good butter!"

During the late 1800s, creameries began to process local milk into butter and cheese. Butter then became known as either 'dairy butter' (made on the farm) or 'creamery butter' (produced in a creamery). Beginning in about 1890, parchment paper was used to wrap 1-pound rectangular blocks of butter. Early in the 20th century, as the creamery industry became more and more mechanized, cardboard cartons came into use.

Peki's Journal

People put their hands over their mouths and laugh, trying to look in the opposite direction, but also wanting to alert their friends or family, and speak in hushed tones, "there's a midget." When I make eye contact, they seem embarrassed. I can read lips. It's an acquired skill, developed over the years. There are times when these retards don't even pretend to hide their ridicule. I'll pass a store in the mall, someone will spot me, point, snicker, and jeer. My existence is a joke to folks. To them, I'm not human, I'm a separate species. It's used in a clinical capacity. In medical journals, the language is somewhere along the lines of "this male dwarf." Do they say "this female autistic" or "this male cerebral palsy?" No. Of course not. It's usually "this person" with "fill in the condition." When I was a kid I could understand crap better than most my age. I sensed and saw others reacting differently to me. My mother would insist I was the same as everybody else. I knew she was saying this to make me feel good, to boost my fragile ego. She made sure I participated in activities I'd otherwise avoid. She cared for me and was determined not to shield me from the world. In public places someone would say "isn't he cute," but occasionally it was crueler. Coming to terms with being a little person has been a very long process. Complicated by society's prejudice. It's a kick in the groin when I'm treated with contempt or my picture is taken without my consent. People believe my life on this planet is a farce. I've since stopped internalizing my anger and started externalizing it, where it belongs. My independence and self-sufficiency have served me well — though I am small in stature, I'm accomplishing big things. I have Achondroplasia, a genetic mutation that results in shorter limbs and a standing height of four feet. There are countless challenges associated with Dwarfism. I experience chronic health issues, from bone and joint pain to bow legs and a narrow spinal column. I have undergone three surgeries on my neck and back to widen it. The communal problems are equally extensive. School was especially difficult, with peers and teachers who teased and bullied me. I've grown to accept my diversity. I make a distinction between the shit I can change and the shit I cannot change. I realize that I can't do anything about my height, but I can do something about my beliefs, attitudes, thoughts, and connection to spirit. I've learned how to control my temper when I want to rip some stranger's head off for being a rude asshole. I mean, there is a difference between innocent curiosity and an individual being a moron. I practice patience. I have a thicker skin lately. An insult will come out of the blue and take my breath away. Inwardly, I'll cope with the torment. Outwardly, I will be stoic. I will pretend it isn't happening. I'd weep and wish someone else was the subject of the nasty comment. I'm often the target. I played soccer as a teenager. Attributed to my limited leg span, I couldn't run, only I could pass and shoot. Nonetheless, I was an outcast on the team. My mates refused to embrace me as one of their own. I was a liability, a hindrance. It was fucking heartbreaking. The indignities I suffered were numerous. I was told that a nurse exclaimed, "Holy Jesus in heaven!" when I was born. I arrived a month late. Mama was shocked and upset. I can't blame her. She knew how hard my existence would be. She was right. She is as tall as I am small and has been my protector from the beginning. She has made it possible for me to live whatever life I choose. She raised me. Expectations for me to succeed, despite my disabilities, were not lowered. They stayed high. She never permitted me to hide. She wouldn't cut me any slack. She's my cheerleader and my critic. Fight or flight. It's up to me. I am the main attraction daily. Getting prescription pills and going grocery shopping — it's as if I'm a pseudo-celebrity, without fame or money, naturally, and men, women, and children are my paparazzi. Anonymity is not achievable. I might lose my career or my home only I'll never lose my dignity. I won't take it. I refuse to suck it up. It's part of my nature. Eleanor Roosevelt said, "You must do the thing you think you cannot do." Obstacles are hurdles I jump over with mental athleticism. I can physically go around or under them. I will be forever on the receiving end of protracted gazes. Fine. I have dreams of harmonious humanity. I nurture the precious part of who I am: the soul. I'm normal. I have the same feelings and desires as you. Why should I tolerate the taunting? There's nothing wrong with me. It has taken me a lifetime not to trust the opinions of others. Those who don't matter. If a person doesn't respect you, or appreciate you for who you are, because of your appearance or whatever, then they're not worth befriending. If you don't get the job on account of the way you look then that job isn't worth it. Don't be so quick to judge. Instead of identifying my handicap as a crutch, I use it to set myself apart from the rest and turn it into a unique characteristic about myself. I accomplish tasks with relative confidence and ease, although admittedly I need to stand on a bucket to reach the sink, employ a wastebasket to get to a cabinet, or use the bathtub's water to brush my teeth in a hotel room. It doesn't faze me. I am forced to adapt. There aren't any options. My old car was modified to fit my frame, with pedal extensions and safety features such as disarmed airbags. Chairs and stools at the apartment and work are right-sized, pimped-out to accommodate me. I've pursued a profession in butter-making and selling. This is what I want to do for the rest of my life: produce my special, delectable mantequilla. I'm ok with myself. Culturally, Dwarfism generally receives negative attention, dating back to 19th-century mythology. In art, film, and literature, dwarfs are typically depicted as nonhuman, mythical, or even divine. There is a fine line between how little people are portrayed and how they prefer to be perceived. I can't change my anatomical defects, but I can increase my vocational expertise. I apply myself with focus and commitment. I cannot control how folks respond to me, only I can control how I respond to them. If one experiences oppression and discrimination, one can go where less exists — change one's locality. That's why we live in this parallel universe, the Fifth Dementia. I've gotten a new wardrobe and hairstyle that flatter me. I look into my heart and see my magnificence. My beauty shines from the inside out. According to a report from the Regional Dysplasia Clinics, achondroplasia occurs in 1 in every 25,000 births. It doesn't matter. It happened. I'm here and walking tall! Hahaha!

Abril Amor

She is a duck-faced Monstro, her whalish shape a result of nature's maldesign. She has gourd tits and her bicepses are very similar to her forearms, seemingly going to her hands without any wrist intervention. Abril's bedraggled fauxhawk is shiny, like a seal's coat, mostly from anxiety sweat. She is a wacko evangelical and chronic procrasturbator who considers herself an intimate writer of literary fiction (with its high-and-low diction), making a mind-meld that is freakily Vulcan with the reader. She is preternaturally good at creating Dunning-Kruger in her audience. Of course, as an option, one can absorb her pages by osmosis. She wears these welfare glasses and has jumbo teeth, fleshly chins, and a ciggy-boozy laugh, with a preference for Parcheesi. She is the self-proclaimed high priestess of moon-barking and napkin-shredding. She smells strangely of margarine. Following her compulsory pudendacure (trimmed to a triangle), she clumps along the sidewalk, with its aggregate of pedestrians, stumps up the street, wind-whipped, dodging cars, under a rash-red sun, finally getting onto the Mainssieuxian road under the woods, feeling frilly and girly, amped up on crank, bouncing on endorphins, tense as a cocked gun, having left her lover, Violeta Bisquick, the patron saint of suffering, a switchblade-slender, coked-out dumb blond, a Fellinian Satyriconette constantly looking catatonic, her front flat as an ironing board, always untweezed, paste-pale, with chiffonade hair, anteater nose, gummous mouth, and dopey grin, after bonking her in the abandoned truck in an unused parking lot. Her armpits, with scrubbing-brush tufts, reeked of an overused washcloth, her feet with a weird-ass sewage odor, enough to turn the stomach. Although Abril was rough, she was impelled by no malice. They were thick as thieves. Make no mistake. The doors, covered in obscene graffiti, were like the walls of a fortress. The intimacy was intense. The two gyrated in the Chevy like fish in a glass bowl. Abril, who took the lead in the coital dance, could barely repress a cry of joy when she came. They hung around not unlike mussels on a rock, then slept like logs. The repose the vehicle offered was comforting. It provided them with momentary relaxation from their worries. When Abril woke, she saw the penile centipede, scuttering with pubic legs on the hood, which really discomposed her. She has a splitting headache and her inner loins are sore, on her way to visit the transvestitured sponger, Rafa Chendo, this ramrod-rigid valet who lives in a hovel adjacent to a luxurious house of ill fame, the guy with a room-service smile, yodel voice, love handles, limp noodle, pelvic problems, hippopotamus-humongous rear end, and the complexion of commode porcelain, to score. She is endowed with a bird's sense of direction. He has the intelligence quotient of a traffic cone. She is certain of his proclivities and knows he has no malevolent intentions. He's gotten crabs so often that he's become a human brine. There is a sexual abnormality embodied in him. She is sure of it. The grandmaster of melodrama, he's painted and paunchy, with sweeping eyelashes, his profile endued with a neo-Hellenic elegance. He was well-brought-up, and possesses social affability. She is unmoved by civilities and is impervious to the vanities of the population. When it comes to her background, she is of humble extraction. She is a frequenter of his sordid world, not a citizen of it. He is inflexible and dignified, confident and terse, with a pugnacious instinct and bellicose humor, and let's not forget the distinguished poses and hideous memory. Purplish waves rise and fall in a mystic dance under the incitement of a sudden breeze. Abril feels like white bread, sloppy seconds, a goddam doormat for guys. She should turn back. She visualizes her blinders as being windows, lids their shades, and she drifts off, her slumber borne on the tidal flow of tiredness. A ship sets sail. She waddles obesely, her blinkers glistening with perfervid daydreams. She introduces her imagination to the idea that Rafa cares for her. He has a profoundly ingrained habit of not returning her phone calls. Her heart is heavy. Hope for a better life lies in a brighter morrow. Peki compliments the dragon tat on her calf.

Marisa's Diary

My cherished Peki was, unequivocally, a wanted and planned baby. Make no mistake about this. I thankfully had a healthy pregnancy, followed by two doctors: a general practitioner and an obstetrician. I had 3 ultrasonographs: in the first, second, and third trimesters and did several blood tests. Everything was always all right. He was born in the early hours of the 29th of August. I had an epidural when I was 4 cm dilated and it was natural childbirth after 4 hours of active labor. He had 2930 g, 46.5 cm long, and 36 cm head perimeter (6 pounds,18.1 inches long, and 14 inches head perimeter). We, my husband and I, both felt full of joy! In his first hours of life, everything seemed to be okay, but at the same time, something was strange. I examined the baby that we had expected for 9 months. I remember looking at him when my husband held him in his arms. And I noticed his hands: long fingers but very wide open. Weird. He was so tiny! His clothes didn't fit him well. On the second night, while looking at him sleeping on my bed, I stopped and stretched his arms along his body. And his hands didn't reach his legs. Not even close. I measured my arms and they did reach my thighs. I wondered what was up. But at the same time, nothing was or could be too odd. I was happy and tired too. He was a quiet baby and had a good appetite. During the 3 days we stayed in the hospital maternity, Peki was seen by 4 pediatricians. A few hours after going home, the third doctor came to discharge him from the hospital. The doctor began to observe him, extended his arms and after some seconds of silence she said, "This child has short limbs." Then and there, I didn't think that something could be wrong. That doctor did a transfontanellar ultrasound (through an open space of his skull), and said that he was okay and that Peki should have to have a follow-up. I started to put all the things that I noticed and the doctor's comments together. My heart started to slowly break... A sadness affected us significantly and we just could not enjoy every single moment with our son without thinking that something could be tremendously wrong. We soon went to his pediatrician and told him what happened. He did not notice anything abnormal until we mentioned the hospital pediatrician's suspicions. He advised us to see a geneticist. One week later we went to Lisbon for an appointment with a geneticist. At first, the doctor said, "What are these parents doing here with this beautiful baby?!" After several minutes of talking about what happened, Peki was once again over an observation table. I was about to stop my heart from beating at that the point when the doctor started "dissecting and cutting" piece by piece all my hope saying, "Rizomelic shortening, trident hands, frontal prominence, small nose... " The doctor ended by saying that Peki had skeletal dysplasia, but it probably could be hypochondroplasia and for that, be a minor problem. Maybe it was achondroplasia. 50-50 chance. He had to do exams. I struggled for breath. I felt destroyed inside, couldn't believe what was occurring. My sweet baby boy had a rare condition. A few days after, he had his first complete skeletal x-ray and a blood sample was taken from him for a genetic test. During the time without the genetic test result, I refused to search for anything related to achondroplasia. That period was lived in limbo. We were not living those moments with our newborn child as planned. We waited 1 month until the diagnosis came. Peki had achondroplasia. The end of a story and the beginning of a new one. Achondroplasia, a new word... meaning unknown in our lives. Our journey started, unexpectedly, without our dream destiny but now with an expected dream as the destination. Peki was an infant like all babies. He slept and ate well, cried, shat, laughed, and smiled at every/anything. He stopped and stared at his lovely mother, me, haha, that in a tick was kissing her and telling her stories, while he pulled out his toys "because he doesn't want to play more with this one!" Well, I hope to be able to help and enlighten you about the life of a babe with achondroplasia and about the life of a family whom achondroplasia visited. Here is what I've learned over time:

Achondroplasia is the most recognizable form of short stature, characterized by disproportionate short stature with prevalence rates of about 1:10,000 to 1:30,000 per live births. The cause of achondroplasia was identified to be a gain-of-function mutation in the gene for the fibroblast growth factor receptor 3 (FGFR-3) and is known to be an autosomal dominant trait. Achondroplasia is characterized by short stature, short limbs, and rhizomelic disproportion, macrocephaly, and midfacial retrusion. Other characteristics are a small chest, thoracolumbar kyphosis, lumbar hyperlordosis, limited elbow extension, short fingers, and trident configuration of the hands. Patients may also show hypermobile hips and knees, bowing of the mesial segment of the legs as well as hypotonia. Affected patients experience various orthopedic and neurological complications and might face multiple medical and non-medical challenges in their daily life. Treat your child according to their age and developmental level, not their size. A 2-year-old should not still use a bottle, for example, even if she's the size of a 1-year-old. And, if you expect a 6-year-old to clean up his room, don't make an exception because your child is small. Make changes to your child's environment to promote independence. Simple, inexpensive options include light switch extenders or step-stools. Treat your child's skeletal dysplasia as a difference, not a problem. Your attitude and expectations can greatly influence your child's self-esteem. Ask how your child wants to refer to their dwarfism. Some people prefer "little person" or "person of short stature." Try your best to stay calm and positive when responding to other people's reactions. Address questions or comments as directly as possible, then point out something special about your child. Your kid will see that you notice the qualities that make them unique. This helps prepare your child for responding to these situations when you're not there. If your child is teased at school, don't overlook it. Talk to teachers and administrators to make sure your child is getting the support they need. Offer to work with the school to educate others about dwarfism. Help your youngster learn about their condition and possible health care needs as your child gets older and more independent. Encourage your child to find a hobby or activity to enjoy. Check with your doctor about any sports to avoid. Music, art, computers, writing, or photography are also wonderful options to explore. Stay active together as a family. If needed, choose or adapt the activity so your child can join. About 80 percent of people born with achondroplasia have average-sized parents. This means that the genetic mutation that causes achondroplasia occurs during conception when the mother's egg is fertilized by the father's sperm. It is not known why this genetic mutation occurs, or how the mutation translates into the characteristics of achondroplasia.

Twenty percent of people born with achondroplasia inherit the faulty gene from an affected parent. If one parent has achondroplasia, then their child has a 50 percent chance of inheriting the gene for the condition. If both parents have achondroplasia, their child has: A one in four risk of inheriting the faulty gene from both parents, which causes a fatal condition known as 'double dominant' or homozygous achondroplasia. Children born with this variation generally don't live beyond 12 months of age. A 50 percent chance of inheriting one copy of the gene for the condition, and therefore having achondroplasia.A one in four chance of not inheriting the gene, and having normal stature. Children with achondroplasia face a number of difficulties, including: Breathing difficulties – including snoring and sleep apnoea (the regular cessation of breathing during sleep), caused by narrowed nasal passages. Ear infections – caused by narrowed Eustachian tubes (tubes leading from the ears to the throat) and nasal passages. Bowed legs – the legs are initially straight, but over time (in some cases) they become bowed once the child starts walking. Increased lumbar lordosis – a backward curve in the lower spine. Reduced muscle strength – the child has a softer muscle tone than normal and needs to be adequately supported until the muscle groups are ready to support the neck and spine. Hydrocephalus – the child has an increased risk of hydrocephalus (one in 100), which is an accumulation of cerebrospinal fluid inside the skull that can lead to head enlargement. Narrow foramen magnum – the child has a smaller than normal opening at the base of the skull (foramen magnum), where the spinal cord begins. This can sometimes press against the brain stem and cause symptoms including apnoea (cessation of breathing) and neurological signs. Problems faced by adults with achondroplasia can include: Nerve compression – the nerves in the lower back or lumbar region are squashed, which can cause symptoms such as numbness or tingling in the legs. Obesity – most adults experience difficulties in maintaining a healthy weight for their height. Crowded teeth – the upper jaw is typically small, which causes the teeth to overcrowd. Higher risk pregnancies – pregnant women with achondroplasia need expert antenatal care. Cesarean section is the usual mode of delivery. There is no cure for achondroplasia. Human growth hormone has no place in its management, as the condition is not caused by a lack of growth hormone. Treatment focuses on the prevention, management, and treatment of medical complications as well as social and family support. This may include: Surgery – may be advised to relieve pressure on the nervous system, generally at the base of the skull and lower back, or to open obstructed airways by removing the adenoids. Dental and orthodontic work – to correct malocclusion and ensure dental health. Support from other health care providers – including geneticists, neurologists, and pediatricians. There are currently preliminary trials on a medication called vosoritide to treat the symptoms of achondroplasia, but these are only in the initial stages.

Flowery Marisa

The head of the female efflorescent creature, named Marisa, with a puckered brow and twitching mouth, brought about by the dawning's drowse, her gray hair full of fragments of ancient stones and the shells of prehistoric snails, droops on her bodily peduncle, in her bed circumscribed by reeds, the floral being's fetuses shrimp-shaped and with frightfully pitiable, weary eyes. They must have been waiting to be born for many years. A form in the middle of withered terrain, called Peki, studies her from afar. His head is troubled and his heart is torn. With an animalistic yawn, she spreads her leafage, lustrous and warm, and with a glossy olive-green hue, naturally and unconcernedly as if she were in front of a lover instead of her son, and gently strokes his knuckles. He rejects the caress by pulling his hand away. She issues a hopeless sigh. The faintest flicker of longing wavers across his countenance. The reckless, indiscreet contact, to him, was ill-advised and intrusive. His filmy mane hangs loose on his shoulders, goatee triangulated. His unformulated attraction for her remains unrevealed. He refuses to be outwitted in familial/military strategy. Peace and power are bonded by a reluctant compromise. She's clever, but he's no idiot. She drives him crazy. She has observed him from his infancy. He can't confide in her; he keeps his own counsel. He draws back several steps in a lapse of time too rapid for its passage to be registered and utters inarticulate sounds of bemusement. Here the invisible with all the visual logic becomes visible.

A curious straw-colored vapor drifts from the precipices and swallows the valley. The endless salt-marsh estuary merges with the heavens – it's either the universe before the birth of the country or the one where the ground is not conceived by the Creator. The flower with a woman's face, white as sea foam, one belonging to Marisa, in which, without much effort, it is feasible to make out abnormal anatomy, either that of a vegetable, or a human: veinal stalks, bloody juice, numerous wrinkles, indicating the swiftly shriveling, inner gleaming, which turns out to be the only possible measure. These embryonic buds grow in translucent cocoons, which are awaited by the same contemplative stillness and infinitely long burgeoning in the sphere where the earth is not conceived. In the province where there's nothing else to behold except the swamp, one's sight illumines this impenetrable depth of turbid water. Peki smells a sepulchral sourness. He flutters around the gynaecoid bloom like a moth would a flame. His clenched fists are held taut at his sides. He represses his feelings. He is not unlike a dammed weir. Saliva dribbles down his chin. He is reduced to a bewildered state. The nightmare has added years to her age. Her tender maternal indulgences he is not the least bit appreciative of. It rains wood shavings. The sun, directly above the strip of damp, mossy woodland, ripples with heat as though it's a reflection in a lake, a pebble thrown into it. He pulls his tunic tighter to counteract the chill. There's a redolence of sweet fungus. Verbally does she drag the string of sarcasm. He is corpse-cold. The tension in his nerves is eased a little by staying clear of her. Ashes sprinkle. The two get to know, intimately, each other's peculiarities on a mortal and botanical level. Impulsively he kneels and pats the soil surrounding her stem and plucks her. A four-footed, rail-thin, strawberry blond girl, with the rump of an ass, wearing a romper and waders, caterwauls and canters.

In the clammy, arch-roofed chamber of prodigious size, with a woolen curtain over the square of a window, the motherly blossom bends forward in the decorative china container and he quickly kisses her feverish forehead. He contemplates her fizzog with a reproachful expression. Then they exchange reprehensible and ravishing stories of the wildest mysteries, tales originally told by hysterical demons centuries ago. He is motionless like a decoy duck. Gusts wail and whistle in the cavernous room. He is seated on a fragrant fir log, respiring laboriously, monotonously.

Emotions satisfy the demands of the situation. Palpable oxygen has this semenoid odor. A yellow haze thickens. This dreamworld is at once intensely real and grotesquely fabulous. Is he soundly asleep or fully awake? Suddenly, her petalous fingers grope for his wrist. Whereupon he finds himself stripped and exposed, comfortably ensconced in the goatskin chair, watching her go through various metamorphoses. The weather-beaten place holds the scents of Arabian oils and Syrian spices. A phallic lance, painted and polished, leans against the rocky wall, an oil lamp hanging suspended by an iron chain in its crack. Her arm-leaves, in the pallid radiance, make gestures at once respectful and impersonal. Her perennial petals are as soft as butterfly wings. Her voice is so low as to be nearly inaudible. She is proud, pure, and simple. He feels free from responsibility and concern. He'd dug her up. It is incumbent upon him to replant her, relocate her to a more salubrious clime. She is stationary, unique, and vulnerable in her unconsciousness. His conscience limits the potentiality of an erotic experience. The psychic quality of their relationship is a revelation to him. He has a sensation of relief when she inexplicably wilts before his very eyes. And it is done. He clambers on the slumberous raft and floats off whence he came. The mist is a living and breathing eidolon.

Under a victorious moon, Marisa's fragile lids lift in a refuge in time and space. She surfaces from the abyssal depths of deep sleep, splashing like a fish in the urn. She, perched like some exotic bird on the shelf, awakens to Peki's presence and emits an agitated cry. In a single pulse beat, she is contemplatively calm. They are opposites, as night and day, sound and silence, creation and destruction, birth and death... His acceptance of the darkness of exhibitionistic onanism is presented by the chance of the occasion, with a fantastic opportunity to assert itself. His mental energy is drained to the dregs. The mere idea of masturbating in front of her helpless old loveliness is overwhelming. Her tone is tender. He resists succumbing to an overpowering passion in the blackest recesses of his fathomless soul. He maintains self-control over his romantic cravings, thinking of an ecstatic, scurrilous union. How long can he hold out? Can he continue to curb these primordial instincts? She brushes the rugged contours of his cheeks with her quivering leafage. This is an irresistible enticement. He looks at her with reverence. A flame of primeval lust flares in his loins. He is afraid he might blunder and make a fool of himself in any ill-considered and clumsy attempt at wit. His blood is in ferment. His would-be prey stirs him up in an immemorial predacious fervor. Will their erotic emanations stop before they've begun? There's a delirious intensity of emotion, both under the influence of one another. He wishes to ravish her into docility. He swoons, unable to retain his balance, and he falls to the stone floor with a thud. His bogus long hair covers his pale visage — shadow on snow. He envelops himself in a burgundy coverlet, heart thumping as if a hundred bugbears had been pursuing him. She is humble and upright. His amatory desires are still subdued. A fire burns brightly on the hearth. She talks easily and naturally. There are traces of awkwardness and embarrassment in his inflection. He plunks on the portentously big bench after mechanically moving the hoes and rakes out of the way. The squash pie he had prepared is not exactly unpalatable. She revels in every succulent minute of this richly dramatic scene with him, acting as though the entire scenario is perfectly normal, which is disconcerting to him. She has the scent of an aromatic peel of a particular species of fruit he cannot pinpoint...

They clash on the battlement of a boulder, its lichen like integument. There is a hesitant suspension of the conflict. Torrential lava is ejaculated from the volcano. Quartziferous overcast. A vocalic ceasefire is agreed upon. He yens to submit to her embrace, and yet is awed with terror at the prospect. She bewitches him with her evil eyes. His skin has a fishy scaly texture to it. Peki and Marisa are installed on the rock side by side in a religious quietness. There's forced restraint and reserved power. Golden refulgence flickers and fluctuates. The breeze is an impalpable instrument accompanying their voices. Insubstantial vaporous remnants, not unlike scattered revenants, linger in the alders, their ribs of brown bark with saxifrage on it, under the influence of the wind and its secret stress. He looks at her profile in astonishment. Neither one gains any advantage in the balance of their relations. She throws a puzzled glance at him. The exultation he experiences is beyond the boundaries of sanity, attributing his excitement to the newfound connection to his madre. His concentrated scrutiny of her he devotes his attention to without so much as a second's hesitation. She recites the Latin language of an exorcist rite, and regards the lightness of his step. He repels the most significant temptation to which he has ever been subject. He divines his affection for her. As if heeding the dictates of a heathen faith, he prays he will make her his own. He slackens his speed to keep pace with his preoccupied encephalon on the path, fern-shadowed, with its twists and turns. He assesses the imponderable vacuity of the azure. The wet grass is the final legacy of the precip. Illumined dewdrops glisten like millions of dazzling diamonds. Bushes are adventurous enough to bear raspberries. Treacherous portents are engendered in the murk. Sprays of brambles and spread pine needles indicate human arrangement. Her senses are unnaturally acute. It's as though she's in sync with the chemical substratum of planetary integrands, her superconscious essence with fluidity and solidity. She can feel this within, for she is a phenomenon of Nature, an accidental miracle of transcendent glory. Stars are a blaze of gems, their resplendence otherworldly.

Peki's unexplainable transformation back to himself, in the conquering light, is a shock that pushes him over the brink. It is enough to plunge him into nihility. Jerking off in the washroom, he, bent like a bow, in spasmodic rapture, envisages Marisa vividly, his lascivious imagination producing her, as caprice prescribes, revealed in her previous incarnation, secured in shackles and sexual congress with him in a caliginous bocardo. He rubs her ovine face and kneads her uddered midsection. Syllables proceed from her mouth. He supplies sounds surpassing the reach of words. He feels the vibration of triumphant gratification. His verbal endearments pour forth. She's an obsession who possesses him. She lifts his spirits, brightens his soul, and redeems his sorrows. Men increase her obliviousness to humanly loves and hates. He sees himself loving her for the rest of his days. She galvanizes him with a fascinated curiosity. He is concerned exclusively with these explicit visions. There's a reckless ambition to the make-believe, the participants bound in a frenzy of ardor. Shuddering convulses contort Peki's deformed body as he climaxes, the termination of his desire complete. He suspends his judgment on the subject of Marisa's present state… The soaker reminds him of jets of arterial blood. He auscultates African drumming and strains of chanting coming from the harbor, growing louder and wilder, on the outer edge of this territory, where there are gods and monsters, forest aboriginals, and desert daughters. The dominion is a heart of darkness. The flaming orb above is at its zenith. His psychical vitality is at its nadir. In a twinkling, his memory is seized upon by recollections of her and is caught up in delight. He cannot keep up with the cosmic changes.

A male's head comes out of a clay pot, his neck rising upward like the stalk of an uncanny hybrid herb. Delicate spicules cover his flesh and dome, giving him a cactaceous appearance while also suggesting Christ's crown of thorns or other similar martyrs. With wide oculi, flattened nose, and full lips, the thing has an expression that is both observant and indifferent. The vase is embellished with an image of an Amazon slaying a man, referring to the Greek myth of women warriors whose conflation of feminine and masculine traits matches that of human and plant forms. Glugging Gallic wine, Peki feels led to him by an unseen entity, like a lamb to the slaughter. An absorbed fascination draws him closer. He coasts on the wave crest of oceanic consciousness. His muscles relax and tighten. He experiences guileless wonder and profound suspicion. Sporadic gusts of dialogue commence and eventually reach vortices of conversation. They are both under the influence of a different atmosphere, the enchanted continent of the imagination, separated from that anxious cosmos.

A gigantic hot-air eyeball has morphed into an aberrant balloon in the fog, undulant and opaque, its dead stare directed toward the vault as it rises above the vista. Instead of a basket containing passengers, it carries a severed head on a silver platter, much like that of St. John the Baptist in the Biblical story of Salome. The fronds of a palm-ish annual are perceptible, and the sky, its blue intensifying itself, solidifying itself, is full of lanate clouds. It sees, beyond reality, nature, and the discernible. The bodiless brumal alien, inescapable and insistent, is possessed of its own indefinite identity. Peki evaluates these entities, engrossed in their schemes, like a pair of potential treacherous and unscrupulous enemies, as if they're following a laid plan of their own. He gives little enough thought to their respective departures. He feels like a husk without its seed.

Following the bouquet wassail that Marisa was a participant in, Peki, enamored, inspects her with romantic intentions, perturbation in his senses. Are her connate abilities of captivation divine or demonic? He lacks words to speak and casts a supplicating look at her creased front. He croaks like a raven, worked up into a queer calefaction. Their shadows are hideously distorted. Her perennial pulchritude seems to suck out of him the pith and marrow of his resistance. Her reverberating tone is one of authority. Her volume increases. Her luminous brown eyes are filled with tears, her contrived smile radiant. He has the sensation of being a spawn of hell, an archdevil in human shape, situated on sacred dirt. The glade's undergrowth impedes the gales' impact on them. Her annual appearance strikes his sentience with the force of a blow, one that will leave the imprint of a psychological bruise. Her stem shivers and her leaves flap. An indifferent sun scorches them. He feels like a crab without its shell. She absorbs and arrests his focus. He hears a chorus of voices, these subhuman chantings in his skull. He collects his cogitations and listens. A leggy doll, a large lady of gawky stature garbed in a soothsayer's garments, rides a stag, hastening at a gallop. The horse then pauses and rears. She settles into the saddle. There are multitudinous accurst inhabitants on this infected planet. Ice pellets are not unlike homicidal arrows. A sparely built, curly-haired lad is engaged in reading and writing and drawing a picture and sharpening a weapon, emitting long-drawn, heart-stricken blubs, the apparition of an albinotic hound lounging on his lap, under a mistletoe-bearing branch. Doves and pigeons, in frantic apprehension, are intermingled and indistinguishable on a terrace. The avian scene is presented to Peki over slabs of ancient masonry. He feels like a dead and buried heretic. Marisa is in a trance of atrophied dormancy. The region is blighted by pestilence. Jackdaws, evolved, squawk. Absolute nothingness is appalling and reassuring, so remote from ordinary reality. Twilight is august and lovely. Landscape recalls a lugubrious frontispiece to a picture book. Inky empyrean is smudged with cirri. He ruminates on the Butyrum. Solitariness is the linchpin of his art. It is a supernatural skill, creating something from nothing, his mind making up the madness of mantequilla. With uncompromising gusto and fierce audacity, he concocts butter with a velocity of action in perfect isolation and mystic rhapsody, confined rigorously within the limits of the lab. He picks his pitted nose and wonders if his ambition to succeed has retarded, at least to a degree, his purposes instead of advancing them. His singular sensibility prohibits him from complying with society's rules, standards, and ethics. He won't conform to the culture. With his business, he wishes to pull the plug of blandness from the sump of the metropolis. The laboratory is relatively spare, one usually associated with a recluse. He's more or less withdrawn from the world. His memories are congested. He is bedeviled by an angel — Marisa! Is she a developing copulatrix? Peki's below lust and above love. He eccentrically ambles, balances his teepee of a hat on his nut, repeats her name like a mantra, and wants to vacate the premises of life.

Caught in Marisa's gaze, in the declining sunshine, Peki has the sensation of being a fish feeling the hook at the end of the line. She has a crabapple kisser. He shakes as though he has palsy. He wants to pull his scanty strands out by the roots. The racket from the city increases, intensifies, and heightens. Face hot like he was slapped, he drools like a goon. A stammer is activated in her presence. His unconventional conduct is enhanced. A wistful grin crosses his lips, animal's ears flapping, unwieldy pate oscillating. He's immobile not unlike an inanimate automaton. The shadow is a simulacrum of its maker. They exchange confidences on their jaunt in a well-treed (stripped of fronds) hilly locale. He's a dwarven Dante and she's a florid Beatrice in an unparadisiacal idyll. Townies, bullet-headed, troll-faced, slack-jawed, shovel-mouthed, in their bumpkinry, are parodies of themselves in a burlesque of socialization. An odor of decay mingles with poultry, bourbon, and honeysuckle. Thank the Lord the lethiferous storm has come and gone. There is an infinite firmament and ocean. A revolting priest's disciples and pupils, dressed in the skins of beasts, in the disheveled brilliance, depart from an unfinished church, the group encircled by the leaps and bounds of bald poodles. The mountain mist, white as chalk, has an effect as if it is produced by witchcraft. Seaweed is reminiscent of horsehair. Uncivilized marauders' communal existence is foreign to him. For some unknown reason, his right arm hurts a good deal. His left one has gone numb. His resoluteness in keeping his hands to himself is a rallying cry of admiration, a trumpet call of restraint. The realization of his ownership of her causes more disgust than satisfaction. He imagines the connection of their sexes, an encounter he's been anticipating. He advances from the cave's opening like water searching out its level. His wayward movements coincide with erratic cerebrations. Will she sacrifice her floral virginity for him? This would be the supreme consummation of their mutual fondness. She is affectionate, patient, and considerate. He's crazed with fright. They must support each other in the risky enterprise. If Marisa were to decline the opportunity to coitionally conjoin, Peki'd heed her without protest and wouldn't sulk. He would not make a desperate appeal. If they got together he'd take responsibility for the consequence, his moral complacency receiving a jolt. And this suits him just startlingly fine. His heart hops up and down like a rabbit, watering her, and she enunciates "aaahhh… " She intends on remaining free, although she is under his inviolable protection from those prehistoric invaders who eat people's eyes out of their sockets. She stays being herself, lolling carelessly and lazily in the vaselet, with its distinctive verdurous design, in devotion to herself. There's an emotive colloquy between them. Its sounds like birdie chatter. Peki's ursine lamps zero in on the dangling creepers, looking like navel strings. His senses are somewhat satisfied, the cosmos of his consciousness placid. The chunks of wood on the floor have burnt themselves out. They've been extinct for hours. Marisa is sunk in the undersea of snooze. She is the prominent personage of his contemplations. The resonant tide leaves its sound behind like the transitory laudation of a susurration. Here is nowhere surrounded by nothing. Cicadas beckon dusk. His flatulence has the sonancy of a bat squeak.

Marisa snores like a cat. She's stretched and still, lying in her back. Her tress, Stygian as Juvenal's black swan, tents her face, and her gown enshrines her body. She is a bloom that has blossomed into her normal anatomical arrangement. The oriental sun is bowled up. The fulgor is gamboge-yellow and vermilion-red. She opens her peepers wide, sits up after a satisfying slumber, and hastily looks around as Peki is slipping on his sandals. She expresses herself freely, kneeling and squeezing the cypress wood bedpost. There is an exchange of wordless gazes and gestures. And he chop-gesticulates, hunched like a hawk. Humble of cerebrum, they tomfoolerize one another. She has excellent composure, and is majestically and maternally commanding. His cloth belt wags in the zephyr like a satyr's tail. Guilt for ogling her spears him as if he's an eel. She has an emphatic resolve to move and finds that she can't refrain from literally jumping out of bed. She has a vole's beady eyes and a hawberry mouth. She's reckless and respondent. She is happier than anyone deserves to be. She's a fleeting fancy of his dreams. He pours himself a libation of rum, thinks of the tortoise of the day and the hare of the night, epiphanizing the fact that time drags in the light and speeds up in the dark. His elbows are akimbo. She is a magnetic mystery that draws him to her. His limpid pies rove in scrutiny over her. He feels weighted down, like Atlas carrying the globe. He's pinchpussed. His eczema is not unlike burial earth. Her yap is cemented shut. She is redolent of soap and mint. Her head is at a prayerful angle. Her lips evoke those cherry-flavored Gummy Worm candies. Her smirk seems premeditated. She has a visage out of Vermeer that breaks hearts. He plops himself, skewbacked, into the warped cane chair, in the mustard-colored emanation, wearing his mussed jim-jams, muttering to himself, employing a villageois vocabulary. His hair is braided in tight corn-row plaits. He's got this Stalin beard. He chaws on a gumball. Cranked music disturbs the peace. Streets are not paved. Puddles are egg-brown. In the rundown outdistrict these stripped vehicles, overcome by wisteria, are humped on cinderblocks. A steeple's bell bongs mournfully. The coppery sun disappears into the horizon, the hue of fowl guano, like a dot. These sumptuous, ornate neo-biblical murals hang in the circular, voluminous quarters. Marisa, spoon-headed and newt-eyed, her cheeks poppy-rubied and jelly-soft, stands in icy silence, with a cryptic moue, has her coffee, and smokes. Peki's hermitic loneliness is gone. He stinks of pitilessly boiled Brussels sprouts. His intonation is shattered by gasps. He is a mite of a man. Tear-shaped petals bestrew the rug.

A turbulent incident transpires in the tobacco-stained anteroom, a curious area with bow windows and ornamental debris. Peki has a goblinish grimace, irate at Marisa's despotic sentiment. Her extreme language lashes like a whip. His cerebral levee breaks and torrential invectives gush. She stands erect, a starveling frighteningly gaunt, with a strikingly ugly countenance, ghastly pallor, and high forehead, with an air of agitated restlessness, wearing a fancy costume and nonchalantly combing the disordered mass of her gray wavy mop in the mahogany-framed looking-glass over the mantelpiece. There is a sallowness to her cheeks. She articulates with a suspicious accent. Her lips protrude like fungi from bark. She puzzles and perturbs him. The hall-clock tick-tocks. Her lean limbs are of surprising grace. He regards, with mackerel-hued, languid oculi, her peaked face, and prominent nose as if for the first time. Her flesh appears to be composed of a substance like translucent water. She, in a perpendicular position, gives his bushy eyebrows a furtive glance and smooths out her shawl, rust-tinted not unlike polyanthus. She straightens herself and squares her shoulders, in an attitude of one who sees and listens, and organizes the blue and white hyacinths in the earthenware bowl on the round table in the snug parlor. Then she hugs herself as though to assure herself of her identity. He is as uncontrollable as a mad dog. Heretofore suppressed emotions burst forth. He feels sliced and diced, cut open and exposed, gouged and scooped, insides on the outside, like a vivisected toad. He attempts to conceal his bulging tummy, one similar to Napoleon's, with his forearms, docile as a lamb, contrasting his sardonic leer, wishing he could hide his monstrous lineaments like they're abominably menacing. His facial features are massive and unrefined. He mentally forms this visual image in his mind. He has carried her through his life like a camel. Cowled, she reminds him of a hooded snake, the forked tongue flickering out of her trap. Her shadow is contorted. She has a low, meditative modulation. There is a youthful glossiness to her tresses, carefully parted. She, in the detestable kitchen, finishes her coffee and lights a cigarette in the chestnut-colored illumination. Her body odor carries the vague taste of saturated silage in its savor. She has a statuesque pompous pose, in a maid's cap and apron, at the mullioned panes. Her butt's filmy smoke forms patterns. There's been episodic ebbing and flowing. He grasps her with the five senses. His befogged brain isn't operating properly. Her extraordinary physiognomy is furrowed with amiable wrinkles. He tries to be flexible, obliging with her, and makes an effort to get his thoughts into focus. His orbs are half-shut. He feels bound up in an easy affiliation with her, a whimsical harmony. Her integument is like parchment, taut on her feeble, bony structure. He derives satisfaction from the sight of her. His pensile eyelids bat. She has a creamy, detached manner, snacking on raisins and almonds. Language rolls out of her mouth, not unlike a sheet of satin. He studies her with a sympathetic magnifying glass, her flaws and frailties exaggerated. She releases a silky sough, followed by meaningless monosyllables. She plays hopscotch on the floor's quadrilateral tiles. Her odd behavior disturbs his mental equanimity. Her busted sentences sound like they are delivered courtesy of a broken apparatus. The aperture through which he views her is at once microscopic and telescopic. She can be an aggravating threat and an invigorating challenge. She dominates his field of vision. She says he has the "haunches of a mare," and that he is "queer-shaped." His physical and psychological balance is off. His habitual disposition reasserts itself. His encephalon is composed of chemicals out of which his impressions are compounded. He brushes his pointed beard. The overloaded bookcases give the space, quiet and simple, a reading-room aspect. It is a sanctuary, the material objects containing almost mystical importance, especially the Victorian-era watercolor masterpieces hanging here and there. He's motionless and mute in the oak-paneled study, by the Jacobean door, as if he's planted in a gloppy pool of paralyzing, primal silence. The countryside, vaporously blurred, is a feverish panorama. Fireflies are evocative of sparks caused by iron being struck against flint. Plants' fronds are the size of elephants' ears. Red coal of the moon smolders in the hearth of heaven.

Enduring a worrying turn of the brain, with constitutional nervousness, anxious expression, and jittery hands, Peki indulges in an excess of concentrated cogitation. He looks as though something was unexpectedly inflicted upon him and he was off-guard. He frequently feels like a survivor swimming away from a shipwreck, and that the laboratory is an island he reaches, and he eats fruit and drinks fresh water. He mulls over the evolutionary stages of planetary existence. He floats upon an ocean of emotion, fearing he might drown in it. A mask of serenity covers a disconcerted temperament, maintaining the facade in a private act of the will. Marisa slouches and sensually bites her underlip. Her blinders sparkle wickedly. She cannot stop the grin extracted from her frontage. Her laugh tintinnabulates not unlike a peal of bells. She's animated and excited, full of exclamations, yabbering on breathlessly, the cadences of her infection changing. He finds the monotony of her speech endearing. She pauses to blow her nails dry. She is practically and wondrously dippy. Her skin is the color of light emanating from the candles on an altar. The bell-pull of her braided ponytail brushes against his neck when she whirls. It has this webby texture. Her perfume has a candy scent. She stares enigmatically at him as if he is a faraway mirage on a distant horizon. His squinch is conjunctivine. He is cognizant of the suspense between them. Her shadow, in all likelihood, will be cast across his life forever. She is of a somewhat different stripe. Without her, he is lost, outside civilization and looking in. He slumps into the beanbag chair, munching on a pop tart, like a batrachian into a pond, and analyzes the sabers of her shins. He looks equally eccentric and ecclesiastical in the hooded habit. An eclectic hotchpotch of odds and ends is jammed in the cedar chest. A spectral apparition, Marisa is ill-complexioned and braless, fit out in a football jersey (with faded numbers), thong, fishnet hose, and satin pumps. There is a girlishness to her conduct that feeds his contentment. His heart beating fast, Peki has a hankering to contact the small of her back with his fingertips. He leans backward and forward as though he's going to collapse. Her body, wrinkled as a winter pear, is redolent of a stench of almost immortal influence. His nerves are on edge. He toes the mark when it comes to restraint. Her demilune blinkers. Acumination of her sniffer. Babelicious tits like deer noses. An uprush of lust floods his being, making him unhinged. Their love affair will last an eternity, he thinks. The vault above in its immensity and sublimity and running cloudlets. Astropoetic brilliancy. Cataract of air. Laundry loads on the floor give way to her tread. He conjures up an image of her pudendal piggy bank slit. He believes penetration would be violence. Her armpits have the odor of earthmusk. His chest feels as if it's about to burst. They participate in a neo-moral and quasi-hierological convo. Pieces of scrap paper are infested with her reminders. Still in her scanties, she behaves like an adolescent, rubbing her midriff, gabbing and gossiping and swapping stories with some juvenile neighbor on the phone, the spate of tales exchanged in conceit and competition. Her crochet is voodooed with pins. The shower mat and washcloth are fungoid from overuse.

Scrupulously dressed in a dapple-grey tweed suit, neither too new nor too old, he stumps, gait fitful, by cerulean waters, budding birches, miry ditches, and a hazel copse. Castaway hubcaps lie in a muddy creek. There is a picturesque dusting of pollen on the grass. Dirt is like the ash of a holocaust. Arrowhead leaves drift wistfully on the surface. Fulgurous flecks recall deformed butterflies. A medieval abbey, with its vaulted roof and large, rambling garden, lime trees, yew hedges, and velvety lawn, makes him think of a brilliantly painted doll's house on a humongous scale. Shabby vehicles rattle negligently past him. He feels like a hunted criminal taking refuge. He quickens his pace with swinging steps, these short, rapid strides, propelling himself through a field of clover. Will his inner world be invaded by outer forces? He sports a Satanic expression and scrubs his deeply-sunken eyes and shapeless chin. His enthusiasm finishes rather than grows. He pictures his laboratory, the base of operations, as a foxhole. A trolley clangs its way along a narrow road in a cloud of dust. He thinks of the lab, its monstrous appliances, and accursed instruments, such modern inventions, tyrannous machinery, those noisy mechanisms of pistons and cogwheels, and he experiences malicious exultation when he considers the possibilities. He at times, feels like a demiurgical force, drawing power from Butyrum production, his system of selling the stuff with a craftiness that is slippery and serpentine. He has energetic ambitions and undying vigor. Cars, with throbbing motors, skitter like colossal beetles. Cattle graze in a lush, heavily-grassed pasture, next to an alder-shaded brook. Vulturous planes, with thudding engines, come and go from the nearby airport. Overcast is vellum over a folio of azure. The air insectally whirs. His feet are swollen to the size of an elephant's. A bluebottle buzzes by his ear. It lands on his shoulder and commences cleaning its front legs. His dipteran traveling companion moves slowly and cautiously, in the quest for atomic sustenance. Cumuli float not unlike algae. He has a morose mien, a stream of thoughts turning turbid. He, harassed-looking and grim, muses on his selfish begetters, such sinister progenitors. He watches the glitter of the sun in the hushed noon. He feels as though he is a changeling from a different dimension. It's a pellucid crepuscule. A tethered cow moos. Peki realizes his existence has been industrious and monotonous… before the killings.

Fragmenting showy clouds remind Peki of arum lilies unsheathing their petals. The exercise of his ablution, in the pleasant bathroom, an untidy pile of clothing on the spick-and-span linoleum, is a mechanized complement to his corrupted flights of fancy featuring his eldritch Mama. He sponges himself in the tub. Old-fashioned lithographs and elaborate engravings spruce up the walls. It is breakfast-time and he imagines Marisa has a classical athletic anatomy, not dissimilar to Artemis's. He feels like a heathen god, imposing and commanding, with a self-composed attitude almost negated by his short stature. He fantasizes without cessation or intermission. Her frontal is lined and indented, body wan and anorectic, tragic eyes peering forth helplessly from their sockets, mouth tightened in dolor. She believes that she is unobserved in the isolated library. He envisions her stripped bare. He hears the conspiring whisper of her voice. He deposits himself in the French antique armchair. His hobgoblinish jocularity does not cheer her up. She stares at the Hindoo idol, with a bulging belly, surmounting its jade pedestal, in a hypnotic trance. He fixes his sorrowful peepers upon her, more fussy and fidgety than usual, trembly lambency serpentining through the parlor windows, covered with muslin curtains. She isn't wearing much, a close-fitting slip, on her housecleaning maneuvers, and he feels nonplussed and teased. Her callused feet smell of cooked sausages. Her limbs are white as new-sawn ivory. A rainbow registers over the sward expanse. Crows croak in a battery of mighty maples. A prismatic cloud spins like a pinwheel in slo-mo. It is a broiling afternoon. Marisa hopfrogs over a mound of undies on the lemonwood floor with a porcine squeal, acting as though she has got the lead part in a dumbshow, amphitheatrically hamboning, bosom and bottom walloping up and down, and her legs sickeningly snap like a wishbone awkwardly pulled by two people. She is ok and is heedless of time. There are arborescent veins on her ankles. She's seraphically nimble. He gawps at her valentine-shaped heinie, the wings of her shoulder blades. Her hair is drawn back from her temples and knotted in a bun behind her head. She got a fat lip at dawn from bumping into the door's frame, whereupon she tripped in a ricochet over a parallel pile of towels. He waddles like a grebe, sucks on his bulbous thumb, flatus with the sound of misexploding fireworks, and slides into grave meditation. Then he enjoys a midday meal of bread and honey and brown ale, gazing at the herbaceous terrace, plowed orchard beyond, loamy banks with a bevy of voluble birds, the trim, jerrybuilt toolshed circumscribed by splendid jonquils, daffodils, and crocuses, a picturesque dairy farm with its pigs and poultry, and the parish church, a proud edifice, lonely and unfrequented, and its sham-Gothic ornamentation, in impish chicaneries of luminosity and shade. It is gusty and grey, fitting the bill with his mood. This place, he thinks, is a paradisal retreat, generously furnished, far from the madding pell-mell of normal life. No more grave-digging and undertaking for him; it's butter or bust. The illusion of his mother grows not unlike a living thing, arousing him by its reality. He watches and waits, patiently and dutifully… for what, exactly? He composes his cast. There's a slight alteration of his position. His movements make him visible. He has the eyes of an expiring jackal. A barrage of images blasts his brain like artillery shells. His cobnut-brown mitts are spread fanwise in his lap, oculi clear as the waters of a spring. Marissa is in a state of impetuous excitement, sweeping and mopping, mumbling dreamily to herself. Her rapid speech becomes vulgarized. He appraises her voluptuous throat and young knockers. His perverted mind allows for much equivocal indulgence. There is a long silence. They are faithful in their correlative focus. No one says a word. There isn't a sound. In his geographical chimera, this is an Earthly Zion. Wallpaper is the color of woodsmoke. Her corner-crimped paperback is splayed on the dresser. The shopping list is written in her spidery scrawl. The weather fully turns for the worse. She is hydrophobic and valetudinary. The rutted road of his life is smoothed by her existence. The sky dissolves in cirri. Oxygen smells of rain. His sight is tense with search. She scampers, arrayed in a rubber hat, claret slicker, flirty cheekies, and high boots, and subsequently skips along and kicks acorns by a corroded tractor of indistinct make in an otherwise empty field. Overtaken by nerves, he watches her through the steamy pane, muses on his cracked esse. The thunderstorm wages warfare. Downpour hammers in sheets. She squelches in wide strides. She puts her hands into a megaphone and shouts something incomprehensible to him. There's a glut of precipitation. Hellebore-hued celestial sphere is besmeared in ruined cumuli.

Marisa extends her activities, scurrying about like a mouse trying to find a hole in a pantry. She lunges into her chores as a diver plunges into the water. Meanwhile, Peki, sedentary in the horsehair chair in the sober den, sitting like a walrus-assed Buddha, with dirigible hips and blimp bust, pecks on an apple tart and sips a foamy liquor. Using her digits as tweezers, she picks a scab on her elbow and glowers at him with ferocious eyes as if with ineffable disdain. His peepers run riot over her scrawny physique, appealing to him, having a provocative effect on his senses. Her sexiness is overpowering, her form absolute in its imperfection. Without her, he would feel like a bodiless silhouette. Her bubble-bum wags like a flagged canine's tongue. His pipe lit, he examines her with obsessive intentness. By hook or by crook he promises himself he'll have her. He has an insatiable craving for her. His mismatched pies blink, sizing up her drawbridge-long tootsie-wootsies as she blathers on about fame and fortune being the roots of all evil, squill-hooter squashed up. She sounds in-an-ivory-tower pedantic, like a narcotized educatress, tub-thumper-enthusiastic, voice raised and punishingly authoritative, emphasizing points (unpindownable) that seem to have no acute resolution. No issue is diminished, no dilemma is ignored, and nothing of note is overlooked. She's unbearable and impregnable. He beholds the animated event with indecent lamps. In her preoccupation, he is a blur to her. She is apparently sexless, an androgyne poised, for the nonce, in an abstracted coma, beside the makeshift partition. She's a hairsplitter breaking problems down into subsections. Her arms bend not unlike lilac branchlets bearing an excess of moisture. Her charm is cast upon him, heightening his interest in her. Everything encompassing them is rendered rich and mellow as though seen through a diffused aureate coruscation. He surveys her hawk's beak, elfish, ironic smile, quaint chin, slender neck, and indefinite profile. He is taken in all manner of erotic considerations. Her visage has a permanent lethargic pout. He has the look of a sly ravening incubus. She makes these recurring attempts at adjusting her ruffled coral babydoll. She rejects his offer of assistance. His infatuation with her will remain unconfessed. Will his regard for her be reciprocated? A scandalous and shameless ardency seizes him. He has this Machiavellian expression, envisages himself grabbing those legs, and they slip out of his grasp like eels. He beholds her jaundiced complexion. She keeps to a nutso and self-referent fixity of topic, prating on to no consequence, scoffing valentine candies. Their interaction is comparable to that of a rough and tumble vaudeville skit. The upper atmosphere has a glaucous grayness. A warm fire burns in the grate. Biscuits are heaped in a tin. The wind veers and whistles across the slate roof, solidly constructed, on the sturdily built structure. The abode is ill-lighted. Because of her, the universe becomes indistinct. His environment is negligible and tedious. He's a grinning skull. His pecker stiffens and his eyebrows rise. He puffs out his cheeks, tugs on his trim beard, and turns upon her a steady indulgent appraisal. The dirgeful breezes rustle through the tops of the trees. She gives him a look of complicated significance, and not unmixed with complex disapproval and satiric condescension. The malversation is a waste in the spatial and temporal present. She is in perpetual motion, vying to verbally correct various personal difficulties, and he watches her in a kind of autoscopic delirium. His grip on reality is slight and arbitrary. She is an undernourished Amazon and he is a godforgone pygmy idling in her circumference in the enfeebled illumination. His orbs roll like BBs in a bumper car. He's both delighted and surprised that she acknowledges him. He is as wooden as a Dutch clog. Eating marshmallows and drinking soda, he experiences a sensation of agreeable reassurance. He is seated with deprecatory intensity and speaks in a dry, measured voice. She sure knows how to rub his disabilities in his face, and precisely where to stick the knife in. He submits to his uneasiness. There is an inchoate seepage to the discussion. It is a travesty of a talk. Still hot to trot, Peki feels like Dante in the Inferno. Morals commit him to a certain caution. Marisa has a gracious reticence. Her tinea'd feet are the pigment of boiled veal. She announces she has to diddle with herself upside-down to come. He combs his ramiform mustache, endeavoring to interpret her cataleptic moue. The edge of her wordage is as exact as cut glass. He has an inconsequential crush on her. Pissburnt-hued phosphorescence. She blows her steep nose into a Kleenex tissue. Her yawns are eye-watering. The sinewy, Pekingese-faced, unperspirable Valkyrie has a reasonably rampant posture and a hard simper. She pats her pet mink who left Eurasia in the form of a coat. Blustering gusts whimper in utility pole wires. Bugs create a buzz of intrigue on the screen. Cloud cover is the color of oatmeal. She is, after a coprophagous interlude, jumping-jacks out of the stuffy room, and his prick rushes upward like a rocket blasting into outer space.

Peki, an exiled amorist, with a dapper Van Dyke beard, sits around not unlike a spare dick, twiddling his metaphorical thumbs, at this vesper hour, staring fixedly into the starless space and umbrageous skyline, and partaking of tepid milk and frosted cakes. A river sludges along through a shambling meadow, sallow weeds on the banks. Sinople sun. A freight train chugs on the tracks. A cloister of buildings, plain beige affairs, have fallen into disrepair. Which one is the prototype from which every other one is copied? He feels squeezed dry like a sponge. He is heavier than water and lighter than air. The organic light isolates him. He's crouched on a willow stump, in an alert attitude. His physical description at this juncture is beyond even the most skillful Byzantine artists. He notices these unintelligible shapes and outlandish transformations. He abandons himself to the mindly orgy of the ideal and impassioned coupling with Her which he has been fantasizing about for a lifetime. Before he was alone on an island and the surf was coming in. Domestic Rome was burning. He was at the bottom of the barrel. Now he is on top of the world. He currently has clarity, and he sees it was all smoke and mirrors. There's an elemental presence. He senses it. He yearns for untroubled sleep. He feels like a somnambulist emerging from repose. The mold has hardened. The bolt is shot.

Giovana Hoyos

Peki stands on the steep, risky steps and evaluates these sort of pulsating fluorescent signs, some mangy curs timidly nosing around on the topsoil, at a rudderless, rotting boat, ill-defined outlines of edifices, downcast bushes, and the worm-eaten door's wood in the flea-bitten attic of an apartment over a defunct cage of a law office in a shantytown. Giovana Hoyos, a towering transsexual, shining in dissolving light, is a starveling, scrawny as a sick mule, with kinky flaxen hair, defeated eyes, and varicose veins. He proclaims his mother said he was a full-fledged dullard, a piece of shit. She has him on a short rein. Dishes are piled up on the kitchen table. Her abdominal wineskin droops. She is redolent of lye and perspiration, has an inexpressive mannequin's face, cutis taut with fatigue, pianoing a computer keyboard, writing on a pad as if she's tattooing, slides off the davenport like spaghetti from a plate. He pees in a pestilential toilet. A cripple, lame in the knees, she moves as an unchecked blood clot in a vein. Her tress looks like an owl's nest. She puts on a Hawaiian undershirt, shawl, and bikinis and sits in an exhausted chair. Snot runs from her nostrils like blood from headless necks. The teeth in her saturated mouth are like stones in a river. Plastic curtains and rancid food. Used tires are stacked on the aluminum roof of a jerrybuilt building. Adults holler. Children bawl. There is a cacophony that has no name. It's hard as a punch. Giovana is barefoot and knocks back rotgut in cantering shadows. She sings, or shrieks, as a perishing parrot. She ignores him as if he ceased to exist. Peki feels disconnected from a dream. He's sunburned, reddened as a carnival Indian. She untangles her mop with her fingers. Dwellers crawl on the city like ants on a cake. Fogbank is like gaseous sludge. Spate whiffs of ammonia. Her curvy hips have the sensuous rhythms of wavelets. The vacant lot is ash gray. Crystalliferous frost on the panes. Fragmented plaster in the drafty room. Branches dangle as the legs of the hanged. Peacocky harlots, syphilitic imperatrixes, prance on benumbed, parallel streets in flowering carnations of steam. Their ruinous bordello is circumscribed by osseous scaffolding. Her hug is devoid of conviction, kiss lacks sincerity. He cheeps as a parakeet. She points the asthma spray at her oral cavity. He licks a fudge popsicle. Tide laps the shore. Sticky strips are stained with flies. Ferries dock and depart.

"How are you?" She asks.

"If I could fly I'd say I'm ducky," he responds. "And you?"

"If I'm a fish I say I'm doing swimmingly."

Wibeke Lovelock

The columnar giantess, named Wibeke, with a hair-on-fire voice, looking like a cross between Tilda Swinton and Draco Malfoy, the style of her mop as if it is the result of the work of an inept topiarian, her eyes cartoonishly out on stalks, wears a sally hat, flounced dress crisp not unlike blotting paper, and gigantic jodhpurs, the godforgone fashionista sitting stiff as a poker in a ladder-back chair at the fold-top card table. The professional sousaphonist worships in this church (a crumbling, darkly-lit nightmare-scape) and enjoys playing her instrument in the annual Catholicon. The place, containing railroad furnishings, smells like stale bread. Her dental braces resemble a hedgerow fence. She relishes being single. She doesn't want to be Queen Dido, getting shot by Cupid's arrow. With mind-pretzeling problems, she is flustered as a flicker in a petrified forest. The rain sounds like a running urinal. The priest, built like Mr. Potato Head, has a putty-ball nose, humid eyes, and the paws of an agouti. He studies her like a portraitist attempting to capture his model. The man, garbed in loud plaid peejays, ignorant as a felt galosh, in his customary horndoggery, looks at women like Doritos: he can't eat just one. If you took his brain and put it in a hamster it would go backward on the wheel. His ass bird-whistles. He misshoves a Hostess Cupcake into his nutcracker mouth, his antic eyes all over her. And she seeks a relocation activity. A Dostoevskian neurotic, Wibeke, in a social setting, can alter the tone of her personality as a flatfish can change its skin coloration to match the surrounding habitat. She's a few noodles short of a casserole. She is as loopy as a crosseyed bull rider. She has a mundungus malodor. The lingua franca she uses is as precise as cut glass. The aspiring authoressette has this sub-memorable, room-temperature character. She lives cheek to jowl. Often she feels like a square peg trying to fit into a round hole. The young lady is an under-appreciated anecdotalist and is unbudgeable in her opinionating. She operatically shops, following the sale signs like a comical stage sleuth. She has a chip on her shoulder the size of a Mack truck. Her chronic hiccuping sounds like a cuckoo clock. She always appears arranged in an attitude of contrition, shrinking into herself, becoming smaller. The grass waves like water. Wibeke, calm as you please, clad in herringbone tweeds, whelmed by the heather and bilberry, doesn't remember how she arrived on this island, with its mysterious properties, a paradise with its pleasures and punishments. She had sprung up like Minerva in a riddle of liquiform radiance. Seen by the floating ocular balloon, she is introduced to the illumination. She is motionless and moving, exuding force and energy, standing in a Buddhistic state of contemplation, changing and unchanging, consumed and unconsumed. Ache sings in her spine, a note clear and pure as one in vocalic music. Petals are confettied in the gusts. Showers sound like scratching itches. Several grackles gutturally croak in the snapdragons and marigolds. It is hot and muggy. In this environment, Wibeke feels akin to a fly in amber. She twists the rings on her fingers. Starboard-leaning, she walks with a turkey strut. Her oversized bottom is seemingly more upholstered than clothed. Winds sing with a castrati's soprano lilt. Feeling as though she is having a NyQuil-induced fever dream, she sucks on the phallic outgrowths of a native plant to drink the seminal nectar. Then she converses with a crudely constructed camera-obscura-ish wooden box with an oral aperture. A viscid membrane covers the lens. A canine apparition has on a papier-mâché rictus mask of her former lover's face. It acts as a canary in a coal mine. There is freakish botany, this hormone-changing vegetation, everywhere in the lush erotic Arcadia, with its almost human sexuality. There are penile trees and vaginate shrubs. Buds on leaves are reminiscent of jewels. The sap is like sperm. Foliage suggests flesh. A lactescent ambrosia spurts from genitalic herbage in the tropical terrain. Dishabille, beside the cactus appendages, Wibeke gnashes with gusto on scrotal fruits covered in pubic fuzz. Her bosom is fritter-flat. The cellulite makes the backs of her wallop-thighs look like gnocchi boards. Her body is the equivalent of bleak winter with no signs of spring bloom. Mother nature challenges the gender binary. These Lost Boys and Girls, in leafy loincloths, shipwrecked and stranded here after the nautical boot camp, their Querellean drill instructor having drowned, fight and flirt on the beach, in this cyclone of colorful feathers, the kids egged on by a crystal skull cliff entity, the thing like a disco bogeyman, in the variegated light. Genitalial prostheses, male and female, suddenly fall from the radish-crimson sky into the sand. Clouds scud free. There are miltoid sprinkles. Wibeke knows it is time to leave. She wheezes like a bagpipe, straitjacketed in the atmosphere, whereupon she steps slowly on testicular pebbles. Like lust, regret seeks not understanding but satisfaction. She is poised like a ballerina waiting for the orchestra to strike up. Two disembodied breasts stare up at her from the ground. A penis reminds her of a wan eel. Her boat is on the shore. Its sail is hairy. Peki, seated on a nearby boulder, waves to her.

Brain and Butter

There is a watershed moment when it concerns the health advantages of saturated fats. Although there are still some naysayers out there who would tell you all fat is bad, regardless of whether saturated or not, don't listen to them. It is bilge. The science on this subject is rock-hard and the benefits of incorporating more saturated fat into the diet are comprehensive. Here's why saturated fat is so important: every cell in your body has a protective outer layer called the cell wall or cell membrane. This cell wall contains both fat and water. The type of fat found on the cell wall is, not surprisingly, saturated fat. Both the fat and water are arranged in such a way to permit both water-soluble and fat-soluble nutrients to gain access to the interior of the cell through certain parts of the cell membrane. So, dear diary reader, if you are immedicably dehydrated, your cells may not be able to receive the water-soluble nutrients obtained from your diet. And if you don't have enough fat in your diet (saturated fat), the fat-soluble nutrients won't have any way to access your cells either. Every cell membrane requires saturated fat and even more importantly, your brain is made of 60% fat. That makes it even more important to ensure you are getting enough fat in your diet to have healthy cells and a sharp mind. In fact, there has been significant research into the benefits of including saturated fat and the reduction of Alzheimer's Disease, Dementia, and age-related cognitive decline. The best sources of saturated fat are cold-pressed coconut oil, animal fats (from clean, grass-fed, or pastured animals), raw cream and/or butter, and uncured bacon. And there you have it.

Eloise Sheasby

She is almost Sophoclean in her sorrow. She gets out of this hot tub made from the bisected torso of an immense alien as if she's Athena rising from her bath, the polychromatic centrifugent dream diminishing in her mind. Eloise Sheasby is lean and green as an asparagus spear, with a bicycle seat-shaped haircut, miscarved woodcut countenance, crafty viridian eyes, feral teeth the yellow of Nebraskan corn, and apple blossom skin. Her curls resemble onion parings. After toweling off, she dresses in a sleeveless jersey, a celadon skirt with a side-flap, and bold shoes. Her knee-socks are rolled down. The clothes cling to her like varnish. She is spectacularly alone. She feels like a remnant of life. She doesn't have a definite position in the universe unless she is observed, like an electron. A lovelorn troubled soul, she's down in the doldrums. She has one eye on oblivion. The siren song of suicide is louder than any symphony. Music is Eloise's guardian angel, enveloping her with its wings, and protecting her from reality. In the orchestra, she is a strong cellist: Artemis with her bow among the Oreads. The air seems to vibrate with heat. Swallows twitter. A butterfly settles on a sunflower. The overcast is cabbage-white. These bovine creatures with geodes for faces browse in the meadow. Ravens create a wild vortex above. The horizon has labial pinks and violent violets. The proto-monstrous Killian Hadfield, mouse-eared and rubber-lipped, a popular big fish in an insular small pond, has a mafaldine mane. His shampoo smells of eucalyptus. He is as slender as a stalk of rhubarb. His flesh is pallid as bloater paste and cheveril-soft. In Eloise's company, he manages to keep his monomaniacal lust in check. Their words are toxic as acetoarsenite. Killian is swollen with desire. The egg of his head is cracked. His voice sounds heliated. Hot tears burn her cheeks while she gazes at the gentle blades of his back, his rear end reminiscent of a cottage loaf. He is a bored robot, roaming the hothouse-humid room in an existentially mechanized mood, agreeing with himself in his sadistic actions, thus obeying the principle law of Kant's Categorical Imperative. His hormones churn. The apartment reminds her of some recreational center, with its cement-block walls, the corners tricked out with furniture. Nothing coheres in this bizarrerie. A migraine fits around Eloise's head like a crown of thorns. Suffering a schism between reality and irreality, she perspires badly. She has a numbed skull, high in the sky on puffy clouds of narcotics. She's ossified with a hangover. The vicious circle she finds herself in has parallels with Russell's Paradox. Killian says that she is "slippery when wet." When she starts cramming rhododendron leaves down her throat, staring at him as though she's searching for a message, he boots her to the curb. Stars are glistening and tinsel. Flashing lightning evokes the cerulean electric sparks shooting in different directions from the wires of a trolley car. There is a rumbling of distant thunder. Eloise sees an abstract heaven and hears the murmurations of the wind. She recalls the woods she wandered through, and the toys she played with, as a child. Cicadas buzz. Moss drips. During the Witch's Sabbath, under an albescent moon, in the assassin weather, amid the outré flora and fauna, Eloise, feeling not unlike the residuum of relevance, throws a noosed rope over a hemlock bough. If Goethe's suggestion that turning outward to the world is health, and turning inward is sickness, then she is in dire straits. She pauses for just a yoctosecond, whereupon she hangs herself. Peki comes across her and cuts her up.

Peki and Marisa

Looking like a sloe-eyed booze-bag, Peki isn't feeling particularly maniacal or murdery today. He collapses onto his bed and dozes off. The sun falls behind the mounts. After a while, there's an eerie light in the semi-darkness of his digs. Marisa springs up like a shroom and stealthily approaches his covered compact form in his crepuscular, cluttered room. Lying on his side, his heart knocks in his chest. He pretends to be asleep, in half-expectancy of enchantment. She stops dead in the gloom when she thinks he has seen her. Appearing free and comely, she kneels. Strands of her hair brush his brow and cheek. Her breath plays on his snout and ear. He is unsure of what's in store. He wants to savor the wondrous alien salty juice of her sex. Desire awakens in his groin and spreads to his thighs. She strokes his temple. Already he is hard. He shuts his eyes and forces himself to relax. She has on a baggy jersey and lilac-colored underwear. Her wrists are heavy with faux gold bracelets. She speaks, sounding as if she's casting a spell. Her touch is warm and lingering. She is still when he caresses her haunches with his knuckles. She laughs out loud with delight when he tickles her waist. A mongrel yips pointlessly amid the orange and lemon trees. The city is a sea of fluorescence. There is a discernible abstract pattern to the constellations... Unexpectedly, Marisa undresses, staring at him as though to hypnotize him. Peki's gut contracts with nervousness. His pinkie inches toward her butthole. She tolerates this proximity with displeasure. She quells his anxieties. For him, gratitude burgeons where bitterness had been. He is speechless. She's a sibylline and vibrant creature. Her back is redolent of mint and rose. She is like a star that the earth stole from heaven. The nocturnal encounter transports them elsewhere. She takes over the mattress, causing some initial disgruntlement in him. Her sweat smells of walnut oil. She rests her chin on his shoulder. He lets her somatic odors overwhelm him. He believes that she's won over by his unbounded enthusiasm for her body. She is the corporeal creation of a magnificent feast that he must taste. He consistently falls for her appeal and vivaciousness. She floats on the floor like a swan drifting on a lake. Her feet reek of garlic. She is quite exquisite. Her perfume is an orgy of undefinable aromas. She's avidly animated with energy he never would have thought possible at this witching hour. He's wild-eyed, carried away by jubilation. Fumes of her cologne fill his head, exhilarating him. Her natural stink is rich and heady. She's confident and victorious in advance. Her nipples are the size of meatballs. Cicadas sweep across the night with the scythe of stridulous song. Gusts have the sonance of maddened women wailing. An owl screeches as though bereaved. Another whoops. The moon wanes. Police congregate on the curb. Marisa wanders about, disorientating his senses. Her ass is white and round not unlike a Circassian chicken. Peki eagerly awaits the magic moment of her osculations and tactions placed upon his person. And he salivates. She seems to be oblivious to the stifling temperature. She establishes the makeout session, with its rushes and hesitations. He catches a glimpse of the hoary wedge of her pubic hair, superbly trimmed. She whispers such marvelous and poetic things. Her modulation is charged with passion and woe. She kneads her belly, sensations rippling through it. Then she composes herself, seated cross-legged on the pastel cushions. He blinks, dizzy with euphoria. She stands mesmerized by her reflection in the mirror situated on the cherrywood dresser. Her image smirks knowingly at him. She looks mightily bemused by the task of brushing her tresses. He gazes at her genitalia. The osprey flies to its nest. Whereupon Marisa is gone. Was she ever here? Is Peki dreaming? Birds set themselves to chirping when the dawn comes.

Peki Zambrano seemingly has the shelf life of a Ding Dong in a fallout shelter.

An unnatural stillness settles in the apartment. The weather is fair. The air stirs. Peki murmurs direfully like a man of apocalyptic disposition. Marisa's moodiness at such an odd time bodes him no good. He thinks of her being innocent of torment and beguiled by the pristine novelty of peace. Shaped by the years and nature, she has flowered into such adorability that it is difficult for him to remain at ease. Her presence, however spellbinding, causes him collywobbles. His forlorn oculi rest on her, and he experiences the pangs of pleasure. The points of lust prick at his loins. He tries to suppress his delight. He's dry-mouthed with stimulation. She is supremely sensuous. She's neither ugly nor pretty. She is beloved because of her great luminousness, generous spirit, sweet manner, and stick figure. Also, her smarts and humor help make her captivating. A phosphorescence shines out of her body and phiz. She's made lovely by her age. He dogs her faithfully, scrutinizing the line of her nose, and the arch of her eyebrows. She permanently populates his daydreams. He attempts to catch her eye. His expression is one of long-ing and embarrassment. She proceeds through the shady rooms, acting as if he is absent. She plonks herself down on the windowsill, suspires portentously, heartily wanting to be alone. The metropolis is an infer-nal paradise of pollution and discord. The leadership that once pledged so much to its citizenry has declined into tumultuous tyranny. Disease and starvation have infected the populace. Winds sound not unlike birth cries. Peki's aware that in his existence he has accomplished nothing remarkable until he got his establishment up and running. He is poised upon the brink of excellence in this life. He knows he cannot neglect his work and follow Marisa around like a shadow, or a spaniel, straggling behind and whimpering pathetically. He ambles as though he's about his business. He is rather unprepossessing in his appearance. He wipes the perspiration futilely from her forehead. He believes she's becoming more comfortable in her own skin with each day that passes. Her bubbies are pendulous. He wants her to give him head. He is bewitched. She bris-tles with indignation at his juvenescent overtures. Her attitude has some scorn and sarcasm… He suffers a private discomfiture on account of her rebuke. Her sensuality sows distress in his world. Her rejections would make many tragical stories. He finds himself in the improbable position of having to apologize for his indefensible behavior. He twists the ends of his mustache. The breezes are knife-edged. Dull and heavy cirri collect above. Marisa's so cute that the neighbors fight over her. He is tempted to veil her! She should adopt this forced chasteness. He imagines her picking him up with these sizable tongs from a safe distance and putting him in the garbage can. She's quickly wearied by his gabbling and begins to pay little attention to him. Mother and son can marry, it occurs to him, and he chuckles because it is a hypothetical impossibility experienced as a sensible actuality. The froth of his cappuccino rises in the unfeasibly tiny cup. She's seated awkwardly, showing sympathetic faces and fiddling with the plastic leaves of a plant. Her deodorant has the fragrance of amber. Not entirely without vanity, he checks himself out in the pane. She puts her arms around his neck and smacks him fondly. Her pajamas are made out of finely woven cotton, the nearly transparent top and bottom items, embroidered with crescent moons and girthy suns, setting off her physique to the best advantage, enhancing her desirability. The blinds are semi-closed. Stupendous sultriness. Lunar desert. Shabby gathering of ruffians. Peki observes her with regret and resignation in his breast. He feels like a monstrous midget whose ill aspect hits her with horror. She plays frivolous games in which she is so naturally engaged, cruelly excluding him. Her disdain is palpable. He feels privileged to watch her prance around. His heart lunges violently in his chest. Her features are fetching. He handles vacuous melancholia like one yearning for nostalgia for that which has never transpired. Distracted by lovesickness, he reverts, through sheer will, to thoughts of his profession, and everything that entails, and yet is intermittently reminded of his mission (of seduction) in the matter of his Mama. His cheeks flush and his mind starts to whirl. She is a snake, sloughing him off. He plays the self-pity card, previously successful, but she isn't budging in her stance. He bites his tongue and bides his time. She'll cave. He is demented with exhaustion, pushing himself hither and thither between home and the lab. He gets into the cheesecake like a tortoise into vegetables. It has been an unblooded week. He brings to bear his prodigious powers of braggadocio. It's all about brain and brawn, thought and thew. Peki negotiates his way through a crush of humanity — a shark among the shoal.

Birds are exuberantly hued. Sun's a sparkling ruby in the charcoal-colored sky. The clammy air stinks of a public urinal. Newspapers are stacked in tottering columns in the crash pad. The cabinets and fridge have nothing that he would dignify calling edible food. It is a poignant experience for Peki to see the chapel being reduced to rubble. Where is he? What's he supposed to be thinking about? He must've digressed somewhat. The closed pub is uninhabited except for ghosts. It's their haunt now. The megapolis is in the most appalling and abject disarray... He recalls the small place, a charming and interesting salon, he rented. It was eminently satisfactory. Marisa provided him with comfort and consolation. Fucked up and feeling young and silly, she danced gracelessly. At first, she was paralyzed with booze, dope, and hilarity. Mother and son's drunken discourse went on for a while until he commenced fondling her. She was incoherent with discombobulation, the events leaving her shaken. She had raccoon rings around her eyes, her tresses were disheveled, and her pallor was like it was the result of shock. She could barely walk, her shoulders heaving, taking in great gulps of oxygen. Peki was uncharacteristically remote as a German. She endured a series of humiliations, during a drinking party, at his hands. She felt as if she was abducted and abased. She was in disillusionment and despair. He accused her of changing faiths as often as he does his socks. He forced her to her knees and held her head by the hair. Then he ordered her to suck his shaft. She struggled and shouted, failing to comply. He stamped on the soles of her feet. The attack was a shambles and broke down amid her recriminations. His offenses weren't able to subvert her defenses, inevitably and predictably. Her heart pounded so hard she thought she was going to die. Insensible, she fell over onto her side. Then she crawled a short way before vomiting. The church was an apocalypse of wreckage. Poppy-reddish effulgence of dawn and Marisa came to in a pool of her piss and feces. She remembered the assault and wept. She swore aloud that she'd disown him. She called him a "boor," and spat at him. She hysterically demanded that he leave. Peki steadfastly refused. The argument, for her, was already all but lost. A cigar dangled lackadaisically out of the corner of his mouth, looking at her with no apparent regret. He remarked laconically that she was "pitiful." She was disgusted and dismayed. She took the opportunity to announce her independence. He ended up washing her in the bathroom, acting as though he was the hero of the hour. She sat, slumped, on the tub's edge. All was quiet till he touched her inappropriately. She was exasperated by his nerviness. She gave in. She wasn't in a position to resist. His love for her became ever deeper. Her incisors were not unlike ivorine daggers. She was badly bruised. Her body and head ached, and she was feeling demoralized and unwell. He was someone familiar she wanted to forget. He stank of horse and hay. His voice was (impossibly) full of compassion. She chanted. He listened. Was she was extemporizing a prayer to protect herself from further harm? Even in her sorrowful state, he regarded her with envy, for she was tall and had no hump. He cast an evil eye on her... She unselfconsciously scrubbed her privates. Her breath smelled of herbs. There was a vocalic cessation on her part to take note of whether he was focused on her. She stood against him, as day against night. She regarded him as a savage. There was a wavering sensation in her stomach. And he recognized the distress in her lineaments. He considered her intriguingly charismatic. He imagined her in her nubility. She sought assistance and assurance from him. There is a substantial proportion of marketers in the shopping center. Destitute families are queued at a military canteen. Peki tells Marisa that he is becoming better at the waltz and the tango. Impulsive and enthusiastic, he chugs and tokes with virile verve. Her fanny has caught his attention. They talk away in reminiscence, discussing their relationship and his store. His is a profitable enterprise. He is amazed by what he has done behind her back. He behaves as if he gallantly ran the gauntlet of the competition. He forges ahead and doesn't look back. He speaks passionately to her of his ambition for his operation. She's surprised and gladdened to see him running his business so efficiently, and getting rich by effort and acumen. He is doing unexpectedly well. The domestic arrangement for her is enslavement. She feels like a time-server. She wishes to be captivating and free. She is courted by him. He mulls over the idea of a marriage proposal and gets discouraged because he knows she will decline. It's late, only he's too wound up to sleep. He wants to mess around.

Houri Serobyan

Attributed to the murders, tremors of the foreboding rise and run through the megapolis. Warm and gentle zephyrs whisk. Objectors are vitriolic. The authorities are under repeated and relentless attack by the public and the press. Folks want results. And fast. There are manifold links in the chain of blame. The acid of officialdom incompetence corrodes the metal of morale. This will not go unnoticed by history. Society is irreparably changed for the worse because of these sanguinary catastrophes. Peki is a victim and victimizer. He is newly liberated from his former oppressor: life. He has looted possessions and torched dwellings. He kills without qualm. He doesn't give a second thought to the systematic manner in which new ways are devised to torture men and women to death as unhurriedly as possible. He butchers for butter. He slaughters for currency. It is his campaign of extermination. Every ethnic background is fair game. No race is excluded. He drives himself hither and thither without rest. Innumerable hopeless souls have suffered and died for his mantequilla. His tactics include various practiced techniques, treating the chosen ones with particular brutality. Some of the horrors that he has perpetuated are too gruesome to describe. He is motivated by hatred and the desire for luxury. The despondency and desperation that he inflicts are unimaginable. In addition, he is crippling the economy. Citizens aren't spending. They are remaining at home. Jobs are lost. Inflation infects the market. Mom-and-pop stores are paying the heaviest price. They have little choice but to close up shop, for they cannot afford rent and employees. Everyone will always need Butyrum. It's the household staple. Peki is eliminating individuals and incidentally making room for refugees. He is personally bringing about forced migration because of the homicides. He has left behind him plenty of devastated families. It is impossible to know how many civilians he has dispatched. He obeys his laws and administers his affairs. He has survived intact on account of guile. His ambition results in more disaster for the population. He has managed to stay smart after the latest bloodshed and is determined to lay low for a patch. He wishes to repress the grisly images from his mind. Recollections recur frequently and unpredictably. Sometimes he awakens with a jolt, eyes staring, heart thumping... He concentrates hard on keeping his brain blank. He has done such heinous things and is solely culpable for stupendous carnage. He commits atrocities as though in a rage for revenge. Often he dreams of recruiting reserves to help him. It causes him much frustration. He feels as if he is on the front line without a regiment. The violations of his madre overtop and outplay all of it in his noggin. He has such horren-dous flashbacks and nightmares. The breadbasket of the skyline disgorges a varicolored and glistening cascade of entrails — a rainbow. He looks at the impassable mountains, then resumes waxing his mustache so that there's a stylish upturn to the tips. He has a sense of fate, knowing that his business is a part of it, and occasionally becomes captious in its per-secution. He pushes the wire-rimmed spectacles further up his snout and contemplates his destiny and experiences a pang of dread. Tears trickle. He wipes his lamps with his sleeve. His flesh is becoming leathery from all weather. He notices the unromantic scar on his middle. A month ago, he was slashed with a razor courtesy of an Armenoid lady, who was named Houri, with the face of a bull terrier and tumbling shaggy locks. She was shorter and stockier than the norm. She was dark-haired-and-eyed, unibrowed, broad-shouldered, and golden-skinned. He conjures up her bowed head, milk chiclets, and a pink tongue in his noodle. An expression of puzzlement passed over her physog when his blade was thrust into her gut. She waved his hand as if in a gesture of exasperation. He rag-dolled her like she was made of stuffed felt. He crucified her to a cedar and disemboweled her. Whereupon he scraped up her excrement, took out a purse from his sash, and put the ordure in it. He repeated the action and drew the string right. He put his lips to it. His throat constricted. It had a specific scent. He promised that wherever he went, he'd take it with him, reminding him of her. Abruptly he was overcome with emotion. His heart felt heavy like it was granite, and he sat on the low wall circumscribing a flower bed. He sported a stricken mien and his mitts were limp on his lap. He gazed at the gritty soil. A large tortoise crept laboriously by. He experienced guilt and regret. He knew he had to get cracking because the countryside was seething with bandits. Reaching the town, he was struck by how quiet it was since the mandatory curfew. Today has been excellent in terms of sales, sticks, and tubs of his product. The police are ubiquitary. He is laying low tonight. Common sense has conquered temptation. Peki scans the cops skeptically.

The War

The stench of cadavers was overwhelming. Fresh air would have been a welcome change. The attack on the German camp by the Spanish was a fiasco. It was as if the Krauts were anticipating the Spaniards' arrival. Peki managed somehow to get out in time, just when all hell broke loose, but sustained an injury when a piece of shrapnel struck him. Fortunately, it hit his pocket watch. Still, he received a painful bruise. Troops were cut down by sharpshooters. Many died from normal foolhardy courage, refusing to retreat, stubbornly standing their ground. He had no problem being a coward. Blood rushed in his veins. The soldiers were outnumbered. They never had a chance and were subjected to an apocalyptic barrage. It was a shambolic campaign. The assault was disastrous. The operation seemingly had no clear objective. He had rigid regard for his personal safety. The bombardment was intense, and there were countless casualties. The area erupted in flames. The battle predictably established itself. Howitzers fired. Bullets buzzed. Men fought like rats. Shells whistled and thumped. There was damage, shock, and death. Infantry and nature were raked by machine guns. Stars shone like parachute flares. Peki was a wandering ghost. His soul left his body months before. He wanted to go to his good home, exist mildly, and make love to Marisa. His head and heart were filled only with a desire to be with his madre. He dreamed of her seductive company. Debilitating dysentery made him bad-tempered, and he vented on the peasants, male and female, who were unfortunate enough to cross his path. He was sick and weary. He was tired in limb, stamina, and spirit. Disease tightened its grip on him.

He crept about. There was a stink of excrement, piss, sweat, and cordite, making him queasy as he trudged through the thicket. Dead bodies of his brethren were piled in a trench, alive with feeding larvae. He passed by, gagging. His bones ached as though they were broken. His jaws clattered his gnashers together. Explosives meowed. Pistols barked. The dying screamed. Warriors disappeared not unlike phantoms. Men create chaos like a corpse does maggots. Crickets were sawing. There was white light and black shadows. Frogs croaked. Peki's solitude possessed sadness. He was in a great deal of trouble, for he was supposed to be training as an assistant for a sapper and a sniper, and there he was, aimlessly slogging through the jungle. He wasn't missing his patrol and guard duties. He was desperately distancing himself from that military mayhem. He would think up an excuse later on. His gums were bleeding and his teeth were decaying. The oxygen was made into water by the tempest of a downpour. He was like a fish swimming in it. The torrent was violent. It was like God above was toying with humanity below. He was so ill with malaria that he was unable to think straight. He was constantly shitting his life into the bushes. He had to excrete so fiercely that he didn't have the time to dig even the shallowest of latrines. In the ragged trees, grubs fed on mortified members of a platoon, some left in strange poses. The storm roared like a wild beast. The rain and wind felt multiplied. Foxholes were brimming with aqua pura. The wounded who were incapacitated in them drowned. Villagers scavenged among the shriveled corpses in the ruins of a temporary fortress. Peki took potshots at them and they dispersed. Bullets sang. He traipsed in the mud. The weather was insane. He figured it was the end of the world. A dead mule, packages of supplies, and rucksacks floated on the river. He was as despairing as the damned. His drenched, shredded uniform weighed heavily on him. Reality was not unlike a dagger stuck in his midsection and twisting. He shook, his stomach grumbling for sustenance. The fetor of rottenness was making him nauseous. His mouth tasted of aluminum. His lungs burned with every breath. He became weirdly bright-eyed and hoarse-voiced. He witnessed the aftermath of a horse that stepped on a landmine and he retched, staggering in whirlwinds of smoke and dust. There was a loud noise, followed by a huge cloud, mushroom-shaped, on the horizon. The flavor of combat had settled dull on his tongue. Migratory cucks flew and quacked in the scarlet empyrean. He shot one, and it spun in midair as if it was afflicted by madness. In a cave, he sat before the bonfire, clutching his rifle upright in the correct position, unsure of what his next move would be. Spare divisions on both sides rounded up their fallen brothers in the oleander, thyme, and myrtle. Peki watched from high ground as they were treated like slaves, or dogs, by their smug superiors. Moist sighs dried on his lips. Observant, he stood, paralyzed. Then he marched back and forth on the brittle grass. He knew he had to return to base or he would be considered a deserter. He'd never dishonor himself. He decided to write a note, fitted in the space of a large turtle's shell, and prodded it in the direction of the officers and his comrades. It read: 'I'm sorry.' Whereupon he traversed a beach with trepidation, as though expecting it to be booby-trapped when he chanced upon these donkeys that were tethered together on a line in the spinney. They chewed on heaps of hay. The Jerries hid them in there and probably left them behind to come back for them at some point. Peki couldn't allow this. He knew what he had to do. After thoroughly combing and patting them, he, with sorrow in his heart, shot some of them. When he ran out of ammo, he slit the remaining animals' throats. The actions, although necessary (the burros are primarily used to carry provisions up hilly terrain) affected him very much. He had no part in the theater of war. He evacuated blood and slime on the sand.

Ethel Merman

Ethel is (allegedly) a mermaid who is transitioning into a merman. She was a part-time harem-cleaner and leech-gatherer. She very much resembled a heron with an orangey thatch. It was in a lopsided serai where Peki met her. The building, in the vicinity of shady lovely pine wood, was beside the ruins of a pump house with peeled paint and running water. The caravansery's exterior was a dignified structure of the incongruent neoclassical design. The path leading up to the joint was cheaply but cleverly made of pebbles. It had a mosaicked courtyard, protected by a wrought-iron grille, that had undergone recent renovation. The round-roofed construction was wonderfully sensible, made in stone. It had a proper door and windows. The brick chimney was practical. Its interior had carved furniture, decorated walls, and colorful carpets. A canary in a cage was suspended from the ceiling. An incensuous scent permeated the oxygen. The roads in that area were only wide enough for the passing of a couple of humans. The firmament was a jolly shade of cornflower blue. Peki was terrified that he may have initially given her a sense of present unease and imminent unpleasantness due to his dwarfism. Truth is, Ethel felt sorry for him, like you would for a washed-up boxer or an overloaded mule. She got these vibes that he suffered in his soul but admired his independent spirit. He paled in her presence, afraid she'd think he was uneducated and had no culture. He lives an exhausting and eventful life indeed. Sometimes he contemplates hurling himself over a precipice rather than yielding to psychological and physical pain. He endures ridicule in his existence, in spite of his prosperity in butter production. He suffers much humiliation and, to be honest, some of it is his fault, being smug, which automatically gets people's dander up. He gazed at her as if in dumb and uncomprehending awe. The welkin was damselfly-crimson. Peki was concerned that he came across as being an amiable, grubby fellow with a disconcerting habit of constantly talking about himself. He took a fancy to Ethel the moment he saw her, bent over and scrubbing the toilet with a soapy sponge. She wore an olivaceous jumpsuit and tatty sneakers. And he went to her like a swallow for a fly. He clattered not unlike a tortoise in the restroom. He spoke to her, the echo of his voice resounding with half a second's delay. Every once in a while he feels like he's performing. If the scenario was a quintessential Ship of Theseus, swapping and refitting planks until it is impossible to say where the performer ends and performance begins, he was an actor who could conjure a sea-ready vessel at will for whatever each new situation demands. The noise coming from upstairs was at once irritating and thrilling. They mutually decided to take a stroll together on the forest floor, pausing here and there amid the rock and sand, through the shrubs of holly. They hiked higgledy-piggledy up a slope of the hill. The sun was hibiscus-red. Chickens roosted in the trees. Gaudy beetles crawled on the marl. Flotilla of ducks was in formation on the pond. Martens rummaged in the reeds. Turtles glided in the pool. Rubbery-looking frogs squelched. There was a beehive in a hollowed spruce. There were competitive avian tunes. The day darkened as though in displeasure. Peki's backside produced a sound akin to thunder. The booming became so regular that she hardly heard it after a while. He permitted the scruffy children, of unknown provenance, to rollick unmolested. He forsook his perversity under those circumstances. He had caused unspeakable damage to uncountable kids. A group of adults was vigilant when it came to their youngsters, their arms folded, in the perfect attitude of parental focus. He has done tremendous harm to many individuals... Cigarello smoke curled from Ethel's mouth. She dabbed her lips upon his brow. Entwinement of vine tendrils. Delicious breezes blew through the herbage, providing relief from the execrable swelter. It was the hottest time of the year. The aroma of overripe figs was invigorating. The pair was tired, dusty, and thirsty from the travel. The concave mesa was like a vast amphitheater. They peeled awkwardly under a verdurous canopy. Stripping was an example of how swiftly societal standards fall away the further one gets from civilization. He was horrified that she would consider him so hideous without a stitch on that she couldn't bear to behold him. He was OK with her, which meant a lot. Man and woman were hopelessly tangled in the sexual act near a drinking fountain. Gasping, he sounded like an asthmatic donkey. They copulated in a dank cave that had an odor of moldering laundry. It was a most unpleasant miasma. Her flesh smelled and tasted of coconut and Windex. After the romp, he felt refreshed. Their conversation was curiously amusing and satisfying. He tickled her throat with an apricot leaf. She had a snack of nuts and raisins. He declined her offer for a portion... It is an insignificant metropolis of famine and disease, a bewilderingly intractable labyrinth. The smog leaves one feeling disorientated and unhealthy. Peki is spreading slaughter and destruction from one end of the city to the other. The city is a sickness with no cure in sight. Marisa, leavening bread with a rolling pin on a lapboard, weeps like a widow. He maintains his composure. He's fired up about making more Butyrum. He works hard and creates excellent products. His homicidal exercise helps him maintain his robustness. His commodity is a cut above the rest. He probably earns upwards of eighty percent profit simply by selling his wares directly to the public. He has the occasional giveaway in the store. It doesn't hurt to generate goodwill when it concerns the customers. Generosity is great. His job has him inspired. Masturbating in the broom closet, forming a mental picture of Ethel, he warbles like a bird. She is covered in crabs in the mud at the bottom of the harbor.

Wizzy Boo-Saleeba

Wizzy, a dystonian, fist-faced, raving maenad with a duck-cut hairstyle and pinwheel eyes, the very paragon of misrule, dwells in a dirt castle. Her rented room is a broom closet. The other tenants are driven batshit crazy because of the ice-hearted fruit loop's bad behavior. For instance, she will stomp to and fro in the mud-ugly foyer like some demented imperatrix, screaming like a banshee, countenance blood-red, breathing sounding not unlike a typhoon… The neighbors aren't exactly well-balanced themselves. They are often subjected to her violent outbursts of temper. Wizzy has a Tartarish cruel streak and the moral compass of an ill-maintained Wendy's grease trap. She wouldn't piss up your ass if your guts were on fire. Mania governs her life. She smokes like a salmon and rings a flatulent peal. Her rump is harder than tungsten carbide. The lady is a proud firebug and pickpocket. Her soul is a blighting frost. Wizzy exists in a nightmarish grayout. Employed as a doughnut fryer downtown, she despises her fellow workers as Juno did the Trojans. The economy is dead like a dinosaur. Winds blow. Waves crash. The city is rat-ridden, rainswept, and fogbound. It's Alice's Wonderland, the place and its people swelling and shrinking in the pea soup. After snorting Hexen, Wizzy, frockless, and wearing waders, has vomitable thoughts, chthonically trundling down the desolate street as if it is the last frontier. She feels like a zombie on the treadmill. She is fed up with the scene, the social suckage. She'd never be saved from the dung-heap. Her body odor smells of rank herring. Her pupils leap in tiny increments, hitting or missing any target and creating a series of incidental movements. There are burned-out structures, boarded-up businesses, homeless families, delayed buses, unobtainable taxis, piles of rubble, graffiti everywhere, umpteen lowlifes, and canceled trains. Wizzy, on DMT, sees the effete Harlequin, with a skinned-rabbit expression, seated out front of a creepy dive that was once a pet store, the jester enjoying a fizzy drink, fish, and chips. She capers akin to a jackanapes over to him. His flesh is soft as quince. Her tongue scorpion-stings. She is given to snipe and sass. Her voice is ear-shattering. He stares stonily straight ahead while she spews omnidirectional venom. Mad as a sack of rabid polecats, she knuckles him on the brow, kicks his shin, and clips him on the ear. Then, eyes closed, in deep silence, she leans forward, her bare form pleated like a chilled prawn. Her integument is as white as leprosy. She bites the air, wringing her hands, arms rotating like a windmill, lunging at space, legs making these dervishly motions, the young woman fully unhinged. The foul language she uses whirls like whipcord. There's a gale-force fight between them. And she punts the poor man into the gutter, whereupon she, visage scored with sorrow, sits on the wooden bench in the railway station. Push had come to shove. Her derma layer appears deader than tree bark. The brain in her head is a pit in a plum. She lives in darkness and dampness like a fungus. "Hey," Peki says.

Peki's Journal

I had a baffling dream last night, in which I was sleeping in a kiddie pool, using this drinking straw as a snorkel that was strategically placed inside a hollowed-out waffle for its "tasty oxygen."

Arianne

Peki, attired in a sailor suit, visits Arianne for the first time in months. She greets him at the door with a slap, whereupon she bends, unbuckles, unzips, and blows him. Then they cuddle on the plain couch. A stream rushes and leaps. Lupine and vulpine clouds coast along the darkened hilly landscape. Black velvet night changes, incrementally, the topography. Moon's a pale wafer. A gust sighs. She speaks about submitting herself to prostitution, being concerned about venereal diseases, and goes into explicit detail on the callous, albeit necessary, medical examinations, and the damage done to her body. Her tone is resentful, rueful. She feels, plying her trade, like a marionette, jerked about on strings manipulated by johns, putting on a performance directed by them, accepting their abominable practices. Because she is heavyset, she invites and repulses the clientage in equal quantities. Her boobs are not unlike balloons of liquid. She is a big bird of paradise. With them, there is domination (him) and submission (her). He's relieved he wore a rubber. She is a working girl, a fallen woman. This is a burden she bears. To her, whoring is much better than slaving in a sweatshop. She's lying on her stomach, can't think clearly. Digestion takes place for her. His facial expression is one of distant focus, like a kid who concentrates on sports in class instead of on the lesson. They are ardently close on the begrimed mattress, flesh to flesh, consumed by desire. The heart in his chest bangs like a hammer in a forge. He ganders at her pretty profile in the granular lambency. He grabs the hummocks of her thighs. They are stuck together as if connected by magnets. She is handsome, supine in coffee-brown bikini briefs. With consummate persistence, he rolls them off. She mutters something breathlessly. He takes an active interest in her throat. Her inflection is warm and rich as she yanks off her emerald-green socks. Her buttocks are blancmange-white. Her breasts are not like massive soft-boiled eggs. She's hot-flanked. Protozoan cirri breed and transform. Arianne calls herself a "semi-intelligent elephant." Peki shushes her and says she is a "sensuous goddess with human loveliness." She stimulates his attention. He just hopes he doesn't repel hers. She rises, scents herself with perfume, steps into ludicrous, feet-warping high heels that distort her stride, wraps a feather boa around her neck, puts on a faux fur coat, and shimmies seductively like some sacred temple dancer in a silent movie. She is gaudy as a peacock, strutting. The heart in his chest booms like an organ in a church. He observes her zigzag trot, now barefoot, into the drab pantry to get a snack. His remembrances of her, from their previous fling, are important and structural as the bones of a skeleton. Her body odor smells like a combination of turnip and pear. They conjoin in voluntary and involuntary ways, inadvertently creating dramas, humorous and horrible. The pair converse earnestly and frivolously. She has a paradoxical propensity, in the sack, to advance and retreat, depending on the circumstances. He creeps and crawls on her suety trunk like a perverted baby. Their sex has its thrills and dangers. The two share real and imaginary amative adventures in the hay, with continuous inventive willpower. They discuss things with common sense. Her sleek yellow hair is reminiscent of refracted luminosity on the pillows. Her tumefied lips are rosy pink. The day is a bleak disaster. He laps her henna pubes. She cheeps like a chicken when he thumbs her clitoris, and fingers her vulva. His voice is cricket-chirrupy. She has a lunch of cocoa and biscuits. He has a dish of ice cream and a currant bun. She has an expressive intonation. Keen on hygiene, she washes and brushes. He watches. Her fingers and toes are recollective of rolling pins. She physically evokes a doll with a chubby china face and a stuffed shapely body. She sits up straight on the nest of blankets and sheets and pops pumpkin seeds into her mouth. He has the questioning look of a puppy, discerning her comings and goings. Her anklet's glass beads glisten. There is a rubbish heap in the corner. Her hands are evocative of hams. Arianne, with the strap-on dildo wrapped round her waist, poses Peki on the rocking chair. She moves like a puppet, thrusting into him. He mouse-squeaks, penetrated thus. Sodomizing him, yanking his unit, she is sly and sinister. She makes soothing sounds when he, a grim goblin, vents gruff grunts, moans and groans, and, finally, dispenses these sick screams. Reamed, he struggles, bites, and scratches. He yowls so loudly it's as though her ears are going to burst. He squirms and spits like an infuriated feline. It is over. He recovers from the skewering, facedown on the floor in the privacy of shade. His respirations have the sonancy of bellows. His bazoo bleeds. She pulls the silk curtain across the barred window so he can gather himself in peace. He holds on to the stool. In so much pain, he's about to fall into a faint. Her division of the last slice of sponge cake is even, in her estimation. He snorts PCP off the toilet cover using a segment of drinking straw, and slugs Glenmorangie whiskey.

Peki executes cunnilingus on Arianne at breakfast. She fellates him at bathtime. Spitting words out as randomly as bingo balls, he tells her he's fanatical about Oxycontin and benzodiazepines, including Valium, Klonopin, and Ativan, as well as Adderall and Provigil. He glistens like a gastropod, body odor like the sour-smelling smoke of a burning trash fire.

Blitzed, Peki views the mayflies as fairy folk. He has a vivid memory of cutting down the scarecrow, with a Halloween mask frontage, a person of indeterminate age and gender, and tries hard to forget.

After supper, the couple hoof over fells and fens. Peki scurries like a beetle. Arianne stomps not unlike an ogress. Her party dress doesn't quite fit. The weather switches from sunshiny to stormy. He is drunk on tequila and wired on high-grade cocaine.

She's young and wild, free and powerful, full of tenuous fears and hopes. He, on the other hand, is a man of rigorous ambition that is occasionally dispiriting. Arianne makes a kidney pie in the buff, save for those darned socks. Peki's behavior is odd and shocking, lurking on the stairs, staring at her like an owl and masturbating. At the stove, aproned, she gazes mildly at him, brow corrugated with bafflement. He stops beating off, shuts his fly, and sips the steaming broth. Her stillness wavers between composure and inertness. When it concerns her, physically and psychologically, he is a discoverer and an uncoverer. Sometimes he feels as if there's too much concealing and pretending between them. She pads about, going from fridge to oven. She flattens herself against the wall and cackles. Meaningfully and casually, he gooses her and she yips and elbows him. Her skin has a velvet softness. She squats, rummaging in a drawer, nether regions splayed, and breathes deeply. When she takes a trip into the bathroom, he listens at the keyhole. He hears a susurration and, seconds later, a storm of pooping and pissing. He whacks off, trying for quietness. He considers himself a clever creature… He gulps brandy from a flask. His fierce imagination recoils, picturing them sexing, with delights and terrors, making ungodly noises, and shaking so severely that their molars rattle. A loss of selves is created by romance. They are deranged, mad, mating. Meanwhile, she, an anatomic abstraction in the luminescence, treading on slippered feet, malaise apparent, prepares a gin and tonic in an enameled mug. The kitchen, her natural atmosphere, is a cauldron of her creativity. He admits he feels as though his life is incomplete, not unlike a chessboard missing a bishop and a knight. There are pigeons in the yard. Peki is waiting for the opportunity for a shagging session to present itself. He gawps at her like he's afraid she'll vanish. He wants to see her on weekends and holidays but knows this is infeasible. He attempts to be affectionate, but she shrugs him off like a buzzing mosquito. There is something marbly about her middle, something soapy about her tootsies. Their hug is sleepy and slippery, forms whitely gleaming. Arianne puts on a leaf-greenish sweatshirt and matching boxsies, becoming edgy and wary of him. Her cooking is inventive. He offers assistance. She declines. He eats sorbet and drinks soda. She gets out a plate of shortbread and fruitcake. She carries herself well and does everything she has to, rightly and easily. The quarters are cramped. She is a Pre-Raphaelite stunner, proportions flawless. Her bountiful flesh is milky whitish. He plops in the sagging basket chair, looking lost and left out. The pecker in his pants is like a frightened snake ready to strike. She is seemingly scared stiff. Her lips blanch and she looks into space. He reveres her clean-cut countenance, her spectacular buxomness. A blush flares up her neck and cheeks. Her disposition fluctuates alarmingly. Resisting extreme acts, involving human waste, she puts a significant strain on his patience and disrupts his planned progress. Peki surveys the smoke-stained ceiling, distracted momentarily, troubled by his responsibility for his mother's many needs. Arianne is evasive, even shy, and smirks a secret smirk. They play in bed like sparring partners in a gym... They embark on a country walk, in the raw, carrying backpacks, and discuss cinema and botany. A flock of boys and girls move in separate gaggles on the main trail. The lovers, now dressed, whisk past them. They stride away in the wacky weather, dodge the illicit snares and traps, and avoid poachers and picnickers. She lets out a cry, stepping careful lover a broken-necked gosling in a shallow quarry. He pricks up his ears when she gets super opinionated about politics. Waterdrops on a spiderweb wink in the midnight-bluish brilliance. In dungaree overalls and paisley bandana, she could pass for a paintress. She is so lovely to look at! He keeps it casual in a beanie, sunglasses, hoodie, army fatigue shorts, and sneakers. Trees' boughs cast dappled shadows over them. Slatey sky. The duo becomes more candid as they grow more intimate. Overexcited in their openness, they impart to each other frank details of feelings when it comes to their unconventional relationship. A rainbow has these gem colors: amber, jacinth, emerald, sapphire, and ruby. The two talk about the affairs of the heart. He gets such moral support from her. He is very comfortable and confident when he's with her. She does not view him as a freak, loner, contemplative, or withdrawn from the world. She accepts him, unconditionally, for who he is. She respects the path he has chosen. She experiences pain and pleasure with him. The specter of possibilities haunts her...

Like a skater, Peki views the bumps and dips of the business landscape stretching before him as a space for free expression, and where others see obstacles, he sees opportunities. He has a sense of adventure. He will dive headfirst and see if there's water in the pool later. Michael Caine's version of a classic tune, Brenda Lee's 'I'm Sorry,' is on the transistor. Ravens caw on a branchlet. A crab crawls in a pot of boiling water. The megalopolis is spiraling into squalor and decay. Its criminal ecosystem thrives on corruption and poverty.

Peki envisions a situation with Arianne that is wonderfully lovey-dovey, impossible, and secret, their bodies crashing like hammers, both howling like drills, libidinousness primitive. Her snatch is a gulf opening. She is good-looking, in full bloom. His mind races like a hamster running on a wheel. She takes his penis in her mouth like a mongoose takes a snake. She starts to shake, draws sobbing breaths, twat hurt, on the flowery eiderdown. Her muff requires a clipping. The bush shows signs of rebellion. He fusses over her and admires her. Garbed in a peppermint-green union suit, he is in an aura of alcohol, brain spinning like a rodent in a cage. He cracks an acorn, seated in an unupholstered dumpy chair, beside the oil lamp covered with an etched canvas shade on a writing desk, in a darkish corner, gazing down at the floorboards while she, large-eyed, grilles fish and boils veggies, deliberate and resourceful in the preparation. Ladies' magazines are piled on the table. She is fond of reading articles and studying photos and drawings on glossy pages. Her fleshly amplitude and pretty bust are beguiling. She's contained in a lacy jacket, collar standing up, and shaping bodice covered with coiling Chinese dragons. She puts her lank hair up. He scrutinizes her curvy physique and bright white derma layer. She pays half attention to him. Every inch of him resents his reduction of significance. Her heels' hue is somewhere between maroon and umber. Vines in the humid gusts optically evoke umbilical cords floating and twining in fluid. Birds are clumped in separate clutches of squirrels. Elders mix with the young next to the sepia-brown river. The flat is charmingly spartan, the room Itself snug and stifling. The furniture is tasteful. A sheet is thrown over the coffee table, tiny and heavy, made of ornamental ironwork, like a pall over a coffin. It is as if he has ended up in some other world. This unreal environment becomes more real by the minute. He partakes of a cup of consommé, a shrimp patty, and a meringue confection. To him, after ingesting shrooms and imbibing absinthe, the can is a tomb of Snow White, the kitchenette a palace of Sleeping Beauty. She proceeds not unlike a faultless mechanical doll. Arianne is mortified and aggravated to the depth of her soul when Peki, almost tripping over the fragile gilt chair, gropes her. She doesn't know what to think or say. Her suspirations siss icily. She sets the dishes in the sink's sudsy water to soak. By accident or design, she bumps into him, retrieving the cherries and plums, kept in a porcelain bowl, out of the refrigerator. And he fondles her neither carefully nor carelessly. Holding her, he experiences a sense of awe and a flood of blood in his frontal. She talks animatedly about quadratic equations, leaning in an accidental-appearing way. They stumble companionably, tossed about on waves of arousal. Their conversation is kind of formal. Ceasing to be timid, she shrinks back and clumsily pushes him, unbalancing him. She mentions the fact that his greasy mane is a mess, his wardrobe a travesty. Her shampoo smells of apple blossom. They twirl cheerfully. He tells her fibs. There's a sort of slow silence. She informs him that she has a gig tonight at an avant-garde cabaret with a circus atmosphere. The staff's genderless. His response vacillates between anger and amusement. He is chilly in her embrace and does not heat up. He speaks in a small voice. Spritz makes a gentle hissing sound. Effulgence insinuates itself through the blinds. Hail is like trickling coins. Peki feels as though he's under a spell. Or a curse. Arianne's modulation, delivering an apology, is amiably monotonous. She enjoys his molestations, against her expectations. Stripteasing is bread-and-butter work, she explains, and she does it to the best of her ability. He clasps her firmly. She is responsive to his leading, ready to follow him in the variations of positions. Her knees tremble. She hints suggestively and articulates in a funny inflection. She sighs and settles into his arms. They float dreamily. His compliments about her comeliness sound entirely sincere. He resists the temptation to grasp her globate hips. Her hands, hot and strong, tighten on his shoulders. A magician, she conjures up a vibrator, that, to him, is an unexpected flight of fancy. Their woopie-making reminds her of round-abouts and helter-skelters when she was a gal. Her mouth is foxy red. He strokes her wide waist and fine skin, caressing her rounded haunches, beside the framed full-length looking-glass. His fuzzy knuckles touch her bare back. Together, they sway as a single creature. Rosebuds on the washstand. China-blue celestial sphere. He is sleepy and thoughtful. Arianne takes concentrated steps on the ceramic tiles. Peki envisages

Marisa, looking skinny and sexless, her tummy flat as a board. She manages to be at once graceful and ungainly. Her integument is turning grayish and papery. He is a nature beast with an insatiable appetite for her that can never be satisfied.

Arianne gets a voluminous nosebleed. She resembles a stoat. Nymph-naked, she stumbles over her words and swallows a sob. She's broadminded and bosomy. Peki, standing stiffly, suddenly sits like a stone in the stubby chair as if an agony has come upon him and he can't bear to move. Suddenly, he touches, tentatively, her instep. Her pallid face goes whiter. She blurts out a brittle chuckle. Both had drunk too much. He takes a gander at the rolls of her belly. Her boudoir buzzes and hums with their yatter. He came here to find her, only to end up feeling lost. Her emotional state continually changes — she can be stormy and intimidating one minute, respectful and charismatic the next. The dawn rises and they can see the sea. Overcast is steel-bright with the sun emerging, by degrees, in the clouds. She swims out of the comforter like a mermaid from the ocean. Sweating, her hair is plastered to her head. She blinks, her lids bruised from the horseplay the evening before. Her stomach is swollen and hurts. This isn't the first time that he overdid it. And it won't be the last. Diddled with, she mews. The spirit moves him and so he fiddles with her like a mechanic tinkering with a motor. He slaps and shakes her in the wooden box bed. He perches on the corner of the mattress. She sniffles and uses her kerchief. She is spanked into a quavering caterwaul. Her slightly flaccid fundament reminds him of the wrinkled face of an ancient ape. Her fat feet are raw-looking. Their kinky fadoodling is becoming normal. She shifts her painful bulk, catching her breath. She has tears in her eyes and a choke in her throat. He is steadfastly concerned, directly and indirectly, with cunningly controlling the order, and disorder, of her existence. She is emotionally invaded, and violated almost violently. Fleshy gratification, for him, occurs. He dispenses a series of semi-truths and serious lies. He wants to behave well, but cannot. She sports a quizzical moue. Wanking, his semen bubbles up like hot geysers gushing out of a lava field. Showers have a varnish malodor. Surly, Arianne serves him baked beans with a spoonful of molasses and pork rind, frankfurters with ketchup, mustard, and relish. She flows along like water in a riverbed. Peki, seated in the basket chair, stares distractedly out of the window. He keeps his own counsel. His private projects are his business, not hers. He combs his long, unruly mane, thinking of the city, that immense hive of energy. She beholds his intent gaze. She's nervously depressed, restless in his company at this juncture. She hides things well. She fibs splendidly. They've been unhealthily bound up in each other. She is less approachable and more reticent, he notices. She's beginning to dread being in the same space with him. Her inner landscape seems to shift by the hour. He is changing, hugely, who she is. She pretends to be sick so he'll stay clear of her. It's a ploy that fails miserably. She's closed off, perturbing him to the max. She is so cold that even margarine would melt in her mouth! Resisting his overtures will, in all probability, make the situation more precarious. He has a fixed, sinister grin, digging his bratwurst fingers into her. Her voice is cool. Felt up, she kisses him coldly and speaks with anxious warmth. He senses her turmoil of feeling, which confuses him. He has an eager expression. She's tense as an overstrung bow. She is sinking in the quicksand of despondency and refuses his hands to help pull her out. To be introduced to such abuse, with no warning or preparation, is stunning. She respires rapidly while he besieges her body. She feels threatened and enraged and tries to keep calm, to no avail. He is furious because she constantly abandons her devotion to him by dancing and prostituting herself. A glowering girl, she shuffles her feet. She has gotten significantly stouter since he last saw her… The place is minimally furnished. Peki can hear the urban rattle from the forsythia-yellow-walled garden. Arianne greets him as if he is the returning prodigal, and playfully ruffles his tangled, jungly beard. A rambling edifice and a severe dwelling are nearby. She quacks away not unlike Mother Goose on methamphetamines. They dine on sandwiches and sweetmeats. He accidentally backs into her, his derrière on hers like a moon on a planet. She has on a simple dress. He's serviceably clothed. Theirs is a rather rackety discussion about E.T.A Hoffmann. And they chat a great deal about the cosmos. The record of Glenn Close's wretched cover version of Tool's 'Forty Six & 2' spins on the turntable. When she gets into a heated vocal sparring match with her mastodon of a boss at the club, Steeves Njoku-Sample, on her dated cellphone, he pictures his bony, barefoot Mama, with her wiry, graying mop, pointy, witchy chin, wearing a snug shirt and sweeping skirt, and has a ramrod. A booze-hound and drug addict, his life is a smashing disaster.

Japanese woodcuts are startlingly luridly pornographic. Arianne can't stand the mess and muddle but is too lazy right now to get up and clean. She has a purposeful lack of purpose. She is heavy and hot, on top of Peki, in the dappled sunshine. He's smilingly tolerant and breathless on the ruglet, in their little world and its simple secrets, one that is also confining and constrictive. He loves her thick hands and feet, her thin, silky hair, and her big body. She is passionate, mysterious, and intriguing. She's becoming increasingly fed up with his prying customs of investigation and suspicion when it concerns her occupations. He is a trickster, showman, alien, a different creature from somewhere else. He's dressed in baggy breeches, a tweed blazer, and a floppy hat. She wears a jacket and trousers. Their mutual open-mindedness is both a blessing and a curse. They are people of fierce affections and spontaneous actions. She is flirtatious. He's quiet. She experiences a mixture of excitement and revulsion when she couples with him. He is short, stalwart, bearded, and mustached. Her gaze is exquisitely porcelain. She denudes herself, straddles a Gothic chair, and a sinuous worm, with rubious eyes, grinning mouth, and curving teeth, shoots out of her gaping butthole, not unlike a bottle rocket, flies in circles, and explodes in a chromatic rain. The psychedelics, he concludes. His limbs disintegrate into variegated segments. He stares at her ass whitely. His intestines feel like coiled constrictors. She spreads her rear cheeks for her sphincter to receive a smack. He puckers up. She sure is sweet and evil. Her pubical patch is like a hedgehog's spines. She suggests in mine that he should lap her clam. And he bows with deliberate grace, getting on bended knee, but not before he does a paradoxically stately and drunken dance. She sways like a growing plant, kneading his hunched back like a hump of bread dough. She puts an academic cap on and swims on him like a swan on a river. He peers through her strands like a prisoner through a jail's bars. Tongued, she gestures like a conductor to an orchestra. She hangs on to the door's frame like an attire item in a wardrobe, belt-whipped. The dusky room is lit by a skylight. Arianne is like a schoolgirl punished by the sadistic master. He puts on a hangman's mask and wields a fake executioner's sword. His scrutiny of her is neither friendly nor unfriendly. Her belly contracts, back tightens. She is embarrassed, enjoying the analingus, Peki proceeding delicately and diligently. She chooses her words wisely, vocabulary poetical, anally probed. She appreciates his effort. Her strain is endured. She feels diminished and misused. He controls the deviant narrative, directing the scenario as if it's the structure of a play. The pair are resolutely irrational. He looks at her tush like it is a trap for some unknown reason. She suffers stolidly. His lips curl in a dissolute smile. Her sturdy and wan beauty enraptures him. His peepers are black as coal, complexion cockerel-red. She screams at the top of her lungs, thrashing madly, brutally fisted. She hadn't bargained for this anguish. Her pigtails are tugged like the tides by the moon. He smacks her jubblies with glee. His hand comes out of her hind like a butterfly from a chrysalis. She slumps forward pale and vanishing, tummy inflating and deflating like a dudelsack. Humiliated, she flushes and looks away. He smirks like a cherub. She climaxes, whimpers, and goes limp like a marionette. Her cough is dry. She feels his pinkie electric when it contacts her ribs. Her skin is warm. He feeds her cream cakes and coconut coffee. She is a shape-changer in the flickering brilliancy. He applies an ointment on her abrasions as though it is a placatory peace offering. And they have bourbon and cucumber and prate composedly. The two ride (bikes, in the lanes) and stride nude through the copse. He imagines them being Adam and Eve in the Garden. She believes that sometimes he can be a snake in the grass. They take a dip in the deep pond, with luminously green water, in the vicinity of the high, forbidding manor, with a bright courtyard, a splashing and chortling fountain, carved with foliage, dragonflies, reptiles, snails, and a crescent moon surrounded by stars, in its center, in the ruddy gold refulgence that pours like liquid. He sees hallucinatory flashes of color that soon fade. He waits for his vision to adjust. The sun is a translucent skull. It's the shrooms. The vault is duck-egg-blue. The Holy Land is a concentration camp. Her movements are thoughtful and precise, possess the peculiar qualities of a puppet's, her mien purely expressive. She is an emotional being living an essential existence. He walks like a (manikin) shadow several paces behind her. She is larger than him in every direction. They drink chocolate and eat pastry. He tries dowsing with a hazel fork, just for kicks, and both are surprised when the dead wood pitches and pulls him toward her lady parts. Peki ruminates on Marisa, real and unreal, past and present. He senses that their apartment is one through a looking-glass, and has gone through the mirror and refuses to return. Arianne finds repose. Playing a part, he sinks his teeth into the role like it's steak tartare and he's eating for two.

It is a gray day thus far. She is a raucous, meaty seductress with a vampire mouth in the uterine room. She has a rhythmic sensuality. Arianne is the charmer and Peki is the snake. She's a supple Valkyrie. All she needs is a horned helmet and breastplate! She is so young and alive. He is afraid of aging and dying. His backside's belch sounds like an automobile's tooting horn. She is vivacious and sultry. Verdurous tendrils clamber and tumble on the mossy structure. The lovers get sentimental and silly and celebrate their union with gusto. A blush rises to her chubby cheeks. Despite the swelter, he wears an opera cloak over floating robes and handmade sandals. After a leaden morning, the afternoon becomes broiling and brilliant. There are plumbing problems, the pipes with rust and clog. Jars of jam and jelly are on the counter. She yawns, and stretches her arms like elastics. Her axillae have an acrid malodor. She becomes incommunicable to her companion. She examines her slightly bitten nails. He pretends not to notice. There's remoteness and iciness to her. She has lightless pies. She shells peas and makes marmalade. Occasionally she will cock-block him, and he'll feel like the fox ranging round the chicken coop, attempting to find some way in, almost always failing. Their relationship has its passions and dramas. She is dressed in a military tunic and camouflage skirt. She scrubs the pots and pans with a steel wool pad. He catches her around the waist, sits her on his avuncular knee, and rocks her. She's tongue-tied and at a loss, smiling enigmatically. She sure can be confident and gullible, smart and stupid, easy and difficult. She is erected, stretched, and pinned down not unlike a tent. Her abdomen is slackening. Decorously he compliments her on her fine, full figure, mitts fumbling urgently at her behind. And her flesh pricks. She appears pink-complected and flustered and looks out the uneven lancet window-pane, glazed and opaque. The makeshift bookcase is made out of brick and plank; his handiwork. Skeletally scrawny, red-faced women roar like toddlers on the goat-cropped grass, squabbling on unspoiled and pleasant land. He would exterminate them expeditiously, given the chance. And to hell with the prospect of extracting their fat for Butyrum... Peki and Arianne, with packs on their backs, traipse through the elven wood. A goshawk pecks at a dead marten in these pristine plants on the side of a well-trodden footpath. They bask in the full fields and running rivulets, gorge on fruit and vegetables, glug beer and champagne, hike, and sing up and down slopes. Midsummer is muggy, leafy, and inviting. They wander in nature, sink their toes into the soil, and make out. They build this mountainous bonfire, a flickering construction, and dance maniacally around it, backward and forward. He oils the wheels of amorousness with his advances. Intercoursing on the campion and sorrel, in their hiding place in the somber coppice, they, muck-encrusted, light-bedizened, squeal like bagpipes. Her hands fan above his head akin to fish fighting the current. Bright birds in the close trees watch them. The winged fairies, without a stitch on, hovering like hummingbirds, are probably minacious. Fog is a menacing phantom. Shrubbery is shaped by the winds. Peter Pan, the little boy who wouldn't grow up, rollicks with Mowgli, the jungle child, both with wilting daisy chains around their necks, on a boulder, in the hollyhocks, marigolds, and honeysuckle. They are very feral and perfectly beautiful. Their spoken language is baby talk. Peki knows he is tripping. The lads pass a hookah pipe back and forth, the wisps of smoke turning into crinite caterpillars that crawl on the indigoid oxygen, whereupon the youths throw Benjamin Bunny around like a football in the untamed and changing boscage. Then they climb redwoods, not unlike monkeys, and dive simultaneously into a mud bath of a swimming pool encompassed by rotten saplings. A pack of roaming wolves ignores them. Evergreens are draped in a network of frondescent scaffolding. Arianne sneezes and excuses herself. The sweethearts, in their underpants, dive into the depths of a lake. They worship the sun, air, earth, and water, play japes and jests on each other, executing practical jokes at unpredictable times. The pair mess about in a boat, tied to a rickety pier, extending over the aqua pura. Peki twists Arianne into grotesque shapes, and she is beefier. He is proudly polymorphously perverse, and will never construct a psychological or physical dam against carnal excess. Before, he was a broken man. Now, he is put together. The clock ticks at different speeds for them. His life is usually more fast-paced, whereas hers is more of a slow-burn. She believes she might be hopelessly in love with him. Her pulse clicks like a metronome. Her straight strawberry-blonde hair is blowing in the breeze. She has stubble on her shins. Her bush has thickened and coarsened. Trails stretch ahead. The orchard is boundless and shining. She recites lyric poetry from memory while he paws at her. It is intensely satisfying for them. Her attractiveness rouses his admiration.

Time is elasticized. Their schedules are flexible. They natate in the mere, day and night. Peki and Arianne are both baked aureate-fawn, in perpetual motion, prancing in the thicket, walking, running, and leaping through fruitful trees, salubrious becks, dirty paths, and sweet-scented flowers, bitten by horseflies. They stuff down uncooked sausages and apple crumble, in the misty curtain, before plunging into the lagoon, the color of dishwashing water, holding hands, surfacing separately, and shrieking. He holds her and she wriggles out of his grasp like an eel. He dives in off the bank. She bellyflops from a branch. Waist-deep, he suggests some teeny-weeny Triton. They submit to the blaze of the sun. She puts on a slip and knickers while he puts on a Quakerish top. She does these dance movements and gymnastic exercises, glossy tress tied in a ponytail. The deluge is whelming. Boughs flail and leaves hiss in the gales. Peki and Arianne bolt for cover, in the ropes and spirals and whip-lashes of the driving trenches, into a barn. It is clammy and uncomfortable. The soaker soughs. Her hay fever is acting up. She strides with stamps of her bare soles on the dusty floor. Her bum looks like it has a case of acne. His oral cavity tastes of tin. Their bathing suits are sodden and smelly, spread on gardening implements to dry properly. They glance furtively at each other. He bends her back onto a bale of straw. She has loose bowels and strained bladder, goes in an empty pottle. Crouched, her moue is sensual, behavior appetitive. Although gripped and smooched and off-balance, she unfalteringly excretes and micturates. His organ lolls. She takes three steps back, on her heels, whispering inaudibly. She's being skittish when he pokes her paunch. Her speech is soft and slow. His mind is replete with distasteful images of her getting savagely beaten. She is cuddled and kissed. Her gestures are more normal, and less mannered. Her expression, knees cupped by him, is one of satisfaction, her poised calm a total turn-on for him. She's smooth and glowing. They're lubriciously exact and flourishing. The twosome's earthy and fiery. Her lip and tum muscles relax. She says neither no nor yes to the fondling. He thrives on spontaneous intimacy. She catches her breath, heaving. She is wet and hot. He gets the party started. She accepts his lead and gives head. She treats him like a sultan in a harem. She is a puppet with strings to pull. Light and shadow gave meaning to their bodies. He has a chiseled, frozen phiz, inscrutable. Their affection grows not unlike a vegetable from ardorseeds. She talks in a swallowed voice. Suddenly, everything goes black, and he is blinded, like a moth's wing or peacock's tail are sightless, and he passes out. Too much rum. The vista is vacant and swollen. He comes to within minutes... Peki considers himself a superb businessman and an even better salesman. He sees the store as being like a gallery for hanging art, the shop a showplace where his work, Butyrum, can be displayed and sold. The exhibition shelves and cabinets have plate-glass handles with brass knobs, elegant and modern. The checkout counter is a long table of pale wood, the cash register old-fashioned. He's the prime mover behind this setup. The only drawback is the retarded tick-tock of the grandfather clock against the far wall. Its replacement is essential. He is thankful he has dependable help in managing, his assistants quite capable. He's considering the potential prospect of renting a studio for classes on mantequilla making. He'd provide milk, lamb pie, and bread for the students. In addition, he is mulling over the idea of lecturing the butter enthusiasts. He is rigid and rigorous. Peki reads and dreams before hitting the road. He needed to get out and he got out. He felt as if he was living in an atmospheric tale of doomed passion. He has his own life and responsibilities that cannot be disregarded any longer. Although her moods range from morose to manic, he still adores Arianne. She had become disagreeable and domineering in their (impermanent) living arrangement. He had to get a move on. There was a relief, and disappointment, that he didn't maintain that state of affairs. Too much compromise and consultation. Remembrances are like a kaleidoscope — reshaped, reordered. Sun in the overcast: gold in gray.

Brydie Ogle

She senses tension in the atmosphere like a kind of breath-holding. The cryogenically resurrected, satanically intense, Dido-tall Brydie Ogle lives in abstract misery. Her existence satisfies Aristotle's definition of tragedy, that everyone suffers. Despair echoes through her. Her mind is a tempest. Only a miracle could calm this storm. The hectic-haired, knife-hearted, club-footed mudlark is dazed in dreamy self-absorption, wabbling through the woods under a grilling sun. She pretends she is a dryad with a reddish mane in her barken environment. To her, the imagination is quantum physics — it is both a particle and a wave in simultaneity. It can be difficult to measure its dynamic force, the aesthetic propulsion of images and ideas, and gauge its powerful momentum. Birds trill. Crickets chirp. Brydie lives in an airtight bell jar, breathlessly claustrophobic, making any human connection practically impossible. Self-regard is the pool she swims in. When sober and straight, she functions on confidence, and revels in her facility to impress. The weathered brickwork of the building's side is painted with brushstrokes of bloodstains: an evidential mural of violence unbridled. Brydie ghosts in and out of relationships with men and women. She is at the end of her tether. She has fallen so low that she can't fall any lower. She goes into self-preservation mode on a daily basis. She has the beak of a toucan, huge eyes a clear blue like noonlight through saltwater, and a candle-pale complexion. Her long hair is buttercup-colored. She is very self-conscious about her limp. She perceives herself as badly flawed. Mist vaporizes. Church bells are haranguingly clangy. The city is disordered and devastated. These are precarious times. An airplane roars overhead. The river is fast-flowing. There is a sordid garden and reeking well. Brydie remembers smothering her scapegrace ex-boyfriend with his urostomy pouch in his house, a bedraggled clapboard affair, on the apple farm. Raytheon Boatwright-Swingle, with an entrancing, egregious beauty, had lard-white flesh and a coconut fuzz cut. The past always party-crashes the present. The future is a Grand Inquisitor. Breaking up with him was on par with Dionysius conquering Apollo. The fight was a volcanic eruption, the two spouting fire and magma. She was Phoebe. He was Silvius. Love is a goddamn wrecking ball, she thinks. Suddenly, she feels an insistent pulsation in the air at odd intervals... The piss-poor Jasper Hobkirk, so ancient that he farts dirt, is pudding-headed, beaver-faced, chin-heavy, and mountain-pony solid, with a hardcore smoker's sallowness. He wears a sprig of a wig and has the constitution of a diseased ferret. The number of the beast is tattooed on his throat. His skin appears to be in the early stage of putrefaction. In his cups, he mutters curses and blinks like an owl. Half strutting and half stumbling like an overfed grouse, he follows the incandescent girl, emaciated and elongated, down the sidewalk, studying her valentine-shaped buttocks. She has a fine bone structure and smells like rain. The near-midget with bugle ears and avocet's bill hits on her, scurrying crabwise, his spoken language floribundant. Brydie sits against the tree that looks like it was sketched by Fragonard and draws her knees to her chest and her nails to her teeth. Then she becomes a lotus, unfurled, revealing her complicated blossoms. Her absence in the world is a sort of presence, thanks to Peki.

Peki and Marisa

Two distinct and contradictory smells assault his nares: sewage and petroleum. The place is a pigpen. His posterior unleashes an ear-piercing volley of gassy, bestial shrieks. The gooz sounds like a pig is getting slaughtered. A parish is evocative of a sinister erection. Rooks scold from branches. The weather is shifty and tricky. Sun's a shining shield. There is scarcely any traffic. Fulgor pours like the golden sands of an hourglass. Peki's heart almost ceases to beat, glimpsing Marisa's infantile pout. She fixes upon him a satiric scowl. Her knickers are in a twist. She enshrouds him like mist. He vents a puzzled sigh and a melodious chuckle. She was tending the gale-maltreated garden in the dead-bright coruscation, following the aimless and lengthy mouse hunt. He flounces. She slinks. She is, by a mile, flawed: she humors too much, has a monstrous vanity, breaks promises, and is disinclined to take chances. Every so often he swears he could thropple her on the spot. Situations, good and bad, occur quickly. Episodes, negative and positive, happen so fast. Speed contracts time. Is she his responsibility or is it the other way around? She is thoroughly unchangeable and gracilescent. Her buns recall Cupid's cheeks. Her worst fault — she attempts to please herself before others. Her virtues are her vices. Self-conscious, as usual, he feels like a dullard. Insecurity bore a hole in him which never closes up. In spite of the crib's confines, they have lost awareness of both spatial and temporal ambit and remain in their chosen quadrant. He coughs and sneezes, and experiences a strange emotional phenomenon. The floor beneath his feet seems somehow porous and insubstantial. She is a sentient Phidian sculpture, acting like a child, using a duster on the window's woodwork. She straightens her body to rest her taxed muscles, without taking further notice of him, thus enabling him to scrutinize the suppleness of her flanks. Finding her fascinating, he forgets everything. She has an original personality. Her girlishness is suspended like a gossamer cloudlet. She suspires hard and fast and marches with rapid steps. He wants to hold and caress her. Her skin is moss-soft. Making love to her would be like going through a magic gate that leads to a fantastic land of coital gratification, a mysterious dreamworld of unfamiliar soil and alien sky, basically like being on a different planet. The cot, according to his caprice, has been left bare of a spread; however, there is a greasy towel on it. He concentrates on the adjustment of the cogs and wheels of his mind. Shade puts him in swart solitariness. Lust pierces his loins like the actual stabbing of a spear. Motionless at the banister, he feels as if he is hemmed in, lost in weird contemplation. Doors in the remotest wall of his brain unexpectedly open and echoing voices proceed from those recesses. She's a gauche oddity. She possesses a curious interest for him, and he hesitates as to whether to run up and grope her. He gawks at her young bosom as though from across a fathomless gulf. Tensions are unnaturally strained. He wishes to have robust, reckless, obliterating sex with her. The image gives him a voluptuous thrill. He ruminates over the verticals of fantasy and the verticals of fervor. She is hot and panting. Something is violently vibratory deep down in his groin. He glances about from port to stern. A benevolent grimace is seen on her grim features. He stares at her, not unlike a territorial bulldog at a hare on the lawn. They are like a couple of departed souls having reached their final destination, and are spirits free to wander the earth. It is a fun show starring mother and son. Peki carries his Butter Book like a Muslim holds the Koran. Sedulously he strokes his beard as cerebrations pass in his head like avian shadows over terra firma. He gladsomely connects with Marisa. Will this last forever and ever? He observes her as though she's an object. They blether, broach proscribed subjects, embark on drives on side roads, read books, listen to records, and walk through the woods... Driven by the unconscious cunning of a predator, he obstinately pursues her, a glimmer of boyish eagerness in his face. She is imperseverant and preposterous, putters in the pad. He hankers after her. His lack of confidence is an ugly, pathological facet of need. Her body is bioluminescent beneath her transpicuous teddy. He imagines fumbling with her brassiere's clasps like he would with a gate's latches. Drizzle sounds not unlike the rustling of reapers' scything. Tribulations have been overcome. They've gotten much closer lately, thick as thistles, prevailing over setbacks, vanquishing challenges. He wishes they'll be inseparable, which is, it might be mentioned, an impossibility. He remembers the memorable picnic (after visiting the museums and monuments) of quiche and hooch next to the secluded ravine (its continual misenunciations relaxing) and the picturesque sunset, its beauty uncomplicated. A model of steadfastness, he kept his pintle at half-mast. There were no secret kisses or incautious touches. He burned with shame. They swelled in summer's fictile inflections. She encouraged him, as a confidence boost, to spruce up his establishment... Every unconvincing apology, every contrived dollop of flattery, every toe-curlingly misjudged platitude, seems as if it has been concocted by Peki in some secret bio-warfare lab for assaulting Marisa's mind with pure, toxic nonsense. She grackles her complaints out and retires. The burg is blighted but bearable. The forlorn bough of a lime tree appears to reach out toward a bush with heart-shaped leaves, on the side entrance of the confectioner's store. Its proprietor, an amiable apparition, occasionally inflicts a blustering friendliness on Peki. Pantochromatic neon lights of the grocery. Moon's a carbuncular excrescence. He has been flying high on dope for a while; every released arrow must rest eventually. He wishes he could put his problems in a blender and shake them into nonexistence. A nearby shivaree is blaring. He takes a spin in a cab. A Caucasoid, crinite fatty named Spece Mims-Santoso, scar-faced and with a medieval mullet, possessing a slippery surface charm, is at the wheel. He claims he's a "grade-A bastard," and that he "romped with a party boy with a peroxide-blond beatnik mop and goatee." At the crack of dawn, the grass takes the dew.

Flue-hued hillocks. Turnip patch. Aeviternal alps. Empyrean dulls. Temps soar. The television blasts. The radiator is like a tombstone. The buckling parquet wants repair badly. The shutters are slanted. Several shades are pulled. Shadows are ominous. His levels of discomfiture rise

394

and fall. Peki, submersed in the sofa, can read Marisa's mind like a map! He wants to bring her tightly to his heart. A wanton excitement shivers through his nerves. Chills quicken up his spine. Will his presence assist in driving away the sour mood that obsesses her? Is he a disturbance in her atmosphere? He's a joke who isn't laughing. He snickers at his elation. He is simply smitten with her. His fire consumes him but doesn't illuminate anything. He yearns to grab her and yet not lose his hold on their unique relationship. In for a penny, in for a pound, he thinks... They are a fair pair! He refuses to suit action with his urge. Resisting his impulses is like steering a craft away from reefs. It's an occultly way of avoiding possible disaster. She exuberantly preaches her gospel, practicing jiu-jitsu, glomming peaches. She is dressed in a demoniacally snug tube-top, bell-bottoms, and ballet slippers. Her unexpected bawling winds down to a whimper. His throat constricts. He ingests clam chowder and imbibes gin-and-tonic while she plucks her monobrow. She's as lucid, hot, and antic as a candle's flame. She lights him up. Her behavioral inconsistencies, he supposes, are unresolvable; nevertheless, she remains for him an invigorating option to the dire extremes of murder-for-fat and business-building. Work ethic and intestinal fortitude inform success. The shop was once a lonely place. Now it is a hot spot. The store is the sole source of income and protection against impoverishment. He's been busy as a piper. Prospects are exciting. Nothing can diminish his ardor for her. He's not sure if he's waiting for something to happen for them or for something not to happen. The tunnel of probability has narrowed. They promised one another they'd live together 'til death did them part. Marisa's eyes are spurtling with retinal speckles in the sepulchral room. She glares at, into, and then through him. Peki wants to bear hug her as if to squeeze the life out of her and peck those convected bow-lips. Her countenance collapses as though she got shot. Her mood changes are so sudden. She outpaces herself in mumbles and flies a kite in front of the rotating fan. Are her moans and groans vented in pleasure or pain? He can't distinguish the difference. It feels as if they are far apart, at opposite ends of infinity itself. Domestic dramas reach proportions he never thought possible. Her breathy vox is titillating. He admires her for everything she is and everything she isn't. She has an infrigidation of attitude.

Her axillae reek of broccoli. He checks his watch in mid-stride. Did she take her pills today? Her tempestuous emotions are unpredictable. He dodges and pivots through her degrading remarks, ones he will remember to forget. Dead-still, jaw muscles tense, he's stunned by the dismay on her stricken visage. His whole heart is parted into halves when it concerns tries at consolation. He shudders along the wainscoting. She wants him no more than she would a rat! Her blinders are dazed. A boisterous scarf is wrapped around her goosey neck. Wisteria-gray firmament. There is an absurd piling up of misinterpretations between them. Volumes bound in vellum are stacked on the dresser, with its oblong dimension and discolored wood. A mass of memories, secret and personal, circulates in his cranium. He has a bowed back and she has a grizzled head. He gets some medicinal relief from the stabbing pain in his midsection as though an arrowhead, embedded in the abdomen, was slowly pulled out. Her corn-yellow toenails need clipping. Her feet have the bitter aroma of elder leaves. His older and blood-related querida gives him a feeling, permeating every part of him, different from anything he's ever known before. She is touchingly anorectic. The sight of her liquefies his bones within him. He feels something much deeper than passion. She's a will-o'-the wisp entity, alive and tangible, a living, breathing ignis fatuus. She makes her surroundings enchanted and transparent with her diffused essence. He paces up and down the room. Minutes slip by. She is a tad bit inhuman. His tearless blinkers for a moment become fastened upon emptiness as if he's analyzing a mental image. She draws a long breath. Light and shadow waver together. The drapes flap not unlike pterodactylous wings. A sewing machine is situated on the hutch. A china bowl, brimming with bluebells and primroses, is balanced on the mantelpiece. These gauzy curtains wave in the eddying gusts. Entanglement of aspens. Campion-pink welkin. Every aspect of her form, each flicker on her fizzog, tantalizes him. Her anacreontic language evaporates into the midsummer air. The prospect of a venereous dalliance with her exhilarates him. Tripping, in the larder, he finds himself in an ornate palace ballroom, located in a cliffside sanitarium, with its fading grandeur, overhung by an immense chandelier, and has phantasmagorical visions of an assembly of strapping, shaven-headed young men and women playing volleyball on a makeshift court. Stripped down to their underwear, the game degenerates into bonkers roughhousing, and finally into a gonzo wrestling match, with lots of grunting and catcalling. There is cartoonish wailing and thrashing. Wile E. Coyote referees, moving in loony parkourish fashion. Peki views his mother as having the hide of a beast, plumage of a bird, and the scales of a fish. Marisa admits she feels homely and old. His praise of her cheapens on the tongue. He juggles thoughts like balls. They play checkers, wordlessly and unemphatically, crunching breadsticks, both hunched in bibs, shoveling down meat and pudding in swoons of satisfaction. There's strategic subterfuge and fitful murmuring. His commentary is elliptical. Her glances are hesitant. Her mug is margarine-pigmented. In his opinion, there are multiple domains, one inside the other, not unlike Chinese boxes. His lamps plunge into the shallows of her svelte frame, the depths of her oculi. She resembles a grinning skeleton, and bends like a reed in a brook. She extricates herself from his febrile osculations and tactions. Her unwillingness to accept his advances releases his pent-up frustration. They lock horns. They cross swords. It is oral cockfighting. It's Russian roulette with words. He, appearing really angry now, hallouminating and smellucinating, on psycho jello and hungover as a duck, speaks with evident vexation. If this pad is an Eden, is he the snake? He chokes his chicken in the spence.

Tripping too much lately on psychedelics, Peki doesn't trust his eyes. So, he looks at the almost-fridge and possible-hamper with skepticism. He needs to eat a proper meal. And get fresh air. He's black-robed. He has got to get out of these silly clothes! His abundant shaggy hair holds dandruff. His toenails resemble potato chips. Marisa provocatively postures and pouts at him. He finds her to be as attractive as she is insensible. She makes his existence infinitely more interesting. He resists the impulse to grope her. Her flesh is slippery and sweating. He is hopelessly and helplessly enamored of her. He stuffs himself with sauced-and-cheesed linguini. Wild-eyed-and-haired, she tells him that she'd nearly died when she was in her mid-twenties, bleeding from a back-alley abortion… She is so skinny she looks like she was just released from a prison camp. She wears the bead necklace he bought for her. He's unusually attached. She is unnaturally detached. Full now, he feels swollen to bursting, a full-term gravid guy. He wishes he could be civilized, dignified, scholarly, a man fluent in many tongues. His features are distorted by stress. She wears a jumper with no brassiere or panties on underneath. She's being a cold fish toward him. She can be a deft conversationalist, quick-witted and spellbinding. He pictures the spheres of her titties, those typhlotic, ocular nipples, the constellation of freckles on her shoulders. He makes a pass at her. She cringes as if he could contaminate her by getting too close. He will not lose faith as a consequence of her rejection. With her, he is perpetually heated. She knows how to turn him off. She's nasty and daffy at the same time. Their partnership has its problems and dangers. His mouth is open like a flower. He leans on the mediocre, run-of-the-mill, man-sized carving of Christ on the Cross. Chaos reigns in his cranium. His gunky orbs gleam not unlike puddles of oil. He thinks of her genitalia medusa. Then he, squinnied, takes a gander at the shelf of curiosities, including a fetal skeleton, things collected higgledy-piggledy, lingering over the human testicles in a jar of formaldehyde, and these outdated artifacts. Puce sky. Sulfur emanation. Marisa smiles like a skull, peaceful as a corpse, disregarding him, sitting cross-legged on the rug. She eats vanilla yogurt, manipulating the plastic spoon with fastidious fingers. Whereupon she pads round the flat with a defiant, assessing expression. Peki shifts and settles on the radiator and scrutinizes her well-cut, chocolate-brown mop, umber brows and lashes, and strong-featured, bony face. His brain unravels like knitting. He feels as though he's suspended upside down from life like a gnomic Houdini. He considers himself the mover and shaker in their relationship. They part in the apartment. She fits herself into a wine-hued trouser suit. He changes into hospital overalls. She pisses and moans about the dust and darkness. He is economical with his spoken sentences. She insists she caught a virus from him and threatens to sue him. And she flits around the cleaning crew, conjoined twins with stunted limbs and prosthetic buttocks, in the bowels of the building. She drinks soda pop from a urinary bottle. Raindrops have the scent of wood shavings. Fog rolls over the river. Moon's a shocking pink, sea a royal blue. Searchlights snake in the city.

The drawing-room, furnished somewhere between the modernist and the clinical, feels airless. Her lined face blazing in brilliance, Marisa tends to the cacti diligently in the interest of efficiency. Plants occupy the window-sills. She takes care of them too, watering them with disproportionate urgency, and talking to them like they're infants. For Peki, it's a welcome sight, to see her up and about, because for most of the previous week she was bedridden with non-existent medical crises (she is a spasmodic hypo-chondriac). Her collapse was spectacular. She supposedly had high blood pressure, heart palpitations, blue labial lips, muscle spasms, and unstable balance. He was free as the wind, without work, keeping an eye on her. He found the respite from the establishment to be restorative. He knew full well that her illnesses were imagined. The shrill, mesmeric complaints were vehemently kept up. She was pathetically tremulous and weeping. She can be a cantankerous old bitch on occasion! He felt nagged and put upon. She was needy, whiny. His insectoid madre stayed wrapped in her chrysalis sheets seemingly forever. And he never felt more little and lost, not unlike a child. She glowered at him accusingly as if it was his fault she wasn't well. Psychosomatic, he told himself. He was feeling under the weather with allergies. He stayed home to look after her. He was confident the shop could manage without him. After all, he hires only capable people. Experience breeds competence. There was, however, this one night in which he went off at some unearthly hour to whip up the latest batch of Butyrum… The illumination has a spun-silk quality. The flowerbed teems with color. A skyscraper is a shining citadel. The sun is carnation-colored. Zephyrs sound like aggrieved voices. Rain on the warm asphalt has the sound of a steaming iron hissing on the board. The town's din sharpens and fades. Swifts swoop. A heated argument goes on beyond the flimsy wall. The apartment is brimful with rage. Precipitation jangles on the macadam. The discomfort was her occupation. Sickness would no longer employ her. She forced herself to barf into the chamber pot as a final concession to illness. Her phenomenal recovery gave respectability and serenity to her. She regained her vitality in no time. Ice cubes chuckle in Peki's drained tulip glass. He is a creeper looking to her as a place to adhere. A twinge in his jaw is turning into a toothache. He sits on the tweed couch and puts his feet up on the melamine table. Marisa appears to be a bit washed-out, rummaging relentlessly in the cupboards. He glances at her, cursory, electric, desiring contact. His molar shrills silently in his mouth. He thinks he has an abscess. The pain is distracting him from essential concentration. Oh, for relief from the dental anguish… She gazes at him as though she's out in the desert, beholding what may or may not be a mirage. She is lavishly, perhaps even grotesquely, cosmeticized, with the goth mascara and magenta lipstick, putzing around in the bathroom that evokes a time capsule in a science fiction movie. She wears a cerise angora sweater and vermeil bikinis. She yells obscenities at specks of dust. She leafs through these glossy mags you'd unusually find in a doctor's office. Her dermis is apparently desiccated. Her breasts are rounded and her buttocks are lively. She puts in huge hoop earrings. She has a few freckles on her shoulders. She believes in faith healing. Her spiritual nature is why her cure is so marvelous, indeed miraculous. Staring at her, he feels as though he's clinically dead, having stopped breathing, and only an orgasm can bring him back. It is a wonderful experience, maybe even life-changing. His overtures are impeded by his canine agony. She explains, with several narrative flourishes, that when she was incapacitated she had an out-of-body experience, she floated up, up, and away, in indescribable light, blindingly bright, and saw herself lying on the mattress. Suddenly, she drops her panties like a banana peel. He draws the drapes, crosses the threshold, kneels, and endeavors to get himself off. He washes her nether regions clean with a damp washcloth, at the same instant beating off. His idea of heaven — scrubbing her down and whacking off. He blushes, reminding her of a Red Indian in a Western film. She verbalizes that her abrupt sickness happened for a reason: it brought them together. She knows this moment was meant. She mops at her brow with a hankie. Then she takes encapsulated painkillers from tinfoil and gulps them. One can feel the temperature change in the atmosphere. The furniture's polish gleams. There's much bargaining going on at the bazaar. Peki explores Marisa's private parts with his tongue and fingers. He licks the fleshy, salmon-pink cabbage of her cunt, enjoying its taste and intricacies. She says her sleep was uneasy, with creatures from her dream, and visions from her nightmare, lingering in her head. He replies his slumber too was turbulent, that he was drowning in tossing waves of imagery, and when he came to, he regarded the lampshade as if it was a life jacket. He approaches her ass and retreats, for it stinks of an unattended drain. She breathes soft and sweet. He tries not to dwell on his ravaged teeth. He rubs her feet. It is as though the soles are made of a rough, inflexible, indestructible material. He wants very badly to tell her about the heavyset, buzzcut skank he drilled and degraded, the ho he offed and whose suet he used to make more butter with. Mating, mother and son call it "lubricating the domestic machinery." Finished, they bake a cake. Whereupon he makes a beaker of joe for her. The clement weather persists. This is their lovely residence, a pleasant spot. Though homely, it has good vibrations.

Peki, in a cotton loincloth and work boots, pops a Vicodin and Ambien and notices Marisa's tootsies are blistered, probably from the stilettos. He has a panic attack, thinking that she may need a change, and could announce she's getting a place of her own. She just came up from the cave-cellar of the edifice. Frog-agile, he attends to her foots. They smell of steam. She smiles her smile in a harsh phosphorescent pool. He fondles her triangular tits. She feels hopeless and helpless. The stream of her tears glistens. He gets a glimpse of the corkscrew curl of her belly-button. Her respirations sound like bamboo rustling in the drafts. Her limbs are gawkily bent as he applies the ointment to her chafed heels. She observes the firmness to his body, pale and waxy like a bean. He has a monstrous, mountainous head. To her, his nostril hairs are like feelers that sprouted in them. She glances at the sooty wing of a raven in flight. Her gestures shift shape in the splendor. The mizzle is delicate as veiling. Wind sounds like monotonous plaints. Peki caresses the concavity of her stomach. Marisa soughs. His perspective gives her hands a resemblance to the claws of some rare species of aquatic creature. She teases her tresses into shape, staring with blind intelligence. Her mop represents a kind of perpetuity, predictably unchanging in style and color. She becomes quiet, seemingly unalive. Her nates have a dung pat malodor. She laughs sonorously when he furtively kisses her knee. He grumbles not unlike a ghost. She is schizophrenic and hallucinating. His intonation acquires a certain scratchiness and clarity. Full of love and consideration, he takes care of her toes, crouching on the ancient uneven floor. She declares she sometimes feels as if she is commanded into confinement in this fortress building. She evaluates his squatting haunches with repugnance and something approximating pity. She has a spring in her step, readying the pickled pork for supper. She takes a moment to ponder over the blooms below, sentient beings to her, their health and multiplicity. Some blossoms look spent. He has a sort of arachnoid scuttle to his gait. He lights an incense stick. She makes herself a poached egg and a slice of toast. There is quarreling going on in the next flat. Skyline in the overcast contracts like a brace. Winds die down. Leaves sweat dew. The trees are silent, living their lives. The nearby bushes are tamed and tied, along with the peripheral population of shrubs. Irises are tucked into their beds of dirt, baking in the sun, soaking in the scintillation. Fronds of a fern brush slightly against the pane. The homeless, with bowed ribs, cluster in an entryway, with its conoid canopy, like huddled bats, their begging bowls set up like drums on the sidewalk. The courtyard is busy and yapping. Gusts sigh through the heather. A steel mill stands empty, sad, and cold. Mother and son sit companionably on the anonymous bed with its discreet blankets. The golden-brown room has a scum-white ceiling, pigeon-blue paneling, user-friendly TV and stereo, a tandem of leatherette chairs at a Formica table, and a connecting blood-red john. Marisa's cheeks are ruddy. Her bust is small and soft and dry. Peki combs his cobwebby chest hair. Her armpits whiff of sour cooking. Her integument is stretched over bone. The two listen to the scraping songs of the cicadas and debate over third-world hunger, the local economy, and fossil fuels. The moon loses its translucent pinkness. She's characteristically blank when he molests her. They get recumbent rhythmically. He touches her like a lover. Her breath reeks of garlic. She is flushed from many handlings. His grin takes up his entire physiognomy. She's still as stone. The perspiration evaporates on her skin like water on a rock. Her middle glistens like porcelain. She appears wasted, fragile. Her wrinkles make her face resemble a map. Her eyes are sunken into their sockets. Light and shadow dictate her form. He essays to be accommodating, and adaptable, with her. Her flesh, to him, feels like smoked fish. He clings to her, not unlike a limpet. They hear voices that are indistinguishable but irate. He unzips his fly and produces a limp mickey. And her russet lips tighten. She rises to mess with the shower curtain and rubber bathmat. The tub is spotlessly clean.

After an onanistic episode, jacking off in the bath, in the metalline lambency, Peki employs the old-fashioned combover to conceal his baseball-sized bald spot. He'd been visited by spirits in his slumber, his soul sucked out of him… The rims of his peepers are reddened. He can't get rid of the dream in which a village cast him out, but not before stoning him. In his smock, he is shaped like a sack of grain. He looks puffy and pimply. He moves lazily, lounges around languidly, his tasks completed, in the simmering heat. His mouth is compressed. When he attempts to cuddle with Marisa, starkers, on the drab sofa, it is as if an imperceptible sword is wedged between them. She is customarily broody. He views the crescentoid sweat on her abdominal curve. Her lips are pursed in a peevish scowl. What he wants from her is unnatural. His behavior, to her, is abnormal. Her derma layer is earth-warm. Her skeletal hands are seemingly signaling. She's acting as if she's correct and virtuous. Her bunghole has the mephitis of an unhatched egg, the chick curled inside and rotting. The stench of the escaping gases makes him queasy. Tourists are vigorous and noisy outside. Peki pictures her as a fast-moving pallid worm, wiry and venomous, in a pumpkin field, under a waxing moon. He will trap her, using himself both as the bough and the bait. He mulls over ways and means. What he hungers for is difficult and dangerous. His countenance is persimmon-pigmented with passion. The hush is substantial. Words are unnecessary. His gaze is calculating. In this apartment, Marisa has the sensation of being a bee in its honeycomb and drowning in the sweet, sticky, amber fluid. Her posterior has the spongy texture of a mushroom. He reaches toward her, sallow and intent. He teases, impotent, infatuated. Her midriff is springy. She mewls. Her eyes are serious. He smacks her backside and her yap opens so wide she could swallow the moon whole. She ventilates a choked wail, followed by a huge yelp. Grabbing her from behind, he sounds like an enraged beast. The train of events has left the station. Egrets and cormorants are feathered, flying demons. Marisa chops up the dinner vegetables. She sports a secretive smirk. She inclines her head. Discalceated, she, nervy, pads with a cocky strut, her arms swinging. She is sickening, shriveling. Peki has pig eyes. His gape is dropped. His expression is like a kid's, expecting to receive a toy or candy from a parent. He feels as though his gut is on the verge of exploding. His insides squiggle. His chest feels like a furnace. Her shadow skitters raggedly across the carpet. His rod has risen with a life of its own. His prepuce is suggestive of the hood of a charmed snake. The boner judders. He's eager and embarrassed. The sun, pus-yellow, is misshapen in the clouds. Peki tells her he slept badly, and experienced these appalling nightmares. He looks plumped and burnished. His walking is a hunched plodding. He makes self-pitying moans, suffering from diarrhea. His cardiac organ feels like a hot stone. Marisa's hair is plaited down the nape of her neck. He believes it will be sinful and punishable to paw her. His puss puckers. He skips not unlike a goat after her. "This place is cursed," she snaps. "Can the evil be detected?" He snarls. She describes being with him as "a low-grade infection. You're not really sick, but you don't feel well either." The luminosity spurting through the window is temporarily blocked by his back's hump. His slippers flap on the floor, his hair standing erect, like Wile E. Coyote after being detonated by Road Runner. It's easier to change direction when you're moving, he thinks. It is harder to start again once you stop. He feels that if he died tomorrow no one would shed a tear. He wants to be respected and feared by his peers. His mitts will get rusty with blood. He is motivated to murder in the name of mantequilla...

Sonechka Yurov and Maxim Zlodeev

The rectilinear modernist house, with its askew geometry, minimalist decor, chilly courtyards bounded by vast vertiginous walls, and corridors that extend like some sort of open-plan death row, is precariously perched upon the edge of a cliff overlooking the scarce and smoldering heath. Here, form is fluid and the senses are susceptible to outside influence: nothing is at all what it seems. It is a fairytale realm that has the materiality of a stage set but one filtered through an insomniac's delirium. The Baroque pillars and arches are trompe l'oeil. A vaulted ceiling is inlaid with these mother of pearl stag beetles and winged serpents. Drops of blood from a diminutive corpse hit the stone slabs like cannonballs. There are macabre servants, male and female, scurrying. Bats hang from the beams like wineskins in a cellar. The city of demons below reminds one of Milton's Pandemonium beehive. Buildings resemble tombs of the pharaohs under the slate-blue sky. Cacophonous ravens hover ominously on the opaque horizon. Sonechka Yurov, with a sharp, bony body and pointed face, is a triple-jointed, wax-white, morphing sprite with knotted hair. She squawks these rambling monologues, with a limited vocabulary, and squats on the rafters like a bird of prey. Then she prowls a shadow-slashed arcade and climbs a steep Escheresque staircase cradling a phantom (stillborn?) infant. She feels as if she's trapped on a conveyor belt that's taking her to her fate. She thinks trust is an invitation to treachery. Love can be a criminal pact or a motive for revenge. Power is untempered by mercy. As her crimes escalate, her suffering increases, and her fantastic imagination grows ever more inventive. The forensic business of regicide and its aftermath — knockabout farce. Sonechka is enterprising and conniving. She's cold-hearted and single-minded in her ambition. The body count piled up, false accusations flew, and paranoia reached a fever point in the castle. She is steely in her resolve and sneaky in her planning. Her embrace of evil progressively impairs her vision and darkens the world. She seizes what she seeks. She is set in her ways. The chimerical umbilical cord swims like a water moccasin in midair. She seethes, rants, and raves, summoning storms of eloquence from intimate whispers in her grotesque soliloquy. She has a shifting vocal palette. Her heartbeat is an apocalyptic hammering. She has this Gollumly two-sided discussion with herself, the duologue issued with surgical-strike delivery. She croaks her lines like a crow. Dripping liquid crashes onto the floor with a thunderous sound. Three silhouette figures share her voice in the chorus. She has fallen into a pit of madness. Her posture is reminiscent of a vulture who is hunched over from dehydration. She bellows and barks. Wasps beat about her head, burr against her skin. Wild in her cups, she regards the river in flood. Gales create a cloud of petalous wings. The concussions of hail on the windows and roof increase in number and volume. Sonechka, cocooned in a silk shift, propped on starched pillows and bound up in pristine coverlets like a mummy, is peaked, somewhat nauseous, staring into vacancy. She has a creamy second chin and capacious bosom when she's supine. Attributed to depression, she has been rising late and retiring early. She woke from a dream in which she was flying over a forest and sailing on the sea. Beads of sweat dot her upper lip and streak her hairline. The atmosphere has birth odors, bloody and milky. Her breathing is faint. She has huge, keen eyes.

Maxim Zlodeev, sleek as an otter, a sable-coated, branch-armed creature with vulnerable orbs and tea-brown teeth, is mysteriously drawn to Sonechka. He finds the door to her attic room invitingly ajar. A fire flickers in the hearth. Punctured by mosquitoes, he feels like a human pincushion. His lips are pale, cheeks colorless, and he is modestly clothed. Puppet images of them sexing part the curtains of his inner eye. A buff ermine darts around the candle flame. Lightning's crackles sound like beetles being crushed underfoot. He feels not unlike a moldering mushroom when he is not in her company. It's as if his life has no aim or value. He adores her crane-neck and wiry limbs. She dances for her mate like a peacock. His thoughts are a torment to him. He trembles while he divests himself of the earth-hued trousers. Maxim's disproportionate, prominent buttocks appear anatomically unrelated to his trim waist and slender thighs. His jet-black mane, falling in a wavy runnel over his shoulders, arouses a sense of wonder in her, at its abundance and luxuriance. The bark on his flesh seeps like fresh scabs. He possesses an equine brute strength and a skittish spirit. Sonechka rewards his amorous gaze with a slow smile. Perspired, he feels as though he is slimed with a glutinous substance. He smells the fragrant breath of flowers. He came into this place as a shipwrecked stranger. He hurries and avails himself of her, quick as a lizard on a rock. He gathers the courage to touch her breasts, her belly, and her back, and she emits shivering cries. He is licked, kissed, bitten, caressed, soothed, and smoothed. They plummet onto the plump mattress like falling angels to consummate their union. The coupling, for both, is glorious and painful. Maxim admires the intricate excellence of her physique, her panting mouth. Sonechka is cygnet-soft and sugar-sweet. He speaks vaguely, making imprecise promises, and she resists the urge to pressure for lucidity. They are like two interconnecting cogs. The pair throb and ache. Lovemaking becomes a natural force. There's poetry and propulsion to their movements. His twiggy thumb inadvertently tickles her navel. Her chortle sounds like a laugh and a sob together in her throat. The vein in his temple visibly pulses. His legs are wound in hers. Her bare feet reek of fried onions. His shouts sound strangled. There is a heightened sense of unreality for him as if he is a watcher, not a participant. His intonation is a melodic mumble. On top of her, he feels like soil smutching snow. She issues a series of incoherent choking noises. He explores her private places delicately with stick-fingers. Whereupon they call like babes, climaxing simultaneously. After a long, tender silence, Sonechka and Maxim play a complex game with dice and consume coffee and biscuits. And they sleep uneasily. He rouses at dawn to discover she is gone and that he is a rotted tree planted in the ground with fruit growing on his boughs. He hears a baby bawling...

Denizens actuate like automata, mechanized inventions whirring like clockwork, their movements haphazard. There are sundry dim passages in this mazy residence, cool concourses, and marble floors. Peki, returning from some recreational shooting and hunting, bearing the burden of a bleeding turkey, plans on getting rid of the thistles and thorns on each side of the structure tomorrow. The yews need some TLC. His camo apparel is sanguineously spattered. He explains how he traveled far and wide to reach this destination, having embarked on the journey with a bundle of provisions and attire, slumbering on sandy shores, in grassy means, and jungly woods, listening to the birds and monkeys. He believes his arrival here is undeniable evidence of divine providence. Chugging sparkling wine from a goblet, he auscultates a splashing fountain. He appreciates the sumptuous architecture. The luminescence is rosy-fawn. A fluffy kitten meows and meanders. His nightmare needled with complicated eyes, gnashing mandibles, active feelers, twitching antennae, and stabbing stingers; creepy-crawlies from the shades. Sonechka is dressed like a shepherdess, her pleated skirts rustling. She admits she's not a sociable being, instead is a natural solitary. She detests the severe system of governmental authority's constraints, rules, and regulations. His melon is full of crawling mist from the skunkweed. He picks up the scent of the fruit, savor of the beef, the tang of the vin ordinaire. He could make it all vanish in a twinkling. He notices she has an extensive wardrobe. The ebony table is spread with a fabulous feast. A fire burns in the grate. Heaven is silver-blue. Sleet on the panes sounds not unlike tinkling bells. Insects seem irritable. Procession of herons in the orchard. Downpour looks like harpstrings. There is a remorseless, random purposefulness of Mother Nature. It's as if the stormy weather is unleashing its vindictive fury. A rubber plantation has pygmean slaves. Tissue paper flutters in a squall like butterflies. Peki, wearing a cotton habit, is captivated by her unique comeliness. She is fitted in a beige girdle. Her straw hat has a limp ribbon around it. He abstractedly studies her wristbones. He senses a kind of suppressed ferocity in her. His powers of thought are temporarily paralyzed. He is relieved to be putting his wholesale bloodlust tendencies on the back-burner, and wallowing in the leisure, and relaxation. Sonecha has dancing pies and a succulent smirk. His mouth waters at the sight of her. He loves her large, appealing eyes. He wishes he didn't have weak principles and had a kindly disposition. The bile in his gullet feels like gravy boiling. The temperature steadily rises. She's impeded from progress because he gooses her. He is afraid his duff looks like an ugly death's-head. He is a glutton for her. In the hay, she is ductile, flexible, and malleable by licentiousness. He is open to happy accidents in the sack. He sucks like a newborn infant at her teat. He has amoeban swallowing and swimming motions on her. She spreads her asscheeks, so he is more or less obliged to dig in. She dispenses a weird half-human whine. Electric shocks are sent through her entire being. She's a delectable hob. Her squeaky sounds make him think of a fingernail on satin. He is a romantic wild man. They indulge in a harmless wrestling bout, a playful phenomenon, and plunge into the Turkish carpet like a couple of Icaruses. As competitive as they are, the roughhousing never disintegrates into combative chaos. Peki decides to diddle with her, and gauges her response. His nerve cells receive stimuli… Sonechka's orifices are studded with rubies and sapphires. She tries to instruct him on how to be gentle, only it's futile, like trying to teach an unsighted person the concepts of perspective. He pauses and looks thoughtfully downwards, not meeting her lamps. Without more ado, he helps himself to her hips. His feet are hard as hoofs. Her respirations have the sonance of a ruffling pigeon. With a vice-grip on his pizzle, she verbalizes she wishes he had a snout, tusks, and bristles. He snorts like a famished foal. Her smacks sting like snakes. His movement fast and decisive, he pierces her as well as any knight in armor. Her slightly acidic armpit odor wafts into his nares. He has a highly developed sense of smell. Her hand is busy on his cock and balls. He eats her out untidily until her juices run out of the corners of his mouth. She delivers an inarticulate squawk. The couple's like actors in a passionate drama. Their coition is violence. He is fed and nurtured. Sitting on the rattan chaise longue, she, grave-faced, pays assiduous attention to the recherche objects on the shelf. She has livid bruises on her. They play dominoes. This joint is a purple-hazed funhouse, he thinks and smiles.

Peki's the devil but he's no charmer. Sonechka brings up her doctor, a middle-aged misanthrope, this weaselly physician whose quackery extends to stretching her on a rack and molesting her under the guise of gynecology. He spews nihilistic aphorisms, his porcelain nurse's babble lost in his vocalic hurly-burly. Expressions pass over his phiz like cirri over the sun. Ideas growing in his crown are like seeds sprouting under the soil. She is silky-white, with these avian mannerisms, all tense muscles, and sharpened angles. She's hesitant to continue, fearing she's impinging on his preoccupied consciousness. His lips are parted. There is an edge in her inflection. She has on a cinereous cloak and horn-rimmed spectacles. He appreciates being in her sphere of influence. She jumps neatly onto the futon like a cat. She is enchanting. Her spell he doesn't want to snap. He's reflected in the pupil of her eye. They have liquids and solids. Her stories are lively and vivid. Her imagination is most fertile. They're not unlike two pale peas in a pod. Her waist is slavishly seized upon. Her fingers trace his bodily crannies and crevices. Digitally entered and exited, he lets out a great sigh and leans against the bolster. His breath is uneven, his cheeks anemic. There's a discernible submissive droop to his spine. He feels something like pins and needles run through his intestines. The shock, the surprise… Sonechka wipes his tears and tends his belly. She listens to his moans and groans in the absolute darkness. Peki's haunches look like gleaming cabbages. Blood bangs in his head. She is overcome by a fusion of awe, admiration, and apprehension. She appraises the pigling-snoutish nature of his nose. Her drilling is slow and deliberate. It arouses in him some disproportionate shame. He has a sense of impotence, powerlessness. The rimming moves along its inevitable track… Restricted in the corset, her compressed flesh is exquisite. He's full of nervous energy when she mounts him from behind. His heartbeat has the faint echo of galloping. Her athletic legs remind him of cathedral pillarets. Her hand negotiates his olid scrotum. She has aromas of lavender and lemon. Her modulation is soft and dreamy. His rump is mysterious and moony. Jabbed in his hole, he springs like he was stung. His visage is hot and ruddy. He shudders and feels sick. Savagely thumbed, he looks to be in a state of open-mouthed idiocy. He is frozen, like a rabbit cornered by a hound. He swears to himself. Blood sounds not unlike water rushing in his ears. He throbs with emotion. He honks, grunts, brays, and yawps. Her neck is flooded with a flush of furious scarlet as her indexer insinuates into his keister's crack. He winces and whimpers. They make a salty, musky redolence. He's humiliated. She is empowered. He gives a stifled bellow. The duad gobbles up bread and cheese and glugs gin and tonic.

The lagoon is apparently is as wide as the English Channel. Dandelions remind one of umbrellas. A waterfall sounds symphonic. Peki realizes he has become increasingly sedentary. Worms ripple on potato leaves. Plants and vegetables flourish mightily. Pollen is like sawdust. Overcast is a smoky gray. Bees visit flowers. The perimeter wall is engraved with serpentiform beasts and hieroglyphic scribblings. He sets off at a good trot, through the drowsy trees and dreaming garden. The tenebrosity is terrible and devouring. And he flutters away like a leaf blown across a cloister in a wind to begin a new adventure...

The War

Silences are loud and sounds are even louder. Nothing has the right proportion. The ceilings are too high, and the stairways too long. Normal is abnormal. Voices emerge as if from the bottom of a well. Spaces are empty that should be full and vice versa. The mundane is scary, and the scariness seduces. Nothing feels kosher. Peki remembers the warfare. He could feel the softness of his Mama's mouth on his lips, the gentleness of her breath on his chin. He held her liliaceous body and pawed the apples of her breasts. Her sweat tasted of sugar mixed with salt. Blood rushed to his face, making a blush. His whole being burned. Marching wearily, he decided to take a break and accompany a craggy Japanese woman who was plucking and strumming a mandolin, with his toy tin drum. Her place was a fleapit. She had the learned air of a college professor. He was barely covered in the remnants of his uniform. He raised an eloquent eyebrow when he was spoken to. The two succeeded in engendering a private language they sincerely believed to be melodic. Notes were words. Playing music restored his morale. He was revived and was ready to resume his stomping. Allied battleships were in the harbor. It was virtually guaranteed that America would enter the fray soon enough. Peki tramped on, consulting an inaccurate map, to find and bury his country's dead warriors. He seethed in frustration. He had not heard a peep from his superiors on the radio for a while. It was like they didn't know what all the fighting was for anymore. His life was in limbo. He footslogged many unnecessary miles because of the dated charts, which made him livid. He was petrified with consternation when he consulted his compass. He was lost. He hadn't received information or instructions on what to do next. When he last communicated with officers, he got the feeling that they expected defeat and felt guilty for thinking this way. Divisions were exploited. Troops died. He found himself embroiled in a campaign of viciousness with the higher-ups. Hundreds of thousands of innocent individuals were destroyed in the interests of the political agendas of other nations. He was just doing his duty. His conscience was clear, determined to live up to his expectations. He was carrying out orders, sloppily, for he lacked direction, haphazardly fulfilling his function. His diet was meager. The scope of his mission to recover the corpses of his comrades was becoming beyond his endurance. He was downcast. Who would put these wrongs to right? Patterns emerged in the strife, only he was finding it more difficult to recognize them. He no longer relied on his commanders for supplies and munitions. He was on his own. Among his superiors, he was a pigeon amid cats. Reality frustrated his ambition to fantasize. Flights of fancy lent wings to his imaginings. His full-time maneuvering left him war-worn-and-torn. He suffered months of insomnia. Sleep was a pipe dream. He was famished, thirsty, tired, blistered, disgruntled, and horny. As if he didn't have enough problems to cope with, the countryside was plagued with bands of people who engaged in brigandage. He got a sense of relief when the sky clouded over. A warm wind developed. A deformed girl wheeled a pancake on a stick in a doorway. A quiet and intensely curious group of children watched him as he went. He was an adult, yet was as small as them. Several kids had distorted shapes, maimed from the conflict. Eyes scrutinized him, unblinkingly and intently. Peki welcomed the sight of a neoclassical fountain (newly bestowed upon the region), in proximity to scores of whitewashed gravestones. He suspired with benign fatigue and came to a shambolic halt, dropping his gear on the ground. He headed for it to wash and drink up. A couple of rangy mongrels copulated in the vicinity. He strode with resolution. He surveyed the onlookers, who stared at him as though he were some grotesque statuette in a museum. He gestured at them, looking like he was swatting flies. He promenaded in a proper military manner. Pleasantries were exchanged, even though there was a language barrier to be surmounted. He smartly created a respectable impression. He vied to evince undeviating purpose and indomitable manfulness, stepping with implacable efficiency. He treaded with pride and conviction. He enjoyed his confident display of infantry swagger. Although sunburned, tattered, and dusty, despite his diminutive size, he still exhibited a pertinent soldierly bearing. A begrimed boy pranced in ape of his gait, in the natural amphitheater formed by hummocks. And he stood at ease. Whereupon he restarted his strut and observed the locals' discomfiture. He was outnumbered and trepidatious. The ice was never broken. Times were hard for them. Peki gazed at them with rascally seriousness, affected surprise, and sat on a bench under a tree. He sighed through gritted teeth before singing a tune with a certain amount of lachrymosity in the lyrics. Conscientiously he sashayed like he was being ceremoniously honored. He beamed, as though in enlightenment when he chanced upon a bare room of a courtyard in the center of town. The shelter was eminently suitable for his needs, especially when juxtaposed with the jungle. Smelling aromatic smoke, he unpacked his bedroll and settled down. He thought of making (languid) love to Marisa and listened to the nightingales. Deserters infested the area. Outlaws further exacerbated the misery of the populace. Some of the displaced stole, others begged. Separatist factions freely antagonized one another. The chaotic approach remained steadfastly unchanged. Would the succession of humiliations inflicted on humanity ever end? It was inevitable that a rebellion would manifest, and resistance would be organized. It was inconceivable to Peki that a conflict could begin over such petty nonsense. Empires wanted more power. He was cognizant of the rulers' fantastic obstinacy. It blew his mind.

The tatterdemalion Spanish troops proceeded with incidental comic effect, establishing a zone of interest. It was like a death march. A substantial portion of those soldiers was sick to some degree. The commanding officer, a slim man of average height, a lieutenant colonel whose authoritative air made him appear taller than he was, distributed a diatribe. He had blood on his hands, having slaughtered people who were suspected of supplying the enemy with edibles. His complex machinations got him into this position of power. His life would be abbreviated by a misdirected bullet that wound up in his temple. The battalion was set off on a complicatedly nebulous conciliation mission, peacemaking efforts that might turn the tide of the war, according to some. Another platoon unrolled from the garrison. Peki felt weak and dizzy, leaning on a railing to catch his breath in the swelter. His respirations rattled like the sound of dice. He was supposed to communicate with headquarters. He'd tell them later on that it was the great distance that prevented radio contact from occurring. He was completely cut off from the army, just like he was from society back home. There was no assurance of inclusion either. He didn't have the slightest idea what was happening in the world. He wanted to be useful to his side, and he was relieved that he found a role that saved him from desperate straits. His job at this juncture was to check boats, coming and going in the port, for smuggled goods. To put it bluntly: he controlled the contraband. He acquitted himself so well that he was astounded by his proficiency at an assignment that only shortly before he had deemed too difficult. He read the facial expressions and body language of crews like X-rays, knowing who was bringing/taking things in and out illegally and who wasn't, based on a sixth sense, even before boarding the craft. He managed to achieve and maintain the self-esteem that is essential to a handicapped person measuring himself against his fellow fighters. He kept busy, believing that torpidity is detrimental to morale and performance. His ship scrutinies were akin to high-spirited attacks. He was obligated to live on fish, fruit, and vegetables, supplemented by kindhearted peasants when his rations ran out. He developed a taste for their food. The locals regarded him with a blend of admiration (for his work ethic) and perplexity (for his physical appearance)... Chickens pecked about in a wickerwork cage in the middle of a relatively clear space on the dock. Peki scattered a handful of seeds for them to browse on. Cargo crates were stacked pretty much everywhere. Many villagers were starving and ragged, dissolving in the general bedlam. Rebels popped up like toadstools. Radicals inaugurated a campaign of terror against the occupying forces, Spain and Germany. The government made these token attempts to restore order but lacked the proper strategy to pull it off. Renegade infanteers and civilian rioters only made matters worse. The damage was irreparable. Meanwhile, the provincial bigwigs held dinner parties. It was an anomalous situation, to be sure. This left Peki in a state of outraged disbelief, whereas for some of his compatriots it was acceptable. There was an intractable shortage of everything. He had ancient angst ingrained in his psyche. He was always on edge, as though in expectancy of an imminent assault. Peki retired to a shady spot to gripe to himself in private. Motionless, prone on the grass, he ached with tedium. He was very still, as if stone dead, experiencing a childish fury. He periodically visited a house of license, to better decompress. The brothel had a Byzantine style of decoration — the interior and exterior. The pathetic inhabitants were anxious because of a deficiency of clientry. What consolidated the relationship between the dwarf and the madam (who was infamously perfidious and unreasonable) was the tips he often left. Initially, she seemed as though she was trying to frustrate his ardent aspirations. Her sway over him was absolute. He told her he was plagued by grotesque nightmares and she tsked and rubbed his nuque. This was territory he wished to occupy. He savored the odors and soaked in the environment. The opium he smoked there was expected potent, and consequently, he spiraled downward into addiction. He spread the word about the gorgeous girls to his brethren, not unlike a disease. He recollected a priest in the hall resembling a humongous bat. Vehemently he inhaled a cigarette and exhaled. He was frightened and disturbed by the unnatural quietness. When he finished, he ground the stub into the soil with his fingers and paused for a minute before resuming his duties. His flesh felt glassy from the sun, and his eyes were glittering.

Elena Azorin

Peki sits (with a slouched posture) in a coffin-cubicle, poring over inventory numbers, scribbling furiously on stained paper with a stubby pencil, hearing the rats hastening hither-thither. Files are stacked beside the mound of invoices on the crooked desk. There are many cardboard boxes and wooden crates. He must unpack the latest shipment of supplies. He employs a defunct sewing machine as a footstool. There are more bugs in the backroom than he can count. He has the nagging suspicion that things aren't in their proper spots. Plaster particles are like flakes of skin from psoriasis. Sun's decapitated by the drapery. Wispy, chromatic cumuli drift as bright streamers in the pageant of the sky. The concourse is devoted to a freak show. Rattletraps are stuck in gridlock in a brumal dream. Destitute, drunk, and dim-witted people pour forth from every conceivable direction. Hobbledehoys make quite a hullabaloo. An enchanting flower lady, the teenaged Elena Azorin, with a mussed coffee-brown mop, enigmatic eyes, the face of a beautiful basset hound, longish lashes fluttering like insectival pennons, clothed in denim overalls, nerdy rims repaired inadequately with duct tape, asks Peki if she can set up her products on his portion of the sidewalk. Immediately smitten, he answers yes. She is a graceless tomboy, in all probability chilly-cold as coastal mist, an elemental naturalist hovering vaporously between heaven and earth. She is high on grass. She, in animalianly unassertive, is pockmarked and possesses a numbskull's smile. Moles on her biceps remind him of spots on a butterfly's wings. He imagines his satyrish strokes tickling the shell-whorl of her umbilicus. She girlishly giggles. He experiences such incredible contentment of brain and body. Cogitations overbrim the confines of his coconut. He pictures her nonexistent tush wriggling on his lap before she gets up as though it was screwed into it... He has a memory of the magnificent manatee, Vanesa, sensually sashaying, her lumpen hips jiggling like equine ears, becoming a fatty, pulpy, sanguinary mess at the whitewashed wall, in the antiseptic light. Afterward, he felt cleansed, purged, his soul, a second self, phenomenally transformed. Emotion poured out of his pores like perspiration. He misses Marisa. Domestic and occupational ebbings and flowings were proceeding as usual. She chain-smoked cigarillos, unintentionally putting on a panto-mimic production. She was bizarrely obnoxious, swilled gin out of a beer mug, and had a consumptive pallidness. His anger seethed and fer-mented. The psychological pain he suffers without her is more acute than his physical anguish. He thinks of himself as Prometheus and her as the Vulture. She tugged the nerves in him. She was part of a dumb show that sang choral songs. Mind and matter fuse in caliginous paranormal copu-lation. Leven is like firefly antennae in the India ink evening. Peddlers and hawkers, beggars and tramps, circulate among the factory strikers. Stray cats advance and retreat, the instinct of vagary influencing them, amid riotous juveniles. He has a maniacal hatred of adolescents, mostly because they ceaselessly plague him. A valuable contingent of cops. Collegiate lads and lasses congregate on a grassy eminence, and make a hurly-burly of discourse. The disinfectant smells like nail polish. Earlier on, the place had a cadaverous odor. Elena inspects the establishment like a supervisor. Peki slips on a chemical substance but manages to keep his balance. Hail is as spat olive pits. Whores mix with nuns and torrentially stream down the street. Cornfield is beyond the hawthorn hedge. Figures of his victims flood his encephalon, these forms merging, many becom-ing one. They were poor creatures fighting for their lives, squiggling not unlike eels, in their death throes. He found out, at the time, that he derived a malignant pleasure from dispatching them. He knows he will, in the long run, meet his doom. A wounded coil of a man, his face is furrowed as breeze-blown sand. He heeds their pitiful pleas. He feels, in his existence, like a trapped beast, tortured prisoner, racked dissenter. He is crucified on the Cross of life. His self-loathing is hardly deep-rooted.

In the deep fathoms of his consciousness, he believes he's not evil, not some fiend. Hairs on his nape move as snails' horns stirred by drafts. He is despairingly condemned. Darkness is black like blood. Insectile shards are on the sill. Elena's companionship satisfies his entire being. Peki finds her to be winsome. He focuses on her delicate curves with concentrated fetish-worship. She has well-proportioned, long legs. He pictures them contained in damask fishnet stockings. His covetous libidinousness is overwhelming. He gets a whiff of the aromatic aromas of the flowers on her straw hat. She holds what might be a thrush's nest. An exquisite excitement comes to him. The erotic sensations are poignant. The probable piquancy of her pouchy breasts is irresistible. Will she prostrate herself on the rug if he requests that she do so? He's disgusted by his lechery. He has stored feelings for her, like wine in a cellar. Her modulation is akin to undulatory music to his ears. She's in a condition of rumpled allurement. Her essence holds a symbolic signification. Ostentatiously he sparks a cigar and takes a drag theatrically. She reclines on the step-ladder, adorably fit as a fiddle, and unkempt. His oculi, rapturously viewing the visible world, observing everything with equal interest, are inflamed from a recent bout of insomnia and his pestiferous kidneys ache. Thunderous growling. They walk together at lunch, in the dirty-milk beams, under an ashen celestial sphere. The pearlescent lake is still as if it's water in a toilet. She's sincerely charming but is perhaps mentally retarded. He isn't sure. He peruses his dog-eared copy of Nietzsche's 'Will To Power.' The two play cards and throw dice. He recalls his mother calling him a "chicken-hearted dwarf-bird." He felt cut into pieces, and took to liquor. He fantasizes about her, visualizing her like the painter Goya would, her sublime suffering captured splendidly on canvas, in his mind's eye. Elena gives him a vulval rose (petals throbbing as gills in the gust). He has the urge to press upon her a febrile smooch. A wild and mysterious exhilaration could lead to unmitigated disaster if they are not careful! An electric charge of lust is sent through him. His swooning adoration and shaking idolatry aren't noticed by her. His pulse beats are not unlike lightning bolts. Desire channels through every part of him, reaching the center of his core. He is tempted to tell her he's always anxious to try a new experiment, however extreme, and, on a whim, he decided to introduce human fatty tissue to batches of butter. No. This would be a grave mistake. It's much too soon. The whole murderous affair fills him with a sick elation. He feels as though he's putting the final touches on edible works of modern art. He can't believe his luck, going from the road to nowhere to the primrose path. Word of his updated business has spread like wildfire. His lab is a hiding place for him. The metropolis stinks like Satan. Peki's string of recent performances was indubitably monstrous, like a grisly parody of a person under a profound spell of creative inspiration, mug a dusky crimson. His life is undergoing tremendous upheaval. He feels not unlike a madman, a ridiculous person. Elena comments, flirtatiously, on his Roman nose and bulbiform brow. She likes that he is bearded and broad-shouldered. His desire rises from incalculable depths. She absorbs his attention. His entire life is a black crater, an abyss, and he gazes into it with an uncertain, and unholy, eye. He'd arrived at this point by a circuitous route. She tells him her father, Roberto (Peki's former boss), has gone missing. She suspects foul play. The police have no leads in the case. She has hired a private investigator, Jaime Velasco, to look into things. And his heartbeat skips. He gulps inadvertently demonstratively. She is spindly and waxen as a church candle, passes like a ghost. Peki reads in the newspaper that some bodies have been discovered in the marsh. Because of the murders, there's a mandatory curfew. He is distressed because he doesn't know whether his blood pressure is up or down. He crumples like a melted crayon. Death, he thinks, is life's great equalizer. He thrives as the cockroach.

Peki and Elena sit together on the park bench, resembling lovebirds sharing a perch, their communications secretive, conveyed as coded messages. Cupid shoots his arrows in random directions, and these two happen to be stuck. With her, he's no longer living with the handbrake on, he can finally hit the accelerator. His clothes are wrinkled, his hair unbrushed. He has the phizog of a Pekingese. It's the snub nose that does it. She has concave cheeks. He has a rancid taste in his oral cavity. The scant strands overlay his scalp. He'd bet her tummy is tight as a snare drum. His perineal rash is bothersome. Stench of garbage. He recollects Marisa sprawling on the tiling, stretching obliquely, exposing her shriveled midsection.

Vehicular horns sounded as laments of the mortally wounded. Clean laundry hung on lines and dirty dishes were piled in the sink. Blood crept into his veins. His arm rested on her torso like an oar on a kayak. She stammered as though she had suffered a stroke and was learning to speak all over again, reconstructing language in the archaeology of vocabulary. To him, the encroaching storm was a nebulose threat. He imagines that he was riding her like a surfer on a wave. Her pubic hair was like a deceased hedgehog. Acid in his gullet frothed up into his throat and he picked at the shells of his ears. Encarmined rakes of her nails tapped on his kneecaps. His hands ebbed and flowed on her, like dead doves on the surf. He fumbled for his fly... and came up empty. She was cold and still not unlike a corpse on an autopsy table. Incandescent daggers stuck them. She was an ugly bitch, he thought. He wished she had a curvaceous build. She had a faint mustache and survived pancreatic cancer. She was off her rocker. He slumped in the (stolen) dentist's chair. The apple of her backside parted when she did an Eastern dance. He visualized himself breaking on her like a tidal wave on a sea wall. Decency emphasizes the distance of their mother-son relationship. Alcohol and drugs eliminate it. Night took the place of day. Peki impulsively grabbed his groin. His hay feverish sneeze sounds like the snort of a walrus, shivering as if he's undergoing a seizure. A locomotive whistles. Whitecaps sound like catcalls. Thunderous growls. Thalassic sighs. His eyes are neutral, ears as wilted lilies, mouth like a spoiled tangerine. His cheeks are chunky and his legs are bowed. Elena has an anomalous artichoke for a nose. Before her, his life was a slow waltz. Currently, with her, it's a pulsating salsa. He thinks of the folks he'd hacked up with the machete. Is he a basket case? No, he's a businessman, and people's adipose tissue is an ingredient of paramount importance to produce his product. They were like slaughtered hogs in an abattoir. The scabrous store is frequently overwhelmed with shoppers! An excellent problem to have! The ruins of the storeroom hold a Pompeii of unsold merchandise — stuff made without the secret sauce, so to speak. Does Elena even give a plug nickel about him? He's unsure. His gnashers make a grinding sound as a gearbox. She's so emaciated it's as if she's on a starvation diet. He breaks the glassy silence. Their hugging and kissing are like gym exercises. The boniness of her body is concerning. Their gooey lips unglue at the eroding fountain, with its discernible deficiency of water. She is a joy to be around. Her limbs are like the branches of a willow. Canine yelping startles her. Pupils are engaged in a military march alongside their teachers. She's quiet and respectful as though she's attending a wake. He is rigid as a ramrod and extremely fretful. Sun's a lucent lump. He sips cognac out of the thermos. She's huddled against him like a rag doll. He feels like an amoeba, a worthless nonentity, a no-hoper, a pathetic thing. She is uncoordinated not unlike a calf. A haggard gardener prunes shrubs with shears. The mucous membrane of cloud cover. She compliments his Roman centurion sandals. He remembers Marisa, in a bathing suit, taking a tranquilizer with vodka, strutting as though in a henhouse, rummaging through dresser drawers, combing through folders, and plopping in a beat-up easy chair, body odor with this cuttlefish noisomeness, combined with dank soil. She pulled on torn jeans, and he pictured her vaginal trough. She had empty, mistrusting peepers. No, reader, dead ones. They glazed over in the glimmer. She moved as a puppet on strings, and chugged cherry brandy. Her pterodactyloid tootsies were in holey stockings. She swaggered as if she were barefoot on pieces of glass from broken bottles. Peki's globular ox eyes glittered and he hawked phlegm. He coped with racking anxiety attacks and accompanying spasms, his sweat as the goop of entrails. Garms were bestrewed like tidal debris. He is not at peace with himself. He absentmindedly looks at the penial lighthouse, in its admirable erectility. Car comings and goings... unabated. His horn-rimmed glasses are humorously askew and his arteries pound mercilessly. Asthmatoid gusts, pelagic soughs.

Peki and Marisa

Marisa is so immobile on the divan it's as though she's taxidermized. She suffers from an incurable personality disorder. Her throat is decorated with an ornamented necklace. Her gracile body is sheathed in a strapless dress as if she is all set for a titillating enterprise. Her pies are luminiferous, as though in anticipation of pleasure. Hairs sprout from her moles. Peki has the yen to make a declaration of lubricious intent. She has him under her spell. He pictures her as nature intended her to be. He feels reaped and harvested. He's enamored of her virtues. Her bush is finer than gossamer. He is afraid the syphilis canker on his lip will scare her off. Whenever she makes contact with him it is like an electric shock. His flattering remarks are so rhapsodic she thinks he's being mordacious. Junk food has corrupted his digestive system. He is forced to eat on the fly. Keeping the butter churning is becoming increasingly problematic. He knows he should take care of his health. He has got to stay clear of his usual haunts. He doesn't care about fame and fortune, he just wants a successful, lasting business. He fears he'll pass away unloved and unrespected, that no one would mourn him when he's gone. His venereal afflictions have compromised his immune system. He willfully disregarded the efficacy of rubber protection against gonorrhea. Although weakened, he still has the strength to break his victims like candy canes. He goes to Mass on Sundays, confessing his iniquities to wipe the slate clean, for spiritual renewal, and soulful refreshment. He cannot stand living in sustained insecurity and distrust any longer, feeling dissatisfaction about his meaningless existence. Sometimes he feels as if he's going prematurely senile. He was born abnormal. He entered this world with the expression of a thoughtful philosopher. He didn't bawl when the doctor smacked his bippy. The birth guck was sanguine and ivory and sweet-smelling, not unlike tinea. The nurses found him to be uncommonly undemanding. His intellectual apparatus is clicking. Marisa's sexiness makes him priapic. She drives him loco. He sees her and it's like a burro-kick to the gonads and hornet-stings to the eyes. Occasionally he wants to beat the living daylights out of her. He remembers playing hide-and-seek and peek-a-boo with her as a little boy... It was a privilege to prepare the bath for her. He appraised her anatomical curvatures and would try to think of something else. He'd study her mouth and imagine kissing it, their tongues snaking. He was engulfed in a cyclone of arousal, perspiring waterfalls. She made his dry seasons wet. He walked in a dream, disconnected from reality. He was in love with life because of her. Everything he did was done for her. He waited on her hand and foot. With her, he was sublimely contented and jutting with health. She made the overcrowded and unpleasant neighborhood tolerable. She was entertaining company and had a gift for generosity.

Whacked-out on Butyrum, Peki casts reticence aside like a henley. It causes his erection to detumesce and his psychosexual energy to diminish. It has similar effects upon the psyche to acid or mushrooms, altering his consciousness exponentially. The paranormal phenomena are interesting. He's been consuming prodigious quantities of late, inducing a terrific state of affairs in his being, although some bad trips have imbued him with irrational horror. Marisa hasn't helped much when it comes to his state of mind. Pushing others away is second nature to her, and she flings herself into her daily routine of cosmetic application as if donning a face shield of preservation. Peki patiently navigates his mother's nippy rejections and fickle requirements while edging into her confidence.

A scabrous and bloated vagrant, in refuse and on rocks, changes into a sightly sylph, the rubbish bins turning into a carriage drawn by lions. A dog gives birth to kittens. Cirri remind him of the unraveling bandages of a mummy. It is a sultry and woeful twilight. Peki sweats rivers. He has this nagging feeling that everything is ending and that nothing will ever be the same. Potholed streets are in their typical deformation. Pimps make suggestive remarks and prosties give prurient invitations. He treats them with the contempt they deserve. He is an object of curiosity and random ridicule. He adjusts the magnum in its holster in his vest and wears an expression of stern reproach. He possesses an air of a man reconciled to ugliness, corporeally speaking of the recollection of insults. The moon is full and shining. It is so hot he could bake a loaf of bread by setting it on the sidewalk. The humidity makes him feel as though he is in a sauna. The city isn't exactly a model of civilization. He has so much bitterness and so many regrets... Crows perched on wires look like bored vedettes. Direful rain. Ravenous and insatiable skeeters. Such stupefying coalescence...

Peki showers to irrigate away the excreta of his daily life, dries himself off with a freshly laundered towel, and bathrobes and slippers himself. His knit cap is optically suggestive of a long white condom. He has a role in this universe decreed for him by fate: making mantequilla.

Chutcha

Their sexual congress requires feats of superhuman strength, stamina, and cunning, the participants leaving the pursuit to the basic whim or an aesthetic inclination. Peki, grinning composedly, feels, for some unknown reason, that Chutcha's adoration is automatic, unseeing, and abstract. She is softened and open to him on the pompous bed with miraculous curtains, situated dead center in the fretted chamber. She's light as oxygen. Her breasts are the size of larks' eggs. She blanches when other women would blush. He resists digital penetration, trembling slightly in the still space of the bright room, threaded with ribbony effulgence. He is travel-worn and speaks lyrically. Compliments spring naturally to his lips. She becomes perspiry and incoherent, appearing sallow in the refulgence. She stares intently, respiring quietly. Her flanks are ruddy as pomegranates. He gazes soulfully at her. The chess game and music box on the desk briefly capture his attention. Chutcha is porcelain-skinned and fine-boned, her eyes icy pools, their lashes long and corners wrinkled. Her dyed mop is black as soot, straight, and in a fringe. She quivers with nerves. She's cattish and silent. Her breaths waver. Man and woman are melted and merged in a furnace of flames. He has the powerful lungs of a glassblower. She seems brittle and restless beneath him, her voice small. The couple's amorously adaptable in the rumpled sheets. He can hardly prevent himself from feeling her body. There are cerise marks on her flesh as if it was scored. The hollow of her neck is bruised. Both experience a fantastic mixture of pain and pleasure. The two simmer with passion, their sentences unfinished. His mouth speaks to her muff. Initially, she was intensely shy when he groped her in the stairwell, saying very little, but then shortly thereafter she laughed and cried at once. He enjoys her albinic warmth, her secret silkiness. An agonizing ecstasy takes possession of her. She feels as though her being is liquefied. He slides over her like an avalanche. She is afraid of annihilation. He grasps her narrow hips. She pants into cushions. He optically savors the swellings and subsidings of her tummy, reminiscent of the ocean's surface. She stimulates his senses. They talk like tentative children. She clings to him, not unlike seaweed to a rock. They delight in extreme sensations. There's a ferocity to their lovemaking. Venetian blinds create a lucent latticework on the tiled floor, slowly changing its shape according to the dictates of the sun. Heat's oppressive. Humidity is merciless. Transparent bowls and bottles are on the counter. The vault is orangey and purplish. Peki purses his chops up to Chutcha's sphincteric pucker as if about to blow into the trumpet of doom. Her derriere's hole takes in a blast of hot breath and she lets out a high-pitched whinny. Then she falls onto her side on the mattress. She sure can be melodramatic. She could make an epic out of ordering a chalupa at Taco Bell. She experiences a scorching choking sensation in her throat. His countenance is illuminated by the red-hot glow of the molten spheres of her spanked hindquarters, the blazing tulips of her tits lowering. Her stomach runs with sweat and her brow drips. She is apprehensive, her ass suspended above him, thinking it will be taste-less and unappetizing. She bends and crumples when her rear orifice is tongued. She believes her bottom is a bland expanse and her hips have rolls of creamy fat. She's limp and listless. She gets up and can barely stagger to the bathroom. Later on, they postcoitally languish in inactivity beside the lamp's lambency in the gloaming. She is pencil-slender, derma layer cherry-pink after the copulation. The pair bask in a state of comfort and contentment. The sprinkles' aroma reminds him of wood shavings. Seated on the sill of her wonderfully wrought crash pad, he imagines the building resembling a beehive, its apartments hexagonal cells. Wrens and finches wheel in the cardinal-red vista with dove-white clouds. He is squat and stalwart as an oak stump. The showers sound like the tinkling of a xylophone. Thunder and lightning sound like bass-drummers and cymbal-clashers are making experimental percussive music... The trip to

Chutcha's place was arduous but worth it. He went through dark forests and grassy plains, in breezy weather and unexpected storms. The overcast looks as though it is molded from sugar. The maze of corridors is cool and deep as a well. Sitting in a good chair, he regards the sprouting garden and sluggish meanders of the cirri. She stumbles somewhat drunkenly in the dazzling air of her cavernous joint. Her feet look like dying leaves. His unreal city shimmers in the distance. It calls. He won't answer. Not yet. He lives his life on the furthest edge.

The ocean is a turmoil of movement. The moon grows from crescent to round. Peki's wrapped in a camel-hair djellaba. Chutcha is rigged out in a flowing shift and snug-fitting trousers. The warmth feels like glass. He studies the drifting feathers of cumuli in the quicksilver-colored upper atmosphere and the barren, inhospitable mounts. A waterfall, far off, whispers. The swirling sea makes a simulacrum of the sky. His blood stirs and his blinkers shine. She, lissom and pasty, rises awkwardly from the rocking chair as if with the aid of a system of pulleys. He looks fixedly at her while she changes into a button jersey and harem pants, a sash around her waist, and heels. Her mercury-hued nombril ring nictates. She has a pouty mouth and plump lips. There is a noticeable diminution of his anodyne grin. She has this pert nose, pronounced cheekbones, and jutting ribs. Her manga eyes are surrounded by spiky lashes. He glances askance at her uplifted chin and cheery smile. Her breath is redolent of sour milk. She watches the motorway madness below. Cloudlets are shoals of silvery fish swimming on high. She progresses like a self-propelled shooting star. Whizzing wasps. Scintillant spots — a swarm of brilliant bees erratically mobile on the paneling. She writhes not unlike an eel in his embrace, and leaps akin to a salmon. She ostensibly metamorphoses into a shimmering form and twirls like a top. He is tripping badly. The crustacean keyhole crawls up and down, its carapace with a grainy glitter as though speckled with sand. He nips at her nape and sips at her saliva, wanting to suck away her feculent substance. Her melons bob and sink without a trace. She looks nibbled and disheveled. She is, paradoxically, ephemeral and solid. He scratches the itches that scrabble on him like fire ants. He's a tree trunk with gripping roots. The blue of the heavens turns dull and then null. Whereupon he hallucinates a cheetah chasing a fawn on the ceiling. A fireworks display on the horizon. Cascade of chiaroscuro in slo-mo on the wall. Chutcha's bare limbs waggle in teasing syncopated rhythms. She throws aside her exiguous brassiere and bikini briefs. Peki finds himself finned and scaly... She verbalizes he has "magnificent pendulous genitals." Basking sharks wiggle on the linoleum. The front door is lyre-shaped. He advances in a steady, dignified gait, increases his pace to a trot, and they are intertwined like rushing waves. They break and roll in... Day has faded and night takes them into blackness. The brightened world becomes beautiful oblivion.

Rooks coalesce in the empyrean like ebon Catherine wheels. She plays with him like a feline toys with her prey. He observes her hourglass-shaped torso and cupped omphalos. Her cut-price belly-chain hangs, forlorn and vulgar. Her lily-white feet smell like baking yeast dough. Clenbuterol is potent, he determines. Stars cover the welkin like the eyes of a peacock. Lakelet has a mirrory lacquerish sheen to it. The splendor is too lucid to look at. Peki's gasps sound as if they're coming from infinity's depths. Seated in the churchy chair, he wears a cable-knit sweater and periwinkle slacks. His throat feels as though he swallowed silt. He's taken with her, briefly and forever. She offers her nether regions to him like raw oysters on a perfect paten. He brags, with her blowing him, that, when it concerns butter, it's like he's "spinning straw into silk." He revels in being wild and unattached. She has bristly-scratchy stubbly outcrops on her armpits. Her breadbasket has the puffed, risen shape of a teacake. Her breath reminds him of toasted sugar. He admires her round, unpainted mouth. She bends swiftly and without precaution. Her pubic pelt is soft not unlike fox fur. She starts to give him head. Her lamps have retreated into their cavernous sockets. He thrusts fiercely. It is a protracted episode with staccato and shaking tempos. She gets stark naked. Her backside hellhole... he gets closer... drawn in... can't turn away... Chutcha is mildly attentive. On angel dust, he views a phantasmagoric, kaleidoscopic sphinx. Stars in the firmament bring to mind amoebas in pondwater. The roof is coal-glossy. Dust motes brilliantly blink like microwave LED displays. Clouds take up the entire sky-span. Ghost-susurrations of wind. She remains in decorous silence in the artificial incandescence, arranging the tubes of pomades and powders on the dresser, and subsequently begins cooking Cornish pasties. He hasn't been dieting sensibly these days. Vile spit, not unlike the substance from some alien world, lingers on the corners of his lips. He adjusts the appropriate knobs on the rinky-dink oil heater. Inebriated, she's dressed in a shirt-jacket and fluid skirt. Mizzle has a graphitic odor. He is not missing his madre, her torpidity, and the domestic dramas. Vividly he pictures her paper-thin skin, curved beak, taut gob, and stained-umber faux chiclets. He's a creature of habit, and the violent lovemaking with her is one he's addicted to. He relishes remembering the intimate relations, romping, nudity, and intoxicants. Wet weather is volatile, recurring. Attributable to the ancient windows and doors, the apartment is dank and drafty. Peki unwinds on the unfolded settee. Contemplations of departure lessen in their intensity and don't resuscitate. His intestines feel as if they are wound on a spindle. With the heartburn, his chest feels like an iron box, a roaring flame within. The soles of Chutcha's tootsie-wootsies give the impression of tough vellum. Consistently she teases and pleases him. Intercourse with her is inevitable, like sleeping and waking, for instance. The standard lamp isn't working properly; it keeps flickering. Doorsteps and windowsills are emphasized with mineral deposits. He is an audience of one, watching and listening to the cherubim dancing and the seraphim singing in outer space.

Relationships are about luck and risk to him, but sometimes he's like a high-stakes gambler amassing a big pile of chips and then frittering it away on a series of small, pointless bets. Peki lies on the pool table, in his birthday suit, props his head on a cushion, and dozes off to sumo wrestling on the HD boob tube.

Sorrow makes him insubstantial to himself. His waking (and sleeping) dreams are constantly tormenting him. Coils of pain unwind in his gut. His pings and pangs are like beaks and claws pecking and clawing at his innards. He appears waxen and peaked. His middle feels as if it is gangrenous. He discerns the continual sequences of light and shadow. His parchment eyelids are crinkled. Pedestrians progress. He imagines a dog house in the diminutive yard as being a witch's cottage in a fairy-tale. Laundry dances on lines in the gusts. Mephitis of the megalopolis is deathly. His perspiration feels as though it is congealed. Toilet water resembles gruel in a bowl. The bathroom has the scent of disinfectant. Drizzle has the smell of singed filament. Headstones tilt in the grave-yard. Peki draws the blinds and wishes he lived in a respectable suburb. His walk has a limping rhythm. Thoughts of self-doubt fall upon him like a pack of hounds, ripping at him. The furnishings and objects have uncanny life. Chutcha flits not unlike a moth in the gaunt kitchen, painted hospital-green. She takes a necessary coffee break before getting back to the crazy cookery. She has an anxious and vague expression when he proclaims that sex is a mode of physical and psychological destruction. At this point, he talks about when he had measles and mumps. Preferring silence to speech, she sits rigorously upright on the stool after a culinary tragedy (something along the lines of ruining the "melt-in-your-mouth cheese"). He feels snubbed and doesn't know why. His sweat is like scum. Utensils are a monstrous mangle in the stained sink. Her fingers are white worms, her toes little grubs. Her hand is soap-slippery when he attempts to hold it. He comes on to her to liven things up. She's stiff as a board. The brilliancy in her orbs is like glassy threads found in marbles. Her facial expression looks like she tasted something terrible. His saliva is gluey. He tries to bunny-hug her, only she wriggles and winces. She regards his actions as impermissible. She stands like an angelic effigy in rayon petticoats, appalled and distressed by his audacity. The rays are scorched-yellow, coming through the sash windows with lacy curtains. Seagulls shriek raucously. Sleet hitting the slate roof makes the clunking notes of piano keys when the strings are dead. Peki wears a wry grimace well. Chutcha makes stew and soufflé. And her cold-shouldering is vexing. When he speaks to her, she just nods occasionally. Her belly button is an asymmetric whorl with a fleshy sill. He has an intense interest in her cobweb skin, evaluating her with hooded eyes. She nibbles on a biscuit like a mouse on a crust. She refuses to submit herself to his judgment. He wants her to admit him to her confidence. His brow is creased into dolefulness, thinking of his frail, bird-bony mama... A solid shell can be filled up with a new substance... He is weary of the world, afraid in every moment that he might misstep and bring destruction down on him and his mother. Occasionally he is a step ahead of everyone else, only to find he's two steps behind. He's got murder on his mind. He is a planter of devious seeds.

Is he a man too big for his britches, destined to be and punished for it accordingly? His snaky sheath of a getup suits his personality perfectly.

Life to Peki is trying to untangle a web of his own weaving. The amphetamines put him on a high for an hour. Dan Rather's heinous cover of Spencer Davis Group's 'I'm a Man' is on the transistor. He is proud of the fact that he's assiduous and inventive when it comes to mantequilla production and sales, and is determined to improve these skills whenever possible. Already ideas float in the vastity of space and time. He has plenty of tricks of the trade in the butter business. On the meds, he feels numb, experiencing the petrifaction of his vital functions. He is prepared to face death, even if it is right around the next bend. Hooded and booted, he feels as if he has undergone an inexplicable transfiguration, becoming wholly inanimate. He reeks of a canine lavatory and compost bin combined. He sees colors with no color and shapes with no shape. Getting a sniff of baby talc snaps him out of his spell. The bathroom's plumbing clanks and shudders. Peki uses a loofah sponge and pumice stone in the imposing tub. Ruddy veinlets stand out on his knobby feet. He finds relief in the lukewarm water. His digits cling to his balls, not unlike lichen to rocks. His sore muscles, aching tendons, tender ligaments, and tense sinews start to relax. This is his resting place. Dandruff's clustered in his hair, and he thinks that it's eggs laid by a mutant louse or pearls secreted by shellfish. His hair is stringy and matted and so he shampoos it. He feels like a lumpy old man, inert and weighed down. He's tempted to insert a pinkie into his rump's cavity but changes his mind. He smells carbon from exhaust pipes and moisture in the air. Breezes are fitful. Peki towels off and dresses in a granite-gray Etruscan gown (crackling with static cling) and khaki slippers. Sheets of lightning and crashes of thunder in the welkin. His arthritic joints are flaring up. Chutcha wears only a raincoat. Her integument has the milky sheen of marble. She smiles at him, her crystalline gnashers gleaming. Her body odor stinks of organic decay. With the cellulite, her lower haunches and upper thighs look as though they're riddled with needle holes. Perverted visions are caught in his head like flies in amber. She is clammy and fleshy. His pounding heart sounds like a knocking on metal as he touches his scrotum, hard as stone, with nervy fingers. He studies her discarded panties on the Persian rug in the cinnabar half-light. Then he begins to beat off, imagining himself strangling her, kept in a girdle, with the pair. The sensations he experiences are outlandish. Her arms whirl like a nebula, her fantastic form struggling. In his fantasy, he wounds her with a whip, and slashes her with a knife. He jerks off in fits and starts, pausing to get into a corselet, and recommences wanking. The duo obeys the laws of physics in his stark raving daydream. Acid bile churns in his stomach sac. He is clay-pale. Drifting dust motes coruscate like ground glass. Chutcha gazes at the statues of portly child angels in varying conditions of disrepair, a concrete fountain, an anthill bearing semblance to a volcano, and puddles of petrol. Leafless yews are speckled and drip. Stars look like jagged flakes of silica. She has apple cheeks and arched lips. Her teeth glint in the gloom. She's in a state of stoical inertia in front of the full-length mirror. The window is ajar. She shines in the wet and the wind. She observes herself and the weather. Her breath has the fetor of rotting cabbage. She seemingly stares with unseeing eyes.

Sunrise has the splendid shade of heliotrope. Sarah Palin's abysmal rendition of Blondie's 'Rapture' is on the ghetto blaster on the writing desk. Chutcha can be a patience-tester, larking about the furniture pieces. She has a wheezy laugh, greeting him warmly. In the hellish radiance, she stripteases with a music hall flourish. They exchange glances like partners engaged in an evil enterprise. She smirks like she's going to tell him a real rib-tickler. Peki's lust is so grand and fatal that he wills himself to retreat and draw the blinds. Then he churns back to rest his lips on hers. Without her, in life, he feels as if he is at a ball wearing a mask. With her, he can comfortably remove it to reveal his identity. They have no code of conduct. Her bob, abbreviated into bangs, is jagged, her voice scratchy. Her maquillage and wardrobe are enviable. He longs to take a steaming bubble bath with her in that squat tub. He belches repellently. He wonders whether his madre would even care if he never returned. Will he reap the whirlwind of being away? He ruminates on unrecapturable time, wanting back the previous weeks he spent with Marisa. His adventures lately verge on the folkloric, accounts that need no exaggeration. He ingests sardines and imbibes usque, listening to the maritime din. The battered and rangy janitor swings roguishly up the stairs. Smoky apricot sunset. Municipal stillness is interrupted by the concert-going multitudes. There's high drama next door, the neighbors yelling at the tops of their lungs and thumping around. Whereupon the flat abruptly goes grave-silent. Peki reflects on erasing the gentleman, Chema Casablanc, who resembled a middle-aged Benjamin Franklin. The chap wore formal attire and evidently disdained grooming. He had a masculine stride and a feminine mouth. The bloke was hardly a product on the market of desire. Peki managed to hover unnoticed, maintaining his distance. He made sure he kept to the shadows, remaining invisible to public observance. The weather was dirty. Rain's raking attack on the tarnished megapolis was relentless. The squalls howled as though amused. Street beggars appeared and disappeared like apparitions. Juvenile trulls plied their trade of compensated sex on the sidewalk. A white-collar john was disarranged from a passionate encounter with a beanpole of an adolescent. Peki, regions below stirred, with a predator's patience, pinned and assaulted Chema, a mischief-maker and pickpocket, on the pavement, and mulled over the ways and means with which to proceed in wasting him. Part of him wished for a quick end for the guy, the other wanted some slow suffering. So he found a happy medium. Instrumentation devised for torture was used with expert precision. The scalpel served its purpose. His skills were sharpened on the whetstone of practice. He couldn't conceal his contempt. He was more annoyed than alarmed when the victim fought back, struggling defensively against the perpetrator's offensive onslaught. Discomfort was inflicted on the prey's prat and genitals before he was whacked. The poor bastard was stabbed and strangled. And it looked like an intricate, demented dance behind the dumpster. The cement was stained black with blood. Rats watched and waited among the garbage cans. Graffiti on the brick walls of the alley were faded by the elements.

Peki smiled grimly, eyes desolate, savagely crippling him with punches to the liver and kidneys. It was a state of grace for the abuser. He was reluctant to breathe for a few seconds, rectally possessed. Chema looked away as if to avert his gaze from an impending accident he couldn't bear to witness. He held his pants tightly at the waist, as though, by clairvoyant means, he was aware of the dwarf's perverted intentions when it came to his anus, ahead of time. His ass was defiant, wagging this way and that. Peki vented an exasperated sigh and struck him in the face with his fist to create an imbalance. He whispered in his ear and mounted him from the rear. He was determined to satisfy his insatiable appetite for carnal abasement. It was an out-of-body occurrence, seeing himself brandishing his pintle like he was a spectator at an obscene conjuring performance. Aflame, his hands moved languorously to the womanly, congealed-creamy buttocks after pulling those extravagant panties down. He, borne on a wave of cruelty, imagined flogging him, giving him such a thrashing… He was sweat-sodden in an erotic swamp. He was transgressing the limits he set for himself. The master overwhelmed the pupil. He penetrated him and climaxed in a pulsebeat. The orgasm was this sustained, unendurable explosion. He spoke in a tearful tone, expecting him to resist a second rape, but he was already dead. Chema had delicate features and a substantial physique. He stank of fried potato. Peki rolled him up in an eloquent blanket. He had enough suet to make five batches of Butyrum! The stakes were higher. The danger was clearer.

Peki and Chutcha, out on an evening stroll, capriciously break into a trackside salon of imposing swank located in an Art Deco building. Disquieting photos of geriatric nudes are framed and hung on the partitions. Her countenance is veiled with perspiration. Her high-heeled swagger is devastating. Her respirations are just audible. Garbed in a Pierrot costume he found in the closet, he gapes, sparks up a cheroot, and has a woody. He feels as if his mental seam has loosened. His mortal illusions are out of control. He lays his rubber coat on the footstool and experiences lustrous hallucinations in an unmappable noplace. His nipples are rigid and exhibit minds of their own. His eyes are hypnotically fixed on this misbehaving, divine creature of the Orient. Her visage and body are mesmerizing. She is lean and attentive. She is constricted in the corset, and yet he can scarcely breathe. Her husky voice makes her sound world-weary. Her strut is calculated to titillate. She inspects the hosiery before she rolls it off. Their flirtatious dialogue flows. She's acting like a wicked little ingenue. Systematically, she gets naked. She notices his Johnson is expressively stiff. In an instant of lucidity, he realizes his lascivious instincts will prevail. He kneels on the lace pillow, lapping her clitoral bud and parting her labia. Her feet have the aroma of lilac. He doesn't perform. He simply is. There's no type to revert to. They are word-less for a while. Peki's mitts grip her backside. Sexual protocols don't exist for these lovers. His middle finger in her tight sphincter hurts and doesn't hurt her. Chutcha squinches her face up and cries. Anal integ-rity be damned. She is customarily not given to rectal intrusion, but for him, she makes an exception. He had a psychic prediction about this very scenario. Their passion is gloriously ferocious. Tongue-kisses and heated organs. Gilt furnishings. They lose track of time. They make a firm coital connection. Their coupling recalls a rodeo ride. He ramrods her from behind on the duvet. She whines when she comes in a pungent spate, eyebrows raised. Her juices are deliciously drinkable. She calls him her "numbskull buckaroo." And she soaks in the tub and tokes. There are vocal excursions into anecdotes and humor between them. They tell each other relationship war stories and leave out the collateral damage. One bends the other's ear. He is always an audience for her confidences. He never gets bored hearing about her difficulties. The oxygen's vivid with his expelled noxious gaseous odors. The celestial sphere is clear as a department store window. Air's hazed by pollutants. Starlings line up on the telephone wires. The sun, an electrical yellow, overtakes the azure. Rainbow's colors are brighter than expected. Cirri pile on the horizon. Draping sheet of a deluge. Peki looks like a postulant in a habit. He's absurdly enthusiastic about mantequilla and all its promise. He relishes the deep intimacy with the revolutionary project of making butter, a delirium, or a dream. With no interference from authority, community and church, he continues to submit himself to a homicidal imperative to produce Butyrum. For him, this is a welcome relief from the laborious daily grind. He radiates authority in matters concerning his profession.

He is safe and well. He hopes a gourmet meal is on the menu. Chutcha prepares Pasta e Fagioli. He has a dishful of peanuts. Moon glares off the lake. Sky's smudged with soiled cumuli. Yashmak of spritz.

Their dance, this glimmering morn, is almost a carnal one in the blazingly lambent space. They step in rhythm to his hummed waltz. Peki senses that something is coming to an end. He has nothing on save for military jackboots and an infantry helmet. Chutcha's aspect beams as if from a sudden awakening. Hers is a presence demanding to be observed. Her presence has the calming effect of a narcotic and his has the reality-enhancing power of a psychedelic. She is the subject of his attention. Her expression of availability is a source of comfort to him. He fancies her curvaceous form. He directs his ear to her middle as though it's endeavoring to explain the reason for its grumbling. He's exhilarated in seeing her navel, who wouldn't be. He melts in her company like an ice carving. He has intentions of the perverse variety. Her laddered stockings are things of adoration in the prevailing luminosity. She pleasures with lip service. She is a comely crumpet. For him, she fills the bill. She's the wonder of his world. She has an impossible sweetness to her personality. He knows full well he is not her only admirer. She used to earn fistfuls of currency by being a sculptor's model. He can picture her, chiseled into existence, being a stony figurative statue in some marbly corridor, with symbolic imagery, in a respected art gallery. He's a closet death merchant, shape-shifter, an enigma, a sage, a revolutionary, a quack... These are not confidable tidbits. It's like Chutcha's intimate apparel has consciousness and complies with its impulses by moving around. Peki looks at her umbilicus with a brightness of eye. He makes these commanding beckoning gestures. She unabashedly pantomimes these unvoiceably lewd demonstrations... Extravagant acts of degradation happen. He sports a depraved smirk. There is complicated stringery to her thong bikini. Her clam, this pearly aft, invites close inspection. Their inflections modulate. He cups her breasts like Justice holds her scales. He's a smoothie pulling his shenanigans. Her flesh is white as frost. She is surrounded by a luminous aura. His features acquire a derangement in the luminescence. Her position undergoes a certain adjustment on the ottoman.

Her soughs occupy his blood and bones. Eaten out, she levitates, floats above his head, then returns calmly to the floor for further cunnilingus. Lambency enters through the blinds at an extremely oblique angle. A bowl of oatmeal steams on the breakfast table beside fresh flowers and a bottle of plonk in the tea room. The shot glass is spotless. Clouds drift this sultry eve. Chutcha's cheekbones are like dams holding back a flood of tears. Peki's arousal rises like a river. Whereupon it rushes in waves. Her heinie is presentable, and he grabs it in a no-nonsense manner. She turns dominant, and he becomes submissive as if the dramatic roles in a play's production have been unexpectedly reassigned by the director. He feels like an exile and has no idea why. The storm weakens as though it cost its strength to roil. An obsidian smoothness to the overcast. Streets below explode in unruliness. Unintelligible patter comes from a pair of voluptuous ladies in pantsuits and platforms boarding an omnibus in the dazzle of the main square. The couple can still hear the mindless verbal exchanges from the third story. Chutcha hangs up the phone on her ex-beau, a parasitic vine that clung to the tree of her life. She didn't trust the slothful dude as far as she could throw a grand piano. She felt as if his hankie was always damp with chloroform. Peki misses home not unlike a refugee. He envisions the apartment as an empty shell. He and his mama observed a truce from their fighting with a finicky hug. Both sought peace of mind. There was palpable friction, dark energy. The opacity of their behavior ultimately transmuted to clarity. He must steer himself into her gravitational field. His raspberry sounds not unlike a low, vicious snarl. And day draws to night.

Laerke

Closing credits scroll on the TV screen for the 'Three's Crummier' sitcom. 'Magnum P.U.' show starts. Peki slumbers and nightmares that precipitation plummets like falling swords. He skitters on a steep hill like a parasite on the back of an unstirring beast and takes shelter in a cabin that's built into a mount, walled and roofed with earth and rock. The atrium is more like a panopticon. He shakes with exertion and emotion in the ruddy-gold light. His snaky getup suits him perfectly. Laerke, an avian, arachnidan, primate-ish gorgon, is a one-woman triumvirate of wickedness, with serpents for hair and brush-bristly eyebrows. She is in a fit of contortion, crawling over herself like a confused crab, limbs getting caught on themselves. Her frame curls around itself, her voice scraping the bottom of her register. She slinks about and bends, folding herself into a piece of human origami. Linguistically inept, her intonation scratches oddly in her petrifying larynx. She twists her arms and legs into unexpected positions. She chuckles, the sound sort of pebbly. She is something that is alien and contradictory. Physical conventions can't control her, and in the weirdest parody of Myerhold's theory of biomechanic performance, she, impossibly nimble and spindly, displaces her anatomic parts from their joints and reels herself back and rushes around, revealing her essence through motion as much as oration. She shrugs herself into shape. Ants scurry on her ankles. She hisses between her teeth. Her bottle-green cockatrice eyes electrically flicker. She has a Milky Way in each iris. Her veins are full of magma. She is redolent of peaty whiskey and burned bread. Her dermis is speckled and splotched. This is a dead place. The scenery outside is a primal chaos of Ice Age glaciers. Pewtery storm clouds gather in the labradorite-colored heavens. Inhuman beings roam on a carpet of celandine and mulch of mold, near the mussel-blue sea. A ghostly lace of lightning briefly nets the gunmetal overcast. Inside, fungi on the ceiling grow at visible speeds. Molluskan eyes peer out of an oyster shell. A magpie struts. This cauldron is alive with marine creatures. A crystalloid adder coils on the hearth. Breezes sound like the whispering of grasshoppers. Water gurgles. Peki is plagued by strange sights and false visions. Laerke talks in such a tonality that it seems as though her words are being exorcised from a demon living within her body rather than coming from her. She gyrates in an elastic mockery of ecstasy. Her crowing antics, the caws, croaks, and animalism, are maddening. Her spoken language sounds not unlike an incantatory recitation. She swirls like smoke. She grinds a chunk of meat in the mill of her jaws, preparing the mud bath. This forsaken world is like a snow globe being shaken up at the trickster's will, her multiple personalities the flakes, whirling beyond even the creator's control, coating everything and everyone, beholden to actions all their own. Suddenly, she strips down to her satin knickers and tosses the capacious mantlet aside. He gazes at her trout-dappled flesh. Her navel is nonexistent. She has granitoid incisors and flinty molars. Her orbs become charcoal blurs. She is oceanically heaving and restless. And he unexplainably finds in himself the burgeoning desire to sleep with her, out of arousal and curiosity, but resists the urge easily enough. He touches her wrist; it's both hot and cold. Her skin flakes like that of a reptile's when it rubs against a stone. She stares impassively at him. Then they couple, and surge like air currents. The sex has the rhythm and rapidity of a waterfall. The environment appears to have been constructed on a soundstage. The space has a vertiginous quality. The room, looking like it was built by theater designer Edward Gordon Craig, is sculpted out of light and shadow in angles sharp enough to draw blood, a vacuum-sealed, artificial nowhere. There is dripping and knocking and pounding. These fragmental mental pictures remain, like the shards of a dream, one Peki is happy to have awakened from. The screw is tightened. He races like a cirrus in wind, watched dispassionately by the globe of the midnight sun, along the ring road, never seen here again.

440

Hedley Fries-Parrot

She moves toward the town like an ocean disturbance. Her fraudulent eyelashes resemble those radial spokes coming from a comic strip's sun. Her brain is lit up as if by black light. Garish litter skitters. A bus, plastered with advertisements, toddlerishly totters. Weather systems move in these parts as though with free will. Her muddy olive dress color coordinates with her mop. Hedley, narcoleptic, anatomically complicated, with a Boerboel's head breadth, root-white face really difficult to characterize, it being weirdly configured, has brittle poise and warped nympholepsy. She has this faint mildew fetor. She has a kind of akimbo bearing and an obvious overbite. Her nostrils are dissimilar in size and shape, an anomaly that's never sat well with her. She's often discalceated. Mental marvel she isn't. She is somewhat slow and afraid of her own shadow. She is self-immolating, and withstands the daily dread of living. She treats her existence like she's setting up a microwave according to the package's directions. Her mind is branched, webbed, and tangled with linkages. Her leisure interests include playing the bassoon and creating Play-Doh statuettes, the pieces intentionally malformed, making them sitting bolt upright at the wobbly desk in her unkempt place which reeks of an old bathmat. The rats and roaches infesting the building are evidently atomically mutated. Hedley sculpts with precision and intensity whenever the opportunity presents itself, but usually pores over facts and figures by day, and is a taxi dispatcher at night, the tedium and despair just horrendous. At the present time, she is working on a fecaloid figurine version of Michelangelo's David. She wears a stained apron and vivid kerchief and nothing else behind closed doors. She struggles with might and main against her urges... Her response to strong stimuli is throwing up. The young woman is kindhearted. Pigeons commence a mass exodus from the long backless stone bench, precipitated by charging children. There are zigzags of leven. Thunder's booms are regular as respirations. Sea has the blue of flame.

Mucilaginous dankness imbues the storm cellar. Cumuli are mushroom chromatic. The rain is tentative. The cadence of Hedley's speech keeps changing. There's an ammonial tang to her armpits. Avian chitters harmonize briefly and diverge once again. Drencher turns sideways in the berserk gusts. Her shitty artworks are arresting in their exceptional craftsmanship, arranged in hyaline cases. Some are spectacular. She, in stocking feet, moves on the antistatic ruglet hydraulically. Her derma layer is infantly alabaster. She's getting chunky to the point of clinical intervention. She has a core understanding of who she is. She has pendent abdominal parts. Hailstones are grape-sized. Yusuf Cornelius, her subject, with a bell-shaped coconut and tallow pageboy with uneven bangs, looks paralyzed with indecision, his integument gleaming like gravel at noon, wearing only sheer hose and a pair of pumps. He stresses his syllables and is snarky. Torrent is concussive. Surfeit of vehicular din is annoying. Hedley constructs exquisite egesta busts that are literally remarkable. She is a consummate pro when it comes to manufacturing poo effigies. She has a history of substance issues and tons of personal baggage. She gets hunched into herself, methodically carving the caca, her chef's hat crumpled, the sitter squirming on the stool, beside the lamp that's comparable to one of those heated deals over a buffet's entrees. The basement stinks powerfully of body and feces. Her gray matter generates high-speed thought. She spends large blocks of time meticulously making these doo-doo representations, attempting to achieve creative triumphs. She has tunnel vision and is like a train on a straight track. Warmth assembles. The rotating fan makes a stack of bills' envelopes on an end table riffle. The joint, a rented ranch-style duplex, situated in a cul-de-sac with abrasive asphalt, is airless and narrow. The worn mat at the front door bids 'WELC.' Hedley shifts in the davenport, tooties up on the padded rocker. The clock is kneebucklingly heavy. Watermarks mar segments of the paneling. Hedley tries to establish a rapport to put her model Yusuf at ease. It would help if she put attire on. He is slumped not unlike a scolded schoolkid, and serious as a heart attack. He is thickset and has sideburns. He had arrived with a rigid moue and hiphugger Wranglers. He notices the notes for projects are cascades of wordage on pages. Her spine is true and her ankles are crossed. Her sucked-in oculi are expressive and alive. When she abuses herself he unhesitatingly absconds. Whereupon she withdraws into monkish solitude, her preferred state. She brushes her substandard-topiary tresses. Her shoulder blades bear semblance to butt cheeks.

Hedley underwent a back-alley abortion when she was a teenager. Her twin brother, the stolid, kind of saurianish Harold, was the father. They managed to maintain a steady dating relationship until he ODed. The shock and loss she experienced were surreal. He used to suck his thumb and wet the bed well into his twenties. She would sing lullabies to him, sometimes atonally. His breath had a vomitus mephitis to it. He had the facial expression of someone who was being simultaneously demonically possessed and being fried in the electric chair. Their pata-pata was well-nigh choreographic in its routine. His blinders were smeary and empty of everything. He had a resonant voice. His reserve verged on the remote. His body odor reminded her of burnt leaves. His ears looked like little balled fists. The siblings would get on the swing set, climb on the jungle gym, and fall on the wood chips, in the vicinity of the stand of sickly trees. They moved smoothly. The monochrome room, fluorescent-lit, with a single kite-shaped pane, sans curtain and shade, one of institutional quality, they shared as youths, felt pressurized. The walls were painted an emetic green, the ceiling a creamy brindle. When there was parental argufying, she would stop her ears and he would cover his blinkers. Their quarreling was competitive and primitive. TV programs would be on, serving as background noise. Their folks would give the impression of being stuporous and uptight. When Harold found out what she'd done, without his consent, he threw a haymaker at Hedley that didn't connect.

Two mutts, one piebald, the other with matted fur, both collarless and tagless, stray animals in all probability, are conjoined, copulating on a lawn that recalls a junkyard, next to an untended garden surrounded by a shabby wire fence. The mating mongrels fight for dominance, the bottom scrabbling on the sucrose sand, the top loping with it, still hitched. Hedley, driving her battered Beetle (purchased when she was an Avon Lady years ago) on the cold street in the seedy district, her lineaments less distinct because of the slightly tinted windows, pulls over to the curb to watch the amative canine adventure. It's pouring like the absolute dickens. To her, the road, with the lines of lamps along its length, is like a runway. The soaker is wicked dense and persistent. The sagging sky is leaden and sad. She thinks of her occasional boyfriend, Thrun Slaggert, afflicted with rosacea, the guy reminding her of a Great Ape with road rash. The pairing feral pooches' ribcages show. Their eyes are cruel and hurt and hard. Their humping is compelling and diverting. It's as though some tremendous type of evil force has possessed them. Coitally attached, they stagger blindly, and sport stoic expressions. Vault's red fades to pink.

Curse words are written in spray paint on the industrial-chemical factory's brick wall. The graffiti is an impressionistic mash of letters and sketches. Mega mouths of cement pipes puke cocoa-brown sludge and an apricot-hued liquid into the river. Hedley's flatus sounds like an apish hooting. She impulsively does these mime-ish kinesics. It becomes deathly quiet in her car, the soundlessness as though she is submerged in deep water. The events in her life seem unpleasant and contextless, like flashes of imagery, disturbing and unforgettable, in a bad dream's fragmented narrative, appearing and disappearing nightmarishly, the episodic occurrences with a strange peripheralness. She can be deficient in attention. In her fantasy she pictures Thrun stripped and slapped by a crinigerous wrestler of gross corpulence, the man dressed in a burning pink unitard, and pushed into a vat of mayonnaise and quacked at by a mechanical duck called McJunkins, and she uses paste as a lubricant to practice onanism, her head cocked over to one side, like a dog's when it listens to a whistle, one humans cannot hear. Peki feeds the curs. Hedley gets out of the heap.

Peki heaves a great sigh. Love, he thinks, is lust's faithful spouse. His whole being is racked by rheumatism. This place is a breath of fresh air, figuratively speaking, at least in comparison to the apartment's atmosphere, the flat gloomier than a graveyard. Marisa has been timid and withdrawn, the very picture of despair, and refusing to take her medications. It is as if the role of the mother is too much for her. Her despondency pervaded the pad. She will always be his guiding light. She is his North Star. She orients his world to where she is. Right now he feels like he's in a much stronger position than he has been in a long time. He is getting his voice back and reclaiming who he is. His biggest hope for the future is to continue to figure out who he is on his own. He's been a part of a couple for so long that finding out who he is outside of a relationship is hard and traumatic. It's like taking cod liver oil — it's good for him, but he doesn't like how it tastes. Maybe she's fed up with him making the decisions, always getting in the last word. The fecal stench mercilessly assails his olfactory organ. The repellent odor seems to envelop him. He has spent untold uninterrupted hours, day and night, producing Butyrum till he got debilitating cramps. He is the new king of butter. The weight of the crown isn't too heavy to bear. He feels as though he is walking on the razor's edge... He has felt sullen and lazy lately; a dreadful period, blessedly brief. The modest parlor contains undistinguished, second-hand furnishings. Heaps of newspapers form a veritable labyrinth, making a systematically arranged chaos. He notices that each stack corresponds to a single year. He views people below as performers in a play and the city as a theater. Hedley can be vain as a peacock. He feeds her ego with fawning and flattery, to increase his chances of getting laid. Ass-kissing, dispensing such saccharin compliments, it is surprising that the syrup on his tongue doesn't make it stick to the roof of his mouth. Her sweat is rose water? He is acting like some pompous dandy. He's concerned she may become bored, or worse, get scared. Because he is attracted to her, he won't move so much as an inch toward the door, despite the nauseating stink infiltrating the pad. She's a queer bird. She is also quick-witted and has a peculiar accent. Her perspiry nombril, the center of interest in her form, shines not unlike a diamond. She's hardly the paragon of good health. The aromatic lotion on her skin has this woodsy scent, a forestial fragrance in early spring. Her features are harmonious without being lovely, and yet her countenance has a certain charm, in cosmetic powder and paint. She makes a deep impression on him. He wishes to drink wine and invade her body and discuss a thousand things. He listens raptly to her ramblings. She puts on the cruel waspie almost as a form of self-inflicted punishment. He envisages her vaginal juice as being an inflammable element, their venereal sparks the necessary providers to set it alight. Her words drum through his head. She has the potential to change his world radically... for better or for worse? He stares at her like a leopard at a gazelle. She gulps a fizzy liquid, sweetish and acidic. He imagines her sharpening her claws against his flanks. It will be a painful process but an inevitable one. His insect's eyes are bloodshot. Cars on the highway travel at breakneck speed. Sex with her would be a dream and he's full of vigor. Peki's confident he is capable of conquering her. He wants to take advantage of the situation... and her. Hedley is so wrinkled from her long shower that she looks like a golden raisin. She accepts a resounding smooch on her cheek and she returns the favor, leaving him surprised and smiling, and awakening his desire. A peculiar tingle runs down his vertebrae. The sensation is familiar to him. A friendship is beginning between them. He hopes they maintain the momentum they've established. He is rapturously relaxed, buzzed on booze and stoned on pot. He's developing a passion to come and live here. She energizes and inspires him. He feels up her behind before he thumbs her ass, a deplorable propensity of his. She stands stupefied, blinders glazed, shivering with either discomfort or arousal, he isn't sure. He gently and deftly manipulates her genitals, and her totality goes into a hot spasm. He regards her pruny hands and feet. Her breasts and buttocks jut out. She is rigid and silent as he tongues her with the same facility he shows in digitally probing her private parts. They discuss fleeting life, and the finality of death. He grasps her ample hips. She has an exceptionally keen mind when she's messed up on junk, speaking with wisdom and accuracy on diverse topics. He radiates something approximating the obscene. He takes a large swallow of the vino; it is rather harsh and dry. The alcohol lubricates his brain and whets his appetence. The burgundy is splendidly rough and lacks subtlety. Hedley possesses a well-proportioned physique. And her expression tells of woe and resignation. Her paleness makes her peepers appear darker. She is cute without being extraordinarily comely.

Citizens move hurriedly on the streets, headed in different directions. She makes bacon and eggs for them, admitting her finances are unstable, hence the "meager fare." They continue their conversation. Peki watches her at the stove. Both are a bit tipsy and quite high. She mentions her economic situation while he fingers her vulva and licks her clitoris. He's relieved to know his aptitude for seduction hasn't atrophied. He is very stimulated by her. He confesses he has crude manners and can be a cynic and a scoundrel. Her coral panties fit her snugly. He regards the shock of pubic hair. Her pussy reeks of rancid tripe. She launches into this tirade that doesn't spare her former beaus, accusing them of using her like merchandise and tossing her aside like the packaging. He laps her genitalia, calling them "ignorant fools," and claiming to be "the remedy against these idiots." The two come together. She senses the moment has arrived for them to part. He has other ideas. He isn't completely inclined to relinquish so easily the recently acquired thighs of hers from his mitts. Plus, he is not finished devouring her duff. He turns her aversion to amative action into wearisome compliance. With poise, he rides her as a horse at a gallop.

The War

The natives gazed at Peki with curiously mild interest, as though he were some animalic creature that roamed from a menagerie. He gave indications of displeasure by staring daggers at them. His ears burned with embarrassment because he looked not unlike shit. Enraged, he called them "sheep." He was no longer fighting for what he believed in; he was merely a marionette manipulated by the puppeteer powers. He wished to rule over his own life and not be anyone else's pawn. He existed in the erosion of time. His aspirations in the world were crushed by the reality in which he was living. Half the country was laid to waste. He was alone in that backward place. He believed he was as daft as a brush from adversity. The evil of the enemy crawled forth. Hurried exhumations were underway in the graveyard. People were digging up their loved ones to take them with them. They were hastening before the intervention of darkness. The civilians were cutting and running. It was clear they weren't coming back. It was, for him, unforgettably appalling seeing and smelling the decomposed bodies. Unoccupied coffins were set aside like large models. It was a macabre scene that was transpiring. Remains of the dead became precious cargo. Repelled, he regarded them balefully. The deceased should stay buried. Japanese soldiers altercated on a lawn. A youthful woman with a pleasantly plump belly confronted one and was struck flush in the face by the butt of a rifle and she folded with a groan under a lime tree in the first light of dawn. The rosy sun ascended from behind a mountain. Chickens flapped and squawked, surrounded by flimsy fencing. Donkeys pulled preposterous loads of personal belongings in carts. These were times of want and depression. There were deaths on the streets. It would be different to describe the panic. Peki's heart sank, surveying them, in such unwell condition, visible proof of the repercussions of war. Rebels were oddly subdued. There were the young and the old, the manic and the idiots. A column of asylum seekers progressed as if by a process of uncanny telepathic unanimity. A familial drama unfolded. Parents argued. Their kids were amused. A gangling male and female acted as intermediaries. Peki auscultated senescent inanities. A village was being evacuated. He was confounded by the constant turning of events. He had advanced maybe twenty paces when he viewed a griseous, withered middle-aged man (wisps of hair countable) yelling at his haggard mule that wouldn't budge an inch. It let out a low moan when it was repeatedly whipped with a branch. Its owner was perhaps as light as a straw. Peki found himself increasingly upset by the way the wretched beast was being maltreated and was moved to action, belting the guy in the solar plexus, knocking the wind out of him, and he fell over face-first onto the terra firma. His nose bled and his cheek was cut and he wore a puzzled expression. His upper lip quivered. The unexpected disrespect nonplussed him. A stout lady attended to him, helping him to his feet. The incident produced a negative effect on those who were present. It provoked emotion that was exhibited in the witnesses. Peki released the animal from its reins and prodded its hindquarters with his elbow and it cantered off into the woods. He hoped it would get lost and never find its way back to the bastard. And that was the end of that. Peki thought of his relationship with Marisa — romantic, unreputable, and glorious. He formed a mental image of her in his head. He mulled aloud over memories of Her, recollecting the two of them gasping and giggling in their profane conspiracy of affection and intimacy. He choked back tears. Aimless and AWOL, he traversed a great distance, anticipating another unappetizing meal. He had no delusions about the hard decision awaiting him. He would have to return to the base at some point. And what about the brutalities he committed? He bore a bundle of supplies on his back, his robes looking priestly, barely better than rags. He chanted in this rich baritone like he was meditating while on the move. "Mary Mother of Jesus Christ," he said in a cracked voice that echoed from brick walls. He had a haunted and unhappy physiognomy, hiking through the serene and scented pine forest. Suddenly, he saw the mule up ahead in an expanse, grazing peacefully on the banks of a stream. Peki, starving, withdrew his pistol and aimed it. The thing looked at him. It recognized him. He pulled the trigger. There was a pop. It fell, making a disturbing gurgling sound before it died. It was his dinner. He studied his reflection in the water with special intensity. Birds winged up into the empty sky. He negotiated through the tombs and thorns. He held his essentials tight on his lap and slept in a lemon tree like an ape.

The anvil-headed, dwarven Peki Zambrano's heartbeat boomed and echoed like a giant drum in his chest cavity. It sounded almost tribal, ritualistic. He was called the 'cuckoo's egg' of the Spanish side by his comrades. His efforts hatched in the nest of solitariness. He was a self-professed 'Isolato.' Shellshocked, the man shook like a dog just from the water. His face had the emaciation of the Knight in The 'Seventh Seal,' and was cloaked in the medieval habit of Death in that same movie. He was enswathed with ectoplasmic sweat. Perhaps it was the magic mushrooms. These strange excrescences, perforations, and secretions had mysteriously manifested on his skin. A penile weapon emerged out of a vaginoid fold hidden in his armpit. The abnormity of his body eventually came to seem horrendous. Peki stalked with an Oedipal limp on the war-ravaged countryside. He had a phthisical cough. In this verdurous region, he chanced upon an epicene faun flirting with a full-figured woman who resembled the Mona Lisa. The creature explored her omphalos with its fingers, as though it were an orifice requiring such retractive foreplay, or as if he was preparing not to plant a kiss so much as to implant one.

Peki beached his boat and went ashore to join his Spanish compatriots in the fray against the German enemy. The sand was hot. There was a glint in his pies that was like the prospect of inebriety. He evidenced agitation and excitement. He lingered and dealt with his weird wonderment. He tried to suppress his toothache with a big swig of a vodka martini from his flask. Entering the skirmish, he anticipated a hostile reception from the other soldiers. Instead, after their initial surprise, they welcomed him with open arms. He resisted the temptation to flee for a while. Within an hour, terror-stricken, he had a stratagem in his noggin that was apparently both crazy and the only possible course of action, and he hurtled through the mounting commotion of an unpremeditated departure. At first, he was gobsmacked by his decision, and then he panicked. He was too discombobulated and hurried to reconsider. He didn't have the habit of obedience to authority. The troops had a cattle mentality, in his opinion. That was their business. The barrage was unbelievable. He was attempting to organize himself during the bombardment. He was shaking his body and slapping his face. Behind the stack of sandbags, he dashed back and forth, in turmoil, in a curious manner, collecting as much food, water, and equipment as he could carry. He spun around and fell when a piece of shrapnel whizzed by his ear. He felt like he was possessed. The almond and walnut trees offered some protection… Peki flew the coop, abandoning his brothers in the battle with the Kaiser. He was horrified by the foolish measures of bailing on his brethren, and the dangerous misadventures he was undoubted going to bring about. He paused for a minute, to endeavor to think sensibly. He was faced with an impossible choice. What he was doing wrenched his heart. He wanted to leave that place. The combat kept dragging him back, against his will. Not in this instance. Common sense to abscond won him over. His hands were tied, as though by an invasion rope. Surreptitiously he left the encampment. Ultimately, the unit was wiped out. He was a deserter once more. And alive. How would he have ended up? Fate was fickle, after all. A thunderous explosion caused him to fall off a rocky outcrop and he bounced off the grassy ground as if he was made of rubber. Whereupon he rolled and plummeted straight down and smashed into a slope's scree. He was lying there, unmoving for a moment, until he got up and shouted curses, imbued with white rage. He swore, his vox filling with sobs. Finally, he smiled a little bit, for he was free at last. The stones had scraped his flesh and the thorns had scratched it. His fatigues were torn. He wiped the blood from his lamps using his sleeve. The townlet was half-vacated. Peki looked at it like he could make it populate by sufficiently tenacious scrutiny. He pictured Marisa. He cherished her out of necessity and fear.

He was afraid of being alone, without her in his life. He treasured her with his body and brain. It wasn't a normal relationship between mother and son. Peki craved peace and contentment with her. He missed her. There was a hole in his heart that was in the shape of his madre. He remembered her every time he masturbated. His sorrow was unbearable. She was the pleasure of existence. To be honest, she wasn't particularly interesting, funny, or intelligent. She didn't have much education or creativity. She wasn't busy enough to not have vanities. She lived in a box and was always destined to be ordinary. Her biography, if it was ever written, would be completed in a short chapter. She made no impact on the cosmos. But the fact is that she was exceedingly sexy. She had complications in her personality and no malice. She was sweet of soul. He was not wise to the world. She assisted him in navigating his way through it. He enjoyed listening to the catchy melody of her lingua franca. He learned her language. He vowed to die with her name on his lips, her image reflected in his eyes. She occupied his dreams, at night and by day. He knew in his core that she was expecting him to arrive. He promised himself he would be a restrained and dignified gentleman. He would emphasize waddling confidently and holding his head high. He was a tad concerned about his sow's rear. A pack of mongrel revolutionaries wandered the landscape. Haggard, Peki haunted the foothills. His gaze was hard, like metal. His oculi were overflowing with tears and his voice choked as he talked to himself. He made the most difficult decision of his life. He was filthy, hungry, and enervated, but in good spirits, imagining her. He sat down heavily at the trunk of an orange tree, taking a much-needed breather before setting off in the wake of the refugees, secure in the knowledge that he had to survive to see his Mama again. They'd meet again if the Lord willed it. His feet were blistered.

Hercules and Omphale

Attributable to the angel dust and joy juice, Peki believes he is Hercules and Hedley is Omphale.

Omphale's beauty could give Michelangelo's statue of David an erection. She looks out the window of the charming little house at the Dead Sea and the olive grove below. Then her aligned teeth, white as ivory, cast coruscation upon Hercules when she smiles. He regards the oval of her face. Set afire, lust inflaming him, he directs a lascivious gaze toward her without the slightest discretion. Perfectly plump, she appears as though she was sculpted by Phidias. She's rather ingenious and impish. Her big breasts could suckle an army. She possesses prodigious intelligence. He is vigorous and not very bright. He's a master of martial arts and has a predilection for perverted habits. His impressive eyes can pierce straight through anything they see. Although he has harmonious features, his unhandsome visage resembles Tancred's. Their orbs blaze with desire, effusively embracing with fevered passion, whereupon she strokes his proud phallus. His scrotum is bald as a hard-boiled egg and smells of damp rope. He seizes her like a shipwreck survivor would a piece of floating wood and they make love madly. The couple kiss, grab, touch, bite, and suck as if their lives depend on it. They are happy as hummingbirds. This Pantagruelian feast is spread on the rectangular table and an uncomfortable armchair behind them. The fulgor starts to diminish, bringing the shadows of objects into being. Hercules, copulating with Omphale on the bed, connects with space, passing over a threshold that leads to a shortcut across time. He caresses her flaccid stomach and pinches her rosy nipples. She clings to him like moss to a rock. Her porcelaneous flesh is lustrous. She sinks her fingernails into his back. He licks every millimeter of her body, giving special attention to her buttocks, working her up to a fever pitch. She winds herself about him, not unlike a python. Her skin has a jasmine aroma. His testicles are fruit ripened to excitement. He is scorched with heat. Akin to assiduous students, the two study each other quickly, guided by both curiosity and instinct. There is so much pleasure and so much pain. The pair weather their storm. And her womb receives his semen. He crows like a cock. She feels as though she is born again, emerging from an enormous egg to behold a new world. The roads the lovers have traveled are as diametrically opposed as Arcadia and Abaddon. Hercules and Omphale consume red wine and a leg of lamb and sleep like logs. The rain, urine-redolent, is wrathful.

Peki and Marisa

When it comes to his field, Peki stands apart from – if not above – the madding crowd. He successfully fuses the practice of shock tactics on the sales floor and the aura of art. There is madness in his method. The upshot of this sorcery is twofold. Firstly he is guaranteed a large if a brazenly self-selecting group of sensation-hungry customers right out of the gate. Secondly, the negative press he gets usually ends up working in his favor. For every scandalized consumer who walks out of his at-your-own-risk shop, another shopper gets bolder: entry to the booby hatch with butter as a badge of honor. He possesses the power to turn rosy cheeks porcelain, and transform smiling faces into contorted vizards of disquiet. His mantequilla inspires fanatical confidence and devotion among his community of regulars. He makes the stuff with the assiduity and dedication that are testament to his belief in the product, the meanings of which are even mysterious to him. The majority of his earnings are spent on maintaining his establishment. He brings in enough funds to supply an entire chain of stores. In his time and place, the main attraction of butter production lies in his license to perpetrate iniquity. This is amply shown by the fact that as soon as the spread loses its special taste, the number of buyers of the commodity dwindles exponentially. He feels justified in what he's doing. The Devil's heart is delighted. He displaces from his head and heart uncertainty and compassion. The Butyrum is fuel for his fire. He is reinventing the wheel. His clarity stems from his conviction. The success of his exploits serves to increase his confidence beyond the boundaries of basic self-belief. The necessity of his invention decides his courses of action. Avoiding the police is on par with dodging bullets. He experiences the sensation of being an improbable survivor. He is leading a double life. He's gaining precarious popularity on his block. He must order a new amputation saw.

Peki awakens refreshed from a deep sleep. His nuts itch in an ominous manner. He resists the urge to scratch them. His pate feels a draft where Marisa sheered away his strands. And he micturates into the toilet, his urine with the stagnant stink of marsh water. His mouth is dry and his palms are damp. Bloated with constipation, he sits on the hassock, studiously composing a soon-to-be-celebrated recipe as if it's a symphony, unburdened by the idiosyncrasies of his vocation, thus freed to go crazy with creativity. His hams are ink-stained, looking like a mechanic's grimy hands. He is robed in a surgical gown and wears his Nolex watch. He pauses to scrutinize his madre's vibrant grin, pointed boobs, immaculate white silk of her skin, and pictures her shrunken, mummified... an impossible image. She has these imaginary gynecological conundrums. He sensitively diagnoses her "health problems" as hypochondria and/or mental disorder — his technical terms. He treats her "condition" with verbal placebos and unprofessionally identifies her paranoid delusions. Marisa sips corn syrup for the impetigo and scabies she doesn't have. She's been subsisting on Turkish delight. She is reluctant to share her sweets. Her breadbasket is tighter than a snare drum. He appraises her bony limbs and unpadded ribs... She contemplatively blows on an invigorating cup of scalding brew. Her eyes flicker. She uses toilet paper cardboard rolls as a substitute for plastic curlers. He's petrified of her meeting and dating someone new, perhaps marrying for money and influence. Her jotted notes, written in flourished whirls, are posted everywhere. He peruses them whenever he gets a chance. Farting, he intelligently understands the foreign tongue of his sphincter, whereas his Mama personally comprehends not a single syllable. His midsection is cruelly distended. He feels as though something solid and amorphous is in there. Traffic pursues its cumbersome way across the viaduct, reminding him of a rush-hour version of a biblical exodus. He ingests large quantities of Percocet and imbibes sherry. Then he recollects tearing off the wings of a butterfly when he was a kid, whereupon he fired marbles at it with a slingshot, his heart pumping with guilty excitement, experiencing both relief and disappointment when he exhausted his ammunition without ever hitting the thing. Later on, he focused on it with a magnifying glass, the sun's light concentrated on it, burning it. He watched it writhe on the marl, beheld its torment. He stopped when the insect began to smoke. It was dead. There was no bird, cat, or dog safe from his makeshift catapult. He tries to not dwell on his ferocious destructiveness, the atrocities committed with an aberrant precision. He's a barbarian living in civilization. Within him, there is a simple conflict between good and evil. He is a Black Plague ravaging this country. He imperils the health of the nation. He is cancer corrupting the people, proving himself refractory to a cure. Hey, he's attempting to accomplish a greater good with the Butyrum, boosting the local economy. It is like a dentist performing a root canal, a surgeon carrying out an operation, causing pain to relieve a patient for the long haul. The wind has a melodic embellishment of grace notes. Peki remembers the buxom "Negress" with crescentoid spectacles and tuba-ish intonation, and palpating her flesh, kneading the stupendous folds of blubber. She had a cynical glint in her eye. She let out a sigh that sounded not unlike resignation. Meanwhile, he was adrift in a sea of passion. Her body odor stank of roasting beef. She had a winning smirk and alcoholic halitosis. He had purchased carnal ecstasy. She was left in a cold fury when he climaxed and didn't tip. Tripping on LSD, he saw pedestrians as an Egyptian army swallowed up by the Red Sea. He discerned direction from the stars' scintillation. He sure was appreciative of the supplied navigational information. His designation was undecided. In the heat, he felt akin to some burning heretic, not spared the flames of hell in the hereafter. There was an overflow of slum-dwellers and diseased fugitives in those classical ruins. His laughter was coarse and his muttering sounded like priestly invocations. The measured tread of his sandals was drowned out by the unnerving din of gridlock. Gales sounded not unlike the cries of dissembled orgasms. He mumbled curses, his heart dully thudding. With indigestion, it felt as if he had a blazing torch in his tummy. He heard the majestic strains of hymns and psalms…

Peki's aroused from somnolence by the merry mayhem in the plaza. Stark-naked, he scratches his itchy pubes region, his facial expression one of enlightenment, and feigns impatience and indignation, dealing with Marisa, in the rufous effulgence. He excavates dingleberries from his umbilicus. His yap gapes in a yawn that exposes his ginger gums and damaged teeth. He arises from the sill and stretches, his rippling muscles flexing. He visualizes them lying together nude in a tangled heap. His heartbeat sounds like handclaps. His trap floods with saliva at the thought of her divesting herself of the dress. Her pubic hair, in his fantasy, is made of spiderwebs. She paces back and forth as if caged. He's touchy-feely. She is impassive and tolerant. She looks raptly into empty space in the fullness of time. His intuition tells him that she's paying attention and that she's perversely deceptive. He has the primeval urge to leap and subdue her. Showers have the sonance of the brassy tinkles of distant bells. Breezes sound like monotonous incantations. Surf of speculation (concerning the murder mysteries) breaks on folks in the courtyard. Rumors abound about mountain ranger patrols increasing in the sierras within the week. Peki gets lewdly inebriated. Marisa sings sentimental songs, a few with ebulliently obscene lyrics. Her antiperspirant smells of incense. Her trance snaps when he pinches her tochus. She is disconcerted by his overtures. If only she was capable of constructing a makeshift fortification… She's stiff and straight as an ancient musket. His behavior is familiar and discomforting. He eructates excuses and justifications for exceeding the relationship boundaries. There is incredulity in her intonation. He wonders whether or not he is being toyed with. Color rises to his countenance. He pauses to consider her slight frame. She accuses him of being a "false proprietor who fools no one." A silence falls on mother and son. Peki burns with irritation at her rejection and comment. His ears flush with embarrassment. He lays the plans for seduction. Marisa shrugs her bony shoulders and mimes a feeble gesture with both hands. He puts on what seems to be clerical garb while she slips into her battered and beloved sporty slides. He treasures her gaunt build and leporine lineaments. Oxygen's thick and sticky as guava jam. Refulgent beams speak to him in a language unknown to anyone else. The splendor makes a supernatural spectacle in the parlor. They preach their gospel. He gives vent to guttural grunts. She massages his sore hump. His shins hurt for some reason. His oculi glint with malice when she adopts a lofty carriage that belies her perturbation. She ostensibly has no identity, not unlike a mannequin. Her knees shake. Skyline is the pigment of lapis lazuli. Peki's peripheral vision detects a glimmer of movement: cockroaches on the kitchen floor spread out, advancing like a formation of an infantry unit. He pictures volleys of Raid and land mines of Black Flag Roach Motels, spray-salvos halting the relentless march, the scavenging insects hastening for shelter as their instincts dictate. He mutters the lengthy and orotund national anthem. The city is a field of wheat and he is the reaper in its midst. He is polluting the place. Is he the unwitting accomplice of Satan? He has such evil in his heart. The homicides he perpetuates are ceremonies of the Devil. He lacks compassion and sows brutality. He grows frigid and grim. He thrives on tainting love and tarnishing joy. His soul is stone. Attributed the drought, the pond has been reduced to a puddle. Puissant weather. Peki is the Spirit Creator of a New World, with boldness and enterprise. He's a gnome of flesh and blood and ethereal matter. He shall not be dismayed nor deterred. Not only is he puncturing the skin, but he is also shattering bones. He is determined to ensure that every knife thrust and gunshot counts when it comes to the killings. Occasionally he aims to accommodate the idiosyncrasies of the weaponry. The map of the world will become at some point made out of mantequilla. He is murdering citizens to rise to prominence, subjecting souls to the suffering of hell. He commits barbarities in butter's name. He contemplates the future — is he destined to be dispatched or continue to stack horror upon horror, inflicting misery on society? He gets intoxicated by the claret of bloodshed. He bows his head to the Butyrum. He has become a savage, rapist, and a marauder. He's afraid that sooner or later fingers will point accusatorially at him. He wishes he could take a breath of fresh air to alleviate his brandy-actuated queasiness, only a fetid odor is all there is. At night, the moon and stars are sufficient enough for him to see her. They consume the wildfowl he got from the unpleasant swamp.

A smidge of calm descends upon him, his inflection quavering. She intones Glory Bes. The prospect of imminent intimacy between them paralyzes her soul. Marisa slows her delivery down to a snail's pace.

A sense of disheartenment burrows into her chest. At this rate, it will take hours before she's finished with her Hail Marys. She feels as if her encephalon is a clump of quivering jelly. Peki intensifies his degree of concentration. She is stalling, he thinks, attempting to avoid the inevitable. He glances at his watch and sighs with exasperation. He sees them screwing at a speed comparable to that of an express train. She murmurs something about the ascension of the Holy Spirit. Her throat is parched with fright and repetition. She rambles on about the Apostles' Creed. She is heavy with resignation. Her recitations reach implausible lengths. She says the Our Father in a singsong modulation. He's soaking wet with sweat. It would appear that these delays have dampened his lust. "Blessed is the Fruit of Thy Womb, Jesus," she says. These words weigh on him. Stevedores joke and chat with one another on the docks. The metropolis is an immeasurable rambling machine. Gusts whine like fired bullets. Health and safety officers are in the process of inspecting the sanitary situation in the apartment building. Unpredictable police are near and far. He winces at the idea of interacting with them. Downpour is sharper than knives and cuts the cutis. Winds whip the rain and one gets blinded. Vapor arrives from nowhere. In the window washer, you essentially breathe the water. His amative advances spurned, Peki looks at it as a personal betrayal on her part. In his orbs, Marisa's refusal diminishes him. This redoubles the weight on his sturdy shoulders of being the one to bring them closer together. And he has failed miserably. She emphasizes his strategic maneuver was not a pleasant surprise. He looks shocked, reproached for the unsolicited come-ons. He's deified by his love for her and deranged by her dismissal. He has assumed the role of dom, giving her the part of the sub by an incidental method that isn't quite clear to her, but that nonetheless seems solidified. She sends out a bottle of bourbon as a peace offering. After a delayed reaction, he accepts. He makes a pass at her, only she shoots him down, puffing vehemently on a cigarillo, disdainfully ignoring his malign glare. He swallows his pride, knowing he'll shit it out. He would slice his gut open to get it if he has to. His lichen-yellow chiclets render his grin grotesque. Maybe she will come to him in a dream. She puts her hands protectively over her nether regions. Even as a blank slate she's riveting. He smokes rubber. Peki is beginning to believe that he has miraculous invincibility and exceptional power. His perceived aura of preternatural invulnerability is real. "I'm no ordinary man," he repeats to himself. He thinks of the corpse he'd hacked with a sword, the lady left in a flooded plain for the crows to feast on. In his mind, shadows of the dead loom. Sickness begins to strike his stomach. He was bitten and stung by ravenous bugs. He slaughtered a steer and wrapped pieces of it into the leaves of a palm. He recognized the triumph of persistence over the orderless forces of nature, his resolve strengthened when it should have been weakened by the weather. He felt as though he was dissolving in his perspiration, leaning over the precipice to watch the woman wending her way along the plateau below. He waved vigorously at the figure. Inwardly he felt soldierly. The fatigues he wore were an outward sign. His sunburned face resembled a rock stained red from iron. He went up the long and gentle slope behind the bald, zoftig dame, who was oblivious. He turned up, inconspicuously, and pounded her with a lathi like a pestle grinding ingredients in a mortar. His virility was challenged as she was pugnacious. The combatants fought in a verdant grove, in the vicinity of an irrigation canal. He was prepared for a short and victorious task and wasn't disappointed by the outcome. He pitched his tent on a raised and level area, above an abandoned mineshaft of the Incas. Quarrelsome birds defended their branches in a prospect of trees. He reckoned there were plants probably unknown to botanical science... Stilly twilight. Peki contemplates fixedly Marisa's form in front of him. Considering her, he favors an approach from the rear. It will be unexpected, and therefore successful. She gasps in dismay when he implements the stratagem. His penis becomes a banana. She is so cold that his balls retreat into his body. She's so glacial that his hair is encrusted with ice. He reels like a drunkard. The pisco is putrid. His eyes pop from his head. There is a lengthy and depressed hush in the lances of illumination.

Ida Tonne

Scandinavian moppet Ida's regressive autism has taken her capacity for speech. She practically needs orbital ocular reattachment surgery after the amount of involuntary eye-rolling, reacting thus to Peki's bloviating. Behind the war memorial, she listens impassively to him bitching about unabating larceny and industrial rapine in the community. His rejoinders smack unmistakably as sarcasm. She is bored of his dramas acted aplenty in her line of vision. She disconcerts drivers by dashing in and out of cars. He is faster than the flash of a meat cleaver in grabbing her, giving free rein to his baser instincts. A tidal wave of callousness has overtaken him. He longs to bathe in her golden shower. He stares at her in silence. Outrageously she flirts with him. A paroxysm of exasperation captures him. His boutade is risible. She is cunning and evasive, nimbly skipping sideways to avoid his grasp. She disgustingly displays a predilection for exhibitionism, wearing an expression of extreme joy on her pretty phiz. She reeks of pork. His piss stenches a corpse. There is an invasion of vultures. After her Saint Vitus' dance, Ida smears canine excrement on her mouth so Peki won't dare smooch her. She is carmine about the ears, curtsying sarcastically and spitting on the sod. She has on a rain slicker and wellington boots. He grins dumbly. He keeps the sombrero on, afraid she'll see his balding patch. He's dressed in khaki. She twists her lips sardonically. He blinks hard and shakes his head as if to clear it of confusion. She is unnaturally polite. He summons up enough courage to proposition her. She puts a wad of chewing tobacco between her cheek and gum and hops from one foot to another while singing a naughty song. His sangfroid becomes strained. He feels like a pathetic thing, inspecting the livid scar on her midriff, intrigued by it. The inexorable wind blows in its habitual noncommittal fashion. Peki mops his brow with his shirt's sleeve. Ida has a runny nose. She is a puzzle left for him to solve. She is unable to restrain the tears of her humiliation. His shoulders heave as he makes these soothing noises. When he is at last relieved, he exultantly exclaims, "holy moly!" And she shakes with suppressed grief. He takes her hand and squeezes it comfortingly. He feels like a hideous freak. Her countenance clouds over and she crumples once again into blubbing. An awful desire wells up in him. He feels like a grotesque creature. He mutters the last sentence of the Hail Mary. Her oculi are fastened motionlessly on the poor monster as he blabs on about bodily functions and secretions. Buzzards retire to the rooftops. There is a mass intrusion of vacationists, taken on guided tours of the megalopolis. A cop walking the beat looks like a boar, his incisors like tusks. A lovely sailor saunters on by in the honey-brown light. A hummingbird, this exquisitely jeweled avian, shows off, hovering, thence flying upward and downward, darting forward and backward, and finally looping in a circle. Its feathers refract through every hue of the spectrum. It settles on a branchlet and busily preens itself. The girl is gone... Peki is the second coming of the Lord of butter, the new voice sounding out in the wilderness. He doesn't see eye to eye with his colleagues; he has his gaze fixed on the next innovative batch. His peers' ears are permanently pricked in the hope of hearing what he is up to. His place is a dense star for lesser shops to orbit. Customarily he acts as the conscience of the business owners, achieving prosperousness because he won't be forestalled by concessions by those in power. Running the establishment, his demeanor and approach is somewhere between Che Guevara, Attila the Hun, and Fidel Castro. He is accountable for folks disappearing off the face of the earth and reappearing six feet underground. Sometimes his bloodlust is more motivation for killing people than the mantequilla. He is in the prime of his life, disturbed but not defeated by it. The megapolis is in a frenzy of distress on account of the many unsolved murder cases. The jar he "borrowed forevermore" from a medical university is filled with formalin. A colon holed not unlike a colander, varicolored cancers the size of a golf ball, and a fetus, the forlorn result of a miscarriage, a misbegotten victim, bob in the solution. He ingurgitates roughly half of the contents and grimaces. He had pinched it when the African American security guard gawped at a cute young lesbian couple, his eyes popping with amazement. An elderly dumper truck is parked in the breakdown lane. Peki waddles briskly to work off the anomalous effects that the baklava has on his metabolism. He swaggers into the throng. The poisons he has been taking are causing delusions. His paunch resembles a soccer ball that has gone out of shape. He feels as though he is the Devil's miracle or God's mistake. On the go, he looks at his reflection in the grocer's window. "How the mighty are fallen," he mumbles, and falls headlong over a fire hydrant.

Zara and Hugo

In Peki's possession are cannabis, testosterone, basuco, methamphet-amine, and Viaplex, which is used to treat erectile dysfunction. He sits in a generic house in a featureless town in an unidentified location. After losing a toenail, he has phantom pains and is in a delirious state. Distant thunder sounds like the krump of a mortar shell being fired. His respirations have the rasp of scales being scraped off fish. He remembers chomping on the splendidly enormous mango and avocado on the deserted paradise of a plateau and admiring the rice field and platano plantation below when he heard the sound of wet slaps, followed by a male's yelps and a female's shrieks. He removed his automatic from its holster and unsheathed his machete, experiencing a sinking sensation in his stomach as he advanced. A New Zealand couple, named Zara and Hugo, in their early twenties, cavorted in private on the banana grasses, fornicating in infeasible positions. The two smeared each other with the guts of various fruits they'd found. She was as thin as he was thick. Both were redheads and had crewcuts. She had the face of a sala-mander. He was rubicund and rotund, eclipsing the shrub. The grinding pelvic rotations accelerated in improbable rapidity. Peki witnessed the lascivious display in alternate detachment and undisguised enjoyment. The lovers' bodies juddered in an erotic earthquake. Their fucking was like a fray. He became overwhelmed with stupefaction at the salacious spectacle. He knelt on the clay and began jacking off, thrilled in his voy-eurism. They stopped dead in their tracks when he manifested out of the foliage. Their surprise was followed by fury, caused by having been interrupted. Their sorrowfully aborted sex was his fault. He strode toward them and introduced himself with an operatic flourish, arriving like a warhorse summoned by the bugle. They gauged skeptically the compact individual by whom they were confronted. His fatigues were lamentably loose-fitting, boots too big, and the beret is worn at a rakish angle. He was euphoric from the coca. He was distracted for a split second by the rainbow colors at his vision's periphery. His pintle was as erect as a grenadier. The pair leaped up and smiled sheepishly. They attempted in vain to cover their nether parts with their hands, looking around, frantically, for potential escape routes. The discourse between them was intense. His integument broke out into a deluge of diaphoresis. Both were still and silent, mouths agape. His lewd verbiage shocked the susceptible kids' sensibilities. He felt parboiled in the heat. The haze vibrated. He endured hallucinations incomprehensible and horrifying. He deliquesced in the inferno of psychedelic abstraction. Trees were transformed into rare and wondrous things. An incorporeal skeletal black stallion left at the gallop. Pebbles were metamorphosed into marmosets. He was persecuted by stinging bugs. He sang breathily in an altered state. It was a metaphysical cosmos where nothing was solid. Telephone poles belly danced in a pasquinade of seduction. Mailboxes flowed not unlike liquid. Gusts chanted. A scene of brutality transpired in the luxuriant growth. Peki thrashed them, his orbs rotating in their sockets. Zara and Hugo prayed, howled, wept, and pleaded. The scenario was evocative of a sadomasochistic bacchanalia. Strenuously they begged him to let them leave. He was anxious to avoid lengthy explanations for their behavior. He slit her nose with a switchblade, and an uncontrollable sanguinary stream spilled. Pop-eyed with pain, she pressed a kerchief he gave her to the wound. He spoke icily. He beat them about the head with a bat while they endeavored to shield themselves with their arms. They crossed themselves vigorously. A rapturous grimace spread across his rictus. They were fallen cherubim. His visage was set with the zealous delight of murderous rage. The twosome squealed like pigs, their limbs flailing. He roped them to a spruce. The flagellant used a bullwhip to draw claret rivulets of blood from their flesh. The victims' screeches supplied him with vocalized intimations of the torments of purgatory. Hugo had a seraphic voice.

Zara had a charming lisp. Their matching pink pajamas and slippers were piled on the argil. He sought fulfillment and consolation, flogging them, observing the blood springing from their skin. They were severed from life by death. Afterward, he tried to resuscitate the dignity of the original occasion of sightseeing by apologizing to himself and taking out the binoculars. The violence of this land is legendary. He was just adding to it. He surveyed the human carnage and sobbed. The insatiable swelter crept into his being and melted his heart. Mirages quivered and illusory high-rises materialized. He beheld a pastoral idyll. He felt as if he had gotten third-degree burns from the sun. He was slow as an ox. He fell unconscious in the shade. He lurched to his feet and leaned heavily on a sapling for support. He persevered because dusk provided cool relief… and opportunities for the homicidal rampage. His energy was sustained by exemplary zest. On the way home, he came across broken children and ravaged parents. There was much poverty and desperation. Peki imagined crucifying himself in an imitation of Christ. He glowed in anticipation of a fiesta at the bordello, the drunkenness, and orgiastic excess… He lapsed into a perturbed unconsciousness… He hears Stockhausen on the stereo, loving the strident levels of musical cacophony. His shining pate vanishes in combed-over strands. He puckers up his face from the unusual effects of the uncut crack upon his unpracticed psyche. His sweat has a sweet aroma. He believes he has an impressive chestful of hair. He chugs a jug of aniseed water, stuck in the pit of dejection. Negligently inert, he alas decides to ransack his brains for Butyrum ideas until inspiration hits him. He is a warlock on account of his marvelous mantequilla inventions. He is aimless in glum reflection. His enthusiasm for committing mortal sin can only be extinguished if he gets busted. Thanks to his butter, he transcends all glory. Harrowing cogitations formulate themselves in his mind. He thinks of syphilis and gonorrhea and wants to cry. He is the Prince of Darkness. In a stupor, he slumps in the seat. He sleeps like a baby, saliva drooling onto the cushion. He wakes, gulps jujubes, and subsequently has nightmarish visions, induced by the hotness and stimulants.

Billie Rufer

Law enforcement is the cock block/beaver dam to a true celebration of his prosperity. Peki is scared of being arrested and condemned for his sins. The cheap effects in the store are so bad even Ed Wood would have asked for reshoots, so he has to make improvements in that area. He writes concepts for his product on a pad, his pen flowing with his brain. Schemes swirl in his skull. His encephalon is in edifying lucidity; however, he wishes to retire to his bed. He scribbles furiously. This is Satan's work. He has committed uncountable atrocities. In the fungal space of the forsaken greenhouse, with its roof of woven palm, he molders in dank silence. Concepts waft in his cranium like smoke. He devours guava. A padded jacket is around his waist. He's garbed in a clerical gown and priestly shoes. His stocking cap is fraying about the rim. His armpits are redolent of bitter fruits. He bolts a plantain with appreciation and swigs the gourd of soda. The sun sets on the peaks. The world is at the point of dusk. A summit contains his spirit. His pies mist with sorrow, experiencing horrendous loneliness. He hunches his shoulders, reconciling himself to the idea of a night spent here. His jockeys muddle with his socks on the futon mattress. Stars brighten as matches flared. A shorthaired, flea-bitten tabby cat with one missing eye stealthily struts on through. Peki reads a pornographic magazine, pondering the glossy photos of the splayed lovelies, his saucered peepers catching flashes of radiance. He can't recollect much of anything from the previous week. The blackouts are getting worse. His waistcoat reeks of an infant accident. A basalt dildo on a vinyl thong is found on the floor. He fails to connect the dots.

He must've done a disgraceful deed in the lost period. The grinding of his teeth sounds not unlike the scratching of a mouse. He recalls being bombed on lamp oil, engaged, in a friendly fashion, in a wrestling match in the oppressive jungle. She was Billie. Her hair was like a bird's nest and she lived in a dormant volcano. She had an alpaca aspect. Wrinkles of caducity divided her youngness. She had this grayish pallor. The thatch of her tress had streaks of silver. There was salt, slime, and dust everywhere. The songbirds and howler monkeys performed their numbers. Her speech soothed like susurration. She wore a kaftan to the ground and was discalced. He had on a dunce's hat and nothing else. The names of his victims were tattooed on his integument. Usually, she walked with a leopard and secured the trails. He got emotional because she was so uniquely comely. His ears were clogged and his throat was sore. He believed they had become one another's souls. His being felt like a calcified shell. She told tales the whole time, ancient stories of her people. She was like the light and the breeze than they themselves. Her fingernails were like meat hooks. She treaded through the trees, imitating, accurately, the animals. They focused their attention on the spume of the sea. A sylph had a child's body, a hawk's head, and a fish's tail, playing with a bamboo flute on the beach. A harpy cheepily distributed information. Cumulus clouds were sky-hills he wanted to climb. There were rolling mounts in the velvety darkness. Peki noticed that Billie bled between her legs. She gave birth to probability. The ethereal lady turned bread to skin and wine to blood. She talked about breeding dogs and danced and sang. There were lots of questions on his part and few answers on hers. Miracles were executed upon a high place, a chalet built upon a steep rocky prominence. The noxious fumes of burning fat assailed his nares. She smacked her lips in the wilderness. He digested her anecdotes in quiescence, affecting an expression of resignation. He felt injured in the chest. His mind dwelled on the temptation of the flesh. She became thunder and lightning when he came on to her. Instinctively he knew that practical application of his suggestion, conveyed by dint of sign language, would lead to deplorable consequences. Vehemently he protested his innocence. She demanded proof. He had none. She offered him free passage and was perfidiously slain. Then he threw himself on a funeral pyre and arose with a merry heart. He said goodbye to the deserted and diseased townsfolk assembled at a gaily painted bus, a statue of The Virgin Mary in the driver's seat... At dawn, bathing in the creek, Peki pretends he is being baptized. He studies his reflection in the water until he doesn't recognize it. Insects sound like a sawmill. A flock of macaws soars overhead. Something unidentifiable concerns him. It is like a persistent voice, nagging him, barely within earshot. The predator scours the slums and sewers for prey. Whereupon he roams the countryside, doing things for which he'd be incarcerated in the burg. Cirri billow like a mass of pondweed or rotten fabric.

Hedley

Toad-puffy, Peki wets his whistle in the vegetable garden. His passage, from there to here, is comparable to that of a Horseman of the Apocalypse. He has the sensation that his domestic existence is stained with indelible ink. Marisa is currently living in seclusion. Serves her right for treating him with such disdain. He didn't leave her high and dry; she's got enough to get by on. The shop brings in a comfortable income. She's been in a constant bad mood, tense not unlike a feline ready to pounce, and endlessly complaining. She sobbed like some village lass as he packed his bags. Meanwhile, he appeared as if he had fallen into a trance, or had a frightful secret he was on the verge of sharing. He is so tired of the quarreling, sick of the games, disgusted by her outbursts, and weary of the apartment and its stifling environment. He is absorbed in rumination, pondering on the potential for his business. He was planning on unveiling the Butyrum for a long time, weighing every detail, suffering grinding days and sleepless nights, praying to any higher power that would hear him until his larynx went, and waiting for what seemed to be an eternity for a sign: the harlot, Cristina Cabo, the one who laughed at him. He disposed of her and used her adipose tissue to make a batch of butter. Sampling the stuff, he experienced the most exceptional taste that ever reached his palate. Mother's milk in the form of mantequilla. Customers unwittingly endorsed this undertaking, and he realized from that point on that there wasn't anyone or anything that could stop him. And he wept with joy. Inspiration, he thinks, is the axis around which any idea should rotate. He envisages his peers encompassing him to do him homage and honor, congratulating him on his success. He is the symbol around which butter revolves. In reality, his competition would relish dragging him through the mud. These odious imbeciles, a negligible circle of shits, would revel in demeaning him, mocking his product, and ridiculing his store. He would make them swallow their crap. He wouldn't be able to wait to shut the dolts up once and for all! Their dressings-down verge on the violent. Hedley is reflected in the pupils of his nostalgic eyes, gleaming like sapphires. In a singsong voice, she recites vulgar, ornate verses, contemplating the imposing cathedral in the main square, which is the heart of the city. It is a construction made by masterful masons… Peki may have a torturous mind, but he gets the poesy. He is culturally confident, wise and clever from the books he's read and the music he's listened to. Her dentition is regular. Her moue is almost imperceptible. She's rigidly upright and elongated. Her anatomic outlines, under the cover of garb, hint at soft curves. He considers her sober fizzog and slightly curvilinear shape. She is so fascinating that he prolongs their discourse to enjoy her while she speaks. Her companionship is valuable, and he doesn't have to pay for it. She holds him spellbound. He looks at her as though she is the embodiment of a message he uncoded. Their words flow like the waters of a river. He avoids mentioning his madre like a leper. They drink out of the bottle as if celebrating a victory. The meal she has prepared is fit for the gods. She jumps rope, utilizing a grapevine, under laurel leaves. He, beneath the starry heavens, dances about exuberantly, the bald spot in the middle of his head showing. A young couple has a heated dispute, the veins in their necks bulging. The nightmarish individuals, these unfortunate creatures, wearing rags, are so emaciated they could slip cleanly through Peki's finger ring as easily as diving through a hoop. They are damnable visions. The living skeletons surpass anything human, their bones, because the flesh is so taut, are practically countable. Their expressions are in a perpetual grimace. They have sunken eyes and withered dermis. The ayahuasca (a psychoactive tea) he'd glugged cause his mind to conjure the teratoid corpses. The figments are indicative of his brain's proclivities. He's in a sorry state. The haunting figures make a lamentable spectacle on the paved street. And he goes on a blow binge.

472

Peki compares himself to the crippled Hephaestus, hammering together his warped and magnificent product. His brain beats like his heart. Lust, he thinks, is a salve for loneliness. After a self-administered electroconvulsive shock treatment (with the assistance of a hemorrhoidal human, a chronic stutterer who plays the harp), he returns to Hedley's place.

Hedley appears livid as if confronted by Death itself. Peki ambulates around her digs, a pleasant townhouse, while she stays intractably seated in an old easy chair. Vexed, her disquiet manifests in communications of unconstrained gestures. She can be a fury when pushed. His brain can't make up its mind if she's real or not. His organs of visual perception aren't reliable at this juncture. He talks in a stentorian intonation, querulous and prolix, delirious on psychedelics. He walks like a foreigner who has lost his way. For a change, he is clad simply and neatly. His attitude is pompous and affected. His belch sounds like it's expelled from the middle of his gullet. His spiel is an endless syllabled rosary. Following his rant, he reflects. The vacuum of his Mama's absence is meaningful. A striking procession of ideas goes through his skull. Furrows form on his brow. His peepers are protuberant. He muses on his establishment. In his business, his back against the wall, he came out swinging with bare fists, a brave warrior with intestinal fortitude and inexhaustible energy. He has made a career virtually out of nothing, building it from the ground up. He is in a stupor because of the liquor and narcotics. He's sick to death of the filth and poverty of the metropolis. A violinated ditty is auscultated. The instrument is out of tune, played by an aged guy on the corner, installed on the curb and under the pressure of the sun's shafts. He has a repugnant mouth and decayed teeth. He is as thin as a reptile and has bulging pies and a ferrety face. The music takes a part of the manikin's soul, just as he cuts pieces of fat from his victims. A juggler converses with a harlequin, both on break from entertaining pedestrians. Light slumbers on his countenance. He feels shaken like a rag doll. He's dying for a breath of fresh air to cast out his doldrums. There are damp stains on the paneling of the vast boudoir. A desk is situated underneath the pane. Portraits of people, rendered excellently in pen and ink, hang on the wine-painted walls. Peki's unexpected modesty is moving to her. Hedley showers praise on him. She is stewed to the gills, glugging Hennessy like OJ. In rough shape, she is also on illegal substances. He is dead tired. He hasn't had a single bite of food in a bit, shut up in his room drinking and drugging. These insectoid images swarm in his cranium. He stares at her with deep affection. He rouses himself from absorption to regard her thick thighs. He observes in her a desolation he identifies with. They look like despairing lovers. She is uniquely alluring and sturdy. Her plenteous rosy skin is partly covered by some Roman tunic. She excites his blood. She is attractive and seductive. He wants to rub her buttocks like the relics of a saint. Her bosom is bounteous. She has a come-hither smile. Booze slides into his stomach. Her legs, built not unlike oak beams, get his attention. Her belly is as ample as human desire. He causes her to split her sides laughing at his quick jokes. She's noisily flirty. Her keester is as large and round as a wheel on Apollo's chariot. Her hair is tied back in a pigtail. Her oculi are wide and vivacious and radiate charm. He occupies himself by ogling her beefy hips and meaty feet, running the risk of being taken for a perverted fetishist. The laces of her sandals twine above her ankles and nest her calves. Her nose is short and straight. She is a divine being adored on this earth. He's transfixed by her expression. The effects of the intoxicants enliven their convo. She gazes with conspiratorial eyes at him. She is very much an affable person. She is known to be tyrannized by poor habits. Under the influence, he looks at her as though through opera glasses. He envisions his trunk hammering on hers as on an anvil during sex. His pisser is an arrow meant to be shot at a target — her twat. She drifts off. Sober-faced, he gets a sniff of impoverishment, a combination of a thousand abnormal odors, the sources unidentifiable and intimate, assembled in the clammy air. He notices the river's flow. It is a mad world, he thinks. She has a tousled shock and heavy sweat and succulent snatch. The morning was relatively warm. Now it is extraordinarily hot. It is fully dark. The back road is impressively lit, owed to the new streetlamps. The heat hasn't diminished in its intensity.

Hedley's nude derrière leads him to her the way a lighthouse's beacon guides a ship to port. Peki is dressed in his customary peculiar apparel. His flatus sounds like peals of laughter. He welcomes her companionship.

He had been sealing himself up in the lab for so long and not wanting to see anybody. When he first popped up here, at the garret, her temporary lodgings, he was so begrimed with soil after digging a grave To deposit his latest victim that it took a few baths to become clean again... He believes he is a contamination incarnate. He knows he is a monster. The devil exists. Like Lucifer, he is not sorry for the atrocious sins he has committed. He has suffered many tragedies. He's on intimate terms with sorrow. He honestly doesn't know how he survived. He fails to banish the blasphemous thoughts from his head. There is an explosion at the gunpowder factory in a poor district. Rubbish spins about in a whirlwind. Teenage girls, in their private school attire, empty-headed young ladies to him, and so full of themselves, make the racket of a flock of hens, under a faint sun. Urchins, assembling in the center of town, resemble angels. Militiamen chat up fishwives. Peki's eyes are riveted on Hedley, his mug turning scarlet. Perspiring copiously, he ogles her with true pleasure. His boner reaches higher than the Tower of Babel. Her bare feet reek of ringworm and burning wood. He gorges on her with a voracious appetite, accompanying his kisses with caresses, taking advantage of intervals to speak freely about this, that, and the other thing. Butt-fucked on the towel, she guffaws uproariously at the remarks spoken by him into her ear. His fingers, agile and lively, move frantically up and down her spinal cord. She titters, her toes curled. He enjoys her to the point of exhaustion. The sodomy has a slowness that occurs only in dreams. His lips brush hers. The intercourse is exasperatingly arhythmic. Sucking him off, she makes these mellifluent noises, the notes like they're falling asleep on his prick. Shivers race on his vertebrae when she tongues his hole and laps his gonads. She allows a glorious assault on her body. Their mouths meet, humming like bees. She has a missing incisor. The pair pump like people possessed. Their orbs are wet with tears of bliss. She is at once oddly encouraging and defiant. He holds her hands as if they are pricy jewels. This is a perverse game he wants to win. She fulfills his wishes. He loves her firm flesh. The attic apartment has the sour and stale odor of a public library. There's enough produce on the counter to supply a grocery store. Hedley glides like a ghost. Peki snorts lines of her dandruff, a fair quantity, off a glossy mag while she has liqueurs. She is sweet and serene, wearing knee breeches and a halter top, ensconced on the varnished bench. Her coiffure is fantastic, in his estimation. She has the air of a celestial. He strokes his dick. The couple sing and dance as though attending a carnival, chorusing jubilantly. The marble floor is polished, the colored slabs arranged in geometrical shapes. The ceiling is decorated with lavish moldings of plaster covered in Klimtian gold leaf. A chunklet of shade looks like the sinister shape of a guillotine's blade. He feels as if he's on the razor's edge, for the situation with his rivals is touchy. It is difficult and dangerous. They'd gladly devour him and spit him out. He won't let it happen. He is too industrious and clever. Competition between him and his colleagues is fierce. He is enemy number one. He continues to survive their slander and lies. He must watch his step at all times. He could get knifed to death by some adversarial fanatic. His opponents are driven by envy. They act like he has stolen the credit for innovation that they deserve! He cannot reconcile himself to their frankly ludicrous conduct. They glare at him at conventions with hatred in their eyes. He just keeps his trap shut. They despise him. So what? He'll live. He doesn't have ill-gotten gains; quite to the contrary. He is piling up a fortune for himself and makes no apologies. As far as problems go, he has encountered several on his way to wealth. There were leaks in numerous places in his life. He is surprised his stupendous store never sank! The holes are plugged. A deplorable dwarf has become a famous businessman. He is a friend of the folks. He's adored by the plebs and the politicians. He spares neither effort nor resources to provide premium stuff for his shoppers. Experimentation ideations occupy his encephalon. Hey, he is revolutionizing mantequilla production and sales. And his counterparts are left in the dust. They are the tortoises and he is the hare in this lopsided race. The knowledge that has eluded everyone for decades on end now belongs solely to him. Although he certainly didn't discover the spread, he can explain what its discovery means for civilization. He is ambitious for glory, eager for his name to go down in history. His product circulates like coins among the inhabitants of the megapolis. Word of his commodity is spreading not unlike fire. He is carrying out his obligation to the clientele. His preposterous plans are panning out. Dawn is mild and gray. The megalopolis is sad. Peki is lying in the small bed. Hedley is at his side, snoring under the sheet. She has a voluptuous figure and magnificent tits. Her curves could arouse the interest of any male or female. An absurd idea crosses his mind to masturbate on her exposed foot. He dismisses it and slips into his tricolored trousers. The gilded-framed mirror contains his reflection. He is apparently ingenuous and noble. He thinks his profile hardly mitigates his ugliness. He evaluates himself as though he is some revolting specimen at a zoo. The room has identical large windows, three chaise longues, and a square and clumsy table. People multiply on the patio below, not unlike mushrooms in autumn. He quaffs cognac out of a cup, absorbed in thought. Then he plunks himself on the commode and takes a dump. The crap looks like sloppily stacked firewood. He pores over the minute details of the next batch of Butyrum, just as a theater director goes over the script before the performance of a play. His lamps are reddened with fatigue. Wrinkles furrow his forehead. The sun is red like an apple. He is tempted to permit her the privilege of witnessing one of the most amazing phenomena ever to have taken place in the fascinating science that is art: the making of butter, a poetic product, an essential edible substance. She would applaud enthusiastically and bow from the waist.

Peki had this bizarre dream, in which he was using artificial saliva as eyedrops while being chased on side streets by Mary Tyler Moore, who was trying to throw her hat onto his head as if it was in some weird on-the-move version of ring toss. A terrible migraine torments him. The pain won't subside, in spite of the myriad remedies attempted, including warm/cold compresses, fruit rinds, fresh meats, a heating pad, and an ice pack... all in vain. There is a stubbornness to his attitude, battling through the monstrous headache, refusing to yield so much as a centimeter in his resolve. He scratches his itchy balls. Sometimes, when it comes to making his product, he's spinning his wheels when he needs to hit the ground running. Despite the run of problems he has encountered along the way, owing to the dangers inherent in his homicidal activities, he is overseeing a profitable establishment. If his profession was school, as far as academic achievement goes, he would give himself high honors for execution and low marks for discipline. He requires fat. People have it. As though in obedience to an obscure guiding principle, he goes to perfervid lengths to ensure his quarries don't suffer too much. He takes great care to skirt any subject whose demise might be stimulating to him. He thinks of his barbarous deeds... A series of memories come to his mind, the majority of them unpleasant. He always has a strange feeling the disposing of his victims' bodies, whether sinking them in a swamp or stuffing them in a dumpster, as if he's abandoning babies on the doorstep of an orphanage just after they're born. He keeps a ferret's eye out for the cops. The punishment he metes out to his prey... His life has taken a radical turn that has made him more content than he ever suspected he could be. His existence has purpose and meaning. Butter has cleared the path for him. He has embarked on a fabulous journey fighting for his product. On the other hand, his managerial effort has lessened by a fair amount. In fact, he barely invests much of himself when on the sales floor, which is a rare sighting recently. He finds this part of the job tedious. The shop is prospering wildly. The refrigerated stockroom is chockablock with Butyrum. Shelves occupy the entire area out back. Things are improving considerably in the place. He remembers being on the point of going under. Lately, he has been slipping in and out of the joint like a shadow. He loves giving a boot up the behinds of his rivals. They are extremely embittered and incompetent. He finds these contests with adversarial operations exciting, with the giving-and-taking, as though their livelihoods depend on it. Strength and will prevail. It is not unlike chess in super slow motion. Consumers are the spectators cheering them on. Their ardor does not influence the results. And there are no rematches. He unquestionably deserves to celebrate his victories. He deems himself the most daring and original thinker (out of the box) of his generation, fusing ancient and modern ideas to create something new. He endeavors to maintain that balance. What he does is not for the timid or the fainthearted. The standard system, the across-the-board approach to mantequilla creation, upheld and preserved by the division of powers in the field, is antiquated. He's becoming a living legend in the city. No one can hold a candle to him. His scandalous conduct (firsthand acquaintances with a goodly number of ladies of the night, lest we forget his propensity for complete dissipation) does not affect his status one iota. His boorish behavior causes a veritable furor in the aristocratic and bourgeois circles around town. He makes many enemies. He swears to change the future of Spain and perhaps the whole world. He toils like a mule and acts like a madman. These are insane times and he's fitting in perfectly. He shoulders the burden of innovation. Periodically he feels hopeless, akin to a eunuch trying to impregnate, or a useless idler. He thinks of his forewoman on all fours. Lively as a child, fiery as the devil, short and stocky, fair-haired and rosily-complected, Valeria, his assistant manager, cleaves the air when she stomps in her clodhoppers. Her wit is sharper than a Ginsu, and she has an inclination for rebellion and fits of temper; however, she is dependable and competent, thus invaluable. She never complains when she has to work OT. She goes about each shift as if it were her last. It is always full speed ahead. When off the clock, she can be as docile as a lamb. Her eyes dominate her frontage. She has a head reminiscent of a cannonball and a birdie bill. Her face is flat and full as the moon and her derma layer is ruined by smallpox. She is raspy-voiced. Once a week they play handball on a nearby gymnasium's court. Peki is lightning-fast and it wouldn't be an exaggeration to say he is almost unbeatable. He feels a religious veneration for his employees. They represent the best the country has to offer. They don't have a dishonest bone in their body. These apprentices would never swindle their master. The urban area is an illimitable pigsty. Citizens are like rats. A rash of disturbances is taking place. Peki and Hedley attack the booze and narcotics with the same gusto they had shown in fornicating a while before. They jabber, animated by the stimulants. She is dressed in snowy colors. He's wearing austere clothing. His mouth is an obscene mound. He has a majestic bearing, only his homeliness is as absolute as death. He writes spicy and piquant poetry, teeming with erotic imagery, for her, penned with eloquence and detail that leaves little for the reader's imagination. The style is elegantly sober. He is off like a shot...

Life wrings Peki out like a towel it is trying to hand dry, straining to get every drop out of him. Almost every night, after he is finished a hard day's labor, Hedley attempts to be supportive of his efforts. At the laboratory, he feels like a mole living in a garden. A hermit, hermetically sealed in that place, a Holy Land, his big head is crammed with thoughts. One can't fathom the sheer volume of Butyrum, an unsurpassable product, he has concocted in that place! He struts around as if he is the only person in the universe who prepares butter! He wishes to be left alone in peace, busying himself with making mantequilla. It compliantly permits itself to be fussed with, and demanded nothing from him in return, revealing its secrets, in the creation process, changing its states of taste and texture, transformed into the splendid yellow edible fatty substance. He has the vitality to toil and handle the loneliness into which his concepts, increasingly radical and irreverent as time passes, are leading him, effectively alienating his madre, who has wound up warier of him than the plague... He broods about his remembrances. Marisa, with nothing on, was supine on the mattress, panting with pleasure. It was like death was waiting around the corner for her she looked so wasted. The aroma of her genitals pleased him. She unleashed peals of laughter when he tickled her hip. He wished to drill her throat with his penis, then bury it in her vagina. She uttered this nonsensical shit. A tremendous vision (a mirage?), she suggested a human ostrich. He stood in the passageway that had the shape of a semicircular arch. Similar rooms were bare and gloomy and illuminated by these crude tallow candles. There was a set of roughhewn chairs... Horny, he hyperventilated, and his lungs could scarcely take in a breath of oxygen. His heart throbbed. His erection vibrated not unlike a tuning fork. His dart-all-day eyes and grasp-at-air of a hand all aggravated. Time flowed at a different speed, as in dreams. He saw with her eyes, heard with her ears, thought with her brain, felt with her hands... two minds were one... Was he crazy as a loon? Her inflection sounded enfeebled as though it was issued from a sickbed. She seemed frail, swallowed by a sheet. A moue materialized on her lips. His tool was stiffened by the proximity of her. He stepped in a mechanical, maybe military motion. Enervated, feeling like he was at death's door, he collapsed like a house without a foundation. In her arms he was relieved, refreshed, feeling as if his moral burdens were lifted. Dawn caught them unawares, both still in deep conversation and sex. During intercourse, they listed together from side to side like a ship at sea. They were so immersed in intimacy that the flies didn't even dare buzz for fear of disturbing them. Words

poured forth frantically from their mouths. Their mating was powerful and emotional. She was submissive and reserved and had a semblance of humility and discretion. He squeezed her like a sponge. The copulation was a mix of comedy and opera. She struggled under him as a feline pinned. Coming in simultaneity, she cried out at the top of her lungs, drowning out his hoots. Mother and son were plastered. The syllables fell like snowflakes. Her questions went unanswered. Moon was a dead-white eyeball. The horizon was a rosy pink. Yelling at Marisa, Peki sounded like Moses pillorying a Jew. She admitted she saw him as a parasite encysted in the flat that should be extirpated. Nothing he said was worth a hill of beans. He was a powder keg on the brink of exploding in that insane asylum of an apartment. She was dour and phlegmatic. It was a catastrophe for him being so closely related to her. She was myopic and inane. It was as though she wasn't seeing him, her orbs gazing at what was going on in her noggin. She blew on the scalding liquid steaming in the stoup. She repeated his speech like a parrot. Stupefied on her medications, her head was emptier than a tramp's stomach. She acted as if he was a deadly bore. The argument was aggressive and penetrating. They waged a war and fought for the same cause: their petty interests. He had the sensation of being Perseus confronted by a monster. They got involved in a Byzantine discussion. When they started to trade insults, he left...
Hedley is endeavoring to be more patient with Peki and less critical than his mother. It is a real challenge. He is tense and expectant. His gut is round as a melon. With the acid reflux, his midsection feels like a boiler about to blow. The vein in his temple is on the cusp of bursting. He is grotesque and yet she is spellbound. His incredibly ugly frontal is somehow appealing to her. His expression of lugubriousness is as characteristic of him as his small size. He stares into space and farts at the four winds. He has a lively interest in erotic acrobatics with her. She racks her noodle in search of the right thing to say to him. She has a dignified bearing. He feels like a living fossil next to her. From her lofty height, she remarks his avid glances. The slum is becoming too crowded. The worst scum seemingly populates this section. Some of the swine here are his worst enemies. He floats in the air like a bubble. He recollects the nightmare in which he had castrated himself with his own bare hands. He has the

481

fever dreams of a madman. He has this sensation of his being in incompleteness, like a song being cut off before its final notes. Home is where his heart is. He imagines Marisa's face, looking literally crushed at times, like her cheekbones have shattered, like something inside has collapsed, structural integrity breached. The deterioration continues… She is a misty wisp that threatens to solidify. The guttural beats and white noise pierces through quiescence and isolated sounds not unlike a mournful wail and a knife plunging through flesh echo, producing a distinct sense of discomfort. He runs as though he's chasing someone, or like he's trying to beat the clock, or as if he's fleeing in a total fight-or-flight panic.

The Concubine

Romina, with coffee-colored locks, has the inexhaustible grace of the Virgin. Grinning cheerfully, she is clad in a classy outfit of blue velvet, striding with a firm step down the sumptuous corridor of the immense edifice after servicing an ill-shaved, elderly CEO with no ears on a crude table. She is so adorable she could turn a sculpture's head. She chomps on sweetmeats and roasted chestnuts and cradles a rag doll with this tiny wig. Peki espies her swaggering in stilettos on the esplanade. Ardor, he concludes, degrades a person's reason and disables his/her senses. His throat dry, he downs his canteen of tap water. Peddlers abound and mill about. Serious as a singer debuting at the opera, he pushes through the throng, intent on doing her grave harm, his hand grasping the horny handle of the dagger concealed in his toga, black as pitch, worried that he is as conspicuous as a beggar at a royal hall, and approaches her. Crippled by insecurity, her gentleness brings him out of his paralysis. Alone with her, in the redwoods and evergreens, he gives a cattish leap, grabs her shoulder, pulls her toward him, close to his chest, and thrusts the blade into her side. She cries out and staggers, pressing her palm to the wound. She loses her balance. Then he removes the blade and plunges it into her abdomen, the cutter delivered into her gut lightning-swift. She reels. He stabs her thrice in the back and she stumbles, neighing. Everything happens in the span of an instant. Standing stock-still, he considers the weapon, pleased that it fulfilled the function it was meant to serve. He watches her, floundering, whining, and bleeding, overcome by pain and panic, as though he is in disbelief at what he has done. Her injuries will surely prove to be mortal ones. He sinks into a state of anxiety. Children caper in the piazza. A manure cart is drawn by an ox. Thunder sounds not unlike the roll of drums. Peki kneels before Romina and raises his eyes to the skies, commending her cunt to her Creator. He whispers a promise to soon alleviate her torment. She looks dejected, her eyes brimming with tears. She utters the words "Mummy" and "Daddy," leaving him deeply disturbed. He places a crucifix before her lips to devotedly kiss. She nods weakly and whimpers. Though disconcerted, he is determined not to lose his composure. He concentrates on her indifferent expression, lying in a pool of her blood. It seems as though she no longer exists. Is her soul far away, at the pearly gates? She emits an emotionless shout. He believes his sin doesn't deserve a confession. After all, he's merely a butter fanatic inflamed by a passion for the product. And now the procedure to extract her suet is to be repeated, step by step, rung by rung, as enshrined by tradition. Any detail, whether minor or major, that's left out could disturb his work. He performs the solemn task with self-control and a steady pulse, looking hypnotized. Whereupon he has a vision of himself chained in a dungeon, his already-deformed body further mangled by torture, these cruel punishments inflicted upon him for the monstrous crimes against humanity he has committed. The law would no doubt prescribe a death sentence in his case. He would surely suffer before being executed. There would be no chance for appeal, no opportunity for clemency, and no plea of insanity would be heard by any judge and jury. He'd be condemned to die a slow death. He is waging a war on the competition, and he sees victory with increasing clarity, knowing that he will cause the collapse of the many-year reign of the powerful margarine companies. The silence of the Mexican victim communicates itself to the perpetrator. She's so tanned that she reminds him of some bronze Greek statue. He feels both guilt and pity. A long rosary hangs from his wrist. Nervously he paws at her bounteous bosom. She prays with her eyes half-closed. Her face is acneously pitted under the layers of pancake. She inhales and exhales clouds of steam from her widened nostrils when chunks of flesh the size of grapefruit are sliced from her tummy and tushie.

Peki's mien is a mix of pleasure, fear, and amazement, digging into the blubber of her stomach. Romina gasps and groans. The instrument he employs is made with superb craftsmanship. He has a hankering for onion soup with grated cheese, spicy beef in slices of fried bread, and dessert as pastry slathered in blackberry jelly. He speaks quietly, wanting to show respect for her. She breathes rapidly. This atrocity is occurring. He is solely responsible. He's astonished that she is still alive. Holy Christ. Unfortunately, he doesn't have time to wait for her to properly perish. It is important to take from her what is required. The shop must survive. He finds himself in a good predicament. To wit, the product is being picked off the shelves like fruit from trees. And the stock is running low. She is the string he is forced to tug on to undo the knot. Her anatomy has splendidly balanced proportions. The lines of her contours are like they were laid down by an expert geometer. The carving of her ass is abrupt and sadistic. She lets out an earsplitting peal of agony. He guffaws as if he heard the funniest joke in his whole life. She sighs and shudders. Her resistance flees, yielding its place to acceptance. He takes a swig of a nip of mint lacquer. The sweet liquid is tasty. Drinking on the job is rarely an issue for him. He breaks into hearty laughter, given to boasting, going on about the Butyrum while tirelessly operating on her hips. He doesn't wait for her reply, hacking into her nates with a meat cleaver. He inspects every part that he removes of her, testing the portion with his nose, dilating his nostrils in a mistrustful manner. Slaughtering the innocent is becoming a daily and nightly ritual. He performs gruesome surgery on her breasts and buttocks. He will bet she is a warm and generous lady. He surveys her large lamps, enormous mouth, and little limbs. He could down her in a single gulp. His fervent wish is to fuck her. Darkness plummets. It is a sultry evening. Peki's more inexpressive than ever. Suddenly, Romina sports a sarcastic smile, followed by a sneer of disgust. She talks in a snide tone of voice. He clasps her to him and holds her tight as she fades. She is light as a feather. The sounds she distributes are the songs of a siren to drive the dwarfish Odysseus crazy. The cadence is precise, the harmony celestial, and the melody delightful. He observes her voluptuous volume, experiencing a queer sensation, faintly illuminated in the moon's glow. He brutally yanks off her skimpy underpants (rolled at her thighs) and mounts her. His virile member pierces her, nestling inside her, and he pumps with prodigious speed. His rhythm is in time to his craving. They heave frantically. Their movements are violent. His apron is splattered with her blood. Does she think he's irredeemably ugly? He wonders. Her delectable neck smells of peaches. She has a kind calf's eyes and is short in stature. Her skin is apple-fresh-and-smooth. A set of dimples are formed in her cheeks. Her hind is round and sturdy. Her avid lips are on his. Her feet have the texture of parchment. For him, it's like lying on a cloud of cotton. They couple with a robustness that can only come from knowing that they are eternal. Her knockers are dry as grapes left out in the sun. He explodes when she tongues his pucker. It is an intense and prolonged climax. His nuts feel like globs of phosphorus bursting in the oxygen after having been taken from a vessel of oil. Orgasming, his being is burnt to cinders. He is instantaneously incinerated. He tries to calm her, console her, speaking in this cavernous vox, but she too is reduced to ashes. Her tresses are tangled. He spends minutes in rapt appreciation of her. His fundament is an angel sounding a terrible trumpet. They fornicate until they are exhausted. Dawn breaks and she is deceased. He has what he needs from her. She will subsist in his yellow spread. He views the constellation of Orion. Cars advance clumsily and implacably on the strip of road. Peki traverses a broad, flat expanse after pitting Romina's remains, along with her rag doll, in a flimsy burial pit. They could've been mistaken for a pair of cuddling lovers. He whistles a popular tune. The heart of the sun palpably beats. Locusts engulf the verdure. He is scared the earth might swallow him up. He feels as though his hard flesh has softened like it's made of wax. Hail is not unlike a rain of bullets. Peki dines in a tavern, partaking in a delicious dish. His head feels like an egg slowly cracking. The ideas for mantequilla are incubated in his cerebrum. Images of Romina repeat themselves monotonously in his melon. She occupies his thoughts and therefore thrills him. The picture of her nests in his encephalon like a grub in a pear. Her fat will enrich the Butyrum to the heights of the sublime. Her eyes were green as olives... He vows to prosper in civilization, adapting to the modern era, and leaving the primitive age behind. Writing in his notebook, he describes in a succinct, cryptic style, the number of ingredients he wants to include in the next butter batch. He scarfs down crawfish and champagne. Back home, his gonads exquisitely empty, his mind totally at peace, he sips boiling-hot poppy tea and falls fast asleep, to regain the strength the slut sapped. When he wakes in the morning, shaken by his imperious and perverted mother, he sobs bitterly and deliberately slams his brow against the bedside table. He feels as though he's sliding downward as if on a corkscrew's spiral. Romana was soft as tapioca. There's a persistent hum of hovering flies. He notices the rotten plants and maggots in the fruit.

Peki's Journal

Adjusting lifestyles always affects our attitude toward nutrition. Values and/ or intimacy associated with the foods we as a society eat, have largely been washed away by a desire for easier and less time-consuming preparations. We have traded in our 'larder' for refrigerators and keep foods for lengths of time unimaginable seventy-five years ago. What we eat these days is based on convenience. Inherently, ready-to-eat foods are what we'll reach for when we feel the need to "fill the gap." Aspartame, monosodium glutamate, synthesized vitamins, and a host of preservatives are present in these foods to extend shelf life, increase flavor, suggest healthfulness, and increase the saleability to the demographics. With the trend of local, organic, and natural foods, now is the time to get back to basics by incorporating a fundamental nutritional building block – a staple in every professional cook's kitchen at home and work – butter. Compared to margarine, butter serves more as an icon of a nation that sustains the family farm and the related values of this lifestyle. Certainly not as lucrative as margarine, butter is a natural product made from cream to which salt is often added for its preservative qualities. The cream is pasteurized and churned or shaken until it becomes semi-solid, at which point the buttermilk is separated. Fifteen to twenty percent of butter is milk solids and salt, held in an emulsion by naturally present lecithin, which also assists in the absorption of fat-soluble vitamins. Because of the presence of milk solids, butter has a refrigerated shelf life of up to one month, or at room temperature for a few hours. Slightly warmed butter is unmatched as a spread for flavor, but also naturally presents unprocessed vitamins and other qualities. The most easily absorbed... I have to go.

Abby Domen and Ha-Joon

The building suggests an Aztec structure. Surrounding edifices are like Egyptian pyramids. Peki feels like a "birdbrained mofo" on the mind-altering chemicals. Decked out in a tailor-made suit and alligator cowboy boots, he consumes wormwood bellywash in a stein. Thoroughly wasted, he's losing his sense of scale. In his existence, he keeps slipping through the loopholes in cosmic laws. He thinks of the highly competitive market that mantequilla has become. He must invest more in machinery to stay above the fray, including electrical generators, hydraulic pumps, stationary engines, and a squadron of trucks for distribution, all requiring consistent maintenance. He enjoys reading the operating manuals that come with the contraptions: info lit. He's in a hypnotic state, picturing the serviceable belts, clutches, shafts, and pulleys. He gets into the nitty-gritty of disassembling and reassembling units. They're like gigantic mechanized puzzles. He regularly drives himself around the bend, imagining the money-making potential of his establishment. His assistant manager, a shrunken old lady, calls, going into a long list of crises at the shop, none of which adds up to a row of beans. He has been a done-to his whole life. Now he is a doer. It is his time to shine. For a heartbeat and a half, he wants to fornicate with Abby, the living human torso, in the mud-colored room. It hacks in a pea-souper of tobacco smoke. Their relationship is coherent, and connected, to an extent. It should be as incommensurate as life and death, only it isn't. He watches the loco motorists on the wet roads. An argumentative storm brews in the cobbled alley and blows in through the screen. Ferity prevails and humaneness is unknown in the megalopolis.

A flock of turkeys crosses the bush street. Peki has been bottled up in the lab, cut off from the rest of civilization, so getting out and living a little is a good thing. This place is like a penthouse suite in comparison to the apartment! He has a desperate thirst for brandy but he's out of booze. The adjacent package store is a monument of modest height. He is not in the mood for moderation. There is the departure of the day and the arrival of the night. Minutes are snakes coiling in and around themselves. Robins populate a fig. Lightning bugs put on their luminescent show. Shadows have depth. Abby is hunkered in the corner. Next to it, he feels not unlike a humdrum college professor beside a circus freak. Indivisible illumination rushes through the ancient skylight, with wrought-iron guesswork, and weathered windows. Sleet dashes at the glass. Ha-Joon's hand, nails like claws, lands on his wrist like a falcon. Peki gazes at her, believing that her body and blood are bread and wine. Playfully he flicks stogie ash at her. She snickers and smirks enigmatically. He apparently falls into a trance, leaning on the granite pillar, fiddling mindlessly with the telescope on the tripod. After freebasing, he feels as though he's growing taller. She is a Korean parlormaid escort, dinky and trim as can be. She collects her clothing at the mahogany door, beside the triumphal cactus sculpture standing in a wicker-chariot. She appears poised to fly, an angel in her Asianness, her shoulder blades like small wings, the young girl prepared for something. Her oculi remind him of those luminous beetles. The threesome, for her, was frightful. The trunk is fugly. And furry. It stinks of burning flesh. It sits still on these burlap sacks. The drizzle is more or less unremitting. Cops attend to the strikers' hostilities. Voices are audible, both close and distant. Ha-Joon's visage, with the makeup, could conceivably pass for a mask. She regards her compact john with some semblance of amusement before systematically washing the dishes and stirring the chowder, baring her décolletage in a plunging purplish pantsuit. Peki wants to have sex with her and raise hell at the local taproom in simultaneity, only instead settling for snorting lines and shooting up. She is a picker at a banana plantation and a tree-shaker in an orange grove. This prostitution gig provides her with respectable supplemental income to assist in supporting herself. She is so pale you could read the paper by her. And her megawatt smile could light up an entire city block.

Peki gives Ha-Joon a nice chunk of change plus a bonus. She is cute in every way, dressed as a fandango gal. He's cranked up from breathing glue fumes and huffing spray paint. Sweat oozes from his pores and saturates his skin. He feels self-conscious about his humpback and harelip, which indicates a minor palatal defect. His armpits reek of horse droppings. She purrs, calling his weenie a "third leg." When it concerns his cock, her maw is never satisfied. He is crusty-nosed. They do the fox-trot, looking like lovebirds. These nights have been sleepless, the days dedicated to debauchery and substances illegal. Jagged rooftops are in his vision. Windows frame the scenery. The megapolis seems embattled and wretched. Dumb scabs are shipped in cattle cars, under an open sky, to steal workers' jobs, in his estimation. Heat and humidity occupy and own the environment. Cirri subdue the splendor. The bonking is a wacky exercise. She's heartbroken, if not crushed, to be excluded from the fun. She'd be appreciative to join in. She has an aspect of adolescent impatience. A dwarf drilling a torso, in intensities of lucency, is quite the phenomenon. She is never one to forgo a good fuck. She curses their souls. They make absurd music, or is she tone-deaf? She refrains herself as though it's a long-practiced personal task. Abby shivers, stationary, like a helpless victim, screwed in the umbilicus. They whirl in the den, small and spare as if carried by a tornado. She sports a shit-eating grin all over her face, attentive in the shade of the study. Ha-Joon has an infectious heck-with-it attitude. She sticks these acupuncture needles in Abby's so that it looks like a porcupine. She hoofsteps in high heels, keeping a wary eye open for nosy neighbors and assorted vermin. Peki's hands prayerfully support her posterior before he brews herbs. Her moue is amiable. He sniffs coffee grounds from the bottom of an urn using a drinking straw, his demeanor oddly jovial. She has a lift of spirit. They have a long and pleasant confabulation in the kitchen as she prepares the champagne and pheasant. She dreams of engendering a family, furthering her race. She stares at him as though he's a snake-oil salesman. Scintillation is noticeably on the wane. Roach motels are strategically set up around the joint. He wants to photograph her degradation. He has an edacity for brutality that is difficult to satisfy. He is developing a rep for unspeakable sex. Peki pictures his rivals, a mental rogues' gallery.

He customarily has an expression of unreachable contempt whenever his competitors are mentioned. The butter trade is wrong. He is making it right. An unfortunate unbalance exists. He deems himself to be a man of practice, not of hypothesis. He feels his place will grow in the city like a flower in a glebe. He won't flinch when confronted with adversity. More must die. There's unfinished business. He thinks of the cadavers he is responsible for and cringes. The dead are unquiet in his head. He and his mother will be high and mighty. To distract himself, he remembers the ashen land, broken country, the treeless and shelterless trails, to get here. He dug latrines and pitched tents. He went around the base camps of both sides of the warring factions. Rounds of spent ammo buzzed not unlike bugs. He was jittery and running for cover. Searchlights set up on towers swept the terrain relentlessly. There was an engagement, with cannonballs, between the militiamen, in ragged army camouflage and insomniac, unshaven police officers in stained uniforms in these godforsaken canyons. He sought safety and silence. This one time he slumbered on bluebells and bunchgrass in a meadow. And he slept on packed earth, against a cemetery gate, in an abandoned farmhouse. He felt like a sitting duck during a shootout in a coalfield. Day degenerates into the night. Peki tiptoes into the boudoir and snuggles next to Ha-Joon on the cushiony mattress. She attends for a while to his meat.

Ha-Joon's attire screams insurance company manager. She appears bored out of her skull. Her excuse for not smoking and drinking is flimsy as a cat's chew toy. The rain comes, cooling things off, like a form of compassion. God's pity? This week will be memorable for its high temps. Maudlin, Peki, with a claret cast and bulging eyes, plods lopsidedly. He glugs grappa and gorges on beef jerky. He expects that any minute now Abby's pelage, like hay, will spontaneously burst into flames and travel with impunity. Ha-Joon feels like fair game in this atmosphere, out in the open and susceptible to strange occurrences. Is considers herself a special target and acts as if she is a poor little victim at their mercy. The light, shining on her, is not unlike a spotlight, calling attention to her, and at the same time blinding her to them, putting her in a vulnerable position. She is drably appareled and yet is appealing. Lordy, his appreciation for her has gone to the edge of unhealthy obsession. Babe she is. She's playing serious hooky from her other vocations. The young lady is a freelancer pro. At the brothel she was formerly employed at, the crabby, fubsy madam became stingy with the budget allocations, and Ha-Joon decided to be an independent operator, vacating the premises to turn her own tricks, defining her clientage and negotiating her fees for service, the entire amount earned going into her purse instead of the majority of it going into the madam's bank account. She is in charge of her revenue flow. She doesn't have to fork over property rent and deal with interest from business loans. She invests in herself and is counting on this gamble to pay dividends. She sold her van and bought a camel. There are alternate versions of her shown in the mirrors of the hall, a space-time track, like stars being a reflection of the Earth. Heat is suffocating. The baleful mizzle gradually dissolves and visibility is marginally improved. The hirsute trunk is asleep on its... Breezes slur, as though with exhaustion. Vaporous eventide. The nation swelters. There is a letup in the precip. The first streetlamps turn on in the spoil-scarred metropolis. Amassment of cicadae stridencies. Moisture spits in spasms. The lightning leaps over the steel bridge. Thunder bams! Collective of shadows one could actually touch. Peki grabs Ha-Joon and grins as if he's getting away with something. She takes a deep breath, as though she is about to enter a burning building to fight the fire. She's mounted, fore and aft, by Abby (front), and Peki (rear). And she is penetrated and controlled. They are forthright and friendly. Peki practically plows right through her and comes out the other side. She is rather easy to read. She is a fille de joie Virgin Mary, sculpted by Michelangelo, magically, or miraculously, animated. She's Pieta perfect. Banging her, he tells her sordid tales. She has a lovely lizard face, is red-eyed and tensed up. She keeps her countenance composed. He drools down his shirt. She inhales and exhales carefully, pretending not to be in pain. He makes the noises of animalian victory. DP'd, she feels as if she is in the middle of hell. Pallid smudge of her phiz is screwed up in anguish as he propels himself, repeatedly, with fierceness. Her indignity is a hole she cannot see to the bottom of. Agonized, she tries not to sob. Her spoken words are weighted with sadness. She grunts and trembles. He assures her, pounded and pumped, that she'll be safe from harm. She's fairly miserable, double-teamed. They are so frigging hot that it is like they are grapes shriveling to raisins. It's as if the sinister luminary, blazing with unmatched intensity, has landed in the living room and is consciously bent on the trio's destruction. She complains about the mistreatment in stricken suspirations. He announces he is about to cum like a train conductor. Shooting his spunk in her breech, he sounds like a rooster cutting loose at cockcrow. Sun's bright, calescent, and calamitous. Mountains are masses of umber. Razor-sharp coastline stretches for miles. It is a nearly full moon. The closet is crammed with contraband. Is Abby a fugitive from justice? Peki chews and swallows a box of Hot Tamale candies while Ha-Joon bounces back and forth from the hydrogen-burning stove to the patent fridge. In the carmine emanation, his perspiration is evocative of molten lava during the period of geologic upheaval. He crouches and holds a harmonica to Abby's belly button oral cavity so it can properly play a ditty. She gazes at them puzzledly. They are so unusual and yet so familiar. The torso politely returns to its customary silence, its integument like turbulent water abruptly brought still. Man and woman share a smoke. Their vocalic ejaculations are shot at length. They are liberated and unreflective... The skyline's glow has grown phosphorescent. The city stinks of decay, urine, and feces. She preps the onion, cabbage, and beet soup.

Peki stands with his arms folded under his pectorals. He feels like the victim of witchcraft, spellbound by Ha-Joon. He's dressed in liver-brown robes and a peaked cap. She is wearing blue jeans, sloganeering tee-shirt, and these sort of boat-ish clogs. Her hair is braided in pigtails. She trots conceitedly, not unlike a hen. Maybe he should wring her neck! They chitchat for a timeless time. Depraved thoughts rise in his brain like the gases of fermented beans stored in a receptacle. There is a furrowing to her brow and a pout to her mouth. She's smoldering and sullen when he strips her. Whereupon he ties her wrists with hemp cords, binds her ankles using linen bands, and pummels her a little. She has tight buttcheeks that could crack walnuts. She experiences animal fear. She wants to refuse sex in favor of celibacy like the incorruptible Jesus Christ rejected sustenance for starvation in John Milton's 'Paradise Regained.' Her being is threatened with occupation, like a town by the opposing military. He is a foreign power ruling her. His maneuvering is comparable to the Blitz. He stares at her orifices like a potential homebuyer peering in at every aperture. Then he moves finely in her front like water in a river. And she wiggles akin to a bowel cooking on a grill. He tunnels into her land. He infiltrates, to destroy. He watches her with his whole attention. He feels as if his blood is boiling and his cutis is bubbling it is so roasting. The knobs of his knees ache. Showers are susurrant. A hexagonal aluminum cage is situated in the corner. Abby's reluctant to communicate, content to spectate. Perhaps it's a form of courtesy, staying quiet out of deference, the thing changing position in the cat bed. It emits a faint pleasured hum. She has the feeling that it is a puppet master, pulling the strings in this salacious show like gravity governs the movement of heavenly bodies. Ha-Joon falls into torment, hurrying the humiliation by succumbing to him, her pain natural and possible. She is slit-eyed and golden. Reamed, she feels as though her bottom is burning in excruciating flame. Her tongue is a knoll. Sweat runs down her spine. This is a loss of herself. She once belonged to herself. Now she's husked. She feels like dust, swept, and a stain, wiped. Agony ripples through her uninterrupted. He snorts, and pumps. She is buggered, anguished. Peki's lusterless lock is coiled around her neck like a flung rope. They bathe in the swelter. He hears the clatter in her throat. She lies like a discarded garment. Her bum-hole is a red rose, its stubble the thorns. Their brief talkative breaks are hectic. He thrusts with jerky ease. His mane, she notices, is dyed oven-black. The soles of her feet are heated like irons. He plunges into her organ as casually as he would dive into a pool. After coming, he skips and jumps, scuttling away like a woodlouse from an ax-split log. Pillows she shores against her ruin. He returns, draped in a poncho, to pick her up, putting her on the couch like an instrumentalist places his clarinet into its case. Is it dawn or dusk? She wonders. Abby, from the spotless kitchen, looks at them like they're tourist attractions. Its crinigerous stomach is sulky. Its language has become more fluent and idiomatic as the afternoon ages. It whistles a soothing Viennese waltz. The modestly opulent room has Bauhaus-derived furnishings, characterless ceilings and walls, and neon-strip lighting. The digital clock-radio glows puce. An intractable towerscape, made up of a multitude of Brueghel's vertiginous Babels, glitters in the ochreous effulgence. The building they currently occupy is shaped like a cigar. Below, there are a few elms and acacias, a herbaceous border, and nameless flowers. Other skyscrapers are graceless erections. The river resonates with rattles under a great bridge. The azure whines with a plane. Surrounding structures are canyons. The sprinkles sigh and give up the ghost. Serpentiform gridlock slithers and becomes inert. In this parallel universe, Peki feels not unlike a rat in an orientation maze. The vista's line sinuates, from his vantage point, and is straightened out, as if the slack is yanked. His perspiry integument is petrol-iridescent in the refulgence. He has the sensation that he came halfway around the world just to get here. He pours scotch on ice. Scissor-blades of brilliance snip through the slats of the blinds. The cathedral city, solid and durable, sprawls, lit with an infernal flare. The Milky Way is barely visible through the pollution. The hot weather has gone on unduly long, the extreme heat and humidity the worst in living memory. Peki's dermis feels baked like poorly-cured leather. He quaffs a liter of honey water. He and Ha-Joon blether like children. Parts of her body hurt badly. She has such a lovely, long face. Her expression is not dissimilar to a lake, the shifting depth of emotion shimmering beneath the surface. She wishes to put the carving knife to his jugular… It's like he bears the burden of a tremendous weight on his back, as though his hump is a boulder. The vault seems unreal. The day continues to be scorching. Covered in a pelisse, she readies the rice-wine-and-cakes. The deluge, cracking and rushing, sounds like a conflagration. The trio's like the three sides of a triangle… Peki has a vision in his mind of being eaten by avian and vermicular creatures, his bones left unburied. His heart feels like wilted kale. He yearns to be home with his madre. An image of her develops in his head, but it's only a negative. The dogged silence is getting to him. It is a wet and windy twilight.

The ship's-galley-sized study, in the well-proportioned, rambling structure, is a warm and welcoming place. Furniture has these strong folky hues. Ha-Joon's peepers are narrowed, lips closed, cast composed. Peki, saffron-seraped, is excluded by her absorption. Her flesh is reminiscent of creamy paper. She is cross-legged and shoeless on the ottoman.

Her heels are crushed-strawberry-pink. And her blouse has these leg o' mutton sleeves. She complied with his request that she stay in her undies. A Gucci bag and a Cabbage Patch Kid are beside her. Her physiognomy expresses indignation. Her feet smell of bonfires. She didn't appreciate the day-long degradations. Not at all. She believes that Abby, as a bystander, is complicit in her maltreatment. Though iffy about them, she continues to accommodate them. The two sleep in the cozy attic. She's frosty and wordless, looking at them fixedly through artsy metal-rimmed glasses. Her taciturnity is an aspect of her reticent nature, Peki assumes. She can be unshakably schoolmistressy. She has an uncertain temper. A force-field emanates from her being. Their connection is broken because of the uncultured brute's behavior. She thaws eventually, enlivened by his energy, moved by his hyperactive imagination. She looks at his lank hair, and his hunched shoulders. He has yellow-clay skin. His body odor has the odor of dirty wool. Sometimes he feels like a kite and she is winding the reel. He's ensconced on the L-shaped table. Lances of coruscation remind him of the long buff tentacles of a jellyfish. He utilizes knitting needles as chopsticks, digging into the Chinese takeout carton. What a fantastic feast! He had tossed the fork into the sink as though it was a crude implement. There's an eddy of quiescence. They discuss the economically unstable industrial town until Abby, a springy thing, bounces onto the bench, verbalizing it'd put a hand over its oral-omphalos when it speaks, if it had one, as a manner of politeness. It thinks it's rude to show anyone else the lint in its nombril while it's talking. It modifies its intonation, vocalizing it doesn't want to be marginalized in civilization. It has a miasma of stale urine, which turns Peki on. He glances at its navel-mouth and gets a semi-woody. Flotsam and jetsam of his cogitations. He is relaxed here, well-fed and well-entertained, coming freely in and out, so he cannot complain. Is he invading her space? Tripping his balls off, he cavorts like a mutant under a mushroom cumulus and yells he doesn't wish to vanish from the cosmos. He grabs the banister as if for support. He and Ha-Joon feverishly exchange ideas in the imitation farmhouse kitchen, slightly urbanized, gleaming with claret and copper. He's tense. She is limp. He pictures himself rugger-tackling her, his phallus slipping into her like a thread through a bead. She has a vulnerable countenance, and is breathy and cheeky. He clasps the mug of vodka-spiked cocoa like a mechanical drummer holds his toy snare. The din of the megalopolis is distressing to his ears. The aural torture is too much to handle. He makes a foray for food and drink. She tucks into the plums and carrots. Her armpits whiff of damp ashes. Abby is saved by the solitary and sensuous pleasure of seeing itself in the cobwebby and cracked mirror. The grass is marshy after the drencher. Abby is a barometer. Its nipples know when the temperature or the pressure is about to drop. The trunk aches when the clouds come. Its spinal cord is a lightning conductor. The torso forecasted the soaker. It says it needs a normal life, some understanding, and social activities. It shares its insecurities, secret goals, and hope for improved relations with society. Its blather is vague and unfocused. It has a non-resonant inflection. It strains to maintain its upright and immobile bulk. Its intonation is deliberate and desperate-sounding. Always hiding, it insists, is not a way of life. The creature is pathologically afraid of being alone. It is next to a potted rubber plant. It has a case of agoraphobia and its blood-sugar level is low. A kestrel glides in the murky sky. The main road, wide and lethal, carves the expressway. Rhododendrons round the pond. Abby is lonely and embarrassed after losing its job as a checkout clerk at the local library. It hated taking the bus, but it was the sensible option to get to work. No available seat would arouse terror. It saw commuters as menacing. It was constantly mocked by people. It suffers from insomnia. The thing shuffles tentatively. Uselessly erect, it beholds its malformed reflection in the biscuit tin. It is giddy in the humans' company. It has an independent identity, carefully created. It has nervous mannerisms. A boob tube addict, it sits passively in front of the box. 'Dr. No-No,' a James Bong flick starring Sean Crockery, has just started. Ha-Joon warns that the characters on screen are "false friends." It sees her serpentining, hind-wagging figure. Its mamillae are rigid. With circumspection and tact, Peki fits the halter top and bicycle shorts, stinking of tobacco, on it. He changes into a smelly sweater and corduroy pants. The lavatory is like a cell, with books and pastel tissues brightening it. Sun is an angry red. The air has an ancient bitterness and fustiness. The storm hisses and clamors. The street's sodium lighting shines through the pane.

The den is tastefully decorated, with its velvet chairs, odalisque reading lamps, and Persian carpet. There is a collection of complicated prints and photographs on a pretty bureau. A paperweight, braille machine, and ink-well are based on a desk. The rainbow has the chromatic intensity of a detonated paintbox. Thunder sounds like a battery of percussion. Hail's metallic clicking on the windows sounds not unlike a mechanical type-writer. Strewn clothes come in wacky colors. Peki feels unattractive next to Ha-Joon. He feels a deep sense of inadequacy. Nevertheless, compliments trip off his tongue. He wolf-whistles at her. She averts her gaze as if alarmed by him. His pies wander. His chest bursts. Her brassiere is birch-silver, her panties catkins-hazel. His dipstick reverberates in involuntary paroxysms. The previous several days it's been nothing but collisions of personal-ity. She is tracksuited, feet contained incongruous high-heels. She calls her makeup "war paint." Her impeccable tresses are stiff and set. She's breathtaking. He experiences this sharp decline in the supply of oxygen to the lungs and brain. He feels as though he is seizing up with electric shock. She jolts his heart into boom. She is gawky and grinning. Her skin has a youthful sheen of good health. She moseys importantly. Her voice sounds cultivated, speaking, using her fairytale vocabulary. He realizes he is becoming too serious, a worrier. He reveals his stained gnashers in an expectant smile. He's got her in the optical crosshairs. She presents a stable target. His orbs are suffused with blood. His extravagant lip lifts from incisors. She pootles confidently. He wishes to bury his nose between her batty's cheeks and to sniff her natures. His pinguid strands are clustered on his forehead. He galumphs, arms aslant, legs bowed. Abby, gracefully isolated, is tweeded, in the bathroom that is like a large closet, staring at the ruffled peaty water of the basin below, encircled by pussy willows. A portly collie streaks by unleashed. Floral bumps of buds poke through the soil like pox-pimples emerging through powder. There's a chalk drawing on the sidewalk, done as it might be by a child, of a vase full of flow-ers, in carmine or vermilion, and a featureless oviform face, subdued and demure, beside it. The adjoining building reminds it of a colossal Rubik's Cube. Sun's poppy-scarlet in the powder-blue sky. Cirri are iron-grey. The torso goes from side to side like a metronome. The aircon makes an engine-hum. Sleet goes tappety on the panes. Ha-Joon's pristine toenails are painted rose-pink. She has a cello mouth, carved cheekbones, and an outstanding brow. She springs lithely. Her flesh is the creamy color of a cappuccino's froth. She has a precise modulation. She looks at Peki like she can read his thoughts. With warmth and directness, he tells her he wants her to blow him. His woolen hat is pulled well down over his dome. He's garbed in a combat jacket, faded, ripped jeans, and brand-new laced trainers. He is, to all appearances, barrel-bodied and no-necked. Something seems undefinably wrong with him, toddling with this exaggerated caution, his movements shaky and excessive. Is he drunk? Stoned? She has no clue. His creep turns into a jog, the steps unvarying. He actuates at a brisk pace. Capering, he looks not unlike a mental leprechaun. On PCP, he is a deformed dwarf hemmed in by a group of infantas in a Velazquezian 'Las Meninas' animated artwork. His blank mien changes into a scornful leer. He holds his todger like a totem. It vibrates in rhythm with her twitching eyelids. Swish of the downpour. In the indigo dusk, Ha-Joon is rigid with independence and then relaxes into consent. Peki scuttles crabwise. His knees are splayed and his hips swivel as he putters. He possesses an extraordinary virility, a fierce impulse. They carry on, making pervasive and raucous noises. There are various sounds but no voices. Her stomach churns like a washer, switches into a spin-cycle, until, at last, it rests and simmers. She listens to the drumming tattoo of his heartbeat. She flails and flops, throated thus, and gags. Her ululations explode. Grinding notes can be heard, and plashy titters, mingled with high-pitched squeaks, grunts, snorts, and squawks. Rammed ruthlessly, she delivers a woodwind squeal. She is supine and luminous. Her limbs dangle beyond the confines of the coffee table. Her blue-black mop is fanned across a not-too-clean pair of shorts. Her begonia-pinkish soles. Lobelia-cobalt of her irises. Her hair and dermis: inky and ivory. The abrasions on her have the purple hue of bilberry juice. She sees his bitten-down fingernails, and fern-green tube socks. Her queef is a fluttery burr. The town is mythical and lunatic. Autos honk like geese. In hindsight, Peki thinks that he made fellatial implorations he never should have ventured on. His flatus banshee-screams.

Traffic makes a roaring and wheezing racket, rhythmically swelling into a cacophonic crescendo. Rainbow has these screaming colors. The entire space has turned into an Aladdin's Cave, the burgeoning mess into treasure chests. Tattered wallpaper — sensational tapestries. Unopened mail is elastic banded and paper clipped in tidy heaps on saucers near a constellation of crayons on the counter. Bills are scattered. Sequined insects fly with their gauzy wings. Pivoting panes are set into the roof. Venetian blinds are terra cotta. A sulfurous butterfly zips by the screen. The sun is infrared one minute, ultraviolet the next. Peki, on angel dust, experiences a subdued passion that carries with it an invigorating nip. He listens to the rain's frenetic rattle and menacing whine and evaluates Ha-Joon's soot-colored bob, caught up in a tortoiseshell comb, ping-pong-ball-sized eyes, straight, salient conk, clearcut chin, concertina neck, and tiddly, marguerite-whitish feet. She is clad in a royal-blue jumper. She took off the mulberry cocktail dress with embroidered sage-green annuals in disgust. And forget about the parachute pants. He has on a black-eyed-Susan-orange trench coat, its collar like a choirboy's, the shoulder pads similar to the bony plates of a stegosaurus, and lizard-skin shoes. Abrasions are violaceous stains on her shins. She chews on sunflower seeds. He discovers she was once a dedicated cricketer and a wood-engraver with skill and accuracy. She was well-paid. Topazine earrings hang from her lobes. His mane's hanging strands evoke tendrils of unearthly creepers. He togs himself in tartan trousers. She slips into a snazzy swimsuit. Her contusions remind him of a dragon's scales. She is in a friendly enough mood at the moment. He imagines them merged not unlike amalgamated soap chips. He swallows cod-liver capsules. The cavern is chromatically becrazed. Feather duster. Peacock fan. The celestial sphere is a swimming pool-bluish. The semen in his drawers is like sinus fluid in a skull pocket or a snail trail across cotton material. He clasps his rig like a captured eel, fantasizing about licking her cherry-crimson clitoris, an icon of the cult of cunt, and lapping her poppy-red bunghole while clutching her glossy haunches. She looks like a superficial blend of Botticelli's Venus, Kali, and the Mona Lisa. The waste paper basket metamorphoses into the Temple of Artemis. Sometimes Peki feels as if he's an accommodating cuckold and she's the indulgent harridan. He must shove off in a twinkling. He unties his knot of emotion, feeling unsettled because he is being driven away by her indifference. He has a chip on his shoulder. She represents order. He is chaotic. His confidence, once expanding, is now diminishing. Is he disrupting her self-centered isolation? He has an air of a rueful lad, changing into the fisherman's smock and candy-striped stockings. His dry tongue feels like a dead leaf. He's failing in executing his balancing act, between home and here. Ha-Joon sips her chilled Sauvignon, in a lemon-yellow tank top and lime-green pleated skirt. Her socks have null and neutral tones. Her hair on this day resembles a hedgehog. In the shade, it could be mistaken for a plant in a pot. She has the frontage of a colt, contemplating his cubic physique. Her blush is sugar-pink. She is reliable and resourceful, he opines. Her frontal is unsmiling and judicious. A messenger on a motorbike wipes out. Megapolis is very dense and disagreeable. Rush hour is tortoise-paced. He auscultates its jangly noise. Stores have discos' dayglo. The moon is a mandala. He is slightly flushed. His heart ticks like a clock. He muses on the mantequilla. He is mad and obsessed. The night is a black hole. He's silhouetted obsidian on the pavement, plodding through puddles.

Special Thanks

Marylynn, Derek, Velma, Ester, Lupe, Paco, Chita, Zuki, Gus, Crummy, Mittens, Red, and Fruity.

About the Author

Christopher S. Peterson has been seriously dreaming since he was a bambino, immersing himself in Icarusian flights of fancy. He enjoys reading, film, music, animals, working out, football, hockey, and living in nerdvana. He has been published in several lit mags few people have read. He was properly educated at Wildwood Elementary School in Burlington, Massachusetts, and currently lives in Atlanta, Georgia with his black cats.

Christopher S. Peterson

Butter,
or
the Dairy
of a
Madman

Book Two

Fomite

Writing a review on social media sites for readers will help the progress of independent publishing. To submit a review, go to the book page on any of the sites and follow the links for reviews. Books from independent presses rely on reader-to-reader communications.

For more information or to order any of our books, visit:
fomitepress.com/our-books.html

More novels and novellas from Fomite...

Joshua Amses — *During This, Our Nadir*
Joshua Amses — *Ghats*
Joshua Amses — *Raven or Crow*
Joshua Amses — *The Moment Before an Injury*
Raymond Barfield — *Dreams of a Spirit Seer*
Charles Bell — *The Married Land*
Charles Bell — *The Half Gods*
Jaysinh Birjepatel — *Nothing Beside Remains*
Jaysinh Birjepatel — *The Good Muslim of Jackson Heights*
David Borofka — *The End of Good Intnetions*
David Brizer — *Cacademonomania*
David Brizer — *The Secret Doctrine of V. H. Rand*
David Brizer — *Victor Rand*
L. M Brown — *Hinterland*
Paula Closson Buck — *Summer on the Cold War Planet*
L.enny Cavallaro — *Paganini Agitato*
Dan Chodorkoff — *Loisaida*
Dan Chodorkoff — *Sugaring Down*
David Adams Cleveland -— *Time's Betrayal*
Paul Cody— *Sphyxia*
Jaimee Wriston Colbert — *Vanishing Acts*
Roger Coleman — *Skywreck Afternoons*
Stephen Downes — *The Hands of Pianists*
Marc Estrin — *Et Resurrexit*
Marc Estrin — *Hyde*
Marc Estrin — *Kafka's Roach*
Marc Estrin — *Proceedings of the Hebrew Free Burial Society*
Marc Estrin — *Speckled Vanities*
Marc Estrin — *The Annotated Nose*
Marc Estrin — *The Penseés of Alan Krieger*
Zdravka Evtimova — *Asylum for Men and Dogs*

Fomite

Fomite

Frederick Ramey — *Comes A Time*
Howard Rappaport — *Arnold and Igor*
Joseph Rathgeber — *Mixedbloods*
Kathryn Roberts — *Companion Plants*
Robert Rosenberg — *Isles of the Blind*
Fred Russell — *Rafi's World*
Ron Savage — *Voyeur in Tangier*
David Schein — *The Adoption*
Charles Simpson — *Uncertain Harvest*
Lynn Sloan — *Midstream*
Rana Shubair — *And No Net Ensnares Me*
Lynn Sloan — *Principles of Navigation*
L.E. Smith — *The Consequence of Gesture*
L.E. Smith — *Travers' Inferno*
L.E. Smith — *Untimely RIPped*
Robert Sommer — *A Great Fullness*
Caitlin Hamilton Summie — *Geographies of the Heart*
Tom Walker — *A Day in the Life*
Susan V. Weiss —*My God, What Have We Done?*
Peter M. Wheelwright — *As It Is on Earth*
Peter M. Wheelwright — *The Door-Man*
Suzie Wizowaty — *The Return of Jason Green*

Made in the USA
Columbia, SC
08 January 2025

51292081R00309